To Mother
Love Merry Christmas

DATE DUE

1-2			
2-19			
3-9			
3-20			
4-20			
5-9			
7-16			
10-10			
11-23			
12-29			
2-19			
7-12			
2-17			
GAYLORD			PRINTED IN U.S.A.

Agatha Christie

FIVE CLASSIC MURDER MYSTERIES

Agatha Christie

FIVE CLASSIC MURDER MYSTERIES

The Secret Adversary

The Murder of Roger Ackroyd

The Boomerang Clue

The Moving Finger

Death Comes as the End

AVENEL BOOKS · NEW YORK

This Omnibus edition was previously published in separate volumes under the titles:

Published 1985 by Avenel Books, distributed by Crown Publishers, Inc., One Park Avenue, New York, New York 10016, by arrangement with Dodd, Mead & Company.

Composition and typesetting done in England, printing and binding done in the United States of America.

Library of Congress Cataloging in Publication Data

Christie, Agatha, 1890-1976.
Agatha Christie, five classic murder mysteries.

Contents: The secret adversary—The murder of Roger Ackroyd—The boomerang clue—[etc.]
1. Detective and mystery stories, English.
I. Title.
PR6005.H66A6 1985 823′.912 84-24429
ISBN: 0-517-46852-2

h g f e d c

Contents

Shamrock Public Library

The Secret Adversary

Prologue

IT WAS 2 P.M. on the afternoon of May 7, 1915. The *Lusitania* had been struck by two torpedoes in succession and was sinking rapidly, while the boats were being launched with all possible speed. The women and children were being lined up awaiting their turn. Some still clung desperately to husbands and fathers; others clutched their children closely to their breasts. One girl stood alone, slightly apart from the rest. She was quite young, not more than eighteen. She did not seem afraid, and her grave, steadfast eyes looked straight ahead.

"I beg your pardon."

A man's voice beside her made her start and turn. She had noticed the speaker more than once amongst the first-class passengers. There had been a hint of mystery about him which had appealed to her imagination. He spoke to no one. If anyone spoke to him he was quick to rebuff the overture. Also he had a nervous way of looking over his shoulder with a swift, suspicious glance.

She noticed now that he was greatly agitated. There were beads of perspiration on his brow. He was evidently in a state of overmastering fear. And yet he did not strike her as the kind of man who would be afraid to meet death!

"Yes?" Her grave eyes met his inquiringly.

He stood looking at her with a kind of desperate irresolution.

"It must be!" he muttered to himself. "Yes—it is the only way." Then aloud he said abruptly: "You are an American?"

"Yes."

"A patriotic one?"

The girl flushed.

"I guess you've no right to ask such a thing! Of course I am!"

"Don't be offended. You wouldn't be if you knew how much there was at stake. But I've got to trust someone—and it must be a woman."

"Why?"

"Because of 'women and children first.'" He looked round and lowered his voice. "I'm carrying papers—vitally important papers. They make all the difference to the Allies in the war. You understand? These papers have *got* to be saved! They've more chance with you than with me. Will you take them?"

The girl held out her hand.

"Wait—I must warn you. There may be a risk—if I've been followed. I don't think I have, but one never knows. If so, there will be danger. Have you the nerve to go through with it?"

The girl smiled.

"I'll go through with it all right. And I'm real proud to be chosen! What am I to do with them afterward?"

"Watch the newspapers! I'll advertise in the personal column of the *Times*, beginning 'Shipmate.' At the end of three days if there's nothing—well, you'll know I'm down and out. Then take the packet to the American Embassy, and deliver it into the Ambassador's own hands. Is that clear?"

"Quite clear."

"Then be ready—I'm going to say good-bye." He took her hand in his. "Good-bye. Good luck to you,' he said in a louder tone.

Her hand closed on the oilskin packet that had lain in his palm.

The *Lusitania* settled with a more decided list to starboard. In answer to a quick command, the girl went forward to take her place in the boat.

1

The Young Adventurers, Ltd.

"TOMMY, OLD THING!"

"Tuppence, old bean!"

The two young people greeted each other affectionately, and momentarily blocked the Dover Street Tube exit in doing so. The adjective "old" was misleading. Their united ages would certainly not have totaled forty-five.

"Not seen you for simply centuries," continued the young man. "Where are you off to? Come and chew a bun with me. We're getting a bit unpopular here—blocking the gangway as it were. Let's get out of it."

The girl assenting, they started walking down Dover Street toward Piccadilly.

"Now then," said Tommy, "where shall we go?"

The very faint anxiety which underlay his tone did not escape the astute ears of Miss Prudence Cowley, known to her intimate friends for some mysterious reason as "Tuppence." She pounced at once.

"Tommy, you're stony!"

"Not a bit of it," declared Tommy unconvincingly. "Rolling in cash."

"You always were a shocking liar," said Tuppence severely, "though you did once persuade Sister Greenbank that the doctor had ordered you beer as a tonic, but forgotten to write it on the chart. Do you remember?"

Tommy chuckled.

"I should think I did! Wasn't the old cat in a rage when she found out? Not that she was a bad sort really, old Mother Greenbank! Good old hospital—demobbed like everything else, I suppose?"

Tuppence sighed.

"Yes. You too?"

Tommy nodded.

"Two months ago."

"Gratuity?" hinted Tuppence.

"Spent."

"Oh, Tommy!"

"No, old thing, not in riotous dissipation. No such luck! The cost of living—ordinary plain, or garden living nowadays is, I assure you, if you do not know——"

"My dear child," interrupted Tuppence, "there is nothing I do *not* know about the cost of living. Here we are at Lyons', and we will each of us pay for our own. That's it!" And Tuppence led the way upstairs.

The place was full, and they wandered about looking for a table, catching odds and ends of conversation as they did so.

"And—do you know, she sat down and *cried* when I told her she couldn't have the flat after all." "It was simply a *bargain*, my dear! Just like the one Mabel Lewis brought from Paris——"

"Funny scraps one does overhear," murmured Tommy. "I passed two Johnnies in the street today talking about someone called Jane Finn. Did you ever hear such a name?"

But at that moment two elderly ladies rose and collected parcels, and Tuppence deftly ensconced herself in one of the vacant seats.

Tommy ordered tea and buns. Tuppence ordered tea and buttered toast.

"And mind the tea comes in separate teapots," she added severely.

Tommy sat down opposite her. His bared head revealed a shock of exquisitely slicked-back red hair. His face was pleasantly ugly—nondescript, yet unmistakably the face of a gentleman and a sportsman. His brown suit was well cut, but perilously near the end of its tether.

They were an essentially modern-looking couple as they sat there. Tuppence had no claim to beauty, but there was character and charm in the elfin lines of her little face, with its determined chin and large, wide-apart gray eyes that looked mistily out from under straight black brows. She wore a small bright green toque over her black bobbed hair, and her extremely short and rather shabby skirt revealed a pair of uncommonly dainty ankles. Her appearance presented a valiant attempt at smartness.

The tea came at last, and Tuppence, rousing herself from a fit of meditation, poured it out.

"Now then," said Tommy, taking a large bite of bun, "let's get up-to-date. Remember, I haven't seen you since that time in hospital in 1916."

"Very well." Tuppence helped herself liberally to buttered toast. "Abridged biography of Miss Prudence Cowley, fifth daughter of Archdeacon Cowley of Little Missendell, Suffolk. Miss Cowley left the delights (and drudgeries) of her home life early in the war and came up to London, where she entered an officers' hospital. First month: Washed up six hundred and forty-eight plates every day. Second month: Promoted to drying aforesaid plates. Third month: Promoted to peeling potatoes. Fourth month: Promoted to cutting bread and butter. Fifth month: Promoted one floor up to duties of wardmaid with mop and pail. Sixth month: Promoted to waiting at table. Seventh month: Pleasing appearance and nice manners so striking that am promoted to waiting on the Sisters! Eighth month: Slight check in career. Sister Bond ate Sister Westhaven's egg! Grand row! Wardmaid clearly to blame! Inattention in such important matters cannot be too highly censured. Mop and pail again! How are the mighty fallen! Ninth month: Promoted to sweeping out wards, where I found a friend of my childhood in Lieutenant Thomas Beresford (bow, Tommy!), whom I had not seen for five long years. The meeting was affecting! Tenth month: Reproved by matron for visiting the pictures in company with one of the patients, namely: the aforementioned Lieutenant Thomas Beresford. Eleventh and twelfth months: Parlormaid duties resumed with entire success. At the end of the year left hospital in a blaze of glory. After that, the talented Miss Cowley drove successively a trade delivery van, a motor-lorry and a general. The last was the pleasantest. He was quite a young general!"

"What blighter was that?" inquired Tommy. "Perfectly sickening the way those brass hats drove from the War Office to the Savoy, and from the Savoy to the War Office!"

"I've forgotten his name now," confessed Tuppence. "To resume, that was in a way the apex of my career. I next entered a Government office. We had several very enjoyable tea parties. I had intended to become a land girl, a postwoman, and a bus conductress by way of rounding off my career—but the Armistice intervened! I clung to the office with the true limpet touch for many long months, but, alas, I was combed out at last. Since then I've been looking for a job. Now then—your turn."

"There's not so much promotion in mine," said Tommy regretfully, "and a great deal less variety. I went out to France again, as you know. Then they sent me to Mesopotamia, and I got wounded for the second time, and went into hospital out there. Then I got stuck in Egypt till the Armistice happened, kicked my heels there some time longer, and, as I told you, finally got demobbed. And, for ten long, weary months I've been job hunting! There aren't any jobs! And, if there were, they wouldn't give 'em to me. What good am I? What do I know about business? Nothing."

Tuppence nodded gloomily.

"What about the colonies?" she suggested.

Tommy shook his head.

"I shouldn't like the colonies—and I'm perfectly certain they wouldn't like me!"

"Rich relations?"

Again Tommy shook his head.

"Oh, Tommy, not even a great-aunt?"

"I've got an old uncle who's more or less rolling, but he's no good."

"Why not?"

"Wanted to adopt me once. I refused."

"I think I remember hearing about it," said Tuppence slowly. "You refused because of your mother——"

Tommy flushed.

"Yes, it would have been a bit rough on the mater. As you know, I was all she had. Old boy hated her—wanted to get me away from her. Just a bit of spite."

"Your mother's dead, isn't she?" said Tuppence gently.

Tommy nodded.

Tuppence's large grey eyes looked misty.

"You're a good sort, Tommy. I always knew it."

"Rot!" said Tommy hastily. "Well, that's my position. I'm just about desperate."

"So am I! I've hung out as long as I could. I've touted round. I've answered advertisements. I've tried every mortal blessed thing. I've screwed and saved and pinched! But it's no good. I shall have to go home!"

"Don't you want to?"

"Of course I don't want to! What's the good of being sentimental? Father's a dear—I'm awfully fond of him—but you've no idea how I worry him! He has that delightful early Victorian view that short skirts and smoking are immoral. You can imagine what a thorn in the flesh I am to him! He just heaved a sigh of relief when the war took me off. You see, there are seven of us at home. It's awful! All housework and mothers' meetings! I have always been the changeling. I don't want to go back, but—oh, Tommy, what else is there to do?"

Tommy shook his head sadly. There was a silence, and then Tuppence burst out:

"Money, money, money! I think about money morning, noon and night! I dare say it's mercenary of me, but there it is!"

"Same here," agreed Tommy with feeling.

"I've thought over every imaginable way of getting it too," continued Tuppence. "There are only three! To be left it, to marry it, or to make it. First is ruled out. I haven't got any rich elderly relatives. Any relatives I have are in homes for decayed gentlewomen! I always help old ladies over crossings, and pick up parcels for old gentlemen, in case they should turn out to be eccentric millionaires. But not one of them has ever asked me my name—and quite a lot never said 'Thank you.'"

There was a pause.

"Of course," resumed Tuppence, "marriage is my best chance. I made up my mind to marry money when I was quite young. Any thinking girl would! I'm not sentimental, you know." She paused. "Come now, you can't say I'm sentimental," she added sharply.

"Certainly not," agreed Tommy hastily. "No one would ever think of sentiment in connection with you."

"That's not very polite," replied Tuppence. "But I dare say you mean it alright. Well, there it is! I'm ready and willing—but I never meet any rich men! All the boys I know are about as hard up as I am."

"What about the general?" inquired Tommy.

"I fancy he keeps a bicycle shop in time of peace," explained Tuppence. "No, there it is! Now *you* could marry a rich girl."

"I'm like you. I don't know any."

"That doesn't matter. You can always get to know one. Now, if I see a man in a fur coat come out of the Ritz I can't rush up to him and say: "Look here, you're rich. I'd like to know you.'"

"Do you suggest that I should do that to a similarly garbed female?"

"Don't be silly. You tread on her foot, or pick up her handkerchief, or something like that. If she thinks you want to know her she's flattered, and will manage it for you somehow."

"You overrate my manly charms," murmured Tommy.

"On the other hand," proceeded Tuppence, "my millionaire would probably run for his life! No—marriage is fraught with difficulties. Remains—to *make* money!"

"We've tried that, and failed," Tommy reminded her.

"We've tried all the orthodox ways, yes. But suppose we try the unorthodox. Tommy, let's be adventurers!"

"Certainly," replied Tommy cheerfully. "How do we begin?"

"That's the difficulty. If we could make ourselves known, people might hire us to commit crimes for them."

"Delightful," commented Tommy. "Especially coming from a clergyman's daughter!"

"The moral guilt," Tuppence pointed out, "would be theirs—not mine. You must admit that there's a difference between stealing a diamond necklace for yourself and being hired to steal it."

"There wouldn't be the least difference if you were caught!"

"Perhaps not. But I shouldn't be caught. I'm so clever."

"Modesty always was your besetting sin," remarked Tommy.

"Don't rag. Look here, Tommy, shall we really? Shall we form a business partnership?"

"Form a company for the stealing of diamond necklaces?"

"That was only an illustration. Let's have a—what do you call it in bookkeeping?"

"Don't know. Never did any."

"I have—but I always got mixed up, and used to put credit entries on the debit side, and vice versa—so they fired me out. Oh, I know—a joint venture! It struck me as such a romantic phrase to come across in the middle of musty old figures. It's got an Elizabethan flavor about it—makes one think of galleons and doubloons. A joint venture!"

"Trading under the name of the Young Adventurers, Ltd.? Is that your idea, Tuppence?"

"It's all very well to laugh, but I feel there might be something in it."

"How do you propose to get in touch with your would-be employers?"

"Advertisement," replied Tuppence promptly. "Have you got a bit of paper and a pencil? Men usually seem to have. Just like we have hairpins and powderpuffs."

Tommy handed over a rather shabby green notebook, and Tuppence began writing busily.

"Shall we begin: 'Young officer, twice wounded in the war——'"

"Certainly not."

"Oh, very well, my dear boy. But I can assure you that that sort of thing might touch the heart of an elderly spinster, and she might adopt you, and then there would be no need for you to be a young adventurer at all."

"I don't want to be adopted."

"I forgot you had a prejudice against it. I was only ragging you! The papers are full up to the brim with that type of thing. Now listen—how's this? 'Two young adventurers for hire. Willing to do anything, go anywhere. Pay must be good.' (We might as well make that clear from the start.) Then we might add: 'No reasonable offer refused'—like flats and furniture."

"I should think any offer we get in answer to that would be a pretty *un*reasonable one!"

"Tommy! You're a genius! That's ever so much more chic. 'No unreasonable offer refused—if pay is good.' How's that?"

"I shouldn't mention pay again. It looks rather eager."

"It couldn't look as eager as I feel! But perhaps you are right. Now I'll read it straight through. 'Two young adventurers for hire. Willing to do anything, go anywhere. Pay must be good. No unreasonable offer refused.' How would that strike you if you read it?"

"It would strike me as either being a hoax, or else written by a lunatic."

"It's not half so insane as a thing I read this morning beginning 'Petunia' and signed 'Best Boy.'" She tore out the leaf and handed it to Tommy. "There you are. *Times*, I think. Reply to Box so-and-so. I expect it will be about five shillings. Here's half a crown for my share."

Tommy was holding the paper thoughtfully. His face burned a deeper red.

"Shall we really try it?" he said at last. "Shall we, Tuppence? Just for the fun of the thing?"

"Tommy, you're a sport! I knew you would be! Let's drink to success." She poured some cold dregs of tea into the two cups.

"Here's to our joint venture, and may it prosper!"

"The Young Adventurers, Ltd.!" responded Tommy.

They put down the cups and laughed rather uncertainly. Tuppence rose.

"I must return it to my palatial suite at the hostel."

"Perhaps it is time I strolled round to the Ritz," agreed Tommy with a grin. "Where shall we meet? And when?"

"Twelve o'clock tomorrow. Piccadilly Tube station. Will that suit you?"

"My time is my own," replied Mr. Beresford magnificently.

"So long, then."

"Good-bye, old thing."

The two young people went off in opposite directions. Tuppence's hostel was situated in what was charitably called Southern Belgravia. For reasons of economy she did not take a bus.

She was halfway across St. James's Park, when a man's voice behind her made her start.

"Excuse me," it said. "But may I speak to you for a moment?"

2

Mr. Whittington's Offer

TUPPENCE TURNED SHARPLY, but the words hovering on the tip of her tongue remained unspoken, for the man's appearance and manner did not bear out her first and most natural assumption. She hesitated. As if he read her thoughts, the man said quickly:

"I can assure you I mean no disrespect."

Tuppence believed him. Although she disliked and distrusted him instinctively, she was inclined to acquit him of the particular motive which she had at first attributed to him. She looked him up and down. He was a big man, clean shaven, with a heavy jowl. His eyes were small and cunning, and shifted their glance under her direct gaze.

"Well, what is it?" she asked.

The man smiled.

"I happened to overhear part of your conversation with the young gentleman in Lyons'."

"Well—what of it?"

"Nothing—except that I think I may be of some use to you."

Another inference forced itself into Tuppence's mind:

"You followed me here?"

"I took that liberty."

"And in what way do you think you could be of use to me?"

The man took a card from his pocket and handed it to her with a bow.

Tuppence took it and scrutinized it carefully. It bore the inscription, "Mr. Edward Whittington." Below the name were the words "Esthonia Glassware Co.," and the address of a city office. Mr. Whittington spoke again:

"If you will call upon me tomorrow morning at eleven o'clock, I will lay the details of my proposition before you."

"At eleven o'clock?" said Tuppence doubtfully.

"At eleven o'clock."

Tuppence made up her mind.

"Very well. I'll be there."

"Thank you. Good evening."

He raised his hat with a flourish, and walked away. Tuppence remained for some minutes gazing after him. Then she gave a curious movement of her shoulders, rather as a terrier shakes himself.

"The adventures have begun," she murmured to herself. "What does he want me to do, I wonder? There's something about you, Mr. Whittington, that I don't like at all. But, on the other hand, I'm not the least bit afraid of you. And as I've said before, and shall doubtless say again, little Tuppence can look after herself, thank you!"

And with a short, sharp nod of her head she walked briskly onward. As a result of further meditations, however, she turned aside from the direct route and entered a post office. There she pondered for some moments, a telegraph form in her hand. The thought of a possible five shillings spent unnecessarily spurred her to action, and she decided to risk the waste of ninepence.

Disdaining the spiky pen and thick, black treacle which a beneficent Government had provided, Tuppence drew out Tommy's pencil which she had retained and wrote rapidly: "Don't put in advertisement. Will explain tomorrow." She addressed it to Tommy at his club, from which in one short month he would have to resign, unless a kindly fortune permitted him to renew his subscription.

"It may catch him," she murmured. "Anyway, it's worth trying."

After handing it over the counter she set out briskly for home, stopping at a baker's to buy three penny-worth of new buns.

Later, in her tiny cubicle at the top of the house she munched buns and reflected on the future. What was the Esthonia Glassware Co., and what earthly need could it have for her services? A pleasurable thrill of excitement made Tuppence tingle. At any rate, the country vicarage had retreated into the background again. The morrow held possibilities.

It was a long time before Tuppence went to sleep that night, and, when at length she did, she dreamed that Mr. Whittington had set her to washing up a pile of Esthonia Glassware, which bore an unaccountable resemblance to hospital plates!

It wanted some five minutes to eleven when Tuppence reached the block of buildings in which the offices of the Esthonia Glassware Co. were situated. To arrive before the time would look over-eager. So Tuppence decided to walk to the end of the street and back again. She did so. On the stroke of eleven she plunged into the recesses of the building. The Esthonia Glassware Co. was on the top floor. There was a lift, but Tuppence chose to walk up.

Slightly out of breath, she came to a halt outside the ground glass door with the legend painted across it "Esthonia Glassware Co."

Tuppence knocked. In response to a voice from within, she turned the handle and walked into a small rather dirty outer office.

A middle-aged clerk got down from a high stool at a desk near the window and came toward her inquiringly.

"I have an appointment with Mr. Whittington," said Tuppence.

"Will you come this way, please." He crossed to a partition door with "Private" on it, knocked, then opened the door and stood aside to let her pass in.

Mr. Whittington was seated behind a large desk covered with papers. Tuppence felt her previous judgment confirmed. There was something wrong about Mr. Whittington. The combination of his sleek prosperity and his shifty eye was not attractive.

He looked up and nodded.

"So you've turned up all right? That's good. Sit down, will you?"

Tuppence sat down on the chair facing him. She looked particularly small and demure this morning. She sat there meekly with downcast eyes whilst Mr. Whittington sorted and rustled amongst his papers. Finally he pushed them away, and leaned over the desk.

"Now, my dear young lady, let us come to business." His large face broadened into a smile. "You want work? Well, I have work to offer you. What should you say now to £100 down, and all expenses paid?" Mr. Whittington leaned back in his chair, and thrust his thumbs into the arm-holes of his waistcoat.

Tuppence eyed him warily.

"And the nature of the work?" she demanded.

"Nominal—purely nominal. A pleasant trip, that is all."

"Where to?"

Mr. Whittington smiled again.

"Paris."

"Oh!" said Tuppence thoughtfully. To herself she said: "Of course, if father heard that he would have a fit! But somehow I don't see Mr. Whittington in the rôle of the gay deceiver."

"Yes," continued Whittington. "What could be more delightful? To put the clock back a few years—a very few, I am sure—and re-enter one of those charming *pensionnats de jeunes filles* with which Paris abounds——"

Tuppence interrupted him.

"A *pensionnat*?"

"Exactly. Madame Colombier's in the Avenue de Neuilly."

Tuppence knew the name well. Nothing could have been more select. She had had several American friends there. She was more than ever puzzled.

"You want me to go to Madame Colombier's? For how long?"

"That depends. Possibly three months."

"And that is all? There are no other conditions?"

"None whatever. You would, of course, go in the character of my ward, and you would hold no communication with your friends. I should have to request absolute secrecy for the time being. By the way, you are English, are you not?"

"Yes."

"Yet you speak with a slight American accent?"

"My great pal in hospital was a little American girl. I dare say I picked it up from her. I can soon get out of it again."

"On the contrary, it might be simpler for you to pass as an American. Details about your past life in England might be more difficult to sustain. Yes, I think that would be decidedly better. Then——"

"One moment, Mr. Whittington! You seem to be taking my consent for granted."

Whittington looked surprised.

"Surely you are not thinking of refusing? I can assure you that Madame Colombier's is a most high-class and orthodox establishment. And the terms are most liberal."

"Exactly," said Tuppence. "That's just it. The terms are almost too liberal, Mr. Whittington. I cannot see any way in which I can be worth that amount of money to you."

"No?" said Whittington softly. "Well, I will tell you. I could doubtless obtain someone else for very much less. What I am willing to pay for is a young lady with sufficient intelligence and presence of mind to sustain her part well, and also one who will have sufficient discretion not to ask too many questions."

Tuppence smiled a little. She felt that Whittington had scored.

"There's another thing. So far there has been no mention of Mr. Beresford. Where does he come in?"

"Mr. Beresford?"

"My partner," said Tuppence with dignity. "You saw us together yesterday."

"Ah, yes. But I'm afraid we shan't require his services."

"Then it's off!" Tuppence rose. "It's both or neither. Sorry—but that's how it is. Good morning, Mr. Whittington."

"Wait a minute. Let us see if something can't be managed. Sit down again, Miss——" He paused interrogatively.

Tuppence's conscience gave her a passing twinge as she remembered the archdeacon. She seized hurriedly on the first name that came into her head.

"Jane Finn," she said hastily; and then paused openmouthed at the effect of those two simple words.

All the geniality had faded out of Whittington's face. It was purple with rage, and the veins stood out on the forehead. And behind it all there lurked a sort of incredulous dismay. He leaned forward and hissed savagely:

"So that's your little game, is it?"

Tuppence, though utterly taken aback, nevertheless kept her head. She had not the faintest comprehension of his meaning, but she was naturally quick-witted, and felt it imperative to "keep her end up" as she phrased it.

Whittington went on:

"Been playing with me, have you, all the time, like a cat and mouse? Knew all the time what I wanted you for, but kept up the comedy. Is that it, eh?" He was cooling down. The red color was ebbing out of his face. He eyed her keenly. "Who's been blabbing? Rita?"

Tuppence shook her head. She was doubtful as to how long she could sustain this illusion, but she realized the importance of not dragging an unknown Rita into it.

"No," she replied with perfect truth. "Rita knows nothing about me."

His eyes still bored into her like gimlets.

"How much do you know?" he shot out.

"Very little indeed," answered Tuppence, and was pleased to note that Whittington's uneasiness was augmented instead of allayed. To have boasted that she knew a lot might have raised doubts in his mind.

"Anyway," snarled Whittington, "you knew enough to come in here and plump out that name."

"It might be my own name," Tuppence pointed out.

"It's likely, isn't it, that there would be two girls with a name like that?"

"Or I might just have hit upon it by chance," continued Tuppence, intoxicated with the success of truthfulness.

Mr. Whittington brought his fist down upon the desk with a bang.

"Quit fooling! How much do you know? And how much do you want?"

The last five words took Tuppence's fancy mightily, especially after a meager breakfast and a supper of buns the night before. Her present part was of the adventuress rather than the adventurous order, but she did not deny its possibilities. She sat up and smiled with the air of one who has the situation thoroughly well in hand.

"My dear Mr. Whittington," she said, "let us by all means lay our cards upon the table. And pray do not be so angry. You heard me say yesterday that I proposed to live by my wits. It seems to me that I have now proved I have some wits to live by! I admit I have knowledge of a certain name, but perhaps my knowledge ends there."

"Yes—and perhaps it doesn't," snarled Whittington.

"You insist on misjudging me," said Tuppence, and sighed gently.

"As I said once before," said Whittington angrily, "quit fooling, and come to the point. You can't play the innocent with me. You know a great deal more than you're willing to admit."

Tuppence paused a moment to admire her own ingenuity, and then said softly:

"I shouldn't like to contradict you, Mr. Whittington."

"So we come to the usual question—how much?"

Tuppence was in a dilemma. So far she had fooled Whittington with complete success, but to mention a palpably impossible sum might awaken his suspicions. An idea flashed across her brain.

"Suppose we say a little something down, and a fuller discussion of the matter later?"

Whittington gave her an ugly glance.

"Blackmail, eh?"

Tuppence smiled sweetly.

"Oh no! Shall we say payment of services in advance?"

Whittington grunted.

"You see," explained Tuppence still sweetly, "I'm so very fond of money!"

"You're about the limit, that's what you are," growled Whittington, with a sort of unwilling admiration. "You took me in all right. Thought you were quite a meek little kid with just enough brains for my purpose."

"Life," moralized Tuppence, "is full of surprises."

"All the same," continued Whittington, "someone's been talking. You say it isn't Rita. Was it——? Oh, come in."

The clerk followed his discreet knock into the room, and laid a paper at his master's elbow.

"Telephone message just come for you, sir."

Whittington snatched it up and read it. A frown gathered on his brow.

"That'll do, Brown. You can go."

The clerk withdrew, closing the door behind him. Whittington turned to Tuppence.

"Come tomorrow at the same time. I'm busy now. Here's fifty to go on with."

He rapidly sorted out some notes, and pushed them across the table to Tuppence, then stood up, obviously impatient for her to go.

The girl counted the notes in a businesslike manner, secured them in her handbag, and rose.

"Good morning, Mr. Whittington," she said politely. "At least, *au revoir*, I should say."

"Exactly, *Au revoir!*" Whittington looked almost genial again, a reversion that aroused in Tuppence a faint misgiving. "*Au revoir*, my clever and charming young lady."

Tuppence sped lightly down the stairs. A wild elation possessed her. A neighboring clock showed the time to be five minutes to twelve.

"Let's give Tommy a surprise!" murmured Tuppence, and hailed a taxi.

The cab drew up outside the tube station. Tommy was just within the entrance. His eyes opened to their fullest extent as he hurried forward to assist Tuppence to alight. She smiled at him affectionately, and remarked in a slightly affected voice:

"Pay the thing, will you, old bean? I've got nothing smaller than a five-pound note!"

3
A Set Back

THE MOMENT WAS not quite so triumphant as it ought to have been. To begin with, the resources of Tommy's pockets were somewhat limited. In the end the fare was managed, the lady recollecting a plebeian twopence, and the driver, still holding the varied assortment of coins in his hand, was prevailed upon to move on, which he did after one last hoarse demand as to what the gentleman thought he was giving him?

"I think you've given him too much, Tommy," said Tuppence innocently. "I fancy he wants to give some of it back."

It was possibly this remark which induced the driver to move away.

"Well," said Mr. Beresford, at length able to relieve his feelings, "what the—dickens, did you want to take a taxi for?"

"I was afraid I might be late and keep you waiting," said Tuppence gently.

"Afraid—you—might—be—late! Oh Lord, I give it up!" said Mr. Beresford.

"And really and truly," continued Tuppence, opening her eyes very wide, "I haven't got anything smaller than a five-pound note."

"You did that part of it very well, old bean, but all the same the fellow wasn't taken in—not for a moment!"

"No!" said Tuppence thoughtfully, "he didn't believe it. That's the curious part about speaking the truth. No one does believe it. I found that out this morning. Now let's go to lunch. How about the Savoy?"

Tommy grinned.

"How about the Ritz?"

"On second thoughts, I prefer the Piccadilly. It's nearer. We shan't have to take another taxi. Come along."

"Is this a new brand of humor? Or is your brain really unhinged?" inquired Tommy.

"Your last supposition is the correct one. I have come into money, and the shock has been too much for me! For that particular form of mental trouble an eminent physician recommends unlimited hors d'œvre, Lobster à l'américane, Chicken Newberg, and Pêche Melba! Let's go and get them!"

"Tuppence, old girl, what has really come over you?"

"Oh, unbelieving one!" Tuppence wrenched open her bag. "Look here, and here, and here!"

"Great Jehosaphat! My dear girl, don't wave Fishers aloft like that!"

"They're not Fishers. They're five times better than Fishers, and this one's ten times better!"

Tommy groaned.

"I must have been drinking unawares! Am I dreaming, Tuppence, or do I really behold a large quantity of five-pound notes being waved about in a dangerous fashion?"

"Even so, O King! *Now*, will you come and have lunch?"

"I'll come anywhere. But what have you been doing? Holding up a bank?"

"All in good time. What an awful place Piccadilly Circus is. There's a huge bus bearing down on us. It would be too terrible if they killed the five-pound notes!"

"Grill room?" inquired Tommy, as they reached the opposite pavement in safety.

"The other's more expensive," demurred Tuppence.

"That's mere wicked wanton extravagance. Come on below."

"Are you sure I can get all the things I want there?"

"That extremely unwholesome menu you were outlining just now? Of course you can—or as much as is good for you, anyway."

"And now tell me," said Tommy, unable to restrain his pent-up curiosity any longer, as they sat in state surrounded by the many hors d'œvre of Tuppence's dreams.

Miss Cowley told him.

"And the curious part of it is," she ended, "that I really did invent the name of Jane Finn! I didn't want to give my own because of poor father—in case I should get mixed up in anything shady."

"Perhaps that's so," said Tommy slowly. "But you didn't invent it."

"What?"

"No. *I* told it to you. Don't you remember, I said yesterday I'd overheard two people talking about a female called Jane Finn? That's what brought the name into your mind so pat."

"So you did. I remember now. How extraordinary——" Tuppence tailed off into silence. Suddenly she aroused herself. "Tommy!"

"Yes?"

"What were they like, the two men you passed?"

Tommy frowned in an effort at remembrance.

"One was a big fat sort of chap. Clean shaven, I think—and dark."

"That's him," cried Tuppence, in an ungrammatical squeal. "That's Whittington! What was the other man like?"

"I can't remember. I didn't notice him particularly. It was really the outlandish name that caught my attention."

"And people say that coincidences don't happen!" Tuppence tackled her Pêche Melba happily.

But Tommy had become serious.

"Look here, Tuppence, old girl, what is this going to lead to?"

"More money," replied his companion.

"I know that. You've only got one idea in your head. What I mean is, what about the next step? How are you going to keep the game up?"

"Oh!" Tuppence laid down her spoon. "You're right, Tommy, it is a bit of a poser."

"After all, you know, you can't bluff him forever. You're sure to slip up sooner or later. And, anyway, I'm not at all sure that it isn't actionable—blackmail, you know."

"Nonsense. Blackmail is saying you'll tell unless you are given money. Now, there's nothing I could tell, because I don't really know anything."

"Hm," said Tommy doubtfully. "Well, anyway, what *are* we going to do? Whittington was in a hurry to get rid of you this morning, but next time he'll want to know something more before he parts with his money. He'll want to know how much *you* know, and where you got your information from, and a lot of other things that you can't cope with. What are you going to do about it?"

Tuppence frowned severely.

"We must think. Order some Turkish coffee, Tommy. Stimulating to the brain. Oh, dear, what a lot I have eaten!"

"You have made rather a hog of yourself! So have I for that matter, but I flatter myself that my choice of dishes was more judicious than yours. Two coffees." (This was to the waiter.) "One Turkish, one French."

Tuppence sipped her coffee with a deeply reflective air, and snubbed Tommy when he spoke to her.

"Be quiet. I'm thinking."

"Shades of Pelmanism!" said Tommy, and relapsed into silence.

"There!" said Tuppence at last. "I've got a plan. Obviously what we've got to do is to find out more about it all."

Tommy applauded.

"Don't jeer. We can only find out through Whittington. We must discover where he lives, what he does—sleuth him, in fact! Now I can't do it, because he knows me, but he only saw you for a minute or two in Lyons'. He's not likely to recognize you. After all, one young man is much like another."

"I repudiate that remark utterly. I'm sure my pleasing features and distinguished appearance would single me out from any crowd."

"My plan is this," Tuppence went on calmly, "I'll go alone tomorrow. I'll put him off again like I did today. It doesn't matter if I don't get any more money at once. Fifty pounds ought to last us a few days."

"Or even longer."

"You'll hang about outside. When I come out I shan't speak to you in case he's watching. But I'll take up my stand somewhere near, and when he comes out of the building I'll drop a handkerchief or something, and off you go!"

"Off I go where?"

"Follow him, of course, silly! What do you think of the idea?"

"Sort of thing one reads about in books. I somehow feel that in real life one will feel a bit of an ass standing in the street for hours with nothing to do. People will wonder what I'm up to."

"Not in the city. Every one's in such a hurry. Probably no one will even notice you at all."

"That's the second time you've made that sort of remark. Never mind, I forgive you. Anyway, it will be rather a lark. What are you doing this afternoon?"

"Well," said Tuppence meditatively. "I *had* thought of hats! Or perhaps silk stockings! Or perhaps——"

"Hold hard," admonished Tommy. "There's a limit to fifty pounds! But let's do dinner and a show tonight at all events."

"Rather."

The day passed pleasantly. The evening even more so. Two of the five-pound notes were now irretrievably dead.

They met by arrangement the following morning and proceeded cityward. Tommy remained on the opposite side of the road while Tuppence plunged into the building.

Tommy strolled slowly down to the end of the street, then back again. Just as he came abreast of the building, Tuppence darted across the road.

"Tommy!"

"Yes. What's up?"

"The place is shut. I can't make anyone hear."

"That's odd."

"Isn't it? Come up with me, and let's try again."

Tommy followed her. As they passed the third floor landing a young clerk came out of an office. He hesitated a moment, then addressed himself to Tuppence.

"Were you wanting the Esthonia Glassware?"

"Yes, please."

"It's closed down. Since yesterday afternoon. Company being wound up, they say. Not that I've ever heard of it myself. But anyway the office is to let."

"Th—thank you," faltered Tuppence. "I suppose you don't know Mr. Whittington's address?"

"Afraid I don't. They left rather suddenly."

"Thank you very much," said Tommy. "Come on, Tuppence."

They descended to the street again where they gazed at one another blankly.

"That's torn it," said Tommy at length.

"And I never suspected it," wailed Tuppence.

"Cheer up, old thing, it can't be helped."

"Can't it, though!" Tuppence's little chin shot out defiantly. "Do you think this is the end? If so, you're wrong. It's just the beginning!"

"The beginning of what?"

"Of our adventure! Tommy, don't you see, if they are scared enough to run away like this, it shows that there must be a lot in this Jane Finn business! Well, we'll get to the bottom of it. We'll run them down! We'll be sleuths in earnest!"

"Yes, but there's no one left to sleuth."

"No, that's why we'll have to start all over again. Lend me that bit of pencil. Thanks. Wait a minute—don't interrupt. There!" Tuppence handed back the pencil, and surveyed the piece of paper on which she had written with a satisfied eye: "What's that?"

"Advertisement."

"You're not going to put that thing in after all?"

"No, it's a different one." She handed him the slip of paper.

Tommy read the words on it aloud:

"WANTED, any information respecting Jane Finn. Apply Y.A."

4
Who Is Jane Finn?

THE NEXT DAY passed slowly. It was necessary to curtail expenditure. Carefully husbanded, forty pounds will last a long time. Luckily the weather was fine, and "walking is cheap," dictated Tuppence. An outlying picture house provided them with recreation for the evening.

The day of disillusionment had been a Wednesday. On Thursday the advertisement had duly appeared. On Friday letters might be expected to arrive at Tommy's rooms.

He had been bound by an honorable promise not to open any such letters if they did arrive, but to repair to the National Gallery, where his colleague would meet him at ten o'clock.

Tuppence was first at the rendezvous. She ensconsed herself on a red velvet seat, and gazed at the Turners with unseeing eyes until she saw the familiar figure enter the room.

"Well?"

"Well," returned Mr. Beresford provokingly. "Which is your favorite picture?"

"Don't be a wretch. Aren't there *any* answers?"

Tommy shook his head with a deep and somewhat overacted melancholy.

"I didn't want to disappoint you, old thing, by telling you right off. It's too bad. Good money wasted." He sighed. "Still, there it is. The advertisement has appeared, and—there are only two answers!"

"Tommy, you devil!" almost screamed Tuppence. "Give them to me. How could you be so mean!"

"Your language, Tuppence, your language! They're very particular at the National Gallery. Government show, you know. And do remember, as I have pointed out to you before, that as a clergyman's daughter——"

"I ought to be on the stage!" finished Tuppence with a snap.

"That is not what I intended to say. But if you are sure that you have enjoyed to the full the reaction of joy after despair with which I have kindly provided you free of charge, let us get down to our mail, as the saying goes."

Tuppence snatched the two precious envelopes from him unceremoniously, and scrutinized them carefully.

"Thick paper, this one. It looks rich. We'll keep it to the last and open the other first."

"Right you are. One, two, three, go!"

Tuppence's little thumb ripped open the envelope, and she extracted the contents.

"DEAR SIR,

"Referring to your advertisement in this morning's paper, I may be able to be of some use to you. Perhaps you could call and see me at the above address at eleven o'clock tomorrow morning.

"Yours truly,
"A. CARTER."

"27 Carshalton Gardens," said Tuppence, referring to the address. "That's Gloucester Road way. Plenty of time to get there if we tube."

"The following," said Tommy, "is the plan of campaign. It is my turn to assume the offensive. Ushered into the presence of Mr. Carter, he and I wish each other good morning as is customary. He then says: 'Please take a seat, Mr.—er?' To which I reply promptly and significantly: 'Edward Whittington!' whereupon Mr. Carter turns purple in the face and gasps out: 'How much?' Pocketing the usual fee of fifty pounds, I rejoin you in the road outside, and we proceed to the next address and repeat the performance."

"Don't be absurd, Tommy. Now for the other letter. Oh, this is from the Ritz!"

"A hundred pounds instead of fifty!"

"I'll read it:

"DEAR SIR,

"Re your advertisement, I should be glad if you would call round somewhere about lunchtime.

"YOURS TRULY,
"JULIUS P. HERSHEIMMER."

"Ha!" said Tommy. "Do I smell a Boche? Or only an American millionaire of unfortunate ancestry? At all events we'll call at lunchtime. It's a good time—frequently leads to free food for two."

Tuppence nodded assent.

"Now for Carter. We'll have to hurry."

Carshalton Terrace proved to be an unimpeachable row of what Tuppence called "ladylike looking houses." They rang the bell at No. 27, and a neat maid answered the door. She looked so respectable that Tuppence's heart sank. Upon Tommy's request for Mr. Carter, she showed them into a small study on the ground floor where she left them. Hardly a minute elapsed, however, before the door opened, and a tall man with a lean hawklike face and a tired manner entered the room.

"Mr. Y. A.?" he said, and smiled. His smile was distinctly attractive. "Do sit down, both of you."

They obeyed. He himself took a chair opposite to Tuppence and smiled at her encouragingly. There was something in the quality of his smile that made the girl's usual readiness desert her.

As he did not seem inclined to open the conversation, Tuppence was forced to begin.

"We wanted to know—that is, would you be so kind as to tell us anything you know about Jane Finn?"

"Jane Finn? Ah!" Mr. Carter appeared to reflect. "Well, the question is, what do *you* know about her?"

Tuppence drew herself up.

"I don't see that that's got anything to do with it."

"No? But it has, you know, really it has." He smiled again in his tired way, and continued reflectively. "So that brings us down to it again. What do *you* know about Jane Finn?

"Come now," he continued, as Tuppence remained silent. "You must know *something* to have advertised as you did?" He leaned forward a little, his weary voice held a hint of persuasiveness. "Suppose you tell me. . . ."

There was something very magnetic about Mr. Carter's personality. Tuppence seemed to shake herself free of it with an effort, as she said:

"We couldn't do that, could we, Tommy?"

But to her surprise, her companion did not back her up. His eyes were fixed on Mr. Carter, and his tone when he spoke held an unusual note of deference.

"I dare say the little we know won't be any good to you, sir. But such as it is, you're welcome to it."

"Tommy!" cried out Tuppence in surprise.

Mr. Carter slewed round in his chair. His eyes asked a question.

Tommy nodded.

"Yes, sir, I recognized you at once. Saw you in France when I was with the Intelligence. As soon as you came into the room, I knew——"

Mr. Carter held up his hand.

"No names, please. I'm known as Mr. Carter here. It's my cousin's house, by the way. She's willing to lend it to me sometimes when it's a case of working on strictly unoffical lines. Well, now"—he looked from one to the other—"who's going to tell me the story?"

"Fire ahead, Tuppence," directed Tommy. "It's your yarn."

"Yes, little lady, out with it."

And obediently Tuppence did out with it, telling the whole story from the forming of the Young Adventurers Ltd., downward.

Mr. Carter listened in silence with a resumption of his tired manner. Now and then he passed his hand across his lips as though to hide a smile. When she had finished he nodded gravely.

"Not much. But suggestive. Quite suggestive. If you'll excuse my saying so, you're a curious young couple. I don't know—you might succeed where others have failed. . . . I believe in luck, you know—always have. . . ."

He paused a moment, and then went on.

"Well, how about it? You're out for adventure. How would you like to work for me? All quite unofficial, you know. Expenses paid, and a moderate screw?"

Tuppence gazed at him, her lips parted, her eyes growing wider and wider.

"What should we have to do?" she breathed.

Mr. Carter smiled.

"Just go on with what you're doing now. *Find Jane Finn.*"

"Yes, but—who *is* Jane Finn?"

Mr. Carter nodded gravely.

"Yes, you're entitled to know that, I think."

He leaned back in his chair, crossed his legs, brought the tips of his fingers together, and began in a low monotone:

"Secret diplomacy (which, by the way, is nearly always bad policy!) does not concern you. It will be sufficient to say that in the early days of 1915 a certain document came into being. It was the draft of a secret agreement—treaty—call it what you like. It was drawn up ready for signature by the various representatives, and drawn up in America—at that time a neutral country. It was dispatched to England by a special messenger selected for that purpose, a young fellow called Danvers. It was hoped that the whole affair had been kept so secret that nothing would have leaked out. That kind of hope is usually disappointed. Somebody always talks!

"Danvers sailed for England on the *Lusitania*. He carried the precious papers in an oilskin packet which he wore next his skin. It was on that particular voyage that the *Lusitania* was torpedoed and sunk. Danvers was among the list of those missing. Eventually his body was washed ashore, and identified beyond any possible doubt. But the oilskin packet was missing!

"The question was, had it been taken from him, or had he himself passed it on into another's keeping? There were a few incidents that strengthened the possibility of the latter theory. After the torpedo struck the ship, in a few moments during the launching of the boats, Danvers was seen speaking to a young American girl. No one actually saw him pass anything to her, but he might have done so. It seems to me quite likely that he entrusted the papers to this girl, believing that she, as a woman, had a greater chance of bringing them safely to shore.

"But if so, where was the girl, and what had she done with the papers? By later advice from America it seemed likely that Danvers had been closely shadowed on the way over. Was this girl in league with his enemies? Or had she, in her turn, been shadowed and either tricked or forced into handing over the precious packet?

"We set to work to trace her out. It proved unexpectedly difficult. Her name was Jane Finn, and it duly appeared among the list of the survivors, but the girl herself seemed to have vanished completely. Inquiries into her antecedents did little to help us. She was an orphan, and had been what we should call over here a pupil teacher in a small school out West. Her passport had been made out for Paris, where she was going to join the staff of a hospital. She had offered her services voluntarily, and after some correspondence they had been accepted. Having seen her name in the list of the saved from the *Lusitania*, the staff of the hospital were naturally very surprised at her not arriving to take up her billet, and at not hearing from her in any way.

"Well, every effort was made to trace the young lady—but all in vain. We tracked her across Ireland, but nothing could be heard of her after she set foot in England. No use was made of the draft treaty—as might very easily have been done—and we therefore came to the conclusion that Danvers had, after all, destroyed it. The war entered on another phase, the diplomatic aspect changed accordingly, and the treaty was never redrafted. Rumours as to its existence were emphatically denied. The disappearance of Jane Finn was forgotten and the whole affair was lost in oblivion."

Mr. Carter paused, and Tuppence broke in impatiently:

"But why has it all cropped up again? The war's over."

A hint of alertness came into Mr. Carter's manner.

"Because it seems that the papers were not destroyed after all, and that they might be resurrected today with a new and deadly significance."

Tuppence stared. Mr. Carter nodded.

"Yes, five years ago, that draft treaty was a weapon in our hands; today it is a weapon against us. It was a gigantic blunder. If its terms were made public, it would mean disaster . . . It might possibly bring about another war—not with Germany this time! That is an extreme possibility, and I do not believe in its likelihood myself, but that document undoubtedly implicates a number of our statesmen whom we cannot afford to have discredited in any way at the present moment. As a party cry for Labour it would be irresistible, and a Labour Government at this juncture would, in my opinion, be a grave disability for British trade, but that is a mere nothing to the *real* danger."

He paused, and then said quietly.

"You may perhaps have heard or read that there is Bolshevist influence at work behind the present labour unrest?"

Tuppence nodded.

"That is the truth. Bolshevist gold is pouring into this country for the specific purpose of procuring a Revolution. And there is a certain man, a man whose real name is unknown to us, who is working in the dark for his own ends. The Bolsheviks are behind the labour unrest—but this man is *behind the Bolshevists*. Who is he? We do not know. He is always spoken of by the unassuming title of 'Mr. Brown.' But one thing is certain, he is the master criminal of this age. He controls a marvelous organization. Most of the Peace propaganda during the war was originated and financed by him. His spies are everywhere."

"A naturalized German?" asked Tommy.

"On the contrary, I have every reason to believe he is an Englishman. He was pro-German, as he would have been pro-Boer. What he seeks to attain we do not know—probably supreme power for himself, of a kind unique in history. We have no clue as to his real personality. It is reported that even his own followers are ignorant of it. Where we have come across his tracks, he has always played a secondary part. Somebody else assumes the chief role. But afterward we always find that there has been some nonentity, a servant or a clerk, who has remained in the background unnoticed, and that the elusive Mr. Brown has escaped us once more."

"Oh!" Tuppence jumped. "I wonder——"

"Yes?"

"I remember in Mr. Whittington's office. The clerk—he called him Brown. You don't think——"

Carter nodded thoughtfully.

"Very likely. A curious point is that the name is usually mentioned. An idiosyncrasy of genius. Can you describe him at all?"

"I really didn't notice. He was quite ordinary—just like anyone else."

Mr. Carter sighed in his tired manner.

"That is the invariable description of Mr. Brown! Brought a telephone message to the man Whittington, did he? Notice a telephone in the outer office?"

Tuppence thought.

"No, I don't think I did."

"Exactly. That 'message' was Mr. Brown's way of giving an order to his subordinate. He overheard the whole conversation of course. Was it after that that Whittington handed you over the money, and told you to come the following day?"

Tuppence nodded.

"Yes, undoubtedly the hand of Mr. Brown!" Mr. Carter paused. "Well, there it is, you see what you are pitting yourselves against? Possibly the finest criminal brain of the age. I don't quite like it, you know. You're such young things, both of you. I shouldn't like anything to happen to you."

"It won't," Tuppence assured him positively.

"I'll look after her, sir," said Tommy.

"And *I'll* look after *you*," retorted Tuppence, resenting the manly assertion.

"Well, then, look after each other," said Mr. Carter, smiling. "Now let's get back to business. There's something mysterious about this draft treaty that we haven't fathomed yet. We've been threatened with it—in plain and unmistakable terms. The Revolutionary element as good as declare that it's in their hands, and that they intend to produce it at a given moment. On the other hand, they are clearly at fault about many of its provisions. The Government consider it as mere bluff on their part, and, rightly or wrongly, have stuck to the policy of absolute denial. I'm not so sure. There have been hints, indiscreet allusions, that seem to indicate that the menace is a real one. The position is much as though they had got hold of an incriminating document, but couldn't read it because it was in cipher—but we know that the draft treaty wasn't in cipher—couldn't be in the nature of things—so that won't wash. But there's *something*. Of course, Jane Finn may be dead for all we know—but I don't think so. The curious thing is *they're trying to get information about the girl from us*."

"What?"

"Yes. One or two little things have cropped up. And your story, little lady, confirms my idea. They know we're looking for Jane Finn. Well, they'll produce a Jane Finn of their own—say at a *pensionnat* in Paris." Tuppence gasped, and Mr. Carter smiled. "No one knows in the least what she looks like, so that's all right. She's primed with a trumped-up tale, and her real business is to get as much information as possible out of us. See the idea?"

"Then you think"—Tuppence paused to grasp the supposition fully—"that it *was* as Jane Finn that they wanted me to go to Paris?"

Mr. Carter smiled more wearily than ever.

"I believe in coincidences, you know," he said.

5
Mr. Julius P. Hersheimmer

"WELL," SAID TUPPENCE, recovering herself, "it really seems as though it were meant to be."

Carter nodded.

"I know what you mean. I'm superstitious myself. Luck, and all that sort of thing. Fate seems to have chosen you out to be mixed up in this."

Tommy indulged in a chuckle.

"My word! I don't wonder Whittington got the wind up when Tuppence plumped out that name! I should have myself. But look here, sir, we're taking up an awful lot of your time. Have you any tips to give us before we clear out?"

"I think not. My experts, working in stereotyped ways, have failed. You will bring imagination and an open mind to the task. Don't be discouraged if that too does not succeed. For one thing there is a likelihood of the pace being forced."

Tuppence frowned uncomprehendingly.

"When you had that interview with Whittington, they had time before them. I have information that the big *coup* was planned for early in the new year. But the Government is contemplating legislative action which will deal effectually with the strike menace. They'll get wind of it soon, if they haven't already, and it's possible that they may bring things to a head. I hope it will myself. The less time they have to mature their plans the better. I'm just warning you that you haven't much time before you, and that you needn't be cast down if you fail. It's not an easy proposition anyway. That's all."

Tuppence rose.

"I think we ought to be businesslike. What exactly can we count upon you for, Mr. Carter?"

Mr. Carter's lips twitched slightly, but he replied succinctly:

"Funds within reason, detailed information on any point, and *no official recognition*. I mean that if you get yourselves into trouble with the police, I can't officially help you out of it. You're on your own."

Tuppence nodded sagely.

"I quite understand that. I'll write out a list of the things I want to know when I've had time to think. Now—about money——"

"Yes, Miss Tuppence. Do you want to say how much?"

"Not exactly. We've got plenty to go with for the present, but when we want more——"

"It will be waiting for you."

"Yes, but—I'm sure I don't want to be rude about the Government if you've got anything to do with it, but you know one really has the devil of a time getting anything out of it! And if we have to fill up a blue form and send it in, and then, after three months, they send us a green one, and so on—well, that won't be much use, will it?"

Mr. Carter laughed outright.

"Don't worry, Miss Tuppence. You will send a personal demand to me here, and the money, in notes, shall be sent by return of post. As to salary, shall we say at the rate of three hundred a year? And an equal sum for Mr. Beresford, of course."

Tuppence beamed upon him.

"How lovely. You are kind. I do love money! I'll keep beautiful accounts of our expenses—all debit and credit, and the balance on the right side, and a red line drawn sideways with the totals the same at the bottom. I really know how to do it when I think."

"I'm sure you do. Well, goodbye, and good luck to you both."

He shook hands with them, and in another minute they were descending the steps of 27 Carshalton Terrace with their heads in a whirl.

"Tommy! Tell me at once, who is 'Mr. Carter?'"

Tommy murmured a name in her ear.

"Oh!" said Tuppence, impressed.

"And I can tell you, old bean, he's IT!"

"Oh!" said Tuppence again. Then she added reflectively. "I like him, don't you? He looks so awfully tired and bored, and yet you feel that underneath he's just like steel, all keen and flashing. Oh!" She gave a skip. "Pinch me, Tommy, do pinch me. I can't believe it's real!"

Mr. Beresford obliged.

"Ow! That's enough! Yes, we're not dreaming. We've got a job!"

"And what a job! The joint venture has really begun."

"It's more respectable than I thought it would be," said Tuppence thoughtfully.

"Luckily I haven't got your craving for crime! What time is it? Let's have lunch—oh!"

The same thought sprang to the minds of each. Tommy voiced it first.

"Julius P. Hersheimmer!"

"We never told Mr. Carter about hearing from him."

"Well, there wasn't much to tell—not till we've seen him. Come on, we'd better take a taxi."

"Now who's being extravagant?"

"All expenses paid, remember. Hop in."

"At any rate, we shall make a better effect arriving this way," said Tuppence, leaning back luxuriously. "I'm sure blackmailers never arrive in buses!"

"We've ceased being blackmailers," Tommy pointed out.

"I'm not sure I have," said Tuppence darkly.

On inquiring for Mr. Hersheimmer, they were at once taken up to his suite. An impatient voice cried "Come in" in answer to the page boy's knock, and the lad stood aside to let them pass in.

Mr. Julius P. Hersheimmer was a great deal younger than either Tommy or Tuppence had pictured him. The girl put him down as thirty-five. He was of middle height, and squarely built to match his jaw. His face was pugnacious but pleasant. No one could have mistaken him for anything but an American, though he spoke with very little accent.

"Get my note? Sit down and tell me right away all you know about my cousin."

"Your cousin?"

"Sure thing. Jane Finn."

"Is she your cousin?"

"My father and her mother were brother and sister," explained Mr. Hersheimmer meticulously.

"Oh!" cried Tuppence. "Then you know where she is?"

"No!" Mr. Hersheimmer brought down his fist with a bang on the table. "I'm darned if I do! Don't you?"

"We advertised to receive information, not to give it," said Tuppence severely.

"I guess I know that. I can read. But I thought maybe it was her back history you were after, and that you'd know where she was now?"

"Well, we wouldn't mind hearing her back history," said Tuppence guardedly.

But Mr. Hersheimmer seemed to grow suddenly suspicious.

"See here," he declared. "This isn't Sicily! No demanding ransom or threatening to crop her ears if I refuse. These are the British Isles, so quit the funny business, or I'll just sing out for that beautiful big British policeman I see out there in Piccadilly."

Tommy hastened to explain.

"We haven't kidnapped your cousin. On the contrary, we're trying to find her. We're employed to do so."

Mr. Hersheimmer leant back in his chair.

"Put me wise," he said succinctly.

Tommy fell in with this demand in so far as he gave him a guarded version of the disappearance of Jane Finn, and of the possibility of her having been mixed up unawares in "some political show." He alluded to Tuppence and himself as "private inquiry agents" commissioned to find her, and added that they would therefore be glad of any details Mr. Hersheimmer could give them.

That gentleman nodded approval.

"I guess that's all right. I was just a mite hasty. But London gets my goat! I only know little old New York. Just trot out your questions and I'll answer."

For the moment this paralyzed the Young Adventurers, but Tuppence, recovering herself, plunged boldly into the breach with a reminiscence culled from detective fiction.

"When did you last see the dece—your cousin, I mean?"

"Never seen her," responded Mr. Hersheimmer.

"What?" demanded Tommy, astonished.

Hersheimmer turned to him.

"No, sir. As I said before, my father and her mother were brother and sister, just as you might be"—Tommy did not correct this view of their relationship—"but they didn't always get on together. And when my aunt made up her mind to marry Amos Finn, who was a poor schoolteacher out West, my father was just mad! Said if he made his pile, as he seemed in a fair way to do, she'd never see a cent of it. Well, the upshot was that Aunt Jane went out West and we never heard from her again.

"The old man *did* pile it up. He went into oil, and he went into steel, and he played a bit with railroads, and I can tell you he made Wall Street sit up!" He paused. "Then he died—last fall—and I got the dollars. Well, would you believe it, my conscience got busy! Kept knocking me up and saying: What about your Aunt Jane, way out West? It worried me some. You see, I figured it out that Amos Finn would never make good. He wasn't the sort. End of it was, I hired a man to hunt her down. Result, she was dead, and Amos Finn was dead, but they'd left a daughter—Jane—who'd been torpedoed in the *Lusitania* on her way to Paris. She was saved alright, but they didn't seem able to hear of her over this side. I guessed they weren't hustling any, so I thought I'd come along over, and speed things up. I phoned Scotland Yard and the Admiralty first thing. The Admiralty rather choked me off, but Scotland Yard were very civil—said they would make inquiries, even sent a man round this morning to get her photograph. I'm off to Paris tomorrow, just to see what the Prefecture is doing. I guess if I go to and fro hustling them, they ought to get busy!"

The energy of Mr. Hersheimmer was tremendous. They bowed before it.

"But say now," he ended, "you're not after her for anything? Contempt of court, or something British? A proud-spirited young American girl might find your rules and regulations in war time rather irksome, and get up against it. If that's the case, and there's such a thing as graft in this country, I'll buy her off."

Tuppence reassured him.

"That's good. Then we can work together. What about some lunch? Shall we have it up here, or go down to the restaurant?"

Tuppence expressed a preference for the latter, and Julius bowed to her decision.

Oysters had just given place to Sole Colbert when a card was brought to Hersheimmer.

"Inspector Japp, C.I.D. Scotland Yard again. Another man this time. What does he expect I can tell him that I didn't tell the first chap? I hope they haven't lost that photograph. That Western photographer's place was burned down and all his negatives destroyed—this is the only copy in existence. I got it from the principal of the college there."

An unformulated dread swept over Tuppence.

"You—you don't know the name of the man who came this morning?"

"Yes, I do. No, I don't. Half a second. It was on his card. Oh, I know! Inspector Brown. Quiet, unassuming sort of chap."

6
A Plan of Campaign

A VEIL MIGHT with profit be drawn over the events of the next half-hour. Suffice it to say that no such person as "Inspector Brown" was known to Scotland Yard. The photograph of Jane Finn, which would have been of the utmost value to the police in tracing her, was lost beyond recovery. Once again "Mr. Brown" had triumphed.

The immediate result of this setback was to effect a *rapprochement* between Julius Hersheimmer and the Young Adventurers. All barriers went down with a crash, and Tommy and Tuppence felt they had known the young American all their lives. They abandoned the discreet reticence of "private inquiry agents," and revealed to him the whole history of the joint venture, whereat the young man declared himself "tickled to death."

He turned to Tuppence at the close of the narration.

"I've always had a kind of idea that English girls were just a mite moss-grown. Old-fashioned and sweet, you know, but scared to move round without a footman or a maiden aunt. I guess I'm a bit behind the times!"

The upshot of these confidential relations was that Tommy and Tuppence took up their abode forthwith at the Ritz, in order, as Tuppence put it, to keep in touch with Jane Finn's only living relation. "And put like that," she added confidentially to Tommy, "nobody could boggle at the expense!"

Nobody did, which was the great thing.

"And now," said the young lady on the morning after their installation, "to work!"

Mr. Beresford put down the *Daily Mail*, which he was reading, and applauded with somewhat unnecessary vigor. He was politely requested by his colleague not to be an ass.

"Dash it all, Tommy, we've got to *do* something for our money."

Tommy sighed.

"Yes, I fear even the dear old Government will not support us at the Ritz in idleness for ever."

"Therefore, as I said before, we must *do* something."

"Well," said Tommy, picking up the *Daily Mail* again, "*do* it. I shan't stop you."

"You see," continued Tuppence. "I've been thinking——"

She was interrupted by a fresh bout of applause.

"It's all very well for you to sit there being funny, Tommy. It would do you no harm to do a little brain work too."

"My union, Tuppence, my union! It does not permit me to work before 11 A.M."

"Tommy, do you want something thrown at you? It is absolutely essential that we should without delay map out a plan of campaign."

"Hear, hear!"

"Well, let's do it."

Tommy laid his paper finally aside. "There's something of the simplicity of the truly great mind about you, Tuppence. Fire ahead. I'm listening."

"To begin with," said Tuppence, "what have we to go upon?"

"Absolutely nothing," said Tommy cheerily.

"Wrong!" Tuppence wagged an energetic finger. "We have two distinct clues."

"What are they?"

"First clue, we know one of the gang."

"Whittington?"

"Yes. I'd recognize him anywhere."

"Hum," said Tommy doubtfully, "I don't call that much of a clue. You don't know where to look for him, and it's about a thousand to one against your running against him by accident."

"I'm not so sure about that," replied Tuppence thoughtfully. "I've often noticed that once coincidences start happening they go on happening in the most extraordinary way. I dare say it's some natural law that we haven't found out. Still, as you say, we can't rely on that. But there *are* places in London where simply everyone is bound to turn up sooner or later. Piccadilly Circus, for instance. One of my ideas was to take up my stand there every day with a tray of flags."

"What about meals?" inquired the practical Tommy.

"How like a man! What does mere food matter?"

"That's all very well. You've just had a thundering good breakfast. No one's got a better appetite than you have, Tuppence, and by teatime you'd be eating the flags, pins and all. But, honestly, I don't think much of the idea. Whittington mayn't be in London at all."

"That's true. Anyway, I think clue No. 2 is more promising."

"Let's hear it."

"It's nothing much. Only a Christian name—Rita. Whittington mentioned it that day."

"Are you proposing a third advertisement: Wanted, female crook, answering to the name of Rita?"

"I am not. I propose to reason in a logical manner. That man, Danvers, was shadowed on the way over, wasn't he? And it's more likely to have been a woman than a man——"

"I don't see that at all."

"I am absolutely certain that it would be a woman, and a good-looking one," replied Tuppence calmly.

"On these technical points I bow to your decision," murmured Mr. Beresford.

"Now, obviously this woman, whoever she was, was saved."

"How do you make that out?"

"If she wasn't, how would they have known Jane Finn had got the papers?"

"Correct. Proceed, O Sherlock!"

"Now there's just a chance, I admit it's only a chance, that this woman may have been 'Rita.'"

"And if so?"

"If so, we've got to hunt through the survivors of the *Lusitania* till we find her."

"Then the first thing is to get a list of the survivors."

"I've got it. I wrote a long list of things I wanted to know, and sent it to Mr. Carter. I got his reply this morning, and among other things it encloses the official statement of those saved from the *Lusitania*. How's that for clever little Tuppence?"

"Full marks for industry, zero for modesty. But the great point is, is there a 'Rita' on the list?"

"That's just what I don't know," confessed Tuppence.

"Don't know?"

"Yes. Look here." Together they bent over the list. "You see, very few Christian names are given. They're nearly all Mrs. or Miss."

Tommy nodded.

"That complicates matters," he murmured thoughtfully.

Tuppence gave her characteristic "terrier" shake.

"Well, we've just got to get down to it, that's all. We'll start with the London area. Just note down the addresses of any of the females who live in London or roundabout, while I put on my hat."

Five minutes later the young couple emerged into Piccadilly, and a few seconds later a taxi was bearing them to The Laurels, Glendower Road, N.7, the residence of Mrs. Edgar Keith, whose name figured first in a list of seven reposing in Tommy's pocketbook.

The Laurels was a dilapidated house, standing back from the road with a few grimy bushes to support the fiction of a front garden. Tommy paid off the taxi, and accompanied Tuppence to the front door bell. As she was about to ring it, he arrested her hand.

"What are you going to say?"

"What am I going to say? Why, I shall say—Oh dear, I don't know. It's very awkward."

"I thought as much," said Tommy with satisfaction. "How like a woman! No foresight! Now just stand aside, and see how easily the mere male deals with the situation." He pressed the bell. Tuppence withdrew to a suitable spot.

A slatternly-looking servant, with an extremely dirty face and a pair of eyes that did not match, answered the door.

Tommy had produced a notebook and pencil.

"Good morning," he said briskly and cheerfully. "From the Hampstead Borough Council. The new Voting Register. Mrs. Edgar Keith lives here, does she not?"

"Yaas," said the servant.

"Christian name?" asked Tommy, his pencil, poised.

"Missus's? Eleanor Jane."

"Eleanor," spelt Tommy. "Any sons or daughters over twenty-one?"

"Naow."

"Thank you." Tommy closed the notebook with a brisk snap. "Good morning."

The servant volunteered her first remark:

"I thought perhaps as you'd come about the gas," she observed cryptically, and shut the door.

Tommy rejoined his accomplice.

"You see, Tuppence," he observed. "Child's play to the masculine mind."

"I don't mind admitting that for once you've scored handsomely. I should never have thought of that."

"Good wheeze, wasn't it? And we can repeat it ad lib."

Lunchtime found the young couple attacking a steak and chips in an obscure hostelry with avidity. They had collected a Gladys Mary and a Marjorie, been baffled by one change of address, and had been forced to listen to a long lecture on universal suffrage from a vivacious American lady whose Christian name had proved to be Sadie.

"Ah!" said Tommy, imbibing a long draught of beer, "I feel better. Where's the next draw?"

The notebook lay on the table between them. Tuppence picked it up.

"Mrs. Vandemeyer," she read, "20 South Audley Mansions. Miss Wheeler, 43 Clapington Road, Battersea. She's a lady's maid, as far as I remember, so probably won't be there, and, anyway, she's not likely."

"Then the Mayfair lady is clearly indicated as the first port of call."

"Tommy, I'm getting discouraged."

"Buck up, old bean. We always knew it was an outside chance. And, anyway, we're only starting. If we draw a blank in London, there's a fine tour of England, Ireland and Scotland before us."

"True," said Tuppence, her flagging spirits reviving. "And all expenses paid! But, oh, Tommy, I do like things to happen quickly. So far, adventure has succeeded adventure, but this morning has been dull as dull."

"You must stifle this longing for vulgar sensation, Tuppence. Remember that if Mr. Brown is all he is reported to be, it's a wonder that he has not ere now done us to death. That's a good sentence, quite a literary flavor about it."

"You're really more conceited than I am—with less excuse! Ahem! But it certainly is queer that Mr. Brown has not yet wreaked vengeance upon us. (You see, I can do it too.) We pass on our way unscathed."

"Perhaps he doesn't think us worth bothering about," suggested the young man simply.

Tuppence received the remark with great disfavor.

"How horrid you are, Tommy. Just as though we didn't count."

"Sorry, Tuppence. What I meant was that we work like moles in the dark, and that he has no suspicion of our nefarious schemes. Ha ha!"

"Ha ha!" echoed Tuppence approvingly, as she rose.

South Audley Mansions was an imposing looking block of flats just off Park Lane. No. 20 was on the second floor.

Tommy had by this time the glibness born of practice. He rattled off the formula to the elderly woman, looking more like a housekeeper than a servant, who opened the door to him.

"Christian name?"

"Margaret."

Tommy spelt it, but the other interrupted him.

"No, *gue*."

"Oh, Marguerite; French way, I see." He paused, then plunged boldly. "We had her down as Rita Vandemeyer, but I suppose that's incorrect?"

"She's mostly called that, sir, but Marguerite's her name."

"Thank you. That's all. Good morning."

Hardly able to contain his excitement, Tommy hurried down the stairs. Tuppence was waiting at the angle of the turn.

"You heard?"

"Yes. Oh, *Tommy!*"

Tommy squeezed her arm sympathetically.

"I know, old thing. I feel the same."

"It's—it's so lovely to think of things—and then for them really to happen!" cried Tuppence enthusiastically.

Her hand was still in Tommy's. They had reached the entrance hall. There were footsteps on the stairs above them, and voices.

Suddenly, to Tommy's complete surprise, Tuppence dragged him into the little space by the side of the lift where the shadow was deepest.

"What the——"

"Hush!"

Two men came down the stairs and passed out through the entrance. Tuppence's hand closed tighter on Tommy's arm.

"Quick—follow them. I daren't. He might recognize me. I don't know who the other man is, but the bigger of the two was Whittington."

7

The House in Soho

WHITTINGTON AND HIS companion were walking at a good pace. Tommy started in pursuit at once, and was in time to see them turn the corner of the street. His vigorous strides soon enabled him to gain upon them, and by the time he, in his turn, reached the corner the distance between them was sensibly lessened. The small Mayfair streets were comparatively deserted, and he judged it wise to content himself with keeping them in sight.

The sport was a new one to him. Though familiar with the technicalities from a course of novel reading, he had never before attempted to "follow" anyone, and it appeared to him at once that, in actual practice, the proceeding was fraught with difficulties. Supposing, for instance, that they should suddenly hail a taxi? In books, you simply leapt into another, promised the driver a sovereign—or its modern equivalent—and there you were. In actual fact, Tommy foresaw that it was extremely likely there would be no second taxi. Therefore he would have to run. What happened in actual fact to a young man who ran incessantly and persistently through the London streets? In a main road he might hope to create the illusion that he was merely running for a bus. But in these obscure aristocratic byways he could not but feel that an officious policeman might stop him to explain matters.

At this juncture in his thoughts a taxi with flag erect turned the corner of the street ahead. Tommy held his breath. Would they hail it?

He drew a sigh of relief as they allowed it to pass unchallenged. Their course was a zigzag one designed to bring them as quickly as possible to Oxford Street. When at length they turned into it, proceeding in an easterly direction, Tommy slightly increased his pace. Little by little he gained upon them. On the crowded pavement there was little chance of his attracting their notice, and he was anxious if possible to catch a word or two of their conversation. In this he was completely foiled; they spoke low and the din of the traffic drowned their voices effectually.

Just before the Bond Street Tube station they crossed the road, Tommy, unperceived, faithfully at their heels, and entered the big Lyons'. There they went up to the first floor, and sat at a small table in the window. It was late, and the place was thinning out. Tommy took a seat at the table next to them, sitting directly behind Whittington in case of recognition. On the other hand, he had a full view of the second man and studied him attentively. He was fair, with a weak, unpleasant face, and Tommy put him down as being either a Russian or a Pole. He was probably about fifty years of age, his shoulders cringed a little as he talked, and his eyes, small and crafty, shifted unceasingly.

Having already lunched heartily, Tommy contented himself with ordering a Welsh rarebit and a cup of coffee. Whittington ordered a substantial lunch for himself and his companion; then, as the waitress withdrew, he moved his chair a little closer to the table and began to talk earnestly in a low voice. The other man joined in. Listen as he would, Tommy could only catch a word here and there; but the gist of it seemed to be some directions or orders which the big man was impressing on his companion, and with which the latter seemed from time to time to disagree. Whittington addressed the other as Boris.

Tommy caught the word "Ireland" several times, also "propaganda," but of Jane Finn there was no mention. Suddenly, in a lull in the clatter of the room, he got one phrase entire. Whittington was speaking. "Ah, but you don't know Flossie. She's a marvel. An archbishop would swear she was his own mother. She gets the voice right every time, and that's really the principal thing."

Tommy did not hear Boris's reply, but in response to it Whittington said something that sounded like: "Of course—only in an emergency. . . ."

Then he lost the thread again. But presently the phrases became distinct again whether because the other two had insensibly raised their voices, or because Tommy's ears were getting more attuned, he could not tell. But two words certainly had a most stimulating effect upon the listener. They were uttered by Boris and they were: "Mr. Brown."

Whittington seemed to remonstrate with him, but he merely laughed.

"Why not, my friend? It is a name most respectable—most common. Did he not choose it for that reason? Ah, I should like to meet him—Mr. Brown."

There was a steely ring in Whittington's voice as he replied:

"Who knows? You may have met him already."

"Bah!" retorted the other. "That is children's talk—a fable for the police. Do you know what I say to myself sometimes? That he is a fable invented by the Inner Ring, a bogy to frighten us with. It might be so."

"And it might not."

"I wonder . . . or is it indeed true that he is with us and amongst us, unknown to all but a chosen few? If so, he keeps his secret well. And the idea is a good one, yes. We never know. We look at each other—*one of us is Mr. Brown*—which? He commands—but also he serves. Among us—in the midst of us. And no one knows which he is. . . ."

With an effort the Russian shook off the vagary of his fancy. He looked at his watch.

"Yes," said Whittington. "We might as well go."

He called the waitress and asked for his bill. Tommy did likewise, and a few moments later was following the two men down the stairs.

Outside, Whittington hailed a taxi, and directed the driver to go to Waterloo.

Taxis were plentiful here, and before Whittington's had driven off another was drawing up to the curb in obedience to Tommy's peremptory hand.

"Follow that other taxi," directed the young man. "Don't lose it."

The elderly chauffeur showed no interest. He merely grunted and jerked down his flag. The drive was uneventful. Tommy's taxi came to rest at the departure platform just after Whittington's. Tommy was behind him at the booking office. He took a first-class single ticket to Bournemouth. Tommy did the same. As he emerged, Boris remarked, glancing up at the clock: "You are early. You have nearly half an hour."

Boris's words had aroused a new train of thought in Tommy's mind. Clearly Whittington was making the journey alone, while the other remained in London. Therefore he was left with a choice as to which he would follow. Obviously, he could not follow both of them unless——Like Boris, he glanced up at the clock, and then to the announcement board of the trains. The Bournemouth train left at 3:30. It was now ten past. Whittington and Boris were walking up and down by the bookstall. He gave one doubtful look at them, then hurried into an adjacent telephone box. He dared not waste time in trying to get hold of Tuppence. In all probability she was still in the neighborhood of South Audley Mansions. But there remained another ally. He rang the Ritz and asked for Julius Hersheimmer. There was a click and a buzz. Oh, if only the young American was in his room! There was another click, and then "Hello" in unmistakable accents came over the wire.

"That you, Hersheimmer? Beresford speaking. I'm at Waterloo. I've followed Whittington and another man here. No time to explain. Whittington's off to Bournemouth by the 3:30. Can you get there by then?"

The reply was reassuring.

"Sure. I'll hustle."

The telephone rang off. Tommy put back the receiver with a sigh of relief. His opinion of Julius's power of hustling was high. He felt instinctively that the American would arrive in time.

Whittington and Boris were still where he had left them. If Boris remained to see his friend off, all was well. Then Tommy fingered his pocket thoughtfully. In spite of the carte blanche assured to him, he had not yet acquired the habit of going about with any considerable sum of money on him. The taking of the first-class ticket to Bournemouth had left him with only a few shillings in his pocket. It was to be hoped that Julius would arrive better provided.

In the meantime, the minutes were creeping by: 3:15, 3:20, 3:25, 3:27. Supposing Julius did not get there in time. 3:29. . . . Doors were banging. Tommy felt cold waves of despair pass over him. Then a hand fell on his shoulder.

"Here I am, son. Your British traffic beats description! Put me wise to the crooks right away."

"That's Whittington—there, getting in now, that big dark man. The other is the foreign chap he's talking to."

"I'm on to them. Which of the two is my bird?"

Tommy had thought out this question.

"Got any money with you?"

Julius shook his head, and Tommy's face fell.

"I guess I haven't more than three or four hundred dollars with me at the moment," explained the American.

Tommy gave a faint whoop of relief.

"Oh, Lord, you millionaires! You don't talk the same language! Climb aboard the lugger. Here's your ticket. Whittington's your man."

"Me for Whittington!" said Julius darkly. The train was just starting as he swung himself aboard. "So long, Tommy." The train slid out of the station.

Tommy drew a deep breath. The man Boris was coming along the platform toward him. Tommy allowed him to pass and then took up the chase once more.

From Waterloo Boris took the tube as far as Piccadilly Circus. Then he walked up Shaftesbury Avenue, finally turning off into the maze of mean streets round Soho. Tommy followed him at a judicious distance.

They reached at length a small dilapidated square. The houses there had a sinister air in the midst of their dirt and decay. Boris looked round, and Tommy drew back into the shelter of a friendly porch. The place was almost deserted. It was a cul-de-sac, and consequently no traffic passed that way. The stealthy way the other had looked round stimulated Tommy's imagination. From the shelter of the doorway he watched him go up the steps of a particularly evil-looking house and rap sharply, with a peculiar rhythm, on the door. It was opened promptly, he said a word or two to the doorkeeper, then passed inside. The door was shut to again.

It was at this juncture that Tommy lost his head. What he ought to have done, what any sane man would have done, was to remain patiently where he was and wait for his man to come out again. What he did do was entirely foreign to the sober common sense which was, as a rule, his leading characteristic. Something, as he expressed it, seemed to snap in his brain. Without a moment's pause for reflection he, too, went up the steps, and reproduced as far as he was able the peculiar knock.

The door swung open with the same promptness as before. A villainous-faced man with close-cropped hair stood in the doorway.

"Well?" he grunted.

It was at that moment that the full realization of his folly began to come home to Tommy. But he dared not hesitate. He seized at the first words that came into his mind.

"Mr. Brown?" he said.

To his surprise the man stood aside.

"Upstairs," he said, jerking his thumb over his shoulder, "second door on your left."

8

The Adventures of Tommy

TAKEN ABACK THOUGH he was by the man's words, Tommy did not hesitate. If audacity had successfully carried him so far, it was to be hoped it would carry him yet farther. He quietly passed into the house and mounted the ramshackle staircase. Everything in the house was filthy beyond words. The grimy paper, of a pattern now indistinguishable, hung in loose festoons from the wall. In every angle was a gray mass of cobweb.

Tommy proceeded leisurely. By the time he reached the bend of the staircase, he had heard the man below disappear into a back room. Clearly no suspicion attached to him as yet. To come to the house and ask for "Mr. Brown" appeared indeed to be a reasonable and natural proceeding.

At the top of the stairs Tommy halted to consider his next move. In front of him ran a narrow passage, with doors opening on either side of it. From the one nearest him on the left came a low murmur of voices. It was this room which he had been directed to enter. But what held his glance fascinated was a small recess immediately on the right, half concealed by a torn velvet curtain. It was directly opposite the left-handed door and, owing to its angle, it also commanded a good view of the upper part of the staircase. As a hiding place for one or, at a pinch, two men, it was ideal, being about two feet deep and three feet wide. It attracted Tommy mightily. He thought things over in his usual slow and steady way, deciding that the mention of "Mr. Brown" was not a request for an individual, but in all probability a password used by the gang. His lucky use of it had gained him admission. So far he had aroused no suspicion. But he must decide quickly on his next step.

Suppose he were boldly to enter the room on the left of the passage. Would the mere fact of his having been admitted to the house be sufficient? Perhaps a further password would be required, or, at any rate, some proof of identity. The doorkeeper did not know all the members of the gang by sight, but it might be different upstairs. On the whole it seemed to him that luck had served him very well so far, but that there was such a thing as trusting it too far. To enter that room was a colossal risk. He could not hope to sustain his part indefinitely; sooner or later he was almost bound to betray himself, and then he would have thrown away a vital chance in mere foolhardiness.

A repetition of the signal knock sounded on the door below, and Tommy, his mind made up, slipped quickly into the recess, and cautiously drew the curtain farther across so that it shielded him completely from sight. There were several rents and slits in the ancient material which afforded him a good view. He would watch events, and any time he chose could, after all, join the assembly, modeling his behavior on that of the new arrival.

The man who came up the staircase with a furtive, soft-footed tread was quite unknown to Tommy. He was obviously of the very dregs of society. The low beetling brows, and the criminal jaw, the bestiality of the whole countenance were new to the young man, though he was a type that Scotland Yard would have recognized at a glance.

The man passed the recess, breathing heavily as he went. He stopped at the door opposite, and gave a repetition of the signal knock. A voice inside called out something, and the man opened the door and passed in, affording Tommy a momentary glimpse of the room inside. He thought there must be about four or five people seated round a long table that took up most of the space, but his attention was caught and held by a tall man with close-cropped hair and a short, pointed, naval-looking beard, who sat at the head of the table with papers in front of him. As the newcomer entered he glanced up, and with a correct, but curiously precise enunciation, which attracted Tommy's notice, he asked:

"Your number, comrade?"

"Fourteen, guv'nor," replied the other hoarsely.

"Correct."

The door shut again.

"If that isn't a Hun, I'm a Dutchman!" said Tommy to himself. "And running the show darned systematically too—as they always do. Lucky I didn't roll in. I'd have given the wrong number, and there would have been the deuce to pay. No, this is the place for me. Hullo, here's another knock."

This visitor proved to be of an entirely different type to the last. Tommy recognized in him an Irish Sinn Feiner. Certainly Mr. Brown's organization was a far-reaching concern. The common criminal, the well-bred Irish gentleman, the pale Russian, and the efficient German master of the ceremonies! Truly a strange and sinister gathering! Who was this man who held in his finger these curiously variegated links of an unknown chain?

In this case, the procedure was exactly the same. The signal knock, the demand for a number, and the reply "Correct."

Two knocks followed in quick succession on the door below. The first man was quite unknown to Tommy, who put him down as a city clerk. A quiet, intelligent-looking man, rather shabbily dressed. The second was of the working classes, and his face was vaguely familiar to the young man.

Three minutes later came another, a man of commanding appearance, exquisitely dressed, and evidently well born. His face, again, was not unknown to the watcher, though he could not for the moment put a name to it.

After his arrival there was a long wait. In fact Tommy concluded that the gathering was now complete, and was just cautiously creeping out from his hiding place, when another knock sent him scuttling back to cover.

This last-comer came up the stairs so quietly that he was almost abreast of Tommy before the young man had realized his presence.

He was a small man, very pale, with a gentle almost womanish air. The angle of the cheekbones hinted at his Slavonic ancestry, otherwise there was nothing to indicate his nationality. As he passed the recess, he turned his head slowly. The strange light eyes seemed to burn through the curtain; Tommy could hardly believe that the man did not know he was there and in spite of himself he shivered. He was no more fanciful than the majority of young Englishmen, but he could not rid himself of the impression that some unusually potent force emanated from the man. The creature reminded him of a venomous snake.

A moment later his impression was proved correct. The newcomer knocked on the door as all had done, but his reception was very different. The bearded man rose to his feet, and all the others followed suit. The German came forward and shook hands. His heels clicked together.

"We are honored," he said. "We are greatly honored. I much feared that it would be impossible."

The other answered in a low voice that had a kind of hiss in it:

"There were difficulties. It will not be possible again, I fear. But one meeting is essential—to define my policy. I can do nothing without—Mr. Brown. He is here?"

The change in the German's voice was audible as he replied with slight hesitation:

"We have received a message. It is impossible for him to be present in person." He stopped, giving a curious impression of having left the sentence unfinished.

A very slow smile overspread the face of the other. He looked round at a circle of uneasy faces.

"Ah! I understand. I have read of his methods. He works in the dark and trusts no one. But, all the same, it is possible that he is among us now. . . ." He looked round him again, and again that expression of fear swept over the group. Each man seemed eyeing his neighbor doubtfully.

The Russian tapped his cheek.

"So be it. Let us proceed."

The German seemed to pull himself together. He indicated the place he had been occupying at the head of the table. The Russian demurred, but the other insisted.

"It is the only possible place," he said, "for—Number One. Perhaps Number Fourteen will shut the door?"

In another moment Tommy was once more confronting bare wooden panels, and the voices within had sunk once more to a mere undistinguishable murmur. Tommy became restive. The conversation he had overheard had stimulated his curiosity. He felt that, by hook or by crook, he must hear more.

There was no sound from below, and it did not seem likely that the doorkeeper would come upstairs. After listening intently for a minute or two, he put his head round the curtain. The passage was deserted. Tommy bent down and removed his shoes, then, leaving them behind the curtain, he walked gingerly out on his stockinged feet, and kneeling down by the closed door he laid his ear cautiously to the crack. To his intense annoyance he could distinguish little more; just a chance word here and there if a voice was raised, which merely served to whet his curiosity still farther.

He eyed the handle of the door tentatively. Could he turn it by degrees so gently and imperceptibly that those in the room would notice nothing? He decided that with great care it could be done. Very slowly, a fraction of an inch at a time, he moved it round, holding his breath in his excessive care. A little more—a little more still—would it never be finished? Ah! at last it would turn no farther.

He stayed so for a minute or two, then drew a deep breath, and pressed it ever so slightly inward. The door did not budge. Tommy was annoyed. If he had to use too much force, it would almost certainly creak. He waited until the voices rose a little, then he tried again. Still nothing happened. He increased the pressure. Had the beastly thing stuck? Finally, in desperation, he pushed with all his might. But the door remained firm, and at last the truth dawned upon him. It was locked or bolted on the inside.

For a moment or two Tommy's indignation got the better of him.

"Well, I'm damned!" he said. "What a dirty trick!"

As his indignation cooled, he prepared to face the situation. Clearly the first thing to be done was to restore the handle to its original position. If he let it go suddenly, the men inside would be almost certain to notice it, so, with the same infinite pains, he reversed his former tactics. All went well, and with a sigh of relief the young man rose to his feet. There was a certain bulldog tenacity about Tommy that made him slow to admit defeat. Checkmated for the moment, he was far from abandoning the conflict. He still intended to hear what was going on in the locked room. As one plan had failed, he must hunt about for another.

He looked round him. A little farther along the passage on the left was a second door. He slipped silently along to it. He listened for a moment or two, then tried the handle. It yielded, and he slipped inside.

The room, which was untenanted, was furnished as a bedroom. Like everything else in the house, the furniture was falling to pieces, and the dirt was, if anything, more abundant.

But what interested Tommy was the thing he had hoped to find, a communicating door between the two rooms, up on the left by the window. Carefully closing the door into the passage behind him, he stepped across to the other and examined it closely. The bolt was shot across it. It was very rusty, and had clearly not been used for some time. By gently wriggling it to and fro, Tommy managed to draw it back without making too much noise. Then he repeated his former maneuvers with the handle—this time with complete success. The door swung open—a crack, a mere fraction, but enough for Tommy to hear what went on. There was a velvet *portière* on the inside of this door which prevented him from seeing, but he was able to recognize the voices with a reasonable amount of accuracy.

The Sinn Feiner was speaking. His rich Irish voice was unmistakable:

"That's all very well. But more money is essential. No money—no results!"

Another voice which Tommy rather thought was that of Boris replied:

"Will you guarantee that there *are* results?"

"In a month from now—sooner or later as you wish—I will guarantee you such a reign of terror in Ireland as shall shake the British Empire to its foundations."

There was a pause, and then came the soft, sibilant accents of Number One:

"Good! You shall have the money. Boris, you will see to that."

Boris asked a question:

"Via the Irish Americans, and Mr. Potter as usual?"

"I guess that'll be all right!" said a new voice, with a transatlantic intonation, "though I'd like to point out, here and now, that things are getting a mite difficult. There's not the sympathy there was, and a growing disposition to let the Irish settle their own affairs without interference from America."

Tommy felt that Boris had shrugged his shoulders as he answered:

"Does that matter, since the money only nominally comes from the States?"

"The chief difficulty is the landing of the ammunition," said the Sinn Feiner. "The money is conveyed in easily enough—thanks to our colleague here."

Another voice, which Tommy fancied was that of the tall, commanding-looking man whose face had seemed familiar to him, said:

"Think of the feelings of Belfast if they could hear you!"

"That is settled, then," said the sibilant tones. "Now, in the matter of the loan to an English newspaper, you have arranged the details satisfactorily, Boris?"

"I think so."

"That is good. An official denial from Moscow will be forthcoming if necessary."

There was a pause, and then the clear voice of the German broke the silence:

"I am directed by—Mr. Brown, to place the summaries of the reports from the different unions before you. That of the miners is most satisfactory. We must hold back the railways. There may be trouble with the A.S.E."

For a long time there was a silence, broken only by the rustle of papers and an occasional word of explanation from the German. Then Tommy heard the light tap-tap of fingers, drumming on the table.

"And—the date, my friend?" said Number One.

"The 29th."

The Russian seemed to consider:

"That is rather soon."

"I know. But it was settled by the principal Labour leaders, and we cannot seem to interfere too much. They must believe it to be entirely their own show."

The Russian laughed softly, as though amused.

"Yes, yes," he said. "That is true. They must have no inkling that we are using them for our own ends. They are honest men—and that is their value to us. It is curious—but you cannot make a revolution without honest men. The instinct of the populace is infallible." He paused, and then repeated, as though the phrase pleased him: "Every revolution has had its honest men. They are soon disposed of afterward."

There was a sinister note in his voice.

The German resumed:

"Clymes must go. He is too far-seeing. Number Fourteen will see to that."

There was a hoarse murmur.

"That's alright, guv'nor." And then after a moment or two: "Suppose I'm nabbed."

"You will have the best legal talent to defend you," replied the German quietly. "But in any case you will wear gloves fitted with the fingerprints of a notorious housebreaker. You have little to fear."

"Oh, I ain't afraid, guv'nor. All for the good of the cause. The streets is going to run with blood, so they say." He spoke with a grim relish. "Dreams of it, sometimes, I does. And diamonds and pearls rolling about in the gutter for anyone to pick up!"

Tommy heard a chair shifted. Then Number One spoke:

"Then all is arranged. We are assured of success?"

"I—think so." But the German spoke with less than his usual confidence.

Number One's voice held suddenly a dangerous quality:

"What has gone wrong?"

"Nothing; but——"

"But what?"

"The Labour leaders. Without them, as you say, we can do nothing. If they do not declare a general strike on the 29th——"

"Why should they not?"

"As you've said, they're honest. And, in spite of everything we've done to discredit the Government in their eyes, I'm not sure that they haven't got a sneaking faith and belief in it."

"But——"

"I know. They abuse it unceasingly. But, on the whole, public opinion swings to the side of the Government. They will not go against it."

Again the Russian's fingers drummed on the table.

"To the point, my friend. I was given to understand that there was a certain document in existence which assured success."

"That is so. If that document were placed before the leaders, the result would be immediate. They would publish it broadcast throughout England, and declare for the Revolution without a moment's hesitation. The Government would be broken finally and completely."

"Then what more do you want?"

"The document itself," said the German bluntly.

"Ah! It is not in your possession? But you know where it is?"

"No."

"Does anyone know where it is?"

"One person—perhaps. And we are not sure of that even."

"Who is this person?"

"A girl."

Tommy held his breath.

"A girl?" The Russian's voice rose contemptuously. "And you have not made her speak? In Russia we have ways of making a girl talk."

"This case is different," said the German sullenly.

"How—different?" He paused a moment, then went on: "Where is the girl now?"

"The girl?"

"Yes."

"She is——"

But Tommy heard no more. A crashing blow descended on his head, and all was darkness.

9

Tuppence Enters Domestic Service

WHEN TOMMY SET forth on the trail of the two men, it took all Tuppence's self-command to refrain from accompanying him. However, she contained herself as best she might, consoled by the reflection that her reasoning had been justified by events. The two men had undoubtedly come from the second floor flat, and that one slender thread of the name "Rita" had set the Young Adventurers once more upon the track of the abductors of Jane Finn.

The question was what to do next? Tuppence hated letting the grass grow under her feet. Tommy was amply employed, and debarred from joining him in the chase, the girl felt at a loose end. She retraced her steps to the entrance hall of the mansions. It was now tenanted by a small lift boy, who was polishing brass fittings, and whistling the latest air with a good deal of vigor and a reasonable amount of accuracy.

He glanced round at Tuppence's entry. There was a certain amount of the gamin element in the girl, at all events she invariably got on well with small boys. A sympathetic bond seemed instantly to be formed. She reflected that an ally in the enemy's camp, so to speak, was not to be despised.

"Well, William," she remarked cheerfully, in the best approved hospital-early-morning style, "getting a good shine up?"

The boy grinned responsively.

"Albert, miss," he corrected.

"Albert be it," said Tuppence. She glanced mysteriously round the hall. The effect was purposely a broad one in case Albert should miss it. She leaned toward the boy and dropped her voice: "I want a word with you, Albert."

Albert ceased operations on the fittings and opened his mouth slightly.

"Look! Do you know what this is?" With a dramatic gesture she flung back the left side of her coat and exposed a small enameled badge. It was extremely unlikely that Albert would have any knowledge of it—indeed, it would have been fatal for Tuppence's plans, since the badge in question was the device of a local training corps originated by the archdeacon in the early days of the war. Its presence in Tuppence's coat was due to the fact that she had used it for pinning in some flowers a day or two before. But Tuppence had sharp eyes, and had noted the corner of a three-penny detective novel protruding from Albert's pocket, and the immediate enlargement of his eyes told her that her tactics were good, and that the fish would rise to the bait.

"American Detective Force!" she hissed.

Albert fell for it.

"Lord!" he murmured ecstatically.

Tuppence nodded at him with the air of one who has established a thorough understanding.

"Know who I'm after?" she inquired genially.

Albert, still round-eyed, demanded breathlessly:

"One of the flats?"

Tuppence nodded and jerked a thumb up the stairs.

"No. 20. Calls herself Vandemeyer. Vandemeyer! Ha! ha!"

Albert's hand stole to his pocket.

"A crook?" he queried eagerly.

"A crook? I should say so. Ready Rita they call her in the States."

"Ready Rita," repeated Albert deliriously. "Oh, ain't it just like the pictures!"

It was. Tuppence was a great frequenter of the cinema.

"Annie always said as how she was a bad lot," continued the boy.

"Who's Annie?" inquired Tuppence idly.

"'Ouse-parlormaid. She's leaving today. Many's the time Annie's said to me: 'Mark my words, Albert, I wouldn't wonder if the police was to come after her one of these days.' Just like that. But she's a stunner to look at, ain't she?"

"She's some peach," allowed Tuppence carelessly. "Finds it useful in her layout, you bet. Has she been wearing any of the emeralds, by the way?"

"Emeralds? Them's the green stones, isn't they?"

Tuppence nodded.

"That's what we're after her for. You know old man Rysdale?"

Albert shook his head.

"Peter B. Rysdale, the oil king?"

"It seems sort of familiar to me."

"The sparklers belonged to him. Finest collection of emeralds in the world. Worth a million dollars!"

"Lummee!" came ecstatically from Albert. "It sounds more like the pictures every minute."

Tuppence smiled, gratified at the success of her efforts.

"We haven't exactly proved it yet. But we're after her. And"—she produced a long-drawn-out wink—"I guess she won't get away with the goods this time."

Albert uttered another ejaculation indicative of delight.

"Mind you, sonny, not a word of this," said Tuppence suddenly. "I guess I oughtn't to have put you wise, but in the States we know a real smart lad when we see one."

"I'll not breathe a word," protested Albert eagerly. "Ain't there anything I could do? A bit of shadowing, maybe, or such like?"

Tuppence affected to consider, then shook her head.

"Not at the moment, but I'll bear you in mind, son. What's this about the girl you say is leaving?"

"Annie? Regular turn up, they 'ad. As Annie said, servants is someone nowadays, and to be treated accordingly, and, what with her passing the word round, she won't find it so easy to get another."

"Won't she?" said Tuppence thoughtfully. "I wonder——"

An idea was dawning in her brain. She thought a minute or two, then tapped Albert on the shoulder.

"See here, son, my brain's got busy. How would it be if you mentioned that you'd got a young cousin, or a friend of yours had, that might suit the place. You get me?"

"I'm there," said Albert instantly. "You leave it to me, miss, and I'll fix the whole thing up in two ticks."

"Some lad!" commented Tuppence, with a nod of approval. "You might say that the young woman could come in right away. You let me know, and if it's O.K. I'll be round tomorrow at eleven o'clock."

"Where am I to let you know to?"

"Ritz," replied Tuppence laconically. "Name of Cowley."

Albert eyed her enviously.

"It must be a good job, this tec business."

"It sure is," drawled Tuppence, "especially when old man Rysdale backs the bill. But don't fret, son. If this goes well, you shall come in on the ground floor."

With which promise she took leave of her new ally, and walked briskly away from South Audley Mansions, well pleased with her morning's work.

But there was no time to be lost. She went straight back to the Ritz and wrote a few brief words to Mr. Carter. Having dispatched this, and Tommy not having yet returned—which did not surprise her—she started off on a shopping expedition which, with an interval for tea and assorted creamy cakes, occupied her until well after six o'clock, and she returned to the hotel jaded, but satisfied with her purchases. Starting with a cheap clothing store, and passing through one or two secondhand establishments, she had finished the day at a well-known hairdresser's. Now, in the seclusion of her bedroom, she unwrapped that final purchase. Five minutes later she smiled contentedly at her reflection in the glass. With an actress's pencil she had slightly altered the line of her eyebrows, and that, taken in conjunction with the new luxuriant growth of fair hair above, so changed her appearance that she felt confident that even if she came face to face with Whittington he would not recognize her. She would wear elevators in her shoes, and the cap and apron would be an even more valuable disguise. From hospital experience she knew only too well that a nurse out of uniform is frequently unrecognized by her patients.

"Yes," said Tuppence aloud, nodding at the pert reflection in the glass, "you'll do." She then resumed her normal appearance.

Dinner was a solitary meal. Tuppence was rather surprised at Tommy's non-return. Julius, too, was absent—but that to the girl's mind was more easily explained. His "hustling" activities were not confined to London, and his abrupt appearances and disappearances were fully accepted by the Young Adventurers as part of the day's work. It was quite on the cards that Julius P. Hersheimmer had left for Constantinople at a moment's notice if he fancied that a clue to his cousin's disappearance was to be found there. The energetic young man had succeeded in making the lives of several Scotland Yard men unbearable to them, and the telephone girls at the Admiralty had learned to know and dread the familiar "Hullo!" He had spent three hours in Paris hustling the Prefecture, and had returned from there imbued with the idea, possibly inspired by a weary French official, that the true clue to the mystery was to be found in Ireland.

"I dare say he's dashed off there now," thought Tuppence. "All very well, but this is very dull for *me!* Here I am bursting with news, and absolutely no one to tell it to! Tommy might have wired, or something. I wonder where he is. Anyway, he can't have 'lost the trail' as they say. That reminds me——" And Miss Cowley broke off in her meditations, and summoned a small boy.

Ten minutes later the lady was ensconced comfortably on her bed, smoking cigarettes and deep in the perusal of *Garnaby Williams, the Boy Detective*, which, with other three-penny works of lurid fiction, she had sent out to purchase. She felt, and rightly, that before the strain of attempting further intercourse with Albert, it would be as well to fortify herself with a good supply of local color.

The morning brought a note from Mr. Carter:

"DEAR MISS TUPPENCE,

"You have made a splendid start, and I congratulate you. I feel, though, that I should like to point out to you once more the risks you are running, especially if you pursue the course you indicate. Those people are absolutely desperate and incapable of either mercy or pity. I feel that you probably underestimate the danger, and therefore warn you again that I can promise you no protection. You have given us valuable information, and if you choose to withdraw now no one could blame you. At any rate, think the matter over well before you decide.

"If, in spite of my warnings, you make up your mind to go through with it, you will find everything arranged. You have lived for two years with Miss Dufferin, The Parsonage, Llanelly, and Mrs. Vandemeyer can apply to her for a reference.

"May I be permitted a word or two of advice? Stick as near to the truth as possible—it minimizes the danger of 'slips.' I suggest that you should represent yourself to be what you are, a former V.A.D., who has chosen domestic service as a profession. There are many such at the present time. That explains away any incongruities of voice or manner which otherwise might awaken suspicion.

"Whichever way you decide, good luck to you.

"Your sincere friend,

"MR. CARTER."

Tuppence's spirits rose mercurially. Mr. Carter's warnings passed unheeded. The young lady had far too much confidence in herself to pay any heed to them.

With some reluctance she abandoned the interesting part she had sketched out for herself. Although she had no doubts of her own powers to sustain a role indefinitely, she had too much common sense not to recognize the force of Mr. Carter's arguments.

There was still no word or message from Tommy, but the morning post brought a somewhat dirty postcard with the words: "It's O.K." scrawled upon it.

At ten-thirty Tuppence surveyed with pride a slightly battered tin trunk containing her new possessions. It was artistically corded. It was with a slight blush that she rang the bell and ordered it to be placed in a taxi. She drove to Paddington, and left the box in the cloak room. She then repaired with a handbag to the fastnesses of the ladies' waiting room. Ten minutes later a metamorphosed Tuppence walked demurely out of the station and entered a bus.

It was a few minutes past eleven when Tuppence again entered the hall of South Audley Mansions. Albert was on the lookout, attending to his duties in a somewhat desultory fashion. He did not immediately recognize Tuppence. When he did, his admiration was unbounded.

"Blest if I'd have known you! That rig-out's top-hole."

"Glad you like it, Albert," replied Tuppence modestly. "By the way, am I your cousin, or am I not?"

"Your voice too," cried the delighted boy. "It's as English as anything! No, I said as a friend of mine knew a young gal. Annie wasn't best pleased. She's stopped on till today—to oblige, *she* said, but really it's so as to put you against the place."

"Nice girl," said Tuppence.

Albert suspected no irony.

"She's style about her, and keeps her silver a treat—but, my word, ain't she got a temper. Are you going up now, miss? Step inside the lift. No. 20 did you say?" And he winked.

Tuppence quelled him with a stern glance, and stepped inside.

As she rang the bell of No. 20 she was conscious of Albert's eyes slowly descending beneath the level of the floor.

A smart young woman opened the door.

"I've come about the place," said Tuppence.

"It's a rotten place," said the young woman without hesitation. "Regular old cat—always interfering. Accused me of tampering with her letters. Me! The flap was half undone anyway. There's never anything in the wastepaper basket—she burns everything. She's a wrong 'un, that's what she is. Swell clothes, but no class. Cook knows something about her—but she won't tell—scared to death of her. And suspicious! She's on to you in a minute if you as much as speak to a fellow. I can tell you——"

But what more Annie could tell, Tuppence was never destined to learn, for at that moment a clear voice with a peculiarly steely ring to it called:

"Annie!"

The smart young woman jumped as if she had been shot.

"Yes, ma'am."

"Who are you talking to?"

"It's a young woman about the situation, ma'am."

"Show her in then. At once."

"Yes, ma'am."

Tuppence was ushered into a room on the right of the long passage. A woman was standing by the fireplace. She was no longer in her first youth, and the beauty she undeniably possessed was hardened and coarsened. In her youth she must have been dazzling. Her pale gold hair, owing a slight assistance to art, was coiled low on her neck, her eyes, of a piercing electric blue, seemed to possess a faculty of boring into the very soul of the person she was looking at. Her exquisite figure was enhanced by a wonderful gown of indigo charmeuse. And yet, despite her swaying grace, and the almost ethereal beauty of her face, you felt instinctively the presence of something hard and menacing, a kind of metallic strength that found expression in the tones of her voice and in that gimletlike quality of her eyes.

For the first time Tuppence felt afraid. She had not feared Whittington, but this woman was different. As if fascinated, she watched the long cruel line of the red curving mouth, and again she felt that sensation of panic pass over her. Her usual self-confidence deserted her. Vaguely she felt that deceiving this woman would be very different to deceiving Whittington. Mr. Carter's warning recurred to her mind. Here, indeed, she might expect no mercy.

Fighting down that instinct of panic which urged her to turn tail and run without further delay, Tuppence returned the lady's gaze firmly and respectfully.

As though that first scrutiny had been satisfactory, Mrs. Vandemeyer motioned to a chair.

"You can sit down. How did you hear I wanted a house-parlormaid?"

"Through a friend who knows the lift boy here. He thought the place might suit me."

Again that basilisk glance seemed to pierce her through.

"You speak like an educated girl?"

Glibly enough, Tuppence ran through her imaginary career on the lines suggested by Mr. Carter. It seemed to her, as she did so, that the tension of Mrs. Vandemeyer's attitude relaxed.

"I see," she remarked at length. "Is there anyone I can write to for a reference?"

"I lived last with a Miss Dufferin, The Parsonage, Llanelly. I was with her two years."

"And then you thought you would get more money by coming to London, I suppose? Well, it doesn't matter to me. I will give you £50—£60—whatever you want. You can come in at once?"

"Yes, ma'am. Today, if you like. My box is at Paddington."

"Go and fetch it in a taxi, then. It's an easy place. I am out a good deal. By the way, what's your name?"

"Prudence Cooper, ma'am."

"Very well, Prudence. Go away and fetch your box. I shall be out to lunch.

The cook will show you where everything is."

"Thank you, ma'am."

Tuppence withdrew. The smart Annie was not in evidence. In the hall below a magnificent hall porter had relegated Albert to the background. Tuppence did not even glance at him as she passed meekly out.

The adventure had begun, but she felt less elated than she had done earlier in the morning. It crossed her mind that if the unknown Jane Finn had fallen into the hands of Mrs. Vandemeyer, it was likely to have gone hard with her.

10

Enter Sir James Peel Edgerton

TUPPENCE BETRAYED NO awkwardness in her new duties. The daughters of the archdeacon were well grounded in household tasks. They were also experts in training a "raw girl," the inevitable result being that the raw girl, once trained, departed elsewhere where her newly acquired knowledge commanded a more substantial remuneration than the archdeacon's meagre purse allowed.

Tuppence had therefore very little fear of proving inefficient. Mrs. Vandemeyer's cook puzzled her. She evidently went in deadly terror of her mistress. The girl thought it probable that the other woman had some hold over her. For the rest, she cooked like a chef, as Tuppence had an opportunity of judging that evening. Mrs. Vandemeyer was expecting a guest to dinner, and Tuppence accordingly laid the beautifully polished table for two. She was a little exercised in her own mind as to this visitor. It was highly possible that it might prove to be Whittington. Although she felt fairly confident that he would not recognize her, yet she would have been better pleased had the guest proved to be a total stranger. However, there was nothing for it but to hope for the best.

At a few minutes past eight the front door bell rang, and Tuppence went to answer it with some inward trepidation. She was relieved to see that the visitor was the second of the two men whom Tommy had taken upon himself to follow.

He gave his name as Count Stepanov. Tuppence announced him, and Mrs. Vandemeyer rose from her seat on a low divan with a quick murmur of pleasure.

"It is delightful to see you, Boris Ivanovitch," she said.

"And you, madame!" He bowed low over her hand.

Tuppence returned to the kitchen.

"Count Stepanov, or some such," she remarked, and affecting a frank and unvarnished curiosity: "Who's he?"

"A Russian gentleman, I believe."

"Come here much?"

"Once in a while. What d'you want to know for?"

"Fancied he might be sweet on the missus, that's all," explained the girl, adding with an appearance of sulkiness: "How you do take one up!"

"I'm not quite easy in my mind about the soufflé," explained the other.

"You know something," thought Tuppence to herself, but aloud she only said: "Going to dish up now? Right-o."

Whilst waiting at table, Tuppence listened closely to all that was said. She remembered that this was one of the men Tommy was shadowing when she had last seen him. Already, although she would hardly admit it, she was becoming uneasy about her partner. Where was he? Why had no word of any kind come from him? She had arranged before leaving the Ritz to have all letters or messages sent on at once by special messenger to a small stationer's shop near at hand where Albert was to call in frequently. True, it was only yesterday morning that she had parted from Tommy, and she told herself that any anxiety on his behalf would be absurd. Still, it was strange that he had sent no word of any kind.

But, listen as she might, the conversation presented no clue. Boris and Mrs. Vandemeyer talked on purely indifferent subjects: plays they had seen, new dances, and the latest society gossip. After dinner they repaired to the small boudoir where Mrs. Vandemeyer, stretched out on the divan, looked more wickedly beautiful than ever. Tuppence brought in the coffee and liqueurs and unwillingly retired. As she did so, she heard Boris say:

"New, isn't she?"

"She came in today. The other was a fiend. This girl seems alright. She waits well."

Tuppence lingered a moment longer by the door which she had carefully neglected to close, and heard him say:

"Quite safe, I suppose?"

"Really, Boris, you are absurdly suspicious. I believe she's the cousin of the hall porter, or something of the kind. And nobody even dreams that I have any connection with our—mutual friend, Mr. Brown."

"For heaven's sake, be careful, Rita. That door isn't shut."

"Well, shut it then," laughed the woman.

Tuppence removed herself speedily.

She dared not absent herself longer from the back premises, but she cleared away and washed up with a breathless speed acquired in hospital. Then she slipped quietly back to the boudoir door. The cook, more leisurely, was still busy in the kitchen and, if she missed the other, would only suppose her to be turning down the beds.

Alas! The conversation inside was being carried on in too low a tone to permit of her hearing anything of it. She dared not reopen the door, however gently. Mrs. Vandemeyer was sitting almost facing it, and Tuppence respected her mistress's lynx-eyed powers of observation.

Nevertheless, she felt she would give a good deal to overhear what was going on. Possibly, if anything unforeseen had happened, she might get news of Tommy. For some moments she reflected desperately, then her face brightened. She went quickly along the passage to Mrs. Vandemeyer's bedroom, which had long French windows leading on to a balcony that ran the length of the flat. Slipping quickly through the window, Tuppence crept noiselessly along till she reached the boudoir window. As she had thought it stood a little ajar, and the voices within were plainly audible.

Tuppence listened attentively, but there was no mention of anything that could be twisted to apply to Tommy. Mrs. Vandemeyer and the Russian seemed to be at variance over some matter, and finally the latter exclaimed bitterly:

"With your persistent recklessness, you will end by ruining us!"

"Bah!" laughed the woman. "Notoriety of the right kind is the best way of disarming suspicion. You will realize that one of these days—perhaps sooner than you think!"

"In the meantime, you are going about everywhere with Peel Edgerton. Not only is he, perhaps, the most celebrated K.C. in England, but his special hobby is criminology! It is madness!"

"I know that his eloquence has saved untold men from the gallows," said Mrs. Vandemeyer calmly. "What of it? I may need his assistance in that line myself someday. If so, how fortunate to have such a friend at court—or perhaps it would be more to the point to say *in* court."

Boris got up and began striding up and down. He was very excited.

"You are a clever woman, Rita; but you are also a fool! Be guided by me, and give up Peel Edgerton."

Mrs. Vandemeyer shook her head gently.

"I think not."

"You refuse?" There was an ugly ring in the Russian's voice.

"I do."

"Then, by Heaven," snarled the Russian, "we will see——"

But Mrs. Vandemeyer also rose to her feet, her eyes flashing.

"You forget, Boris," she said. "I am accountable to no one. I take my orders only from—Mr. Brown."

The other threw up his hands in despair.

"You are impossible," he muttered. "Impossible! Already it may be too late. They say Peel Edgerton can *smell* a criminal! How do we know what is at the bottom of his sudden interest in you? Perhaps even now his suspicions are aroused. He guesses——"

Mrs. Vandemeyer eyed him scornfully.

"Reassure yourself, my dear Boris. He suspects nothing. With less than your usual chivalry, you seem to forget that I am commonly accounted a beautiful woman. I assure you that is all that interests Peel Edgerton."

Boris shook his head doubtfully.

"He has studied crime as no other man in his kingdom has studied it. Do you fancy that you can deceive him?"

Mrs. Vandemeyer's eyes narrowed.

"If he is all that you say—it would amuse me to try!"

"Good heavens, Rita——"

"Besides," added Mrs. Vandemeyer, "he is extremely rich. I am not one who despises money. The 'sinews of war,' you know, Boris!"

"Money—money! That is always the danger with you, Rita. I believe you would sell your soul for money. I believe——" He paused, then in a low, sinister voice he said slowly: "Sometimes I believe that you would sell—*us*!"

Mrs. Vandemeyer smiled and shrugged her shoulders.

"The price, at any rate, would have to be enormous," she said lightly. "It would be beyond the power of anyone but a millionaire to pay."

"Ah!" snarled the Russian. "You see, I was right!"

"My dear Boris, can you not take a joke?"

"Was it a joke?"

"Of course."

"Then all I can say is that your ideas of humor are peculiar, my dear Rita."

Mrs. Vandemeyer smiled.

"Let us not quarrel, Boris. Touch the bell. We will have some drinks."

Tuppence beat a hasty retreat. She paused a moment to survey herself in Mrs. Vandemeyer's long glass, and be sure that nothing was amiss with her appearance. Then she answered the bell demurely.

The conversation that she had overheard, although interesting in that it proved beyond doubt the complicity of both Rita and Boris, threw very little light on the present preoccupations. The name of Jane Finn had not even been mentioned.

The following morning a few brief words with Albert informed her that nothing was waiting for her at the stationer's. It seemed incredible that Tommy, if all was well with him, should not send any word to her. A cold hand seemed to close round her heart. . . . Supposing . . . She choked her fears down bravely. It was no good worrying. But she leapt at a chance offered her by Mrs. Vandemeyer.

"What day do you usually go out, Prudence?"

"Friday's my usual day, ma'am."

Mrs. Vandemeyer lifted her eyebrows.

"And today is Friday! But I suppose you hardly wish to go out today, as you only came yesterday."

"I was thinking of asking you if I might, ma'am."

Mrs. Vandemeyer looked at her a minute longer, and then smiled.

"I wish Count Stepanov could hear you. He made a suggestion about you last night." Her smile broadened, catlike. "Your request is very—typical. I am satisfied. You do not understand all this—but you can go out today. It makes no difference to me, as I shall not be dining at home."

"Thank you, ma'am."

Tuppence felt a sensation of relief once she was out of the other's presence. Once again she admitted to herself that she was afraid, horribly afraid, of the beautiful woman with the cruel eyes.

In the midst of a final desultory polishing of her silver, Tuppence was disturbed by the ringing of the front door bell, and went to answer it. This time the visitor was neither Whittington nor Boris, but a man of striking appearance.

Just a shade over average height, he nevertheless conveyed the impression of a big man. His face, clean shaven and exquisitely mobile, was stamped with an expression of power and force far beyond the ordinary. Magnetism seemed to radiate from him.

Tuppence was undecided for the moment whether to put him down as an actor or a lawyer, but her doubts were soon solved as he gave her his name: Sir James Peel Edgerton.

She looked at him with renewed interest. This, then, was the famous K.C. whose name was familiar all over England. She had heard it said that he might one day be Prime Minister. He was known to have refused office in the interests of his profession, preferring to remain a simple Member for a Scotch constituency.

Tuppence went back to her pantry thoughtfully. The great man had impressed her. She understood Boris's agitation. Peel Edgerton would not be an easy man to deceive.

In about a quarter of an hour the bell rang, and Tuppence repaired to the hall to show the visitor out. He had given her a piercing glance before. Now, as she handed him his hat and stick, she was conscious of his eyes raking her through. As she opened the door and stood aside to let him pass out, he stopped in the doorway.

"Not been doing this long, eh?"

Tuppence raised her eyes, astonished. She read in his glance kindliness, and something else more difficult to fathom.

He nodded as though she had answered.

"V.A.D. and hard up, I suppose?"

"Did Mrs. Vandemeyer tell you that?" asked Tuppence suspiciously.

"No, child. The look of you told me. Good place here?"

"Very good, thank you, sir."

"Ah, but there are plenty of good places nowadays. And a change does no harm sometimes."

"Do you mean——?" began Tuppence.

But Sir James was already on the topmost stair. He looked back with his kindly, shrewd glance.

"Just a hint," he said. "That's all."

Tuppence went back to the pantry more thoughtful than ever.

11
Julius Tells a Story

DRESSED APPROPRIATELY, TUPPENCE duly sallied forth for her "afternoon out." Albert was in temporary abeyance, but Tuppence went herself to the stationer's to make quite sure that nothing had come for her. Satisfied on this point, she made her way to the Ritz. On inquiry she learnt that Tommy had not yet returned. It was the answer she had expected, but it was another nail in the coffin of her hopes. She resolved to appeal to Mr. Carter, telling him when and where Tommy had started on his quest, and asking him to do something to trace him. The prospect of his aid revived her mercurial spirits, and she next inquired for Julius Hersheimmer. The reply she got was to the effect that he had returned about half an hour ago, but had gone out immediately.

Tuppence's spirits revived still more. It would be something to see Julius. Perhaps he could devise some plan for finding out what had become of Tommy. She wrote her note to Mr. Carter in Julius's sitting room, and was just addressing the envelope when the door burst open.

"What the hell——" began Julius, but checked himself abruptly. "I beg your pardon, Miss Tuppence. Those fools down at the office would have it that Beresford wasn't here any longer—hadn't been here since Wednesday. Is that so?"

Tuppence nodded.

"You don't know where he is?" she asked faintly.

"I? How should I know? I haven't had one darned word from him though I wired him yesterday morning."

"I expect your wire's at the office unopened."

"But where is he?"

"I don't know. I hoped you might."

"I tell you I haven't had one darned word from him since we parted at the depot on Wednesday."

"What depot?"

"Waterloo. Your London and South Western road."

"Waterloo?" frowned Tuppence.

"Why, yes. Didn't he tell you?"

"I haven't seen him either," replied Tuppence impatiently. "Go on about Waterloo. What were you doing there?"

"He gave me a call. Over the phone. Told me to get a move on, and hustle. Said he was trailing two crooks."

"Oh!" said Tuppence, her eyes opening. "I see. Go on."

"I hurried along right away. Beresford was there. He pointed out the crooks. The big one was mine, the guy you bluffed. Tommy shoved a ticket into my hand and told me to get aboard the cars. He was going to sleuth the other crook." Julius paused. "I thought for sure you'd know all this."

"Julius," said Tuppence firmly, "stop walking up and down. It makes me giddy. Sit down in that armchair, and tell me the whole story with as few fancy turns of speech as possible."

Mr. Hersheimmer obeyed.

"Sure," he said. "Where shall I begin?"

"Where you left off. At Waterloo."

"Well," began Julius, "I got into one of your dear old-fashioned first-class British compartments. The train was just off. First thing I knew a guard came along and informed me mighty politely that I wasn't in a smoking carriage. I handed him out half a dollar, and that settled that. I did a bit of prospecting along the corridor to the next coach. Whittington was there right enough. When I saw the skunk, with his big sleek fat face, and thought of poor little Jane in his clutches, I felt real mad that I hadn't got a gun with me. I'd have tickled him up some.

"We got to Bournemouth all right. Whittington took a cab and gave the name of an hotel. I did likewise, and we drove up within three minutes of each other. He hired a room, and I hired one too. So far it was all plain sailing. He hadn't the remotest notion that anyone was on to him. Well, he just sat around in the hotel lounge, reading the papers and so on, till it was time for dinner. He didn't hurry any over that either.

"I began to think that there was nothing doing, that he'd just come on the trip for his health, but I remembered that he hadn't changed for dinner, though it was by way of being a slap-up hotel, so it seemed likely enough that he'd be going out on his real business afterward.

"Sure enough, about nine o'clock, so he did. Took a car across the town—mighty pretty place by the way, I guess I'll take Jane there for a spell when I find her—and then paid it off and struck out along those pine-woods on the top of the cliff. I was there too, you understand. We walked, maybe, for half an hour. There's a lot of villas all the way along, but by degrees they seemed to get more and more thinned out, and in the end we got to one that seemed the last of the bunch. Big house it was, with a lot of piny grounds around it.

"It was a pretty black night, and the carriage drive up to the house was dark as pitch. I could hear him ahead, though I couldn't see him. I had to walk carefully in case he might get on to it that he was being followed. I turned a curve and I was just in time to see him ring the bell and get admitted to the house. I just stopped where I was. It was beginning to rain, and I was soon pretty near soaked through. Also it was almighty cold.

"Whittington didn't come out again, and by and by I got kind of restive, and began to mooch around. All the ground floor windows were shuttered tight, but upstairs, on the first floor (it was a two-storied house) I noticed a window with a light burning and the curtains not drawn.

"Now, just opposite to that window, there was a tree growing. It was about thirty foot away from the house, maybe, and I sort of got it into my head that, if I climbed up that tree, I'd very likely be able to see into that room. Of course, I knew there was no reason why Whittington should be in that room rather than in any other—less reason, in fact, for the betting would be on his being in one of the reception rooms downstairs. But I guess I'd got the hump from standing so long in the rain, and anything seemed better than going on doing nothing. So I started up.

"It wasn't so easy, by a long chalk! The rain had made the boughs mighty slippery, and it was all I could do to keep a foothold, but bit by bit I managed it, until at last there I was level with the window.

"But then I was disappointed. I was too far to the left. I could only see sideways into the room. A bit of curtain, and a yard of wallpaper was all I could command. Well, that wasn't any manner of good to me, but just as I was going to give it up, and climb down ignominiously, someone inside moved and threw his shadow on my little bit of wall—and, by gum, it was Whittington!

"After that, my blood was up. I'd just *got* to get a look into that room. It was up to me to figure out how. I noticed that there was a long branch running out from the tree in the right direction. If I could only swarm about halfway along it, the proposition would be solved. But it was mighty uncertain whether it would bear my weight. I decided I'd just got to risk that, and I started. Very cautiously, inch by inch, I crawled along. The bough creaked and swayed in a nasty fashion, and it didn't do to think of the drop below, but at last I got safely to where I wanted to be.

"The room was medium-sized, furnished in a kind of bare hygienic way. There was a table with a lamp on it in the middle of the room, and sitting at that table, facing toward me, was Whittington right enough. He was talking to a woman dressed as a hospital nurse. She was sitting with her back to me, so I couldn't see her face. Although the blinds were up, the window itself was shut, so I couldn't catch a word of what they said. Whittington seemed to be doing all the talking, and the nurse just listened. Now and then she nodded, and sometimes she'd shake her head, as though she were answering questions. He seemed very emphatic—once or twice he beat with his fist on the table. The rain had stopped now, and the sky was clearing in that sudden way it does.

"Presently, he seemed to get to the end of what he was saying. He got up, and so did she. He looked toward the window and asked something—I guess it was whether it was raining. Anyway, she came right across and looked out. Just then the moon came out from behind the clouds. I was scared the woman would catch sight of me, for I was full in the moonlight. I tried to move back a bit. The jerk I gave was too much for that rotten old branch. With an almighty crash, down it came, and Julius P. Hersheimmer with it!"

"Oh, Julius," breathed Tuppence, "how exciting! Go on."

"Well, luckily for me, I pitched down into a good soft bed of earth—but it put me out of action for the time, sure enough. The next thing I knew, I was lying in bed with a hospital nurse (not Whittington's one) on one side of me, and a little black-bearded man with gold glasses, and medical man written all over him, on the other. He rubbed his hands together, and raised his eyebrows as I stared at him. 'Ah!' he said. 'So our young friend is coming round again. Capital. Capital.'

"I did the usual stunt. Said: 'What's happened?' And 'Where am I?' But I knew the answer to the last well enough. There's no moss growing on my brain. 'I think that'll do for the present, sister,' said the little man, and the nurse left the room in a sort of brisk well-trained way. But I caught her handing me out a look of deep curiosity as she passed through the door.

"That look of hers gave me an idea. 'Now then, doc,' I said, and tried to sit up in bed, but my right foot gave me a nasty twinge as I did so. 'A slight sprain,' explained the doctor. 'Nothing serious. You'll be about again in a couple of days.'"

"I noticed you walked lame," interpolated Tuppence.

Julius nodded, and continued:

"'How did it happen?' I asked again. He replied dryly. 'You fell, with a considerable portion of one of my trees, into one of my newly planted flower beds.'

"I liked the man. He seemed to have a sense of humor. I felt sure that he, at least, was plumb straight. 'Sure, doc,' I said, 'I'm sorry about the tree, and I guess the new bulbs will be on me. But perhaps you'd like to know what I was doing in your garden?' 'I think the facts do call for an explanation,' he replied. 'Well, to begin with, I wasn't after the spoons.'

"He smiled. 'My first theory. But I soon altered my mind. By the way, you are an American, are you not?' I told him my name. 'And you?' 'I am Dr. Hall, and this, as you doubtless know, is my private nursing home.'

"I didn't know, but I wasn't going to put him wise. I was just thankful for the information. I liked the man, and I felt he was straight, but I wasn't going to give him the whole story. For one thing he probably wouldn't have believed it.

"I made up my mind in a flash. 'Why, doctor,' I said, 'I guess I feel an almighty fool, but I owe it to you to let you know that it wasn't the Bill Sikes business I was up to.' Then I went on and mumbled out something about a girl. I trotted out the stern guardian business, and a nervous breakdown, and finally explained that I had fancied I recognized her among the patients at the home, hence my nocturnal adventures.

"I guess it was just the kind of story he was expecting. 'Quite a romance,' he said genially, when I'd finished. 'Now, doc,' I went on, 'will you be frank with me? Have you here now, or have you had here at any time, a young girl called Jane Finn?' He repeated the name thoughtfully. 'Jane Finn?' he said. 'No.'

"I was chagrined, and I guess I showed it. 'You are sure?' 'Quite sure, Mr. Hersheimmer. It is an uncommon name, and I should not have been likely to forget it.'

"Well, that was flat. It laid me out for a space. I'd kind of hoped my search was at an end. 'That's that,' I said at last. 'Now, there's another matter. When I was hugging that darned branch I thought I recognized an old friend of mine talking to one of your nurses.' I purposely didn't mention any name because, of course, Whittington might be calling himself something quite different down here, but the doctor answered at once. 'Mr. Whittington, perhaps?' 'That's the fellow,' I replied. 'What's he doing down here? Don't tell me *his* nerves are out of order?'

"Dr. Hall laughed. 'No. He came down to see one of my nurses, Nurse Edith, who is a niece of his.' 'Why, fancy that!' I exclaimed. 'Is he still here?' 'No, he went back to town almost immediately.' 'What a pity!' I ejaculated. 'But perhaps I could speak to his niece—Nurse Edith, did you say her name was?'

"But the doctor shook his head. 'I'm afraid that, too, is impossible. Nurse Edith left with a patient tonight also.' 'I seem to be real unlucky,' I remarked. 'Have you Mr. Whittington's address in town? I guess I'd like to look him up when I get back.' 'I don't know his address. I can write to Nurse Edith for it if you like.' I thanked him. 'Don't say who it is wants it. I'd like to give him a little surprise.'

"That was about all I could do for the moment. Of course, if the girl was really Whittington's niece, she might be too cute to fall into the trap, but it was worth trying. Next thing I did was to write out a wire to Beresford saying where I was, and that I was laid up with a sprained foot, and telling him to come down if he wasn't busy. I had to be guarded in what I said. However, I didn't hear from him, and my foot soon got all right. It was only ricked, not really sprained, so today I said good-bye to the little doctor chap, asked him to send me word if he heard from Nurse Edith, and came right away back to town. Say, Miss Tuppence, you're looking mighty pale!"

"It's Tommy," said Tuppence. "What can have happened to him?"

"Buck up, I guess he's alright really. Why shouldn't he be? See here, it was a foreign-looking guy he went off after. Maybe they've gone abroad—to Poland, or something like that?"

Tuppence shook her head.

"He couldn't without passports and things. Besides I've seen that man, Boris Something, since. He dined with Mrs. Vandemeyer last night."

"Mrs. Who?"

"I forgot. Of course you don't know all that."

"I'm listening," said Julius, and gave vent to his favorite expression. "Put me wise."

Tuppence thereupon related the events of the last two days. Julius's astonishment and admiration were unbounded.

"Bully for you! Fancy you a menial. It just tickles me to death!" Then he added seriously: "But say now, I don't like it, Miss Tuppence, I sure don't. You're just as plucky as they make 'em, but I wish you'd keep right out of this. These crooks we're up against would as soon croak a girl as a man any day."

"Do you think I'm afraid?" said Tuppence indignantly, valiantly repressing memories of the steely glitter in Mrs. Vandemeyer's eyes.

"I said before you were darned plucky. But that doesn't alter facts."

"Oh, bother *me!*" said Tuppence impatiently. "Let's think about what can have happened to Tommy. I've written to Mr. Carter about it," she added, and told him the gist of her letter.

Julius nodded gravely.

"I guess that's good as far as it goes. But it's for us to get busy and do something."

"What can we do?" asked Tuppence, her spirits rising.

"I guess we'd better get on the track of Boris. You say he's been to your place. Is he likely to come again?"

"He might. I really don't know."

"I see. Well, I guess I'd better buy a car, a slap-up one, dress as a chauffeur and hang about outside. Then if Boris comes, you could make some kind of signal, and I'd trail him. How's that?"

"Splendid, but he mightn't come for weeks."

"We'll have to chance that. I'm glad you like the plan." He rose.

"Where are you going?"

"To buy the car, of course," replied Julius surprised. "What make do you like? I guess you'll do some riding in it before we've finished."

"Oh," said Tuppence faintly, "I *like* Rolls-Royces, but——"

"Sure," agreed Julius. "What you say goes. I'll get one."

"But you can't at once," cried Tuppence. "People wait ages sometimes."

"Little Julius doesn't," affirmed Mr. Hersheimmer. "Don't you worry any. I'll be round in the car in half an hour."

Tuppence got up.

"You're awfully good, Julius. But I can't help feeling that it's rather a forlorn hope. I'm really pinning my faith to Mr. Carter."

"Then I shouldn't."

"Why?"

"Just an idea of mine."

"Oh; but he must do something. There's no one else. By the way, I forgot to tell you of a queer thing that happened this morning."

And she narrated her encounter with Sir James Peel Edgerton. Julius was interested.

"What did the guy mean, do you think?" he asked.

"I don't quite know," said Tuppence meditatively. "But I think that, in an ambiguous, legal, without prejudishish lawyer's way, he was trying to warn me."

"Why should he?"

"I don't know," confessed Tuppence. "But he looked kind, and simply awfully clever. I wouldn't mind going to him and telling him everything."

Somewhat to her surprise, Julius negatived the idea sharply.

"See here," he said, "we don't want any lawyers mixed up in this. That guy couldn't help us any."

"Well, I believe he could," reiterated Tuppence obstinately.

"Don't you think it. So long. I'll be back in half an hour."

Thirty-five minutes had elapsed when Julius returned. He took Tuppence by the arm, and walked her to the window.

"There she is."

"Oh!" said Tuppence with a note of reverence in her voice, as she gazed down at the enormous car.

"She's some pacemaker, I can tell you," said Julius complacently.

"How did you get it?" gasped Tuppence.

"She was just being sent home to some bigwig."

"Well?"

"I went round to his house," said Julius. "I said that I reckoned a car like that was worth every penny of twenty thousand dollars. Then I told him that it was worth just about fifty thousand dollars to me if he'd get out."

"Well?" said Tuppence, intoxicated.

"Well," returned Julius, "he got out, that's all."

12

A Friend in Need

FRIDAY AND SATURDAY passed uneventfully. Tuppence had received a brief answer to her appeal from Mr. Carter. In it he pointed out that the Young Adventurers had undertaken the work at their own risk, and had been fully warned of the dangers. If anything had happened to Tommy he regretted it deeply, but he could do nothing.

This was cold comfort. Somehow, without Tommy, all the savor went out of the adventure, and, for the first time, Tuppence felt doubtful of success. While they had been together she had never questioned it for a minute. Although she was accustomed to take the lead, and to pride herself on her quick-wittedness, in reality she had relied upon Tommy more than she realized at the time. There was something so eminently sober and clear-headed about him, his common sense and soundness of vision were so unvarying, that without him Tuppence felt much like a rudderless ship. It was curious that Julius, who was undoubtedly much cleverer than Tommy, did not give her the same feeling of support. She had accused Tommy of being a pessimist, and it is certain that he always saw the disadvantages and difficulties which she herself was optimistically given to overlooking, but nevertheless she had really relied a good deal on his judgment. He might be slow, but he was very sure.

It seemed to the girl that, for the first time, she realized the sinister character of the mission they had undertaken so lightheartedly. It had begun like a page of romance. Now, shorn of its glamor, it seemed to be turning to grim reality. Tommy—that was all that mattered. Many times in the day Tuppence blinked the tears out of her eyes resolutely. "Little fool" she would apostrophize herself, "don't snivel. Of course you're fond of him. You've known him all your life. But there's no need to be sentimental about it."

In the meantime, nothing more was seen of Boris. He did not come to the flat, and Julius and the car waited in vain. Tuppence gave herself over to new meditations. Whilst admitting the truth of Julius's objections, she had nevertheless not entirely relinquished the idea of appealing to Sir James Peel Edgerton. Indeed, she had gone so far as to look up his address in the *Red Book*. Had he meant to warn her that day? If so, why? Surely she was at least entitled to demand an explanation. He had looked at her so kindly. Perhaps he might tell them something concerning Mrs. Vandemeyer which might lead to a clue to Tommy's whereabouts.

Anyway, Tuppence decided, with her usual shake of the shoulders, it was worth trying, and try it she would. Sunday was her afternoon out. She would meet Julius, persuade him to her point of view, and they would beard the lion in his den.

When the day arrived Julius needed a considerable amount of persuading, but Tuppence held firm. "It can do no harm," was what she always came back to. In the end Julius gave in, and they proceeded in the car to Carlton House Terrace.

The door was opened by an irreproachable butler. Tuppence felt a little nervous. After all, perhaps it *was* colossal cheek on her part. She had decided not to ask if Sir James was "at home," but to adopt a more personal attitude.

"Will you ask Sir James if I can see him for a few minutes? I have an important message for him."

The butler retired, returning a moment or two later.

"Sir James will see you. Will you step this way?"

He ushered them into a room at the back of the house, furnished as a library. The collection of books was a magnificent one, and Tuppence noticed that all one wall was devoted to works on crime and criminology. There were several deep-padded leather armchairs, and an old-fashioned open hearth. In the window was a big rolltop desk strewn with papers at which the master of the house was sitting.

He rose as they entered.

"You have a message for me? Ah"—he recognized Tuppence with a smile—"it's you, is it? Brought a message from Mrs. Vandemeyer, I suppose?"

"Not exactly," said Tuppence. "In fact, I'm afraid I only said that to be quite sure of getting in. Oh, by the way, this is Mr. Hersheimmer, Sir James Peel Edgerton."

"Pleased to meet you," said the American, shooting out a hand.

"Won't you both sit down?" asked Sir James. He drew forward two chairs.

"Sir James," said Tuppence, plunging boldly, "I dare say you will think it is most awful cheek of me coming here like this. Because, of course, it's nothing whatever to do with you, and then you're a very important person, and of course Tommy and I are very unimportant." She paused for breath.

"Tommy?" queried Sir James, looking across at the American.

"No, that's Julius," explained Tuppence. "I'm rather nervous, and that makes me tell it badly. What I really want to know is what you meant by what you said to me the other day? Did you mean to warn me against Mrs. Vandemeyer? You did, didn't you?"

"My dear young lady, as far as I recollect I only mentioned that there were equally good situations to be obtained elsewhere."

"Yes, I know. But it was a hint, wasn't it?"

"Well, perhaps it was," admitted Sir James gravely.

"Well, I want to know more. I want to know just *why* you gave me a hint."

Sir James smiled at her earnestness.

"Suppose the lady brings a libel action against me for defamation of character?"

"Of course," said Tuppence. "I know lawyers are always dreadfully careful. But can't we say 'without prejudice' first, and then say just what we want to."

"Well," said Sir James, still smiling "without prejudice, then, if I had a young sister forced to earn her living, I should not like to see her in Mrs. Vandemeyer's service. I felt it incumbent on me just to give you a hint. It is no place for a young and inexperienced girl. That is all I can tell you."

"I see," said Tuppence thoughtfully. "Thank you very much. But I'm not *really* inexperienced, you know. I knew perfectly that she was a bad lot when I went there—as a matter of fact that's *why* I went——" She broke off, seeing some bewilderment on the lawyer's face, and went on: "I think perhaps I'd better tell you the whole story, Sir James. I've a sort of feeling that you'd know in a minute if I didn't tell the truth, and so you might as well know all about it from the beginning. What do you think, Julius?"

"As you're bent on it, I'd go right ahead with the facts," replied the American, who had so far sat in silence.

"Yes, tell me all about it," said Sir James. "I want to know who Tommy is."

Thus encouraged Tuppence plunged into her tale, and the lawyer listened with close attention.

"Very interesting,' he said, when she finished. "A great deal of what you tell me, child, is already known to me. I've had certain theories of my own about this Jane Finn. You've done extraordinarily well so far, but it's rather too bad of—what do you know him as?—Mr. Carter to pitchfork you two young things into an affair of this kind. By the way, where did Mr. Hersheimmer come in originally? You didn't make that clear?"

Julius answered for himself.

"I'm Jane's first cousin," he explained, returning the lawyer's keen gaze.

"Ah!"

"Oh, Sir James," broke out Tuppence, "what do you think has become of Tommy?"

"H'm." The lawyer rose, and paced slowly up and down. "When you arrived, young lady, I was just packing up my traps. Going to Scotland by the night train for a few days' fishing. But there are different kinds of fishing. I've a good mind to stay, and see if we can't get on the track of that young chap."

"Oh!" Tuppence clasped her hands ecstatically.

"All the same, as I said before, it's too bad of—of Carter to set you two babies on a job like this. Now, don't get offended, Miss—er——"

"Cowley. Prudence Cowley. But my friends call me Tuppence."

"Well, Miss Tuppence, then, as I'm certainly going to be a friend. Don't be offended because I think you're young. Youth is a failing only too easily outgrown. Now, about this young Tommy of yours——"

"Yes." Tuppence clasped her hands.

"Frankly, things look bad for him. He's been butting in somewhere where he wasn't wanted. Not a doubt of it. But don't give up hope."

"And you really will help us? There, Julius! He didn't want me to come," she added by way of explanation.

"H'm," said the lawyer, favoring Julius with another keen glance. "And why was that?"

"I reckoned it would be no good worrying you with a petty little business like this."

"I see." He paused a moment. "This petty little business, as you call it, bears directly on a very big business, bigger perhaps than either you or Miss Tuppence know. If this boy is alive, he may have very valuable information to give us. Therefore, we must find him."

"Yes, but how?" cried Tuppence. "I've tried to think of everything."

Sir James smiled.

"And yet there's one person quite near at hand who in all probability knows where he is, or at all events where he is likely to be."

"Who is that?" asked Tuppence, puzzled.

"Mrs. Vandemeyer."

"Yes, but she'd never tell us."

"Ah, that is where I come in. I think it quite likely that I shall be able to make Mrs. Vandemeyer tell me what I want to know."

"How?" demanded Tuppence, opening her eyes very wide.

"Oh, just by asking her questions," replied Sir James easily. "That's the way we do it, you know."

He tapped with his finger on the table, and Tuppence felt again the intense power that radiated from the man.

"And if she won't tell?" asked Julius suddenly.

"I think she will. I have one or two powerful levers. Still, in that unlikely event, there is always the possibility of bribery."

"Sure. And that's where I come in!" cried Julius, bringing his fist down on the table with a bang. "You can count on me, if necessary, for one million dollars. Yes sir, one million dollars!"

Sir James sat down and subjected Julius to a long scrutiny.

"Mr. Hersheimmer," he said at last, "that is a very large sum."

"I guess it'll have to be. These aren't the kind of folk to offer sixpence to."

"At the present rate of exchange it amounts to considerably over two hundred and fifty thousand pounds."

"That's so. Maybe you think I'm talking through my hat, but I can deliver the goods all right, with enough over to spare for your fee."

Sir James flushed slightly.

"There is no question of a fee, Mr. Hersheimmer. I am not a private detective."

"Sorry. I guess I was just a mite hasty, but I've been feeling bad about this money question. I wanted to offer a big reward for news of Jane some days ago, but your crusted institution of Scotland Yard advised me against it. Said it was undesirable."

"They were probably right," said Sir James dryly.

"But it's all O.K. about Julius," put in Tuppence. "He's not pulling your leg. He's got simply pots of money."

"The old man piled it up in style," explained Julius. "Now, let's get down to it. What's your idea?"

Sir James considered for a moment or two.

"There is no time to be lost. The sooner we strike the better." He turned to Tuppence. "Is Mrs. Vandemeyer dining out tonight, do you know?"

"Yes, I think so but she will not be out late. Otherwise, she would have taken the latchkey."

"Good. I will call upon her about ten o'clock. What time are you supposed to return?"

"About nine-thirty or ten, but I could go back earlier."

"You must not do that on any account. It might arouse suspicion if you did not stay out till the usual time. Be back by nine-thirty. I will arrive at ten. Mr. Hersheimmer will wait below in a taxi perhaps."

"He's got a new Rolls-Royce car," said Tuppence with vicarious pride.

"Even better. If I succeed in obtaining the address from her, we can go there at once, taking Mrs. Vandemeyer with us if necessary. You understand?"

"Yes." Tuppence rose to her feet with a skip of delight. "Oh, I feel so much better!"

"Don't build on it too much, Miss Tuppence. Go easy."

Julius turned to the lawyer.

"Say, then. I'll call for you in the car round about nine-thirty. Is that right?"

"Perhaps that will be the best plan. It would be unnecessary to have two cars waiting about. Now, Miss Tuppence, my advice to you is to go and have a good dinner, a *really* good one, mind. And don't think ahead more than you can help."

He shook hands with them both, and a moment later they were outside.

"Isn't he a duck?" inquired Tuppence ecstatically, as she skipped down the steps. "Oh, Julius, isn't he just a duck?"

"Well, I allow he seems to be the goods all right. And I was wrong about its being useless to go to him. Say, shall we go right back to the Ritz?"

"I must walk a bit, I think. I feel so excited. Drop me in the park, will you? Unless you'd like to come too?"

"I want to get some petrol," he explained. "And send off a cable or two."

"All right. I'll meet you at the Ritz at seven. We'll have to dine upstairs. I can't show myself in these glad rags."

"Sure. I'll get Felix help me choose the menu. He's some head waiter, that. So long."

Tuppence walked briskly along toward the Serpentine, first glancing at her watch. It was nearly six o'clock. She remembered that she had had no tea, but felt too excited to be conscious of hunger. She walked as far as Kensington Gardens and then slowly retraced her steps, feeling infinitely better for the fresh air and exercise. It was not so easy to follow Sir James's advice, and put the possible events of the evening out of her head. As she drew nearer and nearer to Hyde Park corner, the temptation to return to South Audley Mansions was almost irresistible.

At any rate, she decided, it would do no harm just to go and *look* at the building. Perhaps, then, she could resign herself to waiting patiently for ten o'clock.

South Audley Mansions looked exactly the same as usual. What Tuppence had expected she hardly knew, but the sight of its red brick stolidity slightly assuaged the growing and entirely unreasonable uneasiness that possessed her. She was just turning away when she heard a piercing whistle, and the faithful Albert came running from the building to join her.

Tuppence frowned. It was no part of the program to have attention called to her presence in the neighborhood, but Albert was purple with suppressed excitement.

"I say, miss, she's a going!"

"Who's going?" demanded Tuppence sharply.

"The crook. Ready Rita. Mrs. Vandemeyer. She's a-packing up, and she's just sent down word for me to get her a taxi."

"What?" Tuppence clutched his arm.

"It's the truth, miss. I thought maybe as you didn't know about it."

"Albert," cried Tuppence, "you're a brick. If it hadn't been for you we'd have lost her."

Albert flushed with pleasure at this tribute.

"There's no time to lose," said Tuppence, crossing the road. "I've got to stop her. At all costs I must keep her here until——" She broke off. "Albert, there's a telephone here, isn't there?"

The boy shook his head.

"The flats mostly have their own, miss. But there's a box just around the corner."

"Go to it then, at once, and ring up the Ritz Hotel. Ask for Mr.

Hersheimmer, and when you get him tell him to get Sir James and come on at once, as Mrs. Vandemeyer is trying to hook it. If you can't get him, ring up Sir James Peel Edgerton, you'll find his number in the book, and tell him what's happening. You won't forget the names, will you?"

Albert repeated them glibly. "You trust to me, miss, it'll be all right. But what about you? Aren't you afraid to trust yourself with her?"

"No, no, that's all right. *But go and telephone*. Be quick."

Drawing a long breath, Tuppence entered the Mansions and ran up to the door of No. 20. How she was to detain Mrs. Vandemeyer until the two men arrived, she did not know, but somehow or other it had to be done, and she must accomplish the task single-handed. What had occasioned this precipitate departure? Did Mrs. Vandemeyer suspect her?

Speculations were idle. Tuppence pressed the bell firmly. She might learn something from the cook.

Nothing happened and, after waiting some minutes, Tuppence pressed the bell again, keeping her finger on the button for some little while. At last she heard footsteps inside, and a moment later Mrs. Vandemeyer herself opened the door. She lifted her eyebrows at the sight of the girl.

"You?"

"I had a touch of toothache, ma'am," said Tuppence glibly. "So thought it better to come home and have a quiet evening."

Mrs. Vandemeyer said nothing, but she drew back and let Tuppence pass into the hall.

"How unfortunate for you," she said coldly. "You had better go to bed."

"Oh, I shall be all right in the kitchen, ma'am. Cook will——"

"Cook is out," said Mrs. Vandemeyer, in a rather disagreeable tone. "I sent her out. So you see you had better go to bed."

Suddenly Tuppence felt afraid. There was a ring in Mrs. Vandemeyer's voice that she did not like at all. Also, the other woman was slowly edging her up the passage. Tuppence turned at bay.

"I don't want——"

Then, in a flash, a rim of cold steel touched her temple, and Mrs. Vandemeyer's voice rose cold and menacing:

"You damned little fool! Do you think I don't know? No, don't answer. If you struggle or cry out, I'll shoot you like a dog."

The rim of steel pressed a little harder against the girl's temple.

"Now then, march," went on Mrs. Vandemeyer. "This way—into my room. In a minute, when I've done with you, you'll go to bed as I told you to. And you'll sleep—oh yes, my little spy, you'll sleep all right!"

There was a sort of hideous geniality in the last words which Tuppence did not at all like. For the moment there was nothing to be done, and she walked obediently into Mrs. Vandemeyer's bedroom. The pistol never left her forehead. The room was in a state of wild disorder, clothes were flung about right and left, a suitcase and a hat box, half packed, stood in the middle of the floor.

Tuppence pulled herself together with an effort. Her voice shook a little, but she spoke out bravely.

"Come now," she said. "This is nonsense. You can't shoot me. Why, every one in the building would hear the report."

"I'd risk that," said Mrs. Vandemeyer cheerfully. "But, as long as you don't sing out for help, you're all right—and I don't think you will. You're a clever girl. You deceived *me* all right. I hadn't a suspicion of you! So I've no doubt that you understand perfectly well that this is where I'm on top and you're underneath. Now then—sit on the bed. Put your hands above your head, and if you value your life don't move them."

Tuppence obeyed passively. Her good sense told her that there was nothing else to do but accept the situation. If she shrieked for help there was very little chance of anyone hearing her, whereas there was probably quite a good chance of Mrs. Vandemeyer's shooting her. In the meantime, every minute of delay gained was valuable.

Mrs. Vandemeyer laid down the revolver on the edge of the washstand within reach of her hand, and, still eyeing Tuppence like a lynx in case the girl should attempt to move, she took a little stoppered bottle from its place on the marble and poured some of its contents into a glass which she filled up with water.

"What's that?" asked Tuppence sharply.

"Something to make you sleep soundly."

Tuppence paled a little.

"Are you going to poison me?" she asked in a whisper.

"Perhaps," said Mrs. Vandemeyer, smiling agreeably.

"Then I shan't drink it," said Tuppence firmly. "I'd much rather be shot. At any rate that would make a row, and some one might hear it. But I won't be killed off quietly like a lamb."

Mrs. Vandemeyer stamped her foot.

"Don't be a little fool! Do you really think I want a hue and cry for murder out after me? If you've any sense at all, you'll realize that poisoning you wouldn't suit my book at all. It's a sleeping draught, that's all. You'll wake up tomorrow morning none the worse. I simply don't want the bother of tying you up and gagging you. That's the alternative—and you won't like it, I can tell you! I can be very rough if I choose. So drink this down like a good girl, and you'll be none the worse for it."

In her hearts of hearts Tuppence believed her. The arguments she had adduced rang true. It was a simple and effective method of getting her out of the way for the time being. Nevertheless, the girl did not take kindly to the idea of being tamely put to sleep without as much as one bid for freedom. She felt that once Mrs. Vandemeyer gave them the slip, the last hope of finding Tommy would be gone.

Tuppence was quick in her mental processes. All these reflections passed through her mind in a flash, and she saw where a chance, a very problematical chance, lay, and she determined to risk all in one supreme effort.

Accordingly, she lurched suddenly off the bed and fell on her knees before Mrs. Vandemeyer, clutching her skirts frantically.

"I don't believe it," she moaned. "It's poison—I know it's poison. Oh, don't make me drink it"—her voice rose to a shriek—"don't make me drink it!"

Mrs. Vandemeyer, glass in hand, looked down with a curling lip at this sudden collapse.

"Get up, you little idiot! Don't go on driveling there. How you ever had the nerve to play your part as you did I can't think." She stamped her foot. "Get up, I say."

But Tuppence continued to cling and sob, interjecting her sobs with incoherent appeals for mercy. Every minute gained was to the good. Moreover, as she groveled, she moved imperceptibly nearer to her objective.

Mrs. Vandemeyer gave a sharp impatient exclamation, and jerked the girl to her knees.

"Drink it at once!" Imperiously she pressed the glass to the girl's lips.

Tuppence gave one last despairing moan.

"You swear it won't hurt me?" she temporized.

"Of course it won't hurt you. Don't be a fool."

"Will you swear it?"

"Yes, yes," said the other impatiently. "I swear it."

Tuppence raised a trembling left hand to the glass.

"Very well." Her mouth opened meekly.

Mrs. Vandemeyer gave a sigh of relief, off her guard for the moment. Then, quick as a flash, Tuppence jerked the glass upward as hard as she could. The fluid in it splashed into Mrs. Vandemeyer's face, and during her momentary gasp, Tuppence's right hand shot out and grasped the revolver where it lay on the edge of the washstand. The next moment she had sprung back a pace, and the revolver pointed straight at Mrs. Vandemeyer's heart, with no unsteadiness in the hand that held it.

In the moment of victory, Tuppence betrayed a somewhat unsportsmanlike triumph.

"Now who's on top and who's underneath?" she crowed.

The other's face was convulsed with rage. For a minute Tuppence thought she was going to spring upon her, which would have placed the girl in an unpleasant dilemma, since she meant to draw the line at actually letting off the revolver. However, with an effort Mrs. Vandemeyer controlled herself, and at last a slow evil smile crept over her face.

"Not a fool, then, after all! You did that well, girl. But you shall pay for it—oh, yes, you shall pay for it! I have a long memory!"

"I'm surprised you should have been gulled so easily," said Tuppence scornfully. "Did you really think I was the kind of girl to roll about on the floor and whine for mercy?"

"You may do—someday!" said the other significantly.

The cold malignity of her manner sent an unpleasant chill down Tuppence's spine, but she was not going to give in to it.

"Supposing we sit down," she said pleasantly. "Our present attitude is a little melodramatic. No—not on the bed. Draw a chair up to the table, that's right. Now I'll sit opposite you with the revolver in front of me—just in case of accidents. Splendid! Now, let's talk."

"What about?" said Mrs. Vandemeyer sullenly.

Tuppence eyed her thoughtfully for a minute. She was remembering several things. Boris's words, "I believe you would sell—*us!*" and her answer, "The price would have to be enormous," given lightly, it was true, yet might not there be a substratum of truth in it? Long ago, had not Whittington asked: "Who's been blabbing? Rita?" Would Rita Vandemeyer prove to be the weak spot in the armor of Mr. Brown?

Keeping her eyes fixed steadily on the other's face, Tuppence replied quietly:

"Money——"

Mrs. Vandemeyer started. Clearly, the reply was unexpected.

"What do you mean?"

"I'll tell you. You said just now that you had a long memory. A long memory isn't half as useful as a long purse! I dare say it relieves your feelings a good deal to plan out all sorts of dreadful things to do to me, but is that *practical?* Revenge is very unsatisfactory. Everyone always says so. But money" —Tuppence warmed to her pet creed—"well, there's nothing unsatisfactory about money, is there?"

"Do you think," said Mrs. Vandemeyer scornfully, "that I am the kind of woman to sell my friends?"

"Yes," said Tuppence promptly. "If the price was big enough."

"A paltry hundred pounds or so!"

"No," said Tuppence. "I should suggest—a hundred thousand!"

Her economical spirit did not permit her to mention the whole million dollars suggested by Julius.

A flush crept over Mrs. Vandemeyer's face.

"What did you say?" she asked, her fingers playing nervously with a brooch on her breast. In that moment Tuppence knew that the fish was hooked, and for the first time she felt a horror of her own money-loving spirit. It gave her a dreadful sense of kinship to the woman fronting her.

"A hundred thousand pounds," repeated Tuppence.

The light died out of Mrs. Vandemeyer's eyes. She leaned back in her chair.

"Bah!" she said. "You haven't got it."

"No," admitted Tuppence, "I haven't—but I know some one who has."

"Who?"

"A friend of mine."

"Must be a millionaire," remarked Mrs. Vandemeyer unbelievingly.

"As a matter of fact he is. He's an American. He'll pay you that without a murmur. You can take it from me that it's a perfectly genuine proposition."

Mrs. Vandemeyer sat up again.

"I'm inclined to believe you," she said slowly.

There was a silence between them for some time, then Mrs. Vandemeyer looked up.

"What does he want to know, this friend of yours?"

Tuppence went through a momentary struggle, but it was Julius's money, and his interests must come first.

"He wants to know where Jane Finn is," she said boldly.

Mrs. Vandemeyer showed no surprise.

"I'm not sure where she is at the present moment," she replied.

"But you could find out?"

"Oh, yes," returned Mrs. Vandemeyer carelessly. "There would be no difficulty about that."

"Then"—Tuppence's voice shook a little—"there's a boy, a friend of mine. I'm afraid something's happened to him, through your pal Boris."

"What's his name?"

"Tommy Beresford."

"Never heard of him. But I'll ask Boris. He'll tell me anything he knows."

"Thank you." Tuppence felt a terrific rise in her spirits. It impelled her to more audacious efforts. "There's one thing more."

"Well?"

Tuppence leaned forward and lowered her voice.

"Who is Mr. Brown?"

Her quick eyes saw the sudden paling of the beautiful face. With an effort Mrs. Vandemeyer pulled herself together and tried to resume her former manner. But the attempt was a mere parody.

She shrugged her shoulders.

"You can't have learnt much about us if you don't know that *nobody knows who Mr. Brown is. . . .*"

"You do," said Tuppence quietly.

Again the color deserted the other's face.

"What makes you think that?"

"I don't know," said the girl truthfully. "But I'm sure."

Mrs. Vandemeyer stared in front of her for a long time.

"Yes," she said hoarsely, at last, "*I* know. I was beautiful, you see—very beautiful——"

"You are still," said Tuppence with admiration.

Mrs. Vandemeyer shook her head. There was a strange gleam in her electric-blue eyes.

"Not beautiful enough," she said in a soft dangerous voice. "Not—beautiful—enough! And sometimes, lately, I've been afraid. . . . It's dangerous to know too much!" She leaned forward across the table. "Swear that my name shan't be brought into it—that no one shall ever know."

"I swear it. And, once he's caught, you'll be out of danger."

A terrified look swept across Mrs. Vandemeyer's face.

"Shall I? Shall I ever be?" She clutched Tuppence's arm. "You're sure about the money?"

"Quite sure."

"When shall I have it? There must be no delay."

"This friend of mine will be here presently. He may have to send cables, or something like that. But there won't be any delay—he's a terrific hustler."

A resolute look settled on Mrs. Vandemeyer's face.

"I'll do it. It's a great sum of money, and besides"—she gave a curious smile—"it is not—wise to throw over a woman like me!"

For a moment or two, she remained smiling, and lightly tapping her fingers on the table. Suddenly she started, and her face blanched.

"What was that?"

"I heard nothing."

Mrs. Vanmdemeyer gazed round her fearfully.

"If there should be someone listening——"

"Nonsense. Who could there be?"

"Even the walls might have ears," whispered the other. "I tell you I'm frightened. You don't know him!"

"Think of the hundred thousand pounds," said Tuppence soothingly.

Mrs. Vandemeyer passed her tongue over her dried lips.

"You don't know him," she reiterated hoarsely. "He's—ah!"

With a shriek of terror she sprang to her feet. Her outstretched hand pointed over Tuppence's head. Then she swayed to the ground in a dead faint.

Tuppence looked round to see what had startled her.

In the doorway were Sir James Peel Edgerton and Julius Hersheimmer.

13
The Vigil

SIR JAMES BRUSHED past Julius and hurriedly bent over the fallen woman.

"Heart," he said sharply. "Seeing us so suddenly must have given her a shock. Brandy—and quickly, or she'll slip through our fingers."

Julius hurried to the washstand.

"Not there," said Tuppence over her shoulder. "In the tantalus in the dining room. Second door down the passage."

Between them Sir James and Tuppence lifted Mrs. Vandemeyer and carried her to the bed. There they dashed water on her face, but with no result. The lawyer fingered her pulse.

"Touch and go," he muttered. "I wish that young fellow would hurry up with the brandy."

At that moment Julius reentered the room, carrying a glass half full of the spirit which he handed to Sir James. While Tuppence lifted her head the lawyer tried to force a little of the spirit between her closed lips. Finally the woman opened her eyes feebly. Tuppence held the glass to her lips.

"Drink this."

Mrs. Vandemeyer complied. The brandy brought the color back to her white cheeks, and revived her in a marvelous fashion. She tried to sit up—then fell back with a groan, her hand to her side.

"It's my heart," she whispered. "I mustn't talk."

She lay back with closed eyes.

Sir James kept his finger on her wrist a minute longer, then withdrew it with a nod.

"She'll do now."

All three moved away, and stood together talking in low voices. One and all were conscious of a certain feeling of anticlimax. Clearly any scheme for cross-questioning the lady was out of the question for the moment. For the time being they were baffled, and could do nothing.

Tuppence related how Mrs. Vandemeyer had declared herself willing to disclose the identity of Mr. Brown, and how she had consented to discover and reveal to them the whereabouts of Jane Finn. Julius was congratulatory.

"That's alright, Miss Tuppence. Splendid! I guess that hundred thousand pounds will look just as good in the morning to the lady as it did overnight. There's nothing to worry over. She won't speak without the cash anyway, you bet!"

There was certainly a good deal of common sense in this, and Tuppence felt a little comforted.

"What you say is true," said Sir James meditatively. "I must confess, however, that I cannot help wishing we had not interrupted at the minute we did. Still, it cannot be helped, it is only a matter of waiting until the morning."

He looked across at the inert figure on the bed. Mrs. Vandemeyer lay perfectly passive with closed eyes. He shook his head.

"Well," said Tuppence, with an attempt at cheerfulness, "we must wait until the morning, that's all. But I don't think we ought to leave the flat."

"What about leaving that bright boy of yours on guard?"

"Albert? And suppose she came round again and hooked it. Albert couldn't stop her."

"I guess she won't want to make tracks away from the dollars."

"She might. She seemed very frightened of 'Mr. Brown.'"

"What? Real plumb scared of him?"

"Yes. She looked round and said even walls had ears."

"Maybe she meant a dictaphone," said Julius with interest.

"Miss Tuppence is right," said Sir James quietly. "We must not leave the flat—if only for Mrs. Vandemeyer's sake."

Julius stared at him.

"You think he'd get after her? Between now and tomorrow morning. How could he know, even?"

"You forget your own suggestion of a dictaphone," said Sir James dryly. "We have a very formidable adversary. I believe, if we exercise all due care, that there is a very good chance of his being delivered into our hands. But we must neglect no precaution. We have an important witness, but she must be safeguarded. I would suggest that Miss Tuppence should go to bed, and that you and I, Mr. Hersheimmer, should share the vigil."

Tuppence was about to protest, but happening to glance at the bed she saw Mrs. Vandemeyer, her eyes half-open, with such an expression of mingled fear and malevolence on her face that it quite froze the words on her lips.

For a moment she wondered whether the faint and the heart attack had been a gigantic sham, but remembering the deadly pallor she could hardly credit the supposition. As she looked the expression disappeared as by magic, and Mrs. Vandemeyer lay inert and motionless as before. For a moment the girl fancied she must have dreamt it. But she determined nevertheless to be on the alert.

"Well," said Julius, "I guess we'd better make a move out of here anyway."

The others fell in with his suggestion. Sir James again felt Mrs. Vandemeyer's pulse.

"Perfectly satisfactory," he said in a low voice to Tuppence. "She'll be absolutely alright after a night's rest."

The girl hesitated a moment by the bed. The intensity of the expression she had surprised had impressed her powerfully. Mrs. Vandemeyer lifted her lids. She seemed to be struggling to speak. Tuppence bent over her.

"Don't—leave——" she seemed unable to proceed, murmuring something that sounded like "sleepy." Then she tried again.

Tuppence bent lower still. It was only a breath.

"Mr.—Brown——" The voice stopped.

But the half-closed eyes seemed still to send an agonized message.

Moved by a sudden impulse, the girl said quickly:

"I shan't leave the flat. I shall sit up all night."

A flash of relief showed before the lids descended once more. Apparently Mrs. Vandemeyer slept. But her words had awakened a new uneasiness in Tuppence. What had she meant by that low murmur: "Mr. Brown"? Tuppence caught herself nervously looking over her shoulder. The big wardrobe loomed up in a sinister fashion before her eyes. Plenty of room for a man to hide in that. . . . Half-ashamed of herself, Tuppence pulled it open and looked inside. No one—of course! She stooped down and looked under the bed. There was no other possible hiding place.

Tuppence gave her familiar shake of the shoulders. It was absurb, this giving way to nerves! Slowly she went out of the room. Julius and Sir James were talking in a low voice. Sir James turned to her.

"Lock the door on the outside, please, Miss Tuppence, and take out the key. There must be no chance of anyone entering that room."

The gravity of his manner impressed them, and Tuppence felt less ashamed of her attack of "nerves."

"Say," remarked Julius suddenly, "there's Tuppence's bright boy. I guess I'd better go down and ease his young mind. That's some lad, Tuppence."

"How did you get in, by the way?" asked Tuppence suddenly. "I forgot to ask."

"Well, Albert got me on the phone alright. I ran round for Sir James here, and we came right on. The boy was on the lookout for us, and was just a mite worried about what might have happened to you. He'd been listening outside the door of the flat, but couldn't hear anything. Anyhow he suggested sending us up in the coal lift instead of ringing the bell. And sure enough we landed in the scullery and came right along to find you. Albert's still below, and must be just hopping mad by this time." With which Julius departed abruptly.

"Now then, Miss Tuppence," said Sir James, "you know this place better than I do. Where do you suggest we should take up our quarters?"

Tuppence considered for a moment or two.

"I think Mrs. Vandemeyer's boudoir would be the most comfortable," she said at last, and led the way there.

Sir James looked round approvingly.

"This will do very well, and now, my dear young lady, do go to bed and get some sleep."

Tuppence shook her head resolutely.

"I couldn't, thank you, Sir James. I should dream of Mr. Brown all night!"

"But you'll be so tired, child."

"No, I shan't. I'd rather stay up—really."

The lawyer gave in.

Julius reappeared some minutes later, having reassured Albert and rewarded him lavishly for his services. Having in his turn failed to persuade Tuppence to go to bed, he said decisively:

"At any rate, you've got to have something to eat right away. Where's the larder?"

Tuppence directed him, and he returned in a few minutes with a cold pie and three plates.

After a hearty meal, the girl felt inclined to pooh-pooh her fancies of half an hour before. The power of the money bribe could not fail.

"And now, Miss Tuppence," said Sir James, "we want to hear your adventures."

"That's so," agreed Julius.

Tuppence narrated her adventures with some complacence. Julius occasionally interjected an admiring "Bully." Sir James said nothing until she had finished, when his quiet "well done, Miss Tuppence," made her flush with pleasure.

"There's one thing I don't get clearly," said Julius. "What put her up to clearing out?"

"I don't know," confessed Tuppence.

Sir James stroked his chin thoughtfully.

"The room was in great disorder. That looks as though her flight was unpremeditated. Almost as though she got a sudden warning to go from someone."

"Mr. Brown, I suppose," said Julius scoffingly.

The lawyer looked at him deliberately for a minute or two.

"Why not?" he said. "Remember, you yourself have once been worsted by him."

Julius flushed with vexation.

"I feel just mad when I think of how I handed out Jane's photograph to him like a lamb. Gee, if I ever lay hands on it again, I'll freeze on to it like—like hell!"

"That contingency is likely to be a remote one," said the other dryly.

"I guess you're right," said Julius frankly. "And, in any case, it's the original I'm out after. Where do you think she can be, Sir James?"

The lawyer shook his head.

"Impossible to say. But I've a very good idea where she *has* been."

"You have? Where?"

Sir James smiled.

"At the scene of your nocturnal adventures, the Bournemouth nursing home."

"There? Impossible. I asked."

"No, my dear sir, you asked if anyone of the name of Jane Finn had been there. Now, if the girl had been placed there it would almost certainly be under an assumed name."

"Bully for you," cried Julius. "I never thought of that!"

"It was fairly obvious," said the other.

"Perhaps the doctor's in it too," suggested Tuppence.

Julius shook his head.

"I don't think so. I took to him at once. No, I'm pretty sure Dr. Hall's alright."

"Hall, did you say?" asked Sir James. "That is curious—really very curious."

"Why?" demanded Tuppence.

"Because I happened to meet him this morning. I've known him slightly on and off for some years, and this morning I ran across him in the street. Staying at the Métropole, he told me." He turned to Julius. "Didn't he tell you he was coming up to town?"

Julius shook his head.

"Curious," mused Sir James. "You did not mention his name this afternoon, or I would have suggested your going to him for further information with my card as introduction."

"I guess I'm a mutt,' said Julius with unusual humility. "I ought to have thought of the false name stunt."

"How could you think of anything after falling out of that tree?" cried Tuppence. "I'm sure anyone else would have been killed right off."

"Well, I guess it doesn't matter now, anyway," said Julius. "We've got Mrs. Vandemeyer on a string, and that's all we need."

"Yes," said Tuppence, but there was a lack of assurance in her voice.

A silence settled down over the party. Little by little the magic of the night began to gain a hold on them. There were sudden creaks in the furniture, imperceptible rustlings in the curtains. Suddenly Tuppence sprang up with a cry.

"I can't help it. I know Mr. Brown's somewhere in the flat! I can *feel* him."

"Sure, Tuppence, how could he be? This door's open into the hall. No one could have come in by the front door without our seeing and hearing him."

"I can't help it. I *feel* he's here!"

She looked appealingly at Sir James, who replied gravely:

"With due deference to your feelings, Miss Tuppence (and mine as well for that matter), I do not see how it is humanly possible for anyone to be in the flat without our knowledge."

The girl was a little comforted by his words.

"Sitting up at night is always rather jumpy," she confessed.

"Yes," said Sir James. "We are in the condition of people holding a séance. Perhaps if a medium were present we might get some marvelous results."

"Do you believe in spiritualism?" asked Tuppence, opening her eyes wide.

The lawyer shrugged his shoulders.

"There is some truth in it, without a doubt. But most of the testimony would not pass muster in the witness box."

The hours drew on. With the first faint glimmerings of dawn, Sir James drew aside the curtains. They beheld, what few Londoners see, the slow rising of the sun over the sleeping city. Somehow, with the coming of the light, the dreads and fancies of the past night seemed absurd. Tuppence's spirits revived to the normal.

"Hooray!" she said. "It's going to be a gorgeous day. And we shall find Tommy. And Jane Finn. And everything will be lovely. I shall ask Mr. Carter if I can't be made a Dame!"

At seven o'clock Tuppence volunteered to go and make some tea. She returned with a tray, containing the teapot and four cups.

"Who's the other cup for?" inquired Julius.

"The prisoner, of course. I suppose we might call her that?"

"Taking her tea seems a kind of anticlimax to last night," said Julius thoughtfully.

"Yes, it does," admitted Tuppence. "But, anyway, here goes. Perhaps you'd both come, too, in case she springs on me, or anything. You see, we don't know what mood she'll wake up in."

Sir James and Julius accompanied her to the door.

"Where's the key? Oh, of course, I've got it myself."

She put it in the lock, and turned it, then paused.

"Supposing, after all, she's escaped?" she murmured in a whisper.

"Plumb impossible," replied Julius reassuringly.

But Sir James said nothing.

Tuppence drew a long breath and entered. She heaved a sigh of relief as she saw that Mrs. Vandemeyer was lying on the bed.

"Good morning," she remarked cheerfully. "I've brought you some tea."

Mrs. Vandemeyer did not reply. Tuppence put down the cup on the table by the bed and went across to draw up the blinds. When she turned, Mrs. Vandemeyer still lay without a movement. With a sudden fear clutching at her heart, Tuppence ran to the bed. The hand she lifted was cold as ice. . . . Mrs. Vandemeyer would never speak now. . . .

Her cry brought the others. A very few minutes sufficed. Mrs. Vandemeyer was dead—must have been dead some hours. She had evidently died in her sleep.

"If that isn't the cruelest luck," cried Julius in despair.

The lawyer was calmer, but there was a curious gleam in his eyes.

"If it is luck," he replied.

"You don't think—but, say, that's plumb impossible—no one could have got in."

"No," admitted the lawyer. "I don't see how they could. And yet—she is on the point of betraying Mr. Brown, and—she dies. Is it only chance?"

"But how——"

"Yes, *how!* That is what we must find out." He stood there silently, gently stroking his chin. "We must find out," he said quietly, and Tuppence felt that if she was Mr. Brown she would not like the tone of those simple words.

Julius's glance went to the window.

"The window's open," he remarked. "Do you think——"

Tuppence shook her head.

"The balcony only goes along as far as the boudoir. We were there."

"He might have slipped out——" suggested Julius.

But Sir James interrupted him.

"Mr. Brown's methods are not so crude. In the meantime we must send for a doctor, but before we do so, is there anything in this room that might be of value to us?"

Hastily, the three searched. A charred mass in the grate indicated that Mrs. Vandemeyer had been burning papers on the eve of her flight. Nothing of importance remained, though they searched the other rooms as well.

"There's that," said Tuppence suddenly, pointing to a small, old-fashioned safe let into the wall. "It's for jewelry, I believe, but there might be something else in it."

The key was in the lock, and Julius swung open the door, and searched inside. He was some time over the task.

"Well," said Tuppence impatiently.

There was a pause before Julius answered, then he withdrew his head and shut the door.

"Nothing," he said.

In five minutes a brisk young doctor arrived, hastily summoned. He was deferential to Sir James, whom he recognized.

"Heart failure, or possibly an overdose of some sleeping draught." He sniffed. "Rather an odor of chloral in the air."

Tuppence remembered the glass she had upset. A new thought drove her to the washstand. She found the little bottle from which Mrs. Vandemeyer had poured a few drops.

It had been three parts full. Now—*it was empty.*

14
A Consultation

NOTHING WAS MORE surprising and bewildering to Tuppence than the ease and simplicity with which everything was arranged, owing to Sir James's skillful handling. The doctor accepted quite readily the theory that Mrs. Vandemeyer had accidentally taken an overdose of chloral. He doubted whether an inquest would be necessary. If so, he would let Sir James know. He understood that Mrs. Vandemeyer was on the eve of departure for abroad, and that the servants had already left? Sir James and his young friends had been paying a call upon her, when she was suddenly stricken down and they had spent the night in the flat, not liking to leave her alone. Did they know of any relatives? They did not, but Sir James referred him to Mrs. Vandemeyer's solicitor.

Shortly afterward a nurse arrived to take charge, and the others left the ill-omened building.

"And what now?" asked Julius, with a gesture of despair. "I guess we're down and out for good."

Sir James stroked his chin thoughtfully.

"No," he said quietly. "There is still the chance that Dr. Hall may be able to tell us something."

"Gee! I'd forgotten him."

"The chance is slight, but it must not be neglected. I think I told you that he is staying at the Métropole. I should suggest that we call upon him there as soon as possible. Shall we say after a bath and breakfast?"

It was arranged that Tuppence and Julius should return to the Ritz, and call for Sir James in the car. This program was faithfully carried out, and a little after eleven they drew up before the Métropole. They asked for Dr. Hall, and a page-boy went in search of him. In a few minutes the little doctor came hurrying toward them.

"Can you spare us a few minutes, Dr. Hall?" said Sir James pleasantly, "Let me introduce you to Miss Cowley. Mr. Hersheimmer, I think, you already know."

A quizzical gleam came into the doctor's eye as he shook hands with Julius. "Ah, yes, my young friend of the tree episode! Ankle alright, eh?"

"I guess it's cured owing to your skillful treatment, doc."

"And the heart trouble? Ha ha!"

"Still searching," said Julius briefly.

"To come to the point, can we have a word with you in private?" asked Sir James.

"Certainly. I think there is a room here where we shall be quite undisturbed."

He led the way, and the others followed him. They sat down, and the doctor looked inquiringly at Sir James.

"Dr. Hall, I am very anxious to find a certain young lady for the purpose of obtaining a statement from her. I have reason to believe that she has been at one time or another in your establishment at Bournemouth. I hope I am transgressing no professional etiquette in questioning you on the subject?"

"I suppose it is a matter of testimony?"

Sir James hesitated a moment, then he replied:

"Yes."

"I shall be pleased to give you any information in my power. What is the young lady's name? Mr. Hersheimmer asked me, I remember——" He half turned to Julius.

"The name," said Sir James bluntly, "is really immaterial. She would be almost certainly sent to you under an assumed one. But I should like to know if you are acquainted with a Mrs. Vandemeyer?"

"Mrs. Vandemeyer, of 20 South Audley Mansions? I know her slightly."

"You are not aware of what has happened?"

"What do you mean?"

"You do not know that Mrs. Vandemeyer is dead?"

"Dear, dear, I had no idea of it! When did it happen?"

"She took an overdose of chloral last night."

"Purposely?"

"Accidentally, it is believed. I should not like to say myself. Anyway, she was found dead this morning."

"Very sad. A singularly handsome woman. I presume she was a friend of yours, since you are acquainted with all these details."

"I am acquainted with the details because—well, it was I who found her dead."

"Indeed," said the doctor, starting.

"Yes," said Sir James, and stroked his chin reflectively.

"This is very sad news, but you will excuse me if I say that I do not see how it bears on the subject of your inquiry?"

"It bears on it in this way, is it not a fact that Mrs. Vandemeyer committed a young relative of hers to your charge?"

Julius leaned forward eagerly.

"That is the case," said the doctor quietly.

"Under the name of——"

"Janet Vandemeyer. I understood her to be a niece of Mrs. Vandemeyer's."

"And she came to you."

"As far as I can remember in June or July of 1915."

"Was she a mental case?"

"She is perfectly sane, if that is what you mean. I understood from Mrs. Vandemeyer that the girl had been with her on the *Lusitania* when that ill-fated ship was sunk, and had suffered a severe shock in consequence."

"We're on the right track, I think?" Sir James looked round.

"As I said before, I'm a mutt!" returned Julius.

The doctor looked at them all curiously.

"You spoke of wanting a statement from her," he said. "Supposing she is not able to give one?"

"What? You have just said that she is perfectly sane."

"So she is. Nevertheless, if you want a statement from her concerning any events prior to May 7, 1915, she will not be able to give it to you."

They looked at the little man, stupefied. He nodded cheerfully.

"It's a pity," he said. "A great pity, especially as I gather, Sir James, that the matter is important. But there it is, she can tell you nothing."

"But why, man? Darn it all, why?"

The little man shifted his benevolent glance to the excited young American.

"Because Janet Vandemeyer is suffering from a complete loss of memory."

"What?"

"Quite so. An interesting case, a *very* interesting case. Not so uncommon, really, as you would think. There are several well known parallels. It's the first case of the kind that I've had under my own personal observation, and I must admit that I've found it of absorbing interest." There was something rather ghoulish in the little man's satisfaction.

"And she remembers nothing," said Sir James slowly.

"Nothing prior to May 7, 1915. After that date her memory is as good as yours or mine."

"Then the first thing she remembers?"

"Is landing with the survivors. Everything before that is a blank. She did not know her name, or where she had come from, or where she was. She couldn't even speak her own tongue."

"But surely all this is most unusual?" put in Julius.

"No, my dear sir. Quite normal under the circumstances. Severe shock to the nervous system. Loss of memory proceeds nearly always on the same lines. I suggested a specialist, of course. There's a very good man in Paris—makes a study of these cases—but Mrs. Vandemeyer opposed the idea of publicity that might result from such a course."

"I can imagine she would," said Sir James grimly.

"I fell in with her views. There *is* a certain notoriety given to these cases. And the girl was very young—nineteen, I believe. It seemed a pity that her infirmity should be talked about—might damage her prospects. Besides, there is no special treatment to pursue in such cases. It is really a matter of waiting."

"Waiting?"

"Yes, sooner or later, the memory will return—as suddenly as it went. But in all probability the girl will have entirely forgotten the intervening period, and will take up life where she left off—at the sinking of the *Lusitania*."

"And when do you expect this to happen?"

The doctor shrugged his shoulders.

"Ah, that I cannot say. Sometimes it is a matter of months, sometimes it has been known to be as long as twenty years! Sometimes another shock does the trick. One restores what the other took away."

"Another shock, eh?" said Julius thoughtfully.

"Exactly. There was a case in Colorado——" The little man's voice trailed on, voluble, mildly enthusiastic.

Julius did not seem to be listening. He had relapsed into his own thoughts and was frowning. Suddenly he came out of his brown study, and hit the table such a resounding bang with his fist that everyone jumped, the doctor most of all.

"I've got it! I guess, doc, I'd like your medical opinion on the plan I'm about to outline. Say Jane was to cross the herring pond again, and the same thing was to happen. The submarine, the sinking ship, everyone to take to the boats—and so on. Wouldn't that do the trick? Wouldn't it give a mighty big bump to her subconscious self, or whatever the jargon is, and start it functioning again right away?"

"A very interesting speculation, Mr. Hersheimmer. In my own opinion, it would be successful. It is unfortunate that there is no chance of the conditions repeating themselves as you suggest."

"Not by nature, perhaps, doc. But I'm talking about art."

"Art?"

"Why, yes. What's the difficulty? Hire a liner——"

"A liner!" murmured Dr. Hall faintly.

"Hire some passengers, hire a submarine—that's the only difficulty, I guess. Governments are apt to be a bit hidebound over their engines of war. They won't sell to the first comer. Still, I guess that can be got over. Ever heard of the word 'graft,' sir? Well, graft gets there every time! I reckon that we shan't really need to fire a torpedo. If every one hustles round and screams loud enough that the ship is sinking, it ought to be enough for an innocent young girl like Jane. By the time she's got a life-belt on her, and is being hustled into a boat, with a well-drilled lot of artistes doing the hysterical stunt on deck, why—she ought to be right back where she was in May, 1915. How's that for the bare outline?"

Dr. Hall looked at Julius. Everything that he was for the moment incapable of saying was eloquent in that look.

"No," said Julius, in answer to it, "I'm not crazy. The thing's perfectly possible. It's done every day in the States for the movies. Haven't you seen trains in collision on the screen? What's the difference between buying up a train and buying up a liner? Get the properties and you can go right ahead!'

Dr. Hall found his voice.

"But the expense, my dear sir." His voice rose. "The expense! It will be *colossal!*"

"Money doesn't worry me any," explained Julius simply.

Dr. Hall turned an appealing face to Sir James, who smiled slightly.

"Mr. Hersheimmer is very well off—very well off indeed."

The doctor's glance came back to Julius with a new and subtle quality in it. This was no longer an eccentric young fellow with a habit of falling off trees. The doctor's eyes held the deference accorded to a really rich man.

"Very remarkable plan. Very remarkable," he murmured. "The movies—of course! Your American word for the cinema. Very interesting. I fear we are perhaps a little behind the times over here in our methods. And you really mean to carry out this remarkable plan of yours."

"You bet your bottom dollar I do."

The doctor believed him—which was a tribute to his nationality. If an Englishman had suggested such a thing, he would have had grave doubts as to his sanity.

"I cannot guarantee a cure," he pointed out. "Perhaps I ought to make that quite clear."

"Sure, that's alright," said Julius. "You just trot out Jane, and leave the rest to me."

"Jane?"

"Miss Janet Vandemeyer, then. Can we get on the long distance to your place right away, and ask them to send her up; or shall I run down and fetch her in my car?"

The doctor stared.

"I beg your pardon, Mr. Hersheimmer. I thought you understood."

"Understood what?"

"That Miss Vandemeyer is no longer under my care."

15
Tuppence Receives a Proposal

JULIUS SPRANG UP.

"What?"

"I thought you were aware of that."

"When did she leave?"

"Let me see. Today is Monday is it not? It must have been last Wednesday—why, surely—yes, it was the same evening that you—er—fell out of my tree."

"That evening? Before, or after?"

"Let me see—oh yes, afterward. A very urgent message arrived from Mrs. Vandemeyer. The young lady and the nurse who was in charge of her left by the night train."

Julius sank back again into his chair.

"Nurse Edith—left with a patient—I remember," he muttered. "My God, to have been so near!"

Dr. Hall looked bewildered.

"I don't understand. Is the young lady not with her aunt, after all?"

Tuppence shook her head. She was about to speak when a warning glance from Sir James made her hold her tongue. The lawyer rose.

"I'm much obliged to you, Hall. We're very grateful for all you've told us. I'm afraid we're now in the position of having to track Miss Vandemeyer anew. What about the nurse who accompanied her; I suppose you don't know where she is?"

The doctor shook his head.

"We've not heard from her, as it happens. I understood she was to remain with Miss Vandemeyer for a while. But what can have happened? Surely the girl has not been kidnapped."

"That remains to be seen," said Sir James gravely.

The other hesitated.

"You do not think I ought to go to the police?"

"No, no. In all probability the young lady is with other relations."

The doctor was not completely satisfied, but he saw that Sir James was determined to say no more, and realized that to try and extract more information from the famous K.C. would be mere waste of labor. Accordingly, he wished them good-bye, and they left the hotel. For a few minutes they stood by the car talking.

"How maddening," cried Tuppence. "To think that Julius must have been actually under the same roof with her for a few hours."

"I was a darned idiot," muttered Julius gloomily.

"You couldn't know," Tuppence consoled him. "Could he?" She appealed to Sir James.

"I should advise you not to worry," said the latter kindly. "No use crying over spilt milk, you know."

"The great thing is what to do next," added Tuppence the practical.

Sir James shrugged his shoulders.

"You might advertise for the nurse who accompanied the girl. That is the only course I can suggest, and I must confess I do not hope for much result. Otherwise there is nothing to be done."

"Nothing?" said Tuppence blankly. "And—Tommy?"

"We must hope for the best," said Sir James. "Oh yes, we must go on hoping."

But over her downcast head his eyes met Julius's, and almost imperceptibly he shook his head. Julius understood. The lawyer considered the case hopeless. The young American's face grew grave. Sir James took Tuppence's hand.

"You must let me know if anything further comes to light. Letters will always be forwarded."

Tuppence stared at him blankly.

"You are going away?"

"I told you. Don't you remember? To Scotland."

"Yes, but I thought——" The girl hestitated.

Sir James shrugged his shoulders.

"My dear young lady, I can do nothing more, I fear. Our clues have all ended in thin air. You can take my word for it that there is nothing more to be done. If anything should arise, I shall be glad to advise you in any way I can."

His words gave Tuppence an extraordinarily desolate feeling.

"I suppose you're right," she said. "Anyway, thank you very much for trying to help us. Good-bye."

Julius was bending over the car. A momentary pity came into Sir James's keen eyes, as he gazed into the girl's downcast face.

"Don't be too disconsolate, Miss Tuppence," he said in a low voice. "Remember, holiday time isn't always all playtime. One sometimes manages to put in some work as well."

Something in his tone made Tuppence glance up sharply. He shook his head with a smile.

"No, I shan't say any more. Great mistake to say too much. Remember that. Never tell all you know—not even to the person you know best. Understand? Good-bye."

He strode away. Tuppence stared after him. She was beginning to understand Sir James's methods. Once before he had thrown her a hint in the same careless fashion. Was this a hint? What exactly lay behind those last brief words? Did he mean that, after all, he had not abandoned the case; that, secretly, he would be working on it still while——

Her meditations were interrupted by Julius, who adjured her to "get right in."

"You're looking kind of thoughtful," he remarked as they started off. "Did the old guy say anything more?"

Tuppence opened her mouth impulsively, and then shut it again. Sir James's words sounded in her ears: "Never tell all you know—not even to the person you know best." And like a flash there came into her mind another memory. Julius before the safe in the flat, her own question and the pause before his reply, "Nothing." Was there really nothing? Or had he found something he wished to keep to himself? If he could make a reservation, so could she.

"Nothing particular," she replied.

She felt rather than saw Julius throw a sideways glance at her.

"Say, shall we go for a spin in the park?"

"If you like."

For a while they ran on under the trees in silence. It was a beautiful day. The keen rush through the air brought a new exhilaration to Tuppence.

"Say, Miss Tuppence, do you think I'm ever going to find Jane?"

Julius spoke in a discouraged voice. The mood was so alien to him that Tuppence turned and stared at him in surprise. He nodded.

"That's so. I'm getting down and out over the business. Sir James today hadn't got any hope at all, I could see that. I don't like him—we don't gee together somehow—but he's pretty cute, and I guess he wouldn't quit if there was any chance of success—now, would he?"

Tuppence felt rather uncomfortable, but clinging to her belief that Julius had also withheld something from her, she remained firm.

"He suggested advertising for the nurse," she reminded him.

"Yes, with a 'forlorn hope' flavor to his voice! No—I'm about fed up. I've half a mind to go back to the States right away."

"Oh no!" cried Tuppence. "We've got to find Tommy."

"I sure forgot Beresford," said Julius contritely. "That's so. We must find him. But after—well, I've been daydreaming ever since I started on this trip—and these dreams are rotten poor business. I'm quit of them. Say, Miss Tuppence, there's something I'd like to ask you."

"Yes?"

"You and Beresford. What about it?"

"I don't understand you," replied Tuppence with dignity, adding rather inconsequently: "And, anyway, you're wrong!"

"Not got a sort of kindly feeling for one another?"

"Certainly not," said Tuppence with warmth. "Tommy and I are friends—nothing more."

"I guess every pair of lovers has said that sometime or another," observed Julius.

"Nonsense!" snapped Tuppence. "Do I look the sort of girl that's always falling in love with every man she meets?"

"You do not. You look the sort of girl that's mighty often getting fallen in love with!"

"Oh!" said Tuppence, rather taken aback. "That's a compliment, I suppose?"

"Sure. Now let's get down to this. Supposing we never find Beresford and—and——"

"Alright—say it! I can face facts. Supposing he's—dead! Well?"

"And all this business fiddles out. What are you going to do?"

"I don't know," said Tuppence forlornly.

"You'll be darned lonesome, you poor kid."

"I shall be all right," snapped Tuppence with her usual resentment of any kind of pity.

"What about marriage?" inquired Julius. "Got any views on the subject?"

"I intend to marry, of course," replied Tuppence. "That is, if"—she paused, knew a momentary longing to draw back and then stuck to her guns bravely—"I can find someone rich enough to make it worth my while. That's frank, isn't it? I dare say you despise me for it."

"I never despise business instinct," said Julius. "What particular figure have you in mind?"

"Figure?" asked Tuppence, puzzled. "Do you mean tall or short?"

"No. Sum—income."

"Oh, I—I haven't quite worked that out."

"What about me?"

"You?"

"Sure thing."

"Oh, I couldn't!"

"Why not?"

"I tell you I couldn't."

"Again, why not?"

"It would seem so unfair."

"I don't see anything unfair about it. I call your bluff, that's all. I admire you immensely, Miss Tuppence, more than any girl I've ever met. You're so darned plucky. I'd just love to give you a real, rattling good time. Say the word, and we'll run round right away to some high-class jeweler, and fix up the ring business."

"I can't," gasped Tuppence.

"Because of Beresford?"

"No, no, *no!*"

"Well then?"

Tuppence merely continued to shake her head violently.

"You can't reasonably expect more dollars than I've got."

"Oh, it isn't that," gasped Tuppence with an almost hysterical laugh. "But thanking you very much, and all that, I think I'd better say no."

"I'd be obliged if you'd do me the favor to think it over until tomorrow."

"It's no use."

"Still, I guess we'll leave it like that."

"Very well," said Tuppence meekly.

Neither of them spoke again until they reached the Ritz.

Tuppence went upstairs to her room. She felt morally battered to the ground after her conflict with Julius's vigorous personality. Sitting down in front of the glass, she stared at her own reflection for some minutes.

"Fool," murmured Tuppence at length, making a grimace. "Little fool. Everything you want—everything you've ever hoped for, and you go and bleat out 'no' like an idiotic little sheep. It's your one chance. Why don't you take it? Grab it? Snatch at it? What more do you want?"

As if in answer to her own question, her eyes fell on a small snapshot of Tommy that stood on her dressing table in a shabby frame. For a moment she struggled for self-control, and then abandoning all pretence, she held it to her lips and burst into a fit of sobbing.

"Oh, Tommy, Tommy," she cried, "I do love you so—and I may never see you again. . . ."

At the end of five minutes Tuppence sat up, blew her nose, and pushed back her hair.

"That's that," she observed sternly. "Let's look facts in the face. I seem to have fallen in love—with an idiot of a boy who probably doesn't care two straws about me." Here she paused. "Anyway," she resumed, as though arguing with an unseen opponent, "I don't *know* that he does. He'd never have dared to say so. I've always jumped on sentiment—and here I am being more sentimental than anybody. What idiots girls are! I've always thought so. I suppose I shall sleep with his photograph under my pillow, and dream about him all night. It's dreadful to feel you've been false to your principles."

Tuppence shook her head sadly, as she reviewed her back-sliding.

"I don't know what to say to Julius, I'm sure. Oh, what a fool I feel! I'll have to say *something*—he's so American and thorough, he'll insist upon having a reason. I wonder if he did find anything in that safe——"

Tuppence's meditations went off on another tack. She reviewed the events of last night carefully and persistently. Somehow, they seemed bound up with Sir James's enigmatical words. . . .

Suddenly she gave a great start—the color faded out of her face. Her eyes, fascinated, gazed in front of her, the pupils dilated.

"Impossible," she murmured. "Impossible! I must be going mad even to think of such a thing. . . ."

Monstrous—yet it explained everything. . . .

After a moment's reflection she sat down and wrote a note, weighing each word as she did so. Finally she nodded her head as though satisfied, and slipped it into an envelope which she addressed to Julius. She went down the passage to his sitting room and knocked at the door. As she had expected, the room was empty. She left the note on the table.

A small page boy was waiting outside her own door when she returned to it.

"Telegram for you, miss."

Tuppence took it from the salver, and tore it open carelessly. Then she gave a cry. The telegram was from Tommy!

16

Further Adventures of Tommy

FROM A DARKNESS punctuated with throbbing stabs of fire, Tommy dragged his senses slowly back to life. When he at last opened his eyes, he was conscious of nothing but an excruciating pain through his temples. He was vaguely aware of unfamiliar surroundings. Where was he? What had happened? He blinked feebly. This was not his bedroom at the Ritz. And what the devil was the matter with his head?

"Damn!" said Tommy, and tried to sit up. He had remembered. He was in that sinister house in Soho. He uttered a groan and fell back. Through his almost-closed lids he reconnoitered carefully.

"He is coming to," remarked a voice very near Tommy's ear. He recognized it at once for that of the bearded and efficient German, and lay artistically inert. He felt that it would be a pity to come round too soon; and until the pain in his head became a little less acute, he felt quite incapable of collecting his wits. Painfully he tried to puzzle out what had happened. Obviously somebody must have crept up behind him as he listened and struck him down with a blow on the head. They knew him now for a spy, and would in all probability give him short shrift. Undoubtedly he was in a tight place. Nobody knew where he was, therefore he need expect no outside assistance, and must depend solely on his own wits.

"Well, here goes," murmured Tommy to himself, and repeated his former remark.

"Damn!" he observed, and this time succeeded in sitting up.

In a minute the German stepped forward and placed a glass to his lips, with the brief command "Drink." Tommy obeyed. The potency of the draught made him choke, but it cleared his brain in a marvelous manner.

He was lying on a couch in the room in which the meeting had been held. On one side of him was the German, on the other the villainous-faced doorkeeper who had let him in. The others were grouped together at a little distance away. But Tommy missed one face. The man known as Number One was no longer of the company.

"Feel better?" asked the German, as he removed the empty glass.

"Yes, thanks," returned Tommy cheerfully.

"Ah, my young friend, it is lucky for you your skull is so thick. The good Conrad struck hard." He indicated the evil-faced doorkeeper by a nod. The man grinned.

Tommy twisted his head round with an effort.

"Oh," he said, "so you're Conrad, are you? It strikes me the thickness of my skull was lucky for you too. When I look at you I feel it's almost a pity I've enabled you to cheat the hangman."

The man snarled, and the bearded man said quietly:

"He would have run no risk of that."

"Just as you like," replied Tommy. "I know it's the fashion to run down the police. I rather believe in them myself."

His manner was nonchalant to the last degree. Tommy Beresford was one of those young Englishmen not distinguished by any special intellectual ability, but who are emphatically at their best in what is known as a "tight place." Their natural diffidence and caution fall from them like a glove. Tommy realized perfectly that in his own wits lay the only chance of escape, and behind his casual manner he was racking his brains furiously.

The cold accents of the German took up the conversation:

"Have you anything to say before you are put to death as a spy?"

"Simply lots of things," replied Tommy with the same urbanity as before.

"Do you deny that you were listening at that door?"

"I do not. I must really apologize—but your conversation was so interesting that it overcame my scruples."

"How did you get in?"

"Dear old Conrad here." Tommy smiled deprecatingly at him. "I hesitate to suggest pensioning off a faithful servant, but you really ought to have a better watchdog."

Conrad snarled impotently, and said sullenly, as the man with the beard swung round upon him:

"He gave the word. How was I to know?"

"Yes," Tommy chimed in. "How was he to know? Don't blame the poor fellow. His hasty action has given me the pleasure of seeing you all face to face."

He fancied that his words caused some discomposure among the group, but the watchful German stilled it with a wave of his hand.

"Dead men tell no tales," he said evenly.

"Ah," said Tommy, "but I'm not dead yet!"

"You soon will be, my young friend," said the German.

An assenting murmur came from the others.

Tommy's heart beat faster, but his casual pleasantness did not waver.

"I think not," he said firmly. "I should have a great objection to dying."

He had got them puzzled, he saw that by the look on his captor's face.

"Can you give us any reason why we should not put you to death?" asked the German.

"Several," replied Tommy. "Look here, you've been asking me a lot of questions. Let me ask you one for a change. Why didn't you kill me off at once before I regained consciousness?"

The German hesitated, and Tommy seized his advantage.

"Because you didn't know how much I knew—and where I obtained that knowledge. If you kill me now, you never will know."

But here the emotions of Boris became too much for him. He stepped forward waving his arms.

"You hell-hound of a spy," he screamed. "We will give you short shrift. Kill him! Kill him!"

There was a roar of applause.

"You hear?" said the German, his eyes on Tommy. "What have you to say to that?"

"Say?" Tommy shrugged his shoulders. "Pack of fools. Let them ask themselves a few questions. How did I get into this place? Remember what dear old Conrad said—*with your own password*, wasn't it? How did I get hold of that? You don't suppose I came up those steps haphazard and said the first thing that came into my head?"

Tommy was pleased with the concluding words of this speech. His only regret was that Tuppence was not present to appreciate its full flavor.

"That is true," said the working man suddenly. "Comrades, we have been betrayed!"

An ugly murmur arose. Tommy smiled at them encouragingly.

"That's better. How can you hope to make a success of any job if you don't use your brains?"

"You will tell us who has betrayed us," said the German. "But that shall not save you—oh, no! You shall tell us all that you know. Boris, here, knows pretty ways of making people speak!"

"Bah!" said Tommy scornfully, fighting down a singularly unpleasant feeling in the pit of his stomach. "You will neither torture me nor kill me."

"And why not?" asked Boris.

"Because you'd kill the goose that lays the golden eggs," replied Tommy quietly.

There was a momentary pause. It seemed as though Tommy's persistent assurance was at last conquering. They were no longer completely sure of themselves. The man in the shabby clothes stared at Tommy searchingly.

"He's bluffing you, Boris," he said quietly.

Tommy hated him. Had the man seen through him?

The German, with an effort, turned roughly to Tommy.

"What do you mean?"

"What do you think I mean?" parried Tommy, searching desperately in his own mind.

Suddenly Boris stepped forward, and shook his fist in Tommy's face.

"Speak, you swine of an Englishman—speak!"

"Don't get so excited, my good fellow," said Tommy calmly. "That's the worst of you foreigners. You can't keep calm. Now, I ask you, do I look as though I thought there were the least chance of your killing me?"

He looked confidently round, and was glad they could not hear the persistent beating of his heart which gave the lie to his words.

"No," admitted Boris at last sullenly, "you do not."

"Thank God, he's not a mind reader," thought Tommy. Aloud he pursued his advantage:

"And why am I so confident? Because I know something that puts me in a position to propose a bargain."

"A bargain?" The bearded man took him up sharply.

"Yes—a bargain. My life and liberty against——" He paused.

"Against what?"

The group pressed forward. You could have heard a pin drop.

Slowly Tommy spoke.

"The papers that Danvers brought over from America in the *Lusitania*."

The effect of his words was electrical. Everyone was on his feet. The German waved them back. He leaned over Tommy, his face purple with excitement.

"*Himmel!* You have got them, then?"

With magnificent calm Tommy shook his head.

"You know where they are?" persisted the German.

Again Tommy shook his head. "Not in the least."

"Then—then——" angry and baffled, the words failed him.

Tommy looked round. He saw anger and bewilderment on every face, but his calm assurance had done its work—no one doubted but that something lay behind his words.

"I don't know where the papers are—but I believe that I can find them. I have a theory——"

"Pah!"

Tommy raised his hand, and silenced the clamors of disgust.

"I call it a theory—but I'm pretty sure of my facts—facts that are known to no one but myself. In any case what do you lose? If I can produce the papers—you give me my life and liberty in exchange. Is it a bargain?"

"And if we refuse?" said the German quietly.

Tommy lay back on the couch.

"The 29th," he said thoughtfully, "is less than a fortnight ahead——"

For a moment the German hesitated. Then he made a sign to Conrad.

"Take him into the other room."

For five minutes, Tommy sat on the bed in the dingy room next door. His heart was beating violently. He had risked all on this throw. How would they decide? And all the while that this agonized questioning went on within him, he talked flippantly to Conrad, enraging the cross-grained doorkeeper to the point of homicidal mania.

At last the door opened, and the German called imperiously to Conrad to return.

"Let's hope the judge hasn't put his black cap on," remarked Tommy frivolously. "That's right, Conrad, march me in. The prisoner is at the bar, gentlemen."

The German was seated once more behind the table. He motioned to Tommy to sit down opposite to him.

"We accept," he said harshly, "on terms. The papers must be delivered to us before you go free."

"Idiot!" said Tommy amiably. "How do you think I can look for them if you keep me tied by the leg here?"

"What do you expect, then?"

"I must have liberty to go about the business in my own way."

The German laughed.

"Do you think we are little children to let you walk out of here leaving us a pretty story full of promises?"

"No," said Tommy thoughtfully. "Though infinitely simpler for me, I did not really think you would agree to that plan. Very well, we must arrange a compromise. How would it be if you attached little Conrad here to my person. He's a faithful fellow, and very ready with the fist."

"We prefer," said the German coldly, "that you should remain here. One of our number will carry out your instructions minutely. If the operations are complicated, he will return to you with a report and you can instruct him further."

"You're tying my hands," complained Tommy. "It's a very delicate affair, and the other fellow will muff it up as likely as not, and then where shall I be? I don't believe one of you has got an ounce of tact."

The German rapped the table.

"Those are our terms. Otherwise, death!"

Tommy leaned back wearily.

"I like your style. Curt, but attractive. So be it, then. But one thing is essential. I must see the girl."

"What girl?"

"Jane Finn, of course."

The other looked at him curiously for some minutes, then he said slowly, and as though choosing his words with care:

"Do you not know that she can tell you nothing?"

Tommy's heart beat a little faster. Would he succeed in coming face to face with the girl he was seeking?

"I shall not ask her to tell me anything," he said quietly. "Not in so many words, that is."

"Then why see her?"

Tommy paused.

"To watch her face when I ask her one question," he replied at last.

Again there was a look in the German's eyes that Tommy did not quite understand.

"She will not be able to answer your question."

"That does not matter. I shall have seen her face when I ask it."

"And you think that will tell you anything?" He gave a short disagreeable laugh. More than ever, Tommy felt that there was a factor somewhere that he did not understand. The German looked at him searchingly. "I wonder whether, after all, you know as much as we think?" he said softly.

Tommy felt his ascendancy less sure than a moment before. His hold had slipped a little. But he was puzzled. What had he said wrong? He spoke out on the impulse of the moment.

"There may be things that you know which I do not. I have not pretended to be aware of all the details of your show. But equally I've got something up my sleeve that *you* don't know about. And that's where I mean to score. Danvers was a damned clever fellow——" He broke off as if he had said too much.

But the German's face had lightened a little.

"Danvers," he murmured. "I see——" He paused a minute, then waved to Conrad. "Take him away. Upstairs—you know."

"Wait a minute," said Tommy. "What about the girl?"

"That may perhaps be arranged."

"It must be."

"We will see about it. Only one person can decide that."

"Who?" asked Tommy. But he knew the answer.

"Mr. Brown——"

"Shall I see him?"

"Perhaps."

"Come," said Conrad harshly.

Tommy rose obediently. Outside the door his gaoler motioned to him to mount the stairs. He himself followed close behind. On the floor above Conrad opened a door and Tommy passed into a small room. Conrad lit a hissing gas burner and went out. Tommy heard the sound of the key being turned in the lock.

He set to work to examine his prison. It was a smaller room than the one downstairs, and there was something peculiarly airless about the atmosphere of it. Then he realized that there was no window. He walked round it. The walls were filthy dirty, as everywhere else. Four pictures hung crookedly on the wall representing scenes from "Faust." Marguerite with her box of jewels, the church scene, Siebel and his flowers, and Faust and Mephistopheles. The latter brought Tommy's mind back to Mr. Brown again. In this sealed and closed chamber, with its close-fitting heavy door, he felt cut off from the world, and the sinister power of the arch-criminal seemed more real. Shout as he would, no one could ever hear him. The place was a living tomb. . . .

With an effort Tommy pulled himself together. He sank onto the bed and gave himself up to reflection. His head ached badly; also, he was hungry. The silence of the place was dispiriting.

"Anyway," said Tommy, trying to cheer himself, "I shall see the chief—the mysterious Mr. Brown and with a bit of luck in bluffing I shall see the mysterious Jane Finn also. After that——"

After that Tommy was forced to admit the prospect looked dreary.

17
Annette

THE TROUBLES OF the future, however, soon faded before the troubles of the present. And of these, the immediate and pressing was that of hunger. Tommy had a healthy and vigorous appetite. The steak and chips partaken of for lunch seemed now to belong to another decade. He regretfully recognized the fact that he would not make a success of a hunger strike.

He prowled aimlessly about his prison. Once or twice he discarded dignity, and pounded on the door. But nobody answered the summons.

"Hang it all!" said Tommy indignantly. "They can't mean to starve me to death." A newborn fear passed through his mind that this might, perhaps, be one of those "pretty ways" of making a prisoner speak, which had been attributed to Boris. But on reflection he dismissed the idea.

"It's that sour-faced brute Conrad," he decided. "That's a fellow I shall enjoy getting even with one of these days. This is just a bit of spite on his part. I'm certain of it."

Further meditations induced in him the feeling that it would be extremely pleasant to bring something down with a whack on Conrad's egg-shaped head. Tommy stroked his own head tenderly, and gave himself up to the pleasures of imagination. Finally a bright idea flashed across his brain. Why not convert imagination into reality? Conrad was undoubtedly the tenant of the house. The others, with the possible exception of the bearded German, merely used it as a rendezvous. Therefore, why not wait in ambush for Conrad behind the door, and when he entered bring down a chair, or one of the decrepit pictures, smartly on to his head. One would, of course, be careful not to hit too hard. And then—and then, simply walk out! If he met anyone on the way down, well——Tommy brightened at the thought of an encounter with his fists. Such an affair was infinitely more in his line than the verbal encounter of this afternoon. Intoxicated by his plan, Tommy gently unhooked the picture of the Devil and Faust, and settled himself in position. His hopes were high. The plan seemed to him simple but excellent.

Time went on, but Conrad did not appear. Night and day were the same in this prison room, but Tommy's wristwatch, which enjoyed a certain degree of accuracy, informed him that it was nine o'clock in the evening. Tommy reflected gloomily that if supper did not arrive soon it would be a question of waiting for breakfast. At ten o'clock hope deserted him, and he flung himself on the bed to seek consolation in sleep. In five minutes his woes were forgotten.

The sound of the key turning in the lock awoke him from his slumbers. Not belonging to the type of hero who is famous for awaking in full possession of his faculties, Tommy merely blinked at the ceiling and wondered vaguely where he was. Then he remembered, and looked at his watch. It was eight o'clock.

"It's either early morning tea or breakfast," deduced the young man, "and pray God it's the latter!"

The door swung open. Too late, Tommy remembered his scheme of obliterating the unprepossessing Conrad. A moment later he was glad that he had, for it was not Conrad who entered, but a girl. She carried a tray which she set down on the table.

In the feeble light of the gas burner Tommy blinked at her. He decided at once that she was one of the most beautiful girls he had ever seen. Her hair was a full rich brown, with sudden glints of gold in it as though there were imprisoned sunbeams struggling in its depths. There was a wild-rose quality about her face. Her eyes, set wide apart, were hazel, a golden hazel that again recalled a memory of sunbeams.

A delirious thought shot through Tommy's mind.

"Are you Jane Finn?" he asked breathlessly.

The girl shook her head wonderingly.

"My name is Annette, monsieur."

She spoke in a soft, broken English.

"Oh!" said Tommy, rather taken aback. "*Française?*" he hazarded.

"Oui, monsieur. Monsieur parle français?"

"Not for any length of time," said Tommy. "What's that? Breakfast?"

The girl nodded. Tommy dropped off the bed and came and inspected the contents of the tray. It consisted of a loaf, some margarine, and a jug of coffee.

"The living is not equal to the Ritz," he obsered with a sigh. "But for what we are at last about to receive the Lord has made me truly thankful. Amen."

He drew up a chair, and the girl turned away to the door.

"Wait a sec," cried Tommy. "There are lots of things I want to ask you, Annette. What are you doing in his house? Don't tell me you're Conrad's niece, or daughter, or anything, because I can't believe it."

"I do the *service*, monsieur. I am not related to anybody."

"I see," said Tommy. "You know what I asked you just now. Have you ever heard that name?"

"I have heard people speak of Jane Finn, I think."

"You don't know where she is?"

Annette shook her head.

"She's not in this house, for instance?"

"Oh no, monsieur. I must go now—they will be waiting for me."

She hurried out. The key turned in the lock.

"I wonder who 'they' are," mused Tommy, as he continued to make inroads on the loaf. "With a bit of luck, that girl might help me to get out of here. She doesn't look like one of the gang."

At one o'clock Annette reappeared with another tray, but this time Conrad accompanied her.

"Good morning," said Tommy amiably. "You have *not* used Pear's soap, I see."

Conrad growled threateningly.

"No light repartee, have you, old bean? There, there, we can't always have brains as well as beauty. What have we for lunch? Stew? How did I know? Elementary, my dear Watson—the smell of onions is unmistakable."

"Talk away," grunted the man. "It's little enough time you'll have to talk in, maybe."

The remark was unpleasant in its suggestion, but Tommy ignored it. He sat down at the table.

"Retire, varlet," he said, with a wave of his hand. "Prate not to thy betters."

That evening Tommy sat on the bed, and cogitated deeply. Would Conrad again accompany the girl? If he did not, should he risk trying to make an ally of her? He decided that he must leave no stone unturned. His position was desperate.

At eight o'clock the familiar sound of the key turning made him spring to his feet. The girl was alone.

"Shut the door," he commanded. "I want to speak to you."

She obeyed.

"Look here, Annette, I want you to help me get out of this."

She shook her head.

"Impossible. There are three of them on the floor below."

"Oh!" Tommy was secretly grateful for the information. "But you would help me if you could?"

"No, monsieur."

"Why not?"

The girl hesitated.

"I think—they are my own people. You have spied upon them. They are quite right to keep you here."

"They're a bad lot, Annette. If you'll help me, I'll take you away from the lot of them. And you'd probably get a good whack of money."

But the girl merely shook her head.

"I dare not, monsieur; I am afraid of them."

She turned away.

"Wouldn't you do anything to help another girl?" cried Tommy. "She's about your age too. Won't you save her from their clutches?"

"You mean Jane Finn?"

"Yes."

"It is her you came here to look for? Yes?"

"That's it."

The girl looked at him, then passed her hand across her forehead.

"Jane Finn. Always I hear that name. It is familiar."

Tommy came forward eagerly.

"You must know *something* about her?"

But the girl turned away abruptly.

"I know nothing—only the name." She walked toward the door. Suddenly she uttered a cry. Tommy stared. She had caught sight of the picture he had laid against the wall the night before. For a moment he caught a look of terror in her eyes. As inexplicably it changed to relief. Then abruptly she went out of the room. Tommy could make nothing of it. Did she fancy that he had meant to attack her with it? Surely not. He rehung the picture on the wall thoughtfully.

Three more days went by in dreary inaction. Tommy felt the strain telling on his nerves. He saw no one but Conrad and Annette, and the girl had become dumb. She spoke only in monosyllables. A kind of dark suspicion smoldered in her eyes. Tommy felt that if this solitary confinement went on much longer he would go mad. He gathered from Conrad that they were waiting for orders from "Mr. Brown." Perhaps, thought Tommy, he was abroad or away, and they were obliged to wait for his return.

But the evening of the third day brought a rude awakening.

It was barely seven o'clock when he heard the tramp of footsteps outside in the passage. In another minute the door was flung open. Conrad entered. With him was the evil-looking Number 14. Tommy's heart sank at the sight of them.

"Evenin', guv'nor," said the man with a leer. "Got those ropes, mate?"

The silent Conrad produced a length of fine cord. The next minute Number 14's hands, horribly dexterous, were winding the cord round his limbs, while Conrad held him down.

"What the devil——?" began Tommy.

But the slow, speechless grin of the silent Conrad froze the words on his lips.

Number 14 proceeded deftly with his task. In another minute Tommy was a mere helpless bundle. Then at last Conrad spoke:

"Thought you'd bluffed us, did you? With what you knew, and what you didn't know. Bargained with us! And all the time it was bluff! Bluff! You know less than a kitten. But your number's up now all right, you b—— swine."

Tommy lay silent. There was nothing to say. He had failed. Somehow or other the omnipotent Mr. Brown had seen through his pretensions. Suddenly a thought occurred to him.

"A very good speech, Conrad," he said approvingly. "But wherefore the bonds and fetters? Why not let this kind gentlemen here cut my throat without delay?"

"Garn," said Number 14 unexpectedly. "Think we're as green as to do you in here, and have the police nosing round? Not 'alf! We've ordered the carriage for your lordship tomorrow mornin', but in the meantime we're not taking any chances, see!"

"Nothing," said Tommy, "could be plainer than your words—unless it was your face."

"Stow it," said Number 14.

"With pleasure," replied Tommy. "You're making a sad mistake—but yours will be the loss."

"You don't kid us that way again," said Number 14. "Talking as though you were still at the blooming Ritz, aren't you?"

Tommy made no reply. He was engaged in wondering how Mr. Brown had discovered his identity. He decided that Tuppence, in the throes of anxiety, had gone to the police, and that his disappearance having been made public the gang had not been slow to put two and two together.

The two men departed and the door slammed. Tommy was left to his meditations. They were not pleasant ones. Already his limbs felt cramped and stiff. He was utterly helpless, and he could see no hope anywhere.

About an hour had passed when he heard the key softly turned, and the door opened. It was Annette. Tommy's heart beat a little faster. He had forgotten the girl. Was it possible that she had come to his help?

Suddenly he heard Conrad's voice:

"Come out of it, Annette. He doesn't want any supper tonight."

"Oui, oui, je sais bien. But I must take the other tray. We need the things on it."

"Well, hurry up," growled Conrad.

Without looking at Tommy the girl went over to the table, and picked up the tray. She raised a hand and turned out the light.

"Curse you"—Conrad had come to the door—"why did you do that?"

"I always turn it out. You should have told me. Shall I relight it, Monsieur Conrad?"

"No, come on out of it."

"Le beau petit monsieur," cried Annette, pausing by the bed in the darkness. "You have tied him up well, *hein?* He is like a trussed chicken!" The frank amusement in her tone jarred on the boy; but at that moment, to his amazement, he felt her hand running lightly over his bonds, and something small and cold was pressed into the palm of his hand.

"Come on, Annette."

"Mais me voilà."

The door shut. Tommy heard Conrad say:

"Lock it and give me the key."

The footsteps died away. Tommy lay petrified with amazement. The object Annette had thrust into his hand was a small penknife, the blade open. From the way she had studiously avoided looking at him, and her action with the light, he came to the conclusion that the room was overlooked. There must be a peephole somewhere in the walls. Remembering how guarded she had always been in her manner, he saw that he had probably been under observation all the time. Had he said anything to give himself away? Hardly. He had revealed a wish to escape and a desire to find Jane Finn, but nothing that could have given a clue to his own identity. True, his question to Annette had proved that he was personally unacquainted with Jane Finn, but he had never pretended otherwise. The question now was, did Annette really know more? Were her denials intended primarily for the listeners? On that point he could come to no conclusion.

But there was a more vital question that drove out all others. Could he, bound as he was, manage to cut his bonds? He essayed cautiously to rub the open blade up and down on the cord that bound his two wrists together. It was an awkward business, and drew a smothered "Ow" of pain from him as the knife cut into his wrist. But slowly and doggedly he went on sawing to and fro. He cut the flesh badly, but at last he felt the cord slacken. With his hands free, the rest was easy. Five minutes later he stood upright with some difficulty, owing to the cramp in his limbs. His first care was to bind up his bleeding wrist. Then he sat on the edge of the bed to think. Conrad had taken the key of the door, so he could expect little more assistance from Annette. The only outlet from the room was the door, consequently he would perforce have to wait until the two men returned to fetch him. But when they did . . . Tommy smiled! Moving in infinite caution in the dark room, he found and unhooked the famous picture. He felt an economical pleasure that his first plan would not be wasted. There was now nothing to do but to wait. He waited.

The night passed slowly. Tommy lived through an eternity of hours, but at last he heard footsteps. He stood upright, drew a deep breath, and clutched the picture firmly.

The door opened. A faint light streamed in from outside. Conrad went straight toward the gas to light it. Tommy deeply regretted that it was he who had entered first. It would have been pleasant to get even with Conrad. Number 14 followed. As he stepped across the threshold, Tommy brought the picture down with a terrific force on his head. Number 14 went down amidst a stupendous crash of broken glass. In a minute Tommy had slipped out and pulled to the door. The key was in the lock. He turned it and withdrew it just as Conrad hurled himself against the door from the inside with a volley of curses.

For a moment Tommy hesitated. There was the sound of some one stirring on the floor below. Then the German's voice came up the stairs.

"*Gott im Himmel!* Conrad, what is it?"

Tommy felt a small hand thrust into his. Beside him stood Annette. She pointed up a rickety ladder that apparently led to some attics.

"Quick—up here!" She dragged him after her up the ladder. In another moment they were standing in a dusty garret littered with lumber. Tommy looked round.

"This won't do. It's a regular trap. There's no way out."

"Hush! Wait." The girl put her finger to her lips. She crept to the top of the ladder and listened.

The banging and beating on the door was terrific. The German and another were trying to force the door in. Annette explained in a whisper:

"They will think you are still inside. They cannot hear what Conrad says. The door is too thick."

"I thought you could hear what went on in the room?"

"There is a peephole into the next room. It was clever of you to guess. But they will not think of that—they are only anxious to get in."

"Yes—but look here——"

"Leave it to me." She bent down. To his amazement, Tommy saw that she was fastening the end of a long piece of string to the handle of a big cracked jug. She arranged it carefully, then turned to Tommy.

"Have you the key of the door?"

"Yes."

"Give it to me."

He handed it to her.

"I am going down. Do you think you can go halfway, and then swing yourself down *behind* the ladder, so that they will not see you?"

Tommy nodded.

"There's a big cupboard in the shadow of the landing. Stand behind it. Take the end of this string in your hand. When I've let the others out—*pull!*"

Before he had time to ask her anything more, she had flitted lightly down the ladder and was in the midst of the group with a loud cry:

"Mon Dieu! Mon Dieu! Qu'est-ce qu'il y a?"

The German turned on her with an oath.

"Get out of this. Go to your room!"

Very cautiously Tommy swung himself down the back of the ladder. So long as they did not turn round . . . all was well. He crouched behind the cupboard. They were still between him and the stairs.

"Ah!" Annette appeared to stumble over something. She stooped. *"Mon Dieu, voilà la clef!"*

The German snatched it from her. He unlocked the door. Conrad stumbled out, swearing.

"Where is he? Have you got him?"

"We have seen no one," said the German sharply. His face paled. "Who do you mean?"

Conrad gave vent to another oath.

"He's got away."

"Impossible. He would have passed us."

At that moment, with an ecstatic smile Tommy pulled the string. A crash of crockery came from the attic above. In a trice the men were pushing each other up the rickety ladder and had disappeared into the darkness above.

Quick as a flash Tommy leapt from his hiding place and dashed down the stairs, pulling the girl with him. There was no one in the hall. He fumbled over the bolts and chain. At last they yielded, the door swung open. He turned. Annette had disappeared.

Tommy stood spellbound. Had she run upstairs again? What madness possessed her! He fumed with impatience, but he stood his ground. He would not go without her.

And suddenly there was an outcry overhead, an exclamation from the German, and then Annette's voice, clear and high:

"*Ma foi*, he has escaped! And quickly! Who would have thought it?"

Tommy still stood rooted to the ground. Was that a command to him to go? He fancied it was.

And then, louder still, the words floated down to him:

"This is a terrible house, I want to got back to Marguerite. To Marguerite. *To Marguerite!*"

Tommy had run back to the stairs. She wanted him to go and leave her. But why? At all costs he must try and get her away with him. Then his heart sank. Conrad was leaping down the stairs, uttering a savage cry at the sight of him. After him came the others.

Tommy stopped Conrad's rush with a straight blow with his fist. It caught the other on the point of the jaw and he fell like a log. The second man tripped over his body and fell. From higher up the staircase there was a flash, and a bullet grazed Tommy's ear. He realized that it would be good for his health to get out of this house as soon as possible. As regards Annette he could do nothing. He had got even with Conrad, which was one satisfaction. The blow had been a good one.

He leapt for the door, slamming it behind him. The square was deserted. In front of the house was a baker's van. Evidently he was to have been taken out of London in that, and his body found many miles from the house in Soho. The driver jumped to the pavement and tried to bar Tommy's way. Again Tommy's fist shot out, and the driver sprawled on the pavement.

Tommy took to his heels and ran—none too soon. The front door opened and a hail of bullets followed him. Fortunately none of them hit him. He turned the corner of the square.

"There's one thing," he thought to himself, "they can't go on shooting. They'll have the police after them if they do. I wonder they dared to there."

He heard the footsteps of his pursuers behind him, and redoubled his own pace. Once he got out of these byways he would be safe. There would be a policeman about somewhere—not that he really wanted to invoke the aid of the police if he could possibly do without it. It meant explanations, and general awkwardness. In another moment he had reason to bless his luck. He stumbled over a prostrate figure, which started up with a yell of alarm and dashed off down the street. Tommy drew back into a doorway. In a minute he had the pleasure of seeing his two pursuers, of whom the German was one, industriously tracking down the red herring!

Tommy sat down quietly on the doorstep and allowed a few moments to elapse while he recovered his breath. Then he strolled gently in the opposite direction. He glanced at his watch. It was a little after half-past five. It was rapidly growing light. At the next corner he passed a policeman. The policeman cast a suspicious eye on him. Tommy felt slightly offended. Then, passing his hand over his face, he laughed. He had not shaved or washed for three days! What a guy he must look.

He betook himself without more ado to a Turkish Bath establishment which he knew to be open all night. He emerged into the busy daylight feeling himself once more, and able to make plans.

First of all, he must have a square meal. He had eaten nothing since midday yesterday. He turned into an A.B.C. shop and ordered eggs and bacon and coffee. Whilst he ate, he read a morning paper propped up in front of him. Suddenly he stiffened. There was a long article on Kramenin, who was described as the "man behind Bolshevism" in Russia, and who had just arrived in London—some thought as an unofficial envoy. His career was sketched lightly, and it was firmly asserted that he, and not the figurehead leaders, had been the author of the Russian Revolution.

In the centre of the page was his portrait.

"So that's who Number 1 is," said Tommy with his mouth full of eggs and bacon. "Not a doubt about it, I must push on."

He paid for his breakfast and betook himself to Whitehall. There he sent up his name, and the message that it was urgent. A few minutes later he was in the presence of the man who did not here go by the name of "Mr. Carter." There was a frown on his face.

"Look here, you've no business to come asking for me in this way. I thought that was distinctly understood?"

"It was, sir. But I judged it important to lose no time."

And as briefly and succinctly as possible he detailed the experiences of the last few days.

Halfway through, Mr. Carter interrupted him to give a few cryptic orders through the telephone. All traces of displeasure had now left his face. He nodded energetically when Tommy had finished.

"Quite right. Every moment's of value. Fear we shall be too late anyway. They wouldn't wait. Would clear out at once. Still, they may have left something behind them that will be a clue. You say you've recognized Number 1 to be Kramenin? That's important. We want something against him badly to prevent the Cabinet falling on his neck too freely. What about the others? You say two faces were familiar to you? One's a Labor man, you think? Just look through these photos, and see if you can spot him."

A minute later, Tommy held one up. Mr. Carter exhibited some surprise.

"Ah, Westway! Shouldn't have thought it. Poses as being moderate. As for the other fellow, I think I can give a good guess." He handed another photograph to Tommy, and smiled at the other's exclamation. "I'm right, then. Who is he? Irishman. Prominent Unionist M.P. All a blind, of course. We've suspected it—but couldn't get any proof. Yes, you've done very well, young man. The 29th, you say, is the date. That gives us very little time—very little time indeed."

"But——" Tommy hesitated.

Mr. Carter read his thoughts.

"We can deal with the General Strike menace, I think. It's a toss-up—but we've got a sporting chance! But if that draft treaty turns up—we're done. England will be plunged in anarchy. Ah, what's that? The car? Come on, Beresford, we'll go and have a look at this house of yours."

Two constables were on duty in front of the house in Soho. An inspector reported to Mr. Carter in a low voice. The latter turned to Tommy.

"The birds have flown—as we thought. We might as well go over it."

Going over the deserted house seemed to Tommy to partake of the character of a dream. Everything was just as it had been. The prison room with the crooked pictures, the broken jug in the attic, the meeting room with its long table. But nowhere was there a trace of papers. Everything of that kind had either been destroyed or taken away. And there was no sign of Annette.

"What you tell me about the girl puzzled me," said Mr. Carter. "You believe that she deliberately went back?"

"It would seem so, sir. She ran upstairs while I was getting the door open."

"H'm, she must belong to the gang, then; but, being a woman, didn't feel like standing by to see a personable young man killed. But evidently she's in with them, or she wouldn't have gone back."

"I can't believe she's really one of them, sir. She—seemed so different——"

"Good-looking, I suppose?" said Mr. Carter with a smile that made Tommy flush to the roots of his hair. He admitted Annette's beauty rather shamefacedly.

"By the way," observed Mr. Carter, "have you shown yourself to Miss Tuppence yet? She's been bombarding me with letters about you."

"Tuppence? I was afraid she might get a bit rattled. Did she go to the police?"

Mr. Carter shook his head.

"Then I wonder how they twigged me."

Mr., Carter looked inquiringly at him, and Tommy explained. The other nodded thoughtfully.

"True, that's rather a curious point. Unless the mention of the Ritz was an accidental remark?"

"It might have been, sir. But they must have found out about me suddenly in some way."

"Well," said Mr. Carter looking round him, "there's nothing more to be done here. What about some lunch with me?"

"Thanks awfully, sir. But I think I'd better get back and rout out Tuppence."

"Of course. Give her my kind regards and tell her not to believe you're killed too readily next time."

Tommy grinned.

"I take a lot of killing, sir."

"So I perceive," said Mr. Carter dryly. "Well, good-bye. Remember you're a marked man now, and take reasonable care of yourself."

"Thank you, sir."

Hailing a taxi briskly Tommy stepped in, and was swiftly borne to the Ritz, dwelling the while on the pleasurable anticipation of startling Tuppence.

"Wonder what she's been up to. Dogging 'Rita' most likely. By the way, I suppose that's who Annette meant by Marguerite. I didn't get it at the time." The thought saddened him a little, for it seemed to prove that Mrs. Vandemeyer and the girl were on intimate terms.

The taxi drew up at the Ritz. Tommy burst into its sacred portals eagerly, but his enthusiasm received a check. He was informed that Miss Cowley had gone out a quarter of an hour ago.

18
The Telegram

BAFFLED FOR THE moment, Tommy strolled into the restaurant, and ordered a meal of surpassing excellence. His four days' imprisonment had taught him anew to value good food.

He was in the middle of conveying a particularly choice morsel of Sole à la Jeanette to his mouth, when he caught sight of Julius entering the room. Tommy waved a menu cheerfully, and succeeded in attracting the other's attention. At the sight of Tommy, Julius's eyes seemed as though they would pop out of his head. He strode across, and pump-handled Tommy's hand with what seemed to the latter quite unnecessary vigor.

"Holy snakes!" he ejaculated. "Is it really you?"

"Of course it is. Why shouldn't it be?"

"Why shouldn't it be? Say, man, don't you know you've been given up for dead? I guess we'd have had a solemn requiem for you in another few days."

"Who thought I was dead?" demanded Tommy.

"Tuppence."

"She remembered the proverb about the good dying young, I suppose. There must be a certain amount of original sin in me to have survived. Where is Tuppence, by the way?"

"Isn't she here?"

"No, the fellows at the office said she'd just gone out."

"Gone shopping, I guess. I dropped her here in the car about an hour ago. But, say, can't you shed that British calm of yours, and get down to it? What on God's earth have you been doing all this time?"

"If you're feeding here," replied Tommy, "order now. It's going to be a long story."

Julius drew up a chair to the opposite side of the table, summoned a hovering waiter, and dictated his wishes. Then he turned to Tommy.

"Fire ahead. I guess you've had some few adventures."

"One or two," replied Tommy modestly, and plunged into his recital.

Julius listened spellbound. Half the dishes that were placed before him he forgot to eat. At the end he heaved a long sigh.

"Bully for you. Reads like a dime novel!"

"And now for the home front," said Tommy, stretching out his hand for a peach.

"We-el," drawled Julius, "I don't mind admitting we've had some adventures too."

He, in turn, assumed the role of narrator. Beginning with his unsuccessful reconnoitering at Bournemouth, he passed on to his return to London, the buying of the car, the growing anxieties of Tuppence, the call upon Sir James, and the sensational occurrences of the previous night.

"But who killed her?" asked Tommy. "I don't quite understand."

"The doctor kidded himself she took it herself," replied Julius dryly.

"And Sir James? What did he think?"

"Being a legal luminary, he is likewise a human oyster," replied Julius. "I should say he 'reserved judgment.'" He went on to detail the events of the morning.

"Lost her memory, eh?" said Tommy with interest. "By Jove, that explains why they looked at me so queerly when I spoke of questioning her. Bit of a slip on my part, that! But it wasn't the sort of thing a fellow would be likely to guess."

"They didn't give you any sort of hint as to where Jane was?"

Tommy shook his head regretfully.

"Not a word. I'm a bit of an ass, as you know. I ought to have got more out of them somehow."

"I guess you're lucky to be here at all. That bluff of yours was the goods alright. How you ever came to think of it all so pat beats me to a frazzle!"

"I was in such a funk I had to think of something," said Tommy simply.

There was a moment's pause, and then Tommy reverted to Mrs. Vandemeyer's death.

"There's no doubt it was chloral?"

"I believe not. At least they call it heart failure induced by an overdose, or some such claptrap. It's alright. We don't want to be worried with an inquest. But I guess Tuppence and I and even the highbrow Sir James have all got the same idea."

"Mr. Brown?" hazarded Tommy.

"Sure thing."

Tommy nodded.

"All the same," he said thoughtfully, "Mr. Brown hasn't got wings. I don't see how he got in and out."

"How about some high-class thought transference stunt? Some magnetic influence that irresistibly impelled Mrs. Vandemeyer to commit suicide?"

Tommy looked at him with respect.

"Good, Julius. Distinctly good. Especially the phraseology. But it leaves me cold. I yearn for a real Mr. Brown of flesh and blood. I think the gifted young detectives must get to work, study the entrances and exits, and tap the bumps on their foreheads until the solution of the mystery dawns on them. Let's go round to the scene of the crime. I wish we could get hold of Tuppence. The Ritz would enjoy the spectacle of the glad reunion."

Inquiry at the office revealed the fact that Tuppence had not yet returned.

"All the same, I guess I'll have a look round upstairs," said Julius. "She might be in my sitting room." He disappeared.

Suddenly a diminutive boy spoke at Tommy's elbow:

"The young lady—she's gone away by train, I think, sir," he murmured shyly.

"What?" Tommy wheeled round upon him.

The small boy became pinker than before.

"The taxi, sir. I heard her tell the driver Charing Cross and to look sharp."

Tommy stared at him, his eyes opening wide in surprise. Emboldened, the small boy proceeded. "So I thought, having asked for an A.B.C. and a Bradshaw."

Tommy interrupted him:

"When did she ask for an A.B.C. and a Bradshaw?"

"When I took her the telegram, sir."

"A telegram?"

"Yes, sir."

"When was that?"

"About half-past twelve, sir."

"Tell me exactly what happened."

The small boy drew a long breath.

"I took up a telegram to No. 891—the lady was there. She opened it and gave a gasp, and then she said, very jolly like: 'Bring me up a Bradshaw, and an A.B.C., and look sharp, Henry.' My name isn't Henry, but——"

"Never mind your name," said Tommy impatiently. "Go on."

"Yes, sir. I brought them, and she told me to wait, and looked up something. And then she looks up at the clock, and "Hurry up," she says. "Tell them to get me a taxi," and she begins a-shoving on of her hat in front of the glass, and she was down in two ticks, almost as quick as I was, and I seed her going down the steps and into the taxi, and I heard her call out what I told you."

The small boy stopped and replenished his lungs. Tommy continued to stare at him. At that moment Julius rejoined him. He held an open letter in his hand.

"I say, Hersheimmer"—Tommy turned to him—"Tuppence has gone off sleuthing on her own."

"Shucks!"

"Yes, she has. She went off in a taxi to Charing Cross in the deuce of a hurry after getting a telegram." His eye fell on the letter in Julius's hand. "Oh; she left a note for you. That's alright. Where's she off to?"

Almost unconsciously, he held out his hand for the letter, but Julius folded it up and placed it in his pocket. He seemed a trifle embarrassed.

"I guess this is nothing to do with it. It's about something else—something I asked her that she was to let me know about."

"Oh!" Tommy looked puzzled, and seemed waiting for more.

"See here," said Julius suddenly. "I'd better put you wise. I asked Miss Tuppence to marry me this morning."

"Oh!" said Tommy mechanically. He felt dazed. Julius's words were totally unexpected. For the moment they benumbed his brain.

"I'd like to tell you," continued Julius, "that before I suggested anything of the kind to Miss Tuppence, I made it clear that I didn't want to butt in in any way between her and you——"

Tommy roused himself.

"That's alright," he said quickly. "Tuppence and I have been pals for years. Nothing more." He lit a cigarette with a hand that shook ever so little. "That's quite alright. Tuppence always said that she was looking out for——"

He stopped abruptly, his face crimsoning, but Julius was in no way discomposed.

"Oh, I guess it'll be the dollars that'll do the trick. Miss Tuppence put me wise to that right away. There's no humbug about her. We ought to get along together very well."

Tommy looked at him curiously for a minute, as though he were about to speak, then changed his mind and said nothing. Tuppence and Julius! Well, why not? Had she not lamented the fact that she knew no right men? Had she not openly avowed her intention of marrying for money if she ever had the chance? Her meeting with the young American millionaire had given her the chance—and it was unlikely she would be slow to avail herself to it. She was out of money. She had always said so. Why blame her because she had been true to her creed?

Nevertheless, Tommy did blame her. He was filled with a passionate and utterly illogical resentment. It was all very well to *say* things like that—but a *real* girl would never marry for money. Tuppence was utterly cold-blooded and selfish, and he would be delighted if he never saw her again! And it was a rotten world!

Julius's voice broke in on these meditations.

"Yes, we ought to get along together very well. I've heard that a girl always refuses you once—a sort of convention."

Tommy caught his arm.

"Refuses? Did you say *refuses?*"

"Sure thing. Didn't I tell you that? She just rapped out a 'no' without any kind of reason to it. The eternal feminine, the Huns call it, I've heard. But she'll come round right enough. Likely enough, I hustled her some——"

But Tommy interrupted regardless of decorum.

"What did she say in that note?" he demanded fiercely.

The obliging Julius handed it to him.

"There's no earthly clue in it as to where she's gone," he assured Tommy. "But you might as well see for yourself if you don't believe me."

The note, in Tuppence's well-known schoolboy writing, ran as follows:

"DEAR JULIUS,

"It's always better to have things in black and white. I don't feel I can be bothered to think of marriage until Tommy is found. Let's leave it till then.

"Yours affectionately,
"TUPPENCE."

Tommy handed it back, his eyes shining. His feelings had undergone a sharp reaction. He now felt that Tuppence was all that was noble and disinterested. Had she not refused Julius without hesitation? True, the note betokened signs of weakening, but he could excuse that. It read almost like a bribe to Julius to spur him on in his efforts to find Tommy, but he supposed she had not really meant it that way. Darling Tuppence, there was not a girl in the world to touch her! When he saw her—— His thoughts were brought up with a sudden jerk.

"As you say," he remarked, pulling himself together, "there's not a hint here as to what she's up to. Hi—Henry!"

The small boy came obediently. Tommy produced five shillings.

"One more thing. Do you remember what the young lady did with the telegram?"

Henry gasped and spoke.

"She crumpled it up into a ball and threw it into the grate, and made a sort of noise like 'Whoop!' sir."

"Very graphic, Henry," said Tommy. "Here's your five shillings. Come on, Julius. We must find that telegram."

They hurried upstairs. Tuppence had left the key in her door. The room was as she had left it. In the fireplace was a crumpled ball of orange and white. Tommy disentangled it and smoothed out the telegram.

"Come at once, Moat House, Ebury, Yorkshire, great developments—TOMMY."

They looked at each other in stupefaction. Julius spoke first:

"*You* didn't send it?"

"Of course not. What does it mean?"

"I guess it means the worst," said Julius quietly. "They've got her."

"What?"

"Sure thing! They signed your name, and she fell into the trap like a lamb."

"My God! What shall we do?"

"Get busy, and go after her! Right away! There's no time to waste. It's almighty luck that she didn't take the wire with her. If she had we'd probably never have traced her. But we've got to hustle. Where's that Bradshaw?"

The energy of Julius was infectious. Left to himself, Tommy would probably have sat down to think things out for a good half-hour before he decided on a plan of action. But with Julius Hersheimmer about, hustling was inevitable

After a few muttered imprecations he handed the Bradshaw to Tommy as being more conversant with its mysteries. Tommy abandoned it in favor of an A.B.C.

"Here we are. Ebury, Yorks. From King's Cross. Or St. Pancras. (Boy must have made a mistake. It was King's Cross, not *Charing* Cross) 12:50, that's the train she went by. 2:10, that's gone. 3:20 is the next.—and a damned slow train too."

"What about the car?"

Tommy shook his head.

"Send it up if you like, but we'd better stick to the train. The great thing is to keep calm."

Julius groaned.

"That's so. But it gets my goat to think of that innocent young girl in danger!"

Tommy nodded abstractedly. He was thinking. In a moment or two, he said:

"I say, Julius, what do they want her for, anyway?"

"Eh? I don't get you?"

"What I mean is that I don't think it's their game to do her any harm," explained Tommy, puckering his brow with the strain of his mental processes. "She's a hostage, that's what she is. She's in no immediate danger, because if we tumble on to anything, she'd be damned useful to them. As long as they've got her, they've got the whip hand of us. See?"

"Sure thing," said Julius thoughtfully. "That's so."

"Besides," added Tommy, as an afterthought, "I've great faith in Tuppence."

The journey was wearisome, with many stops, and crowded carriages. They had to change twice, once at Doncaster, once at a small junction. Ebury was a deserted station with a solitary porter, to whom Tommy addressed himself:

"Can you tell me the way to the Moat House?"

"The Moat House? It's a tidy step from here. The big house near the sea, you mean?"

Tommy assented, brazenly. After listening to the porter's meticulous but perplexing directions, they prepared to leave the station. It was beginning to rain, and they turned up the collars of their coats as they trudged through the slush of the road. Suddenly Tommy halted.

"Wait a moment." He ran back to the station and tackled the porter anew.

"Look here, do you remember a young lady who arrived by an earlier train, the 12:50 from London? She'd probably ask you the way to the Moat House."

He described Tuppence as well as he could, but the porter shook his head. Several people had arrived by train in question. He could not call to mind one young lady in particular. But he was quite certain that no one had asked him the way to the Moat House.

Tommy rejoined Julius, and explained. Depression was settling down on him like a leaden weight. He felt convinced that their quest was going to be unsuccessful. The enemy had over three hours' start. Three hours was more than enough for Mr. Brown. He would not ignore the possibility of the telegram having been found.

The way seemed endless. Once they took the wrong turning and went nearly half a mile out of their direction. It was past seven o'clock when a small boy told them that "t' Moat House" was just past the next corner.

A rusty iron gate swinging dismally on its hinges! An overgrown drive thick with leaves. There was something about the place that struck a chill to both their hearts. They went up the deserted drive. The leaves deadened their footsteps. The daylight was almost gone. It was like walking in a world of ghosts. Overhead the branches flapped and creaked with a mournful note. Occasionally a sodden leaf drifted silently down, startling them with its cold touch on their cheek.

A turn of the drive brought them in sight of the house. That, too, seemed empty and deserted. The shutters were closed, the steps up to the door overgrown with moss. Was it indeed to this desolate spot that Tuppence had been decoyed? It seemed hard to believe that a human footstep had passed this way for months.

Julius jerked the rusty bell handle. A jangling peal rang discordantly, echoing through the emptiness within. No one came. They rang again and again—but there was no sign of life. Then they walked completely round the house. Everywhere silence, and shuttered windows. If they could believe the evidence of their eyes the place was empty.

"Nothing doing," said Julius.

They retraced their steps slowly to the gate.

"There must be a village handy," continued the young American. "We'd better make inquiries there. They'll know something about the place, and whether there's been anyone there lately."

"Yes, that's not a bad idea."

Proceeding up the road, they soon came to a little hamlet. On the outskirts of it, they met a workman swinging his bag of tools, and Tommy stopped him with a question.

"The Moat House? It's empty. Been empty for years. Mrs. Sweeney's got the key if you want to go over it—next to the post office."

Tommy thanked him. They soon found the post office, which was also a sweet and general fancy shop, and knocked at the door of the cottage next to it. A clean, wholesome looking woman opened it. She readily produced the key of the Moat House.

"Though I doubt if it's the kind of place to suit you, sir. In a terrible state of repair. Ceilings leaking and all. 'Twould need a lot of money spent on it."

"Thanks," said Tommy cheerily. "I dare say it'll be a washout, but houses are scarce nowadays."

"That they are," declared the woman heartily . "My daughter and son-in-law have been looking for a decent cottage for I don't know how long. It's all the war. Upset things terribly, it has. But excuse me, sir, it'll be too dark for you to see much of the house. Hadn't you better wait until tomorrow?"

"That's alright. We'll have a look around this evening, anyway. We'd have been here before only we lost our way. What's the best place to stay at for the night round here?"

Mrs. Sweeny looked doubtful.

"There's the *Yorkshire Arms*, but it's not much of a place for gentlemen like you."

"Oh, it will do very well. Thanks. By the way, you've not had a young lady here asking for this key today?"

The woman shook her head.

"No one's been over the place for a long time."

"Thanks very much."

They retraced their steps to the Moat House. As the front door swung back on its hinges, protesting loudly, Julius struck a match and examined the floor carefully. Then he shook his head.

"I'd swear no one's passed this way. Look at the dust. Thick. Not a sign of a footmark."

They wandered round the deserted house. Everywhere the same tale. Thick layers of dust apparently undisturbed.

"This gets me," said Julius. "I don't believe Tuppence was ever in this house."

"She must have been."

Julius shook his head without replying.

"We'll go over it again tomorrow," said Tommy. "Perhaps we'll see more in the daylight."

On the morrow they took up the search once more, and were reluctantly forced to the conclusion that the house had not been invaded for some considerable time. They might have left the village altogether but for a fortunate discovery of Tommy's. As they were retracing their steps to the gate, he gave a sudden cry, and stopping, picked something up from among the leaves, and held it out to Julius. It was a small gold brooch.

"That's Tuppence's!"

"Are you sure?"

"Absolutely. I've often seen her wear it."

Julius drew a deep breath.

"I guess that settles it. She came as far as here, anyway. We'll make that pub our headquarters, and raise hell round here until we find her. Somebody *must* have seen her."

Forthwith the campaign began. Tommy and Julius worked separately and together, but the result was the same. Nobody answering to Tuppence's description had been seen in the vicinity. They were baffled—but not discouraged. Finally they altered their tactics. Tuppence had certainly not remained long in the neighborhood of the Moat House. That pointed to her having been overcome and carried away in a car. They renewed inquiries. Had anyone seen a car standing somewhere near the Moat House that day? Again they met with no success.

Julius wired to town for his own car, and they scoured the neighborhood daily with unflagging zeal. A gray limousine on which they had set high hopes was traced to Harrogate, and turned out to be the property of a highly respectable maiden lady!

Each day saw them set out on a new quest. Julius was like a hound on the leash. He followed up the slenderest clue. Every car that had passed through the village on the fateful day was tracked down. He forced his way into country properties and submitted the owners of the motors to a searching cross-examination. His apologies were as thorough as his methods, and seldom failed in disarming the indignation of his victims; but, as day succeeded day, they were no nearer to discovering Tuppence's whereabouts. So well had the abduction been planned that the girl seemed literally to have vanished into thin air.

And another preoccupation was weighing on Tommy's mind.

"Do you know how long we've been here?" he asked one morning as they sat facing each other at breakfast. "A week! We're no nearer to finding Tuppence, *and next Sunday is the 29th!*"

"Shucks!" said Julius thoughtfully. "I'd almost forgotten about the 29th. I've been thinking of nothing but Tuppence."

"So have I. At least, I hadn't forgotten about the 29th, but it didn't seem to matter a damn in comparison to finding Tuppence. But today's the 23rd, and time's getting short. If we're ever going to get hold of her at all, we must do it before the 29th—her life won't be worth an hour's purchase afterward. The hostage game will be played out by then. I'm beginning to feel that we've made a big mistake in the way we've set about this. We've wasted time and we're no forrader."

"I'm with you there. We've been a couple of mutts, who've bitten off a bigger bit than they can chew. I'm going to quit fooling right away!"

"What do you mean?"

"I'll tell you. I'm going to do what we ought to have done a week ago. I'm going right back to London to put the case in the hands of your British police. We fancied ourselves as sleuths. Sleuths! It was a piece of damn-fool foolishness! I'm through! I've had enough of it. Scotland Yard for me!"

"You're right," said Tommy slowly. "I wish to God we'd gone there right away.

"Better late than never. We've been like a couple of babes playing 'Here we go round the Mulberry Bush.' Now I'm going right along to Scotland Yard to ask them to take me by the hand and show me the way I should go. I guess the professional always scores over the amateur in the end. Are you coming along with me?"

Tommy shook his head.

"What's the good? One of us is enough. I might as well stay here and nose round a bit longer. Something *might* turn up. One never knows."

"Sure thing. Well, so long. I'll be back in a couple of shakes with a few inspectors along. I shall tell them to pick out their brightest and best."

But the course of events was not to follow the plan Julius had laid down. Later in the day Tommy received a wire:

"Join me Manchester Midland Hotel. Important news—JULIUS."

At 7:30 that night Tommy alighted from a slow cross-country train. Julius was on the platform.

"Thought you'd come by this train if you weren't out when my wire arrived."

Tommy grasped him by the arm.

"What is it? Is Tuppence found?"

Julius shook his head.

"No. But I found this waiting in London. Just arrived."

He handed the telegraph form to the other. Tommy's eyes opened as he read:

"Jane Finn found. Come Manchester Midland Hotel immediately—PEEL EDGERTON."

Julius took the form back and folded it up.

"Queer," he said thoughtfully. "I thought that lawyer chap had quit!"

19
Jane Finn

"MY TRAIN GOT in half an hour ago," explained Julius, as he led the way out of the station. "I reckoned you'd come by this before I left London, and wired accordingly to Sir James. He's booked rooms for us, and will be round to dine at eight."

"What made you think he'd ceased to take any interest in the case?" asked Tommy curiously.

"What he said," replied Julius dryly. "The old bird's as close as an oyster! Like all the darned lot of them, he wasn't going to commit himself till he was sure he could deliver the goods."

"I wonder," said Tommy thoughtfully.

"You wonder what?"

"Whether that was his real reason."

"Sure. You bet your life it was."

Tommy shook his head unconvinced.

Sir James arrived punctually at eight o'clock, and Julius introduced Tommy. Sir James shook hands with him warmly.

"I am delighted to make your acquaintance, Mr. Beresford. I have heard so much about you from Miss Tuppence"—he smiled involuntarily—"that it really seems as though I already know you quite well."

"Thank you, sir," said Tommy with his cheerful grin. He scanned the great lawyer eagerly. Like Tuppence, he felt the magnetism of the other's personality. He was reminded of Mr. Carter. The two men, totally unlike so far as physical resemblance went, produced a similar effect. Beneath the weary manner of the one and the professional reserve of the other, lay the same quality of mind, keen-edged like a rapier.

In the meantime he was conscious of Sir James's close scrutiny. When the lawyer dropped his eyes the young man had the feeling that the other had read him through and through like an open book. He could not but wonder what the final judgment was, but there was little chance of learning that. Sir James took in everything, but gave out only what he chose. A proof of that occurred almost at once.

Immediately the first greetings were over Julius broke out into a flood of eager questions. How had Sir James managed to track the girl? Why had he not let them know that he was still working on the case? And so on.

Sir James stroked his chin and smiled. At last he said:

"Just so, just so. Well, she's found. And that's the great thing, isn't it? Eh! Come now, that's the great thing?"

"Sure it is. But just how did you strike her trail? Miss Tuppence and I thought you'd quit for good and all."

"Ah!" The lawyer shot a lightning glance at him, then resumed operations on his chin. "You thought that, did you? Did you really? H'm, dear me."

"But I guess I can take it we were wrong," pursued Julius.

"Well, I don't know that I should go so far as to say that. But it's certainly fortunate for all parties that we've managed to find the young lady."

"But where is she?" demanded Julius, his thoughts flying off on another tack. "I thought you'd be sure to bring her along?"

"That would hardly be possible," said Sir James gravely.

"Why?"

"Because the young lady was knocked down in a street accident, and has sustained slight injuries to the head. She was taken to the infirmary, and on recovering consciousness gave her name as Jane Finn. When—ah!—I heard that, I arranged for her to be removed to the house of a doctor—a friend of mine, and wired at once for you. She relapsed into unconsciousness and has not spoken since."

"She's not seriously hurt?"

"Oh, a bruise and a cut or two; really, from a medical point of view, absurdly slight injuries to have produced such a condition. Her state is probably to be attributed to the mental shock consequent on recovering her memory."

"It's come back?" cried Julius excitedly.

Sir James tapped the table rather impatiently.

"Undoubtedly, Mr. Hersheimmer, since she was able to give her real name. I thought you had appreciated that point."

"And you just happened to be on the spot," said Tommy. "Seems quite like a fairy tale."

But Sir James was far too wary to be drawn.

"Coincidences are curious things," he said dryly.

Nevertheless Tommy was now certain of what he had before only suspected. Sir James's presence in Manchester was not accidental. Far from abandoning the case, as Julius supposed, he had by some means of his own successfully run the missing girl to earth. The only thing that puzzled Tommy was the reason for all this secrecy. He concluded that it was a foible of the legal mind.

Julius was speaking.

"After dinner," he announced, "I shall go right away and see Jane."

"That will be impossible, I fear," said Sir James. "It is unlikely they would allow her to see visitors at this time of night. I should suggest tomorrow morning about ten o'clock."

Julius flushed. There was something in Sir James which always stirred him to antagonism. It was a conflict of two masterful personalities.

"All the same, I reckon I'll go round there tonight and see if I can't ginger them up to break through their silly rules."

"It will be quite useless, Mr. Hersheimmer."

The words came out like the crack of a pistol, and Tommy looked up with a start. Julius was nervous and excited. The hand with which he raised his glass to his lips shook slightly, but his eyes held Sir James's defiantly. For a moment the hostility between the two seemed likely to burst into flame, but in the end Julius lowered his eyes, defeated.

"For the moment, I reckon you're the boss."

"Thank you," said the other. "We will say ten o'clock then?" With consummate ease of manner he turned to Tommy. "I must confess, Mr. Beresford, that it was something of a surprise to me to see you here this evening. The last I heard of you was that your friends were in grave anxiety on your behalf. Nothing had been heard of you for some days, and Miss Tuppence was inclined to think you had got into difficulties."

"I had sir!" Tommy grinned reminiscently. "I was never in a tighter place in my life."

Helped out by questions from Sir James, he gave an abbreviated account of his adventures. The lawyer looked at him with renewed interest as he brought the tale to a close.

"You got yourself out of a tight place very well," he said gravely. "I congratulate you. You displayed a great deal of ingenuity and carried your part through well."

Tommy blushed, his face assuming a prawnlike hue at the praise.

"I couldn't have got away but for the girl, sir."

"No." Sir James smiled a little. "It was lucky for you she happened to—er—take a fancy to you." Tommy appeared about to protest, but Sir James went on. "There's no doubt about her being one of the gang, I suppose?"

"I'm afraid not, sir. I thought perhaps they were keeping her there by force, but the way she acted didn't fit in with that. You see, she went back to them when she could have got away."

Sir James nodded thoughtfully.

"What did she say? Something about wanting to be taken to Marguerite?"

"Yes, sir. I suppose she meant Mrs. Vandemeyer."

"She always signed herself Rita Vandemeyer. All her friends spoke of her as Rita. Still, I suppose the girl must have been in the habit of calling her by her full name. And, at the moment she was crying out to her, Mrs. Vandemeyer was either dead or dying! Curious! There are one or two points that strike me as being obscure—their sudden change of attitude toward yourself, for instance. By the way, the house was raided, of course?"

"Yes, sir, but they'd all cleared out."

"Naturally," said Sir James dryly.

"And not a clue left behind."

"I wonder——" The lawyer tapped the table thoughtfully.

Something in his voice made Tommy look up. Would this man's eyes have seen something where theirs had been blind? He spoke impulsively:

"I wish you'd been there, sir, to go over the house!"

"I wish I had," said Sir James quietly. He sat for a moment in silence. Then he looked up. "And since then? What have you been doing?"

For a moment, Tommy stared at him. Then it dawned on him that of course the lawyer did not know.

"I forgot that you didn't know about Tuppence," he said slowly. The sickening anxiety, forgotten for a while in the excitement of knowing Jane Finn was found at last, swept over him again.

The lawyer laid down his knife and fork sharply.

"Has anything happened to Miss Tuppence?" His voice was keen-edged.

"She's disappeared," said Julius.

"When?"

"A week ago."

"How?"

Sir James's questions fairly shot out. Between them Tommy and Julius gave the history of the last week and their futile search.

Sir James went at once to the root of the matter.

"A wire signed with your name? They knew enough of you both for that. They weren't sure of how much you had learnt in that house. Their kidnapping of Miss Tuppence is the counter-move to your escape. If necessary they could seal your lips with a threat of what might happen to her."

Tommy nodded.

"That's just what I thought, sir."

Sir James looked at him keenly. "*You* had worked that out, had you? Not bad—not at all bad. The curious thing is that they certainly did not know anything about you when they first held you prisoner. You are sure that you did not in any way disclose your identity?"

Tommy shook his head.

"That's so," said Julius with a nod. "Therefore I reckon someone put them wise—and not earlier than Sunday afternoon."

"Yes, but who?"

"That almighty omniscient Mr. Brown, of course!"

There was a faint note of derision in the American's voice which made Sir James look up sharply.

"You don't believe in Mr. Brown, Mr. Hersheimmer?"

"No, sir, I do not," returned the young American with emphasis. "Not as such, that is to say. I reckon it out that he's a figurehead—just a bogy name to frighten the children with. The real head of this business is that Russian chap Kramenin. I guess he's quite capable of running revolutions in three countries at once if he chose! The man Whittington is probably the head of the English branch."

"I disagree with you," said Sir James shortly. "Mr. Brown exists." He turned to Tommy. "Did you happen to notice where that wire was handed in?"

"No, sir, I'm afraid I didn't."

"H'm. Got it with you?"

"It's upstairs, sir, in my kit."

"I'd like to have a look at it sometime. No hurry. You've wasted a week"—Tommy hung his head—"a day or so more is immaterial. We'll deal with Miss Jane Finn first. Afterward, we'll set to work to rescue Miss Tuppence from bondage. I don't think she's in any immediate danger. That is, so long as they don't know that we've got Jane Finn, and that her memory has returned. We must keep that dark at all costs. You understand?"

The other two assented, and, after making arrangements for meeting on the morrow, the great lawyer took his leave.

At ten o'clock, the two young men were at the appointed spot. Sir James had joined them on the doorstep. He alone appeared unexcited. He introduced them to the doctor.

"Mr. Hersheimmer—Mr. Beresford—Dr. Roylance. How's the patient?"

"Going on well. Evidently no idea of the flight of time. Asked this morning how many had been saved from the *Lusitania*. Was it in the papers yet? That, of course, was only what was to be expected. She seems to have something on her mind, though."

"I think we can relieve her anxiety. May we go up?"

"Certainly."

Tommy's heart beat sensibly faster as they followed the doctor upstairs. Jane Finn at last! The long-sought, the mysterious, the elusive Jane Finn! How wildly improbable success had seemed! And here in this house, her memory almost miraculously restored, lay the girl who held the future of England in her hands. A half groan broke from Tommy's lips. If only Tuppence could have been at his side to share in the triumphant conclusion of their joint venture! Then he put the thought of Tuppence resolutely aside. His confidence in Sir James was growing. There was a man who would unerringly ferret out Tuppence's whereabouts. In the meantime Jane Finn! And suddenly a dread clutched at his heart. It seemed too easy. . . . Suppose they should find her dead . . . stricken down by the hand of Mr. Brown?

In another minute he was laughing at these melodramatic fancies. The doctor held open the door of a room and they passed in. On the white bed, bandages round her head, lay the girl. Somehow the whole scene seemed unreal. It was so exactly what one expected that it gave the effect of being beautifully staged.

The girl looked from one to the other of them with large wondering eyes. Sir James spoke first.

"Miss Finn," he said, "this is your cousin, Mr. Julius P. Hersheimmer."

A faint flush flitted over the girl's face, as Julius stepped forward and took her hand.

"How do, Cousin Jane?" he said lightly.

But Tommy caught the tremor in his voice.

"Are you really Uncle Hiram's son?" she asked wonderingly.

Her voice, with the slight warmth of the Western accent, had an almost thrilling quality. It seemed vaguely familiar to Tommy, but he thrust the impression aside as impossible.

"Sure thing."

"We used to read about Uncle Hiram in the papers," continued the girl, in her low soft tones. "But I never thought I'd meet you one day. Mother figured it out that Uncle Hiram would never get over being mad with her."

"The old man was like that," admitted Julius. "But I guess the new generation's sort of different. Got no use for the family feud business. First thing I thought about, as soon as the war was over, was to come along and hunt you up."

A shadow passed over the girl's face.

"They've been telling me things—dreadful things—that my memory went, and that there are years I shall never know about—years lost out of life."

"You didn't realize that yourself?"

The girl's eyes opened wide.

"Why, no. It seems to me as though it were no time since we were being hustled into those boats. I can see it all now." She closed her eyes with a shudder.

Julius looked across at Sir James, who nodded.

"Don't worry any. It isn't worth it. Now, see here, Jane, there's something we want to know about. There was a man aboard that boat with some mighty important papers on him, and the big guns in this country have got a notion that he passed on the goods to you. Is that so?"

The girl hesitated, her glance shifting to the other two. Julius understood.

"Mr. Beresford is commissioned by the British Government to get those papers back. Sir James Peel Edgerton is an English Member of Parliament, and might be a big gun in the Cabinet if he liked. It's owing to him that we've ferreted you out at last. So you can go right ahead and tell us the whole story. Did Danvers give you the papers?"

"Yes. He said they'd have a better chance with me, because they would save the women and children first."

"Just as we thought," said Sir James.

"He said they were very important—that they might make all the difference to the Allies. But, if it's all so long ago, and the war's over, what does it matter now?"

"I guess history repeats itself, Jane. First there was a great hue and cry over those papers, then it all died down, and now the whole caboodle's started all over again—for rather different reasons. Then you can hand them over to us right away?"

"But I can't."

"What?"

"I haven't got them."

"You—haven't—got them?" Julius punctuated the words with little pauses.

"No—I hid them."

"You *hid* them?"

"Yes. I got uneasy. People seemed to be watching me. It scared me—badly." She put her hand to her head. "It's almost the last thing I remember before waking up in the hospital. . . ."

"Go on," said Sir James, in his quiet penetrating tones. "What do you remember?"

She turned to him obediently.

"It was at Holyhead. I came that way—I don't remember why. . . ."

"That doesn't matter. Go on."

"In the confusion on the quay I slipped away. Nobody saw me. I took a car. Told the man to drive me out of the town. I watched when we got on the open road. No other car was following us. I saw a path at the side of the road. I told the man to wait."

She paused and then went on. "The path led to the cliff, and down to the sea between big yellow gorse bushes—they were like golden flames. I looked round. There wasn't a soul in sight. But just level with my head there was a hole in the rock. It was quite small—I could only just get my hand in, but it went a long way back. I took the oilskin packet from round my neck and shoved it right in as far as I could. Then I tore off a bit of gorse—My! But it did prick—and plugged the hole with it so that you'd never guess there was a crevice of any kind there. Then I marked the place carefully in my own mind, so that I'd find it again. There was a queer boulder in the path just there—for all the world like a dog sitting up begging. Then I went back to the road. The car was waiting, and I drove back. I just caught the train. I was a bit ashamed of myself for fancying things maybe, but, by and by, I saw the man opposite me wink at a woman who was sitting next to me, and I felt scared again, and was glad the papers were safe. I went out in the corridor to get a little air. I thought I'd slip into another carriage. But the woman called me back, said I'd dropped something, and when I stooped to look, something seemed to hit me—here." She placed her hand to the back of her head. "I don't remember anything more until I woke up in the hospital."

There was a pause.

"Thank you, Miss Finn." It was Sir James who spoke. "I hope we have not tired you?"

"Oh, that's alright. My head aches a little, but otherwise I feel fine."

Julius stepped forward and took her hand again.

"So long, Cousin Jane. I'm going to get busy after those papers, but I'll be back in two shakes of a dog's tail, and I'll tote you up to London and give you the time of your young life before we go back to the States! I mean it—so hurry up and get well."

20
Too Late

IN THE STREET they held an informal council of war. Sir James had drawn a watch from his pocket. "The boat train to Holyhead stops at Chester at 12:14. If you start at once I think you can catch the connection."

Tommy looked up, puzzled.

"Is there any need to hurry, sir? Today is only the 24th."

"I guess it's always well to get up early in the morning," said Julius, before the lawyer had time to reply. "We'll make tracks for the depot right away."

A little frown had settled on Sir James's brow.

"I wish I could come with you. I am due to speak at a meeting at two o'clock. It is unfortunate."

The reluctance in his tone was very evident. It was clear, on the other hand, that Julius was easily disposed to put up with the loss of the other's company.

"I guess there's nothing complicated about this deal," he remarked. "Just a game of hide-and-seek, that's all."

"I hope so," said Sir James.

"Sure thing. What else could it be?"

"You are still young, Mr. Hersheimmer. At my age you will probably have learnt one lesson. 'Never underestimate your adversary.'"

The gravity of his tone impressed Tommy, but had little effect upon Julius.

"You think Mr. Brown might come along and take a hand? If he does, I'm ready for him." He slapped his pocket. "I carry a gun. Little Willie here travels round with me everywhere." He produced a murderous-looking automatic, and tapped it affectionately before returning it to its home. "But he won't be needed this trip. There's nobody to put Mr. Brown wise."

The lawyer shrugged his shoulders.

"There was nobody to put Mr. Brown wise to the fact that Mrs. Vandemeyer meant to betray him. Nevertheless, *Mrs. Vandemeyer died without speaking.*"

Julius was silenced for once, and Sir James added on a lighter note:

"I only want to put you on your guard. Good-bye, and good luck. Take no unnecessary risk once the papers are in your hands. If there is any reason to believe that you have been shadowed, destroy them at once. Good luck to you. The game is in your hands now." He shook hands with them both.

Ten minutes later the two young men were seated in a first-class carriage *en route* for Chester.

For a long time neither of them spoke. When at length Julius broke the silence, it was with a totally unexpected remark.

"Say," he observed thoughtfully, "did you ever make a darned fool of yourself over a girl's face?"

Tommy, after a moment's astonishment, searched his mind.

"Can't say I have," he replied at last. "Not that I can recollect, anyhow. Why?"

"Because for the last two months I've been making a sentimental idiot of myself over Jane! First moment I clapped eyes on her photograph my heart did all the usual stunts you read about in novels. I guess I'm ashamed to admit it, but I came over here determined to find her and fix it all up, and take her back as Mrs. Julius P. Hersheimmer!"

"Oh!" said Tommy, amazed.

Julius uncrossed his legs brusquely and continued:

"Just shows what an almighty fool a man can make of himself! One look at the girl in the flesh, and I was cured!"

Feeling more tongue-tied than ever, Tommy ejaculated "Oh!" again.

"No disparagement to Jane, mind you," continued the other. "She's a real nice girl, and some fellow will fall in love with her right away."

"I thought her a very good-looking girl," said Tommy, finding his tongue.

"Sure she is. But she's not like her photo one bit. At least I suppose she is in a way—must be—because I recognized her right off. If I'd seen her in a crowd I'd have said 'There's a girl whose face I know' right away without any hesitation. But there was something about that photo"—Julius shook his head, and heaved a sigh—"I guess romance is a mighty queer thing!"

"It must be," said Tommy coldly, "if you can come over here in love with one girl, and propose to another within a fortnight."

Julius had the grace to look discomposed.

"Well, you see, I'd got a sort of tired feeling that I'd never find Jane—and that it was all plumb foolishness anyway. And then—oh, well, the French, for instance, are much more sensible in the way they look at things. They keep romance and marriage apart——"

Tommy flushed.

"Well I'm damned! If that's——"

Julius hastened to interrupt.

"Say now, don't be hasty. I don't mean what you mean. I take it Americans have a higher opinion of morality than you have even. What I meant was that the French set about marriage in a business-like way—find two people who are suited to one another, look after the money affairs, and see the whole thing practically, and in a businesslike spirit."

"If you ask me," said Tommy, "we're all too damned businesslike nowadays. We're always saying, 'Will it pay?' The men are bad enough, and the girls are worse!"

"Cool down, son. Don't get so heated."

"I feel heated," said Tommy.

Julius looked at him and judged it wise to say no more.

However, Tommy had plenty of time to cool down before they reached Holyhead, and the cheerful grin had returned to his countenance as they alighted at their destination.

After consultation, and with the aid of a road map, they were fairly well agreed as to their direction, so were able to hire a taxi without more ado and drive out on the road leading to Treaddur Bay. They instructed the man to go slowly, and watched narrowly so as not to miss the path. They came to it not long after leaving the town, and Tommy stopped the car promptly, asked in a casual tone whether the path led down to the sea, and hearing it did paid off the man in handsome style.

A moment later the taxi was slowly chugging back to Holyhead. Tommy and Julius watched it out of sight, and then turned to the narrow path.

"It's the right one, I suppose?" asked Tommy doubtfully. "There must be simply heaps along here."

"Sure it is. Look at the gorse. Remember what Jane said?"

Tommy looked at the swelling hedges of golden blossom which bordered the path on either side, and was convinced.

They went down in single file, Julius leading. Twice Tommy turned his head uneasily. Julius looked back.

"What is it?"

"I don't know. I've got the wind up somehow. Keep fancying there's someone following us."

"Can't be," said Julius positively. "We'd see him."

Tommy had to admit that this was true. Nevertheless, his sense of uneasiness deepened. In spite of himself he believed in the omniscience of the enemy.

"I rather wish that fellow would come along," said Julius. He patted his pocket. "Little William here is just aching for exercise!"

"Do you always carry it—him—with you?" inquired Tommy with burning curiosity.

"Most always. I guess you never know what might turn up."

Tommy kept a respectful silence. He was impressed by little William. It seemed to remove the menace of Mr. Brown farther away.

The path was now running along the side of the cliff, parallel to the sea. Suddenly Julius came to such an abrupt halt that Tommy cannoned into him.

"What's up?" he inquired.

"Look there. If that doesn't beat the band!"

Tommy looked. Standing out half obstructing the path was a huge boulder which certainly bore a fanciful resemblance to a "begging" terrier.

"Well," said Tommy, refusing to share Julius's emotion, "it's what we expected to see, isn't it?"

Julius looked at him sadly and shook his head.

"British phlegm! Sure we expected it—but it kind of rattles me, all the same, to see it sitting there just where we expected to find it!"

Tommy, whose calm was, perhaps, more assumed than natural, moved his feet impatiently.

"Push on. What about the hole?"

They scanned the cliff-side narrowly. Tommy heard himself saying idiotically:

"The gorse won't be there after all these years."

And Julius replied solemnly:

"I guess you're right."

Tommy suddenly pointed with a shaking hand.

"What about that crevice there?"

Julius replied in an awestricken voice:

"That's it—for sure."

They looked at each other.

"When I was in France," said Tommy reminiscently, "whenever my batman failed to call me, he always said that he had come over queer. I never believed it. But whether he felt it or not, there *is* such a sensation. I've got it now! Badly!"

He looked at the rock with a kind of agonized passion.

"Damn it!" he cried. "It's impossible! Five years! Think of it! Bird's-nesting boys, picnic parties, thousands of people passing! It can't be there! It's a hundred to one against its being there! It's against all reason!"

Indeed, he felt it to be impossible—more, perhaps, because he could not believe in his own success where so many others had failed. The thing was too easy, therefore it could not be. The hole would be empty.

Julius looked at him with a widening smile.

"I guess you're rattled now alright," he drawled with some enjoyment. "Well, here goes!" He thrust his hand into the crevice, and made a slight grimace. "It's a tight fit. Jane's hand must be a few sizes smaller than mine. I don't feel anything—no—say, what's this? Gee whiz!" And with a flourish he waved aloft a small discolored packet. "It's the goods alright. Sewn up in oilskin. Hold it while I get my penknife."

The unbelievable had happened. Tommy held the precious packet tenderly between his hands. They had succeeded!

"It's queer," he murmured idly, "you'd think the stitches would have rotted. They look just as good as new."

They cut them carefully and ripped away the oilsilk. Inside was a small folded sheet of paper. With trembling fingers they unfolded it. The sheet was blank! They stared at each other, puzzled.

"A dummy?" hazarded Julius. "Was Danvers just a decoy?"

Tommy shook his head. That solution did not satisfy him. Suddenly his face cleared.

"I've got it! *Sympathetic ink!*"

"You think so?"

"Worth trying anyhow. Heat usually does the trick. Get some sticks. We'll make a fire."

In a few minutes the little fire of twigs and leaves was blazing merrily.

Tommy held the sheet of paper near the glow. The paper curled a little with the heat. Nothing more.

Suddenly Julius grasped his arm, and pointed to where characters were appearing in a faint brown color.

"Gee whiz! You've got it! Say, that idea of yours was great. It never occurred to me."

Tommy held the paper in position some minutes longer until he judged the heat had done its work. Then he withdrew it. A moment later he uttered a cry.

Across the sheet in neat brown printing ran the words:

WITH THE COMPLIMENTS OF MR. BROWN.

21

Tommy Makes a Discovery

FOR A MOMENT or two they stood staring at each other stupidly, dazed with the shock. Somehow, inexplicably, Mr. Brown had forestalled them. Tommy accepted defeat quietly. Not so Julius.

"How in tarnation did he get ahead of us? That's what beats me!" he ended up.

Tommy shook his head, and said dully:

"It accounts for the stitches being new. We might have guessed. . . ."

"Never mind the darned stitches. How did he get ahead of us? We hustled all we knew. It's downright impossible for anyone to get here quicker than we did. And, anyway, how did he know? Do you reckon there was a dictaphone in Jane's room? I guess there must have been."

But Tommy's common sense pointed out objections.

"No one could have known beforehand that she was going to be in that house—much less that particular room."

"That's so," admitted Julius. "Then one of the nurses was a crook and listened at the door. How's that?"

"I don't see that it matters anyway," said Tommy wearily. "He may have found out some months ago, and removed the papers, then——No, by Jove, that won't wash! They'd have been published at once."

"Sure thing they would! No, someone's got ahead of us today by an hour or so. But how they did it gets my goat."

"I wish that chap Peel Edgerton had been with us," said Tommy thoughtfully.

"Why?" Julius stared. "The mischief was done when we came."

"Yes——" Tommy hesitated. He could not explain his own feeling—the illogical idea that the K.C.'s presence would somehow have averted the catastrophe. He reverted to his former point of view. "It's no good arguing about how it was done. The game's up. We've failed. There's only one thing for me to do."

"What's that?"

"Get back to London as soon as possible. Mr. Carter must be warned. It's only a matter of hours now before the blow falls. But, at any rate, he ought to know the worst."

The duty was an unpleasant one, but Tommy had no intention of shirking it. He must report his failure to Mr. Carter. After that his work was done. He took the midnight mail to London. Julius elected to stay the night at Holyhead.

Half an hour after arrival, haggard and pale, Tommy stood before his chief.

"I've come to report, sir. I've failed—failed badly."

Mr. Carter eyed him sharply.

"You mean that the treaty——"

"Is in the hands of Mr. Brown, sir."

"Ah!" said Mr. Carter quietly. The expression on his face did not change, but Tommy caught the flicker of despair in his eyes. It convinced him as nothing else had done that the outlook was hopeless.

"Well," said Mr. Carter after a minute or two, "we mustn't sag at the knees, I suppose. I'm glad to know definitely. We must do what we can."

Through Tommy's mind flashed the assurance: "It's hopeless, and he knows it's hopeless!"

The other looked up at him.

"Don't take it to heart, lad," he said kindly. "You did your best. You were up against one of the biggest brains of the century. And you came very near success. Remember that."

"Thank you, sir. It's awfully decent of you."

"I blame myself. I have been blaming myself ever since I heard this other news."

Something in his tone attracted Tommy's attention. A new fear gripped at his heart.

"Is there—something more, sir?"

"I'm afraid so," said Mr. Carter gravely. He stretched out his hand to a sheet on the table.

"Tuppence——?" faltered Tommy.

"Read for yourself."

The typewritten words danced before his eyes. The description of a green toque, a coat with a handkerchief in the pocket marked P.L.C. He looked an agonized question at Mr. Carter. The latter replied to it:

"Washed up on the Yorkshire coast—near Ebury. I'm afraid—it looks very much like foul play."

"My God!" gasped Tommy. *"Tuppence!* Those devils—I'll never rest till I've got even with them! I'll hunt them down! I'll——"

The pity on Mr. Carter's face stopped him.

"I know what you feel like, my poor boy. But it's no good. You'll waste your strength uselessly. It may sound harsh, but my advice to you is: Cut your losses. Time's merciful. You'll forget."

"Forget Tuppence? Never!"

Mr. Carter shook his head.

"So you think now. Well, it won't bear thinking of—that brave little girl! I'm sorry about the whole business—confoundedly sorry."

Tommy came to himself with a start.

"I'm taking up your time, sir," he said with an effort. "There's no need for you to blame yourself. I dare say we were a couple of young fools to take on such a job. You warned us alright. But I wish to God *I*'d been the one to get it in the neck. Good-bye, sir."

Back at the Ritz, Tommy packed up his few belongings mechanically, his thoughts far away. He was still bewildered by the introduction of tragedy into his cheerful commonplace existence. What fun they had had together, he and Tuppence! And now—oh, he couldn't believe it—it couldn't be true! *Tuppence—dead!* Little Tuppence, brimming over with life! It was a dream, a horrible dream. Nothing more.

They brought him a note, a few kind words of sympathy from Peel Edgerton, who had read the news in the paper. (There had been a large headline: EX-V.A.D. FEARED DROWNED.) The letter ended with the offer of a post on a ranch in the Argentine, where Sir James had considerable interests.

"Kind old beggar," muttered Tommy, as he flung it aside.

The door opened, and Julius burst in with his usual violence. He held an open newspaper in his hand.

"Say, what's all this? They seem to have got some fool idea about Tuppence."

"It's true," said Tommy quietly.

"You mean they've done her in?"

Tommy nodded.

"I suppose when they got the treaty she—wasn't any good to them any longer, and they were afraid to let her go."

"Well, I'm darned!" said Julius. "Little Tuppence. She sure was the pluckiest little girl——"

But suddenly something seemed to crack in Tommy's brain. He rose to his feet.

"Oh, get out! You don't really care, damn you! You asked her to marry you in your rotten cold-blooded way, but I *loved* her. I'd have given the soul out of my body to save her from harm. I'd have stood by without a word and let her marry you, because you could have given her the sort of time she ought to have had, and I was only a poor devil without a penny to bless himself with. But it wouldn't have been because I didn't care!"

"See here," began Julius temperately.

"Oh, go to the devil! I can't stand your coming here and talking about 'little Tuppence.' Go and look after your cousin. Tuppence is my girl! I've always loved her, from the time we played together as kids. We grew up and it was just the same. I shall never forget when I was in hospital, and she came in in that ridiculous cap and apron! It was like a miracle to see the girl I loved turn up in a nurse's kit——"

But Julius interrupted him.

"A nurse's kit! Gee whiz! I must be going to Colney Hatch! I could swear I've seen Jane in a nurse's cap too. And that's plumb impossible! No, by gum, I've got it! It was her I saw talking to Whittington at that nursing home in Bournemouth. She wasn't a patient there! She was a nurse!"

"I dare say," said Tommy angrily, "she's probably been in with them from the start. I shouldn't wonder if she stole those papers from Danvers to begin with."

"I'm darned if she did!" shouted Julius. "She's my cousin, and as patriotic a girl as ever stepped."

"I don't care a damn what she is, but get out of here!" retorted Tommy also at the top of his voice.

The young men were on the point of coming to blows. But suddenly, with an almost magical abruptness, Julius's anger abated.

"Alright, son," he said quietly, "I'm going. I don't blame you any for what you've been saying. It's mighty lucky you did say it. I've been the most almighty blithering darned idiot that it's possible to imagine. Calm down"—Tommy had made an impatient gesture—"I'm going right away now—going to the London and North Western Railway depot, if you want to know."

"I don't care a damn where you're going," growled Tommy.

As the door closed behind Julius, he returned to his suitcase.

"That's the lot," he murmured, and rang the bell.

"Take my luggage down."

"Yes, sir. Going away, sir?"

"I'm going to the devil," said Tommy, regardless of the menial's feelings.

That functionary, however, merely replied respectfully:

"Yes, sir. Shall I call a taxi?"

Tommy nodded.

Where was he was going? He hadn't the faintest idea. Beyond a fixed determination to get even with Mr. Brown he had no plans. He re-read Sir James's letter, and shook his head. Tuppence must be avenged. Still, it was kind of the old fellow.

"Better answer it, I suppose." He went across to the writing-table. With the usual perversity of bedroom stationery, there were innumerable envelopes and no paper. He rang. No one came. Tommy fumed at the delay. Then he remembered that there was a good supply in Julius's sitting-room. The American had announced his immediate departure, there would be no fear of running up against him. Besides, he wouldn't mind if he did. He was beginning to be rather ashamed of the things he had said. Old Julius had taken them jolly well. He'd apologize if he found him there.

But the room was deserted. Tommy walked across to the writing-table, and opened the middle drawer. A photograph, carelessly thrust in face upward, caught his eye. For a moment he stood rooted to the ground. Then he took it out, shut the drawer, walked slowly over to an armchair, and sat down still staring at the photograph in his hand.

What on earth was a photograph of the French girl Annette doing in Julius Hersheimmer's writing table?

22
In Downing Street

THE PRIME MINISTER tapped the desk in front of him with nervous fingers. His face was worn and harassed. He took up his conversation with Mr. Carter at the point it had broken off.

"I don't understand," he said. "Do you really mean that things are not so desperate after all?"

"So this lad seems to think."

"Let's have a look at his letter again."

Mr. Carter handed it over. It was written in a sprawling boyish hand.

"DEAR MR. CARTER,

"Something's turned up that has given me a jar. Of course I may be simply making an awful ass of myself, but I don't think so. If my conclusions are right, that girl at Manchester was just a plant. The whole thing was prearranged, sham packet and all, with the object of making us think the game was up—therefore I fancy that we must have been pretty hot on the scent.

"I think I know who the real Jane Finn is, and I've even got an idea where the papers are. The last's only a guess, of course, but I've a sort of feeling it'll turn out right. Anyhow, I enclose it in a sealed envelope for what it's worth. I'm going to ask you not to open it until the very last moment, midnight on the 28th, in fact. You'll understand why in a minute. You see, I've figured it out that those things of Tuppence's are a plant too, and she's no more drowned than I am. The way I reason is this: as a last chance they'll let Jane Finn escape in the hope that she's been shamming this memory stunt, and that once she thinks she's free she'll go right away to the cache. Of course it's an awful risk for them to take, because she knows all about them—but they're pretty desperate to get hold of that treaty. *But if they know that the papers have been recovered by us*, neither of those two girls' lives will be worth an hour's purchase. I must try and get hold of Tuppence before Jane escapes.

"I want a repeat of that telegram that was sent to Tuppence at the Ritz. Sir James Peel Edgerton said you would be able to manage that for me. He's frightfully clever.

"One last thing—please have that house in Soho watched day and night.

"Yours, etc.,
"THOMAS BERESFORD."

The Prime Minister looked up.

"The enclosure?"

Mr. Carter smiled dryly.

"In the vaults of the Bank. I am taking no chances."

"You don't think—" the Prime Minister hesitated a minute—"that it would be better to open it now? Surely we ought to secure the document, that is, provided the young man's guess turns out to be correct, at once. We can keep the fact of having done so quite secret."

"Can we? I'm not so sure. There are spies all round us. Once it's known I wouldn't give that"—he snapped his fingers—"for the life of those two girls. No, the boy trusted me, and I shan't let him down."

"Well, well, we must leave it at that, then. What's he like, this lad?"

"Outwardly, he's an ordinary clean-limbed, rather block-headed young Englishman. Slow in his mental processes. On the other hand, it's quite impossible to lead him astray through his imagination. He hasn't got any—so he's difficult to deceive. He worries things out slowly, and once he's got hold of anything he doesn't let go. The little lady's quite different. More intuition and less common sense. They make a pretty pair working together. Pace and stamina."

"He seems confident," mused the Prime Minister.

"Yes, and that's what gives me hope. He's the kind of diffident youth who would have to be *very* sure before he ventured an opinion at all."

A half smile came to the other's lips.

"And it is this—boy who will defeat the master criminal of our time?"

"This—boy, as you say! But I sometimes fancy I see a shadow behind."

"You mean?"

"Peel Edgerton."

"Peel Edgerton?" said the Prime Minister in astonishment.

"Yes. I see his hand in *this*." He struck the open letter. "He's there—working in the dark, silently, unobtrusively. I've always felt that if anyone was to run Mr. Brown to earth, Peel Edgerton would be the man. I tell you he's on the case now, but doesn't want it known. By the way, I got rather an odd request from him the other day."

"Yes?"

"He sent me a cutting from some American paper. It referred to a man's body found near the docks in New York about three week's ago. He asked me to collect any information on the subject I could."

"Well?"

Carter shrugged his shoulders.

"I couldn't get much. Young fellow about thirty-five—poorly dressed—face very badly disfigured. He was never identified."

"And you fancy that the two matters are connected in some way?"

"Somehow I do. I may be wrong, of course."

There was a pause, then Mr. Carter continued:

"I asked him to come round here. Not that we'll get anything out of him he doesn't want to tell. His legal instincts are too strong. But there's no doubt he can throw light on one or two obscure points in young Beresford's letter. Ah, here he is!"

The two men rose to greet the newcomer. A half whimsical thought flashed across the Premier's mind. "My successor, perhaps!"

"We've had a letter from young Beresford," said Mr. Carter, coming to the point at once. "You've seen him, I suppose?"

"You suppose wrong," said the lawyer.

"Oh!" Mr. Carter was a little nonplussed.

Sir James smiled, and stroked his chin.

"He rang me up," he volunteered.

"Would you have any objection to telling us exactly what passed between you?"

"Not at all. He thanked me for a certain letter which I had written to him—as a matter of fact, I had offered him a job. Then he reminded me of something I had said to him at Manchester respecting that bogus telegram which lured Miss Cowley away. I asked him if anything untoward had occurred. He said it had—that in a drawer in Mr. Hersheimmer's room he had discovered a photograph." The lawyer paused, then continued: "I asked him if the photograph bore the name and address of a Californian photographer. He replied: 'You're on to it, sir. It had.' Then he went on to tell me something I *didn't* know. The original of that photograph was the French girl, Annette, who saved his life."

"What?"

"Exactly. I asked the young man with some curiosity what he had done with the photograph. He replied that he had put it back where he found it." The lawyer paused again. "That was good, you know—distinctly good. He can use his brains, that young fellow. I congratulated him. The discovery was a providential one. Of course, from the moment that the girl in Manchester was proved to be a plant everything was altered. Young Beresford saw that for himself without my having to tell it him. But he felt he couldn't trust his judgment on the subject of Miss Cowley. Did I think she was alive? I told him, duly weighing the evidence, that there was a very decided chance in favor of it. That brought us back to the telegram."

"Yes?"

"I advised him to apply to you for a copy of the original wire. It had occurred to me as probable that, after Miss Cowley flung it on the floor, certain words might have been erased and altered with the express intention of setting searchers on a false trail."

Carter nodded. He took a sheet from his pocket, and read aloud:

> "Come at once, Astley Priors, Gatehouse, Kent. Great developments—TOMMY."

"Very simple," said Sir James, "and very ingenious. Just a few words to alter, and the thing was done. And the one important clue they overlooked."

"What was that?"

"The page boy's statement that Miss Cowley drove to Charing Cross. They were so sure of themselves that they took it for granted he had made a mistake."

"Then young Beresford is now?"

"At Gatehouse, Kent, unless I am much mistaken."

Mr. Carter looked at him curiously.

"I rather wonder you're not there too, Peel Edgerton?"

"Ah, I'm busy on a case."

"I thought you were on your holiday?"

"Oh, I've not been briefed. Perhaps it would be more correct to say I'm preparing a case. Any more facts about that American chap for me?"

"I'm afraid not. Is it important to find out who he was?"

"Oh, I know who he was," said Sir James easily. "I can't prove it yet—but I know."

The other two asked no questions. They had an instinct that it would be mere waste of breath.

"But what I don't understand," said the Prime Minister suddenly, "is how that photograph came to be in Mr. Hersheimmer's drawer?"

"Perhaps it never left it," suggested the lawyer gently.

"But the bogus inspector? Inspector Brown?"

"Ah!" said Sir James thoughtfully. He rose to his feet. "I mustn't keep you. Go on with the affairs of the nation. I must get back to—my case."

Two days later Julius Hersheimmer returned from Manchester. A note from Tommy lay on his table:

"DEAR HERSHEIMMER,

"Sorry I lost my temper. In case I don't see you again, goodbye. I've been offered a job in the Argentine, and might as well take it.

"Yours,

"TOMMY BERESFORD."

A peculiar smile lingered for a moment on Julius's face. He threw the letter into the wastepaper basket.

"The darned fool!" he murmured.

23

A Race Against Time

AFTER RINGING UP Sir James, Tommy's next procedure was to make a call at South Audley Mansions. He found Albert discharging his professional duties, and introduced himself without more ado as a friend of Tuppence's. Albert unbent immediately.

"Things has been very quiet here lately," he said wistfully. "Hope the young lady's keeping well, sir?"

"That's just the point, Albert. She's disappeared."

"You don't mean as the crooks have got her?"

"They have."

"In the Underworld?"

"No, dash it all, in this world!"

"It's a h'expression, sir," explained Albert. "At the pictures the crooks always have a restoorant in the Underworld. But do you think as they've done her in, sir?"

"I hope not. By the way, have you by any chance an aunt, a cousin, a grandmother, or any other suitable female relation who might be represented as being likely to kick the bucket?"

A delighted grin spread slowly over Albert's countenance.

"I'm on, sir. My poor aunt what lives in the country has been mortal bad for a long time, and she's asking for me with her dying breath."

Tommy nodded approval.

"Can you report this in the proper quarter and meet me at Charing Cross in an hour's time?"

"I'll be there, sir. You can count on me."

As Tommy had judged, the faithful Albert proved an invaluable ally. The two took up their quarters at the inn in Gatehouse. To Albert fell the task of collecting information. There was no difficulty about it.

Astley Priors was the property of a Dr. Adams. The doctor no longer practiced, had retired, the landlord believed, but he took a few private patients—here the good fellow tapped his forehead knowingly—"balmy ones! You understand!" The doctor was a popular figure in the village, subscribed freely to all the local sports—"a very pleasant, affable gentleman." Been there long? Oh, a matter of ten years or so—might be longer. Scientific gentleman, he was. Professors and people often came down from town to see him. Anyway, it was a gay house, always visitors.

In the face of all this volubility, Tommy felt doubts. Was it possible that this genial, well-known figure could be in reality a dangerous criminal? His life seemed so open and above-board. No hint of sinister doings. Suppose it was all a gigantic mistake? Tommy felt a cold chill at the thought.

Then he remembered the private patients—"balmy ones." He inquired carefully if there was a young lady amongst them, describing Tuppence. But nothing much seemed to be known about the patients—they were seldom seen outside the grounds. A guarded description of Annette also failed to provoke recognition.

Astley Priors was a pleasant red-brick edifice, surrounded by well-wooded grounds which effectually shielded the house from observation from the road.

On the first evening Tommy, accompanied by Albert, explored the grounds. Owing to Albert's insistence they dragged themselves along painfully on their stomachs, thereby producing a great deal more noise than if they had stood upright. In any case, these precautions were totally unnecessary. The grounds, like those of any other private house after nightfall, seemed untenanted. Tommy had imagined a possible fierce watchdog. Albert's fancy ran to a puma, or a tame cobra. But they reached a shrubbery near the house quite unmolested.

The blinds of the dining-room window were up. There was a large company assembled round the table. The port was passing from hand to hand. It seemed a normal, pleasant company. Through the open window scraps of conversation floated out disjointedly on the night air. It was a heated discussion on country cricket!

Again Tommy felt that cold chill of uncertainty. It seemed impossible to believe that these people were other than they seemed. Had he been fooled once more? The fair-bearded, spectacled gentleman who sat at the head of the table looked singularly honest and normal.

Tommy slept badly that night. The following morning the indefatigable Albert, having cemented an alliance with the greengrocer's boy, took the latter's place and ingratiated himself with the cook at Malthouse. He returned with the information that she was undoubtedly "one of the crooks," but Tommy mistrusted the vividness of his imagination. Questioned, he could adduce nothing in support of his statement except his own opinion that she wasn't the usual kind. You could see that at a glance.

The substitution being repeated (much to the pecuniary advantage of the real greengrocer's boy) on the following day, Albert brought back the first piece of hopeful news. There *was* a French young lady staying in the house. Tommy put his doubts aside. Here was confirmation of his theory. But time pressed. Today was the 27th. The 29th was the much-talked-of "Labour Day," about which all sorts of rumors were running riot. Newspapers were getting agitated. Sensational hints of a Labour *coup d' état* were freely reported. The Government said nothing. It knew and was prepared. There were rumors of dissension among the Labour leaders. They were not of one mind. The more far-seeing among them realized that what they proposed might well be a death-blow to the England that at heart they loved. They shrank from the starvation and misery a general strike would entail, and were willing to meet the Government halfway. But behind them were subtle, insistent forces at work, urging the memories of old wrongs, deprecating the weakness of half-and-half measures, fomenting misunderstandings.

Tommy felt that, thanks to Mr. Carter, he understood the position fairly accurately. With the fatal document in the hands of Mr. Brown, public opinion would swing to the side of the Labor extremists and revolutionists. Failing that, the battle was an even chance. The Government with a loyal army and police force behind them might win—but at a cost of great suffering. But Tommy nourished another and a preposterous dream. With Mr. Brown unmasked and captured he believed, rightly or wrongly, that the whole organization would crumble ignominiously and instantaneously. The strange permeating influence of the unseen chief held it together. Without him, Tommy believed an instant panic would set in; and, the honest men left to themselves, an eleventh-hour reconciliation would be possible.

"This is a one-man show," said Tommy to himself. "The thing to do is to get hold of the man."

It was partly in furtherance of this ambitious design that he had requested Mr. Carter not to open the sealed envelope. The draft treaty was Tommy's bait. Every now and then he was aghast at his own presumption. How dared he think that he had discovered what so many wiser and cleverer men had overlooked? Nevertheless he stuck tenaciously to his idea.

That evening he and Albert once more penetrated the grounds of Astley Priors. Tommy's ambition was somehow or other to gain admission to the house itself. As they approached cautiously, Tommy gave a sudden gasp.

On the second floor window someone standing between the window and the light in the room threw a silhouette on the blind. It was one Tommy would have recognized anywhere! Tuppence was in that house!

He clutched Albert by the shoulder.

"Stay here! When I begin to sing, watch that window."

He retreated hastily to a position on the main drive, and began in a deep roar, coupled with an unsteady gait, the following ditty:

I am a Soldier
A jolly British Soldier;
You can see that I'm a Soldier by my feet . . .

It had been a favorite on the gramophone in Tuppence's hospital days. He did not doubt but that she would recognize it and draw her own conclusions. Tommy had not a note of music in his voice, but his lungs were excellent. The noise he produced was terrific.

Presently an unimpeachable butler, accompanied by an equally unimpeachable footman, issued from the front door. The butler remonstrated with him. Tommy continued to sing, addressing the butler affectionately as "dear old whiskers." The footman took him by one arm, the butler by the other. They ran him down the drive, and neatly out of the gate. The butler threatened him with the police if he intruded again. It was beautifully done—soberly and with perfect decorum. Anyone would have sworn that the butler was a real butler, the footman a real footman—only, as it happened, the butler was Whittington!

Tommy retired to the inn and waited for Albert's return. At last that worthy made his appearance.

"Well?" cried Tommy eagerly.

"It's alright. While they was a-running of you out the window opened, and something was chucked out." He handed a scrap of paper to Tommy. "It was wrapped round a letter-weight."

On the paper were scrawled three words: "Tomorrow—same time."

"Good egg!" cried Tommy. "We're getting going."

"I wrote a message on a piece of paper, wrapped it round a stone, and chucked it through the window," continued Albert breathlessly.

Tommy groaned.

"Your zeal will be the undoing of us, Albert. What did you say?"

"Said we was a-staying at the inn. If she could get away, to come there and croak like a frog."

"She'll know that's you," said Tommy with a sigh of relief. "Your imagination runs away with you, you know, Albert. Why, you wouldn't recognize a frog croaking if you heard it."

Albert looked rather crestfallen.

"Cheer up," said Tommy. "No harm done. That butler's an old friend of mine—I bet he knew who I was, though he didn't let on. It's not their game to show suspicion. That's why we found it fairly plain sailing. They don't want to discourage me altogether. On the other hand, they don't want to make it too easy. I'm a pawn in their game, Albert, that's what I am. You see, if the spider lets the fly walk out too easily, the fly might suspect it was a put-up job. Hence the usefulness of that promising youth, Mr. T. Beresford, who's blundered in just at the right moment for them. But later, Mr. T. Beresford had better look out!"

Tommy retired for the night in a state of some elation. He had elaborated a careful plan for the following evening. He felt sure that the inhabitants of Astley Priors would not interfere with him up to a certain point. It was after that that Tommy proposed to give them a surprise.

About twelve o'clock, however, his calm was rudely shaken. He was told that someone was demanding him in the bar. The applicant proved to be a rude-looking carter well coated with mud.

"Well, my good fellow, what is it?" asked Tommy.

"Might this be for you, sir?" The carter held out a very dirty folded note, on the outside of which was written: "Take this to the gentleman at the inn near Astley Priors. He will give you ten shillings."

The handwriting was Tuppence's. Tommy appreciated her quick-wittedness in realizing that he might be staying at the inn under an assumed name. He snatched at it.

"That's alright."

The man withheld it.

"What about my ten shillings?"

Tommy hastily produced a ten-shilling note, and the man relinquished his find. Tommy unfastened it.

"DEAR TOMMY,

"I knew it was you last night. Don't go this evening. They'll be lying in wait for you. They're taking us away this morning. I heard something about Wales—Holyhead, I think. I'll drop this on the road if I get a chance. Annette told me how you'd escaped. Buck up.

"Yours,

"TWOPENCE."

Tommy raised a shout for Albert before he had even finished perusing this characteristic epistle.

"Pack my bag! We're off!"

"Yes, sir." The boots of Albert could be heard racing upstairs.

Holyhead! Did that mean that, after all—— Tommy was puzzled. He read on slowly.

The boots of Albert continued to be active on the floor above.

Suddenly a second shout came from below.

"Albert! I'm a damned fool! Unpack that bag!"

"Yes, sir."

Tommy smoothed out the note thoughtfully.

"Yes, a damned fool," he said softly. "But so's someone else! And at last I know who it is!"

24
Julius Takes a Hand

IN HIS SUITE at Claridge's, Kramenin reclined on a couch and dictated to his secretary in sibilant Russian.

Presently the telephone at the secretary's elbow purred, and he took up the receiver, spoke for a minute or two, then turned to his employer.

"Someone below is asking for you."

"Who is it?"

"He gives the name of Mr. Julius P. Hersheimmer."

"Hersheimmer," repeated Kramenin thoughtfully. "I have heard that name before."

"His father was one of the steel kings of America," explained the secretary, whose business it was to know everything. "This young man must be a millionaire several times over."

The other's eyes narrowed appreciatively.

"You had better go down and see him, Ivan. Find out what he wants."

The secretary obeyed, closing the door noiselessly behind him. In a few minutes he returned.

"He declines to state his business—says it is entirely private and personal, and that he must see you."

"A millionaire several times over," murmured Kramenin. "Bring him up, my dear Ivan."

The secretary left the room once more, and returned escorting Julius.

"Monsieur Kramenin?" said the latter abruptly.

The Russian, studying him attentively with his pale venomous eyes, bowed.

"Pleased to meet you," said the American. "I've got some very important business I'd like to talk over with you, if I can see you alone." He looked pointedly at the other.

"My secretary, Monsieur Grieber, from whom I have no secrets."

"That may be so—but I have," said Julius dryly. "So I'd be obliged if you'd tell him to scoot."

"Ivan," said the Russian softly, "perhaps you would not mind retiring into the next room——"

"The next room won't do," interrupted Julius. "I know these ducal suites—and I want this one plumb empty except for you and me. Send him round to a store to buy a penn'orth of peanuts."

Though not particularly enjoying the American's free and easy manner of speech, Kramenin was devoured by curiosity. "Will your business take long to state?"

"Might be an all night job if you caught on."

"Very good, Ivan. I shall not require you again this evening. Go to the theater—take a night off."

"Thank you, your excellency."

The secretary bowed and departed.

Julius stood at the door watching his retreat. Finally, with a satisfied sigh, he closed it, and came back to his position in the center of the room.

"Now, Mr. Hersheimmer, perhaps you will be so kind as to come to the point?"

"I guess that won't take a minute," drawled Julius. Then, with an abrupt change of manner: "Hands up—or I shoot!"

For a moment Kramenin stared blindly into the big automatic, then, with almost comical haste, he flung up his hands above his head. In that instant Julius had taken his measure. The man he had to deal with was an abject physical coward—the rest would be easy.

"This is an outrage," cried the Russian in a high hysterical voice. "An outrage! Do you mean to kill me?"

"Not if you keep your voice down. Don't go edging sideways toward that bell. That's better."

"What do you want? Do nothing rashly. Remember my life is of the utmost value to my country. I may have been maligned——"

"I reckon," said Julius, "that the men who let daylight into you would be doing humanity a good turn. But you needn't worry any. I'm not proposing to kill you this trip—that is, if you're reasonable."

The Russian quailed before the stern menace in the other's eyes. He passed his tongue over his dry lips.

"What do you want? Money?"

"No. I want Jane Finn."

"Jane Finn? I—never heard of her!"

"You're a darned liar! You know perfectly who I mean."

"I tell you I've never heard of the girl."

"And I tell you," retorted Julius, "that Little Willie here is just hopping mad to go off!"

The Russian wilted visibly.

"You wouldn't dare——"

"Oh, yes, I would, son!"

Kramenin must have recognized something in the voice that carried conviction, for he said sullenly:

"Well? Granted I do know what you mean—what of it?"

"You will tell me now—right here—where she is to be found."

Kramenin shook his head.

"I daren't."

"Why not?"

"I daren't. You ask an impossibility."

"Afraid, eh? Of whom? Mr. Brown? Ah, that tickles you up! There is such a person, then? I doubted it. And the mere mention of him scares you stiff!"

"I have seen him," said the Russian slowly. "Spoken to him face to face. I did not know it until afterward. He was one of a crowd. I should not know him again. Who is he really? I do not know. But I know this—he is a man to fear."

"He'll never know," said Julius.

"He knows everything—and his vengeance is swift. Even I—Kramenin!—would not be exempt!"

"Then you won't do as I ask you?"

"You ask an impossibility."

"Sure that's a pity for you," said Julius cheerfully. "But the world in general will benefit." He raised the revolver.

"Stop," shrieked the Russian. "You cannot mean to shoot me?"

"Of course I do. I've always heard you Revolutionists held life cheap, but it seems there's a difference when it's your own life in question. I gave you just one chance of saving your dirty skin, and that you wouldn't take!"

"They would kill me!"

"Well," said Julius pleasantly, "it's up to you. But I'll just say this. Little Willie here is a dead cert, and if I was you I'd take a sporting chance with Mr. Brown!"

"You will hang if you shoot me," muttered the Russian resolutely.

"No, stranger, that's where you're wrong. You forget the dollars. A big crowd of solicitors will get busy, and they'll get some highbrow doctors on the job, and the end of it all will be that they'll say my brain was unhinged. I shall spend a few months in a quiet sanatorium, my mental health will improve, the doctors will declare me sane again, and all will end happily for little Julius. I guess I can bear a few months' retirement in order to rid the world of you, but don't you kid yourself I'll hang for it!"

The Russian believed him. Corrupt himself, he believed implicity in the power of money. He had read of American murder trials running much on the lines indicated by Julius. He had bought and sold justice himself. This virile young American, with the significant drawling voice, had the whip hand of him.

"I'm going to count five," continued Julius, "and I guess, if you let me get past four, you needn't worry any about Mr. Brown. Maybe he'll send some flowers to the funeral, but *you* won't smell them! Are you ready? I'll begin. One—two—three—four——"

The Russian interrupted with a shriek:

"Do not shoot. I will do you all you wish."

Julius lowered the revolver.

"I thought you'd hear sense. Where is the girl?"

"At Gatehouse, in Kent. Astley Priors, the place is called."

"Is she a prisoner there?"

"She's not allowed to leave the house—though it's safe enough really. The little fool has lost her memory, curse her!"

"That's been annoying for you and your friends, I reckon. What about the other girl, the one you decoyed away over a week ago?"

"She's there too," said the Russian sullenly.

"That's good," said Julius. "Isn't it all panning out beautifully? And a lovely night for the run!"

"What run?" demanded Kramenin, with a stare.

"Down to Gatehouse, sure. I hope you're fond of motoring?"

"What do you mean? I refuse to go."

"Now don't get mad. You must see I'm not such a kid as to leave you here. You'd ring up your friends on that telephone first thing! Ah!" He observed the fall on the other's face. "You see, you'd got it all fixed. No, sir, you're coming along with me. This your bedroom next door here? Walk right in. Little Willie and I will come behind. Put on a thick coat, that's right. Fur lined? And you a Socialist! Now we're ready. We walk downstairs and out through the hall to where my car's waiting. And don't you forget I've got you covered every inch of the way. I can shoot just as well through my coat pocket. One word, or a glance even, at one of those liveried menials, and there'll sure be a strange face in the Sulfur and Brimstone Works!"

Together they descended the stairs, and passed out to the waiting car. The Russian was shaking with rage. The hotel servants surrounded them. A cry hovered on his lips, but at the last minute his nerve failed him. The American was a man of his word.

When they reached the car, Julius breathed a sigh of relief. The danger zone was passed. Fear had successfully hypnotized the man by his side.

"Get in," he ordered. Then as he caught the other's sidelong glance, "No, the chauffeur won't help you any. Naval man. Was on a submarine in Russia when the Revolution broke out. A brother of his was murdered by your people. George!"

"Yes, sir?" The chauffeur turned his head.

"This gentleman is a Russian Bolshevik. We don't want to shoot him, but it may be necessary. You understand?"

"Perfectly, sir."

"I want to go to Gatehouse in Kent. Know the road at all?"

"Yes, sir, it will be about an hour and a half's run."

"Make it an hour. I'm in a hurry."

"I'll do my best, sir." The car shot forward through the traffic.

Julius ensconced himself comfortably by the side of his victim. He kept his hand in the pocket of his coat, but his manner was urbane to the last degree.

"There was a man I shot once in Arizona——" he began cheerfully.

At the end of the hour's run the unfortunate Kramenin was more dead than alive. In succession to the anecdote of the Arizonaman, there had been a tough from 'Frisco, and an episode in the Rockies. Julius's narrative style, if not strictly accurate, was picturesque!

Slowing down, the chauffeur called over his shoulder that they were just coming into Gatehouse. Julius bade the Russian direct them. His plan was to drive straight up to the house. There Kramenin was to ask for the two girls. Julius explained to him that Little Willie would not be tolerant of failure. Kramenin, by this time, was as putty in the other's hands. The terrific pace they had come had still further unmanned him. He had given himself up for dead at every corner.

The car swept up the drive, and stopped before the porch. The chauffeur looked round for orders.

"Turn the car first, George. Then ring the bell, and get back to your place.

Keep the engine going, and be ready to scoot like hell when I give the word."

"Very good, sir."

The front door was opened by the butler. Kramenin felt the muzzle of the revolver pressed against his ribs.

"Now," hissed Julius. "And be careful."

The Russian beckoned. His lips were white, and his voice was not very steady.

"It is I—Kramenin! Bring down the girl at once! There is no time to lose!"

Whittington had come down the steps. He uttered an exclamation of astonishment at seeing the other.

"You! What's up? Surely you know the plan——"

Kramenin interrupted him, using the words that have created many unnecessary panics.

"We have been betrayed! Plans must be abandoned. We must save our own skins. The girl! And at once! It's our only chance."

Whittington hesitated, but for hardly a moment.

"You have orders—from *him?*"

"Naturally! Should I be here otherwise? Hurry! There is no time to be lost. The other little fool had better come too."

Whittington turned and ran back into the house. The agonizing minutes went by. Then—two figures hastily huddled in cloaks appeared on the steps and were hustled into the car. The smaller of the two was inclined to resist and Whittington shoved her in unceremoniously. Julius leaned forward, and in doing so the light from the open door lit up his face. Another man on the steps behind Whittington gave a startled exclamation. Concealment was at an end.

"Get a move on, George," shouted Julius.

The chauffeur slipped in his clutch, and with a bound the car started.

The man on the steps uttered an oath. His hand went to his pocket. There was a flash and a report. The bullet just missed the taller girl by an inch.

"Get down, Jane," cried Julius. "Flat on the bottom of the car." He thrust her sharply forward, then standing up, he took careful aim and fired.

"Have you hit him?" cried Tuppence eagerly.

"Sure," replied Julius. "He isn't killed, though. Skunks like that take a lot of killing. Are you alright, Tuppence?"

"Of course I am. Where's Tommy? And who's this?" She indicated the shivering Kramenin.

"Tommy's making tracks for the Argentine. I guess he thought you'd turned up your toes. Steady through the gate, George! That's right. It'll take 'em at least five minutes to get busy after us. They'll use the telephone, I guess, so look out for snares ahead—and don't take the direct route. Who's this, did you say, Tuppence? Let me present Monsieur Kramenin. I persuaded him to come on the trip for his health."

The Russian remained mute, still livid with terror.

"But what made them let us go?" demanded Tuppence suspiciously.

"I reckon Monsieur Kramenin here asked them so prettily they just couldn't refuse!"

This was too much for the Russian. He burst out vehemently:

"Curse you—curse you! They know now that I betrayed them. My life won't be safe for an hour in this country."

"That's so," assented Julius. "I'd advise you to make tracks for Russia right away."

"Let me go, then," cried the other. "I have done what you asked. Why do you still keep me with you?"

"Not for the pleasure of your company. I guess you can get right off now if you want to. I thought you'd rather I tooled you back to London."

"You may never reach London," snarled the other. "Let me go here and now."

"Sure thing. Pull up, George. The gentleman's not making the return trip. If I ever come to Russia, Monsieur Kramenin, I shall expect a rousing welcome, and——"

But before Julius had finished his speech, and before the car had finally halted, the Russian has swung himself out and disappeared into the night.

"Just a mite impatient to leave us," commented Julius, as the car gathered way again. "And no idea of saying good-bye politely to the ladies. Say, Jane, you can get up on the seat now."

For the first time the girl spoke.

"How did you 'persuade' him?" she asked.

Julius tapped his revolver.

"Little Willie here takes the credit!"

"Splendid!" cried the girl. The color surged into her face, her eyes looked admiringly at Julius.

"Annette and I didn't know what was going to happen to us," said Tuppence. "Old Whittington hurried us off. *We* thought it was lambs to the slaughter."

"Annette," said Julius. "Is that what you call her?"

His mind seemed to be trying to adjust itself to a new idea.

"It's her name," said Tuppence, opening her eyes very wide.

"Shucks!" retorted Julius. "She may think it's her name, because her memory's gone, poor kid. But it's the one real and original Jane Finn we've got here."

"What——?" cried Tuppence.

But she was interrupted. With an angry spurt, a bullet embedded itself in the upholstery of the car just behind her head.

"Down with you," cried Julius. "It's an ambush. These guys have got busy pretty quickly. Push her a bit, George."

The car fairly leapt forward. Three more shots rang out, but went happily wide. Julius, upright, leant over the back of the car.

"Nothing to shoot at," he announced gloomily. "But I guess there'll be another little picnic soon. Ah!"

He raised his hand to his cheek.

"You are hurt?" said Annette quickly.

"Only a scratch."

The girl sprang to her feet.

"Let me out! Let me out, I say. Stop the car. It is me they're after. I'm the one they want. You shall not lose your lives because of me. Let me go." She was fumbling with the fastenings of the door.

Julius took her by both arms, and looked at her. She had spoken with no trace of foreign accent.

"Sit down, kid," he said gently. "I guess there's nothing wrong with your memory. Been fooling them all the time, eh?"

The girl looked at him, nodded, and then suddenly burst into tears. Julius patted her on the shoulder.

"There, there—just you sit tight. We're not going to let you quit."

Through her sobs the girl said indistinctly:

"You're from home. I can tell by your voice. It makes me homesick."

"Sure I'm from home. I'm your cousin—Julius Hersheimmer. I came over to Europe on purpose to find you—and a pretty dance you've led me."

The car slackened speed. George spoke over his shoulder:

"Crossroads here, sir. I'm not sure of the way."

The car slowed down till it hardly moved. As it did so, a figure climbed suddenly over the back, and plunged head first into the midst of them.

"Sorry," said Tommy, extricating himself.

A mass of confused exclamations greeted him. He replied to them severally:

"Was in the bushes by the drive. Hung on behind. Couldn't let you know before at the pace you were going. It was all I could do to hang on. Now then, you girls, get out!"

"Get out?"

"Yes. There's a station just up that road. Train due in three minutes. You'll catch it if you hurry."

"What the devil are you driving at?" demanded Julius. "Do you think you can fool them by leaving the car?"

"You and I aren't going to leave the car. Only the girls."

"You're crazed, Beresford. Stark staring mad! You can't let those girls go off alone. It'll be the end of it if you do."

Tommy turned to Tuppence.

"Get out at once, Tuppence. Take her with you, and do just as I say. No one will do you any harm. You're safe. Take the train to London. Go straight to Sir James Peel Edgerton. Mr. Carter lives out of town, but you'll be safe with him."

"Darn you!" cried Julius. "You're mad. Jane, you stay where you are."

With a sudden swift movement, Tommy snatched the revolver from Julius's hand, and leveled it at him.

"Now will you believe I'm in earnest? Get out, both of you, and do as I say—or I'll shoot!"

Tuppence sprang out, dragging the unwilling Jane after her.

"Come on, it's alright. If Tommy's sure—he's sure. Be quick. We'll miss the train."

They started running.

Julius's pent-up rage burst forth.

"What the hell——"

Tommy interrupted him.

"Dry up! I want a few words with you, Mr. Julius Hersheimmer."

25
Jane's Story

HER ARM THROUGH Jane's, dragging her along, Tuppence reached the station. Her quick ears caught the sound of the approaching train.

"Hurry up," she panted, "or we'll miss it."

They arrived on the platform just as the train came to a standstill. Tuppence opened the door of an empty first-class compartment, and the two girls sank down breathless on the padded seats.

A man looked in, then passed on to the next carriage. Jane started nervously. Her eyes dilated with terror. She looked questioningly at Tuppence.

"Is he one of them, do you think?" she breathed.

Tuppence shook her head.

"No, no. It's alright." She took Jane's hand in hers. "Tommy wouldn't have told us to do this unless he was sure we'd be alright."

"But he doesn't know them as I do!" The girl shivered. "You can't understand. Five years! Five long years! Sometimes I thought I should go mad."

"Never mind. It's all over."

"Is it?"

The train was moving now, speeding through the night at a gradually increasing rate. Suddenly Jane Finn started up.

"What was that? I thought I saw a face—looking in through the window."

"No, there's nothing. See." Tuppence went to the window, and lifting the strap let the pane down.

"You're sure?"

"Quite sure."

The other seemed to feel some excuse was necessary:

"I guess I'm acting like a frightened rabbit, but I can't help it. If they caught me now they'd——" Her eyes opened wide and staring.

"Don't!" implored Tuppence. "Lie back, and *don't think.* You can be quite sure that Tommy wouldn't have said it was safe if it wasn't."

"My cousin didn't think so. He didn't want us to do this."

"No," said Tuppence, rather embarrassed.

"What are you thinking of?" said Jane sharply.

"Why?"

"Your voice was so—queer!"

"I *was* thinking of something," confessed Tuppence. "But I don't want to tell you—not now. I may be wrong, but I don't think so. It's just an idea that came into my head a long time ago. Tommy's got it too—I'm almost sure he has. But don't *you* worry—there'll be time enough for that later. And it mayn't be so at all! Do what I tell you—lie back and don't think of anything."

"I'll try." The long lashes drooped over the hazel eyes.

Tuppence, for her part, sat bolt upright—much in the attitude of a watchful terrier on guard. In spite of herself she was nervous. Her eyes flashed continually from one window to the other. She noted the exact position of the communication cord. What it was that she feared, she would have been hard put to it to say. But in her own mind she was far from feeling the confidence displayed in her words. Not that she disbelieved in Tommy, but occasionally she was shaken with doubts as to whether anyone so simple and honest as he was could ever be a match for the fiendish subtlety of the arch-criminal.

If they once reached Sir James Peel Edgerton in safety, all would be well. But would they reach him? Would not the silent forces of Mr. Brown already be assembling against them. Even that last picture of Tommy, revolver in hand, failed to comfort her. By now he might be overpowered, borne down by sheer force of numbers. . . . Tuppence mapped out her plan of campaign.

As the train at length drew slowly into Charing Cross, Jane Finn sat up with a start.

"Have we arrived? I never thought we should!"

"Oh, I thought we'd get to London alright. If there's going to be any fun, now is when it will begin. Quick, get out. We'll nip into a taxi."

In another minute they were passing the barrier, had paid the necessary fares, and were stepping into a taxi.

"King's Cross," directed Tuppence. Then she gave a jump. A man looked in at the window, just as they started. She was almost certain it was the same man who had got into the carriage next to them. She had a horrible feeling of being slowly hemmed in on every side.

"You see," she explained to Jane, "if they think we're going to Sir James, this will put them off the scent. Now they'll imagine we're going to Mr. Carter. His country place is north of London somewhere."

Crossing Holborn there was a block, and the taxi was held up. This was what Tuppence had been waiting for.

"Quick," she whispered. "Open the right-hand door!"

The two girls stepped out into the traffic. Two minutes later they were seated in another taxi and were retracing their steps, this time direct to Carlton House Terrace.

"There," said Tuppence, with great satisfaction, "this ought to do them. I can't help thinking that I'm really rather clever. How that other taxi man will swear! But I took his number, and I'll send him a postal order tomorrow, so that he won't lose by it if he happens to be genuine. What's this thing swerving—— Oh!"

There was a grinding noise and a bump. Another taxi had collided with them.

In a flash Tuppence was out on the pavement. A policeman was approaching. Before he arrived Tuppence had handed the driver five shillings, and she and Jane had merged themselves in the crowd.

"It's only a step or two now," said Tuppence breathlessly. The accident had taken place in Trafalgar Square.

"Do you think the collision was an accident, or done deliberately?"

"I don't know. It might have been either."

Hand-in-hand, the two girls hurried along.

"It may be my fancy," said Tuppence suddenly, "but I feel as though there was someone behind us."

"Hurry!" murmured the other, "Oh, hurry!"

They were now at the corner of Carlton House Terrace, and their spirits lightened. Suddenly a large and apparently intoxicated man barred their way.

"Good evening, ladies," he hiccupped. "Whither away so fast?"

"Let us pass, please," said Tuppence imperiously.

"Just a word with your pretty friend here." He stretched out an unsteady hand, and clutched Jane by the shoulder. Tuppence heard other footsteps behind. She did not pause to ascertain whether they were friends or foes. Lowering her head, she repeated a maneuver of childish days, and butted their aggressor full in the capacious middle. The success of these unsportsmanlike tactics was immediate. The man sat down abruptly on the pavement. Tuppence and Jane took to their heels. The house they sought was some way down. Other footsteps echoed behind them. Their breath was coming in choking gasps as they reached Sir James's door. Tuppence seized the bell and Jane the knocker.

The man who had stopped them reached the foot of the steps. For a moment he hesitated, and as he did so the door opened. They fell into the hall together. Sir James came forward from the library door.

"Hullo! What's this?"

He stepped forward, and put his arm round Jane as she swayed uncertainly. He half carried her into the library, and laid her on the leather couch. From a tantalus on the table he poured out a few drops of brandy, and forced her to drink them. With a sigh she sat up, her eyes still wild and frightened.

"It's alright. Don't be afraid, my child. You're quite safe."

Her breath came more normally, and the color was returning to her cheeks. Sir James looked at Tuppence quizzically.

"So you're not dead, Miss Tuppence, any more than that Tommy boy of yours was!"

"The Young Adventurers take a lot of killing," boasted Tuppence.

"So it seems," said Sir James dryly. "Am I right in thinking that the joint venture has ended in success, and that this"—he turned to the girl on the couch—"is Miss Jane Finn?"

Jane sat up.

"Yes," she said quietly, "I am Jane Finn. I have a lot to tell you."

"When you are stronger——"

"No—now!" Her voice rose a little. "I shall feel safer when I have told everything."

"As you please," said the lawyer.

He sat down in one of the big armchairs facing the couch. In a low voice Jane began her story.

"I came over on the *Lusitania* to take up a post in Paris. I was fearfully keen about the war, and just dying to help somehow or other. I had been studying French, and my teacher said they were wanting help in a hospital in Paris, so I wrote and offered my services, and they were accepted. I hadn't got any folk of my own, so it made it easy to arrange things.

"When the *Lusitania* was torpedoed, a man came up to me. I'd noticed him more than once—and I'd figured it out in my own mind that he was afraid of somebody or something. He asked me if I was a patriotic American, and told me he was carrying papers which were just life or death to the Allies. He asked me to take charge of them. I was to watch for an advertisement in the *Times*. If it didn't appear, I was to take them to the American Ambassador.

"Most of what followed seems like a nightmare still. I see it in my dreams sometimes. . . . I'll hurry over that part. Mr. Danvers had told me to watch out. He might have been shadowed from New York, but he didn't think so. At first I had no suspicions, but on the boat to Holyhead I began to get uneasy. There was one woman who had been very keen to look after me, and chum up with me generally—a Mrs. Vandemeyer. At first I'd been only grateful to her for being so kind to me; but all the time I felt there was something about her I didn't like, and on the Irish boat I saw her talking to some queer-looking men, and from the way they looked I saw that they were talking about me. I remembered that she'd been quite near me on the *Lusitania* when Mr. Danvers gave me the packet, and before that she'd tried to talk to him once or twice. I began to get scared, but I didn't quite see what to do.

"I had a wild idea of stopping at Holyhead, and not going on to London that day, but I soon saw that that would be plumb foolishness. The only thing was to act as though I'd noticed nothing, and hope for the best. I couldn't see how they could get me if I was on my guard. One thing I'd done already as a precaution—ripped open the oilskin packet and substituted blank paper, and then sewn it up again. So, if anyone did manage to rob me of it, it wouldn't matter.

"What to do with the real thing worried me no end. Finally I opened it out flat—there were only two sheets—and laid it between two of the advertisement pages of a magazine. I stuck the two pages together round the edge with some gum off an envelope. I carried the magazine carelessly stuffed into the pocket of my ulster.

"At Holyhead I tried to get into a carriage with people that looked alright, but in a queer way there seemed always to be a crowd round me shoving and pushing me just the way I didn't want to go. There was something uncanny and frightening about it. In the end I found myself in a carriage with Mrs. Vandemeyer after all. I went out into the corridor, but all the other carriages were full, so I had to go back and sit down. I consoled myself with the thought that there were other people in the carriage—there was quite a nice-looking man and his wife sitting just opposite. So I felt almost happy about it until just outside London. I had leaned back and closed my eyes. I guess they thought I was asleep, but my eyes weren't quite shut, and suddenly I saw the nice-looking man get something out of his bag and hand it to Mrs. Vandemeyer, and as he did so he winked. . . .

"I can't tell you how that wink sort of froze me through and through. My only thought was to get out in the corridor as quick as ever I could. I got up, trying to look natural and easy. Perhaps they saw something—I don't know—but suddenly Mrs. Vandemeyer said 'Now,' and flung something over my nose and mouth as I tried to scream. At the same moment I felt a terrific blow on the back of my head. . . ."

She shuddered. Sir James murmured something sympathetically. In a minute she resumed:

"I don't know how long it was before I came back to consciousness. I felt very ill and sick. I was lying on a dirty bed. There was a screen round it, but I could hear two people talking in the room. Mrs. Vandemeyer was one of them. I tried to listen, but at first I couldn't take much in. When at last I did begin to grasp what was going on—I was just terrified! I wonder I didn't scream right out there and then.

"They hadn't found the papers. They'd got the oilskin packet with the blanks, and they were just mad! They didn't know whether *I'd* changed the papers, or whether Danvers had been carrying a dummy message, while the real one was sent another way. They spoke of"—she closed her eyes—"torturing me to find out!

"I'd never known what fear—real sickening fear—was before. Once they came to look at me. I shut my eyes and pretended to be still unconscious, but I was afraid they'd hear the beating of my heart. However, they went away again. I began thinking madly. What could I do? I knew I wouldn't be able to stand up against torture very long.

"Suddenly something put the thought of loss of memory into my head. The subject had always interested me, and I'd read an awful lot about it. I had the whole thing at my finger tips. If only I could succeed in carrying the bluff, it might save me. I said a prayer, and drew a long breath. Then I opened my eyes and started babbling in *French!*

"Mrs. Vandemeyer came round the screen at once. Her face was so wicked I nearly died, but I smiled up at her doubtfully, and asked her in French where I was.

"It puzzled her, I could see. She called the man she had been talking to. He stood by the screen with his face in shadow. He spoke to me in French. His voice was very ordinary and quiet, but somehow, I don't know why, he scared me worse than the woman. I felt he'd seen right through me, but I went on playing my part. I again asked where I was, and then went on that there was something I *must* remember—*must* remember—only for the moment it was all gone. I worked myself up to be more and more distressed. He asked me my name. I said I didn't know—that I couldn't remember anything at all.

"Suddenly he caught my wrist, and began twisting it. The pain was awful. I screamed. He went on. I screamed and screamed, but I managed to shriek out things in French. I don't know how long I could have gone on, but luckily I fainted. The last thing I heard was his voice saying: 'That's not bluff! Anyway, a kid of her age wouldn't know enough.' I guess he forgot American girls are older for their age than English ones, and take more interest in scientific subjects.

"When I came to, Mrs. Vandemeyer was sweet as honey to me. She'd had her orders, I guess. she spoke to me in French—told me I'd had a shock and been very ill. I should be better soon. I pretended to be rather dazed—murmured something about the 'doctor' having hurt my wrist. She looked relieved when I said that.

"By and by she went out of the room altogether. I was suspicious still, and lay quite quiet for some time. In the end, however, I got up and walked round the room, examining it. I thought that even if anyone *was* watching me from somewhere, it would seem natural enough under the circumstances. It was a squalid, dirty place. There were no windows, which seemed queer. I guessed the door would be locked, but I didn't try it. There were some battered old pictures on the walls, representing scenes from *Faust*."

Jane's two listeners gave a simultaneous "Ah!" The girl nodded.

"Yes—it was the place in Soho where Mr. Beresford was imprisoned. Of course, at the time I didn't even know if I was in London. One thing was worrying me dreadfully, but my heart gave a great throb of relief when I saw my ulster lying carelessly over the back of a chair. *And the magazine was still rolled up in the pocket!*

"If only I could be certain that I was not being overlooked! I looked carefully round the walls. There didn't seem to be a peephole of any kind—nevertheless I felt kind of sure there must be. All of a sudden I sat down on the edge of the table, and put my face in my hands, sobbing out a 'Mon Dieu! Mon Dieu!' I've got very sharp ears. I distinctly heard the rustle of a dress, and slight creak. That was enough for me. I was being watched!

"I lay down on the bed again, and by and by Mrs. Vandemeyer brought me some supper. She was still sweet as they make them. I guess she'd been told to win my confidence. Presently she produced the oilskin packet, and asked me if I recognized it, watching me like a lynx all the time.

"I took it and turned it over in a puzzled sort of way. Then I shook my head. I said that I felt I *ought* to remember something about it, that it was just as though it was all coming back, and then, before I could get hold of it, it went again. Then she told me that I was her niece, and that I was to call her 'Aunt Rita.' I did obediently, and she told me not to worry—my memory would soon come back.

"That was an awful night. I'd made my plan whilst I was waiting for her. The papers were safe so far, but I couldn't take the risk of leaving them there any longer. They might throw that magazine away any minute. I lay awake waiting until I judged it must be about two o'clock in the morning. Then I got up as softly as I could, and felt in the dark along the left-hand wall. Very gently, I unhooked one of the pictures from its nail—Marguerite with her casket of jewels. I crept over to my coat and took out the magazine, and an odd envelope or two that I had shoved in. Then I went to the wash-stand, and damped the brown paper at the back of the picture all round. Presently I was able to pull it away. I had already torn out the two stuck-together pages from the magazine, and now I slipped them with their precious enclosure between the picture and its brown paper backing. A little gum from the envelopes helped me to stick the latter up again. No one would dream the picture had ever been tampered with. I rehung it on the wall, put the magazine back in my coat pocket, and crept back to bed. I was pleased with my hiding place. They'd never think of pulling to pieces one of their own pictures. I hoped that they'd come to the conclusion that Danvers had been carrying a dummy all along, and that, in the end, they'd let me go.

"As a matter of fact, I guess that's what they did think at first and, in a way, it was dangerous for me. I learnt afterward that they nearly did away with me then and there—there was never much chance of their 'letting me go'—but the first man, who was the boss, preferred to keep me alive on the chance of my having hidden them, and being able to tell where if I recovered my memory.

They watched me constantly for weeks. Sometimes they'd ask me questions by the hour—I guess there was nothing they didn't know about the third degree!—but somehow I managed to hold my own. The strain of it was awful, though . . .

"They took me back to Ireland, and over every step of the journey again, in case I'd hidden it somewhere *en route*. Mrs. Vandemeyer and another woman never left me for a moment. They spoke of me as a young relative of Mrs. Vandemeyer's whose mind was affected by the shock of the *Lusitania*. There was no one I could appeal to for help without giving myself away to *them*, and if I risked it and failed—and Mrs. Vandemeyer looked so rich, and so beautifully dressed, that I felt convinced they'd take her word against mine, and think it was part of my mental trouble to think myself 'persecuted'—I felt that the horrors in store for me would be too awful once they knew I'd been only shamming."

Sir James nodded comprehendingly.

"Mrs. Vandemeyer was a woman of great personality. With that and her social position she would have had little difficulty in imposing her point of view in preference to yours. Your sensational accusations against her would not easily have found credence."

"That's what I thought. It ended in my being sent to a sanatorium at Bournemouth. I couldn't make up my mind at first whether it was a sham affair or genuine. A hospital nurse had charge of me. I was a special patient. She seemed so nice and normal that at last I determined to confide in her. A merciful providence just saved me in time from falling into the trap. My door happened to be ajar, and I heard her talking to someone in the passage. *She was one of them!* They still fancied it might be a bluff on my part, and she was put in charge of me to make sure! After that, my nerve went completely. I dared trust nobody.

"I think I almost hypnotized myself. After a while, I almost forgot that I was really Jane Finn. I was so bent on playing the part of Janet Vandemeyer that my nerves began to play me tricks. I became really ill—for months I sank into a sort of stupor. I felt sure I should die soon, and that nothing really mattered. A sane person shut up in a lunatic asylum often ends by becoming insane, they say. I guess I was like that. Playing my part had become second nature to me. I wasn't even unhappy in the end—just apathetic. Nothing seemed to matter. And the years went on.

"And then suddenly things seemed to change. Mrs. Vandemeyer came down from London. She and the doctor asked me some questions, experimented with various treatments. There was some talk of sending me to a specialist in Paris. In the end, they did not dare risk it. I overheard something that seemed to show that other people—friends—were looking for me. I learnt later that the nurse who had looked after me went to Paris, and consulted the specialist, representing herself to be me. He put her through some searching tests, and exposed her loss of memory to be fraudulent; but she had taken a note of his methods and reproduced them on me. I dare say I couldn't have deceived the specialist for a minute—a man who had made a lifelong study of a thing is unique—but I managed once again to hold my own with them. The fact that I'd not thought of myself as Jane Finn for so long made it easier.

"One night I was whisked off to London at a moment's notice. They took me back to the house in Soho. Once I got away from the sanatorium I felt different—as though something in me that had been buried for a long time was waking up again.

"They sent me in to wait on Mr. Beresford. (Of course I didn't know his name then.) I was suspicious—I thought it was another trap. But he looked so honest, I could hardly believe it. However, I was careful in all I said, for I knew we could be overheard. There's a small hole, high up in the wall.

"But on the Sunday afternoon a message was brought to the house. They were all very disturbed. Without their knowing, I listened. Word had come that he was to be killed. I needn't tell the next part, because you know it. I thought I'd have time to rush up and get the papers from their hiding place, but I was caught. So I screamed out that he was escaping, and I said I wanted to go back to Marguerite. I shouted the name three times very loud. I knew the others would think I meant Mrs. Vandemeyer, but I hoped it might make Mr. Beresford think of the picture. He'd unhooked one the first day—that's what made me hesitate to trust him."

She paused.

"Then the papers," said Sir James slowly, "are still at the back of the picture in that room."

"Yes." The girl had sunk back on the sofa exhausted with the strain of the long story.

Sir James rose to his feet. He looked at his watch.

"Come," he said, "we must go at once."

"Tonight?" queried Tuppence, surprised.

"Tomorrow may be too late," said Sir James gravely. "Besides, by going tonight we have the chance of capturing that great man and super-criminal—Mr. Brown!"

There was dead silence, and Sir James continued:

"You have been followed here—not a doubt of it. When we leave the house we shall be followed again, but not molested, *for it is Mr. Brown's plan that we are to lead him.* But the Soho house is under police supervision night and day. There are several men watching it. When we enter that house, Mr. Brown will not draw back—he will risk all, on the chance of obtaining the spark to fire his mine. And he fancies the risk not great—since he will enter in the guise of a friend!"

Tuppence flushed, then opened her mouth impulsively.

"But there's something you don't know—that we haven't told you." Her eyes dwelt on Jane in perplexity.

"What is that?" asked the other sharply. "No hesitations, Miss Tuppence. We need to be sure of our going."

But Tuppence, for once, seemed tongue-tied.

"It's so difficult—you see, if I'm wrong—oh, it would be dreadful." She made a grimace at the unconscious Jane. "Never forgive me," she observed cryptically.

"You want me to help you out, eh?"

"Yes, please. *You* know who Mr. Brown is, don't you?"

"Yes," said Sir James gravely. "At last I do."

"At last?" queried Tuppence doubtfully. "Oh, but I thought——?" She paused.

"You thought correctly, Miss Tuppence. I have been morally certain of his identity for some time—ever since the night of Mrs. Vandemeyer's mysterious death."

"Ah!" breathed Tuppence.

"For there we are up against the logic of facts. There are only two solutions. Either the chloral was administered by her own hand, which theory I reject utterly, or else——"

"Yes?"

"Or else it was administered in the brandy you gave her. Only three people touched that brandy—you, Miss Tuppence, I myself, and one other—Mr. Julius Hersheimmer!"

Jane Finn stirred and sat up, regarding the speaker with wide astonished eyes.

"At first, the thing seemed utterly impossible. Mr. Hersheimmer, as the son of a prominent millionaire, was a well-known figure in America. It seemed utterly impossible that he and Mr. Brown could be one and the same. But you cannot escape from the logic of facts. Since the thing was so—it must be accepted. Remember Mrs. Vandemeyer's sudden and inexplicable agitation. Another proof, if proof was needed.

"I took an early opportunity of giving you a hint. From some words of Mr. Hersheimmer's at Manchester, I gathered that you had understood and acted on that hint. Then I set to work to prove the impossible possible. Mr. Beresford rang me up and told me, what I had already suspected, that the photograph of Miss Jane Finn had never really been out of Mr. Hersheimmer's possession——"

But the girl interrupted. Springing to her feet, she cried out angrily:

"What do you mean? What are you trying to suggest? That Mr. Brown is *Julius?* Julius—my own cousin!"

"No, Miss Finn," said Sir James unexpectedly. "Not your cousin. The man who calls himself Julius Hersheimmer is no relation to you whatsoever."

26
Mr. Brown

SIR JAMES'S WORDS came like a bombshell. Both girls looked equally puzzled. The lawyer went across to his desk, and returned with a small newspaper cutting, which he handed to Jane. Tuppence read it over her shoulder. Mr. Carter would have recognized it. It referred to the mysterious man found dead in New York.

"As I was saying to Miss Tuppence," resumed the lawyer, "I set to work to prove the impossible possible. The great stumbling block was the undeniable fact that Julius Hersheimmer was not an assumed name. When I came across this paragraph my problem was solved. Julius Hersheimmer set out to discover what had become of his cousin. He went out West, where he obtained news of her and her photograph to aid him in his search. On the eve of his departure from New York he was set upon and murdered. His body was dressed in shabby clothes, and the face disfigured to prevent identification. Mr. Brown took his place. He sailed immediately for England. None of the real Hersheimmer's friends or intimates saw him before he sailed—though indeed it would hardly have mattered if they had, the impersonation was so perfect. Since then he had been hand and glove with those sworn to hunt him down. Every secret of theirs has been known to him. Only once did he come near disaster. Mrs. Vandemeyer knew his secret. It was no part of his plan that that huge bribe should ever be offered to her. But for Miss Tuppence's fortunate change of plan, she would have been far away from the flat when we arrived there. Exposure stared him in the face. He took a desperate step, trusting in his assumed character to avert suspicion. He nearly succeeded—but not quite."

"I can't believe it," murmured Jane. "He seemed so splendid."

"The real Julius Hersheimmer *was* a splendid fellow! And Mr. Brown is a consummate actor. But ask Miss Tuppence if she also has not had her suspicions."

Jane turned mutely to Tuppence. The latter nodded.

"I didn't want to say it, Jane—I knew it would hurt you. And, after all, I couldn't be sure. I still don't understand why, if he's Mr. Brown, he rescued us."

"Was it Julius Hersheimmer who helped you to escape?"

Tuppence recounted to Sir James the exciting events of the evening, ending up: "But I can't see *why*!"

"Can't you? I can. So can young Beresford, by his actions. As a last hope Jane Finn was to be allowed to escape—and the escape must be managed so that she harbors no suspicions of its being a put-up job. They're not averse to young Bereford's being in the neighborhood, and, if necessary, communicating with you. They'll take care to get him out of the way at the right minute. Then Julius Hersheimmer dashes up and rescues you in true melodramatic style. Bullets fly—but don't hit anybody. What would have happened next? You would have driven straight to the house in Soho and secured the documents which Miss Finn would probably have entrusted to her cousin's keeping. Or, if he conducted the search, he would have pretended to find the hiding place already rifled. He would have had a dozen ways of dealing with the situation, but the result would have been the same. And I rather fancy some accident would have happened to both of you. You see, you know rather an inconvenient amount. That's a rough outline. I admit I was caught napping; but somebody else wasn't."

"Tommy," said Tuppence softly.

"Yes. Evidently when the right moment came to get rid of him—he was too sharp for them. All the same, I'm not too easy in my mind about him."

"Why?"

"Because Julius Hersheimmer is Mr. Brown," said Sir James dryly. "And it takes more than one man and a revolver to hold up Mr. Brown. . . ."

Tuppence paled a little.

"What can we do?"

"Nothing until we've been to the house in Soho. If Beresford has still got the upper hand, there's nothing to fear. If otherwise, our enemy will come to find us, and he will not find us unprepared!" From a drawer in the desk, he took a service revolver, and placed it in his coat pocket.

"Now we're ready. I know better than even to suggest going without you, Miss Tuppence——"

"I should think so indeed!"

"But I do suggest that Miss Finn should remain here. She will be perfectly safe, and I am afraid she is absolutely worn out with all she has been through."

But to Tuppence's surprise Jane shook her head.

"No. I guess I'm going too. Those papers were my trust. I must go through with this business to the end. I'm heaps better now anyway."

Sir James's car was ordered round. During the short drive Tuppence's heart beat tumultuously. In spite of momentary qualms of uneasiness respecting Tommy, she could not but feel exultation. They were going to win!

The car drew up at the corner of the square and they got out. Sir James went up to a plainclothesman who was on duty with several others, and spoke to him. Then he rejoined the girls.

"No one has gone into the house so far. It is being watched at the back as well, so they are quite sure of that. Anyone who attempts to enter after we have done so will be arrested immediately. Shall we go in?"

A policeman produced a key. They all knew Sir James well. They had also had orders respecting Tuppence. Only the third member of the party was unknown to them. The three entered the house, pulling the door to behind them. Slowly they mounted the rickety stairs. At the top was the ragged curtain hiding the recess where Tommy had hidden that day. Tuppence had heard the story from Jane in her character of "Annette." She looked at the tattered velvet with interest. Even now she could almost swear it moved—as though *someone* was behind it. So strong was the illusion that she almost fancied she could make out the outline of a form. . . . Supposing Mr. Brown—Julius—was there waiting. . . .

Impossible of course! Yet she almost went back to put the curtain aside and make sure. . . .

Now they were entering the prison room. No place for anyone to hide here, thought Tuppence, with a sigh of relief, then chided herself indignantly. She must not give way to this foolish fancying—this curious insistent feeling that *Mr. Brown was in the house. . . . Hark! What was that? A stealthy footstep on the stairs? There was* someone in the house! Absurd! She was becoming hysterical.

Jane had gone straight to the picture of Marguerite. She unhooked it with a steady hand. The dust lay thick upon it, and festoons of cobwebs lay between it and the wall. Sir James handed her a pocketknife, and she ripped away the brown paper from the back. . . . The advertisement page of a magazine fell out. Jane picked it up. Holding apart the frayed inner edges she extracted two thin sheets covered with writing!

No dummy this time! The real thing!

"We've got it," said Tuppence. "At last. . . ."

The moment was almost breathless in its emotion. Forgotten the faint creakings, the imagined noises of a minute ago. None of them had eyes for anything but what Jane held in her hand.

Sir James took it, and scrutinized it attentively.

"Yes," he said quietly, "this is the ill-fated draft treaty!"

"We've succeeded," said Tuppence. There was awe and an almost wondering unbelief in her voice.

Sir James echoed her words as he folded the paper carefully and put it away in his pocketbook, then he looked curiously round the dingy room.

"It was here that our young friend was confined for so long, was it not?" he said. "A truly sinister room. You notice the absence of windows, and the thickness of the close-fitting door. Whatever took place here would never be heard by the outside world."

Tuppence shivered. His words awoke a vague alarm in her. What if there *was* someone concealed in the house? Someone who might bar that door on them, and leave them to die like rats in a trap! Then she realized the absurdity of her thought. The house was surrounded by police who, if they failed to reappear, would not hesitate to break in and make a thorough search. She smiled at her own foolishness—then looked up with a start to find Sir James watching her. He gave her an emphatic little nod.

"Quite right, Miss Tuppence. You scent danger. So do I. So does Miss Finn."

"Yes," admitted Jane. "It's absurd—but I can't help it."

Sir James nodded again.

"You feel—as we all feel—*the presence of Mr. Brown.* Yes"—as Tuppence made a movement—"not a doubt of it—*Mr. Brown is here. . . .*"

"In this house?"

"In this room. . . . You don't understand? *I am Mr. Brown. . . .*"

Stupefied, unbelieving, they stared at him. The very lines of his face had changed. It was a different man who stood before them. He smiled a slow cruel smile.

"Neither of you will leave this room alive! You said just now we had succeeded! *I* have succeeded! The draft treaty is mine." His smile grew wider as he looked at Tuppence. "Shall I tell you how it will be? Sooner or later the police will break in, and they will find three victims of Mr. Brown—three, not two, you understand, but fortunately the third will not be dead, only wounded, and will be able to describe the attack with a wealth of detail! The treaty? It is in the hands of Mr. Brown. So no one will think of searching the pockets of Sir James Peel Edgerton!"

He turned to Jane.

"You outwitted me. I make my acknowledgments. But you will not do it again."

There was a faint sound behind him, but, intoxicated with success, he did not turn his head.

He slipped his hand into his pocket.

"Checkmate to the Young Adventurers," he said, and slowly raised the big automatic.

But, even as he did so, he felt himself seized from behind in a grip of iron. The revolver was wrenched from his hand, and the voice of Julius Hersheimmer said drawlingly:

"I guess you're caught red-handed with the goods upon you."

The blood rushed to the K.C.'s face, but his self-control was marvelous, as he looked from one to the other of his two captors. He looked longest at Tommy.

"You," he said beneath his breath. *"You!* I might have known."

Seeing that he was disposed to offer no resistance, their grip slackened. Quick as a flash his left hand, the hand which bore the big signet ring, was raised to his lips. . . .

"'*Ave, Cæsar! Te morituri salutant,*'" he said, still looking at Tommy.

Then his face changed, and with a long convulsive shudder he fell forward in a crumpled heap, whilst an odor of bitter almonds filled the air.

27

A Supper Party at the "Savoy"

THE SUPPER PARTY given by Mr. Julius Hersheimmer to a few friends on the evening of the 30th will long be remembered in catering circles. It took place in a private room, and Mr. Hersheimmer's orders were brief and forcible. He gave carte blanche—and when a millionaire gives carte blanche he usually gets it!

Every delicacy out of season was duly provided. Waiters carried bottles of ancient and royal vintage with loving care. The floral decorations defied the seasons, and fruits of the earth as far apart as May and November found themselves miraculously side by side. The list of guests was small and select. The American Ambassador, Mr. Carter, who had taken the liberty, he said, of bringing an old friend, Sir William Beresford, with him, Archdeacon Cowley, Dr. Hall, those two youthful adventurers, Miss Prudence Cowley and Mr. Thomas Beresford, and last, but not least, as guest of honor, Miss Jane Finn.

Julius had spared no pains to make Jane's appearance a success. A mysterious knock had brought Tuppence to the door of the apartment she was sharing with the American girl. It was Julius. In his hand he held a check.

"Say, Tuppence," he began, "will you do me a good turn? Take this, and get Jane regularly togged up for this evening. You're all coming to supper with me at the *Savoy*. See? Spare no expense. You get me?"

"Sure thing," mimicked Tuppence. "We shall enjoy ourselves. It will be a pleasure dressing Jane. She's the loveliest thing I've ever seen."

"That's so," agreed Mr. Hersheimmer fervently.

His fervor brought a momentary twinkle to Tuppence's eye.

"By the way, Julius," she remarked demurely, "I—haven't given you my answer yet."

"Answer?" said Julius. His face paled.

"You know—when you asked me to—marry you," faltered Tuppence, her eyes downcast in the true manner of the early Victorian heroine, "and wouldn't take no for an answer. I've thought it well over——"

"Yes?" said Julius. The perspiration stood on his forehead.

Tuppence relented suddenly.

"You great idiot!" she said. "What on earth induced you to do it? I could see at the time you didn't care a twopenny dip for me!"

"Not at all. I had—and still have—the highest sentiments of esteem and respect—and admiration for you——"

"H'm!" said Tuppence. "Those are the kind of sentiments that very soon go to the wall when the other sentiment comes along! Don't they, old thing?"

"I don't know what you mean," said Julius stiffly, but a large and burning blush had overspread his countenance.

"Shucks!" retorted Tuppence. She laughed, and closed the door, reopening it to add with dignity: "Morally, I shall always consider I have been jilted!"

"What was it?" asked Jane as Tuppence rejoined her.

"Julius."

"What did he want?"

"Really, I think, he wanted to see you, but I wasn't going to let him. Not until tonight, when you're going to burst upon everyone like King Solomon in his glory! Come on! *We're going to shop!*"

To most people the 29th, the much-heralded "Labor Day," had passed much as any other day. Speeches were made in the Park and Trafalgar Square. Straggling processions, singing the "Red Flag," wandered through the streets in a more or less aimless manner. Newspapers which had hinted at a general strike, and the inauguration of a reign of terror, were forced to hide their diminished heads. The bolder and most astute among them sought to prove that peace had been effected by following their counsels. In the Sunday papers a brief notice of the sudden death of Sir James Peel Edgerton, the famous K.C., had appeared. Monday's paper dealt appreciatively with the dead man's career. The exact manner of his sudden death was never made public.

Tommy had been right in his forecast of the situation. It had been a one-man show. Deprived of their chief, the organization fell to pieces. Kramenin had made a precipitate return to Russia, leaving England early on Sunday morning. The gang had fled from Astley Priors in a panic, leaving behind, in their haste, various damaging documents which compromised them hopelessly. With these proofs of conspiracy in their hands, aided further by a small brown diary taken from the pocket of the dead man which had contained a full and damning résumé of the whole plot, the Government had called an eleventh-hour conference. The Labor leaders were forced to recognize that they had been used as a cat's paw. Certain concessions were made by the Government, and were eagerly accepted. It was to be Peace, not War!

But the Cabinet knew by how narrow a margin they had escaped utter disaster. And burnt in on Mr. Carter's brain was the strange scene which had taken place in the house in Soho the night before.

He had entered the squalid room to find that great man, the friend of a lifetime, dead—betrayed out of his own mouth. From the dead man's pocket-book he had retrieved the ill-omened draft treaty, and then and there, in the presence of the other three, it had been reduced to ashes. . . . England was saved!

And now, on the evening of the 30th, in a private room at the Savoy, Mr. Julius P. Hersheimmer was receiving his guests.

Mr. Carter was the first to arrive. With him was a choleric-looking old gentleman, at sight of whom Tommy flushed up to the roots of his hair. He came forward.

"Ha!" said the old gentleman, surveying him apoplectically. "So you're my nephew, are you? Not much to look at—but you've done good work, it seems. Your mother must have brought you up well after all. Shall we let bygones be bygones, eh? You're my heir, you know; and in future I propose to make you an allowance—and you can look upon Chalmers Park as your home."

"Thank you, sir, it's awfully decent of you."

"Where's this young lady I've been hearing such a lot about?"

Tommy introduced Tuppence.

"Ha!" said Sir William, eyeing her. "Girls aren't what they used to be in my young days."

"Yes, they are," said Tuppence. "Their clothes are different, perhaps, but they themselves are just the same."

"Well, perhaps you're right. Minxes then—minxes now!"

"That's it," said Tuppence. "I'm a frightful minx myself."

"I believe you," said the old gentleman, chuckling, and pinched her ear in high good humor. Most young women were terrified of the "old bear," as they termed him. Tuppence's pertness delighted the old misogynist.

Then came the timid archdeacon, a little bewildered by the company in which he found himself, glad that his daughter was considered to have distinguished herself, but unable to help glancing at her from time to time with nervous apprehension. But Tuppence behaved admirably. She forbore to cross her legs, set a guard upon her tongue, and steadfastly refused to smoke.

Dr. Hall came next, and he was followed by the American Ambassador.

"We might as well sit down," said Julius, when he had introduced all his guests to each other. "Tuppence, will you——"

He indicated the place of honor with a wave of his hand.

But Tuppence shook her head.

"No—that's Jane's place! When one thinks of how she's held out all these years, she ought to be made the queen of the feast tonight."

Julius flung her a grateful glance, and Jane came forward shyly to the allotted seat. Beautiful as she had seemed before, it was as nothing to the loveliness that now went fully adorned. Tuppence had performed her part faithfully. The model gown supplied by a famous dressmaker had been entitled "A tiger lily." It was all golds and reds and browns, and out of it rose the pure column of the girl's white throat, and the bronze masses of hair that crowned her lovely head. There was admiration in every eye, as she took her seat.

Soon the supper party was in full swing, and with one accord Tommy was called upon for a full and complete explanation.

"You've been too darned close about the whole business," Julius accused him. "You let on to me that you were off to the Argentine—though I guess you had your reasons for that. The idea of both you and Tuppence casting me for the part of Mr. Brown just tickles me to death!"

"The idea was not original to them," said Mr. Carter gravely. "It was suggested, and the poison very carefully instilled, by a past master in the art. The paragraph in the New York paper suggested the plan to him, and by means of it he wove a web that nearly enmeshed you fatally."

"I never liked him," said Julius. "I felt from the first that there was something wrong about him, and I always suspected that it was he who silenced Mrs. Vandemeyer so appositely. But it wasn't till I heard that the order for Tommy's execution came right on the heels of our interview with him that Sunday that I began to tumble to the fact that he was the big bug himself."

"I never suspected it at all," lamented Tuppence. "I've always thought I was so much cleverer than Tommy—but he's undoubtedly scored over me handsomely."

Julius agreed.

"Tommy's been the goods this trip! And, instead of sitting there as dumb as a fish, let him banish his blushes, and tell us all about it."

"Hear! Hear!"

"There's nothing to tell," said Tommy, acutely uncomfortable. "I was an awful mug—right up to the time I found that photograph of Annette, and realized that she was Jane Finn. Then I remembered how persistently she had shouted out that word 'Marguerite'—and I thought of the pictures, and—well, that's that. Then of course I went over the whole thing to see where I'd made an ass of myself."

"Go on," said Mr. Carter, as Tommy showed signs of taking refuge in silence once more.

"That business about Mrs. Vandemeyer had worried me when Julius told me about it. On the face of it, it seemed that he or Sir James must have done the trick. But I didn't know which. Finding that photograph in the drawer, after that story of how it had been got from him by Inspector Brown, made me suspect Julius. Then I remembered that it was Sir James who had discovered the false Jane Finn. In the end, I couldn't make up my mind—and just decided to take no chances either way. I left a note for Julius, in case he was Mr. Brown, saying I was off to the Argentine, and I dropped Sir James's letter with the offer of the job by the desk so that he would see it was a genuine stunt. Then I wrote my letter to Mr. Carter and rang up Sir James. Taking him into my confidence would be the best thing either way, so I told him everything except where I believed the papers to be hidden. The way he helped me to get on the track of Tuppence and Annette almost disarmed me, but not quite. I kept my mind open between the two of them. And then I got a bogus note from Tuppence—and I knew!"

"But how?"

Tommy took the note in question from his pocket and passed it round the table.

"It's her handwriting alright, but I knew it wasn't from her because of the signature. She'd never spell her name 'Twopence,' but anyone who'd never seen it written might quite easily do so. Julius *had* seen it—he showed me a note of hers to him once—but *Sir James hadn't!* After that everything was plain sailing. I sent off Albert posthaste to Mr. Carter. I pretended to go away, but doubled back again. When Julius came bursting up in his car, I felt it wasn't part of Mr. Brown's plan—and that there would probably be trouble. Unless Sir James was actually caught in the act, so to speak, I knew Mr. Carter would never believe it of him on my bare word——"

"I didn't," interposed Mr. Carter ruefully.

"That's why I sent the girls off to Sir James. I was sure they'd fetch up at the house in Soho sooner or later. I threatened Julius with the revolver, because I wanted Tuppence to repeat that to Sir James, so that he wouldn't worry about us. The moment the girls were out of sight I told Julius to drive like hell for London, and as we went along I told him the whole story. We got to the Soho house in plenty of time and met Mr. Carter outside. After arranging things with him we went in and hid behind the curtain in the recess. The policemen had orders to say, if they were asked, that no one had gone into the house. That's all."

And Tommy came to an abrupt halt.

There was silence for a moment.

"By the way," said Julius suddenly, "you're all wrong about that photograph of Jane. It *was* taken from me, but I found it again."

"Where?" cried Tuppence.

"In that little safe on the wall in Mrs. Vandemeyer's bedroom."

"I knew you found something," said Tuppence reproachfully. "To tell you the truth, that's what started me off suspecting you. Why didn't you say?"

"I guess I was a mite suspicious too. It had been got away from me once, and I determined I wouldn't let on I'd got it until a photographer had made a dozen copies of it!"

"We all kept back something or other," said Tuppence thoughtfully. "I suppose secret service work makes you like that!"

In the pause that ensued, Mr. Carter took from his pocket a small shabby brown book.

"Beresford has just said that I would not have believed Sir James Peel Edgerton to be guilty unless, so to speak, he was caught in the act. That is so. Indeed, not until I read the entries in this little book could I bring myself fully to credit the amazing truth. This book will pass into the possession of Scotland Yard, but it will never be publicly exhibited. Sir James's long association with the law would make it undesirable. But to you, who know the truth, I propose to read certain passages which will throw some light on the extraordinary mentality of this great man."

He opened the book, and turned the thin pages.

". . . It is madness to keep this book. I know that. It is documentary evidence against me. But I have never shrunk from taking risks. And I feel an urgent need for self-expression . . . The book will only be taken from my dead body. . . .

". . . From an early age I realized that I had exceptional abilities. Only a fool underestimates his capabilities. My brain power was greatly above the average. I know that I was born to succeed. My appearance was the only thing against me. I was quiet and insignificant—utterly nondescript. . . .

". . . When I was a boy I heard a famous murder trial. I was deeply impressed by the power and eloquence of the counsel for the defense. For the first time I entertained the idea of taking my talents to that particular market. . . . Then I studied the criminal in the dock. . . . The man was a fool—he had been incredibly, unbelievably stupid. Even the eloquence of his counsel was hardly likely to save him. I felt an immeasurable contempt for him. . . . Then it occurred to me that the criminal standard was a low one. It was the wastrels, the failures, the general riffraff of civilization who drifted into crime. . . . Strange that men of brains had never realized its extraordinary opportunities. . . . I played with the idea. . . . What a magnificent field—what unlimited possibilities! It made my brain reel. . . .

". . . I read standard works on crime and criminals. They all confirmed my opinion. Degeneracy, disease—never the deliberate embracing of a career by a far-seeing man. Then I considered. Supposing my utmost ambitions were realized—that I was called to the bar, and rose to the height of my profession? That I entered politics—say, even, that I became Prime Minister of England? What then? Was that power? Hampered at every turn by my colleagues, fettered by the democratic system of which I should be the mere figurehead! No—the power I dreamed of was absolute! An autocrat! A dictator! And such power could only be obtained by working outside the law. To play on the weaknesses of human nature, then on the weaknesses of nations—to get together and control a vast organization, and finally to overthrow the existing order, and rule! The thought intoxicated me. . . .

". . . I saw that I must lead two lives. A man like myself is bound to attract notice. I must have a successful career which would mask my true activities. . . . Also I must cultivate a personality. I modeled myself upon famous K.C.'s. I reproduced their mannerisms, their magnetism. If I had chosen to be an actor, I should have been the greatest actor living! No disguises—no grease paint—no false beards! Personality! I put it on like a glove! When I shed it, I was myself, quiet, unobtrusive, a man like every other man. I called myself Mr. Brown. There are hundreds of men called Brown—there are hundreds of men looking just like me. . . .

". . . I succeeded in my false career. I was bound to succeed. I shall succeed in the other. A man like me cannot fail. . . .

". . . I have been reading a life of Napoleon. He and I have much in common. . . .

". . . I should make a practice of defending criminals. A man should look after his own people. . . .

". . . Once or twice I have felt afraid. The first time was in Italy. There was a dinner given. Professor D——, the great alienist, was present. The talk fell on insanity. He said, 'A great many men are mad, and no one knows it. They do not know it themselves.' I do not understand why he looked at me when he said that. His glance was strange. . . . I did not like it. . . .

". . . The war has disturbed me. . . . I thought it would further my plans. The Germans are so efficient. Their spy system, too, was excellent. The streets are full of these boys in khaki. All empty-headed young fools. . . . Yet I do not know. . . . They won the war. . . . It disturbs me. . . .

". . . My plans are going well. . . . A girl butted in—I do not think she really knew anything. . . . But we must give up the Esthonia. . . . No risks now. . . .

". . . All goes well. The loss of memory is vexing. It cannot be a fake. No girl could deceive ME! . . .

". . . The 29th. . . . That is very soon. . . ." Mr. Carter paused.

"I will not read the details of the *coup* that was planned. But there are just two small entries that refer to the three of you. In the light of what happened they are interesting.

". . . By inducing the girl to come to me of her own accord, I have succeeded in disarming her. But she has intuitive flashes that might be dangerous. . . . She must be got out the way. . . . I can do nothing with the American. He suspects and dislikes me. But he cannot know. I fancy my armor is impregnable. . . . Sometimes I fear I have underestimated the other boy. He is not clever, but it is hard to blind his eyes to facts. . . ."

Mr. Carter shut the book.

"A great man," he said. "Genius, or insanity, who can say?"

There was silence.

Then Mr. Carter rose to his feet.

"I will give you a toast. The Joint Venture which has so amply justified itself by success!"

It was drunk with acclamation.

"There's something more we want to hear," continued Mr. Carter. He looked at the American Ambassador. "I speak for you also, I know. We'll ask Miss Jane Finn to tell us the story that only Miss Tuppence has heard so far—but before we do so we'll drink her health. The health of one of the bravest of America's daughters, to whom is due the thanks and gratitude of two great countries!"

28
And After

"THAT WAS A mighty good toast, Jane," said Mr. Hersheimmer, as he and his cousin were being driven back in the Rolls-Royce to the Ritz.

"The one to the joint venture?"

"No—the one to you. There isn't another girl in the world who could have carried it through as you did. You were just wonderful!"

Jane shook her head.

"I don't feel wonderful. At heart I'm just tired and lonesome—and longing for my own country."

"That brings me to something I wanted to say. I heard the Ambassador telling you his wife hoped you would come to them at the Embassy right away. That's good enough, but I've got another plan. Jane—I want you to marry me! Don't get scared and say no at once. You can't love me right away, of course, that's impossible. But I've loved you from the very moment I set eyes on your photo—and now I've seen you I'm simply crazy about you! If you'll only marry me, I won't worry you any—you shall take your own time. Maybe you'll never come to love me, and if that's the case, I'll manage to set you free. But I want the right to look after you, and take care of you."

"That's what I want," said the girl wistfully. "Someone who'll be good to me. Oh, you don't know how lonesome I feel!"

"Sure thing I do. Then I guess that's all fixed up, and I'll see the archbishop about a special license tomorrow morning."

"Oh, Julius!"

"Well, I don't want to hustle you any, Jane, but there's no sense in waiting about. Don't be scared—I shan't expect you to love me all at once."

But a small hand was slipped into his.

"I love you now, Julius," said Jane Finn. "I loved you that first moment in the car when the bullet grazed your cheek. . . ."

Five minutes later Jane murmured softly:

"I don't know London very well, Julius, but is it such a very long way from the Savoy to the Ritz?"

"It depends how you go," explained Julius unblushingly. "We're going by way of Regent's Park!"

"Oh, Julius—what will the chauffeur think?"

"At the wages I pay him, he knows better than to do any independent thinking. Why, Jane, the only reason I had the supper at the Savoy was so that I could drive you home. I didn't see how I was ever going to get hold of you alone. You and Tuppence have been sticking together like Siamese twins. I guess another day of it would have driven me and Beresford stark staring mad!"

"Oh. Is he——?"

"Of course he is. Head over ears."

"I thought so," said Jane thoughtfully.

"Why?"

"From all the things Tuppence didn't say!"

"There you have me beat," said Mr. Hersheimmer. But Jane only laughed.

In the meantime, the Young Adventurers were sitting bolt upright, very stiff and ill at ease, in a taxi which, with a singular lack of originality, was also returning to the Ritz via Regent's Park.

A terrible constraint seemed to have settled down between them. Without quite knowing what had happened, everything seemed changed. They were tongue-tied—paralyzed. All the old camaraderie was gone.

Tuppence could think of nothing to say.

Tommy was equally afflicted.

They sat very straight and forbore to look at each other.

At last Tuppence made a desperate effort.

"Rather fun, wasn't it?"

"Rather."

Another silence.

"I like Julius," essayed Tuppence again.

Tommy was suddenly galvanized into life.

"You're not going to marry him, do you hear?" he said dictatorially. "I forbid it."

"Oh!" said Tuppence meekly.

"Absolutely, you understand."

"He doesn't want to marry me—he really only asked me out of kindness."

"That's not very likely," scoffed Tommy.

"It's quite true. He's head over ears in love with Jane. I expect he's proposing to her now."

"She'll do for him very nicely," said Tommy condescendingly.

"Don't you think she's the most lovely creature you've ever seen?"

"Oh, I dare say."

"But I suppose you prefer sterling worth," said Tuppence demurely.

"I—oh, dash it all, Tuppence, you know!"

"I like your uncle, Tommy," said Tuppence, hastily creating a diversion. "By the way, what are you going to do, accept Mr. Carter's offer of a Government job, or accept Julius's invitation and take a richly remunerated post in America on his ranch?"

"I shall stick to the old ship, I think, though it's awfully good of Hersheimmer. But I feel you'd be more at home in London."

"I don't see where I come in."

"I do," said Tommy positively.

Tuppence stole a glance at him sideways.

"There's the money, too," she observed thoughtfully.

"What money?"

"We're going to get a check each. Mr. Carter told me so."

"Did you ask how much?" inquired Tommy sarcastically.

"Yes," said Tuppence triumphantly. "But I shan't tell you."

"Tuppence, you are the limit!"

"It has been fun, hasn't it? I do hope we shall have lots more adventures."

"You're insatiable, Tuppence. I've had quite enough adventures for the present."

"Well, shopping is almost as good," said Tuppence dreamily. "Think of buying old furniture, and bright carpets, and futurist silk curtains, and a polished dining table, and divan with lots of cushions——"

"Hold hard," said Tommy. "What's all this for?"

"Possibly a house—but I think a flat."

"Whose flat?"

"You think I mind saying it, but I don't in the least! *Ours*, so there!"

"You darling!" cried Tommy, his arms tightly round her. "I was determined to make you say it. I owe you something for the relentless way you squashed me whenever I've tried to be sentimental."

Tuppence raised her face to his. The taxi proceeded on its course round the north side of Regent's Park.

"You haven't really proposed now," pointed out Tuppence. "Not what our grandmothers would call a proposal. But after listening to a rotten one like Julius's, I'm inclined to let you off."

"You won't be able to get out of marrying me, so don't you think it."

"What fun it will be," responded Tuppence. "Marriage is called all sorts of things, a haven, and a refuge, and a crowning glory, and a state of bondage, and lots more. But do you know what I think it is?"

"What?"

"A sport!"

"And a damned good sport too," said Tommy.

THE END

The Murder of Roger Ackroyd

Can't get interested J.

Cast of Characters

CAROLINE SHEPPARD—A loving older sister with a ferretlike curiosity and the staying power of a bloodhound, she hated to lose at anything—even when the game was murder.

DR. JAMES SHEPPARD—A discreet country doctor with the reticence of a father confessor, he let Caroline have her way, but wasn't sure she'd like the answers.

RALPH PATON—A startlingly handsome devil-may-care rake, Roger Ackroyd's stepson was embarrassingly short of money and the only solution to his problem was a drastic one.

MISS RUSSELL—A handsome somewhat-dried-up housekeeper, she seemed the perfect matron in the Ackroyd household, but the doctor found her too inquisitive about the use of poisons.

MRS. CECIL ACKROYD—A penniless, pretentious widow, she accepted the charity of her brother-in-law unwillingly and vowed she'd do anything to be independent.

FLORA ACKROYD—A golden-haired, creamy-skinned English lass, she was engaged to Ralph and protected his reputation even when she learned about his other life.

HERCULE POIROT—A methodical, mustached little Belgian, the detective had faith in the "gray cells" that would, eventually, lead him to the killer.

PARKER—A humorless, nervous man, he lacked the icewater reactions of a typical butler and convinced Poirot that his interest in the murder was not merely a familial one.

GEOFFREY RAYMOND—A debonair, efficient secretary, he enjoyed his intimate connection with the Ackroyd household, and though he confessed to a weakness for the horses, he made up for his losses in other ways.

MAJOR BLUNT—A courageous, cool-headed big-game hunter, he felt ill at ease in a world that wouldn't let a man solve his problems with a gun.

URSULA BOURNE—A tall, ladylike parlormaid, she seemed too perfect for the role she tried to play and the references she gave were disturbingly silent about the past.

CHARLES KENT—A tall, thin, slightly seedy young man, this nighttime visitor to Fernly Park was a number-one suspect—for something.

1

Dr. Sheppard at the Breakfast Table

MRS. FERRARS DIED on the night of the 16th-17th September—a Thursday. I was sent for at eight o'clock on the morning of Friday the 17th. There was nothing to be done. She had been dead some hours.

It was just a few minutes after nine when I reached home once more. I opened the front door with my latchkey, and purposely delayed a few moments in the hall, hanging up my hat and light overcoat that I had deemed a wise precaution against the chill of an early autumn morning. To tell the truth, I was considerably upset and worried. I am not going to pretend that at that moment I foresaw the events of the next few weeks. I emphatically did not do so. But my instinct told me that there were stirring times ahead.

From the dining room on my left there came the rattle of teacups and the short, dry cough of my sister Caroline. "Is that you, James?" she called.

An unnecessary question, since who else could it be. To tell the truth, it was precisely my sister Caroline who was the cause of my few minutes' delay. The motto of the mongoose family, so Mr. Kipling tells us, is: "Go and find out." If Caroline ever adopts a crest, I should certainly suggest a mongoose rampant. One might omit the the first part of the motto. Caroline can do any amount of finding out by sitting placidly at home. I don't know how she manages it, but there it is. I suspect that the servants and the tradesmen constitute her Intelligence Corps. When she goes out, it is not to gather information, but to spread it. At that, too, she is amazingly expert.

It was really this last named trait of hers which was causing me these pangs of indecision. Whatever I told Caroline now concerning the demise of Mrs. Ferrars would be common knowledge all over the village within the space of an hour and a half. As a professional man, I naturally aim at discretion. Therefore I have got into the habit of continually withholding all information possible from my sister. She usually finds out just the same, but I have the moral satisfaction of knowing that I am in no way to blame.

Mrs. Ferrars' husband died just over a year ago, and Caroline has constantly asserted, without the least foundation for the assertion, that his wife poisoned him. She scorns my invariable rejoinder that Mr. Ferrars died of acute gastritis, helped on by habitual overindulgence in alcoholic beverages. The symptoms of gastritis and arsenical poisoning are not, I agree, unlike, but Caroline bases her accusation on quite different lines.

"You've only got to look at her," I have heard her say. Mrs. Ferrars, though not in her first youth, was a very attractive woman, and her clothes, though simple, always seemed to fit her very well, but all the same, lots of women buy their clothes in Paris and have not, on that account, necessarily poisoned their husbands.

As I stood hesitating in the hall, with all this passing through my mind, Caroline's voice came again, with a sharper note in it. "What on earth are you doing out there, James? Why didn't you come and get your breakfast?"

"Just coming, my dear," I said hastily. "I've been hanging up my overcoat."

"You could have hung up half a dozen overcoats in this time." She was quite right. I could have. I walked into the dining room, gave Caroline the accustomed peck on the cheek, and sat down to eggs and bacon. The bacon was rather cold.

"You've had an early call," remarked Caroline.

"Yes," I said. "King's Paddock. Mrs. Ferrars."

"I know," said my sister.

"How did you know?"

"Annie told me."

Annie is the house parlormaid. A nice girl, but an inveterate talker.

There was a pause. I continued to eat eggs and bacon. My sister's nose, which is long and thin, quivered a little at the tip, as it always does when she is interested or excited over anything. "Well?" she demanded.

"A bad business. Nothing to be done. Must have died in her sleep."

"I know," said my sister again.

This time I was annoyed. "You can't know," I snapped. "I didn't know myself until I got there, and I haven't mentioned it to a soul yet. If that girl Annie knows, she must be a clairvoyant."

"It wasn't Annie who told me. It was the milkman. He had it from the Ferrars' cook."

As I say, there is no need for Caroline to go out to get information. She sits at home, and it comes to her.

My sister continued: "What did she die of? Heart failure?"

"Didn't the milkman tell you that?" I inquired sarcastically.

Sarcasm is wasted on Caroline. She takes it seriously and answers accordingly. "He didn't know," she explained.

After all, Caroline was bound to hear sooner or later. She might as well hear from me. "She died of an overdose of veronal. She's been taking it lately for sleeplessness. Must have taken too much."

"Nonsense," said Caroline immediately. "She took it on purpose. Don't tell me!"

It is odd how, when you have a secret belief of your own which you do not wish to acknowledge, the voicing of it by someone else will rouse you to a fury of denial. I burst immediately into indignant speech. "There you go again," I said. "Rushing along without rhyme or reason. Why on earth should Mrs. Ferrars wish to commit suicide? A widow, fairly young still, very well off, good health, and nothing to do but enjoy life. It's absurd."

"Not at all. Even you must have noticed how different she has been looking lately. It's been coming on for the last six months. She's looked positively hagridden. And you have just admitted that she hasn't been able to sleep."

"What is your diagnosis?" I demanded coldly. "An unfortunate love affair, I suppose?"

My sister shook her head. *"Remorse,"* she said with great gusto.

"Remorse?"

"Yes. You never would believe me when I told you she poisoned her husband. I'm more than ever convinced of it now."

"I don't think you're very logical," I objected. "Surely if a woman committed a crime like murder, she'd be sufficiently cold-blooded to enjoy the fruits of it without any weak-minded sentimentality such as repentance."

Caroline shook her head. "There probably are women like that—but Mrs. Ferrars wasn't one of them. She was a mass of nerves. An overmastering impulse drove her on to get rid of her husband because she was the sort of person who simply cannot endure suffering of any kind, and there's no doubt that the wife of a man like Ashley Ferrars must have had to suffer a good deal—"

I nodded.

"And ever since she's been haunted by what she did. I can't help feeling sorry for her."

I don't think Caroline ever felt sorry for Mrs. Ferrars whilst she was alive. Now that she has gone where (presumably) Paris frocks can no longer be worn, Caroline is prepared to indulge in the softer emotions of pity and comprehension. I told her firmly that her whole idea was nonsense. I was all the more firm because I secretly agreed with some part, at least, of what she had said. But it is all wrong that Caroline should arrive at the truth simply by a kind of inspired guesswork. I wasn't going to encourage that sort of thing. She will go round the village airing her views, and everyone will think that she is doing so on medical data supplied by me. Life is very trying.

"Nonsense," said Caroline, in reply to my strictures. "You'll see. Ten to one she's left a letter confessing everything."

"She didn't leave a letter of any kind," I said sharply, and not seeing where the admission was going to land me.

"Oh!" said Caroline. "So you *did* inquire about that, did you? I believe, James, that in your heart of hearts, you think very much as I do. You're a precious old humbug."

"One always has to take the possibility of suicide into consideration," I said repressively.

"Will there be an inquest?"

"There may be. It all depends. If I am able to declare myself absolutely satisfied that the overdose was taken accidentally, an inquest might be dispensed with."

"And are you absolutely satisfied?" asked my sister shrewdly.

I did not answer, but got up from the table.

2
Who's Who in King's Abbot

BEFORE I PROCEED further with what I said to Caroline and what Caroline said to me, it might be as well to give some idea of what I should describe as our local geography. Our village, King's Abbot, is, I imagine, very much like any other village. Our big town is Cranchester, nine miles away. We have a large railway station, a small post office, and two rival "General Stores." Ablebodied men are apt to leave the place early in life, but we are rich in unmarried ladies and retired military officers. Our hobbies and recreations can be summed up in the one word, "gossip."

There are only two houses of any importance in King's Abbot. One is King's Paddock, left to Mrs. Ferrars by her late husband. The other, Fernly Park, is owned by Roger Ackroyd. Ackroyd has always interested me by being a man more impossibly like a country squire than any country squire could really be. He reminds one of the red-faced sportsmen who always appeared early in the first act of an old-fashioned musical comedy, the setting being the village green. They usually sang a song about going up to London. Nowadays we have revues, and the country squire has died out of musical fashion.

Of course, Ackroyd is not really a country squire. He is an immensely successful manufacturer of (I think) wagon wheels. He is a man of nearly fifty years of age, rubicund of face and genial of manner. He is hand and glove with the vicar, subscribes liberally to parish funds (though rumor has it that he is extremely mean in personal expenditure), encourages cricket matches, Lads' Clubs and Disabled Soldiers' Institutes. He is, in fact, the life and soul of our peaceful village of King's Abbot.

Now, when Roger Ackroyd was a lad of twenty-one, he fell in love with, and married, a beautiful woman some five or six years his senior. Her name was Paton, and she was a widow with one child. The history of the marriage was short and painful. To put it bluntly, Mrs. Ackroyd was a dipsomaniac. She succeeded in drinking herself into her grave four years after her marriage.

In the years that followed, Ackroyd showed no disposition to make a second matrimonial adventure. His wife's child by her first marriage was only seven years old when his mother died. He is now twenty-five. Ackroyd has always regarded him as his own son, and has brought him up accordingly, but he has been a wild lad and a continual source of worry and trouble to his stepfather. Nevertheless we are all very fond of Ralph Paton in King's Abbot. He is such a good-looking youngster for one thing.

As I said before, we are ready enough to gossip in our village. Everybody noticed from the first that Ackroyd and Mrs. Ferrars got on very well together. After her husband's death, the intimacy became more marked. They were also seen about together, and it was freely conjectured that at the end of her period of mourning, Mrs. Ferrars would become Mrs. Roger

Ackroyd. It was felt, indeed, that there was a certain fitness in the thing. Roger Ackroyd's wife had admittedly died of drink. Ashley Ferrars had been a drunkard for many years before his death. It was only fitting that these two victims of alcoholic excess should make up to each other for all that they had previously endured at the hands of their former spouses.

The Ferrars only came to live here just over a year ago, but a halo of gossip has surrounded Ackroyd for many years past. All the time that Ralph Paton was growing up to manhood, a series of lady housekeepers presided over Ackroyd's establishment, and each in turn was regarded with lively suspicion by Caroline and her cronies. It is not too much to say that for at least fifteen years the whole village has confidentially expected Ackroyd to marry one of his housekeepers. The last of them, a redoubtable lady called Miss Russell, has reigned undisputed for five years, twice as long as any of her predecessors. It is felt that but for the advent of Mrs. Ferrars, Ackroyd could hardly have escaped. That—and one other factor—the unexpected arrival of a widowed sister-in-law with her daughter from Canada. Mrs. Cecil Ackroyd, widow of Ackroyd's ne'er-do-well younger brother, has taken up her residence at Fernly Park, and has succeeded, according to Caroline, in putting Miss Russell in her proper place.

I don't know exactly what a "proper place" constitutes—it sounds chilly and unpleasant—but I know that Miss Russell goes about with pinched lips, and what I can only describe as an acid smile, and that she professes the utmost sympathy for "poor Mrs. Ackroyd—dependent on the charity of her husband's brother. The bread of charity is so bitter, is it not? *I* should be quite miserable if I did not work for my living."

I don't know what Mrs. Cecil Ackroyd thought of the Ferrars affair when it came on the tapis. It was clearly to her advantage that Ackroyd should remain unmarried. She was always very charming—not to say gushing—to Mrs. Ferrars when they met. Caroline says that proves less than nothing.

Such have been our preoccupations in King's Abbot for the last few years. We have discussed Ackroyd and his affairs from every standpoint. Mrs. Ferrars has fitted into her place in the scheme.

Now there has been a rearrangement of the kaleidoscope. From a mild discussion to probable wedding presents, we have been jerked into the midst of a tragedy.

Revolving these sundry other matters in my mind, I went mechanically on my round. I had no cases of special interest to attend, which was, perhaps, as well, for my thoughts returned again and again to the mystery of Mrs. Ferrars' death. Had she taken her own life? Surely, if she had done so, she would have left some word behind to say what she contemplated doing? Women, in my experience, if they once reach the determination to commit suicide, usually wish to reveal the state of mind that led to the fatal action. They covet the limelight.

When had I last seen her? Not for over a week. Her manner then had been normal enough considering—well considering everything.

Then I suddenly remembered that I had seen her, though not to speak to, only yesterday. She had been walking with Ralph Paton, and I had been surprised because I had had no idea that he was likely to be in King's Abbot. I thought, indeed, that he had quarreled finally with his stepfather. Nothing had been seen of him down here for nearly six months. They had been walking along, side by side, their heads close together, and she had been talking very earnestly.

I think I can safely say that it was at this moment that a foreboding of the future first swept over me. Nothing tangible as yet—but a vague premonition of the way things were setting. That earnest *tête-à-tête* between Ralph Paton and Mrs. Ferrars the day before struck me disagreeably.

I was still thinking of it when I came face to face with Roger Ackroyd. "Sheppard!" he exclaimed, "Just the man I wanted to get hold of. This is a terrible business."

"You've heard then?"

He nodded. He had felt the blow keenly, I could see. His big red cheeks seemed to have fallen in, and he looked a positive wreck of his usual jolly, healthy self. "It's worse than you know," he said quietly. "Look here, Sheppard, I've got to talk to you. Can you come back with me now?"

"Hardly. I've got three patients to see still, and I must be back by twelve to see my surgery patients."

"Then this afternoon—no, better still, dine tonight. At seven-thirty? Will that suit you?"

"Yes—I can manage that alright. What's wrong? Is it Ralph?" I hardly knew why I said that—except, that it had so often been Ralph.

Ackroyd stared blankly at me as though he hardly understood. I began to realize that there must be something very wrong indeed somewhere. I had never seen Ackroyd so upset before. "Ralph?" he said vaguely. "Oh! no, it's not Ralph. Ralph's in London—Damn! Here's old Miss Ganett coming. I don't want to have to talk to her about this ghastly business. See you tonight, Sheppard. Seven-thirty."

I nodded, and he hurried away, leaving me wondering. Ralph in London? But he had certainly been in King's Abbot the preceding afternoon. He must have gone back to town last night or early this morning, and yet Ackroyd's manner had conveyed quite a different impression. He had spoken as though Ralph had not been near the place for months.

I had no time to puzzle the matter out further. Miss Ganett was upon me, thirsting for information. Miss Ganett has all the characteristics of my sister Caroline, but she lacks that unerring aim in jumping to conclusions which lends a touch of greatness to Caroline's maneuvers. Miss Ganett was breathless and interrogatory.

Wasn't it sad about poor dear Mrs. Ferrars? A lot of people were saying she had been a confirmed drug-taker for years. So wicked the way people went about saying things. And yet, the worst of it was, there was usually a grain of truth somewhere in these wild statements. No smoke without fire! They were saying too that Mr. Ackroyd had found out about it, and had broken off the engagement—because there *was* an engagement. She, Miss Ganett, had proof positive of that. Of course *I* must know all about it—doctors always did—but they never tell?

And all this with a sharp beady eye on me to see how I reacted to these suggestions. Fortunately long association with Caroline has led me to preserve an impassive countenance, and to be ready with small noncommittal remarks.

On this occasion I congratulated Miss Ganett on not joining in ill-natured gossip. Rather a neat counterattack, I thought. It left her in difficulties, and before she could pull herself together, I had passed on.

I went home thoughtful, to find several patients waiting for me in the surgery.

I had dismissed the last of them, as I thought, and was just contemplating a few minutes in the garden before lunch when I perceived one more patient waiting for me. She rose and came toward me as I stood somewhat surprised. I don't know why I should have been, except that there is a suggestion of cast iron about Miss Russell, a something that is above the ills of the flesh.

Ackroyd's housekeeper is a tall woman, handsome but forbidding in appearance. She has a stern eye, and lips that shut tightly, and I feel that if I were an under housemaid or a kitchenmaid I should run for my life whenever I heard her coming. "Good morning, Dr. Sheppard," said Miss Russell. "I should be much obliged if you would take a look at my knee."

I took a look, but truth to tell, I was very little wiser when I had done so. Miss Russell's account of vague pains was so unconvincing that with a woman of less integrity of character I should have suspected a trumped-up tale. It did cross my mind for one moment that Miss Russell might have deliberately invented this affection of the knee in order to pump me on the subject of Mrs. Ferrar's death, but I soon saw that there, at last, I had misjudged her. She made a brief reference to the tragedy, nothing more. Yet she certainly seemed disposed to linger and chat.

"Well, thank you very much for this bottle of liniment, doctor," she said at last. "Not that I believe it will do the least good."

I didn't think it would either, but I protested in duty bound. After all, it couldn't do any harm, and one must stick up for the tools of one's trade.

"I don't believe in all these drugs," said Miss Russell, her eyes sweeping over my array of bottles disparagingly. "Drugs do a lot of harm. Look at the cocaine habit."

"Well, as far as that goes—"

"It's very prevalent in high society."

I'm sure Miss Russell knows far more about high society than I do. I didn't attempt to argue with her.

"Just tell me this, doctor," said Miss Russell. "Suppose you are really a slave of the drug habit. Is there any cure?"

One cannot answer a question like that offhand. I gave her a short lecture on the subject, and she listened with close attention. I still suspected her of seeking information about Mrs. Ferrars.

"Now, veronal, for instance—" I proceeded. But, strangely enough, she didn't seem interested in veronal. Instead she changed the subject, and asked me if it was true that there were certain poisons so rare as to baffle detection.

"Ah!" I said. "You've been reading detective stories." She admitted that she had. "The essence of a detective story," I said, "is to have a rare poison—if possible something from South America, that nobody has ever heard of—something that one obscure tribe of savages used to poison their arrows with.

Death is instantaneous, and Western science is powerless to detect it. That is the kind of thing you mean?"

"Yes. Is there really such a thing?" I shook my head regretfully. "I'm afraid there isn't. There's *curare,* of course." I told her a good deal about curare, but she seemed to have lost interest once more. She asked me if I had any in my poison cupboard, and when I replied in the negative I fancy I fell in her estimation.

She said she must be getting back, and I saw her out at the surgery door just as the luncheon gong went.

I should never have suspected Miss Russell of a fondness for detective stories. It pleases me very much to think of her stepping out of the housekeeper's room to rebuke a delinquent housemaid, and then returning to a comfortable perusal of *The Mystery of the Seventh Death,* or something of that kind.

3

The Man Who Grew Vegetable Marrows

I TOLD CAROLINE at lunch time that I should be dining at Fernly. She expressed no objection—on the contrary—

"Excellent," she said. "You'll hear all about it. By the way, what is the trouble with Ralph?"

"With Ralph?" I said, surprised; "there isn't any."

"Then why is he staying at the Three Boars instead of at Fernly Park?"

I did not for a minute question Caroline's statement that Ralph Paton was staying at the local inn. That Caroline had said so was enough for me.

"Ackroyd told me he was in London," I said. In the surprise of the moment I departed from my valuable rule of never parting with information.

"Oh!" said Caroline. I could see her nose twitching as she worked on this. "He arrived at the Three Boars yesterday morning," she said. "And he's still there. Last night he was out with a girl."

That did not surprise me in the least. Ralph, I should say, is out with a girl most nights of his life. But I did rather wonder that he chose to indulge in the pastime in King's Abbot instead of in the gay metropolis. "One of the barmaids?" I asked.

"No. That's just it. He went out to meet her. I don't know who she is." (Bitter for Caroline to have to admit such a thing.) "But I can guess," continued my indefatigable sister.

I waited patiently.

"His cousin."

"Flora Ackroyd?" I exclaimed in surprise.

Flora Ackroyd is, of course, no relation whatever really to Ralph Paton, but Ralph has been looked upon for so long as practically Ackroyd's own son, that cousinship is taken for granted.

"Flora Ackroyd," said my sister.

"But why not go to Fernly if he wanted to see her?"

"Secretly engaged," said Caroline, with immense enjoyment. "Old Ackroyd won't hear of it, and they have to meet this way."

I saw a good many flaws in Caroline's theory, but I forebore to point them out to her. An innocent remark about our new neighbor created a diversion.

The house next door, The Larches, has recently been taken by a stranger. To Caroline's extreme annoyance, she has not been able to find out anything about him, except that he is a foreigner. The Intelligence Corps has proved a broken reed. Presumably the man has milk and vegetables and joints of meat and occasional whitings just like everybody else, but none of these people who make it their business to supply these things seems to have acquired any information. His name, apparently, is Mr. Porrott—a name which conveys an odd feeling of unreality. The one thing we do know about him is that he is interested in the growing of vegetable marrows.

But that is certainly not the sort of information that Caroline is after. She wants to know where he comes from, what he does, whether he is married, what his wife was, or is, like, whether he has children, what his mother's maiden name was—and so on. Somebody very like Caroline must have invented the questions on passports, I think.

"My dear Caroline," I said. "There's no doubt at all about what the man's profession has been. He's a retired hairdresser. Look at that mustache of his."

Caroline dissented. She said that if the man was a hairdresser, he would have wavy hair—not straight. All hairdressers did.

I cited several hairdressers personally known to me who had straight hair, but Caroline refused to be convinced. "I can't make him out at all," she said in an aggrieved voice. "I borrowed some garden tools the other day, and he was most polite, but I couldn't get anything out of him. I asked him point blank at last whether he was a Frenchman, and he said he wasn't—and somehow I didn't like to ask him any more."

I began to be more interested in our mysterious neighbor. A man who is capable of shutting up Caroline and sending her, like the Queen of Sheba, empty away must be something of a personality.

"I believe," said Caroline, "that he's got one of those new vacuum cleaners—" I saw a meditated loan and the opportunity of further questioning gleaming from her eye. I seized the chance to escape into the garden. I am rather fond of gardening. I was busily exterminating dandelion roots when a shout of warning sounded from close by and a heavy body whizzed by my ear and fell at my feet with a repellent squelch. It was a vegetable marrow!

I looked up angrily. Over the wall, to my left, there appeared a face. An egg-shaped head, partially covered with suspiciously black hair, two immense mustaches, and a pair of watchful eyes. It was our mysterious neighbor, Mr. Porrott. He broke at once into fluent apologies. "I demand of you a thousand pardons, monsieur. I am without defense. For some months now I cultivate the marrows. This morning suddenly I enrage myself with these marrows. I send them to promenade themselves—alas! not only mentally but physically. I seize the biggest. I hurl him over the wall. Monsieur, I am ashamed. I prostrate myself."

Before such profuse apologies, my anger was forced to melt. After all, the wretched vegetable hadn't hit me. But I sincerely hoped that throwing large vegetables over walls was not our new friend's hobby. Such a habit could hardly endear him to us as a neighbor.

The strange little man seemed to read my thoughts. "Ah! no," he exclaimed. "Do not disquiet yourself. It is not with me a habit. But can you figure to yourself, monsieur, that a man may work toward a certain object, may labor and toil to attain a certain kind of leisure and occupation, and then find that, after all, he yearns for the old busy days, and the old occupations that he thought himself so glad to leave?"

"Yes," I said slowly. "I fancy that that is a common enough occurrence. I myself am perhaps an instance. A year ago I came into a legacy—enough to enable me to realize a dream. I have always wanted to travel, to see the world. Well, that was a year ago, as I said, and—I am still here."

My little neighbor nodded. "The chains of habit. We work to attain an object, and the object gained, we find that what we miss is the daily toil. And mark you, monsieur, my work was interesting. The most interesting work there is in the world."

"Yes?" I said encouragingly. For the moment the spirit of Caroline was strong within me.

"The study of human nature, monsieur!"

"Just so," I said kindly. Clearly a retired hairdresser. Who knows the secrets of human nature better than a hairdresser?

"Also, I had a friend—a friend who for many years never left my side. Occasionally of an imbecility to make one afraid, nevertheless he was very dear to me. Figure to yourself that I miss even his stupidity. His *naïveté,* his honest outlook, the pleasure of delighting and surprising him by my superior gifts—all these I miss more than I can tell you."

"He died?" I asked sympathetically.

"Not so. He lives and flourishes—but on the other side of the world. He is now in the Argentine."

"In the Argentine," I said enviously. I have always wanted to go to South America. I sighed, and then looked up to find Mr. Porrott eyeing me sympathetically. He seemed an understanding little man.

"You will go there, yes?" he asked. I shook my head with a sigh. "I could have gone," I said, "a year ago. But I was foolish—and worse than foolish—greedy. I risked the substance for the shadow."

"I comprehend," said Mr. Porrott. "You speculated?"

I nodded mournfully, but in spite of myself I felt secretly entertained. This ridiculous little man was so portentously solemn.

"Not the Porcupine Oilfields?" he asked suddenly.

I stared. "I thought of them, as a matter of fact, but in the end I plumped for a gold mine in Western Australia."

My neighbor was regarding me with a strange expression which I could not fathom. "It is Fate," he said at last.

"What is Fate?" I asked irritably.

"That I should live next to a man who seriously considers Porcupine Oilfields, and also West Australian Gold Mines. Tell me, have you also a penchant for auburn hair?"

I stared at him open-mouthed, and he burst out laughing.

"No, no, it is not the insanity that I suffer from. Make your mind easy. It was a foolish question that I put to you there, for, see you, my friend of whom I spoke was a young man, a man who thought all women good, and most of them beautiful. But you are a man of middle age, a doctor, a man who knows the folly and the vanity of most things in this life of ours. Well, well, we are neighbors. I beg of you to accept and present to your excellent sister my best marrow." He stooped, and with a flourish produced an immense specimen of the tribe, which I duly accepted in the spirit in which it was offered.

"Indeed," said the little man cheerfully, "this has not been a wasted morning. I have made the acquaintance of a man who in some ways resembles my far-off friend. By the way, I should like to ask you a question. You doubtless know everyone in this tiny village. Who is the young man with the very dark hair and eyes, and the handsome face. He walks with his head flung back, and an easy smile on his lips?"

The description left me in no doubt. "That must be Captain Ralph Paton," I said slowly.

"I have not seen him about here before?"

"No, he has not been here for some time. But he is the son—adopted son, rather—of Mr. Ackroyd of Fernly Park."

My neighbor made a slight gesture of impatience. "Of course, I should have guessed. Mr. Ackroyd spoke of him many times."

"You know Mr. Ackroyd?" I said, slightly surprised.

"Mr. Ackroyd knew me in London—when I was at work there. I have asked him to say nothing of my profession down here."

"I see," I said, rather amused by this patent snobbery, as I thought it.

But the little man went on with an almost grandiloquent smirk. "One prefers to remain incognito. I am not anxious for notoriety. I have not even troubled to correct the local version of my name."

"Indeed," I said, not knowing quite what to say.

"Captain Ralph Paton," mused Mr. Porrott. "And so he is engaged to Mr. Ackroyd's niece, the charming Miss Flora."

"Who told you so?" I asked, very much surprised.

"Mr. Ackroyd. About a week ago. He is very pleased about it—has long desired that such a thing should come to pass, or so I understood from him. I even believe that he brought some pressure to bear upon the young man. That is never wise. A young man should marry to please himself—not to please a stepfather from whom he has expectations."

My ideas were completely upset. I could not see Ackroyd taking a hairdresser into his confidence, and discussing the marriage of his niece and stepson with him. Ackroyd extends a genial patronage to the lower orders, but he has a very great sense of his own dignity. I began to think that Porrott couldn't be a hairdresser after all. To hide my confusion, I said the first thing that came into my head. "What made you notice Ralph Paton. His good looks."

"No, not that alone—though he is unusually good-looking, for an Englishman—what your lady novelists would call a Greek God. No, there was something about that young man that I did not understand."

He said the last sentence in a musing tone of voice which made an indefinable impression upon me. It was as though he was summing up the boy by the light of some inner knowledge that I did not share. It was that impression that was left with me, for at that moment my sister's voice called me from the house.

I went in. Caroline had her hat on, and had evidently just come in from the village. She began without preamble. "I met Mr. Ackroyd."

"Yes?" I said.

"I stopped him, of course, but he seemed in a great hurry, and anxious to get away."

I have no doubt but that that was the case. He would feel toward Caroline much as he had felt toward Miss Ganett earlier in the day—perhaps more so. Caroline is less easy to shake off.

"I asked him at once about Ralph. He was absolutely astonished. Had no idea the boy was down here. He actually said he thought I must have made a mistake. I! A mistake!"

"Ridiculous," I said. "He ought to have known you better."

"Then he went on to tell me that Ralph and Flora are engaged."

"I know that too," I interrupted, with modest pride.

"Who told you?"

"Our new neighbor."

Caroline visibly wavered for a second or two, much as a roulette ball might coyly hover between two numbers. Then she declined the tempting red herring. "I told Mr. Ackroyd that Ralph was staying at the Three Boars."

"Caroline," I said, "do you never reflect that you might do a lot of harm with this habit of yours of repeating everything indiscriminately?"

"Nonsense," said my sister. "People ought to know things. I consider it my duty to tell them. Mr. Ackroyd was very grateful to me."

"Well?" I said, for there was clearly more to come.

"I think he went straight off to the Three Boars, but if so he didn't find Ralph there."

"No?"

"No. Because as I was coming back through the wood—"

"Coming back through the wood?" I interrupted.

Caroline had the grace to blush. "It was such a lovely day," she exclaimed. "I thought I would make a little round. The woods with their autumnal tints are so perfect at this time of year."

Caroline does not care a hang for woods at any time of year. Normally she regards them as places where you get your feet damp, and where all kinds of unpleasant things may drop on your head. No, it was good sound mongoose instinct which took her to our local wood. It is the only place adjacent to the village of King's Abbot where you can talk with a young woman unseen by the whole of the village. It adjoins the Park of Fernly.

"Well," I said, "go on."

"As I say, I was just coming back through the wood when I heard voices." Caroline paused.

"Yes?"

"One was Ralph Paton's—I knew it at once. The other was a girl's. Of course I didn't mean to listen—"

"Of course not," I interjected, with patent sarcasm—which was, however, wasted on Caroline.

"But I simply couldn't help overhearing. The girl said something—I didn't quite catch what it was, and Ralph answered. He sounded very angry. 'My dear girl,' he said, 'Don't you realize that it is quite on the cards the old man will cut me off with a shilling? He's been pretty fed up with me for the last few years. A little more would do it. And we need the dibs, my dear. I shall be a very rich man when the old fellow pops off. He's mean as they make 'em, but he's rolling in money really. I don't want him to go altering his will. You leave it to me, and don't worry.' Those were his exact words. I remember them perfectly. Unfortunately, just then I stepped on a dry twig or something, and they lowered their voices and moved away. I couldn't, of course, go rushing after them, so wasn't able to see who the girl was."

"That must have been most vexing," I said. "I suppose, though, you hurried on to the Three Boars, felt faint, and went into the bar for a glass of brandy, and so were able to see if both the barmaids were on duty?"

"It wasn't a barmaid," said Caroline unhesitatingly. "In fact, I'm almost sure that it was Flora Ackroyd only—"

"Only it doesn't seem to make sense," I agreed.

"But if it wasn't Flora, who could it have been?"

Rapidly my sister ran over the list of maidens living in the neighborhood, with profuse reasons for and against. When she paused for breath, I murmured something about a patient, and slipped out. I proposed to make my way to the Three Boars. It seemed likely that Ralph Paton would have returned there by now.

I knew Ralph very well—better, perhaps, than anyone else in King's Abbot, for I had known his mother before him, and therefore I understood much in him that puzzled others. He was, to a certain extent, the victim of heredity. He had not inherited his mother's fatal propensity for drink, but nevertheless he had in him a strain of weakness. As my new friend of this morning had declared, he was extraordinarily handsome. Just on six feet, perfectly proportioned, with the easy grace of an athlete, he was dark, like his mother, with a handsome, sunburnt face always ready to break into a smile. Ralph Paton was of those born to charm easily and without effort. He was self-indulgent and extravagant, with no veneration for anything on earth, but he was lovable nevertheless, and his friends were all devoted to him. Could I do anything with the boy? I thought I could.

On inquiry at the Three Boars I found that Captain Paton had just come in. I went up to his room and entered unannounced. For a moment, remembering what I had heard and seen, I was doubtful of my reception, but I need have had no misgivings.

"Why, it's Sheppard! Glad to see you." He came forward to meet me, hand outstretched, a sunny smile lighting up his face. "The one person I am glad to see in this infernal place."

I raised my eyebrows. "What's the place been doing?"

He gave a vexed laugh. "It's a long story. Things haven't been going well with me, doctor. But have a drink, won't you?"

"Thanks," I said, "I will."

He pressed the bell, then, coming back, threw himself into a chair. "Not to mince matters," he said gloomily, "I'm in the devil of a mess. In fact, I haven't the least idea what to do next."

"What's the matter?" I asked sympathetically.

"It's my confounded stepfather."

"What has he done?"

"It isn't what he's done yet, but what he's likely to do."

The bell was answered, and Ralph ordered the drinks. When the man had gone again, he sat hunched in the armchair, frowning to himself.

"Is it really—serious?" I asked.

He nodded. "I'm fairly up against it this time," he said soberly.

The unusual ring of gravity in his voice told me that he spoke the truth. It took a good deal to make Ralph grave. "In fact," he continued, "I can't see my way ahead. . . . I'm damned if I can."

"If I could help—" I suggested diffidently.

But he shook his head very decidedly. "Good of you, doctor. But I can't let you in on this. I've got to play a lone hand." He was silent a minute and then repeated in a slightly different tone of voice: "Yes—I've got to play a lone hand. . . ."

4

Dinner at Fernly

IT WAS JUST a few minutes before half-past seven when I rang the front door bell of Fernly Park. The door was opened with admirable promptitude by Parker, the butler.

The night was such a fine one that I had preferred to come on foot. I stepped into the big square hall and Parker relieved me of my overcoat. Just then Ackroyd's secretary, a pleasant young fellow by the name of Raymond, passed through the hall on his way to Ackroyd's study, his hands full of papers.

"Good evening, doctor. Coming to dine? Or is this a professional call?" The last was in allusion to my black bag, which I had laid down on the oak chest.

I explained that I expected a summons to a confinement case at any moment, and so had come out prepared for an emergency call. Raymond nodded, and went on his way, calling over his shoulder. "Go into the drawing room. You know the way. The ladies will be down in a minute. I must just take these papers to Mr. Ackroyd, and I'll tell him you're here."

On Raymond's appearance Parker had withdrawn, so I was alone in the hall. I settled my tie, glanced in a large mirror which hung there, and crossed to the door directly facing me, which was, as I knew, the door of the drawing-room.

I noticed, just as I was turning the handle, a sound from within—the shutting down of a window, I took it to be. I noted it, I may say, quite mechanically, without attaching any importance to it at the time.

I opened the door and walked in. As I did so, I almost collided with Miss Russell, who was just coming out. We both apologized.

For the first time I found myself appraising the housekeeper and thinking what a handsome woman she must once have been—indeed, as far as that goes, still was. Her dark hair was unstreaked with gray, and when she had a color, as she had at this minute, the stern quality of her looks was not so apparent. Quite subconsciously I wondered whether she had been out, for she was breathing hard, as though she had been running.

"I'm afraid I'm a few minutes early," I said.

"Oh! I don't think so. It's gone half-past seven, Dr. Sheppard." She paused a minute before saying "I—didn't know you were expected to dinner tonight. Mr. Ackroyd didn't mention it."

I received a vague impression that my dining there displeased her in some way, but I couldn't imagine why.

"How's the knee?" I inquired.

"Much the same, thank you, doctor. I must be going now. Mrs. Ackroyd will be down in a moment. I—I only came in here to see if the flowers were alright."

She passed quickly out of the room. I strolled to the window, wondering at her evident desire to justify her presence in the room. As I did so, I saw what, of course, I might have known all the time had I troubled to give my mind to it, namely, that the windows were long French ones opening on the terrace. The sound I had heard, therefore, could not have been that of a window being shut down.

Quite idly, and more to distract my mind from painful thoughts than for any other reason, I amused myself by trying to guess what could have caused the sound in question.

Coals on the fire? No, that was not the kind of noise at all. A drawer of the bureau pushed in? No, not that.

Then my eye was caught by what, I believe, is called a silver table, the lid of which lifts, and through the glass of which you can see the contents. I crossed over to it, studying the things. There were one or two pieces of old silver, a baby shoe belonging to King Charles I, some Chinese jade figures, and quite a number of African implements and curios. Wanting to examine one of the jade figures more closely, I lifted the lid. It slipped through my fingers and fell.

At once, I recognized the sound I had heard. It was this same table lid being shut down gently and carefully. I repeated the action once or twice for my own satisfaction. Then I lifted the lid to scrutinize the contents more closely.

I was still bending over the open silver table when Flora Ackroyd came into the room. Quite a lot of people do not like Flora Ackroyd, but nobody can help admiring her. And to her friends she can be very charming. The first thing that strikes you about her is her extraordinary fairness. She has the real Scandinavian pale gold hair. Her eyes are blue—blue as the waters of a Norwegian fiord, and her skin is cream and roses. She has square, boyish shoulders and slight hips. And to a jaded medical man it is very refreshing to come across such perfect health. A simple straightforward English girl—I may be old-fashioned, but I think the genuine article takes a lot of beating.

Flora joined me by the silver table, and expressed heretical doubts as to King Charles I ever having worn the baby shoe, "And anyway," continued Miss Flora, "all this making a fuss about things because someone wore or used them seems to me all nonsense. They're not wearing or using them now. The pen that George Eliot wrote *The Mill on the Floss* with—that sort of thing—well, it's only just a pen after all. If you're really keen on George Eliot, why not get *The Mill on the Floss* in a cheap edition and read that?"

"I suppose you never read such old out-of-date stuff, Miss Flora?"

"You're wrong, Dr. Sheppard. I love *The Mill on the Floss.*"

I was rather pleased to hear it. The things young women read nowadays and profess to enjoy positively frighten me.

"You haven't congratulated me yet, Dr. Sheppard," said Flora. "Haven't you heard?" She held out her left hand. On the third finger of it was an exquisitely set single pearl. "I'm going to marry Ralph, you know," she went on. "Uncle is very pleased. It keeps me in the family, you see."

I took both her hands in mine. "My dear," I said, "I hope you'll be very happy."

"We've been engaged for about a month," continued Flora in her cool voice, "but it was only announced yesterday. Uncle is going to do up Cross-stones, and give it to us to live in, and we're going to pretend to farm. Really, we shall hunt all the winter, town for the season, and then go yachting. I love the sea. And, of course, I shall take a great interest in the parish affairs, and attend all the Mothers' Meetings."

Just then Mrs. Ackroyd rustled in, full of apologies for being late.

I am sorry to say I detest Mrs. Ackroyd. She is all chains and teeth and bones. A most unpleasant woman. She has small pale flinty blue eyes, and however gushing her words may be, those eyes of her always remain coldly speculative.

I went across to her, leaving Flora by the window. She gave me a handful of assorted knuckles and rings to squeeze and began talking volubly.

Had I heard about Flora's engagement? So suitable in every way. The dear young things had fallen in love at first sight. Such a perfect pair, he so dark and she so fair. "I can't tell you, my dear Dr. Sheppard, the relief to a mother's heart." Mrs. Ackroyd sighed—a tribute to her mother's heart, whilst her eyes remained shrewdly observant of me. "I was wondering. You are such an old friend of Roger's. We know how much he trusts to your judgment. So difficult for me—in my position, as poor Cecil's widow. But there are so many tiresome things—settlements, you know—all that. I fully believe that Roger intends to make settlements upon dear Flora, but, as you know, he is just a *leetle* peculiar about money. Very usual, I've heard, amongst men who are captains of industry. I wondered, you know, if you could just *sound* him on the subject. Flora is so fond of you. We feel you are quite an old friend, although we have only really known you just over two years."

Mrs. Ackroyd's eloquence was cut short as the drawing-room door opened once more. I was pleased at the interruption. I hate interfering in other people's affairs, and I had not the least intention of tackling Ackroyd on the subject of Flora's settlements. In another moment I should have been forced to tell Mrs. Ackroyd as much.

"You know Major Blunt, don't you, doctor?"

"Yes, indeed," I said.

A lot of people know Hector Blunt—at least by repute. He has shot more wild animals in unlikely places than any man living, I suppose. When you mention him, people say: "Blunt—you don't mean the big-game man, do you?"

His friendship with Ackroyd has always puzzled me a little. The two men are so totally dissimilar. Hector Blunt is perhaps five years Ackroyd's junior. They made friends early in life, and though their ways have diverged, the friendship still holds. About once in two years Blunt spends a fortnight at Fernly, and an immense animal's head, with an amazing number of horns which fixes you with a glazed stare as soon as you come inside the front door, is a permanent reminder of the friendship.

Blunt had entered the room now with his own peculiar, deliberate, yet soft-footed tread. He is a man of medium height, sturdily and rather stockily built. His face is almost mahogany-colored, and is peculiarly expressionless. He has gray eyes that give the impression of always watching something that is happening very far away. He talks little, and what he does say is said jerkily, as though the words were forced out of him unwillingly.

He said now: "How are you, Sheppard?" in his usual abrupt fashion, and then stood squarely in front of the fireplace looking over our heads as though he saw something very interesting happening in Timbuktu.

"Major Blunt," said Flora, "I wish you'd tell me about these African things. I'm sure you know what they all are."

I was afraid Mrs. Ackroyd would begin talking about settlements again, so I made a few hurried remarks about the new sweet pea. I knew there was a new sweet pea because the *Daily Mail* had told me so that morning. Mrs. Ackroyd knows nothing about horticulture, but she is the kind of woman who likes to appear well-informed about the topics of the day, and she, too, reads the *Daily Mail*. We were able to converse quite intelligently until Ackroyd and his secretary joined us, and immediately Parker announced dinner.

My place at table was between Mrs. Ackroyd and Flora, Blunt was on Mrs. Ackroyd's other side, and Geoffrey Raymond next to him. Dinner was not a cheerful affair. Ackroyd was visibly preoccupied. He looked wretched, and ate next to nothing. Mrs. Ackroyd, Raymond, and I kept the conversation going. Flora seemed affected by her uncle's depression, and Blunt relapsed into his usual taciturnity.

Immediately after dinner Ackroyd slipped his arm through mine and led me off to his study. "Once we've had coffee, we shan't be disturbed again," he explained. "I told Raymond to see to it that we shouldn't be interrupted."

I studied him quietly without appearing to do so. He was clearly under the influence of some strong excitement. For a minute or two he paced up and down the room, then, as Parker entered with the coffee tray, he sank into an armchair in front of the fire.

The study was a comfortable apartment. Bookshelves lined one wall of it. The chairs were big and covered in dark blue leather. A large desk stood by the window and was covered with papers neatly docketed and filed. On a round table were various magazines and sporting papers.

"I've had a return of that pain after food lately," remarked Ackroyd casually, as he helped himself to coffee. "You must give me some more of those tablets of yours."

It struck me that he was anxious to convey the impression that our conference was a medical one. I played up accordingly. "I thought as much. I brought some up with me."

"Good man. Hand them over now."

"They're in my bag in the hall. I'll get them."

Ackroyd arrested me. "Don't you trouble. Parker will get them. Bring in the doctor's bag, will you, Parker?"

"Very good, sir."

Parker withdrew. As I was about to speak, Ackroyd threw up his hand. "Not yet. Wait. Don't you see I'm in such a state of nerves that I can hardly contain myself?"

I saw that plainly enough. And I was very uneasy. All sorts of forebodings assailed me.

Ackroyd spoke again almost immediately. "Make certain that window's closed, will you?" he asked.

Somewhat surprised, I got up and went to it. It was not a French window, but one of the ordinary sash type. The heavy blue velvet curtains were drawn in front of it, but the window itself was open at the top.

Parker reentered the room with my bag while I was still at the window.

"That's alright," I said, emerging again into the room.

"You've put the latch across?"

"Yes, yes. What's the matter with you, Ackroyd?" The door had just closed behind Parker, or I would not have put the question.

Ackroyd waited just a minute before replying. "I'm in hell," he said slowly, after a minute. "No, don't bother with those damned tablets. I only said that for Parker. Servants are so curious. Come here and sit down. The door's closed too, isn't it?"

"Yes. Nobody can overhear; don't be uneasy."

"Sheppard, nobody knows what I've gone through in the last twenty-four hours. If a man's house ever fell in ruins about him, mine has about me. This business of Ralph's is the last straw. But we won't talk about that now. It's the other—the other—! I don't know what to do about it. And I've got to make up my mind soon."

"What's the trouble?"

Ackroyd remained silent for a minute or two. He seemed curiously averse to begin. When he did speak, the question he asked came as a complete surprise. It was the last thing I expected. "Sheppard, you attended Ashley Ferrars in his last illness, didn't you?"

"Yes, I did."

He seemed to find even greater difficulty in framing his next question. "Did you never suspect—did it ever enter your head—that—well, that he might have been poisoned?"

I was silent for a minute or two. Then I made up my mind what to say. Roger Ackroyd was not Caroline. "I'll tell you the truth," I said. "At the time I had no suspicion whatever, but since—well, it was mere idle talk on my sister's part that first put the idea into my head. Since then I haven't been able to get it out again. But, mind you, I've no foundation whatever for that suspicion."

"He *was* poisoned," said Ackroyd. He spoke in a dull heavy voice.

"Who by?" I asked sharply.

"His wife."

"How do you know that?"

"She told me so herself."

"When?"

"Yesterday! My God! Yesterday! It seems ten years ago."

I waited a minute, and then he went on. "You understand, Sheppard, I'm telling you this in confidence. It's to go no further. I want your advice—I can't carry the whole weight by myself. As I said just now, I don't know what to do."

"Can you tell me the whole story?" I said. "I'm still in the dark. How did Mrs. Ferrars come to make this confession to you?"

"It's like this. Three months ago I asked Mrs. Ferrars to marry me. She refused. I asked her again and she consented, but she refused to allow me to make the engagement public until her year of mourning was up. Yesterday I called upon her, pointed out that a year and three weeks had now elapsed since her husband's death, and that there could be no further objection to making the engagement public property. I had noticed that she had been very strange in her manner for some days. Now, suddenly, without the least warning, she broke down completely. She—she told me everything. Her hatred of her brute of a husband, her growing love for me, and the—the dreadful means she had taken. Poison! My God! It was murder in cold blood."

I saw the repulsion, the horror, in Ackroyd's face. So Mrs. Ferrars must have seen it. Ackroyd is not the type of the great lover who can forgive all for love's sake. He is fundamentally a good citizen. All that was sound and wholesome and law abiding in him must have turned from her utterly in that moment of revelation.

"Yes," he went on, in a low, monotonous voice, "she confessed everything. It seems that there is one person who had known all along—who has been blackmailing her for huge sums. It was the strain of that that drove her nearly mad."

"Who was the man?"

Suddenly before my eyes there arose the picture of Ralph Paton and Mrs. Ferrars side by side. Their heads so close together. I felt a momentary throb of anxiety. Supposing—oh! But surely that was impossible. I remembered the frankness of Ralph's greeting that very afternoon. Absurd!

"She wouldn't tell me his name," said Ackroyd slowly. "As a matter of fact, she didn't actually say that it was a man. But of course—"

"Of course," I agreed. "It must have been a man. And you've no suspicion at all?"

For answer Ackroyd groaned and dropped his head into his hands. "It can't be," he said. "I'm mad even to think of such a thing. No, I won't even admit to you the wild suspicion that crossed my mind. I'll tell you this much, though. Something she said made me think that the person in question might be actually among my household—but that can't be so. I must have misunderstood her."

"What did you say to her?" I asked.

"What could I say? She saw, of course, the awful shock it had been to me. And then there was the question, what was my duty in the matter? She had made me, you see, an accessory after the fact. She saw all that, I think, quicker than I did. I was stunned, you know. She asked me for twenty-four hours—made me promise to do nothing till the end of that time. And she steadfastly refused to give me the name of the scoundrel who had been blackmailing her. I suppose she was afraid that I might go straight off and hammer him, and then the fat would have been in the fire as far as she was concerned. She told me that I should hear from her before twenty-four hours had passed. My God! I swear to you, Sheppard, that it never entered my head what she meant to do. Suicide! And I drove her to it."

"No, no," I said. "Don't take an exaggerated view of things. The responsibility for her death doesn't lie at your door."

"The question is, what am I to do now? The poor lady is dead. Why rake up past trouble?"

"I rather agree with you," I said.

"But there's another point. How am I to get hold of that scoundrel who drove her to death as surely as if he'd killed her. He knew of the first crime, and he fastened on to it like some obscene vulture. She's paid the penalty. Is he to go scot-free?"

"I see," I said slowly. "You want to hunt him down? It will mean a lot of publicity, you know."

"Yes, I've thought of that, I've zigzagged to and fro in my mind."

"I agree with you that the villain ought to be punished, but the cost has to be reckoned."

Ackroyd rose and walked up and down. Presently he sank into the chair again. "Look here, Sheppard, suppose we leave it like this. If no word comes from her, we'll let the dead things lie."

"What do you mean by word coming from her?" I asked curiously.

"I have the strongest impression that somewhere or somehow she must have left a message for me—before she went. I can't argue about it, but there it is."

I shook my head. "She left no letter or word of any kind?" I asked.

"Sheppard, I'm convinced that she did. And more, I've a feeling that by deliberately choosing death, she wanted the whole thing to come out, if only to be revenged on the man who drove her to desperation. I believe that if I could have seen her then, she would have told me his name and bid me go for him for all I was worth." He looked at me. "You don't believe in impressions?"

"Oh, yes, I do, in a sense. If, as you put it, word should come from her—" I broke off. The door opened noiselessly and Parker entered with a salver on which there were some letters.

"The evening post, sir," he said, handing the salver to Ackroyd. Then he collected the coffee cups and withdrew.

My attention, diverted for a moment, came back to Ackroyd. He was staring like a man turned to stone at a long blue envelope. The other letters he had let drop to the ground. *"Her writing,"* he said in a whisper. "She must have gone out and posted it last night, just before—before—"

He ripped open the envelope and drew out a thick enclosure. then he looked up sharply. "You're sure you shut the window?" he said.

"Quite sure," I said, surprised. "Why?"

"All this evening I've had a queer feeling of being watched, spied upon. What's that?—" He turned sharply. So did I. We both had the impression of hearing the latch of the door give ever so slightly. I went across to it and opened it. There was no one there.

"Nerves," murmured Ackroyd to himself.

He unfolded the thick sheets of paper, and read aloud in a low voice. *"My dear, my very dear Roger—A life calls for a life. I see that—I saw it in your face this afternoon. So I am taking the only road open to me. I leave to you the punishment of the person who has made my life hell upon earth for the last year. I would not tell you the name this afternoon, but I propose to write it to you now. I have no children or near relatives to be spared, so do not fear publicity. If you can, Roger, my very dear Roger, forgive me the wrong I meant to do you, since when the time came, I could not do it after all. . . ."*

Ackroyd, his finger on the sheet to turn it over, paused. "Sheppard, forgive me, but I must read this alone," he said unsteadily. "It was meant for my eyes, and my eyes only." He put the letter in the envelope and laid it on the table. "Later, when I am alone."

"No," I cried impulsively, "read it now."

Ackroyd stared at me in some surprise.

"I beg your pardon," I said, reddening. "I do not mean read it aloud to me. But read it through whilst I am still here."

Ackroyd shook his head. "No, I'd rather wait."

But for some reason, obscure to myself, I continued to urge him. "At least, read the name of the man," I said.

Now Ackroyd is essentially pigheaded. The more you urge him to do a thing, the more determined he is not to do it. All my arguments were in vain.

The letter had been brought in at twenty minutes to nine. It was just on ten minutes to nine when I left him, the letter still unread. I hesitated with my hand on the door handle, looking back and wondering if there was anything I had left undone. I could think of nothing. With a shake of the head I passed out and closed the door behind me.

I was startled by seeing the figure of Parker close at hand. He looked embarrassed, and it occurred to me that he might have been listening at the door. What a fat, smug, oily face the man had, and surely there was something decidedly shifty in his eye.

"Mr. Ackroyd particularly does not want to be disturbed," I said coldly. "He told me to tell you so."

"Quite so, sir. I—I fancied I heard the bell ring."

This was such a palpable untruth that I did not trouble to reply. Preceding me to the hall, Parker helped me on with my overcoat, and I stepped out into the night. The moon was overcast and everything seemed very dark and still. The village church clock chimed nine o'clock as I passed through the lodge gates. I turned to the left toward the village, and almost cannoned into a man coming in the opposite direction.

"This the way to Fernly Park, mister?" asked the stranger in a hoarse voice. I looked at him. He was wearing a hat pulled down over his eyes, and his coat collar turned up. I could see little or nothing of his face, but he seemed a young fellow. The voice was rough and uneducated. "These are the lodge gates here," I said.

"Thank you, mister." He paused, and then added, quite unnecessarily, "I'm a stranger in these parts, you see." He went on, passing through the gates as I turned to look after him.

The odd thing was that his voice reminded me of someone's voice that I knew, but whose it was I could not think.

Ten minutes later I was at home once more. Caroline was full of curiosity to know why I had returned so early. I had to make up a slightly fictitious account of evening in order to satisfy her, and I had an uneasy feeling that she saw through the transparent device.

At ten o'clock I rose, yawned, and suggested bed. Caroline acquiesced.

It was Friday night, and on Friday night I wind the clocks. I did it as usual, whilst Caroline satisifed herself that the servants had locked up the kitchen properly.

It was a quarter past ten as we went up the stairs. I had just reached the top when the telephone rang in the hall below.

"Mrs. Bates," said Caroline, immediately.

"I'm afraid so," I said ruefully.

I ran down the stairs and took up the receiver. "What?" I said. *"What?* Certainly, I'll come over at once."

I ran upstairs, caught up my bag, and stuffed a few extra dressings into it. "Parker telephoning," I shouted to Caroline, "from Fernly. They've just found Roger Ackroyd murdered."

5
Murder

I GOT OUT the car in next to no time, and drove rapidly to Fernly. Jumping out, I pulled the bell impatiently. There was some delay in answering, and I rang again.

Then I heard the rattle of the chain and Parker, his impassivity of countenance quite unmoved, stood in the open doorway.

I pushed past him into the hall. "Where is he?" I demanded sharply.

"I beg your pardon, sir?"

"Your master, Mr. Ackroyd. Don't stand there staring at me, man. Have you notified the police?"

"The police, sir? Did you say the police?" Parker stared at me as though I were a ghost.

"What's the matter with you, Parker? If, as you say, your master has been murdered—"

A gasp broke from Parker. "The master? Murdered? Impossible, sir!"

It was my turn to stare. "Didn't you telephone to me, not five minutes ago, and tell me that Mr. Ackroyd had been found murdered?"

"Me, sir? Oh! No indeed, sir. I wouldn't dream of doing such a thing."

"Do you mean to say it's all a hoax? That there's nothing the matter with Mr. Ackroyd?"

"Excuse me, sir, did the person telephoning use my name?"

"I'll give you the exact words I heard, *'Is that Dr. Sheppard? Parker, the butler at Fernly, speaking. Will you please come at once, sir. Mr. Ackroyd has been murdered.'*"

Parker and I stared at each other blankly. "A very wicked joke to play, sir," he said at last, in a shocked tone. "Fancy saying a thing like that."

"Where is Mr. Ackroyd?" I asked suddenly.

"Still in the study, I fancy, sir. The ladies have gone to bed, and Major Blunt and Mr. Raymond are in the billiard room."

"I think I'll just look in and see him for a minute," I said. "I know he didn't want to be disturbed again, but this odd practical joke has made me uneasy. I'd just like to satisfy myself that he's alright."

"Quite so, sir. It makes me feel quite uneasy myself. If you don't object to my accompanying you as far as the door, sir—"

"Not at all," I said. "Come along." I passed through the door on the right, Parker at my heels, traversed the little lobby where a small flight of stairs led upstairs to Ackroyd's bedroom, and tapped on the study door.

There was no answer. I turned the handle, but the door was locked.

"Allow me, sir," said Parker.

Very nimbly, for a man of his build, he dropped on one knee and applied his eye to the keyhole.

"Key is in the lock alright, sir," he said, rising. "On the inside. Mr.

Ackroyd must have locked himself in and possibly just dropped off to sleep."

I bent down and verified Parker's statement. "It seems alright," I said, "but, all the same, Parker, I'm going to wake your master up. I shouldn't be satisfied to go home without hearing from his own lips that he's quite alright."

So saying, I rattled the handle and called out, "Ackroyd, Ackroyd, just a minute."

But still there was no answer. I glanced over my shoulder. "I don't want to alarm the household," I said hesitantly.

Parker went across and shut the door from the big hall through which we had come. "I think that will be alright now, sir. The billiard room is at the other side of the house, and so are the kitchen quarters and the ladies' bedrooms."

I nodded comprehendingly. Then I banged once more frantically on the door, and stooping down, fairly bawled through the keyhole: "Ackroyd, Ackroyd! It's Sheppard. Let me in."

And still—silence. Not a sign of life from within the locked room. Parker and I glanced at each other. "Look here, Parker," I said. "I'm going to break this door in—or, rather, we are. I'll take the responsibility."

"If you say so, sir," said Parker, rather doubtfully.

"I do say so. I'm seriously alarmed about Mr. Ackroyd." I looked around the small lobby and picked up a heavy oak chair. Parker and I held it between us and advanced to the assault. Once, twice, and three times we hurled it against the lock. At the third blow it gave, and we staggered into the room.

Ackroyd was sitting as I had left him in the armchair before the fire. His head had fallen sideways, and clearly visible, just below the collar of his coat, was a shining piece of twisted metalwork.

Parker and I advanced till we stood over the recumbent figure. I heard the butler draw in his breath with a sharp hiss. "Stabbed from be'ind," he murmured. "'Orrible!" He wiped his moist brow with his handkerchief, then stretched out a hand gingerly toward the hilt of the dagger.

"You mustn't touch that," I said sharply. "Go at once to the telephone and ring up the police station. Inform them of what has happened. Then tell Mr. Raymond and Major Blunt."

"Very good, sir." Parker hurried away, still wiping his perspiring brow.

I did what little had to be done. I was careful not to disturb the position of the body, and not to handle the dagger at all. No object was to be attained by moving it. Ackroyd had clearly been dead some little time.

Then I heard young Raymond's voice, horror-stricken and incredulous, outside. "What do you say? Oh! Impossible! Where's the doctor?"

He appeared impetuously in the doorway, then stopped dead, his face very white. A hand put him aside, and Hector Blunt came past him into the room.

"My God!" said Raymond from behind him; "it's true, then."

Blunt came straight on till he reached the chair. He bent over the body, and I thought that, like Parker, he was going to lay hold of the dagger hilt. I drew him back with one hand. "Nothing must be moved." I explained. "The police must see him exactly as he is now."

Blunt nodded in instant comprehension. His face was expressionless as ever, but I thought I detected signs of emotion beneath the stolid mask. Geoffrey Raymond had joined us now, and stood peering over Blunt's shoulder at the body. "This is terrible," he said in a low voice.

He had regained his composure, but as he took off the pince-nez he habitually wore and polished them I observed that his hand was shaking. "Robbery, I suppose," he said. "How did the fellow get in? Through the window? Has anything been taken?" He went toward the desk.

"You think it's burglary?" I said slowly.

"What else could it be? There's no question of suicide, I suppose?"

"No man could stab himself in such a way," I said confidently. "It's murder right enough. But with what motive?"

"Roger hadn't an enemy in the world," said Blunt quietly. "Must have been burglars. But what was the thief after? Nothing seems to be disarranged."

He looked round the room. Raymond was still sorting the papers on the desk. "There seems nothing missing, and none of the drawers show signs of having been tampered with," the secretary observed at last. "It's very mysterious."

Blunt made a slight motion with his head. "There are some letters on the floor here," he said.

I looked down. Three or four letters still lay where Ackroyd had dropped them earlier in the evening. But the blue envelope containing Mrs. Ferrars's letter had disappeared. I half opened my mouth to speak, but at that moment the sound of a bell pealed through the house. There was a confused murmur of voices in the hall, and then Parker appeared with our local inspector and a police constable.

"Good evening, gentlemen," said the inspector. "I'm terribly sorry for this! A good, kind gentleman like Mr. Ackroyd. The butler says it is murder. No possibility of accident or suicide, doctor?"

"None whatever," I said.

"Ah! A bad business." He came and stood over the body. "Been moved at all?" he asked sharply.

"Beyond making certain that life was extinct—an easy matter—I have not disturbed the body in any way."

"Ah! And everything points to the murderer having got clear away—for the moment, that is. Now then, let me hear all about it. Who found the body?"

I explained the circumstances carefully.

"A telephone message, you say? From the butler?"

"A message that I never sent," declared Parker earnestly. "I've not been near the telephone the whole evening. The others can bear me out that I haven't."

"Very odd, that. Did it sound like Parker's voice, doctor?"

"Well—I can't say I noticed. I took it for granted, you see."

"Naturally. Well, you got up here, broke in the door, and found poor Mr. Ackroyd like this. How long should you say he had been dead, doctor?"

"Half an hour at least—perhaps longer," I said.

"The door was locked on the inside, you say? What about the window?"

"I myself closed and bolted it earlier in the evening at Mr. Ackroyd's request."

The inspector strode across to it and threw back the curtains. "Well, it's open now anyway," he remarked.

True enough, the window was open, the lower sash being raised to its fullest extent.

The inspector produced a pocket torch and flashed it along the sill outside. "This is the way he went alright," he remarked, "*and* got in. See here."

In the light of the powerful torch, several clearly defined footmarks could be seen. They seemed to be those of shoes with rubber studs in the soles. One particularly clear one pointed inward, another, slightly overlapping it, pointed outward.

"Plain as a pikestaff," said the inspector. "Any valuables missing?"

Geoffrey Raymond shook his head. "Not so that we can discover. Mr. Ackroyd never kept anything of particular value in this room."

"H'm," said the inspector. "Man found an open window. Climbed in, saw Mr. Ackroyd sitting there—maybe he'd fallen asleep. Man stabbed him from behind, then lost his nerve and made off. But he's left his tracks pretty clearly. We ought to get hold of *him* without much difficulty. No suspicious strangers been hanging about anywhere?"

"Oh!" I said suddenly.

"What is it, doctor?"

"I met a man this evening—just as I was turning out of the gate. He asked me the way to Fernly Park."

"What time would that be?"

"Just nine o'clock. I heard it chime the hour as I was turning out of the gate."

"Can you describe him?"

I did so to the best of my ability.

The inspector turned to the butler. "Anyone answering that description come to the front door?"

"No, sir. No one has been to the house at all this evening."

"What about the back?"

"I don't think so, sir, but I'll make inquiries."

He moved toward the door, but the inspector held up a large hand. "No, thanks. I'll do my own inquiring. But first of all I want to fix the time a little more clearly. When was Mr. Ackroyd last seen alive?"

"Probably by me," I said, "when I left at—let me see—about ten minutes to nine. He told me that he didn't wish to be disturbed, and I repeated the order to Parker."

"Just so, sir," said Parker respectfully.

"Mr. Ackroyd was certainly alive at half-past nine," put in Mr. Raymond, "for I heard his voice in here talking."

"Who was he talking to?"

"That I don't know. Of course, at the time I took it for granted that it was Dr. Sheppard who was with him. I wanted to ask him a question about some papers I was engaged upon, but when I heard the voices I remembered that he had said he wanted to talk to Dr. Sheppard without being disturbed, and I went away again. But now it seems that the doctor had already left?"

I nodded. "I was at home by a quarter-past nine," I said. "I didn't go out again until I received the telephone call."

"Who could have been with him at half-past nine?" queried the inspector. "It wasn't you, Mr.—er—"

"Major Blunt," I said.

"Major Hector Blunt?" asked the inspector, a respectful tone creeping into his voice.

Blunt merely jerked his head affirmatively.

"I think we've seen you down here before, sir," said the inspector. "I didn't recognize you for the moment, but you were staying with Mr. Ackroyd a year ago last May."

"June," corrected Blunt.

"Just so, June it was. Now, as I was saying, it wasn't you with Mr. Ackroyd at nine-thirty this evening?"

Blunt shook his head. "Never saw him after dinner," he volunteered.

The inspector turned once more to Raymond. "You didn't overhear any of the conversation going on, did you, sir?"

"I did catch just a fragment of it," said the secretary, "and supposing as I did that it was Dr. Sheppard who was with Mr. Ackroyd, that fragment struck me as distinctly odd. As far as I can remember, the exact words were these. 'The calls on my purse have been so frequent of late'—that is what he was saying—'of late, that I fear it is impossible for me to accede to your request. . . .' I went away again at once, of course, so did not hear any more. But I rather wondered because Dr. Sheppard—"

"—Does not ask for loans for himself or subscriptions for others," I finished.

"A demand for money," said the inspector musingly. "It may be that here we have a very important clue." He turned to the butler. "You say, Parker, that nobody was admitted by the front door this evening?"

"That's what I say, sir."

"Then it seems almost certain that Mr. Ackroyd himself must have admitted this stranger. But I don't quite see—"

The inspector went into a kind of daydream for some minutes. "One thing's clear," he said at length, rousing himself from his absorption. "Mr. Ackroyd was alive and well at nine-thirty. That is the last moment at which he is known to have been alive."

Parker gave vent to an apologetic cough which brought the inspector's eyes on him at once. "Well?" he said sharply.

"If you'll excuse me, sir, Miss Flora saw him after that."

"Miss Flora?"

"Yes, sir. About a quarter to ten that would be. It was after that that she told me Mr. Ackroyd wasn't to be disturbed again tonight."

"Did he send her to you with that message?"

"Not exactly, sir. I was bringing a tray with soda and whiskey when Miss Flora, who was just coming out of this room, stopped me and said her uncle didn't want to be disturbed."

The inspector looked at the butler with rather closer attention than he had bestowed on him up to now. "You'd already been told that Mr. Ackroyd didn't want to be disturbed, hadn't you?"

Parker began to stammer. His hands shook. "Yes, sir. Yes, sir. Quite so, sir."

"And yet you were proposing to do so?"

"I'd forgotten, sir. At least I mean, I always bring the whiskey and soda about that time, sir, and ask if there's anything more, and I thought—well, I was doing as usual without thinking."

It was at this moment that it began to dawn upon me that Parker was most suspiciously fluttered. The man was shaking and twitching all over.

"H'm," said the inspector. "I must see Miss Ackroyd at once. For the moment we'll leave this room exactly as it is. I can return here after I've heard what Miss Ackroyd has to tell me. I shall just take the precaution of shutting and bolting the window."

This precaution accomplished, he led the way into the hall and we followed him. He paused a moment, as he glanced up at the little staircase, then spoke over his shoulder to the constable. "Jones, you'd better stay here. Don't let anyone go into that room."

Parker interposed deferentially. "If you'll excuse me, sir. If you were to lock the door into the main hall, nobody could gain access to this part. That staircase leads only to Mr. Ackroyd's bedroom and bathroom. There is no communication with the other part of the house. There once was a door through, but Mr. Ackroyd had it blocked up. He liked to feel that his suite was entirely private."

To make things clear and explain the position, I have appended a rough sketch of the right-hand wing of the house. The small staircase leads, as Parker explained, to a big bedroom (made by two being knocked into one) and an adjoining bathroom and lavatory.

The inspector took in the position at a glance. We went through into the large hall and he locked the door behind him, slipping the key into his pocket. Then he gave the constable some low-voiced instructions, and the latter prepared to depart.

"We must get busy on those shoe tracks," explained the inspector. "But first of all, I must have a word with Miss Ackroyd. She was the last person to see her uncle alive. Does she know yet?"

Raymond shook his head. "Well, no need to tell her for another five minutes. She can answer my questions better without being upset by knowing the truth about her uncle. Tell her there's been a burglary, and ask her if she would mind dressing and coming down to answer a few questions."

It was Raymond who went upstairs on this errand. "Miss Ackroyd will be down in a minute," he said, when he returned. "I told her just what you suggested."

In less than five minutes Flora descended the staircase. She was wrapped in a pale pink kimono. She looked anxious and excited.

The inspector stepped forward. "Good evening, Miss Ackroyd," he said civilly. "We're afraid there's been an attempt at robbery, and we want you to help us. What's this room—the billiard room? Come in here and sit down."

Flora sat down composedly on the wide divan which ran the length of the

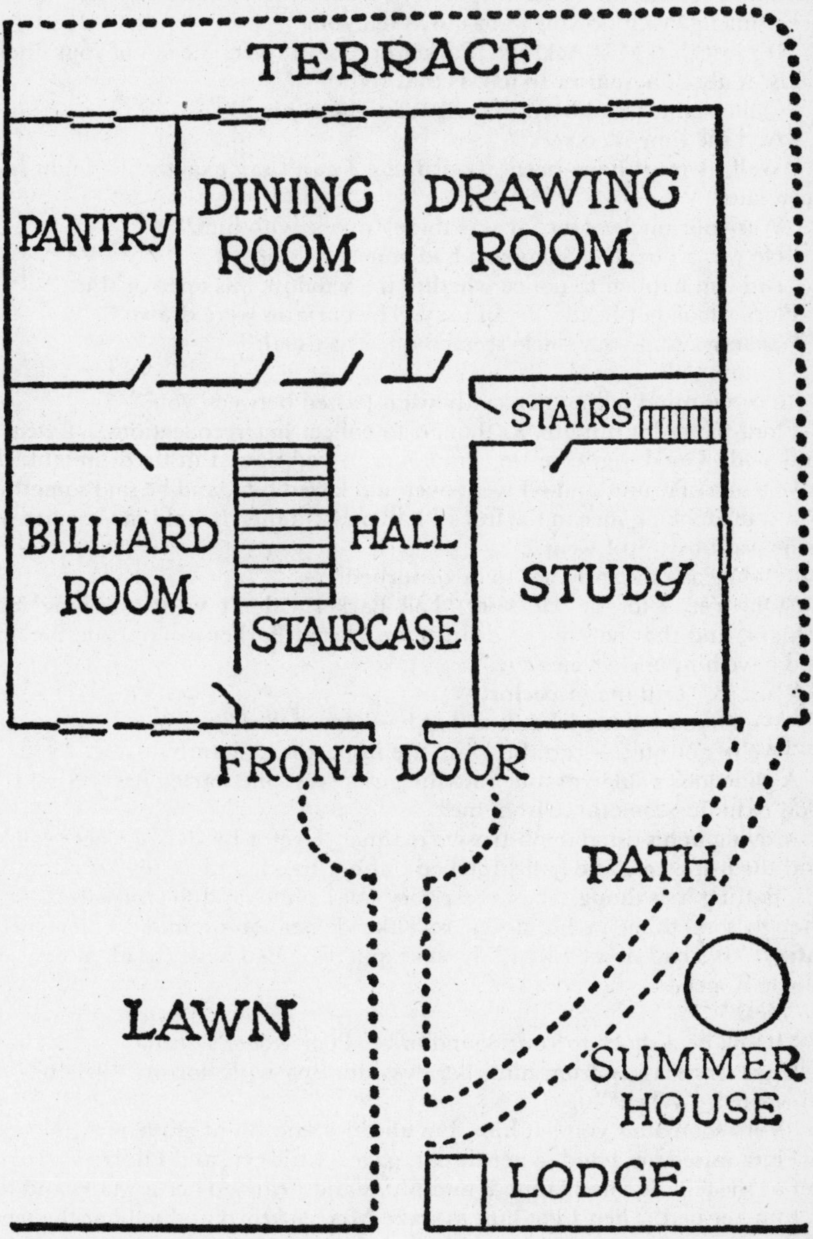
TERRACE
PANTRY
DINING ROOM
DRAWING ROOM
STAIRS
BILLIARD ROOM
HALL
STUDY
STAIRCASE
FRONT DOOR
PATH
LAWN
SUMMER HOUSE
LODGE

wall, and looked up at the inspector. "I don't quite understand. What has been stolen? What do you want me to tell you?"

"It's just this, Miss Ackroyd. Parker here says you came out of your uncle's study at about a quarter to ten. Is that right?"

"Quite right. I had been to say goodnight to him."

"And the time is correct?"

"Well, it must have been about then. I can't say exactly. It might have been later."

"Was your uncle alone, or was there anyone with him?"

"He was alone. Dr. Sheppard had gone."

"Did you happen to notice whether the window was open or shut?"

Flora shook her head. "I can't say. The curtains were drawn."

"Exactly. And your uncle seemed quite as usual?"

"I think so."

"Do you mind telling us exactly what passed between you?"

Flora paused a minute, as though to collect her recollections. "I went in and said, 'Good night, uncle, I'm going to bed now. I'm tired tonight.' He gave a sort of grunt, and—I went over and kissed him, and he said something about my looking nice in the frock I had on, and then he told me to run away as he was busy. So I went."

"Did he ask specially not to be disturbed?"

"Oh! Yes, I forgot. He said: 'Tell Parker I don't want anything more tonight, and that he's not to disturb me.' I met Parker just outside the door and gave him uncle's message."

"Just so," said the inspector.

"Won't you tell me what it is that has been stolen?"

"We're not quite—certain," said the inspector hesitantly.

A wide look of alarm came into the girl's eyes. She started up. "What is it? You're hiding something from me?"

Moving in his usual unobstrusive manner, Hector Blunt came between her and the inspector. She half stretched out her hand, and he took it in both of his, patting it as though she were a very small child, and she turned to him as though something in his stolid, rocklike demeanor promised comfort and safety. "It's bad news, Flora," he said quietly. "Bad news for all of us. Your Uncle Roger—"

"Yes?"

"It will be a shock to you. Bound to be. Poor Roger's dead."

Flora drew away from him, her eyes dilating with horror. "When?" she whispered. "When?"

"Very soon after you left him, I'm afraid," said Blunt gravely.

Flora raised her hand to her throat, gave a little cry, and I hurried to catch her as she fell. She had fainted, and Blunt and I carried her upstairs and laid her on her bed. Then I got him to wake Mrs. Ackroyd and tell her the news. Flora soon revived, and I brought her mother to her, telling her what to do for the girl. Then I hurried downstairs again.

6
The Tunisian Dagger

I MET THE Inspector just coming from the door which led into the kitchen quarters.

"How's the young lady, doctor?"

"Coming around nicely. Her mother's with her."

"That's good. I've been questioning the servants. They all declare that no one has been to the back door tonight. Your description of that stranger was rather vague. Can't you give us something more definite to go upon?"

"I'm afraid not," I said regretfully. "It was a dark night, you see, and the fellow had his coat collar well pulled up and his hat squashed down over his eyes."

"H'm," said the inspector. "Looked as though he wanted to conceal his face. Sure it was no one you know?"

I replied in the negative, but not as decidedly as I might have done. I remembered my impression that the stranger's voice was not unfamiliar to me. I explained this rather haltingly to the inspector.

"It was a rough, uneducated voice, you say?"

I agreed, but it occurred to me that the roughness had been of an almost exaggerated quality. If, as the inspector thought, the man had wished to hide his face, he might equally well have tried to disguise his voice.

"Do you mind coming into the study with me again, doctor? There are one or two things I want to ask you."

I acquiesced. Inspector Davis unlocked the door of the lobby, we passed through, and he locked the door again behind him. "We don't want to be disturbed," he said grimly. "And we don't want any eavesdropping either. What's all this about blackmail?"

"Blackmail?" I exclaimed, very much startled.

"Is it an effort of Parker's imagination? Or is there something in it?"

"If Parker heard anything about blackmail," I said slowly, "he must have been listening outside this door with his ear glued against the keyhole."

Davis nodded. "Nothing more likely. You see, I've been instituting a few inquiries as to what Parker has been doing with himself this evening. To tell the truth, I didn't like his manner. The man knows something. When I began to question him, he got the wind up, and plumped out some garbled story of blackmail."

I took an instant decision. "I'm rather glad you've brought the matter up," I said. "I've been trying to decide whether to make a clean breast of things or not. I'd already practically decided to tell you everything, but I was going to wait for a favorable opportunity. You might as well have it now."

And then and there I narrated the whole events of the evening as I have set them down here. The inspector listened keenly, occasionally interjecting a question.

"Most extraordinary story I ever heard," he said, when I had finished. "And you say that letter has completely disappeared? It looks bad—it looks very bad indeed. It gives us what we've been looking for—a motive for murder."

I nodded. "I realize that."

"You say that Mr. Ackroyd hinted at a suspicion he had that some member of his household was involved? Household's rather an elastic term."

"You don't think that Parker himself might be the man we're after?" I suggested.

"It looks very like it. He was obviously listening at the door when you came out. Then Miss Ackroyd came across him later bent on entering the study. Say he tried again when she was safely out of the way. He stabbed Ackroyd, locked the door on the inside, opened the window, and got out that way, and went around to a side door which he had previously left open. How's that?"

"There's only one thing against it," I said slowly. "If Ackroyd went on reading that letter as soon as I left, as he intended to do, I don't see him continuing to sit on here and turn things over in his mind for another hour. He'd have had Parker in at once, accused him then and there, and there would have been a fine old uproar. Remember, Ackroyd was a man of choleric temper."

"Mightn't have had time to go on with the letter just then," suggested the inspector. "We know someone was with him at half-past nine. If that visitor turned up as soon as you left, and after he went, Miss Ackroyd came in to say goodnight—well, he wouldn't be able to go on with the letter until close upon ten o'clock."

"And the telephone call?"

"Parker sent that alright—perhaps before he thought of the locked door and open windows. Then he changed his mind—or got in a panic—and decided to deny all knowledge of it. That was it, depend upon it."

"Ye-es," I said rather doubtfully.

"Anyway, we can find out the truth about the telephone call from the exchange. If it was put through from here, I don't see how anyone else but Parker could have sent it. Depend upon it, he's our man. But keep it dark—we don't want to alarm him just yet, till we've got all the evidence. I'll see to it he doesn't give us the slip. To all appearances we'll be concentrating on your mysterious stranger."

He rose from where he had been sitting astride the chair belonging to the desk, and crossed over to the still form in the armchair. "The weapon ought to give us a clue," he remarked, looking up. "It's something quite unique—a curio, I should think, by the look of it."

He bent down, surveying the handle attentively, and I heard him give a grunt of satisfaction. Then, very gingerly, he pressed his hands down below the hilt and drew the blade out from the wound. Still carrying it so as not to touch the handle, he placed it in a wide china mug which adorned the mantelpiece.

"Yes," he said, nodding at it. "Quite a work of art. There can't be many of them about."

It was indeed a beautiful object. A narrow, tapering blade, and a hilt of elaborately intertwined metals of curious and careful workmanship. He touched the blade gingerly with his finger, testing its sharpness, and made an appreciative grimace.

"Lord, what an edge," he exclaimed. "A child could drive that into a man—as easy as cutting butter. A dangerous sort of toy to have about."

"May I examine the body properly now?" I asked.

He nodded. "Go ahead."

I made a thorough examination.

"Well?" said the inspector, when I had finished.

"I'll spare you the technical language," I said. "We'll keep that for the inquest. The blow was delivered by a right-handed man standing behind him, and death must have been instantaneous. By the expression on the dead man's face, I should say that the blow was quite unexpected. He probably died without knowing who his assailant was."

"Butlers can creep about as soft-footed as cats," said Inspector Davis. "There's not going to be much mystery about this crime. Take a look at the hilt of that dagger."

I took a look.

"I dare say they're not apparent to you, but I can see them clearly enough." He lowered his voice. *"Fingerprints!"*

He stood off a few steps to judge of his effect.

"Yes," I said mildly. "I guessed that."

I do not see why I should be supposed to be totally devoid of intelligence. After all, I read detective stories, and the newspapaers, and am a man of quite average ability. If there had been toe marks on the dagger handle, now, that would have been quite a different thing. I would then have registered any amount of surprise and awe.

I think the inspector was annoyed with me for declining to get thrilled. He picked up the china mug and invited me to accompany him to the billiard room. "I want to see if Mr. Raymond can tell us anything about this dagger," he explained.

Locking the outer door behind us again, we made our way to the billiard room, where we found Geoffrey Raymond. The inspector held up his exhibit. "Ever seen this before, Mr. Raymond?"

"Why—I believe—I'm almost sure that is a curio given to Mr. Ackroyd by Major Blunt. It comes from Morocco—no, Tunis. So the crime was committed with that? What an extraordinary thing. It seems almost impossible, and yet there could hardly be two daggers the same. May I fetch Major Blunt?" Without waiting for an answer, he hurried off.

"Nice young fellow that," said the inspector. "Something honest and ingenuous about him."

I agreed. In the two years that Geoffrey Raymond has been secretary to Ackroyd, I have never seen him ruffled or out of temper. And he has been, I know, a most efficient secretary.

In a minute or two Raymond returned, accompanied by Blunt. "I was right," said Raymond excitedly. "It *is* the Tunisian dagger."

"Major Blunt hasn't looked at it yet," objected the inspector.

"Saw it the moment I came into the study," said the quiet man.

"You recognized it then?"

Blunt nodded.

"You said nothing about it," said the inspector suspiciously.

"Wrong moment," said Blunt. "Lots of harm done by blurting out things at the wrong time." He returned the inspector's stare placidly enough.

The latter grunted at last and turned away. He brought the dagger over to Blunt. "You're quite sure about it, sir. You identify it positively?"

"Absolutely. No doubt whatever?"

"Where was this—er—curio usually kept? Can you tell me that, sir?"

It was the secretary who answered. "In the silver table in the drawing-room."

"What?" I exclaimed.

The others looked at me.

"Yes, doctor?" said the inspector encouragingly.

"It's nothing."

"Yes, doctor," said the inspector again, still more encouragingly.

"It's so trivial," I explained apologetically. "Only that when I arrived last night for dinner I heard the lid of the silver table being shut down in the drawing room."

I saw profound skepticism and a trace of suspicion on the inspector's countenance. "How did you know it was the silver table lid?"

I was forced to explain in detail—a long tedious explanation which I would infinitely rather not have had to make.

The inspector heard me to the end. "Was the dagger in its place when you were looking over the contents?" he asked.

"I don't know," I said. "I can't say I remember noticing it—but, of course, it may have been there all the time."

"We'd better get hold of the housekeeper," remarked the inspector, and pulled the bell.

A few minutes later Miss Russell, summoned by Parker, entered the room. "I don't think I went near the silver table," she said, when the inspector had posed his question. "I was looking to see that all the flowers were fresh. Oh! Yes, I remember now. The silver table was open—which it had no business to be, and I shut the lid down as I passed." She looked at him aggressively.

"I see," said the inspector. "Can you tell me if this dagger was in its place then?"

Miss Russell looked at the weapon composedly. "I can't say, I'm sure," she replied. "I didn't stop to look. I knew the family would be down any minute, and I wanted to get away."

"Thank you," said the inspector. There was just a trace of hesitation in his manner, as though he would have liked to question her further, but Miss Russell clearly accepted the words as a dismissal, and glided from the room.

"Rather a Tartar, I should fancy, eh?" said the inspector, looking after her. "Let me see. This silver table is in front of one of the windows, I think you said, docotor?"

Raymond answered for me. "Yes, the left-hand window."

"And the window was open?"

"They were both ajar."

"Well, I don't think we need to go into the question much further. Somebody—I'll just say somebody—could get that dagger any time he liked, and exactly when he got it doesn't matter in the least. I'll be coming up in the morning with the chief constable, Mr. Raymond. Until then, I'll keep the key of that door. I want Colonel Melrose to see everything exactly as it is. I happen to know that he's dining out the other side of the county, and, I believe, staying the night. . . ."

We watched the inspector take up the jar. "I shall have to pack this carefully," he observed. "It's going to be an important piece of evidence in more ways than one."

A few minutes later as I came out of the billiard room with Raymond, the latter gave a low chuckle of amusement. I felt the pressure of his hand on my arm, and followed the direction of his eyes. Inspector Davis seemed to be inviting Parker's opinion of a small pocket diary.

"A little obvious," murmured my companion. "So Parker is the suspect, is he? Shall we oblige Inspector Davis with a set of our fingerprints also?" He took two cards from the card tray, wiped them with his silk handkerchief, then handed one to me and took the other himself. Then, with a grin, he handed them to the police inspector. "Souvenirs," he said. "No. 1, Dr. Sheppard; No. 2, my humble self. One from Major Blunt will be forthcoming in the morning."

Youth is very buoyant. Even the brutal murder of his friend and employer could not dim Geoffrey Raymond's spirits for long. Perhaps that is as it should be. I do not know. I have lost the quality of resilience long since myself.

It was very late when I got back, and I hoped that Caroline would have gone to bed. I might know better.

She had hot cocoa waiting for me, and whilst I drank it, she extracted the whole history of the evening from me. I said nothing of the blackmailing business, but contented myself with giving her the facts of the murder.

"The police suspect Parker," I said, as I rose to my feet and prepared to ascend to bed. "There seems a fairly clear case against him."

"Parker!" said my sister. "Fiddlesticks! That inspector must be a perfect fool. Parker indeed! Don't tell me."

With which obscure pronouncement we went up to bed.

7
I Learn My Neighbor's Profession

ON THE FOLLOWING morning I hurried unforgivably over my round. My excuse can be that I had no very serious cases to attend. On my return Caroline came into the hall to greet me. "Flora Ackroyd is here," she announced in an excited whisper.

"What?" I concealed my surprise as best I could.

"She's very anxious to see you. She's been here half an hour." Caroline led the way into our small sitting room, and I followed.

Flora was sitting on the sofa by the window. She was in black and she sat nervously twisting her hands together. I was shocked by the sight of her face. All color had faded away from it. But when she spoke her manner was as composed and resolute as possible. "Dr. Sheppard, I have come to ask you to help me."

"Of course he'll help you, my dear," said Caroline.

I don't think Flora really wished Caroline to be present at the interview. She would, I am sure, have infinitely preferred to speak to me privately. But she also wanted to waste no time so she made the best of it. "I want you to come to The Larches with me."

"The Larches?" I queried, surprised.

"To see that funny little man?" exclaimed Caroline.

"Yes. You know who he is, don't you?"

"We fancied," I said, "that he might be a retired hairdresser."

Flora's blue eyes opened very wide. "Why, he's Hercule Poirot! You know who I mean—the private detective. They say he's done the most wonderful things—just like detectives do in books. A year ago he retired and came to live down here. Uncle knew who he was, but he promised not to tell anyone, because M. Poirot wanted to live quietly without being bothered by people."

"So that's who he is," I said slowly.

"You've heard of him, of course?"

"I'm rather an old fogey, as Caroline tells me," I said, "but I *have* just heard of him."

"Extraordinary!" commented Caroline. I don't know what she was referring to—possibly her own failure to discover the truth.

"You want to go and see him?" I asked slowly. "Now why?"

"To get him to investigate this murder, of course," said Caroline sharply. "Don't be so stupid, James."

I was not really being stupid. Caroline does not always understand what I am driving at. "You haven't got confidence in Inspector Davis?" I went on.

"Of course she hasn't," said Caroline. "I haven't either." Anyone would have thought it was Caroline's uncle who had been murdered.

"And how do you know he would take up the case?" I asked. "Remember he has retired from active work."

"That's just it," said Flora simply. "I've got to persuade him."

"You are sure you are doing wisely?" I asked gravely.

"Of course she is," said Caroline. "I'll go with her myself if she likes."

"I'd rather the doctor came with me if you don't mind, Miss Sheppard," said Flora.

She knows the value of being direct on certain occasions. Any hints would certainly have been wasted on Caroline. "You see," she explained, following directness with tact, "Dr. Sheppard being the doctor, and having found the body, he would be able to give all the details to M. Poirot."

"Yes," said Caroline grudgingly. "I see that."

I took a turn or two up and down the room. "Flora," I said gravely, "be guided by me. I advise you not to drag this detective into the case."

Flora sprang to her feet. The color rushed into her cheeks. "I know why you say that," she cried. "But it's exactly for that reason I'm so anxious to go. You're afraid! But I'm not. I know Ralph better than you do."

"Ralph," said Caroline. "What has Ralph got to do with it?"

Neither of us heeded her.

"Ralph may be weak," continued Flora. "He may have done foolish things in the past—wicked things even—but he wouldn't murder anyone."

"No, no," I exclaimed. "I never thought it of him."

"Then why did you go to the Three Boars last night," demanded Flora, "on your way home—after uncle's body was found?"

I was momentarily silenced. I had hoped that that visit of mine would remain unnoticed. "How did you know about that?" I countered.

"I went there this morning," said Flora. "I heard from the servants that Ralph was staying there—"

I interrupted her. "You had no idea that he was in King's Abbot?"

"No. I was astounded. I couldn't understand it. I went there and asked for him. They told me, what I suppose they told you last night, that he went out at about nine o'clock yesterday evening—and—and never came back."

Her eyes met mine defiantly, and as though answering something in my look, she burst out: "Well, why shouldn't he? He might have gone—anywhere. He may even have gone back to London."

"Leaving his luggage behind?" I asked gently.

Flora stamped her foot. "I don't care. There must be a simple explanation."

"And that's why you want to go to Hercule Poirot? Isn't it better to leave things as they are? The police don't suspect Ralph in the least, remember. They're working on quite another tack."

"But that's just *it,*" cried the girl. "They *do* suspect him. A man from Cranchester turned up this morning—Inspector Raglan, a horrid, weaselly little man. I found he had been to the Three Boars this morning before me. They told me all about his having been there, and the questions he had asked. He must think Ralph did it."

"That's a change of mind from last night, if so," I said slowly. "He doesn't believe in Davis's theory that it was Parker then?"

"Parker indeed," said my sister, and snorted.

Flora came forward and laid her hand on my arm. "Oh! Dr. Sheppard, let us go at once to this M. Poirot. He will find out the truth."

"My dear Flora," I said gently, laying my hand on hers. "Are you quite sure it is the truth we want?"

She looked at me, nodding her head gravely. "You're not sure," she said. "I am. I know Ralph better than you do."

"Of course he didn't do it," said Caroline, who had been keeping silent with great difficulty. "Ralph may be extravagant, but he's a dear boy, and has the nicest manners."

I wanted to tell Caroline that large numbers of murderers have had nice manners, but the presence of Flora restrained me. Since the girl was determined, I was forced to give in to her and we started at once, getting away before my sister was able to fire off any more pronouncements beginning with her favorite words, "Of course."

An old woman with an immense Breton cap opened the door of The Larches to us. M. Poirot was at home, it seemed.

We were ushered into a little sitting room arranged with formal precision, and there, after a lapse of a minute or so, my friend of yesterday came to us.

"Monsieur le docteur," he said, smiling. "Mademoiselle." He bowed to Flora.

"Perhaps," I began, "you have heard of the tragedy which occurred last night."

His face grew grave. "But certainly I have heard. It is horrible. I offer mademoiselle all my sympathy. In what way can I serve you?"

"Miss Ackroyd," I said, "wants you to—to—"

"To find the murderer," said Flora in a clear voice.

"I see," said the little man. "But the police will do that, will they not?"

"They might make a mistake," said Flora. "They are on their way to make a mistake now, I think. Please, M. Poirot, won't you help us? If—if it is a question of money—"

Poirot held up his hand. "Not that, I beg of you, mademoiselle. Not that I do not care for money." His eyes showed a momentary twinkle. "Money, it means much to me and always has done. No, if I go into this, you must understand one thing clearly. *I shall go through with it to the end.* The good dog, he does not leave the scent, remember! You may wish that, after all, you had left it to the local police."

"I want the truth," said Flora, looking at him straight in the eyes.

"All the truth?"

"All the truth."

"Then I accept," said the little man quietly. "And I hope you will not regret those words. Now, tell me all the circumstances."

"Dr. Sheppard had better tell you," said Flora. "He knows more than I do."

Thus enjoined, I plunged into a careful narrative, embodying all the facts I have previously set down. Poirot listened carefully, inserting a question here and there, but for the most part sitting in silence, his eyes on the ceiling.

I brought my story to a close with the departure of the inspector and myself from Fernly Park the previous night.

"And now," said Flora, as I finished, "tell him all about Ralph."

I hesitated, but her imperious glance drove me on.

"You went to this inn—this Three Boars—last night on your way home?" asked Poirot, as I brought my tale to a close. "Now exactly why was that?"

I paused a moment to choose my words carefully. "I thought someone ought to inform the young man of his uncle's death. It occurred to me after I had left Fernly that possibly no one but myself and Mr. Ackroyd were aware that he was staying in the village."

Poirot nodded. "Quite so. That was your only motive in going there, eh?"

"That was my only motive," I said stiffly.

"It was not to—shall we say—reassure yourself about *ce jeune homme?*"

"Reassure myself?"

"I think, M. le docteur, that you know very well what I mean, though you pretend not to do so. I suggest that it would have been a relief to you if you had found that Captain Paton had been at home all the evening."

"Not at all," I said sharply.

The little detective shook his head at me gravely. "You have not the trust in me of Miss Flora," he said. "But no matter. What we have to look at is this—Captain Paton is missing, under circumstances which call for an explanation. I will not hide from you that the matter looks grave. Still, it may admit of a perfectly simple explanation."

"That's just what I keep saying," cried Flora eagerly.

Poirot touched no more upon that theme. Instead he suggested an immediate visit to the local police. He thought it better for Flora to return home, and for me to be the one to accompany him there and introduce him to the officer in charge of the case.

We carried out this plan forthwith. We found Inspector Davis outside the police station looking very glum indeed. With him was Colonel Melrose, the chief constable, and another man whom, from Flora's description of "weaselly," I had no difficulty in recognizing as Inspector Raglan from Cranchester.

I know Melrose fairly well, and I introduced Poirot to him and explained the situation. The chief constable was clearly vexed, and Inspector Raglan looked as black as thunder. Davis, however, seemed slightly exhilarated by the sight of his superior officer's annoyance.

"The case is going to be plain as a pikestaff," said Raglan. "Not the least need for amateurs to come butting in. You'd think any fool would have seen the way things were last night, and then we shouldn't have lost twelve hours." He directed a vengeful glance at poor Davis, who received it with perfect stolidity.

"Mr. Ackroyd's family must, of course, do what they see fit," said Colonel Melrose. "But we cannot have the official investigation hampered in any way. I know M. Poirot's great reputation, of course," he added courteously.

"The police can't advertise themselves, worse luck," said Raglan.

It was Poirot who saved the situation. "It is true that I have retired from the world," he said. "I never intended to take up a case again. Above all things, I have a horror of publicity. I must beg, that in the case of my being able to contribute something to the solution of the mystery, my name may not be mentioned."

Inspector Raglan's face lightened a little.

"I've heard of some very remarkable successes of yours," observed the colonel, thawing.

"I have had much experience," said Poirot quietly. "But most of my successes have been obtained by the aid of the police. I admire enormously your English police. If Inspector Raglan permits me to assist him, I shall be both honored and flattered."

The inspector's countenance became still more gracious.

Colonel Melrose drew me aside. "From all I hear, this little fellow's done some really remarkable things," he murmured. "We're naturally anxious not to have to call in Scotland Yard. Raglan seems very sure of himself, but I'm not quite certain that I agree with him. You see, I—er—know the parties concerned better than he does. This fellow doesn't seem out after kudos, does he? Would work in with us unobstrusively, eh?"

"To the greater glory of Inspector Raglan," I said solemnly.

"Well, well," said Colonel Melrose breezily in a louder voice, "we must put you wise to the latest developments, M. Poirot."

"I thank you," said Poirot. "My friend, Dr. Sheppard, said something of the butler being suspected?"

"That's all bunkum," said Raglan instantly. "These highclass servants get in such a funk that they act suspiciously for nothing at all."

"The fingerprints?" I hinted.

"Nothing like Parker's." He gave a faint smile, and added: "And yours and Mr. Raymond's don't fit either, doctor."

"What about those of Captain Ralph Paton?" asked Poirot quietly.

I felt a secret admiration for the way he took the bull by the horns. I saw a look of respect creep into the inspector's eye.

"I can't help thinking you're mistaken, inspector," said Colonel Melrose warmly. "I've known Ralph Paton from a boy upward. He'd never stoop to murder."

"Maybe not," said the inspector tonelessly.

"What have you got against him?" I asked.

"Went out just on nine o'clock last night. Was seen in neighborhood of Fernly Park somewhere about nine-thirty. Not been seen since. Believed to be in serious money difficulties. I've got a pair of his shoes here—shoes with rubber studs in them. He had two pairs, almost exactly alike. I'm going up now to compare them with those footmarks. The constable is up there seeing that no one tampers with them."

"We'll go at once," said Colonel Melrose. "You and M. Poirot will accompany us, will you not?"

We assented, and all drove up in the colonel's car. The inspector was anxious to get at once to the footmarks, and asked to be put down at the lodge. About half-way up the drive, on the right, a path branched off which led round to the terrace and the window of Ackroyd's study.

"Would you like to go with the inspector, M. Poirot?" asked the chief constable, "or would you prefer to examine the study?"

Poirot chose the latter alternative. Parker opened the door to us. His manner was smug and deferential, and he seemed to have recovered from his panic of the night before.

Colonel Melrose took a key from his pocket, and unlocking the door which led into the lobby, he ushered us through into the study. "Except for the removal of the body, M. Poirot, this room is exactly as it was last night."

"And the body was found—where?"

As precisely as possible, I described Ackroyd's position. The armchair still stood in front of the fire.

Poirot went and sat down in it. "The blue letter you speak of, where was it when you left the room?"

"Mr. Ackroyd had laid it down on this little table at his right hand."

Poirot nodded. "Except for that, everything was in its place?"

"Yes, I think so."

"Colonel Melrose, would you be so extremely obliging as to sit down in this chair a moment. I thank you. Now, M. le docteur, will you kindly indicate to me the exact position of the dagger?"

I did so, whilst the little man stood in the doorway.

"The hilt of the dagger was plainly visible from the door then. Both you and Parker could see it at once?"

"Yes."

Poirot went next to the window. "The electric light was on, of course, when you discovered the body?" he asked over his shoulder.

I assented, and joined him where he was studying the marks on the window sill.

"The rubber studs are the same patterns as those in Captain Paton's shoes," he said quietly.

Then he came back once more to the middle of the room. His eye traveled round, searching everything in the room with a quick, trained glance. "Are you a man of good observation, Dr. Sheppard?" he asked at last.

"I think so," I said, surprised.

"There was a fire in the grate, I see. When you broke the door down and found Mr. Ackroyd dead, how was the fire? Was it low?"

I gave a vexed laugh. "I—I really can't say. I didn't notice. Perhaps Mr. Raymond or Major Blunt—"

The little man opposite me shook his head with a faint smile. "One must always proceed with method. I made an error of judgment in asking you that question. To each man his own knowledge. You could tell me the details of the patient's appearance—nothing there would escape you. If I wanted information about the papers on that desk, Mr. Raymond would have noticed anything there was to see. To find out about the fire, I must ask the man whose business it is to observe such things. You permit—"

He moved swiftly to the fireplace and rang the bell.

After a lapse of a minute or two Parker appeared. "The bell rang, sir," he said hesitantly.

"Come in, Parker," said Colonel Melrose. "This gentleman wants to ask you something."

Parker transferred a respectful attention to Poirot.

"Parker," said the little man, "when you broke down the door with Dr. Sheppard last night, and found your master dead, what was the state of the fire?"

Parker replied without a pause. "It had burned very low, sir. It was almost out."

"Ah!" said Poirot. The exclamation sounded almost triumphant. He went on: "Look round you, my good Parker. Is this room exactly as it was then?"

The butler's eyes swept round. It came to rest on the windows. "The curtains were drawn, sir, and the electric light was on."

Poirot nodded approval. "Anything else?"

"Yes, sir, this chair was drawn out a little more."

He indicated a big grandfather chair to the left of the door between it and the window. I append a plan of the room with the chair in question marked with an X.

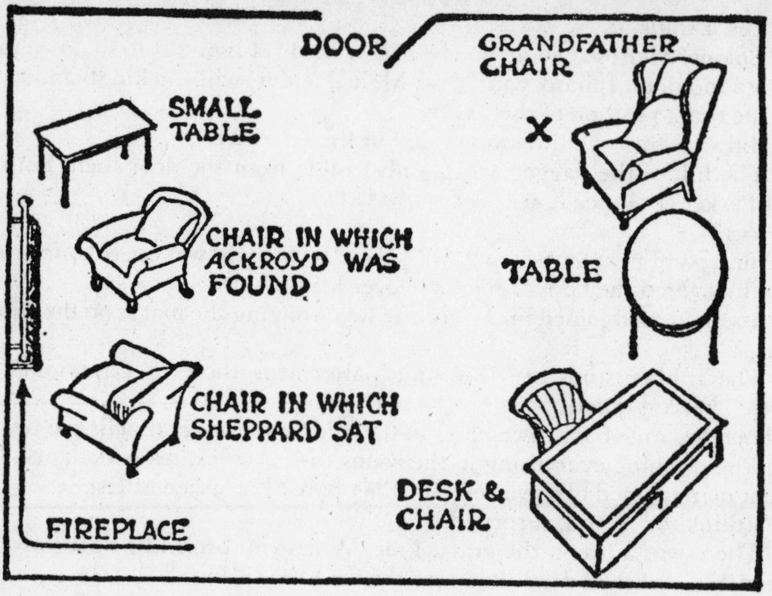

"Just show me," said Poirot.

The butler drew the chair in question out a good two feet from the wall, turning it so that the seat faced the door.

"Voilà ce qui est curieux,"[1] murmured Poirot. "No one would want to sit in a chair in such a position, I fancy. Now who pushed it back into place again, I wonder? Did you, my friend?"

"No, sir," said Parker. "I was too upset with seeing the master and all."

Poirot looked across at me. "Did you, doctor?"

I shook my head.

"It was back in position when I arrived with the police, sir," put in Parker. "I'm sure of that."

"Curious," said Poirot again.

"Raymond or Blunt must have pushed it back," I suggested. "Surely it isn't important?"

"It is completely unimportant," said Poirot. "That is why it is so interesting," he added softly.

"Excuse me a minute," said Colonel Melrose. He left the room with Parker.

"Do you think Parker is speaking the truth?" I asked.

"About the chair, yes. Otherwise I do not know. You will find, M. le docteur, if you have much to do with cases of this kind, that they all resemble each other in one thing."

"What is that?" I asked curiously.

"Everyone concerned in them has something to hide."

"Have I?" I asked, smiling.

---

[1] That's curious!—EDITOR.

Poirot looked at me attentively. "I think you have," he said quietly.

"But—"

"Have you told me everything known to you about this young man Paton?" He smiled as I grew red. "Oh! Do not fear. I will not press you. I shall learn it in good time."

"I wish you'd tell me something of your methods," I said hastily, to cover my confusion. "The point about the fire, for instance?"

"Oh that was very simple. You leave Mr. Ackroyd at—ten minutes to nine, was it not?"

"Yes, exactly, I should say."

"The window is then closed and bolted and the door unlocked. At a quarter past ten when the body is discovered, the door is locked and the window is open. Who opened it? Clearly only Mr. Ackroyd himself could have done so, and for one of two reasons. Either because the room became unbearably hot (but since the fire was nearly out and there was a sharp drop in temperature last night, that cannot be the reason,) or because he admitted someone that way. And if he admitted someone that way, it must have been someone well known to him, since he had previously shown himself uneasy on the subject of that same window."

"It sounds very simple," I said.

"Everything is simple, if you arrange the facts methodically. We are concerned now with the personality of the person who was with him at nine-thirty last night. Everything goes to show that that was the individual admitted by the window, and though Mr. Ackroyd was seen alive later by Miss Flora, we cannot approach a solution of the mystery until we know who that visitor was. The window may have been left open after his departure and so afforded entrance to the murderer, or the same person may have returned a second time. Ah! Here is the colonel who returns."

Colonel Melrose entered with an animated manner. "That telephone call has been traced at last," he said. "It did not come from here. It was put through to Dr. Sheppard at 10:15 last night from a public call office at King's Abbot station. And at 10:23 the night mail leaves for Liverpool."

8

Inspector Raglan Is Confident

WE LOOKED AT each other.

"You'll have inquiries made at the station, of course?" I said.

"Naturally, but I'm not oversanguine as to the result. You know what that station is like."

I did. King's Abbot is a mere village, but its station happens to be an important junction. Most of the big expresses stop there, and trains are shunted, re-sorted, and made up. It has two or three public telephone boxes. At that time of night there local trains come in close upon each other, to catch the connection with the express for the north which comes in at 10:19 and leaves at 10:23. The whole place is in a bustle, and the chances of one particular person being noticed telephoning or getting into an express are very small indeed.

"But why telephone at all?" demanded Melrose. "That is what I find so extraordinary. There seems no rhyme or reason in the ring."

Poirot carefully straightened a china ornament on one of the bookcases. "Be sure there was a reason," he said over his shoulder.

"But what reason could it be?"

"When we know that, we shall know everything. This case is very curious and very interesting."

There was something almost indescribable in the way he said those last words. I felt that he was looking at the case from some peculiar angle of his own, and what he saw I could not tell.

He went to the window and stood there, looking out. "You say it was nine o'clock, Dr. Sheppard, when you met this stranger outside the gate?" He asked the question without turning round.

"Yes," I replied. "I heard the church clock chime the hours."

"How long would it take him to reach the house—to reach this window, for instance?"

"Five minutes at the outside. Two or three minutes only if he took the path at the right of the drive and came straight here."

"But to do that he would have to know the way. How can I explain myself?—It would mean that he had been here before—that he knew his surroundings."

"That is true," replied Colonel Melrose.

"We could find out, doubtless, if Mr. Ackroyd had received any strangers during the past week?"

"Young Raymond could tell us that," I said.

"Or Parker," suggested Colonel Melrose.

"Ou tous les deux,"[1] suggested Poirot, smiling.

Colonel Melrose went in search of Raymond, and I rang the bell once more for Parker.

Colonel Melrose returned almost immediately, accompanied by the young secretary, whom he introduced to Poirot. Geoffrey Raymond was fresh and debonair as ever. He seemed surprised and delighted to make Poirot's acquaintance. "No idea you'd been living among us incognito, M. Poirot," he said. "It will be a great privilege to watch you at work—Hallo, what's this?"

Poirot had been standing to the left of the door. Now he moved aside suddenly, and I saw that while my back was turned he must have swiftly drawn out the armchair till it stood in the position Parker had indicated.

"Want me to sit in the chair whilst you take a blood test?" asked Raymond good-humoredly. "What's the idea?"

"M. Raymond, this chair was pulled out—so—last night when Mr. Ackroyd was found killed. Some one moved it back again into place. Did you do so?"

---

[1] Or Both.—EDITOR.

The secretary's reply came without a second's hesitation. "No, indeed I didn't. I don't even remember that it was in that position, but it must have been if you say so. Anyway, somebody else must have moved it back to its proper place. Have they destroyed a clue in doing so? Too bad!"

"It is of no consequence," said the detective. "Of no consequence whatever. What I really want to ask you is this, M. Raymond: Did any stranger come to see Mr. Ackroyd during this past week?"

The secretary reflected for a minute or two, knitting his brows, and during the pause Parker appeared in answer to the bell. "No," said Raymond at last. "I can't remember anyone. Can you, Parker?"

"I beg your pardon, sir?"

"Any stranger coming to see Mr. Ackroyd this week?"

The butler reflected for a minute or two. "There was the young man who came on Wednesday, sir," he said at last. "From Curtis and Troute, I understood he was."

Raymond moved this aside with an impatient hand. "Oh! Yes, I remember, but that is not the kind of stranger this gentleman means." He turned to Poirot. "Mr. Ackroyd had some idea of purchasing a dictaphone," he explained. "It would have enabled us to get through a lot more work in a limited time. The firm in question sent down their representative, but nothing came of it. Mr. Ackroyd did not make up his mind to purchase."

Poirot turned to the butler. "Can you describe this young man to me, my good Parker?"

"He was fair-haired, sir, and short. Very neatly dressed in a blue serge suit. A very presentable young man, sir, for his station in life."

Poirot turned to me. "The man you met outside the gate, doctor, was tall, was he not?"

"Yes," I said. "Somewhere about six feet, I should say."

"There is nothing in that, then," declared the Belgian. "I thank you, Parker."

The butler spoke to Raymond. "Mr. Hammond has just arrived, sir," he said. "He is anxious to know if he can be of any service, and he would be glad to have a word with you."

"I'll come at once," said the young man. He hurried out. Poirot looked inquiringly at the chief constable.

"The family solicitor, M. Poirot," said the latter.

"It is a busy time for this young M. Raymond," murmured M. Poirot. "He has the air efficient, that one."

"I believe Mr. Ackroyd considered him a most able secretary."

"He has been here—how long?"

"Just on two years, I fancy."

"His duties he fulfills punctiliously. Of that I am sure. In what manner does he amuse himself. Does he go in for *le sport?*"

"Private secretaries haven't much time for that sort of thing," said Colonel Melrose, smiling. "Raymond plays golf, I believe. And tennis in the summer time."

"He does not attend the courses—I should say the running of the horses?"

"Race meetings? No, I don't think he's interested in racing." Poirot nodded and seemed to lose interest. He glanced slowly round the study. "I have seen, I think, all that there is to be seen here."

I, too, looked round. "If those walls could speak," I murmured.

Poirot shook his head. "A tongue is not enough," he said. "They would have to have also eyes and ears. But do not be too sure that these dead things"—he touched the top of the bookcase as he spoke—"are always dumb. To me they speak sometimes—chairs, tables—they have their message!" He turned away toward the door.

"What message?" I cried. "What have they said to you today?"

He looked over his shoulder and raised one eyebrow quizzically. "An opened window," he said. "A locked door. A chair that apparently moved itself. To all three I say, 'Why?' and I find no answer."

He shook his head, puffed out his chest, and stood blinking at us. He looked ridiculously full of his own importance. It crossed my mind to wonder whether he was really any good as a detective. Had his big reputation been built up on a series of lucky chances?

I think the same thought must have occurred to Colonel Melrose, for he frowned. "Anything more you want to see, M. Poirot?" he inquired brusquely.

"You would perhaps be so kind as to show me the silver table from which the weapon was taken? After that, I will trespass on your kindness no longer."

We went to the drawing room, but on the way the constable waylaid the colonel, and after a muttered conversation the latter excused himself and left us together. I showed Poirot the silver table, and after raising the lid once or twice and letting it fall, he pushed open the window and stepped out on the terrace. I followed him.

Inspector Raglan had just turned the corner of the house, and was coming toward us. His face looked grim and satisfied. "So there you are, M. Poirot," he said. "Well, this isn't going to be much of a case. I'm sorry, too. A nice enough young fellow gone wrong."

Poirot's face fell, and he spoke very mildly. "I'm afraid I shall not be able to be of much aid to you, then?"

"Next time, perhaps," said the inspector soothingly. "Though we don't have murders every day in this quiet little corner of the world."

Poirot's gaze took on an admiring quality. "You have been of a marvelous promptness," he observed. "How exactly did you go to work, if I may ask?"

"Certainly," said the inspector. "To begin with—method. That's what I always say—method!"

"Ah!" cried the other. "That, too, is my watchword. Method, order, and the little gray cells."

"The cells?" said the inspector, staring.

"The little gray cells of the brain," explained the Belgian.

"Oh, of course; well, we all use them, I suppose."

"In a greater or lesser degree," murmured Poirot. "And there are, too, differences in quality. Then there is the psychology of a crime. One must study that."

"Ah!" said the inspector, "you've been bitten with all this psychoanalysis stuff? Now, I'm a plain man—"

"Mrs. Raglan would not agree, I am sure, to that," said Poirot, making him a little bow.

Inspector Raglan, a little taken aback, bowed. "You don't understand," he said, grinning broadly. "Lord, what a lot of difference language makes. I'm telling you how I set to work. First of all, method. Mr. Ackroyd was last seen alive at a quarter to ten by his niece, Miss Flora Ackroyd. That's fact number one, isn't it?"

"If you say so."

"Well, it is. At half-past ten, the doctor here says that Mr. Ackroyd has been dead at least half an hour. You stick to that, doctor?"

"Certainly," I said. "Half an hour or longer."

"Very good. That gives us exactly a quarter of an hour in which the crime must have been committed. I make a list of everyone in the house, and work through it, setting down opposite their names where they were and what they were doing between the hour of 9:45 and 10 P.M."

He handed a sheet of paper to Poirot. I read it over his shoulder. It ran as follows, written in a neat script:

Major Blunt—In billiard room with Mr. Raymond. (Latter confirms).
Mr. Raymond—Billiard room. (See above.)
Mrs. Ackroyd—9:45 watching billiard match. Went up to bed 9:55. (Raymond and Blunt watched her up staircase.)
Miss Ackroyd—Went straight from her uncle's room upstairs. (Confirmed by Parker, also housemaid, Elsie Dale.)

Servants:
Parker—Went straight to butler's pantry. (Confirmed by housekeeper, Miss Russell, who came down to speak to him about something at 9:47, and remained at least ten minutes.)
Miss Russell—As above. Spoke to housemaid, Elsie Dale, upstairs at 9:45.
Ursula Bourne (parlormaid)—In her own room until 9:55. Then in Servants' Hall.
Mrs. Cooper (cook)—In Servants' Hall.
Gladys Jones (second housemaid)—In Servants' Hall.
Elsie Dale—Upstairs in bedroom. Seen there by Miss Russell and Miss Flora Ackroyd.
Mary Thripp (kitchenmaid)—Servants' Hall.

"The cook has been here seven years, the parlormaid eighteen months, and Parker just over a year. The others are new. Except for something fishy about Parker, they all seem quite alright."

"A very complete list," said Poirot, handing it back to him. "I am quite sure that Parker did not do the murder," he added gravely.

"So is my sister," I struck in. "And she's usually right." Nobody paid any attention to my interpolation.

"That disposes pretty effectually of the household," continued the inspector. "Now we come to a very grave point. The woman at the lodge—Mary Black—was pulling the curtains last night when she saw Ralph Paton turn in at the gate and go up toward the house."

"She is sure of that?" I asked sharply.

"Quite sure. She knows him well by sight. He went past very quickly and turned off by the path to the right, which is a short cut to the terrace."

"And what time was that?" asked Poirot, who had sat with an immovable face.

"Exactly twenty-five minutes past nine," said the inspector gravely.

There was a silence. Then the inspector spoke again. "It's all clear enough. It fits in without a flaw. At twenty-five minutes past nine, Captain Paton is seen passing the lodge; at nine-thirty or thereabouts, Mr. Geoffrey Raymond hears someone in here asking for money and Mr. Ackroyd refusing. What happens next? Captain Paton leaves the same way—through the window. He walks along the terrace, angry and baffled. He comes to the open drawing-room window. Say it's now a quarter to ten. Miss Flora Ackroyd is saying goodnight to her uncle. Major Blunt, Mr. Raymond, and Mrs. Ackroyd are in the billiard room. The drawing-room is empty. He steals in, takes the dagger from the silver table, and returns to the study window. He slips off his shoes, climbs in, and—well, I don't need to go into details. Then he slips out again and goes off. Hadn't the nerve to go back to the inn. He makes for the station, rings up from there—"

"Why?" said Poirot softly. I jumped at the interruption. The little man was leaning forward. His eyes shone with a queer green light.

For a moment Inspector Raglan was taken aback by the question. "It's difficult to say exactly why he did that," he said at last. "But murderers do funny things. You'd know that if you were in the police force. The cleverest of them make stupid mistakes sometimes. But come along and I'll show you those footprints."

We followed him round the corner of the terrace to the study window. At a word from Raglan a police constable produced the shoes which had been obtained from the local inn. The inspector laid them over the marks. "They're the same," he said confidently. "That is to say, they're not the same pair that actually made these prints. He went away in those. This is a pair just like them, but older—see how the studs are worn down."

"Surely a great many people wear shoes with rubber studs in them?" asked Poirot.

"That's so, of course," said the inspector. "I shouldn't put so much stress on the footmarks if it wasn't for everything else."

"Ah! Well," said the inspector, "it was a dry, fine night, you know. He left no prints on the terrace or on the graveled path. But, unluckily for him, a spring must have welled up just lately at the end of the path from the drive. See here."

A small graveled path joined the terrace a few feet away. In one spot, a few yards from its termination, the ground was wet and boggy. Crossing this wet place there were again the marks of footprints, and amongst them the shoes with the rubber studs.

Poirot followed the path a little way, the inspector by his side. "You noticed the women's footprints?" he said suddenly.

The inspector laughed. "Naturally. But several different women have walked this way—and men as well. It's a regular short cut to the house, you see. It would be impossible to sort out all the footsteps. After all, it's the ones on the window sill that are really important."

Poirot nodded.

"It's no good going farther," said the inspector, as we came in view of the drive. "It's all graveled again here, and hard as it can be."

Again Poirot nodded, but his eyes were fixed on a small garden house—a kind of superior summerhouse. It was a little to the left of the path ahead of us, and a graveled walk ran up to it.

Poirot lingered about until the inspector had gone back toward the house. Then he looked at me. "You must have indeed been sent from the good God to replace my friend Hastings," he said, with a twinkle. "I observe that you do not quit my side. How say you, Dr. Sheppard, shall we investigate the summerhouse? It interests me." He went up to the door and opened it. Inside, the place was almost dark. There were one or two rustic seats, a croquet set, and some folded deck chairs.

I was startled to observe my new friend. He had dropped to his hands and knees and was crawling about the floor. Every now and then he shook his head as though not satisfied. Finally, he sat back on his heels. "Nothing," he murmured. "Well, perhaps it was not to be expected. But it would have meant so much—"

He broke off, stiffening all over. Then he stretched out his hand to one of the rustic chairs. He detached something from one side of it.

"What is it?" I cried. "What have you found?"

He smiled, unclosing his hand so that I should see what lay in the palm of it. A scrap of stiff white cambric.

I took it from him, looked at it curiously, and then handed it back.

"What do you make of it, eh, my friend?" he asked, eyeing me keenly.

"A scrap torn from a handkerchief," I suggested, shrugging my shoulders.

He made another dart and picked up a small quill—a goose quill by the look of it. "And that?" he cried triumphantly. "What do you make of that?"

I only stared.

He slipped the quill into his pocket, and looked again at the scrap of white stuff. "A fragment of a handkerchief?" he mused. "Perhaps you are right. But remember this—*a good laundry does not starch a handkerchief.*" He nodded at me triumphantly, then he put away the scrap carefully in his pocketbook.

9
The Goldfish Pond

WE WALKED BACK to the house together. There was no sign of the inspector. Poirot paused on the terrace and stood with his back to the house, slowly turning his head from side to side. *"Une belle propriété,"*[1] he said at last appreciatively. "Who inherits it?"

His words gave me almost a shock. It is an odd thing, but until that moment the question of inheritance had never come into my head. Poirot watched me keenly. "It is a new idea to you, that," he said at last. "You had not thought of it before—eh?"

"No," I said truthfully. "I wish I had."

He looked at me again curiously. "I wonder just what you mean by that," he said thoughtfully. "Ah! No," as I was about to speak. *"Inutile!*[2] You would not tell me your real thought."

"Everyone has something to hide," I quoted, smiling.

"Exactly."

"You still believe that?"

"More than ever, my friend. But it is not easy to hide things from Hercule Poirot. He has a knack of finding out." He descended the steps of the Dutch garden as he spoke. "Let us walk a little," he said over his shoulder. "The air is pleasant today."

I followed him. He led me down a path to the left enclosed in yew hedges. A walk led down the middle, bordered each side with formal flower beds, and at the end was a round paved recess with a seat and a pond of goldfish. Instead of pursuing the path to the end, Poirot took another which wound up the side of a wooded slope. In one spot the trees had been cleared away, and a seat had been put. Sitting there one had a splendid view over the countryside, and one looked right down on the paved recess and the goldfish pond.

"England is very beautiful," said Poirot, his eyes straying over the prospect. Then he smiled. "And so are English girls," he said in a lower tone. "Hush, my friend, and look at the pretty picture below us."

It was then that I saw Flora. She was moving along the path we had just left and she was humming a little snatch of song. Her step was more dancing than walking, and in spite of her black dress, there was nothing but joy in her whole attitude. She gave a sudden pirouette on her toes, and her black draperies swung out. At the same time she flung her head back and laughed outright.

As she did so a man stepped out from the trees. It was Hector Blunt. The girl started. Her expression changed a little. "How you startled me—I didn't see you."

---

[1] A beautiful estate.—EDITOR.

[2] Useless!—EDITOR.

Blunt said nothing, but stood looking at her for a minute or two in silence.

"What I like about you," said Flora, with a touch of malice, "is your cheery conversation."

I fancy that at that Blunt reddened under his tan. His voice, when he spoke, sounded different—it had a curious sort of humility in it. "Never was much of a fellow for talking. Not even when I was young."

"That was a very long time ago, I suppose," said Flora gravely. I caught the undercurrent of laughter in her voice, but I don't think Blunt did.

"Yes," he said simply, "it was."

"How does it feel to be Methuselah?" asked Flora.

This time the laughter was more apparent, but Blunt was following out an idea of his own. "Remember the Johnny who sold his soul to the devil? In return for being made young again? There's an opera about it."

"*Faust,* you mean?"

"That's the beggar. Rum story. Some of us would do it if we could."

"Anyone would think you were creaking at the joints to hear you talk," cried Flora, half vexed, half amused.

Blunt said nothing for a minute or two. Then he looked away from Flora into the middle distance and observed to an adjacent tree trunk that it was about time he got back to Africa.

"Are you going on another expedition—shooting things?"

"Expect so. Usually do, you know—shoot things, I mean."

"You shot that head in the hall, didn't you?"

Blunt nodded. Then he jerked out, going rather red, as he did so: "Care for some decent skins any time. If so, I could get 'em for you."

"Oh! Please do," cried Flora. "Will you really? You won't forget?"

"I shan't forget," said Hector Blunt. He added, in a sudden burst of communicativeness: "Time I went. I'm no good in this sort of life. Haven't got the manners for it. I'm a rough fellow, no use in society. Never remember the things one's expected to say. Yes, time I went."

"But you're not going at once," cried Flora. "Not—not while we're in all this trouble. Oh! please. If you go—" She turned away a little.

"You want me to stay?" asked Blunt. He spoke deliberately but quite simply.

"We all—"

"I meant you personally," said Blunt, with directness.

Flora turned slowly back again and met his eyes. "I want you to stay," she said, "if—if that makes any difference."

"It makes all the difference," said Blunt.

There was a moment's silence. They sat down on the stone seat by the goldfish pond. It seemed as though neither of them knew quite what to say next.

"It—it's such a lovely morning," said Flora at last. "You know, I can't help feeling happy, in spite—in spite of everything. That's awful, I suppose?"

"Quite natural," said Blunt. "Never saw your uncle until two years ago, did you? Can't be expected to grieve very much. Much better to have no humbug about it."

"There's something awfully consoling about you," said Flora. "You make things so simple."

"Things are simple as a rule," said the big-game hunter.

"Not always," said Flora.

Her voice had lowered itself, and I saw Blunt turn and look at her, bringing his eyes back from (apparently) the coast of Africa to do so. He evidently put his own construction on her change of tone, for he said, after a minute or two, in rather an abrupt manner: "I say, you know, you mustn't worry. About that young chap, I mean. Inspector's an ass. Everybody knows—utterly absurd to think he could have done it. Man from outside. Burglar chap. That's the only possible solution."

Flora turned to look at him. "You really think so?"

"Don't you?" said Blunt quickly.

"I—oh, yes, of course." Another silence, and then Flora burst out: "I'm—I'll tell you why I felt so happy this morning. However heartless you think me, I'd rather tell you. It's because the lawyer has been—Mr. Hammond. He told us about the will. Uncle Roger has left me twenty thousand pounds. Think of it—twenty thousand beautiful pounds."

Blunt looked surprised. "Does it mean so much to you?"

"Mean much to me? Why, it's everything. Freedom—life—no more scheming and scraping and lying—"

"Lying?" said Blunt, sharply interrupting.

Flora seemed taken aback for a minute. "You know what I mean," she said uncertainly. "Pretending to be thankful for all the nasty castoff things rich relations give you. Last year's coats and skirts and hats."

"Don't know much about ladies' clothes; should have said you were always very well turned out."

"It's cost me something, though," said Flora in a low voice. "Don't let's talk of horrid things. I'm so happy I'm free. Free to do what I like. Free not to—" She stopped suddenly.

"Not to what?" asked Blunt quickly.

"I forget now. Nothing important."

Blunt had a stick in his hand, and he thrust it into the pond, poking at something.

"What are you doing, Major Blunt?"

"There's something bright down there. Wondered what it was—looks like a gold brooch. Now I've stirred up the mud and it's gone."

"Perhaps it's a crown," suggested Flora. "Like the one Mélisande saw in the water."

"Mélisande," said Blunt reflectively—"she's in an opera, isn't she?"

"Yes, you seem to know a lot about operas."

"People take me sometimes," said Blunt sadly. "Funny idea of pleasure—worse racket than the natives make with their tom-toms."

Flora laughed. "I remember Mélisande," continued Blunt, "married an old chap old enough to be her father."

He threw a small piece of flint into the goldfish pond. Then, with a change of manner, he turned to Flora. "Miss Ackroyd, can I do anything. About Paton, I mean. I know how dreadfully anxious you must be."

"Thank you," said Flora in a cold voice. "There is really nothing to be done. Ralph will be alright. I've got hold of the most wonderful detective in the world, and he's going to find out all about it."

For some time I felt uneasy as to our position. We were not exactly eavesdropping, since the two in the garden below had only to lift their heads to see us. Nevertheless, I should have drawn attention to our presence before now, had not my companion put a warning pressure on my arm. Clearly he wished me to remain silent.

But now he rose briskly to his feet, clearing his throat. "I demand pardon," he cried. "I cannot allow mademoiselle thus extravagantly to compliment me, and not draw attention to my presence. They say the listener hears no good of himself, but that is not the case this time. To spare my blushes, I must join you and apologize." He hurried down the path with me close behind him, and joined the others by the pond.

"This is M. Hercule Poirot," said Flora. "I expect you've heard of him."

Poirot bowed. "I know Major Blunt by reputation," he said politely. "I am glad to have encountered you, monsieur. I am in need of some information that you can give me."

Blunt looked at him inquiringly.

"When did you last see M. Ackroyd alive?"

"At dinner."

"And you neither saw nor heard anything of him after that?"

"Didn't see him. Heard his voice."

"How was that?"

"I strolled out on the terrace—"

"Pardon me, what time was this?"

"About half-past nine. I was walking up and down smoking in front of the drawing-room window. I heard Ackroyd talking in his study—"

Poirot stopped and removed a microscopic weed. "Surely you couldn't hear voices in the study from that part of the terrace," he murmured.

He was not looking at Blunt, but I was, and to my intense surprise, I saw the latter flush. "Went as far as the corner," he explained unwillingly.

"Ah! Indeed?" said Poirot. In the mildest manner he conveyed an impression that more was needed.

"Thought I saw—a woman disappearing into the bushes. Just a gleam of white, you know. Must have been mistaken. It was while I was standing at the corner that I heard Ackroyd's voice speaking to that secretary of his."

"Speaking to Mr. Geoffrey Raymond?"

"Yes—that's what I supposed at the time. Seems I was wrong."

"Mr. Ackroyd didn't address him by name?"

"Oh, no."

"Then, if I may ask, why did you think—?"

Blunt explained laboriously. "Took it for granted that it *would* be Raymond, because he had said just before I came out that he was taking some papers to Ackroyd. Never thought of it being anybody else."

"Can you remember what the words you heard were?"

"Afraid I can't. Something quite ordinary and unimportant. Only caught a scrap of it. I was thinking of something else at the time."

"It is of no importance," murmured Poirot. "Did you move a chair back against the wall when you went into the study after the body was discovered?"

"Chair? No—why should I?"

Poirot shrugged his shoulders but did not answer. He turned to Flora. "There is one thing I should like to know from you, mademoiselle. When you were examining the things in the silver table with Dr. Sheppard, was the dagger in its place, or was it not?"

Flora's chin shot up. "Inspector Raglan has been asking me that," she said resentfully. "I've told him, and I'll tell you. I'm perfectly certain the dagger was *not* there. He thinks it was and that Ralph sneaked it later in the evening. And—and he doesn't believe me. He thinks I'm saying it to—to shield Ralph."

"And aren't you?" I asked gravely.

Flora stamped her foot. "You, too, Dr. Sheppard! Oh! It's too bad."

Poirot tactfully made a diversion. "It is true what I heard you say, Major Blunt. There is something that glitters in this pond. Let us see if I can reach it."

He knelt down by the pond, baring his arm to the elbow, and lowered it very slowly, so as not to disturb the bottom of the pond. But in spite of all his precautions the mud eddied and swirled, and he was forced to draw his arm out again empty-handed.

He gazed ruefully at the mud upon his arm. I offered him my handkerchief, which he accepted with fervent protestations of thanks. Blunt looked at his watch. "Nearly lunch time," he said. "We'd better be getting back to the house."

"You will lunch with us, M. Poirot?" asked Flora. "I should like you to meet my mother. She is—very fond of Ralph."

The little man bowed. "I shall be delighted, mademoiselle."

"And you will stay, too, won't you, Dr. Sheppard?"

I hesitated.

"Oh, do!"

I wanted to, so I accepted the invitation without further ceremony. We set out toward the house, Flora and Blunt walking ahead.

"What hair," said Poirot to me in a low tone, nodding toward Flora. "The real gold! They will make a pretty couple. She and the dark, handsome Captain Paton. Will they not?"

I looked at him inquiringly, but he began to fuss about a few microscopic drops of water on his coat sleeve. The man reminded me in some ways of a cat. His green eyes and his finicking habits.

"And all for nothing, too," I said sympathetically. "I wonder what it was in the pond?"

"Would you like to see?" said Poirot.

I stared at him. He nodded. "My good friend," he said gently and reproachfully, "Hercule Poirot does not run the risk of disarranging his costume without being sure of attaining his object. To do so would be ridiculous and absurd. I am never ridiculous."

"But you brought your hand out empty," I objected.

"There are times when it is necessary to have discretion. Do you tell your patients everything—everything, doctor? I think not. Nor do you tell your excellent sister everything either, is it not so? Before showing my empty hand,

I dropped what it contained into my other hand. You shall see what that was."

He held out his left hand, palm open. On it lay a little circlet of gold. A woman's wedding ring. I took it from him.

"Look inside," commanded Poirot.

I did so. Inside was an inscription in fine writing: *From R., March 13th.* I looked at Poirot, but he was busy inspecting his appearance in a tiny pocket glass. He paid particular attention to his mustaches, and none at all to me. I saw that he did not intend to be communicative.

10
The Parlormaid

WE FOUND MRS. ACKROYD in the hall. With her was a small dried-up little man, with an aggressive chin and sharp gray eyes, and "lawyer" written all over him.

"Mr. Hammond is staying to lunch with us," said Mrs. Ackroyd. "You know Major Blunt, Mr. Hammond? And dear Dr. Sheppard—also a close friend of poor Roger's. And, let me see—" She paused, surveying Hercule Poirot in some perplexity.

"This is M. Poirot, Mother," said Flora. "I told you about him this morning."

"Oh! Yes," said Mrs. Ackroyd vaguely. "Of course, my dear, of course. He is to find Ralph, is he not?"

"He is to find out who killed uncle," said Flora.

"Oh! My dear," cried her mother. "Please! My poor nerves. I am a wreck this morning, a positive wreck. Such a dreadful thing to happen. I can't help feeling that it must have been an accident of some kind. Roger was so fond of handling queer curios. His hand must have slipped, or something."

This theory was received in polite silence. I saw Poirot edge up to the lawyer, and speak to him in a confidential undertone. They moved aside into the embrasure of the window. I joined them—then hesitated.

"Perhaps I'm intruding," I said.

"Not at all," cried Poirot heartily. "You and I, M. le docteur, we investigate this affair side by side. Without you I should be lost. I desire a little information from the good Mr. Hammond."

"You are acting on behalf of Captain Ralph Paton, I understand," said the lawyer cautiously.

Poirot shook his head. "Not so. I am acting in the interests of justice. Miss Ackroyd has asked me to investigate the death of her uncle."

Mr. Hammond seemed slightly taken aback. "I cannot seriously believe that Captain Paton can be concerned in this crime," he said, "however strong the circumstantial evidence against him may be. The mere fact that he was hard pressed for money—"

"Was he hard pressed for money?" interpolated Poirot quickly.

The lawyer shrugged his shoulders. "It was a chronic condition with Ralph Paton," he said dryly. "Money went through his hands like water. He was always applying to his stepfather."

"Had he done so of late? During the last year, for instance?"

"I cannot say. Mr. Ackroyd did not mention the fact to me."

"I comprehend. Mr. Hammond, I take it that you are acquainted with the provisions of Mr. Ackroyd's will?"

"Certainly. That is my principal business here today."

"Then, seeing that I am acting for Miss Ackroyd, you will not object to telling me the terms of that will?"

"They are quite simple. Shorn of legal phraseology, and after paying certain legacies and bequests—"

"Such as—?" interrupted Poirot.

Mr. Hammond seemed a little surprised. "A thousand pounds to his housekeeper, Miss Russell; fifty pounds to the cook, Emma Cooper; five hundred pounds to his secretary, Mr. Geoffrey Raymond. Then to various hospitals—"

Poirot held up his hand. "Ah! The charitable bequests, they interest me not."

"Quite so. The income on ten thousand pounds' worth of shares to be paid to Mrs. Cecil Ackroyd during her lifetime. Miss Flora Ackroyd inherits twenty thousand pounds outright. The residue—including this property, and shares in Ackroyd and Son—to his adopted son, Ralph Paton."

"Mr. Ackroyd possessed a large fortune?"

"A very large fortune. Captain Paton will be an exceedingly wealthy young man." There was a silence. Poirot and the lawyer looked at each other.

"Mr. Hammond," came Mrs. Ackroyd's voice plaintively from the fireplace.

The lawyer answered the summons. Poirot took my arm and drew me right into the window. "Regard the irises," he remarked in rather a loud voice. "Magnificent, are they not? A straight and pleasing effect."

At the same time I felt the pressure of his hand on my arm, and he added in a low tone: "Do you really wish to aid me? To take part in this investigation?"

"Yes, indeed," I said eagerly. "There's nothing I should like better. You don't know what a dull old fogey's life I lead. Never anything out of the ordinary."

"Good, we will be colleagues then. In a minute or two I fancy Major Blunt will join us. He is not happy with the good mamma. Now there are some things I want to know—but I do not wish to seem to want to know them. You comprehend? So it will be your part to ask the questions."

"What questions do you want me to ask? I asked apprehensively.

"I want you to introduce the name of Mrs. Ferrars."

"Yes?"

"Speak of her in a natural fashion. Ask him if he was down here when her husband died. You understand the kind of thing I mean. And while he replies, watch his face without seeming to watch it. *C'est compris?*"[1]

There was no time for more, for at that minute, as Poirot has prophesied, Blunt left the others in his abrupt fashion and came over to us. I suggested strolling on the terrace, and he acquiesced. Poirot stayed behind.

I stopped to examine a late rose. "How things change in the course of a day or so," I observed. "I was up here last Wednesday, I remember, walking up and down this same terrace. Ackroyd was with me—full of spirits. And now—three days later—Ackroyd's dead, poor fellow, Mrs. Ferrar's dead—you knew her, didn't you? But of course you did."

Blunt nodded his head.

"Had you seen her since you'd been down this time?"

"Went with Ackroyd to call. Last Tuesday, think it was. Fascinating woman—but something queer about her. Deep—one would never know what she was up to."

I looked into his steady gray eyes. Nothing there surely. I went on: "I suppose you'd met her before."

"Last time I was here—she and her husband had just come here to live." He paused a minute and then added: "Rum thing, she had changed a lot between then and now."

"How—changed?" I asked.

"Looked ten years older."

"Were you down here when her husband died?" I asked, trying to make the question as casual as possible.

"No. From all I heard it would be a good riddance. Uncharitable, perhaps, but the truth."

I agreed. "Ashley Ferrars was by no means a pattern husband," I said cautiously.

"Blackguard, I thought," said Blunt.

"No," I said, "only a man with more money than was good for him."

"Oh! Money! All the troubles in the world can be put down to money—or the lack of it."

"Which has been your particular trouble?" I asked.

"I've enough for what I want. I'm one of the lucky ones."

"Indeed."

"I'm not too flush just now, as a matter of fact. Came into a legacy a year ago, and like a fool let myself be persuaded into putting it into some wildcat scheme."

I sympathized, and narrated my own similar trouble.

Then the gong pealed out, and we all went in to lunch. Poirot drew me back a little. *"Eh! Bien?"*[2]

"He's alright," I said. "I'm sure of it."

"Nothing—disturbing?"

"He had a legacy just a year ago," I said. "But why not? Why shouldn't he? I'll swear the man is perfectly square and aboveboard."

"Without doubt, without doubt," said Poirot soothingly. "Do not upset

---

[1] Understand?—EDITOR.

[2] Well?—EDITOR.

yourself." He spoke as though to a fractious child.

We all trooped into the dining room. It seemed incredible that less than twenty-four hours had passed since I last sat at that table.

Afterward, Mrs. Ackroyd took me aside and sat down with me on a sofa.

"I can't help feeling a little hurt," she murmured, producing a handkerchief of the kind obviously not meant to be cried into. "Hurt, I mean, by Roger's lack of confidence in me. That twenty thousand pounds ought to have been left to *me*—not to Flora. A mother could be trusted to safeguard the interests of her child. A lack of trust, I call it."

"You forget, Mrs. Ackroyd," I said, "Flora was Ackroyd's own niece, a blood relation. It would have been different had you been his sister instead of his sister-in-law."

"As poor Cecil's widow, I think my feelings ought to have been considered," said the lady, touching her eyelashes gingerly with the handkerchief. "But Roger was always most peculiar—not to say *mean*—about money matters. It has been a most difficult position for both Flora and myself. He did not even give the poor child an allowance. He would pay her bills, you know, and even that with a good deal of reluctance and asking what she wanted all those fal-lals for—so like a man—but—now I've forgotten what it was I was going to say! Oh, yes, not a penny we could call our own, you know. Flora resented it—yes, I must say she resented it—very strongly. Though devoted to her uncle, of course. But any girl would have resented it. Yes, I must say Roger had very strange ideas about money. He wouldn't even buy new face towels, though I told him the old ones were in holes. And then," proceeded Mrs. Ackroyd, with a sudden leap highly characteristic of her conversation, "to leave all that money—a thousand pounds—fancy, a thousand pounds!—to that woman."

"What woman?"

"That Russell woman. Something very queer about her, and so I've always said. But Roger wouldn't hear a word against her. Said she was a woman of great force of character, and that he admired and respected her. He was always going on about her rectitude and independence and moral worth. I think there's something fishy about her. She was certainly doing her best to marry Roger. But I soon put a stop to that. She's always hated me. Naturally. I saw through her."

I began to wonder if there was any chance of stemming Mrs. Ackroyd's eloquence, and getting away. Mr. Hammand provided the necessary diversion by coming up to say goodbye. I seized my chance and rose also. "About the inquest," I said, "Where would you prefer it to be held? Here, or at the Three Boars?"

Mrs. Ackroyd stared at me with a dropped jaw. "The inquest?" she asked, the picture of consternation. "But surely there won't have to be an inquest?"

Mr. Hammand gave a dry little cough and murmured. "Inevitable. Under the circumstances," in two short little barks.

"But surely Dr. Sheppard can arrange—"

"There are limits to my powers of arrangement," I said dryly.

"If his death was an accident—"

"He was murdered, Mrs. Ackroyd," I said brutally. She gave a little cry.

"No theory of accident will hold water for a minute."

Mrs. Ackroyd looked at me in distress. I had no patience with what I thought was her silly fear of unpleasantness. "If there's an inquest, I—I shan't have to answer questions and all that, shall I?" she asked.

"I don't know what will be necessary," I answered. "I imagine Mr. Raymond will take the brunt of it off you. He knows all the circumstances, and can give formal evidence of identification."

The lawyer assented with a little bow. "I really don't think there is anything to dread, Mrs. Ackroyd," he said. "You will be spared all unpleasantness. Now, as to the question of money, have you all you need for the present? I mean," he added, as she looked at him inquiringly, "ready money. Cash, you know. If not, I can arrange to let you have whatever you require."

"That ought to be alright," said Raymond, who was standing by. "Mr. Ackroyd cashed a check for a hundred pounds yesterday."

"Yes. For wages and other expenses due today. At the moment it is still intact."

"Where is this money? In his desk?"

"No, he always kept his cash in his bedroom. In an old collar-box, to be accurate. Funny idea, wasn't it?"

"I think," said the lawyer, "we ought to make sure the money is there before I leave."

"Certainly," agreed the secretary. "I'll take you up now. . . . Oh! I forgot. The door's locked."

Inquiry from Parker elicited the information that Inspector Raglan was in the housekeeper's room asking a few supplementary questions. A few minutes later the inspector joined the party in the hall, bringing the key with him. He unlocked the door and we passed into the lobby and up the small staircase. At the top of the stairs the door into Ackroyd's bedroom stood open. Inside the room it was dark, the curtains were drawn, and the bed was turned down just as it had been last night. The inspector drew the curtains, letting in the sunlight, and Geoffrey Raymond went to the top drawer of a rosewood bureau.

"He kept his money like that, in an unlocked drawer. Just fancy," commented the inspector.

The secretary flushed a little. "Mr. Ackroyd had perfect faith in the honesty of all the servants," he said hotly.

"Oh! Quite so," said the inspector hastily.

Raymond opened the drawer, took out a round leather collar-box from the back of it, and opening it, drew out a thick wallet. "Here is the money," he said, taking out a fat roll of notes. "You will find the hundred intact, I know, for Mr. Ackroyd put it in the collar-box in my presence last night when he was dressing for dinner, and of course it has not been touched since."

Mr. Hammond took the roll and counted it. He looked up sharply. "A hundred pounds, you said. But there is only sixty here."

Raymond stared at him. "Impossible," he cried, springing forward. Taking the notes from the other's hand, he counted them aloud. Mr. Hammond had been right. The total amounted to sixty pounds. "But—I can't understand it," cried the secretary, bewildered.

Poirot asked a question. "You saw Mr. Ackroyd put this money away last night when he was dressing for dinner? You are sure he had not paid away any of it already?"

"I'm sure he hadn't. He even said, 'I don't want to take a hundred pounds down to dinner with me. Too bulgy.'"

"Then the affair is very simple," remarked Poirot. "Either he paid out that forty pounds sometime last evening, or else it has been stolen."

"That's the matter in a nutshell," agreed the inspector. He turned to Mrs. Ackroyd. "Which of the servants would come in here yesterday evening?"

"I suppose the housemaid would turn down the bed."

"Who is she? What do you know about her?"

"She's not been here very long," said Mrs. Ackroyd. "But she's a nice ordinary country girl."

"I think we ought to clear this matter up," said the inspector. "If Mr. Ackroyd paid that money away himself, it may have a bearing on the mystery of the crime. The other servants alright, as far as you know?"

"Oh, I think so."

"Not missed anything before?"

"No."

"None of them leaving, or anything like that?"

"The parlormaid is leaving."

"When?"

"She gave notice yesterday, I believe."

"To you?"

"Oh no. *I* have nothing to do with the servants. Miss Russell attends to the household matters."

The inspector remained lost in thought for a minute or two. Then he nodded his head and remarked, "I think I'd better have a word with Miss Russell, and I'll see the girl Dale as well."

Poirot and I accompanied him to the housekeeper's room. Miss Russell received us with her usual sangfroid.

Elsie Dale had been at Fernly five months. A nice girl, quick at her duties, and most respectable. Good references. The last girl in the world to take anything not belonging to her.

"What about the parlormaid?"

"She, too, was a most superior girl. Very quiet and ladylike. An excellent worker."

"Then why is she leaving?" asked the inspector.

Miss Russell pursed up her lips. "It was none of my doing. I understand Mr. Ackroyd found fault with her yesterday afternoon. It was her duty to do the study, and she disarranged some of the papers on his desk, I believe. He was very annoyed about it, and she gave notice. At least, that is what I understood from her, but perhaps you'd like to see her yourselves?"

The inspector assented. I had already noticed the girl when she was waiting on us at lunch. A tall girl with a lot of brown hair rolled tightly away at the back of her neck, and very steady gray eyes. She came in answer to the housekeeper's summons, and stood very straight with those same gray eyes fixed on us.

"You are Ursula Bourne?" asked the inspector.

"Yes, sir."

"I understand you are leaving."

"Yes, sir."

"Why is that?"

"I disarranged some papers on Mr. Ackroyd's desk. He was very angry about it, and I said I had better leave. He told me to go as soon as possible."

"Were you in Mr. Ackroyd's bedroom at all last night? Tidying up or anything?"

"No, sir. That is Elsie's work. I never went near that part of the house."

"I must tell you, my girl, that a large sum of money is missing from Mr. Ackroyd's room."

At last I saw her roused. A wave of color swept over her face. "I know nothing about any money. If you think I took it, and that that is why Mr. Ackroyd dismissed me, you are wrong."

"I'm not accusing you of taking it, my girl," said the inspector. "Don't flare up so."

The girl looked at him coldly. "You can search my things if you like," she said disdainfully. "But you won't find anything."

Poirot suddenly interposed. "It was yesterday afternoon that Mr. Ackroyd dismissed you—or you dismissed yourself, was it not?" he asked.

The girl nodded.

"How long did the interview last?"

"The interview?"

"Yes, the interview between you and Mr. Ackroyd in the study?"

"I—I don't know."

"Twenty minutes? Half an hour?"

"Something like that."

"Not longer?"

"Not longer than half an hour, certainly."

"Thank you, mademoiselle."

I looked curiously at him. He was rearranging a few objects on the table, setting them straight with precise fingers. His eyes were shining.

"That'll do," said the inspector.

Ursula Bourne disappeared. The inspector turned to Miss Russell. "How long has she been here? Have you got a copy of the reference you had with her?"

Without answering the first question, Miss Russell moved to an adjacent bureau, opened one of the drawers, and took out a handful of letters clipped together with a patent fastener. She selected one and handed it to the inspector.

"H'm," said he. "Reads alright. Mrs. Richard Folliott, Marby Grange, Marby. Who's this woman?"

"Quite good county people," said Miss Russell.

"Well," said the inspector, handing it back, "let's have a look at the other one, Elsie Dale."

Elsie Dale was a big fair girl, with a pleasant but slightly stupid face. She answered our questions readily enough, and showed much distress and concern at the loss of the money.

"I don't think there's anything wrong with her," observed the inspector, after he had dismissed her.

"What about Parker?"

Miss Russell pursed her lips together and made no reply. "I've a feeling there's something wrong about that man," the inspector continued thoughtfully. "The trouble is that I don't quite see when he got his opportunity. He'd be busy with his duties immediately after dinner, and he's got a pretty good alibi all through the evening. I know, for I've been devoting particular attention to it. Well, thank you very much, Miss Russell. We'll leave things as they are for the present. It's highly probable Mr. Ackroyd paid that money away himself."

The housekeeper bade us a dry good afternoon, and we took our leave. I left the house with Poirot.

"I wonder," I said, breaking the silence, "what the papers the girl disarranged could have been for Ackroyd to have got into such a state about them? I wonder if there is any clue there to the mystery."

"The secretary said there were no papers of particular importance on the desk," said Poirot quietly.

"Yes, but—" I paused.

"It strikes you as odd that Ackroyd should have flown into a rage about so trivial a matter?"

"Yes, it does rather."

"But was it a trivial matter?"

"Of course," I admitted, "we don't know what those papers may have been. But Raymond certainly said—"

"Leave M. Raymond out of it for a minute. What did you think of that girl?"

"Which girl? The parlormaid?"

"Yes, the parlormaid. Ursula Bourne."

"She seemed a nice girl," I said hesitatingly.

Poirot repeated my words, but whereas I had laid a slight stress on the fourth word, he put it on the second.

"She *seemed* a nice girl—yes."

Then, after a minute's silence, he took something from his pocket and handed it to me. "See, my friend, I will show you something. Look there."

The paper he had handed me was that compiled by the inspector and given by him to Poirot that morning. Following the pointing finger, I saw a small cross marked in pencil opposite the name Ursula Bourne.

"You may not have noticed it at the time, my good friend, but there was one person on this list whose alibi had no kind of confirmation. Ursula Bourne."

"You don't think—"

"Dr. Sheppard, I dare to think anything. Ursula Bourne may have killed Mr. Ackroyd, but I confess I can see no motive for her doing so. Can you?" He looked at me very hard—so hard that I felt uncomfortable. "Can you?" he repeated.

"No motive whatsoever," I said firmly.

His gaze relaxed. He frowned and murmured to himself: "Since the blackmailer was a man, it follows that she cannot be the blackmailer, then—"

I coughed. "As far as that goes—" I began doubtfully.

He spun around on me. "What? What are you going to say?"

"Nothing. Nothing. Only that, strictly speaking, Mrs. Ferrars in her letter mentioned a *person*—she didn't actually specify a man. But we took it for granted, Ackroyd and I, that it *was* a man."

Poirot did not seem to be listening to me. He was muttering to himself again. "But then it is possible after all—yes, certainly it is possible—but then—ah! I must rearrange my idea. Method, order; never have I needed them more. Everything must fit in—in its appointed place—otherwise I am on the wrong tack." He broke off, and whirled round upon me again. "Where is Marby?"

"It's on the other side of Cranchester."

"How far away?"

"Oh!—Fourteen miles, perhaps."

"Would it be possible for you to go there? Tomorrow, say?"

"Tomorrow? Let me see, that's Sunday. Yes, I could arrange it. What do you want me to do there?"

"See this Mrs. Folliott. Find out all you can about Ursula Bourne."

"Very well. But—I don't much care for the job."

"It is not the time to make difficulties. A man's life may hang on this."

"Poor Ralph," I said with a sigh. "You believe him to be innocent, though?"

Poirot looked at me very gravely. "Do you want to know the truth?"

"Of course."

"Then you shall have it. My friend, everything points to the assumption that he is guilty."

"What!" I exclaimed.

Poirot nodded. "Yes, that stupid inspector—for he is stupid—has everything pointing his way. I seek for the truth—and the truth leads me every time to Ralph Paton. Motive, opportunity, means. But I will leave no stone unturned. I promised Mademoiselle Flora. And she was very sure, that little one. But very sure indeed."

11
Poirot Pays a Call

I WAS SLIGHTLY nervous when I rang the bell at Marby Grange the following afternoon. I wondered very much what Poirot expected to find out. He had entrusted the job to me. Why? Was it because, as in the case of questioning Major Blunt, he wished to remain in the background? The wish, intelligible in the first case, seemed to me quite meaningless here.

My meditations were interrupted by the advent of a smart parlormaid. Yes, Mrs. Folliott was at home. I was ushered into a big drawing-room, and looked round me curiously as I waited for the mistress of the house. A large bare room, some good bits of old china, and some beautiful etchings, shabby covers and curtains. A lady's room in every sense of the term.

I turned from the inspection of a Bartolozzi on the wall as Mrs. Folliott came into the room. She was a tall woman, with untidy brown hair, and a very winning smile. "Dr. Sheppard," she said hesitatingly.

"That is my name," I replied. "I must apologize for calling upon you like this, but I wanted some information about a parlormaid previously employed by you, Ursula Bourne."

With the utterance of the name the smile vanished from her face, and all the cordiality froze out of her manner. She looked uncomfortable and ill at ease. "Ursula Bourne?" she said hesitatingly.

"Yes," I said. "Perhaps you don't remember the name?"

"Oh, yes, of course. I—I remember perfectly."

"She left you just over a year ago, I understand?"

"Yes. Yes, she did. That is quite right."

"And you were satisfied with her whilst she was with you? How long was she with you, by the way?"

"Ah! A year or two—I can't remember exactly how long. She—she is very capable. I'm sure you will find her quite satisfactory. I didn't know she was leaving Fernly. I hadn't the least idea of it."

"Can you tell me anything about her?" I asked.

"Anything about her?"

"Yes, where she comes from, who her people are—that sort of thing?"

Mrs. Folliott's face wore more than ever its frozen look. "I don't know at all."

"Who was she with before she came to you?"

"I'm afraid I don't remember." There was a spark of anger now underlying her nervousness. She flung up her head in a gesture that was vaguely familiar. "Is it really necessary to ask all these questions?"

"Not at all," I said, with an air of surprise and a tinge of apology in my manner. "I had no idea you would mind answering them. I am very sorry."

Her anger left her and she became confused again. "Oh! I don't mind answering them. I assure you I don't. Why should I? It—it just seemed a little odd, you know. That's all. A little odd."

One advantage of being a medical practitioner is that you can usually tell when people are lying to you. I should have known from Mrs. Folliott's manner, if from nothing else, that she did mind answering my questions—minded intensely. She was thoroughly uncomfortable and upset, and there was plainly some mystery in the background. I judged her to be a woman quite unused to deception of any kind, and consequently rendered acutely uneasy when forced to practice it. A child could have seen through her.

But it was also clear that she had no intention of telling me anything further. Whatever the mystery centering around Ursula Bourne might be, I was not going to learn it through Mrs. Folliott. Defeated, I apologized once more for disturbing her, took my hat and departed.

I went to see a couple of patients and arrived home about six o'clock. Caroline was sitting beside the wreck of tea things. She had that look of suppressed exultation on her face which I know only too well. It is a sure sign with her, of either the getting or the giving of information. I wondered which it had been.

"I've had a very interesting afternoon," began Caroline as I dropped into my own particular easy chair, and stretched out my feet to the inviting blaze in the fireplace.

"Have you?" I asked. "Miss Ganett drop in to tea?"

Miss Ganett is one of the chief of our newsmongers.

"Guess again," said Caroline with intense complacency. I guessed several times, working slowly through all the members of Caroline's Intelligence Corps. My sister received each guess with a triumphant shake of the head. In the end she volunteered the information herself.

"M. Poirot!" she said. "Now what do you think of that?"

I thought a good many things of it, but I was careful not to say them to Caroline. "Why did he come?" I asked.

"To see me, of course. He said that knowing my brother so well, he hoped he might be permitted to make the acquaintance of his charming sister—your charming sister, I've got mixed up, but know what I mean."

"What did he talk about?" I asked.

"He told me a lot about himself and his cases. You know that Prince Paul of Mauretania—the one who's just married a dancer?"

"Yes?"

"I saw a most intriguing paragraph about her in Society Snippets the other day, hinting that she was really a Russian Grand Duchess—one of the Czar's daughters who managed to escape from the Bolsheviks. Well, it seems that M. Poirot solved a baffling murder mystery that threatened to involve them both. Prince Paul was beside himself with gratitude."

"Did he give him an emerald tie pin the size of a plover's egg?" I inquired sarcastically.

"He didn't mention it. Why?"

"Nothing," I said. "I thought it was always done. It is in detective fiction anyway. The super detective always has his rooms littered with rubies and pearls and emeralds from grateful Royal clients."

"It's very interesting to hear about these things from the inside," said my sister complacently.

It would be—to Caroline. I could not but admire the ingenuity of M. Hercule Poirot, who had selected unerringly the case of all others that would appeal to an elderly maiden lady living in a small village.

"Did he tell you if the dancer was really a Grand Duchess?" I inquired.

"He was not at liberty to speak," said Caroline importantly.

I wondered how far Poirot has strained the truth in talking to Caroline—probably not at all. He had conveyed his innuendoes by means of his eyebrows and his shoulders.

"And after all this," I remarked. "I suppose you were ready to eat out of his hand."

"Don't be coarse, James. I don't know where you get these vulgar expressions from."

"Probably from my only link with the outside world—my patients.

Unfortunately my practice does not lie amongst Royal princes and interesting Russian emigrés."

Caroline pushed her spectacles up and looked at me. "You seem very grumpy, James. It must be your liver. A blue pill, I think, tonight."

To see me in my own home, you would never imagine that I was a doctor of medicine. Caroline does the home prescribing both for herself and me. "Damn my liver," I said irritably. "Did you talk about the murder at all?"

"Well, naturally, James. What else is there to talk about locally? I was able to set M. Poirot right upon several points. He was very grateful to me. He said I had the makings of a born detective in me—and a wonderful psychological instinct into human nature."

Caroline was exactly like a cat that is full to overflowing with rich cream. She was positively purring. "He talked a lot about the little gray cells of the brain, and of their functions. His own, he says, are of the first quality."

"He would say so," I remarked bitterly. "Modesty is certainly not his middle name."

"I wish you would not be so horribly American, James. He thought it very important that Ralph should be found as soon as possible, and induced to come forward and give an account of himself. He says that his disappearance will produce a very unfortunate impression at the inquest."

"And what did you say to that?"

"I agreed with him," said Caroline importantly. "And I was able to tell him the way people were already talking about it."

"Caroline," I said sharply, "did you tell M. Poirot what you overheard in the wood that day?"

"I did," said Caroline complacently.

I got up and began to walk about. "You realize what you're doing, I hope," I jerked out. "You're putting a halter round Ralph Paton's neck as surely as you're sitting in that chair."

"Not at all," said Caroline, quite unruffled. "I was surprised *you* hadn't told him."

"I took very good care not to," I said. "I'm fond of that boy."

"So am I. That's why I say you're talking nonsense. I don't believe Ralph did it, and so the truth can't hurt him, and we ought to give M. Poirot all the help we can. Why think, very likely Ralph was out with that identical girl on the night of the murder, and if so, he's got a perfect alibi."

"If he's got a perfect alibi," I retorted, "why doesn't he come forward and say so?"

"Might get the girl into trouble," said Caroline sapiently. "But if M. Poirot gets hold of her, and puts it to her as her duty, she'll come forward of her own accord and clear Ralph."

"You seem to have invented a romantic fairy story of your own," I said. "You read too many trashy novels, Caroline. I've always told you so." I dropped into my chair again. "Did Poirot ask you any more questions?" I inquired.

"Only about the patients you had that morning."

"The patients?" I demanded, unbelievingly.

"Yes, your surgery patients. How many and who they were?"

"Do you mean to say you were able to tell him that?" I demanded.

Caroline is really amazing. "Why not?" asked my sister triumphantly. "I can see the path up to the surgery door perfectly from this window. And I've got an excellent memory, James. Much better than yours, let me tell you."

"I'm sure you have," I murmured mechanically.

My sister went on, checking the names on her fingers. "There was old Mrs. Bennett, and that boy from the farm with the bad finger, Dolly Grice to have a needle out of her finger; that American steward off the liner. Let me see—that's four. Yes, and old George Evans with his ulcer. And lastly—" She paused significantly.

"Well?"

Caroline brought out her climax triumphantly. She hissed in the most approved style—aided by the fortunate number of *s*'s at her disposal. *"Miss Russell!"* She sat back in her chair and looked at me meaningly, and when Caroline looks at you meaningly, it is impossible to miss it.

"I don't know what you mean," I said, quite untruthfully. "Why shouldn't Miss Russell consult me about her bad knee?"

"Bad knee," said Caroline. "Fiddlesticks! No more bad knee than you and I. She was after something else."

"What?" I asked.

Caroline had to admit that she didn't know. "But depend upon it, that was what he was trying to get at, M. Poirot, I mean. There's something fishy about that woman, and he knows it."

"Precisely the remark Mrs. Ackroyd made to me yesterday," I said. "That there was something fishy about Miss Russell."

"Ah!" said Caroline darkly, "Mrs. Ackroyd! There's another!"

"Another what?"

Caroline refused to explain her remarks. She merely nodded her head several times, rolled up her knitting and went upstairs to don the high mauve silk blouse and the gold locket which she calls dressing for dinner.

I stayed there staring into the fire and thinking over Caroline's words. Had Poirot really come to gain information about Miss Russell, or was it only Caroline's tortuous mind that interpreted everything according to her own ideas?

There had certainly been nothing in Miss Russell's manner that morning to arouse suspicion. At least—

I remembered her persistent conversation on the subject of drug-taking and from that she had led the conversation to poisons and poisoning. But there was nothing in that. Ackroyd had not been poisoned. Still, it was odd. . . .

I heard Caroline's voice, rather acid in note, calling from the top of the stairs. "James, you will be late for dinner." I put some coal on the fire and went upstairs obediently.

It is well at any price to have peace in the home.

12
Round the Table

A JOINT INQUEST was held on Monday.

I do not propose to give the proceedings in detail. To do so would only be to go over the same ground again and again. By arrangement with the police, very little was allowed to come out. I gave evidence as to the cause of Ackroyd's death and the probable time. The absence of Ralph Paton was commented on by the coroner, but not unduly stressed.

Afterward, Poirot and I had a few words with Inspector Raglan. The inspector was very grave. "It looks bad, Mr. Poirot," he said. "I'm trying to judge the thing fair and square. I'm a local man, and I've seen Captain Paton many times in Cranchester. I'm not wanting him to be the guilty one—but it's bad whichever way you look at it. If he's innocent, why doesn't he come forward? We've got evidence against him, but it's just possible that that evidence could be explained away. Then why doesn't he give an explanation?"

A lot more lay behind the inspector's words than I knew at the time. Ralph's description had been wired to every port and railway station in England. The police everywhere were on the alert. His rooms in town were watched, and any houses he had known to be in the habit of frequenting. With such a *cordon* it seemed impossible that Ralph should be able to evade detection. He had no luggage, and, as far as anyone knew, no money.

"I can't find anyone who saw him at the station that night," continued the inspector. "And yet he's well known down here, and you'd think somebody would have noticed him. There's no news from Liverpool either."

"You think he went to Liverpool?" queried Poirot.

"Well, it's on the cards. That telephone message from the station, just three minutes before the Liverpool express left—there ought to be something in that."

"Unless it was deliberately intended to throw you off the scent. That might just possibly be the point of the telephone message."

"That's an idea," said the inspector eagerly. "Do you really think that's the explanation of the telephone call?"

"My friend," said Poirot gravely, "I do not know. But I will tell you this: I believe that when we find the explanation of that telephone call we shall find the explanation of the murder."

"You said something like that before, I remember," I observed, looking at him curiously.

Poirot nodded. "I always come back to it," he said seriously.

"It seems to me utterly irrelevant," I declared.

"I wouldn't say that," demurred the inspector. "But I must confess I think Mr. Poirot here harps on it a little too much. We've better clues than that. The fingerprints on the dagger, for instance."

Poirot became suddenly very foreign in manner, as he often did when excited over anything. "M. l'Inspecteur," he said, "beware of the blind—the blind—*comment dire!*[1]—the little street that has no end to it."

Inspector Raglan stared, but I was quicker. "You mean a blind alley?" I said.

"That is it—the blind street that leads nowhere. So it may be with those fingerprints—they may lead you nowhere."

"I don't see how that can well be," said the police officer. "I suppose you're hinting that they're faked? I've read of such things being done, though I can't say I've ever come across it in my experience. But fake or true—they're bound to lead *somewhere.*"

Poirot merely shrugged his shoulders, flinging out his arms wide.

The inspector then showed us various enlarged photographs of the fingerprints, and proceeded to become technical on the subject of loops and whorls.

"Come now," he said at last, annoyed by Poirot's detached manner, "you've got to admit that those prints were made by someone who was in the house that night?"

"Bien entendu,"[2] said Poirot, nodding his head.

"Well, I've taken the prints of every member of the household, every one, mind you, from the old lady down to the kitchenmaid."

"I don't think Mrs. Ackroyd would enjoy being referred to as the old lady. She must spend a considerable amount on cosmetics."

"Everyone's," repeated the inspector fussily.

"Including mine," I said dryly.

"Very well. None of them correspond. That leaves us two alternatives. Ralph Paton, or the mysterious stranger the doctor here tells us about. When we get hold of those two—"

"Much valuable time may have been lost," broke in Poirot.

"I don't quite get you, M. Poirot."

"You have taken the prints of everyone in the house, you say," murmured Poirot. "Is that the exact truth you are telling me there, M. L'Inspecteur?"

"Certainly."

"Without overlooking anyone?"

"Without overlooking anyone."

"The quick or the dead?"

For the moment the inspector looked bewildered at what he took to be a religious observation. Then he reacted slowly. "You mean—"

"The dead, M. l'Inspecteur."

The inspector still took a minute or two to understand.

"I am suggesting," said Poirot placidly, "that the fingerprints on the dagger handle are those of Mr. Ackroyd himself. It is an easy matter to verify. His body is still available."

"But why? What would be the point of it. You're surely not suggesting suicide, M. Poirot?"

---

1 How do you say it?—EDITOR.

2 Of course.—EDITOR.

"Ah! No. My theory is that the murderer wore gloves or wrapped something round his hand. After the blow was struck, he picked up the victim's hand and closed it round the dagger handle."

"But why?"

Poirot shrugged his shoulders again. "To make a confusing case even more confusing."

"Well," said the inspector, "I'll look into it. What gave you the idea in the first place."

"When you were so kind as to show me the dagger and draw attention to the fingerprints. I know very little of loops and whorls—see, I confess my ignorance frankly. But it did occur to me that the position of the prints was somewhat awkward. Not so would I have held a dagger in order to strike. Naturally, with the right hand brought up over the shoulder backward, it would have been difficult to put it in exactly the right position."

Inspector Raglan stared at the little man. Poirot, with an air of great unconcern, flecked a speck of dust from his coat sleeve. "Well," said the inspector, "it's an idea. I'll look into it alright, but don't you be disappointed if nothing comes of it."

He endeavored to make his tone kindly and patronizing. Poirot watched him go off. Then he turned to me with twinkling eyes. "Another time," he observed, "I must be more careful of his *armour propre*.[3] And now that we are left to our own devices, what do you think, my good friend, of a little reunion of the family?"

The "little reunion," as Poirot called it, took place about half an hour later. We sat round the table in the dining room at Fernly—Poirot at the head of the table, like the chairman of some ghastly board meeting. The servants were not present, so we were six in all. Mrs. Ackroyd, Flora, Major Blunt, young Raymond, Poirot, and myself.

When everyone was assembled, Poirot rose and bowed. "Messieurs, mesdames, I have called you together for a certain purpose." He paused. "To begin with, I want to make a very special plea to mademoiselle."

"To me?" said Flora.

"Mademoiselle, you are engaged to Captain Ralph Paton. If anyone is in his confidence, you are. I beg you, most earnestly, if you know of his whereabouts, to persuade him to come forward. One little minute"—as Flora raised her head to speak—"say nothing till you have well reflected. Mademoiselle, his position grows daily more dangerous. If he had come forward at once, no matter how damning the facts, he might have had a chance of explaining them away. But this silence—this flight—what can it mean? Surely only one thing, knowledge of guilt. Mademoiselle, if you really believe in his innocence, persuade him to come forward before it is too late."

Flora's face had gone very white. "Too late!" she repeated, very low.

Poirot leant forward, looking at her. "See now, mademoiselle," he said very gently, "it is Papa Poirot who asks you this. The old Papa Poirot who has much knowledge and much experience. I would not seek to entrap you, mademoiselle. Will you not trust me—and tell me where Ralph Paton is hiding?"

---

[3] Self-esteem.—EDITOR.

The girl rose, and stood facing him. "M. Poirot," she said in a clear voice, "I swear to you—swear solemnly—that I have no idea where Ralph is, and that I have neither seen him nor heard from him either on the day of—of the murder, or since."

She sat down again. Poirot gazed at her in silence for a minute or two, then he brought his hand down on the table with a sharp rap. "*Bien!* That is that," he said. His face hardened. "Now I appeal to these others who sit round this table, Mrs. Ackroyd, Major Blunt, Dr. Sheppard, Mr. Raymond. You are all friends and intimates of the missing man. If you know where Ralph Paton is hiding, speak out."

There was a long silence. Poirot looked to each in turn. "I beg of you," he said in a low voice, "speak out."

But still there was silence, broken at last by Mrs. Ackroyd. "I must say," she observed in a plaintive voice, "that Ralph's absence is most peculiar—most peculiar indeed. Not to come forward at such a time. It looks, you know, as though there were something *behind* it. I can't help thinking, Flora dear, that it was a very fortunate thing your engagement was never formally announced."

"Mother!" cried Flora angrily.

"Providence," declared Mrs. Ackroyd. "I have a devout belief in Providence —a divinity that shapes our ends, as Shakespeare's beautiful line runs."

"Surely you don't make the Almighty directly responsible for thick ankles, Mrs. Ackroyd, do you?" asked Geoffrey Raymond, his irresponsible laugh ringing out. His idea was, I think, to loosen the tension, but Mrs. Ackroyd threw him a glance of reproach and took out her handkerchief.

"Flora has been saved a terrible amount of notoriety and unpleasantness. Not for a moment that I think dear Ralph had anything to do with poor Roger's death. I *don't* think so. But then I have a trusting heart—I always have had, ever since a child. I am loath to believe the worst of anyone. But, of course, one must remember that Ralph was in several air raids as a young boy. The results are apparent long after, sometimes, they say. People are not responsible for their actions in the least. They lose control, you know, without being able to help it."

"Mother," cried Flora, "you don't think Ralph did it?"

"Come, Mrs. Ackroyd," said Blunt.

"I don't know what to think," said Mrs. Ackroyd tearfully. "It's all very upsetting. What would happen to the estate, I wonder, if Ralph were found guilty."

Raymond pushed his chair away from the table violently. Major Blunt remained very quiet, looking thoughtfully at her. "Like shellshock, you know," said Mrs. Ackroyd obstinately, "and I dare say Roger kept him very short of money—with the best intentions, of course. I can see you are all against me, but I do think it is very odd that Ralph has not come forward, and I must say I am thankful Flora's engagement was never announced formally."

"It will be tomorrow," said Flora in a clear voice.

"Flora!" cried her mother, aghast. Flora had turned to the secretary. "Will you send the announcement to the *Morning Post* and the *Times,* please, Mr. Raymond?"

"If you are sure that it is wise, Miss Ackroyd," he replied gravely.

She turned impulsively to Blunt. "You understand," she said. "What else can I do? As things are, I must stand by Ralph. Don't you see that I must?" She looked very searchingly at him, and after a long pause he nodded abruptly.

Mrs. Ackroyd burst out into shrill protests. Flora remained unmoved. Then Raymond spoke. "I appreciate your motives, Miss Ackroyd. But don't you think you're being rather precipitate? Wait a day or two."

"Tomorrow," said Flora, in a clear voice. "It's no good, Mother, going on like this. Whatever else I am, I'm not disloyal to my friends."

"M. Poirot," Mrs. Ackroyd appealed tearfully, "can't you say anything at all?"

"Nothing to be said," interpolated Blunt. "She's doing the right thing. I'll stand by her through thick and thin."

Flora held out her hand to him. "Thank you, Major Blunt," she said.

"Mademoiselle," said Poirot, "will you let an old man congratulate you on your courage and your loyalty? And you will not misunderstand me if I ask you—ask you most solemnly—to postpone the announcement you speak of for at least two days more?"

Flora hesitated.

"I ask it in Ralph Paton's interest as much as in yours, mademoiselle. You frown. You do not see how that can be. But I assure you that it is so. *Pas de blagues.*[4] You put the case into my hands—you must not hamper me now."

Flora paused a few minutes before replying. "I do not like it," she said at last, "but I will do what you say." She sat down again at the table.

"And now, *messieurs et mesdames,*" said Poirot rapidly. "I will continue with what I was about to say. Understand this, I mean to arrive at the truth. The truth, however ugly in itself, is always curious and beautiful to the seeker after it. I am much aged, my powers may not be what they were." Here he clearly expected a contradiction. "In all probability this is the last case I shall ever investigate. But Hercule Poirot does not end with a failure. *Messieurs et mesdames,* I tell you, I mean to *know.* And I shall know—in spite of you all."

He brought out the last words provocatively, hurling them in our face as it were. I think we all flinched back a little, excepting Geoffrey Raymond, who remained good humored and imperturbable as usual. "How do you mean—in spite of us all?" he asked, with slightly raised eyebrows.

"But—just that, monsieur. Every one of you in this room is concealing something from me." He raised his hand as a faint murmur of protest arose. "Yes, yes, I know what I am saying. It may be something unimportant—trivial—which is supposed to have no bearing on the case, but there it is. *Each one of you has something to hide.* Come, now, am I right?" His glance, challenging and accusing, swept round the table. And every pair of eyes dropped before his. Yes, mine as well.

---

[4] No tricks now.—EDITOR.

"I am answered," said Poirot, with a curious laugh. He got up from his seat. "I appeal to you all. Tell me the truth—the whole truth." There was a silence. "Will no one speak?" He gave the same short laugh again. *"C'est dommage,"*[5] he said, and went out.

13
The Goose Quill

THAT EVENING, AT Poirot's request, I went over to his house after dinner. Caroline saw me depart with visible reluctance.

Poirot greeted me hospitably. He had placed a bottle of Irish whiskey (which I detest) on a small table, with a soda water siphon and a glass. He himself was engaged in brewing hot chocolate. It was a favorite beverage of his, I discovered later.

He inquired politely after my sister, whom he declared to be a most interesting woman.

"I'm afraid you've been giving her a swelled head," I said dryly. "What about Sunday afternoon?"

He laughed and twinkled. "I always like to employ the expert," he remarked obscurely, but he refused to explain the remark.

"You got all the local gossip anyway," I remarked. "True, and untrue."

"And a great deal of valuable information," he added quietly.

"Such as—?"

He shook his head. "Why not have told me the truth?" he countered. "In a place like this, all Ralph Paton's doings were bound to be known. If your sister had not happened to pass through the wood that day somebody else would have done so."

"I suppose they would," I said grumpily. "What about this interest of yours in my patients?"

Again he twinkled. "Only one of them, doctor. Only one of them."

"The last?" I hazarded.

"I find Miss Russell a study of the most interesting," he said evasively.

"Do you agree with my sister and Mrs. Ackroyd that there is something fishy about her?" I asked.

"Eh? What do you say—fishy?"

I explained to the best of my ability.

"And they say that, do they?"

"Didn't my sister convey as much to you yesterday afternoon?"

"C'est possible."

---

[5] That's a pity.—EDITOR.

"For no reason whatever," I declared.

"Les femmes," generalized Poirot. "They are marvelous! They invent haphazard—and by miracle they are right. Not that it is that, really. Women observe subconsciously a thousand little details, without knowing that they are doing so. Their subsconcious mind adds these little things together—and they call the result intuition. Me, I am very skilled in psychology, I know these things." He swelled his chest out importantly, looking so ridiculous, that I found it difficult not to burst out laughing. Then he took a small sip of his chocolate, and carefully wiped his mustache.

"I wish you'd tell me," I burst out, "what you really think of it all?"

He put down his cup. "You wish that?"

"I do."

"You have seen what I have seen. Should not our ideas be the same?"

"I'm afraid you're laughing at me," I said stiffly. "Of course, I've no experience of matters of this kind."

Poirot smiled at me indulgently. "You are like the little child who wants to know the way the engine works. You wish to see the affair, not as the family doctor sees it, but with the eye of a detective who knows and cares for no one—to whom they are all strangers and all equally liable to suspicion."

"You put it very well," I said.

"So I give you then, a little lecture. The first thing is to get a clear history of what happened that evening—always bearing in mind that the person who speaks may be lying."

I raised my eyebrows. "Rather a suspicious attitude."

"But necessary—I assure you, necessary. Now first—Dr. Sheppard leaves the house at ten minutes to nine. How do I know that?"

"Because I told you so."

"But you might not be speaking the truth—or the watch you went by might be wrong. But Parker also says that you left the house at ten minutes to nine. So we accept that statement and pass on. At nine o'clock you run into a man—and here we come to what we will call the Romance of the Mysterious Stranger—just outside the Park gates. How do I know that that is so?"

"I told you so," I began again, but Poirot interrupted me with a gesture of impatience.

"Ah! But it is that you are a little stupid tonight, my friend. *You* know that it is so—but how am *I* to know? *Eh bien,* I am able to tell you that the Mysterious Stranger was not a hallucination on your part, because the maid of a Miss Ganett met him a few minutes before you did, and of her too he inquired the way to Fernly Park. We accept his presence, therefore, and we can be fairly sure of two things about him—that he was a stranger to the neighborhood, and that whatever his object in going to Fernly, there was no great secrecy about it, since he twice asked the way there."

"Yes," I said. "I see that."

"Now I have made it my business to find out more about this man. He had a drink at the Three Boars, I learn, and the barmaid there says that he spoke with an American accent and mentioned having just come over from the States. Did it strike you that he had an American accent?"

"Yes, I think he had," I said, after a minute or two, during which I cast my mind back; "but a very slight one."

"*Précisément*. There is also this which, you will remember, I picked up in the summerhouse?"

He held out to me the little quill. I looked at it curiously. Then a memory of something I had read stirred in me.

Poirot, who had been watching my face, nodded. "Yes heroin 'snow.' Drug-takers carry it like this, and sniff it up the nose."

"Diamorphine hydrochloride," I murmured mechanically.

"This method of taking the drug is very common on the other side. Another proof, if we wanted one, that the man came from Canada or the States."

"What first attracted your attention to that summer-house?" I asked curiously.

"My friend the inspector took it for granted that anyone using that path did so as a short cut to the house, but as soon as I saw the summerhouse, I realized that the same path would be taken by anyone using the summer-house as a rendezvous. Now it seems fairly certain that the stranger came neither to the front nor to the back door. Then did someone from the house go out and meet him? If so, what could be a more convenient place than that little summerhouse? I searched it with the hope that I might find some clue inside. I found two, the scrap of cambric and the quill."

"And the scrap of cambric?" I asked curiously. "What about that?"

Poirot raised his eyebrows. "You do not use your little gray cells," he remarked dryly. "The scrap of starched cambric should be obvious."

"Not very obvious to me." I changed the subject. "Anyway," I said, "this man went to the summer-house to meet somebody. Who was that somebody?"

"Exactly the question," said Poirot. "You will remember that Mrs. Ackroyd and her daughter came over from Canada to live here?"

"Is that what you meant today when you accused them of hiding the truth?"

"Perhaps. Now another point. What did you think of the parlormaid's story?"

"What story?"

"The story of her dismissal. Does it take half an hour to dismiss a servant? Was the story of those important papers a likely one? And remember, though she says she was in her bedroom from nine-thirty until ten o'clock, there is no one to confirm her statement."

"You bewilder me," I said.

"To me it grows clearer. But tell me now your own ideas and theories."

I drew a piece of paper from my pocket. "I just scribbled down a few suggestions," I said apologetically.

"But excellent—you have method. Let us hear them."

I read out in a somewhat embarrassed voice. "To begin with, one must look at the thing logically—"

"Just what my poor Hastings used to say," murmured Poirot, "but alas! He never did so."

"*Point No.* 1.—Mr. Ackroyd was heard talking to someone at half-past nine.

"*Point No.* 2.—At some time during the evening Ralph Paton must have come in through the window, as evidenced by the prints of his shoes.

"*Point No.* 3.—Mr. Ackroyd was nervous that evening, and would only have admitted someone he knew.

"*Point No.* 4.—The person with Mr. Ackroyd at nine-thirty was asking for money. We know Ralph Paton was in a scrape.

"*These four points go to show that the person with Mr. Ackroyd at nine-thirty was Ralph Paton. But we know that Mr. Ackroyd was alive at a quarter to ten, therefore it was not Ralph who killed him. Ralph left the window open. Afterward the murderer came in that way.*"

"And who was the murderer?" inquired Poirot.

"The American stranger. He may have been in league with Parker, and possibly in Parker we have the man who blackmailed Mrs. Ferrars. If so, Parker may have heard enough to realize the game was up, have told his accomplice so, and the latter did the crime with the dagger which Parker gave him."

"It is a theory that," admitted Poirot. "Decidedly you have cells of a kind. But it leaves a good deal unaccounted for."

"Such as—?"

"The telephone call, the pushed-out chair—"

"Do you really think the latter important?" I interrupted.

"Perhaps not," admitted my friend. "It may have been pulled out by accident, and Raymond or Blunt may have shoved it into place unconsciously under the stress of emotion. Then there is the missing forty pounds."

"Given by Ackroyd to Ralph," I suggested. "He may have reconsidered his first refusal."

"That still leaves one thing unexplained."

"What?"

"Why was Blunt so certain in his own mind that it was Raymond with Mr. Ackroyd at nine-thirty?"

"He explained that," I said.

"You think so? I will not press the point. Tell me instead, what were Ralph Paton's reasons for disappearing?"

"That's rather more difficult," I said slowly. "I shall have to speak as a medical man. Ralph's nerves must have gone phut! If he suddenly found out that his uncle had been murdered within a few minutes of his leaving him—after, perhaps, a rather stormy interview—well, he might get the wind up and clear right out. Men have been known to do that—act guilty when they're perfectly innocent."

"Yes, that is true," said Poirot. "But we must not lose sight of one thing."

"I know what you're going to say," I remarked: "motive. Ralph Paton inherits a great fortune by his uncle's death."

"That is one motive," agreed Poirot.

"One?"

"*Mais oui.* Do you realize that there are separate motives staring us in the face? Somebody certainly stole the blue envelope and its contents. That is one motive. Blackmail! Ralph Paton may have been the man who blackmailed Mrs. Ferrars. Remember, as far as Hammond knew, Ralph Paton had not applied to his uncle for help of late. That looks as though he were being supplied with money elsewhere. Then there is the fact that he was in some—how do you say—scrape?—which he feared might get to his uncle's ears. And finally there is the one you have just mentioned."

"Dear me," I said, rather taken aback. "The case does seem black against him."

"Does it?" said Poirot. "That is where we disagree, you and I. Three motives—it is almost too much. I am inclined to believe that, after all, Ralph Paton is innocent."

14

Mrs. Ackroyd

AFTER THE EVENING talk that I have just chronicled, the affair seemed to me to enter on a different phase. The whole thing can be divided into two parts, each clear and distinct from the other. Part I ranges from Ackroyd's death on the Friday evening to the following Monday night. It is the straightforward narrative of what occurred, as presented to Hercule Poirot. I was at Poirot's elbow the whole time. I saw what he saw. I tried my best to read his mind. As I know now, I failed in this latter task. Though Poirot showed me all his discoveries—as, for instance, the gold wedding-ring—he held back the vital and yet logical impressions that he formed. As I came to know later, this secrecy was characteristic of him. He would throw out hints and suggestions, but beyond that he would not go.

As I say, up till the Monday evening, my narrative might have been that of Poirot himself. I played Watson to his Sherlock. But after Monday our ways diverged. Poirot was busy on his own account. I got to hear of what he was doing, because in King's Abbot, you get to hear of everything, but he did not take me into his confidence beforehand. And I, too, had my own preoccupations.

On looking back, the thing that strikes me most is the piecemeal character of this period. Everyone had a hand in the elucidation of the mystery. It was rather like a jigsaw puzzle to which everyone contributed his own little piece of knowledge or discovery. But their task ended there. To Poirot alone belongs the renown of fitting those pieces into their correct place.

Some of the incidents seemed at the time irrelevant and unmeaning. There was, for instance, the question of the black boots. But that comes later. . . . To take things strictly in chronological order, I must begin with the summons from Mrs. Ackroyd. She sent for me early on Tuesday morning, and since the summons sounded an urgent one, I hastened there, expecting to find her in extremis.

The lady was in bed. So much did she concede to the etiquette of the situation. She gave me her bony hand, and indicated a chair drawn up to the bedside.

"Well, Mrs. Ackroyd," I said to her, "and what's the matter with you?" I spoke with that kind of spurious geniality which seems to be expected of general practitioners.

"I'm prostrated," said Mrs. Ackroyd in a faint voice. "Absolutely prostrated. It's the shock of poor Roger's death. They say these things often aren't felt at the *time,* you know. It's the reaction afterward."

It is a pity that a doctor is precluded by his profession from being able sometimes to say what he really thinks. I would have given anything to be able to answer. "Bunkum!!" Instead, I suggested a tonic. Mrs. Ackroyd accepted the tonic. One move in the game seemed now to be concluded. Not for a moment did I imagine that I had been sent for because of the shock occasioned by Ackroyd's death. But Mrs. Ackroyd is totally incapable of pursuing a straightforward course on any subject. She always approaches her object by tortuous means. I wondered very much why it was she had sent for me.

"And then that scene—yesterday," continued my patient. She paused as though expecting me to take up a cue.

"What scene?"

"Doctor, how can you? Have you forgotten? That dreadful little Frenchman—or Belgian—or whatever he is. Bullying us all like he did. It has quite upset me. Coming on top of Roger's death."

"I'm very sorry, Mrs. Ackroyd," I said.

"I don't know what he meant—shouting at us like he did. I should hope I know my duty too well to *dream* of concealing anything. I have given the police *every* assistance in my power."

Mrs. Ackroyd paused, and I said, "Quite so." I was beginning to have a glimmering of what all the trouble was about.

"No one can say that I have failed in my duty," continued Mrs. Ackroyd. "I am sure Inspector Raglan is perfectly satisfied. Why should this little upstart of a foreigner make a fuss? A most ridiculous-looking creature he is too—just like a comic Frenchman in a revue. I can't think why Flora insisted on bringing him into the case. She never said a word to me about it. Just went off and did it on her own. Flora is too independent. I am a woman of the world and her mother. She should have come to me for advice first."

I listened to all this in silence.

"What does he think? That's what I want to know. Does he actually imagine I'm hiding something? He—he—positively *accused* me yesterday."

I shrugged my shoulders. "It is surely of no consequence, Mrs. Ackroyd," I said. "Since you are not concealing anything, any remarks he may have made do not apply to you."

Mrs. Ackroyd went off at a tangent, after her usual fashion. "Servants are so tiresome," she said. "They gossip, and talk amongst themselves. And then it gets round—and all the time there's probably nothing in it at all."

"Have the servants been talking?" I asked. "What about?"

Mrs. Ackroyd cast a very shrewd glance at me. It quite threw me off my balance. "I was sure *you'd* know, doctor, if anyone did. You were with M. Poirot all the time, weren't you?"

"I was."

"Then of course you know. It was that girl, Ursula Bourne, wasn't it? Naturally—she is leaving. She *would* want to make all the trouble she could. Spiteful, that's what they are. They're all alike. Now, you being there, doctor, you must know exactly what she did say? I'm most anxious that no wrong impression should get about. After all, you don't repeat every little detail to the police, do you? There are family matters sometimes—nothing to do with the question of the murder. But if the girl was spiteful, she may have made out all sorts of things."

I was shrewd enough to see that a very real anxiety lay behind these outpourings. Poirot had been justified in his premises. Of the six people round the table yesterday, Mrs. Ackroyd at least had had something to hide. It was for me to discover what that something might be.

"If I were you, Mrs. Ackroyd," I said brusquely, "I should make a clean breast of things."

She gave a little scream. "Oh! Doctor, how can you be so abrupt! It sounds as though—as though— And I can explain everything so simply."

"Then why not do so?" I suggested.

Mrs. Ackroyd took out a frilled handkerchief, and became tearful. "I thought, doctor, that you might put it to M. Poirot—explain it, you know—because it's so difficult for a foreigner to see our point of view. And you don't know—nobody could know—what I've had to contend with. A martyrdom—a long martyrdom. That's what my life has been. I don't like to speak ill of the dead—but there it is. Not the smallest bill, but it had all to be gone over—just as though Roger had had a few miserly hundreds a year instead of being (as Mr. Hammond told me yesterday) one of the wealthiest men in these parts." Mrs. Ackroyd paused to dab her eyes with the frilled handkerchief.

"Yes," I said encouragingly. "You were talking about bills?"

"Those dreadful bills. And some I didn't like to show Roger at all. They were things a man wouldn't understand. He would have said the things weren't necessary. And of course they mounted up, you know, and they kept coming in—" She looked at me appealingly, as though asking me to condole with her on this striking peculiarity.

"It's a habit they have," I agreed.

And the tone altered—became quite abusive. "I assure you, doctor, I was becoming a nervous wreck. I couldn't sleep at nights. And a dreadful fluttering round the heart. And then I got a letter from a Scotch gentleman—as a matter of fact there were two letters—both Scotch gentlemen. Mr. Bruce MacPherson was one, and the other was Colin MacDonald. Quite a coincidence."

"Hardly that," I said dryly. "They are usually Scotch gentlemen, but I suspect a Semitic strain in their ancestry."

"Ten pounds to ten thousand on note of hand alone," murmured Mrs. Ackroyd reminiscently. "I wrote to one of them, but it seemed there were difficulties." She paused.

I gathered that we were just coming to delicate ground. I have never known anyone more difficult to bring to the point.

"You see," murmured Mrs. Ackroyd, "it's all a question of expectations, isn't it? Testamentary expectations. And though, of course, I expected that

Roger would provide for me, I didn't *know.* I thought that if only I could glance over a copy of his will—not in any sense of vulgar prying—but just so that I could make my own arrangements." She glanced sideways at me. The position was now very delicate indeed. Fortunately words, ingeniously used, will serve to mask the ugliness of naked facts. "I could only tell this to you, dear Dr. Sheppard," said Mrs. Ackroyd rapidly. "I can trust you not to misjudge me, and to represent the matter in the right light to M. Poirot. It was on Friday afternoon—"

She came to a stop and swallowed uncertainly.

"Yes," I repeated encouragingly. "On Friday afternoon. Well?"

"Everyone was out, or so I thought. And I went into Roger's study—I had some real reason for going there—I mean, there was nothing underhand about it. And as I saw all the papers heaped on the desk, it just came to me, like a flash: 'I wonder if Roger keeps his will in one of the drawers of the desk.' I'm so impulsive, always was, from a child. I do things on the spur of the moment. He'd left his keys—very careless of him—in the lock of the top drawer."

"I see," I said helpfully. "So you searched the desk. Did you find the will?"

Mrs. Ackroyd gave a little scream, and I realized that I had not been sufficiently diplomatic. "How dreadful it sounds. But it wasn't at all like that really."

"Of course it wasn't," I said hastily. "You must forgive my unfortunate way of putting things."

"You see, men are so peculiar. In dear Roger's place, I should not have objected to revealing the provisions of my will. But men are so secretive. One is forced to adopt little subterfuges in self-defense."

"And the result of the little subterfuge?" I asked.

"That's just what I'm telling you. As I got to the bottom drawer, Bourne came in. Most awkward. Of course I shut the drawer and stood up, and I called her attention to a few specks of dust on the surface. But I didn't like the way she looked—quite respectful in manner, but a very nasty light in her eyes. Almost contemptuous, if you know what I mean. I never have liked that girl very much. She's a good servant, and she says Ma'am, and doesn't object to wearing caps and aprons (which I declare to you a lot of them do nowadays,) and she can say, 'Not at home' without scruples if she has to answer the door instead of Parker, and she doesn't have those peculiar gurgling noises inside which so many parlormaids seems to have when they wait at table—Let me see, where was I?"

"You were saying, that in spite of several valuable qualities, you never liked Bourne."

"No more I do. She's—odd. There's something different about her from the others. Too well educated, that's my opinion. You can't tell who are ladies and who aren't nowadays."

"And what happened next?" I asked.

"Nothing. At least, Roger came in. And I thought he was out for a walk. And he said: 'What's all this?' and I said, 'Nothing. I just came in to fetch *Punch.*' And I took *Punch* and went out with it. Bourne stayed behind. I heard her asking Roger if she could speak to him for a minute. I went straight up to my room, to lie down. I was very upset."

There was a pause.

"You will explain to M. Poirot, won't you? You can see for yourself what a trivial matter the whole thing was. But, of course, when he was so stern about concealing things, I thought of this at once. Bourne may have made some extraordinary story out of it, but you can explain, can't you?"

"That is all?" I said. "You have told me everything?"

"Ye-es," said Mrs. Ackroyd. "Oh! Yes," she added firmly.

But I had noted the momentary hesitation, and I knew that there was still something she was keeping back. It was nothing less than a flash of sheer genius that prompted me to ask the question I did. "Mrs. Ackroyd," I said, "was it you who left the silver table open?"

I had my answer in the blush of guilt that even rouge and powder could not conceal. "How did you know?" she whispered.

"It was you, then?"

"Yes—I—you see—there were one or two pieces of old silver—very interesting. I had been reading up the subject and there was an illustration of quite a small piece which had fetched an immense sum at Christy's. It looked to me just the same as the one in the silver table. I thought I would take it up to London with me when I went—and—and—have it valued. Then if it really was a valuable piece, just think what a charming surprise it would have been for Roger?"

I refrained from comments, accepting Mrs. Ackroyd's story on its merits. I even forbore to ask her why it was necessary to abstract what she wanted in such a surreptitious manner. "Why did you leave the lid open?" I asked. "Did you forget?"

"I was startled," said Mrs. Ackroyd. "I heard footsteps coming along the terrace outside. I hastened out of the room and just got up the stairs before Parker opened the front door to you."

"That must have been Miss Russell," I said thoughtfully. Mrs. Ackroyd had revealed to me one fact that was extremely interesting. Whether her designs upon Ackroyd's silver had been strictly honorable I neither knew nor cared. What did interest me was the fact that Miss Russell must have entered the drawing room by the window, and that I had not been wrong when I judged her to be out of breath with running. Where had she been? I thought of the summerhouse and the scrap of cambric.

"I wonder if Miss Russell has her handkerchiefs starched!" I exclaimed on the spur of the moment.

Mrs. Ackroyd's start recalled me to myself, and I rose. "You think you can explain to M. Poirot?" she asked anxiously.

"Oh, certainly. Absolutely."

I got away at last, after being forced to listen to more justifications of her conduct.

The parlormaid was in the hall, and it was she who helped me on with my overcoat. I observed her more closely than I had done heretofore. It was clear that she had been crying. "How is it," I asked, "that you told us that Mr. Ackroyd sent for you on Friday to his study? I hear now that it was *you* who asked to speak to *him*?"

For a minute the girl's eyes dropped before mine. Then she spoke. "I meant to leave in any case," she said uncertainly.

I said no more. She opened the front door for me. Just as I was passing out, she said suddenly in a low voice: "Excuse me, sir, is there any news of Captain Paton?" I shook my head, looking at her inquiringly.

"He ought to come back," she said. "Indeed—indeed he ought to come back." She was looking at me with appealing eyes. "Does no one know where he is?" she asked.

"Do you?" I said sharply.

She shook her head. "No, indeed. I know nothing. But anyone who was a friend to him would tell him this: he ought to come back."

I lingered, thinking that perhaps the girl would say more. Her next question surprised me. "When do they think the murder was done? Just before ten o'clock?"

"That is the idea," I said. "Between a quarter to ten and the hour."

"Not earlier? Not before a quarter to ten?"

I looked at her attentively. She was so clearly eager for a reply in the affirmative. "That's out of the question," I said. "Miss Ackroyd saw her uncle alive at a quarter to ten."

She turned away, and her whole figure seemed to droop.

"A handsome girl," I said to myself as I drove off. "An exceedingly handsome girl."

Caroline was at home. She had had a visit from Poirot and was very pleased and important about it. "I am helping him with the case," she explained.

I felt rather uneasy. Caroline is bad enough as it is. What will she be like with her detective instincts encouraged?

"Are you going round the neighborhood looking for Ralph Paton's mysterious girl?" I inquired.

"I might do that on my own account," said Caroline. "No, this is a special thing M. Poirot wants me to find out for him."

"What is it?" I asked.

"He wants to know whether Ralph Paton's boots were black or brown," said Caroline with tremendous solemnity.

I stared at her. I see now that I was unbelievably stupid about these boots. I failed altogether to grasp the point.

"They were brown shoes," I said. "I saw them."

"Not shoes, James, boots. M. Poirot wants to know whether a pair of boots Ralph had with him at the hotel were brown or black. A lot hangs on it."

Call me dense if you like. I didn't see.

"And how are you going to find out?" I asked.

Caroline said there would be no difficulty about that. Our Annie's dearest friend was Miss Ganett's maid, Clara. And Clara was walking out with the Boots at the Three Boars. The whole thing was simplicity itself, and by the aid of Miss Ganett, who cooperated loyally, at once giving Clara a leave of absence, the matter was rushed through at express speed.

It was when we were sitting down to lunch that Caroline remarked, with would-be unconcern: "About those boots of Ralph Paton's."

"Well," I said, "what about them?"

"M. Poirot thought they were probably brown. He was wrong. They're black." And Caroline nodded her head several times. She evidently felt that she had scored a point over Poirot.

I did not answer. I was puzzling over what the color of a pair of Ralph Paton's boots had to do with the case.

15
Geoffrey Raymond

I WAS TO have a further proof that day of the success of Poirot's tactics. That challenge of his had been a subtle touch born of his knowledge of human nature. A mixture of fear and guilt had wrung the truth from Mrs. Ackroyd. She was the first to react.

That afternoon when I returned from seeing my patients, Caroline told me that Geoffrey Raymond had just left.

"Did he want to see me?" I asked, as I hung up my coat in the hall.

Caroline was hovering by my elbow. "It was M. Poirot he wanted to see," she said. "He'd just come from The Larches. M. Poirot was out. Raymond thought that he might be here, or that you might know where he was."

"I haven't the least idea."

"I tried to make him wait," said Caroline, "but he said he would call back at The Larches in half an hour, and went away down the village. A great pity, because M. Poirot came in practically the minute after he left."

"Came in here?"

"No, to his own house."

"How do you know?"

"The side window," said Caroline briefly.

It seemed to me that we had now exhausted the topic. Caroline thought otherwise. "Aren't you going across?"

"Across where?"

"To The Larches, of course."

"My dear Caroline," I said, "what for?"

"Mr. Raymond wanted to see him very particularly," said Caroline. "You might hear what it's all about."

I raised my eyebrows. "Curiosity is not my besetting sin," I remarked coldly. "I can exist comfortably without knowing exactly what my neighbors are doing and thinking."

"Stuff and nonsense, James," said my sister. "You want to know just as much as I do. You're not so honest, that's all. You always have to pretend."

"Really, Caroline," I said, and retired into my surgery.

Ten minutes later Caroline tapped at the door and entered. In her hand she held what seemed to be a pot of jam. "I wonder, James," she said, "if you would mind taking this pot of medlar jelly across to M. Poirot? I promised it to him. He has never tasted any homemade medlar jelly."

"Why can't Annie go?" I asked coldly.

"She's doing some mending. I can't spare her."

Caroline and I looked at each other. "Very well," I said, rising. "But if I take the beastly thing, I shall just leave it at the door. You understand that?"

My sister raised her eyebrows. "Naturally," she said. "Who suggested you should do anything else?"

The honors were with Caroline.

"If you *do* happen to see M. Poirot," she said, as I opened the front door, "you might tell him about the boots."

It was a most subtle parting shot. I wanted dreadfully to understand the enigma of the boots. When the old lady with the Breton cap opened the door to me, I found myself asking if M. Poirot was in, quite automatically.

Poirot sprang up to meet me, with every appearance of pleasure. "Sit down, my good friend," he said. "The big chair? This small one? The room is not too hot, no?"

I thought it was stifling, but refrained from saying so. The windows were closed, and a large fire burned in the grate.

"The English people, they have a mania for the fresh air," declared Poirot. "The big air, it is all very well outside, where it belongs. Why admit it to the house? But let us not discuss such banalities. You have something for me, yes?"

"Two things," I said. "First—this from my sister." I handed over the pot of medlar jelly.

"How kind of Mademoiselle Caroline. She has remembered her promise. And the second thing?"

"Information—of a kind." And I told him of my interview with Mrs. Ackroyd. He listened with interest, but not much excitement.

"It clears the ground," he said thoughtfully. "And it has a certain value as confirming the evidence of the housekeeper. She said, you remember, that she found the silver table lid open and closed it down in passing."

"What about her statement that she went into the drawing room to see if the flowers were fresh?"

"Ah! We never took that very seriously, did we, my friend? It was patently an excuse, trumped up in a hurry, by a woman who felt it urgent to explain her presence—which, by the way, you would probably never have thought of questioning. I considered it possible that her agitation might arise from the fact that she had been tampering with the silver table, but I think now that we must look for another cause."

"Yes," I said. "Whom she did go out to meet? And why?"

"You think she went to meet someone?"

"I do."

Poirot nodded. "So do I," he said thoughtfully.

There was a pause.

"By the way," I said, "I've got a message for you from my sister. Ralph Paton's boots were black, not brown." I was watching him closely as I gave the message, and I fancied that I saw a momentary flicker of discomposure. If so, it passed almost immediately.

"She is absolutely positive they are not brown?"

"Absolutely."

"Ah!" said Poirot regretfully. "That is a pity." And he seemed quite crestfallen.

He entered into no explanations, but at once started a new subject of conversation. "The housekeeper, Miss Russell, who came to consult you on that Friday morning—is it indiscreet to ask what passed at the interview—apart from the medical details, I mean?"

"Not at all," I said. "When the professional part of the conversation was over, we talked for a few minutes about poisons, and the ease or difficulty of detecting them, and about drug-taking and drug-takers."

"With special reference to cocaine?" asked Poirot.

"How did you know?" I asked, somewhat surprised.

For answer, the little man rose and crossed the room to where newspapers were filed. He brought me a copy of the *Daily Budget,* dated Friday, 16th September, and showed me an article dealing with the smuggling of cocaine. It was a somewhat lurid article, written with an eye to picturesque effect. "That is what put cocaine into her head, my friend," he said.

I would have catechized him further, for I did not quite understand his meaning, but at that moment the door opened and Geoffrey Raymond was announced. He came in fresh and debonair as ever, and greeted us both.

"How are you, doctor? M. Poirot, this is the second time I've been here this morning. I was anxious to catch you."

"Perhaps I'd better be off," I suggested rather awkwardly.

"Not on my account, doctor. No, it's just this," he went on, seating himself at a wave of invitation from Poirot. "I've got a confession to make."

"En vérité?" said Poirot, with an air of polite interest.

"Oh, it's of no consequence, really. But, as a matter of fact, my conscience has been pricking me ever since yesterday afternoon. You accused us all of keeping back something, M. Poirot. I plead guilty. I've had something up my sleeve."

"And what is that, M. Raymond?"

"As I say, it's nothing of consequence—just this. I was in debt—badly, and that legacy came in the nick of time. Five hundred pounds puts me on my feet again with a little to spare." He smiled at us both with that engaging frankness that made him such a likeable youngster.

"You know how it is. Suspicious looking policeman—don't like to admit you were hard up for money—think it will look bad to them. But I was a fool, really, because Blunt and I were in the billiard room from a quarter to ten onward, so I've got a watertight alibi and nothing to fear. Still, when you thundered out that stuff about concealing things, I felt a nasty prick of conscience, and I thought I'd like to get it off my mind." He got up again and stood smiling at us.

"You are a very wise young man," said Poirot, nodding at him with approval. "See you, when I know that anyone is hiding things from me, I suspect that the thing hidden may be something very bad indeed. You have done well."

"I'm glad I'm cleared from suspicion," laughed Raymond. "I'll be off now."

"So that is that," I remarked, as the door closed behind the young secretary.

"Yes," agreed Poirot. "A mere bagatelle—but if he had not been in the billiard room—who knows? After all, many crimes have been committed for the sake of less than five hundred pounds. It all depends on what sum is sufficient to break a man. A question of the relativity, is it not so? Have you reflected, my friend, that many people in the house stood to benefit by Mr. Ackroyd's death? Mrs. Ackroyd, Miss Flora, young Mr. Raymond, the housekeeper, Miss Russell. Only one, in fact, does not, Major Blunt."

His tone in uttering that name was so peculiar that I looked up, puzzled. "I don't quite understand you," I said.

"Two of the people I accused have given me the truth."

"You think Major Blunt has something to conceal also?"

"As for that," remarked Poirot nonchalantly, "there is a saying, is there not, that Englishmen conceal only one thing—their love? And Major Blunt, I should say, is not good at concealments."

"Sometimes," I said, "I wonder if we haven't rather jumped to conclusions on one point."

"What is that?"

"We've assumed that the blackmailer of Mrs. Ferrars is necessarily the murderer of Mr. Ackroyd. Mightn't we be mistaken?"

Poirot nodded energetically. "Very good. Very good indeed. I wondered if that idea would come to you. Of course it is possible. But we must remember one point. The letter disappeared. Still, that, as you say, may not necessarily mean that the murderer took it. When you first found the body, Parker may have abstracted the letter unnoticed by you."

"Parker?"

"Yes, Parker. I always come back to Parker—not as the murderer—no, he did not commit the murder; but who is more suitable than he as the mysterious scoundrel who terrorized Mrs. Ferrars? He may have got his information about Mr. Ferrars's death from one of the King's Paddock servants. At any rate, he is more likely to have come upon it than a casual guest such as Blunt, for instance."

"Parker might have taken the letter," I admitted. "It wasn't till later that I noticed it was gone."

"How much later? After Blunt and Raymond were in the room, or before?"

"I can't remember," I said slowly. "I think it was before—no, afterward. Yes, I'm almost sure it was afterward."

"That widens the field to three," said Poirot thoughtfully. "But Parker is the most likely. It is in my mind to try a little experiment with Parker. How say you, my friend, will you accompany me to Fernly?"

I acquiesced, and we set out at once. Poirot asked to see Miss Ackroyd, and presently Flora came to us.

"Mademoiselle Flora," said Poirot, "I have to confide in you a little secret. I am not yet satisfied of the innocence of Parker. I propose to make a little experiment with your assistance. I want to reconstruct some of his actions on that night. But we must think of something to tell him—ah! I have it. I wish to satisfy myself as to whether voices in the little lobby could have been heard outside on the terrace. Now, ring for Parker, if you will be so good."

I did so, and presently the butler appeared, suave as ever.

"You rang, sir?"

"Yes, my good Parker. I have in mind a little experiment. I have placed Major Blunt on the terrace outside the study window. I want to see if anyone there could have heard the voices of Miss Ackroyd and yourself in the lobby that night. I want to enact that little scene over again. Perhaps you would fetch the tray or whatever it was you were carrying."

Parker vanished, and we repaired to the lobby outside the study door. Presently we heard a chink in the outer hall, and Parker appeared in the doorway carrying a tray with a siphon, a decanter of whiskey, and two glasses on it.

"One moment," cried Poirot, raising his hand and seemingly very excited. "We must have everything in order. Just as it occurred. It is a little method of mine."

"A foreign custom, sir," said Parker. "Reconstruction of the crime they call it, do they not?" He was quite imperturbable as he stood there politely waiting on Poirot's orders.

"Ah! He knows something, the good Parker," cried Poirot. "He has read of these things. Now, I beg you, let us have everything of the most exact. You came from the outer hall—so. Mademoiselle was—where?"

"Here," said Flora, taking up her stand just outside the study door.

"Quite right, sir," said Parker.

"I had just closed the door," continued Flora.

"Yes, miss," agreed Parker. "Your hand was still on the handle as it is now."

"Then *allez,*" said Poirot. "Play me the little comedy."

Flora stood with her hand on the door handle, and Parker came stepping through the door from the hall, bearing the tray. He stopped just inside the door. Flora spoke. "Oh! Parker. Mr. Ackroyd doesn't want to be disturbed again tonight. Is that right?" she added in an undertone.

"To the best of my recollection, Miss Flora," said Parker, "but I fancy you used the word evening instead of night." Then, raising his voice in a somewhat theatrical fashion: "Very good, miss. Shall I lock up as usual?"

"Yes, please."

Parker retired through the door, Flora followed him, and started to ascend the main staircase. "Is that enough?" she asked over her shoulder.

"Admirable," declared the little man, rubbing his hands. "By the way, Parker, are you sure there were two glasses on the tray that evening? Who was the second one for?"

"I always bring two glasses, sir," said Parker. "Is there anything further?"

"Nothing. I thank you."

Parker withdrew, dignified to the last.

Poirot stood in the middle of the hall frowning. Flora came down and joined us. "Has your experiment been successful?" she asked. "I don't quite understand, you know—"

Poirot smiled admiringly at her. "It is not necessary that you should," he said. "But tell me, were there indeed two glasses on Parker's tray that night?"

Flora wrinkled her brows a minute. "I really can't remember," she said. "I think there were. Is—is that the object of your experiment?"

Poirot took her hand and patted it. "Put it this way," he said. "I am always interested to see if people will speak the truth."

"And did Parker speak the truth?"

"I rather think he did," said Poirot thoughtfully.

A few minutes later saw us retracing our steps to the village. "What was the point of that question about the glasses?" I asked curiously.

Poirot shrugged his shoulders. "One must say something," he remarked. "That particular question did as well as any other."

I stared at him.

"At any rate, my friend," he said more seriously, "I know now something I wanted to know. Let us leave it at that."

16
An Evening at Mah Jong

THAT NIGHT WE had a little Mah Jong party. This kind of simple entertainment is very popular in King's Abbot. The guests arrive in galoshes and waterproofs after dinner. They partake of coffee and later of cake, sandwiches, and tea.

On this particular night our guests were Miss Ganett and Colonel Carter, who lives near the church. A good deal of gossip is handed round at these evenings, sometimes seriously interfering with the game in progress. We used to play bridge—chatty bridge of the worst description. We find Mah Jong much more peaceful. The irritated demand as to why on earth your partner did not lead a certain card is entirely done away with, and though we still express criticisms frankly, there is not the same acrimonious spirit.

"Very cold evening, eh, Sheppard?" said Colonel Carter, standing with his back to the fire. Caroline had taken Miss Ganett to her own room, and was there assisting her to disentangle herself from her many wraps. "Reminds me of the Afghan passes."

"Indeed?" I said politely.

"Very mysterious business this about poor Ackroyd," continued the colonel, accepting a cup of coffee. "A deuce of a lot behind it—that's what I say. Between you and me, Sheppard, I've heard the word blackmail mentioned!" The colonel gave me the look which might be tabulated "one man of the world to another." "A woman in it, no doubt," he said. "Depend upon it, a woman in it."

Caroline and Miss Ganett joined us at this minute. Miss Ganett drank coffee whilst Caroline got out the Mah Jong box and poured the tiles upon the table. "Washing the tiles," said the colonel facetiously. "That's right—washing the tiles, as we used to say in the Shanghai Club."

It is the private opinion of both Caroline and myself that Colonel Carter has never been in the Shanghai Club in his life. More, that he has never been farther east than India, where he juggled with tins of bully beef and plum and apple jam during the Great War. But the colonel is determinedly military, and in King's Abbot we permit people to indulge their little idiosyncracies freely.

"Shall we begin?" said Caroline.

We sat round the table. For some five minutes there was complete silence, owing to the fact that there is tremendous secret competition amongst us as to who can build their wall quickest.

"Go on, James," said Caroline at last. "You're East Wind."

I discarded a tile. A round or two proceeded, broken by the monotonous remarks of "Three Bamboos," "Two Circles," "Pung," and frequently from Miss Ganett, "Unpung," owing to that lady's habit of too hastily claiming tiles to which she had no right.

"I saw Flora Ackroyd this morning," said Miss Ganett. "Pung—no—Unpung. I made a mistake."

"Four Circles," said Caroline. "Where did you see her?"

"She didn't see *me,"* said Miss Ganett, with that tremendous significance only to be met with in small villages.

"Ah!" said Caroline interestedly. "Chow."

"I believe," said Miss Gannet, temporarily diverted, "that it's the right thing nowadays to say 'Chee' not 'Chow.'"

"Nonsense," said Caroline. "I have always said 'Chow.'"

"In the Shanghai Club," said Colonel Carter, "they say 'Chow.'" Miss Ganett retired, crushed.

"What were you saying about Flora Ackroyd?" asked Caroline, after a moment or two devoted to the game. "Was she with anyone?"

"Very much so," said Miss Ganett.

The eyes of the two ladies met, and seemed to exchange information. "Really," said Caroline interestedly. "Is that it? Well, it doesn't surprise me in the least."

"We're waiting for you to discard, Miss Caroline," said the colonel. He sometimes affects the pose of the bluff male, intent on the game and indifferent to gossip. But nobody is deceived.

"If you ask me," said Miss Ganett. ("Was that a Bamboo you discarded, dear? Oh! No, I see now—it was a Circle.) As I was saying, if you ask me, Flora's been exceedingly lucky. Exceedingly lucky she's been."

"How's that, Miss Ganett?" asked the colonel. "I'll Pung that Green Dragon. How do you make out that Miss Flora's been lucky? Very charming girl and all that, I know."

"I mayn't know very much about crime," said Miss Ganett, with the air of one who knows everything there is to know, "but I can tell you one thing. The first question that's always asked is: 'Who last saw the deceased alive?' And the person who did is regarded with suspicion. Now, Flora Ackroyd last saw her uncle alive. It might have looked very nasty for her—very nasty indeed. It's my opinion—and I give it for what it's worth, that Ralph Paton is staying away on her account, to draw suspicion away from her."

"Come, now," I protested mildly, "you surely can't suggest that a young girl like Flora Ackroyd is capable of stabbing her uncle in cold blood?"

"Well, I don't know," said Miss Ganett. "I've just been reading a book from the library about the underworld of Paris, and it says that some of the worst women criminals are young girls with the faces of angels."

"That's in France," said Caroline instantly.

"Just so," said the colonel. "Now, I'll tell you a very curious thing—a story that was going around the Bazaars in India. . . ."

The colonel's story was one of interminable length, and of curiously little interest. A thing that happened in India many years ago cannot compare for a moment with an event that took place in King's Abbot the day before yesterday.

It was Caroline who brought the colonel's story to a close by fortunately going Mah Jong. After the slight unpleasantness always occasioned by my corrections of Caroline's somewhat faulty arithmetic, we started a new hand.

"East Wind passes," said Caroline. "I've got an idea of my own about Ralph Paton. Three Characters. But I'm keeping it to myself for the present."

"Are you, dear?" said Miss Gannett. "Chow—I mean Pung."

"Yes," said Caroline firmly.

"Was it alright about the boots?" said Miss Ganett. "Their being black, I mean?"

"Quite alright," said Caroline.

"What was the point, do you think?" asked Miss Ganett.

Caroline pursed her lips, and shook her head with an air of knowing all about it.

"Pung," said Miss Ganett. "No—Unpung. I suppose that now the doctor's in with M. Poirot he knows all the secrets?"

"Far from it," I said.

"James is so modest," Caroline. "Ah! A concealed Kong."

The colonel gave vent to a whistle. For the moment gossip was forgotten. "Your own Wind, too," he said. "*And* you've got two Pungs of Dragons. We must be careful. Miss Caroline's out for a big hand."

We played for some minutes with no irrelevant conversation. "This M. Poirot now," said Colonel Carter, "is he really such a great detective?"

"The greatest the world has ever known," said Caroline solemnly. "He had to come here incognito to avoid publicity."

"Chow," said Miss Ganett. "Quite wonderful for our little village, I'm sure. By the way, Clara—my maid, you know—is great friends with Elsie, the housemaid at Fernly, and what do you think Elsie told her? That there's been a lot of money stolen, and it's her opinion—Elsie's—I mean, that the parlormaid had something to do with it. She's leaving at the month, and she's crying a good deal at night. If you ask me, the girl is very likely in league with a gang. She's always been a queer girl—she's not friends with any of the girls round here. She goes off by herself on her days out—very unnatural, I call it and most suspicious. I asked her once to come to our Girls' Friendly Evenings, but she refused, and then I asked her a few questions about her home and her family—all that sort of thing, and I'm bound to say I consider her manner most impertinent. Outwardly very respectful—but she shut me up in the most barefaced way."

Miss Ganett stopped for breath, and the colonel, who was totally uninterested in the servant question, remarked that in the Shanghai Club brisk play was the inevitable rule.

We had a round of brisk play.

"That Miss Russell," said Caroline. "She came here pretending to consult James on Friday morning. It's my opinion she wanted to see where the poisons were kept. Five Characters."

"Chow," said Miss Ganett. "What an extraordinary idea? I wonder if you can be right."

"Talking of poisons," said the colonel. "Eh—what? Haven't I discarded? Oh! Eight Bamboos."

"Mah Jong!" said Miss Ganett.

Caroline was very much annoyed. "One Red Dragon," she said regretfully, "and I should have had a hand of three doubles."

"I've had two Red Dragons all the time," I mentioned.

"So exactly like you, James," said Caroline reproachfully. "You've no conception of the spirit of the game."

I myself thought I had played rather cleverly. I should have had to pay Caroline an enormous amount if she had gone Mah Jong. Miss Ganett's Mah Jong was of the poorest variety possible, as Caroline did not fail to point out to her.

East Wind passed, and we started a new hand in silence.

"What I was going to tell you just now was this," said Caroline.

"Yes?" said Miss Ganett encouragingly.

"My idea about Ralph Paton, I mean."

"Yes, dear," said Miss Ganett, still more encouragingly. "Chow."

"It's a sign of weakness to Chow so early," said Caroline severely. "You should go for a big hand."

"I know," said Miss Ganett. "You were saying—about Ralph Paton, you know."

"Yes. Well, I've a pretty shrewd idea where he is."

We all stopped to stare at her.

"This is very interesting, Miss Caroline," said Colonel Carter. "All your own idea, eh?"

"Well, not exactly. I'll tell you about it. You know that big map of the county we have in the hall?" We all said Yes.

"As M. Poirot was going out the other day, he stopped and looked at it, and he made some remark—I can't remember exactly what it was. Something about Cranchester being the only big town anywhere near us—which is true, of course. But after he had gone—it came to me suddenly."

"What came to you?"

"His meaning. Of course Ralph is in Cranchester."

It was at that moment that I knocked down the rack that held my pieces. My sister immediately reproved me for clumsiness, but halfheartedly. She was intent on her theory.

"Cranchester, Miss Caroline?" said Colonel Carter. "Surely not Cranchester! It's so near."

"That's exactly it," cried Caroline triumphantly. "It seems quite clear by now that he didn't get away from here by train. He must simply have walked into Cranchester. And I believe he's there still. No one would dream of his being so near at hand." I pointed out several objections to the theory, but when once Caroline has got something firmly into her head, nothing dislodges it.

"And you think M. Poirot has the same idea," said Miss Ganett thoughtfully. "It's a curious coincidence, but I was out for a walk this afternoon on the Cranchester road, and he passed me in a car coming from that direction."

We all looked at each other.

"Why, dear me," said Miss Ganett suddenly. "I'm Mah Jong all the time, and I never noticed it."

Caroline's attention was distracted from her own inventive exercises. She pointed out to Miss Ganett that a hand consisting of mixed suits and too many Chows was hardly worth going Mah Jong on. Miss Ganett listened imperturbably and collected her counters. "Yes, dear, I know what you mean," she said. "But it rather depends on what kind of a hand you have to start with, doesn't it?"

"You'll never get the big hands if you don't go for them," urged Caroline.

"Well, we must all play our own way, mustn't we?" said Miss Ganett. She looked down at her counters. "After all, I'm up, so far."

Caroline, who was considerably down, said nothing.

East Wind passed, and we set to once more. Annie brought in the tea things. Caroline and Miss Ganett were both slightly ruffled as is often the case during one of these festive evenings.

"If you would play a little quicker, dear," said Caroline, as Miss Ganett hesitated over her discard. "The Chinese put down the tiles so quickly it sounds like little birds pattering."

For some few minutes we played like the Chinese.

"You haven't contributed much to the sum of information, Sheppard," said Colonel Carter genially. "You're a sly dog. Hand in glove with the great detective, and not a hint as to the way things are going."

"James is an extraordinary creature," said Caroline. "He can *not* bring himself to part with information." She looked at me with some disfavor.

"I assure you," I said, "that I don't know anything. Poirot keeps his own counsel."

"Wise man," said the colonel with a chuckle. "He doesn't give himself away. But they're wonderful fellows, these foreign detectives. Up to all sorts of dodges, I believe."

"Pung," said Miss Ganett, in a tone of quiet triumph. "And Mah Jong."

The situation became more strained. It was annoyance at Miss Ganett's going Mah Jong for the third time running which prompted Caroline to say to me as we built a fresh wall: "You are too tiresome, James. You sit there like a dead head, and say nothing at all."

"But, my dear," I protested, "I have really nothing to say—that is, of the kind you mean."

"Nonsense," said Caroline, as she sorted her hand. "You *must* know something interesting."

I did not answer for a moment. I was overwhelmed and intoxicated. I had read of there being such a thing as the Perfect Winning—going Mah Jong on one's original hand. I had never hoped to hold the hand myself. With suppressed triumph I laid my hand face upwards on the table. "As they say in the Shanghai Club," I remarked. "Tin-ho—the Perfect Winning!"

The colonel's eyes nearly bulged out of his head.

"Upon my soul," he said. "What an extraordinary thing. I never saw that happen before!"

It was then that I went on, goaded by Caroline's gibes, and rendered reckless by my triumph. "And as to anything interesting," I said. "What about a gold wedding ring with a date and 'From R.' inside?" I pass over the scene that followed. I was made to say exactly where this treasure was found. I was made to reveal the date.

"March 13th," said Caroline. "Just six months ago. Ah!"

Out of the babel of excited suggestions and suppositions three theories were evolved:—

1. That of Colonel Carter: that Ralph was secretly married to Flora. The first or most simple solution.

2. That of Miss Ganett: that Roger Ackroyd had been secretly married to Mrs. Ferrars.

3. That of my sister: that Roger Ackroyd had married his housekeeper, Miss Russell.

A fourth or super-theory was propounded by Caroline later as we went up to bed. "Mark my words," she said suddenly. "I shouldn't be at all surprised if Geoffrey Raymond and Flora weren't married."

"Surely it would be 'From G,' not 'From R' then," I suggested.

"You never know. Some girls call men by their surnames. And you heard what Miss Ganett said this evening—about Flora's carryings on."

Strictly speaking, I had not heard Miss Ganett say anything of the kind, but I respected Caroline's knowledge of innuendoes. "How about Hector Blunt," I hinted. "If it's anybody—"

"Nonsense," said Caroline. "I dare say he admires her—may even be in love with her. But depend upon it a girl isn't going to fall in love with a man old enough to be her father when there's a good-looking young secretary about. She may encourage Major Blunt just as a blind. Girls are very artful. But there's one thing I *do* tell you, James Sheppard, Flora Ackroyd does not care a penny piece for Ralph Paton, and never has. You can take it from me."

I took it from her meekly.

17
Parker

IT OCCURRED TO me the next morning that under the exhilaration produced by Tin-ho, or the Perfect Winning, I might have been slightly indiscreet. True, Poirot had not asked me to keep the discovery of the ring to myself. On the other hand, he had said nothing about it whilst at Fernly, and as far as I knew, I was the only person aware that it had been found. I felt distinctly guilty. The fact was by now spreading through King's Abbot like wildfire. I was expecting wholesale reproaches from Poirot any minute.

The joint funeral of Mrs. Ferrars and Roger Ackroyd was fixed for eleven o'clock. It was a melancholy and impressive ceremony. All the party from Fernly were there.

After it was over, Poirot, who had also been present, took me by the arm, and invited me to accompany him back to The Larches. He was looking very grave, and I feared that my indiscretion of the night before had got round to his ears. But it soon transpired that his thoughts were occupied by something of a totally different nature.

"See you," he said. "We must act. With your help I propose to examine a witness. We will question him, we will put such fear into him that the truth is bound to come out."

"What witness are you talking of?" I asked, very much surprised.

"Parker!" said Poirot. "I asked him to be at my house this morning at twelve o'clock. He should await us there at this very minute."

"What do you think?" I ventured, glancing sideways at his face.

"I know this—that I am not satisfied."

"You think that it was he who blackmailed Mrs. Ferrars?"

"Either that, or—"

"Well?" I said, after waiting a minute or two.

"My friend, I will say this to you—I hope it was he." The gravity of his manner, and something indefinable that tinged it, reduced me to silence.

On arrival at The Larches, we were informed that Parker was already there awaiting our return. As we entered the room, the butler rose respectfully.

"Good morning, Parker," said Poirot pleasantly. "One instant, I pray of you." He removed his overcoat and gloves.

"Allow me, sir," said Parker, and sprang forward to assist him. He deposited the articles neatly on a chair by the door. Poirot watched him with approval.

"Thank you, my good Parker," he said. "Take a seat, will you not? What I have to say may take some time."

Parker seated himself with an apologetic bend of the head.

"Now what do you think I asked you to come here for this morning—eh?"

Parker coughed. "I understood, sir, that you wished to ask me a few questions about my late master—private like."

"Précisément," said Poirot, beaming. "Have you made many experiments in blackmail?"

"Sir!" The butler sprang to his feet.

"Do not excite yourself," said Poirot placidly. "Do not play the farce of the honest, injured man. You know all there is to know about the blackmail, is it not so?"

"Sir, I—I've never—I've never been—"

"Insulted," suggested Poirot, "in such a way before. Then why, my excellent Parker, were you so anxious to overhear the conversation in Mr. Ackroyd's study the other evening, after you had caught the word blackmail?"

"I wasn't—I—"

"Who was your last master?" rapped out Poirot suddenly.

"My last master?"

"Yes, the master you were with before you came to Mr. Ackroyd."

"A Major Ellerby, sir—"

Poirot took the words out of his mouth, "Just so, Major Ellerby. Major Ellerby was addicted to drugs, was he not? You traveled about with him. When he was in Bermuda there was some trouble—a man was killed. Major Ellerby was partly responsible. It was hushed up. But you knew about it. How much did Major Ellerby pay you to keep your mouth shut?"

Parker was staring at him openmouthed. The man had gone to pieces, his cheeks shook flabbily.

"You see, me, I have made inquiries," said Poirot pleasantly. "It is as I say. You got a good sum then as blackmail, and Major Ellerby went on paying you until he died. Now I want to hear about your latest experiment."

Parker still stared.

"It is useless to deny. Hercule Poirot *knows.* It is so, what I have said about Major Ellerby, is it not?"

As though against his will, Parker nodded reluctantly once. His face was ashen pale. "But I never hurt a hair of Mr. Ackroyd's head," he moaned. "Honest to God, sir, I didn't. I've been afraid of this coming all the time. And I tell you I didn't—I didn't kill him." His voice rose almost to a scream.

"I am inclined to believe you, my friend," said Poirot. "You have not the nerve—the courage. But I must have the truth."

"I'll tell you anything, sir, anything you want to know. It's true that I tried to listen that night. A word or two I heard made me curious. And Mr. Ackroyd's wanting not to be disturbed, and shutting himself up with the doctor the way he did. It's God's own truth what I told the police. I heard the word blackmail, sir, and well—" He paused.

"You thought there might be something in it for you?" suggested Poirot smoothly.

"Well—well, yes, I did, sir. I thought that if Mr. Ackroyd was being blackmailed, why shouldn't I have a share of the pickings?"

A very curious expression passed over Poirot's face. He leaned forward. "Had you any reason to suppose before that night that Mr. Ackroyd was being blackmailed?"

"No, indeed, sir. It was a great surprise to me. Such a regular gentleman in all his habits."

"How much did you overhear?"

"Not very much, sir. There seemed what I might call a spite against me. Of course I had to attend to my duties in the pantry. And when I did creep along once or twice to the study it was no use. The first time Dr. Sheppard came out and almost caught me in the act, and another time Mr. Raymond passed me in the big hall and went that way, so I knew it was no use; and when I went with the tray, Miss Flora headed me off."

Poirot stared for a long time at the man, as if to test his sincerity. Parker returned his gaze earnestly. "I hope you believe me, sir. I've been afraid all along the police would rake up that old business with Major Ellerby and be suspicious of me in consequence."

"Eh bien," said Poirot at last. "I am disposed to believe you. But there is one thing I must request of you—to show me your bank-book. You have a bank-book, I presume?"

"Yes, sir, as a matter of fact, I have it with me now." With no sign of confusion, he produced it from his pocket. Poirot took the slim, green-covered book and perused the entries.

"Ah! I perceived you have purchased £500 of National Savings Certificates this year?"

"Yes, sir. I have already over a thousand pounds saved—the result of my connection with—er—my late master, Major Ellerby. And I have had quite a little flutter on some horses this year—very successful. If you remember, sir, a rank outsider won the Jubilee. I was fortunate enough to back it—£20."

Poirot handed him back the book. "I will wish you good-morning. I believe that you have told me the truth. If you have not—so much the worse for you, my friend."

When Parker had departed, Poirot picked up his overcoat once more.

"Going out again?" I asked.

"Yes, we will pay a little visit to the good Mr. Hammond."

"You believe Parker's story?"

"It is credible enough on the face of it. It seems clear that—unless he is a very good actor indeed—he genuinely believes it was Ackroyd himself who was the victim of blackmail. If so, he knows nothing at all about the Mrs. Ferrars business."

"Then in that case—who—"

"Précisément! Who? But our visit to M. Hammond will accomplish one purpose. It will either clear Parker completely or else—"

"Well?"

"I fall into the bad habit of leaving my sentences unfinished this morning," said Poirot apologetically. "You must bear with me."

"By the way," I said, rather sheepishyly, "I've got a confession to make. I'm afraid I have inadvertently let out something about that ring."

"What ring?"

"The ring you found in the goldfish pond."

"Ah! Yes," said Poirot, smiling broadly.

"I hope you're not annoyed? It was very careless of me."

"But not at all, my good friend, not at all. I laid no commands upon you. You were at liberty to speak of it if you so wished. She was interested, your sister?"

"She was indeed. It created a sensation. All sorts of theories are flying about."

"Ah! And yet it is so simple. The true explanation leapt to the eye, did it not?"

"Did it?" I said dryly.

Poirot laughed. "The wise man does not commit himself," he observed. "Is that not so? But here we are at Mr. Hammond's."

The lawyer was in his office, and we were ushered in without any delay. He rose and greeted us in his dry, precise manner.

Poirot came at once to the point. "Monsieur, I desire from you certain information, that is, if you will be so good as to give it to me. You acted, I understand, for the late Mrs. Ferrars of King's Paddock?"

I noticed the swift gleam of surprise which showed in the lawyer's eyes, "Certainly. All her affairs passed through our hands."

"Very good. Now, before I ask you to tell me anything, I should like you to listen to the story Dr. Sheppard will relate to you. You have no objection, have you, my friend, to repeating the conversation you had with Mr. Ackroyd last Friday night?"

"Not in the least," I said, and straightway began the recital of that strange evening.

Hammond listened with close attention.

"That is all," I said, when I had finished.

"Blackmail," said the lawyer thoughtfully.

"You are surprised?" asked Poirot.

The lawyer took off his pince-nez and polished them with his handkerchief. "No," he replied, "I can hardly say that I am surprised. I have suspected something of the kind for some time."

"That brings us," said Poirot, "to the information for which I am asking. If any one can give us an idea of the actual sums paid, you are the man, monsieur."

"I see no object in withholding the information," said Hammond, after a moment or two. "During the past year, Mrs. Ferrars had sold out certain securities, and the money for them was paid into her account and not reinvested. As her income was a large one, and she lived very quietly after her husband's death, it seems certain that these sums of money were paid away for some special purpose. I once sounded her on the subject, and she said that she was obliged to support several of her husband's poor relations. I let the matter drop, of course. Until now, I have always imagined that the money was paid to some woman who had had a claim on Ashley Ferrars. I never dreamed that Mrs. Ferrars herself was involved."

"And the amount?" asked Poirot.

"In all, I should say the various sums totaled at least twenty thousand pounds."

"Twenty thousand pounds!" I exclaimed. "In one year!"

"Mrs. Ferrars was a very wealthy woman," said Poirot dryly. "And the penalty for murder is not a pleasant one."

"Is there anything else that I can tell you?" inquired Mr. Hammond.

"I thank you, no," said Poirot, rising. "All my excuses for having deranged you."

"Not at all, not at all."

"The word derange," I remarked, when we were outside again, "is applicable to mental disorder only."

"Ah!" cried Poirot, "never will my English be quite perfect. A curious language. I should then have said disarranged, *n'est ce pas?*"

"Disturbed is the word you had in mind."

"I thank you, my friend. The word exact, you are zealous for it. *Eh bien,* what about our friend Parker, now? With twenty thousand pounds in hand, would he have continued being a butler? *Je ne pense pas.* It is, of course, possible that he banked the money under another name, but I am disposed to believe he spoke the truth to us. If he is a scoundrel, he is a scoundrel on a mean scale. He has not the big ideas. That leaves us as a possibility, Raymond or—well—Major Blunt."

"Surely not Raymond," I objected. "Since we know that he was desperately hard up for a matter of five hundred pounds."

"That is what he says, yes."

"And as to Hector Blunt—"

"I will tell you something as to the good Major Blunt," interrupted Poirot. "It is my business to make inquiries. I make them. *Eh bien*—that legacy of which he speaks, I have discovered that the amount of it was close upon twenty thousand pounds. What do you think of that?"

I was so taken aback that I could hardly speak. "It's impossible," I said at last. "A well-known man like Hector Blunt."

Poirot shrugged his shoulders. "Who knows? At least he is a man with big ideas. I confess I hardly see him as a blackmailer, but there is another possibility that you have not even considered."

"What is that?"

"The fire, my friend. Ackroyd himself may have destroyed that letter, blue envelope and all, after you left him."

"I hardly think that likely," I said slowly. "And yet—of course, it may be so. He might have changed his mind."

We had just arrived at my house, and on the spur of the moment I invited Poirot to come in and take pot luck.

I thought Caroline would be pleased with me, but it is hard to satisfy one's women folk. It appears that we were eating chops for lunch—the kitchen staff being regaled on tripe and onions. And two chops set before three people are productive of embarrassment.

But Caroline is seldom daunted for long. With magnificent mendacity, she explained to Poirot that although James laughed at her for doing so, she adhered strictly to a vegetarian diet. She descanted ecstatically on the delights of nut cutlets (which I am quite sure she had never tasted) and ate a Welsh rarebit with gusto and frequent cutting remarks as to the dangers of "flesh" foods.

Afterward, when we were sitting in front of the fire and smoking, Caroline attacked Poirot directly. "Not found Ralph Paton yet?" She asked.

"Where should I find him, mademoiselle?"

"I thought, perhaps, you'd found him in Cranchester," said Caroline, with intense meaning in her tone.

Poirot looked merely bewildered. "In Cranchester? But why in Cranchester?"

I enlightened him with a touch of malice. "One of our ample staff of private detectives happened to see you in a car on the Cranchester road yesterday," I explained.

Poirot's bewilderment vanished. He laughed heartily. "Ah, that! A simple visit to the dentist, *c'est tout.* My tooth, it aches. I go there. My tooth, it is at once better. I think of return quickly. The dentist, he says No. Better to have it out. I argue. He insists. He has his way! That particular tooth, it will never ache again."

Caroline collapsed rather like a pricked balloon.

We fell to discussing Ralph Paton.

"A weak nature," I insisted. "But not a vicious one."

"Ah!" said Poirot. "But weakness, where does it end?"

"Exactly," said Caroline. "Take James here—weak as water, if I weren't about to look after him."

"My dear Caroline," I said irritably, "can't you talk without dragging in personalities?"

"You *are* weak, James," said Caroline, quite unmoved. "I'm eight years older than you are—oh! I don't mind M. Poirot knowing that—"

"I should never have guessed it, mademoiselle," said Poirot, with a gallant little bow.

"Eight years older. But I've always considered it my duty to look after you. With a bad bringing up, Heaven knows what mischief you might have got into by now."

"I might have married a beautiful adventuress," I murmured, gazing at the ceiling, and blowing smoke rings.

"Adventuress!" said Caroline, with a snort. "If we're talking of adventuresses—" She left the sentence unfinished.

"Well?" I said, with some curiosity.

"Nothing. But I can think of someone not a hundred miles away." Then she turned to Poirot suddenly. "James sticks to it that you believe someone in the house committed the murder. All I can say is, you're wrong."

"I should not like to be wrong," said Poirot. "It is not—how do you say—my *métier?"*

"I've got the facts pretty clearly," continued Caroline, taking no notice of Poirot's remark, "from James and others. As far as I can see, of the people in the house, only two *could* have had the chance of doing it. Ralph Paton and Flora Ackroyd."

"My dear Caroline—"

"Now, James, don't interrupt me. I know what I'm talking about. Parker met her *outside* the door, didn't he? He didn't hear her uncle saying good night to her. She could have killed him then and there."

"Caroline."

"I'm not saying she *did*, James. I'm saying she *could* have done. As a matter of fact, though Flora is like all these young girls nowadays, with no veneration for their betters and thinking they know best on every subject under the sun, I don't for a minute believe she'd kill even a chicken. But there it is. Mr. Raymond and Major Blunt have alibis. Mrs. Ackroyd's got an alibi. Even that Russell woman seems to have one—and a good job for her it is she has. Who is left? Only Ralph and Flora! And say what you will, I don't believe Ralph Paton is a murderer. A boy we've known all our lives."

Poirot was silent for a minute, watching the curling smoke rise from his cigarette. When at last he spoke, it was in a gentle faraway voice that produced a curious impression. It was totally unlike his usual manner.

"Let us take a man—a very ordinary man. A man with no idea of murder in his heart. There is in him somewhere a strain of weakness—deep down. It has so far never been called into play. Perhaps it never will be—and if so he will go to his grave honored and respected by everyone. But let us suppose that something occurs. He is in difficulties—or perhaps not that even. He may stumble by accident on a secret—a secret involving life or death to someone. And his first impulse will be to speak out—to do his duty as an honest citizen. And then the strain of weakness tells. Here is a chance of money—a great amount of money. He wants money—he desires it—and it is so easy. He has to do nothing for it—just keep silence. That is the beginning. The desire for money grows. He must have more—and more! He is intoxicated by the gold mine which has opened at his feet. He becomes greedy. And in his greed he overreaches himself. One can press a man as far as one likes—but with a woman one must not press too far. For a woman has at heart a great desire to speak the truth. How many husbands who have deceived their wives go comfortably to their graves, carrying their secret with them! How many wives who have deceived their husbands wreck their lives by throwing the fact in those same husbands' teeth! They have been pressed too far. In a reckless moment (which they will afterward regret, *bien entendu*[1]) they fling safety to the winds and turn at bay, proclaiming the truth with great momentary satisfaction to themselves. So it was, I think, in this case. The strain was too great. And so there came your proverb, the death of the goose that laid the golden eggs. But that is not the end. Exposure faced the man of whom we are speaking. And he is not the same man he was—say, a year ago. His moral fiber is blunted. He is desperate. He is fighting a losing battle, and he is prepared to take any means that come to his hand, for exposure means ruin to him. And so—the dagger strikes!"

He was silent for a moment. It was as though he had laid a spell upon the room. I cannot try to describe the impression his words produced. There is something in the merciless analysis, and the ruthless power of vision which struck fear into both of us.

"Afterward," he went on softly, "the danger removed, he will be himself again, normal, kindly. But if the need again arises, then once more he will strike."

---

[1] Of course.—EDITOR.

Caroline roused herself at last. "You are speaking of Ralph Paton," she said. "You may be right, you may not, but you have no business to condemn a man unheard."

The telephone bell rang sharply. I went out into the hall, and took off the receiver. "What?" I said. "Yes. Dr. Sheppard speaking." I listened for a minute or two, then replied briefly. Replacing the receiver, I went back into the drawing-room.

"Poirot," I said, "they have detained a man at Liverpool. His name is Charles Kent, and he is believed to be the stranger who visited Fernly that night. They want me to go to Liverpool at once and identify him."

18
Charles Kent

HALF AN HOUR later saw Poirot, myself, and Inspector Raglan in the train on the way to Liverpool. The inspector was clearly very excited.

"We may get a line on the blackmailing part of the business, if on nothing else," he declared jubilantly. "He's a rough customer, this fellow, by what I heard over the phone. Takes dope, too. We ought to find it easy to get what we want out of him. If there was the shadow of a motive, nothing's more likely than that he killed Mr. Ackroyd. But in that case, why is young Paton keeping out of the way? The whole thing's a muddle—that's what it is. By the way, M. Poirot, you were quite right about those fingerprints. They were Mr. Ackroyd's own. I had rather the same idea myself, but I dismissed it as hardly feasible."

I smiled to myself. Inspector Raglan was so very plainly saving his face.

"As regards this man," said Poirot, "he is not yet arrested, eh?"

"No, detained under suspicion."

"And what account does he give of himself?"

"Precious little," said the inspector, with a grin. "He's a wary bird, I gather. A lot of abuse, but very little more."

On arrival at Liverpool I was surprised to find that Poirot was welcomed with acclamation. Superintendent Hayes, who met us, had worked with Poirot over some case long ago, and had evidently an exaggerated opinion of his powers. "Now we've got M. Poirot here we shan't be long," he said cheerfully. "I thought you'd retired, moosior?"

"So I had, my good Hayes, so I had. But how tedious is retirement! You cannot imagine to yourself the monotony with which day comes after day."

"Very likely. So you've come to have a look at our own particular find? Is this Dr. Sheppard? Think you'll be able to identify him, sir?"

"I'm not very sure," I said doubtfully.

"How did you get hold of him?" inquired Poirot.

"Description was circulated, as you know. In the press and privately. Not much to go on, I admit. This fellow has an American accent alright, and he doesn't deny that he was near King's Abbot that night. Just asks what the hell it is to do with us, and that he'll see us in—before he answers any questions."

"Is it permitted that I, too, see him?" asked Poirot.

The superintendent closed one eye knowingly. "Very glad to have you, sir. You've got permission to do anything you please. Inspector Japp of Scotland Yard was asking after you the other day. Said he'd heard you were connected unofficially with this case. Where's Captain Paton hiding, sir, can you tell me that?"

"I doubt if it would be wise at the present juncture," said Poirot primly, and I bit my lips to prevent a smile. The little man really did it very well.

After some further parley, we were taken to interview the prisoner. He was a young fellow, I should say not more than twenty-two or three. Tall, thin, with slightly shaking hands, and the evidences of considerable physical strength somewhat run to seed. His hair was dark, but his eyes were blue and shifty, seldom meeting a glance squarely. I had all along cherished the illusion that there was something familiar about the figure I had met that night, but if this were indeed he, I was completely mistaken. He did not remind me in the least of anyone I knew.

"Now then, Kent," said the superintendent, "stand up. Here are some visitors come to see you. Recognize any of them?" Kent glared at us sullenly, but did not reply. I saw his glance waver over the three of us, and come back to rest on me.

"Well, sir," said the superintendent to me, "what do you say?"

"The height's the same," I said, "and as far as general appearance goes it might well be the man in question. Beyond that, I couldn't go."

"What the hell's the meaning of all this?" asked Kent. "What have you got against me? Come on, out with it! What am I supposed to have done?"

I nodded my head. "It's the man," I said. "I recognize the voice."

"Recognize my voice, do you? Where do you think you heard it before?"

"On Friday evening last, outside the gates of Fernly Park. You asked me the way there."

"I did, did I?"

"Do you admit it?" asked the inspector.

"I don't admit anything. Not till I know what you've got on me."

"Have you not read the papers in the last few days?" asked Poirot, speaking for the first time.

The man's eyes narrowed. "So that's it, is it? I saw an old gent had been croaked at Fernly. Trying to make out I did the job, are you?"

"You were there that night," said Poirot quietly.

"How do you know, mister?"

"By this." Poirot took something from his pocket and held it out. It was the goose quill we had found in the summer-house.

At the sight of it the man's face changed. He half held out his hand. "Snow," said Poirot thoughtfully. "No, my friend, it is empty. It lay where you dropped it in the summerhouse that night."

Charles Kent looked at him uncertainly. "You seem to know a hell of a lot about everything, you little foreign cock duck. Perhaps you remember this: the papers say that the old gent was croaked between a quarter to ten and ten o'clock?"

"That is so," agreed Poirot.

"Yes, but is it really so? That's what I'm getting at."

"This gentleman will tell you," said Poirot.

He indicated Inspector Raglan. The latter hesitated, glanced at Superintendent Hayes, then at Poirot, and finally, as though receiving sanction, he said, "That's right. Between a quarter to ten and ten o'clock."

"Then you've nothing to keep me here for," said Kent. "I was away from Fernly Park by twenty-five minutes past nine. You can ask at the Dog and Whistle. That's a saloon about a mile out of Fernly on the road to Cranchester. I kicked up a bit of a row there, I remember. As near as nothing to quarter to ten, it was. How about that?"

Inspector Raglan wrote down something in his notebook.

"Well?" demanded Kent.

"Inquiries will be made," said the inspector. "If you've spoken the truth, you won't have anything to complain about. What were you doing at Fernly Park anyway?"

"Went there to meet someone."

"Who?"

"That's none of your business."

"You'd better keep a civil tongue in your head, my man," the superintendent warned him.

"To hell with a civil tongue. I went there on my own business, and that's all there is to it. If I was clear away before the murder was done, that's all that concerns the cops."

"Your name, it is Charles Kent," said Poirot. "Where were you born?"

The man stared at him, then he grinned. "I'm a full-blown Britisher alright," he said.

"Yes," said Poirot meditatively. "I think you are. I fancy you were born in Kent."

The man stared. "Why's that? Because of my name? What's that to do with it? Is a man whose name is Kent bound to be born in that particular county?"

"Under certain circumstances, I can imagine he might be," said Poirot very deliberately. "Under certain circumstances, you comprehend."

There was so much meaning in his voice as to surprise the two police officers. As for Charles Kent, he flushed a brick red, and for a moment I thought he was going to spring at Poirot. He thought better of it, however, and turned away with a kind of laugh. Poirot nodded as though satisfied, and made his way out through the door. He was joined presently by the two officers.

"We'll verify that statement," remarked Raglan. "I don't think he's lying, though. But he's got to come clear with a statement as to what he was doing at Fernly. It looks to me as though we'd got our blackmailer alright. On the other hand, granted his story's correct, he couldn't have had anything to do with the actual murder. He'd got ten pounds on him when he was arrested—rather huge sum. I fancy that forty pounds went to him—the numbers of the notes didn't correspond, but of course he'd have changed them first thing. Mr. Ackroyd must have given him the money, and he made off with it as fast as possible. What was that about Kent being his birthplace? What's that got to do with it?"

"Nothing whatever," said Poirot mildly. "A little idea of mine, that was all. Me, I am famous for my little ideas."

"Are you really?" said Raglan, studying him with a puzzled expression.

The superintendent went into a roar of laughter. "Many's the time I've heard Inspector Japp say that. M. Poirot and his little ideas! Too fanciful for me, he'd say, but always something in them."

"You mock yourself at me," said Poirot, smiling; "but never mind. The old ones they laugh last sometimes, when the young, clever ones do not laugh at all." And nodding his head at them in a sage manner, he walked out into the street.

He and I lunched together at an hotel. I know now that the whole thing lay clearly unravelled before him. He had got the last thread he needed to lead him to the truth.

But at the time I had no suspicion of the fact. I overestimated his general self-confidence, and I took it for granted that the things which puzzled me must be equally puzzling to him. My chief puzzle was what the man Charles Kent could have been doing at Fernly. Again and again I put the question to myself and could get no satisfactory reply. At last I ventured a tentative query. His reply was immediate. *"Mon ami,* I do not think; I know."

"Really?" I said incredulously.

"Yes, indeed. I suppose now that to you it would not make sense if I said that he went to Fernly that night because he was born in Kent?"

I stared at him. "It certainly doesn't seem to make sense to me," I said dryly.

"Ah!" said Poirot pityingly. "Well, no matter. I have still my little idea."

19
Flora Ackroyd

AS I WAS returning from my round the following morning, I was hailed by Inspector Raglan. I pulled up, and the inspector mounted on the step.

"Good-morning, Dr. Sheppard," he said. "Well, that alibi is alright enough."

"Charles Kent's?'

"Charles Kent's. The barmaid at the Dog and Whistle, Sally Jones, she remembers him perfectly. Picked out his photograph from among five others. It was just a quarter to ten when he came into the bar, and the Dog and Whistle is well over a mile from Fernly Park. The girl mentions that he had a lot of money on him—she saw him take a handful of notes out of his pocket. Rather surprised her, it did, seeing the class of fellow he was, with a pair of boots clean dropping off him. That's where that forty pounds went right enough."

"The man still refuses to given an account of his visit to Fernly?"

"Obstinate as a mule he is. I had a chat with Hayes at Liverpool over the wire this morning."

"Hercule Poirot says he knows the reason the man went there last night," I observed.

"Does he?" the inspector said eagerly.

"Yes," I said maliciously. "He says he went there because he was born in Kent." I felt a distinct pleasure in passing on my own discomfiture.

Raglan stared at me for a moment or two uncomprehendingly. Then a grin overspread his weaselly countenance and he tapped his forehead significantly. "Bit gone here," he said. "I've thought so for some time. Poor old chap, so that's why he had to give up and come down here. In the family, very likely. He's got a nephew who's quite off his crumpet."

"Poirot has?" I said, very surprised.

"Yes. Hasn't he ever mentioned him to you? Quite docile, I believe, and all that, but mad as a hatter, poor lad."

"Who told you that?"

Again a grin showed itself on Inspector Raglan's face. "Your sister, Miss Sheppard, she told me all about it."

Really, Caroline is amazing. She never rests until she knows the last details of everybody's family secrets. Unfortunately, I have never been able to instill into her the decency of keeping them to herself.

"Jump in, inspector," I said, opening the door of the car. "We'll go up to The Larches together, and acquaint our Belgian friend with the latest news."

"Might as well, I suppose. After all, even if he is a bit balmy, it was a useful tip he gave me about those fingerprints. He's got a bee in his bonnet about the man Kent, but who knows—there may be something useful behind it."

Poirot received us with his usual smiling courtesy. He listened to the information we had brought him, nodding his head now and then.

"Seems quite O.K., doesn't it?" said the inspector rather gloomily. "A chap can't be murdering someone in one place when he's drinking in the bar in another place a mile away."

"Are you going to release him?"

"Don't see what else we can do. We can't very well hold him for obtaining money on false pretenses. Can't prove a ruddy thing." The inspector tossed a match into the grate in a disgruntled fashion. Poirot retrieved it and put it neatly into a little receptacle designed for the purpose. His action was purely mechanical. I could see that his thoughts were on something very different.

"If I were you," he said at last, "I should not release the man Charles Kent yet."

"What do you mean?" Raglan stared at him.

"What I say. I should not release him yet."

"You don't think he can have had anything to do with the murder, do you?"

"I think probably not—but one cannot be certain yet."

"But haven't I just told you—"

Poirot raised a hand protestingly. *"Mais oui, mais oui,*. I am not deaf—nor stupid, thank the good God! But see you, you approach the matter from the wrong—the wrong—premises, is not that the word?"

The inspector stared at him heavily. "I don't see how you make that out. Look here, we know Mr. Ackroyd was alive at a quarter to ten. You admit that, don't you?"

Poirot looked at him for a moment, then shook his head with a quick smile. "I admit nothing that is not—*proved!"*

"Well, we've got proof enough of that. We've got Miss Flora Ackroyd's evidence."

"That she said goodnight to her uncle? But me—I do not always believe what a young lady tells me—no, not even when she is charming and beautiful."

"But, hang it all, man, Parker saw her coming out of the door."

"No." Poirot's voice rang out with sudden sharpness. "That is just what he did not see. I satisfied myself of that by a little experiment the other day—you remember, doctor? Parker saw her *outside* the door, with her hand on the handle. He did not see her come out of the room."

"But—where else could she have been?"

"Perhaps on the stairs."

"The stairs?"

"That is my little idea—yes."

"But those stairs only lead to Mr. Ackroyd's bedroom."

"Precisely."

And still the inspector stared. "You think she'd been up to her uncle's bedroom? Well, why not? Why should she lie about it?"

"Ah! That is just the question. It depends on what she was doing there, does it not?"

"You mean—the money? Hang it all, you don't suggest that it was Miss Ackroyd who took that forty pounds?"

"I suggest nothing," said Poirot. "But I will remind you of this. Life was not very easy for that mother and daughter. There were bills—there was constant trouble over small sums of money. Roger Ackroyd was a peculiar man over money matters. The girl might be at her wit's end for a comparatively small sum. Figure to yourself then what happens. She has taken the money, she descends the little staircase. When she is half-way down she hears the chink of glass from the hall. She has not a doubt of what it is—Parker coming to the study. At all costs she must not be found on the stairs—Parker will not forget it, he will think it odd. If the money is missed, Parker is sure to remember having seen her come down those stairs. She has just time to rush down to the study door—with her hand on the handle to show that she has just come out, when Parker appears in the doorway. She says the first thing that comes into her head, a repetition of Roger Ackroyd's orders earlier in the evening, and then goes upstairs to her own room."

"Yes, but later," persisted the inspector, "she must have realized the vital importance of speaking the truth? Why, the whole case hinges on it!"

"Afterward," said Poirot dryly, "it was a little difficult for Mademoiselle Flora. She is told simply that the police are here and that there has been a robbery. Naturally she jumps to the conclusion that the theft of the money has been discovered. Her one idea is to stick to her story. When she learns that her uncle is dead she is panic-stricken. Young women do not faint nowadays, monsieur, without considerable provocation. *Eh bien!* There it is. She is bound to stick to her story, or else confess everything. And a young and pretty girl does not like to admit that she is a thief—especially before those whose esteem she is anxious to retain."

Raglan brought his fist down with a thump on the table. "I'll not believe it," he said. "It's—it's not credible. And you—you've known this all along?"

"The possibility has been in my mind from the first," admitted Poirot. "I was always convinced that Mademoiselle Flora was hiding something from us. To satisfy myself, I made the little experiment I told you of. Dr. Sheppard accompanied me."

"A test for Parker, you said it was," I remarked bitterly.

"Mon ami," said Poirot apologetically, "as I told you at the time, one must say something."

The inspector rose. "There's only one thing for it," he declared. "We must tackle the young lady right away. You'll come up to Fernly with me, M. Poirot?"

"Certainly. Dr. Sheppard will drive us up in his car."

I acquiesced willingly.

On inquiry for Miss Ackroyd, we were shown into the billiard room. Flora and Major Hector Blunt were sitting on the long window seat.

"Good-morning, Miss Ackroyd," said the inspector. "Can we have a word or two alone with you?"

Blunt got up at once and moved to the door.

"What is it?" said Flora nervously. "Don't go, Major Blunt. He can stay, can't he?" she asked, turning to the inspector.

"That's as you like," said the inspector dryly. "There's a question or two it's my duty to put to you, Miss, but I'd prefer to do so privately, and I dare say you'd prefer it also."

Flora looked keenly at him. I saw her face grow whiter. Then she turned and spoke to Blunt. "I want you to stay—please—yes, I mean it. Whatever the inspector has to say to me, I'd rather you heard it."

Raglan shrugged his shoulders. "Well, if you will have it so, that's all there is to it. Now, Miss Ackroyd, M. Poirot here has made a certain suggestion to me. He suggests that you weren't in the study at all last Friday night, that you never saw Mr. Ackroyd to say goodnight to him, that instead of being in the study you were on the stairs leading down from your uncle's bedroom when you heard Parker coming across the hall."

Flora's gaze shifted to Poirot. He nodded back at her. "Mademoiselle, the other day, when we sat round the table, I implored you to be frank with me. What one does not tell to Papa Poirot he finds out. It was that, was it not? See, I will make it easy for you. You took the money, did you not?"

"The money," said Blunt sharply.

There was a silence which lasted for at least a minute.

Then Flora drew herself up and spoke. "M. Poirot is right. I took that money. I stole. I am a thief—yes, a common, vulgar little thief. Now you know! I am glad it has come out. It's been a nightmare, these last few days!" she sat down suddenly and buried her face in her hands. She spoke huskily through her fingers. "You don't know what my life had been since I came here. Wanting things, scheming for them, lying, cheating, running up bills, promising to pay—oh! I hate myself when I think of it all! That's what brought us together, Ralph and I. We were both weak! I understood him, and I was sorry—because I'm the same underneath. We're not strong enough to stand alone, either of us. We're weak, miserable, despicable things."

She looked at Blunt and suddenly stamped her foot. "Why do you look at me like that—as though you couldn't believe? I may be a thief—but at any rate I'm real now. I'm not lying any more. I'm not pretending to be the kind of girl you like, young and innocent and simple. I don't care if you never want to see me again. I hate myself, despise myself—but you've got to believe one thing, if speaking the truth would have made things better for Ralph, I would have spoken out. But I've seen all along that it wouldn't be better for Ralph—it makes the case against him blacker than ever. I was not doing him any harm by sticking to my lie."

"Ralph," said Blunt. "I see—always Ralph."

"You don't understand," said Flora hopelessly. "You never will." She turned to the inspector. "I admit everything; I was at my wit's end for money. I never saw my uncle that evening after he left the dinner-table. As to the money, you can take what steps you please. Nothing could be worse than it is now!" Suddenly she broke down again, hid her face in her hands, and rushed from the room.

"Well," said the inspector in a flat tone, "so that's that." He seemed rather at a loss what to do next.

Blunt came forward. "Inspector Raglan," he said quietly, "that money was given to me by Mr. Ackroyd for a special purpose. Miss Ackroyd never touched it. When she says she did, she is lying with the idea of shielding Captain Paton. The truth is as I said, and I am prepared to go into the witness box and swear to it." He made a kind of jerky bow, then turning abruptly, he left the room.

Poirot was after him in a flash. He caught the other up in the hall. "Monsieur—a moment, I beg of you, if you will be so good."

"Well, sir?" Blunt was obviously impatient. He stood frowning down on Poirot.

"It is this," said Poirot rapidly: "I am not deceived by your little fantasy. No, indeed. It was truly Miss Flora who took the money. All the same it is well imagined what you say—it pleases me. It is very good what you have done there. You are a man quick to think and to act."

"I'm not in the least anxious for your opinion, thank you," said Blunt coldly. He made once more as though to pass on, but Poirot, not at all offended, laid a detaining hand on his arm.

"Ah! But you are to listen to me. I have more to say. The other day I spoke of concealments. Very well, all along have I seen what you are concealing. Mademoiselle Flora, you love her with all your heart. From the first moment you saw her, is it not so? Oh! Let us not mind saying these things—why must one in England think it necessary to mention love as though it were some disgraceful secret? You love Mademoiselle Flora. You seek to conceal that fact from the world. That is very good—that is as it should be. But take the advice of Hercule Poirot—do not conceal it from mademoiselle herself."

Blunt had shown several signs of restlessness whilst Poirot was speaking, but the closing words seemed to rivet his attention. "What d'you mean by that?" he said sharply.

"You think that she loves the Capitaine Ralph Paton—but I, Hercule Poirot, tell you that this is not so. Mademoiselle Flora accepted Captain Paton to please her uncle, and because she saw in the marriage a way to escape from her life here which was becoming frankly insupportable to her. She liked him, and there was much sympathy and understanding between them. But love—no! It is not Captain Paton Mademoiselle Flora loves."

"What the devil do you mean?" asked Blunt. I saw the dark flush under his tan.

"You have been blind, monsieur. Blind! She is loyal, the little one. Ralph Paton is under a cloud, she is bound in honor to stick by him."

I felt it was time I put in a word to help on the good work. "My sister told me the other night," I said encouragingly, "that Flora had never cared a penny piece for Ralph Paton, and never would. My sister is always right about these things."

Blunt ignored my well-meant efforts. He spoke to Poirot. "D'you really think—" he began, and stopped. He is one of those inarticulate men who find it hard to put things into words.

Poirot knows no such disability. "If you doubt me, ask her yourself, monsieur. But perhaps you no longer care to—the affair of the money—"

Blunt gave a sound like an angry laugh. "Think I'd hold that against her? Roger was always a queer chap about money. She got in a mess and didn't dare tell him. Poor kid. Poor lonely kid."

Poirot looked thoughtfully at the side door. "Mademoiselle Flora went into the garden, I think," he murmured.

"I've been every kind of a fool," said Blunt abruptly. "Rum conversation we've been having. Like one of those Danish plays. But you're a sound fellow, M. Poirot. Thank you." He took Poirot's hand and gave it a grip which caused the other to wince in anguish. Then he strode to the side door and passed out into the garden.

"Not every kind of a fool," murmured Poirot, tenderly nursing the injured member. "Only one kind—the fool in love."

20
Miss Russell

INSPECTOR RAGLAN HAD received a bad jolt. He was not deceived by Blunt's valiant lie any more than we had been. Our way back to the village was punctuated by his complaints. "This alters everything, this does. I don't know whether you've realized it, Monsieur Poirot?"

"I think so, yes, I think so," said Poirot. "You see, me, I have been familiar with the idea for some time."

Inspector Raglan, who had only had the idea presented to him a short half-hour ago, looked at Poirot unhappily and went on with his discoveries. "Those alibis now. Worthless! Absolutely worthless. Got to start again. Find out what everyone was doing from nine-thirty onward. Nine-thirty—that's the time we've got to hang on to. You were quite right about the man Kent—we don't release *him* yet awhile. Let me see now—nine-forty-five at the Dog and Whistle. He might have got there in a quarter of an hour if he ran. It's just possible that it was *his* voice Mr. Raymond heard talking to Mr. Ackroyd—asking for money which Mr. Ackroyd refused. But one thing's clear—it wasn't he who sent the telephone message. The station is half a mile in the other direction—over a mile and a half from the Dog and Whistle, and he was at the Dog and Whistle until about ten minutes past ten. Dang that telephone call! We always come up against it."

"We do indeed," agreed Poirot. "It is curious."

"It's just possible that if Captain Paton climbed into his uncle's room and found him there murdered, *he* may have sent it. Got the wind up, thought he'd be accused, and cleared out. That's possible, isn't it?"

"Why should he have telephoned?"

"May have had doubts if the old man was really dead. Thought he'd get the doctor up there as soon as possible, but didn't want to give himself away. Yes, I say now, how's that for a theory? Something in that, I should say."

The inspector swelled his chest out impatiently. He was so plainly delighted with himself that any words of ours would have been quite superfluous.

We arrived back at my house at this minute, and I hurried in to my surgery patients, who had all been waiting a considerable time, leaving Poirot to walk to the police station with the inspector.

Having dismissed the last patient, I strolled into the little room at the back of the house which I call my workshop—I am rather proud of the homemade wireless set I turned out. Caroline hates my workshop. I keep my tools there, and Annie is not allowed to wreak havoc with a dustpan and brush. I was just adjusting the interior of an alarm clock which had been denounced as wholly unreliable by the household, when the door opened and Caroline put her head in. "Oh! There you are, James," she said, with deep disapproval. "M. Poirot wants to see you."

"Well," I said, rather irritably, for her sudden entrance had startled me and I had let go of a piece of delicate mechanism, "if he wants to see me, he can come in here."

"In here?" said Caroline.

"That's what I said—in here."

Caroline gave a sniff of disapproval and retired. She returned in a moment or two, ushering in Poirot, and then retired again, shutting the door with a bang.

"Aha! My friend," said Poirot, coming forward and rubbing his hands. "You have not got rid of me so easily, you see!"

"Finished with the inspector?" I asked.

"For the moment, yes. And you, you have seen all the patients?"

"Yes."

Poirot sat down and looked at me, tilting his egg-shaped head on one side, with the air of one who savors a very delicious joke. "You are in error," he said at last. "You have still one patient to see."

"Not you?" I exclaimed in surprise.

"Ah, not me, *bien entendu*. Me, I have the health magnificent. No, to tell you the truth, it is a little *complot* of mine. There is someone I wish to see, you understand—and at the same time it is not necessary that the whole village should intrigue itself about the matter—which is what would happen if the lady were seen to come to my house—for it is a lady. But to you she has already come as a patient before."

"Miss Russell!" I exclaimed.

"*Précisément*. I wish much to speak with her, so I send her the little note and make the appointment in your surgery. You are not annoyed with me?"

"On the contrary," I said. "That is, presuming I am allowed to be present at the interview."

"But naturally! In your own surgery!"

"You know," I said, throwing down the pincers I was holding, "it's extraordinarily intriguing, the whole thing. Every new development that arises is like the shake you give to a kaleidoscope—the thing changes entirely in aspect. Now, why are you so anxious to see Miss Russell?"

Poirot raised his eyebrows. "Surely it is obvious," he murmured.

"There you go again," I grumbled. "According to you everything is obvious. But you leave me walking about in a fog."

Poirot shook his head genially at me. "You mock yourself at me. Take the matter of Mademoiselle Flora. The inspector was surprised—but you—you were not."

"I never dreamed of her being the thief," I expostulated.

"That—perhaps no. But I was watching your face and you were not—like Inspector Raglan—startled and incredulous."

I thought for a minute or two. "Perhaps you are right," I said at last. "All along I've felt that Flora was keeping back something—so the truth, when it came, was subconsciously expected. It upset Inspector Raglan very much indeed, poor man."

"Ah! *Pour ça, oui!*[1] The poor man must rearrange all his ideas. I profited by his state of mental chaos to induce him to grant me a little favor."

"What was that?"

Poirot took a sheet of notepaper from his pocket. Some words were written on it, and he read them aloud.

"The police have, for some days, been seeking for Captain Ralph Paton, the nephew of Dr. Ackroyd of Fernly Park, whose death occurred under such tragic circumstances last Friday. Captain Paton has been found at Liverpool, where he was on the point of embarking for America."

He folded up the piece of paper again. "That, my friend, will be in the newspapers tomorrow morning."

---

[1] As to that, yes!—EDITOR.

I stared at him, dumbfounded. "But—but it isn't true! He's not at Liverpool!"

Poirot beamed on me. "You have the intelligence so quick! No, he has not been found at Liverpool. Inspector Raglan was very loath to let me send this paragraph to the press, especially as I could not take him into my confidence. But I assured him most solemnly that very interesting results would follow its appearance in print, so he gave in, after stipulating that he was, on no account, to bear the responsibility."

I stared at Poirot. He smiled back at me.

"It beats me," I said at last, "what you expect to get out of this."

"You should employ your little gray cells," said Poirot gravely. He rose and came across to the bench. "It is that you have really the love of the machinery," he said, after inspecting the debris of my labors.

Every man has his hobby. I immediately drew Poirot's attention to my home-made wireless. Finding him sympathetic, I showed him one or two little inventions of my own—trifling things, but useful in the house.

"Decidedly," said Poirot, "you should be an inventor by trade, not a doctor. But I hear the bell—that is your patient. Let us go into the surgery."

Once before I had been struck by the remnants of beauty in the housekeeper's face. This morning I was struck anew. Very simply dressed in black, tall, upright and independent as ever, with her big dark eyes and an unwonted flush of color in her usually pale cheeks, I realized that as a girl she must have been startlingly handsome.

"Good morning, mademoiselle," said Poirot. "Will you be seated. Dr. Sheppard is so kind as to permit me the use of his surgery for a little conversation I am anxious to have with you."

Miss Russell sat down with her usual composure. If she felt any inward agitation, it did not display itself in any outward manifestation. "It seems a queer way of doing things, if you'll allow me to say so," she remarked.

"Miss Russell—I have news to give you."

"Indeed!"

"Charles Kent has been arrested at Liverpool."

Not a muscle of her face moved. She merely opened her eyes a trifle wider, and asked, with a tinge of defiance: "Well, what of it?"

But at that moment it came to me—the resemblance that had haunted me all along, something familiar in the defiance of Charles Kent's manner. The two voices, one rough and coarse, the other painfully ladylike—were strangely the same in timbre. It was of Miss Russell that I had been reminded that night outside the gates of Fernly Park. I looked at Poirot, full of my discovery, and he gave me an imperceptible nod.

In answer to Miss Russell's question, he threw out his hands in a thoroughly French gesture. "I thought you might be interested, that's all," he said mildly.

"Well, I'm not particularly," said Miss Russell. "Who is this Charles Kent anyway?"

"He is a man, mademoiselle, who was at Fernly on the night of the murder."

"Really?"

"Fortunately for him, he has an alibi. At a quarter to ten he was at a public house a mile from here."

"Lucky for him," commented Miss Russell.

"But we still do not know what he was doing at Fernly—who it was he went to meet, for instance."

"I'm afraid I can't help you at all," said the housekeeper politely. "Nothing came to *my* ears. If that is all—"

She made a tentative movement as though to rise. Poirot stopped her. "It is not quite all," he said smoothly. "This morning fresh developments have arisen. It seems now that Mr. Ackroyd was murdered, not at a quarter to ten, but *before.* Between ten minutes to nine, when Dr. Sheppard left, and a quarter to ten."

I saw the color drain from the housekeeper's face, leaving it dead white. She leaned forward, her figure swaying. "But Miss Ackroyd said—Miss Ackroyd said—"

"Miss Ackroyd has admitted that she was lying. She was never in the study at all that evening."

"Then—?"

"Then it would seem that in this Charles Kent we have the man we are looking for. He came to Fernly, can give no account of what he was doing there—"

"I can tell you what he was doing there. He never touched a hair of old Ackroyd's head—he never went near the study. He didn't do it, I tell you." She was leaning forward. That iron self-control was broken through at last. Terror and desperation were in her face. "M. Poirot! M. Poirot! Oh, do believe me."

Poirot got up and came to her. He patted her reassuringly on the shoulder. "But yes—but yes, I will believe. I had to make you speak, you know."

For an instant suspicion flared up in her. "Is what you said true?"

"That Charles Kent is suspected of the crime? Yes, that is true. You alone can save him, by telling the reason for his being at Fernly."

"He came to see me." She spoke in a low, hurried voice. "I went out to meet him—"

"In the summerhouse, yes, I know."

"How do you know?"

"Mademoiselle, it is the business of Hercule Poirot to know things. I know that you went out earlier in the evening, that you left a message in the summerhouse to say what time you would be there."

"Yes, I did. I had heard from him—saying he was coming. I dared not let him come to the house. I wrote to the address he gave me and said I would meet in the summerhouse, and described it to him so that he would be able to find it. Then I was afraid he might not wait there patiently, and I ran out and left a piece of paper to say I would be there about ten minutes past nine. I didn't want the servants to see me, so I slipped out through the drawing-room window. As I came back, I met Dr. Sheppard, and I fancied that he would think it queer. I was out of breath, for I had been running. I had no idea that he was expected to dinner that night." She paused.

"Go on," said Poirot. "You went out to meet him at ten minutes past nine.

What did you say to each other?"

"It's difficult. You see—"

"Mademoiselle," said Poirot, interrupting her, "in this matter I must have the whole truth. What you tell us need never go beyond these four walls. Dr. Sheppard will be discreet, and so shall I. See, I will help you. This Charles Kent, he is your son, is he not?"

She nodded. The color had flamed into her cheeks. "No one has ever known. It was long ago—long ago—down in Kent. I was not married. . . ."

"So you took the name of the county as a surname for him. I understand."

"I got work. I managed to pay for his board and lodging. I never told him that I was his mother. But he turned out badly, he drank, then took to drugs. I managed to pay his passage out to Canada. I didn't hear of him for a year or two. Then, somehow or other, he found out that I was his mother. He wrote asking me for money. Finally, I heard from him back in this country again. He was coming to see me at Fernly, he said. I dared not let him come to the house. I have always been considered so—so very respectable. If anyone got an inkling—it would have been all up with my post as housekeeper. So I wrote to him in the way I have just told you."

"And in the morning you came to see Dr. Sheppard?"

"Yes. I wondered if something could be done. He was not a bad boy—before he took to drugs."

"I see," said Poirot. "Now let us go on with the story. He came that night to the summerhouse?"

"Yes, he was waiting for me when I got there. He was very rough and abusive. I had brought with me all the money I had, and I gave it to him. We talked a little, and then he went away."

"What time was that?"

"It must have been between twenty and twenty-five minutes past nine. It was not yet half-past when I got back to the house."

"Which way did he go?"

"Straight out the same way he came, by the path that joined the drive just inside the lodge gates."

Poirot nodded. "And you, what did you do?"

"I went back to the house. Major Blunt was walking up and down the terrace smoking, so I made a detour to get round to the side door. It was then just on half-past nine, as I told you."

Poirot nodded again. He made a note or two in a microscopic pocketbook. "I think that is all," he said thoughtfully.

"Ought I—" she hesitated. "Ought I to tell all this to Inspector Raglan?"

"It may come to that. But let us not be in a hurry. Let us proceed slowly, with due order and method. Charles Kent is not yet formally charged with murder. Circumstances may arise which will render your story unnecessary."

Miss Russell rose. "Thank you very much, M. Poirot," she said. "You have been very kind—very kind indeed. You—you do believe me, don't you? That Charles had nothing to do with this wicked murder?"

"There seems no doubt that the man who was talking to Mr. Ackroyd in the library at nine-thirty could not possibly have been your son. Be of good courage, mademoiselle. All will yet be well."

Miss Russell departed. Poirot and I were left together.

"So that's that," I said. "Every time we come back to Ralph Paton. How did you manage to spot Miss Russell as the person Charles Kent came to meet? Did you notice the resemblance?"

"I had connected her with the unknown man long before we actually came face to face with him. As soon as we found that quill. The quill suggested dope, and I remembered your account of Miss Russell's visit to you. Then I found the article on cocaine in that morning's paper. It all seemed very clear. She had heard from someone that morning—someone addicted to drugs, she read the article in the paper, and she came to you to ask a few tentative questions. She mentioned cocaine, since the article in question was on cocaine. Then, when you seemed too interested, she switched hurriedly to the subject of detective stories and untraceable poisons. I suspected a son or a brother, or some other undesirable male relation. Ah! But I must go. It is the time of the lunch."

"Stay and lunch with us," I suggested.

Poirot shook his head. A faint twinkle came into his eyes. "Not again today. I should not like to force Mademoiselle Caroline to adopt a vegetarian diet two days in succession."

It occurred to me that there was not much which escaped Hercule Poirot.

21
The Paragraph in the Paper

CAROLINE, OF COURSE, had not failed to see Miss Russell come to the surgery door. I had anticipated this, and had ready an elaborate account of the lady's bad knee. But Caroline was not in a cross-questioning mood. Her point of view was that she knew what Miss Russell had already come for and that I didn't.

"Pumping you, James," said Caroline. "Pumping you in the most shameless manner, I've not a doubt. It's no good interrupting. I dare say you hadn't the least idea she was doing it even. Men *are* so simple. She knows that you are in M. Poirot's confidence, and she wants to find out things. Do you know what I think, James?"

"I couldn't begin to imagine. You think so many extraordinary things."

"It's no good being sarcastic. I think Miss Russell knows more about Mr. Ackroyd's death than she is prepared to admit." Caroline leaned back triumphantly in her chair.

"Do you really think so?" I said absently.

"You are very dull today, James. No animation about you. It's that liver of yours."

Our conversation then dealt with purely personal matters.

The paragraph inspired by Poirot duly appeared in our daily paper the next morning. I was in the dark as to its purpose, but its effect on Caroline was immense.

She began by stating, more untruly, that she had said as much all along. I raised my eyebrows, but did not argue. Caroline, however, must have felt a prick of conscience, for she went on: "I mayn't have actually mentioned Liverpool, but I knew he'd try to get away to America. That's what Crippen did."

"Without much success," I reminded her.

"Poor boy, and so they've caught him. I consider, James, that it's your duty to see that he isn't hung."

"What do you expect me to do?"

"Why, you're a medical man, aren't you? You've known him from a boy upward. Not mentally responsible. That's the line to take, clearly. I read only the other day that they're very happy in Broadmoor—it's quite like a high-class club."

But Caroline's words had reminded me of something.

"I never knew that Poirot had an imbecile nephew?" I said curiously.

"Didn't you? Oh, he told me all about it. Poor lad. It's a great grief to all the family. They've kept him at home so far, but it's getting to such a pitch that they're afraid he'll have to go into some kind of institution."

"I suppose you know pretty well everything there is to know about Poirot's family by this time," I said, exasperated.

"Pretty well," said Caroline complacently. "It's a great relief to people to be able to tell all their troubles to someone."

"It might be," I said, "if they were ever allowed to do so spontaneously. Whether they enjoy having confidences screwed out of them by force is another matter."

Caroline merely looked at me with the air of a Christian martyr enjoying martyrdom. "You are so self-contained, James," she said. "You hate speaking out, or parting with any information yourself, and you think everybody else must be just like you. I should hope that I never screw confidences out of anybody. For instance, if M. Poirot comes in this afternoon, as he said he might do, I shall not dream of asking him who it was arrived at his house early this morning."

"Early this morning?" I queried.

"Very early," said Caroline. "Before the milk came. I just happened to be looking out of the window—the blind was flapping. It was a man. He came in a closed car, and he was all muffled up. I couldn't get a glimpse of his face. But I will tell you *my* idea, and you'll see that I'm right."

"What's your idea?"

Caroline dropped her voice mysteriously. "A Home Office expert," she breathed.

"A Home Office expert," I said, amazed. "My dear Caroline!"

"Mark my words, James, you'll see that I'm right. That Russell woman was here that morning after your poisons. Roger Ackroyd might easily have been poisoned in his food that night."

I laughed out loud. "Nonsense," I cried. "He was stabbed in the neck. You know that as well as I do."

"After death, James," said Caroline; "to make a false clue."

"My good woman," I said, "I examined the body, and I know what I'm talking about. That wound wasn't inflicted after death—it was the cause of death, and you need make no mistake about it."

Caroline merely continued to look omniscient, which so annoyed me that I went on: "Perhaps you will tell me, Caroline, if I have a medical degree or if I have not?"

"You have the medical degree, I dare say, James—at least, I mean I know you have. But you've no imagination whatever."

"Having endowed you with a treble portion, there was none left over for me," I said dryly.

I was amused to notice Caroline's maneuvers that afternoon when Poirot duly arrived. My sister, without asking a direct question, skirted the subject of the mysterious guest in every way imaginable. By the twinkle in Poirot's eyes, I saw that he realized her object. He remained blandly impervious, and blocked her bowling so successfully that she herself was at a loss how to proceed.

Having, I suspect, quietly enjoyed the little game, he rose to his feet and suggested a walk. "It is that I need to reduce the figure a little," he explained. "You will come with me, doctor? And perhaps later Miss Caroline will give us some tea?"

"Delighted," said Caroline. "Won't your—er—guest come in also?"

"You are too kind," said Poirot. "But no, my friend reposes himself. Soon you must make his acquaintance."

"Quite an old friend of yours, somebody told me," said Caroline making one last valiant effort.

"Did they?" murmured Poirot. "Well, we must start."

Our tramp took us in the direction of Fernly. I had guessed beforehand that it might do so. I was beginning to understand Poirot's methods. Every little irrelevancy had a bearing upon the whole. "I have a commission for you, my friend," he said at last. "Tonight, at my house, I desire to have a little conference. You will attend, will you not?"

"Certainly," I said.

"Good. I need also all those in the house—that is to say: Mrs. Ackroyd, Mademoiselle Flora, Major Blunt, M. Raymond. I want you to be my ambassador. This little reunion is fixed for nine o'clock. You will ask them yourself?"

"Why don't *you* ask them?" I said.

"Because they will then put the questions: 'Why? What for?' They will demand what my idea is. And, as you know, my friend, I much dislike to have to explain my little ideas until the time comes."

I smiled a little.

"My friend Hastings, he of whom I told you, used to say of me that I was a human oyster. But he was unjust. Of facts, I keep nothing to myself. But to everyone his own interpretation of them."

"When do you want me to do this?"

"Now, if you will. We are close to the house."

"Are you coming in?"

"No, me. I will promenade myself in the grounds. I will rejoin you by the lodge gates in a quarter of an hour's time."

I nodded, and set off on my task. The only member of the family at home proved to be Mrs. Ackroyd, who was sipping an early cup of tea. She received me graciously. "So grateful to you doctor," she murmured, "for clearing up that little matter with M. Poirot. But life is one trouble after another. You have heard about Flora, of course?"

"What exactly?" I asked cautiously.

"This new engagement. Flora and Hector Blunt. Of course not such a good match as Ralph would have been. But after all, happiness comes first. What dear Flora needs is an older man—someone steady and reliable, and then Hector is really a very distinguished man in his way. You saw the news of Ralph's arrest in the paper this morning?"

"Yes," I said, "I did."

"Horrible." Mrs. Ackroyd closed her eyes and shuddered. "Geoffrey Raymond was in a terrible way. Rang up Liverpool. But they wouldn't tell him anything at the police station there. In fact, they said they hadn't arrested Ralph at all. Mr. Raymond insists that it's all a mistake—a—what do they call it?—*canard* of the newspapers. I've forbidden it to be mentioned before the servants. Such a terrible disgrace. Fancy if Flora had actually been married to him."

Mrs. Ackroyd shut her eyes in anguish. I began to wonder how soon I should be able to deliver Poirot's invitation.

Before I had time to speak, Mrs. Ackroyd was off again. "You were here yesterday, weren't you, with that dreadful Inspector Raglan? Brute of a man—he terrified Flora into saying she took that money from poor Roger's room. And the matter was so simple, really. The dear child wanted to borrow a few pounds, didn't like to disturb her uncle since he'd given strict orders against it, but knowing where he kept his notes she went there and took what she needed."

"Is that Flora's account of the matter?" I asked.

"My dear doctor, you know what girls are nowadays. So easily acted on by suggestion. You, of course, know all about hypnosis and that sort of thing. The Inspector shouts at her, says the word 'steal' over and over again, until the poor child gets an inhibition—or is it a complex?—I always mix up those two words—and actually thinks herself that she has stolen the money. I saw at once how it was. But I can't be too thankful for the whole misunderstanding in one way—it seems to have brought those two together—Hector and Flora, I mean. And I assure you that I have been very much worried about Flora in the past: why, at one time I actually thought there was going to be some kind of understanding between her and young Raymond. Just think of it!" Mrs. Ackroyd's voice rose in shrill horror. "A private secretary—with practically no means of his own."

"It would have been a severe blow to you," I said. "Now, Mrs. Ackroyud, I've got a message for you from M. Hercule Poirot."

"For me?" Mrs. Ackroyd looked quite alarmed. I hastened to reassure her, and I explained what Poirot wanted.

"Certainly," said Mrs. Ackroyd rather doubtfully. "I suppose we must come if M. Poirot says so. But what is it all about? I like to know beforehand."

I assured the lady truthfully that I myself did not know any more than she did.

"Very well," said Mrs. Ackroyd at last, rather grudgingly, "I will tell the others, and we will be there at nine o'clock."

Thereupon I took my leave, and joined Poirot at the agreed meeting-place.

"I've been longer than a quarter of an hour, I'm afraid," I remarked. "But once that good lady starts talking it's a matter of the utmost difficulty to get a word in edgeways."

"It is of no matter," said Poirot. "Me, I have been well amused. This park is magnificent."

We set off homeward. When we arrived, to our great surprise Caroline, who had evidently been watching for us, herself opened the door. She put her fingers to her lips. Her face was full of importance and excitement. "Ursula Bourne," she said, "the parlormaid from Fernly. She's here! I've put her in the dining room. She's in a terrible way, poor thing. Says she must see M. Poirot at once. I've done all I could. Taken her a cup of hot tea. It really goes to one's heart to see anyone in such a state."

"In the dining room?" asked Poirot.

"This way," I said, and flung open the door.

Ursula Bourne was sitting by the table. Her arms were spread out in front of her, and she had evidently just lifted her head from where it had been buried. Her eyes were red with weeping.

"Ursula Bourne," I murmured.

But Poirot went past me with outstretched hands. "No," he said, "that is not quite right, I think. It is not Ursula Bourne, is it, my child—but Ursula Paton? Mrs. Ralph Paton."

22
Ursula's Story

FOR A MOMENT the girl looked mutely at Poirot. Then, her reserve breaking down completely, she nodded her head once, and burst into an outburst of sobs.

Caroline pushed past me, and putting her arm round the girl, patted her on the shoulder. "There, there, my dear," she said soothingly, "it will be alright. You'll see—everything will be alright."

Buried under curiosity and scandal-mongering there is a lot of kindness in Caroline. For the moment, even the interest of Poirot's revelation was lost in the sight of the girl's distress.

Presently Ursula sat up and wiped her eyes. "This is very weak and silly of me," she said.

"No, no, my child," said Poirot kindly. "We can all realize the strain of this last week."

"It must have been a terrible ordeal," I said.

"And then to find that you knew," continued Ursula. "How did you know? Was it Ralph who told you?"

Poirot shook his head.

"You know what brought me to you tonight?" went on the girl. *"This—"* She held out a crumpled piece of newspaper, and I recognized the paragraph that Poirot had had inserted. "It says that Ralph has been arrested. So everything is useless. I need not pretend any longer."

"Newspaper paragraphs are not always true, mademoiselle," murmured Poirot, having the grace to look ashamed of himself. "All the same, I think you will do well to make a clean breast of things. The truth is what we need now."

The girl hesitated, looking at him doubtfully.

"You do not trust me," said Poirot gently. "Yet all the same you came here to find me, did you not? Why was that?"

"Because I don't believe that Ralph did it," said the girl in a very low voice. "And I think that you are clever, and will find out the truth. And also—"

"Yes?"

"I think you are kind."

Poirot nodded his head several times. "It is very good that—yes, it is very good. Listen, I do in verity believe that this husband of yours is innocent—but the affair marches badly. If I am to save him, I must know all there is to know—even if it should seem to make the case against him blacker than before."

"How well you understand," said Ursula.

"So you will tell me the whole story, will you not? From the beginning."

"You're not going to send *me* away, I hope," said Caroline, settling herself comfortably in an armchair. "What I want to know," she continued, "is why this child was masquerading as a parlormaid?"

"Masquerading?" I queried.

"That's what I said. Why did you do it, child? For a wager?"

"For a living," said Ursula dryly. And encouraged, she began the story which I reproduce here in my own words.

Ursula Bourne, it seemed, was one of a family of seven—impoverished Irish gentlefolk. On the death of her father, most of the girls were cast out into the world to earn their own living. Ursula's eldest sister was married to Captain Folliott. It was she whom I had seen that Sunday, and the cause of her embarrassment was clear enough now. Determined to earn her living and not attracted to the idea of being a nursery governess—the one profession open to an untrained girl, Ursula preferred the job of parlormaid. She scorned to label herself a "lady parlormaid." She would be the real thing, her reference being supplied by her sister. At Fernly, despite her aloofness which, as has been seen, caused some comment, she was a success at her job—quick, competent, and thorough. "I enjoyed the work," she explained. "And I had plenty of time to myself."

And then came her meeting with Ralph Paton, and the love affair which culminated in a secret marriage. Ralph had persuaded her into that, somewhat against her will. He had declared that his stepfather would not hear of his marrying a penniless girl. Better to be married secretly, and break the news to him at some later and more favorable minute.

And so the deed was done, and Ursula Bourne became Ursula Paton. Ralph had declared that he meant to pay off his debts, find a job, and then, when he was in a position to support her, and independent of his adopted father, they would break the news to him.

But to people like Ralph Paton, turning over a new leaf is easier in theory than in practice. He hoped that his stepfather, whilst still in ignorance of the marriage, might be persuaded to pay his debts and put him on his feet again. But the revelation of the amount of Ralph's liabilities merely enraged Roger Ackroyd, and he refused to do anything at all. Some months passed, and then Ralph was bidden once more to Fernly. Roger Ackroyd did not beat about the bush. It was the desire of his heart that Ralph should marry Flora, and he put the matter plainly before the young man.

And here it was that the innate weakness of Ralph Paton showed itself. As always, he grasped at the easy, the immediate solution. As far as I could make out, neither Flora nor Ralph made any pretense of love. It was, on both sides, a business arrangement. Roger Ackroyd dictated his wishes—they agreed to them, Flora accepted a chance of liberty, money and an enlarged horizon, Ralph, of course, was playing a different game. But he was in a very awkward hole financially. He seized at the chance. His debts would be paid. He could start again with a clean sheet. His was not a nature to envisage the future, but I gather that he saw vaguely the engagement with Flora being broken off after a decent interval had elapsed. Both Flora and he stipulated that it should be kept a secret for the present. He was anxious to conceal it from Ursula. He felt instinctively that her nature, strong and resolute, with an inherent distaste for duplicity, was not one to welcome such a course.

Then came the crucial moment when Roger Ackroyd, always high-handed, decided to announce the engagement. He said no word of his intention to Ralph—only to Flora, and Flora, apathetic, raised no objection. On Ursula, the news fell like a bombshell. Summoned by her, Ralph came hurriedly down from town. They met in the wood, where part of their conversation was overheard by my sister. Ralph implored her to keep silent for a little while longer. Ursula was equally determined to have done with concealments. She would tell Mr. Ackroyd the truth without any further delay. Husband and wife parted acrimoniously.

Ursula, steadfast in her purpose, sought an interview with Roger Ackroyd that very afternoon, and revealed the truth to him. Their interview was a stormy one—it might have been even more stormy had not Roger Ackroyd been already obsessed with his own troubles. It was bad enough, however. Ackroyd was not the kind of a man to forgive the deceit that had been practiced upon him. His rancor was mainly directed to Ralph, but Ursula came in for her share, since he regarded her as a girl who had deliberately tried to "entrap" the adopted son of a very wealthy man. Unforgivable things were said on both sides.

That same evening Ursula met Ralph by appointment in the small summerhouse, stealing out from the house by the side door in order to do so. Their interview was made up of reproaches on both sides. Ralph charged Ursula with having irretrievably ruined his prospects by her ill-timed revelation. Ursula reproached Ralph with his duplicity. They parted at last. A little over half an hour later came the discovery of Roger Ackroyd's body. Since that night Ursula had neither seen nor heard from Ralph.

As the story unfolded itself, I realized more and more what a damning series of facts it was. Alive, Ackroyd could hardly have failed to alter his will—I knew him well enough to realize that to do so would be his first thought. His death came in the nick of time for Ralph and Ursula Paton. Small wonder the girl had held her tongue, and played her part so consistently.

My meditations were interrupted. It was Poirot's voice speaking, and I knew from the gravity of his tone that he, too, was fully alive to the implications of the position.

"Mademoiselle, I must ask you one question, and you must answer it truthfully, for on it everything may hang: What time was it when you parted from Captain Ralph Paton in the summerhouse? Now, take a little minute so that your answer may be very exact."

The girl gave a half laugh, bitter enough in all conscience. "Do you think I haven't gone over that again and again in my own mind? It was just half-past nine when I went out to meet him. Major Blunt was walking up and down the terrace, so I had to go round through the bushes to avoid him. It must have been about twenty-seven minutes to ten when I reached the summer-house. Ralph was waiting for me. I was with him ten minutes—not longer, for it was just a quarter to ten when I got back to the house."

I saw now the insistence of her question the other day. If only Ackroyd could have been proved to have been killed before a quarter to ten, and not after.

I saw the reflection of that thought in Poirot's next question. "Who left the summer-house first?"

"I did."

"Leaving Ralph Paton in the summerhouse?"

"Yes—but you don't think—"

"Mademoiselle, it is of no importance what I think. What did you do when you got back to the house?"

"I went up to my room."

"And stayed there until when?"

"Until about ten o'clock."

"Is there anyone who can prove that?"

"Prove? That I was in my room, you mean? Oh! No. But surely—oh! I see, they might think—they might think—" I saw the dawning horror in her eyes.

Poirot finished the sentence for her. "That it was *you* who entered by the window and stabbed Mr. Ackroyd as he sat in his chair? Yes, they might think just that."

"Nobody but a fool would think any such thing," said Caroline indignantly. She patted Ursula on the shoulder.

The girl had her face hidden in her hands. "Horrible," she was murmuring. "Horrible."

Caroline gave her a friendly shake. "Don't worry, my dear," she said. "M. Poirot doesn't think that really. As for that husband of yours, I don't think much of him, and I tell you so candidly. Running away and leaving you to face the music."

But Ursula shook her head energetically. "Oh, no," she cried. "It wasn't like that at all. Ralph would not run away on his own account. I see now. If he heard of his stepfather's murder, he might think himself that I had done it."

"He wouldn't think any such thing," said Caroline.

"I was so cruel to him that night—so hard and bitter. I wouldn't listen to what he was trying to say—wouldn't believe that he really cared. I just stood there telling him what I thought of him, and saying the coldest cruelest things that came into my mind—trying my best to hurt him."

"Do him no harm," said Caroline. "Never worry about what you say to a man. They're so conceited that they never believe you mean it if it's unflattering."

Ursula went on, nervously twisting and untwisting her hands. "When the murder was discovered and he didn't come forward, I was terribly upset. Just for a moment I wondered—but then I knew he couldn't—he couldn't. . . . But I wished he would come forward and say openly that he'd had nothing to do with it. I knew that he was very fond of Dr. Sheppard, and I fancied that perhaps Dr. Sheppard might know where he was hiding."

She turned to me. "That's why I said what I did to you that day. I thought, if you knew where he was, you might pass on the message to him."

"I?" I exclaimed.

"Why should James know where he was?" demanded Caroline sharply.

"It was very unlikely, I know," admitted Ursula, "but Ralph had often spoken of Dr. Sheppard, and I knew that he would be likely to consider him as his best friend in King's Abbot."

"My dear child," I said, "I have not the least idea where Ralph Paton is at the present moment."

"That is true enough," said Poirot.

"But—" Ursula held out the newspaper cutting in a puzzled fashion.

"Ah! That," said Poirot, slightly embarrassed; "A *bagatelle*, mademoiselle. A *rien de tout*.[1] Not for a moment do I believe that Ralph Paton has been arrested."

"But then—" began the girl slowly.

Poirot went on quickly: "There is one thing I should like to know—did Captain Paton wear shoes or boots that night?"

Ursula shook her head. "I can't remember."

"A pity! But how should you? Now, madame," he smiled at her, his head on one side, his forefinger wagging eloquently, "no questions. And do not torment yourself. Be of good courage, and place your faith in Hercule Poirot."

---

[1] Mere nothing.—EDITOR.

23
Poirot's Little Reunion

"AND NOW," SAID Caroline, rising, "that child is coming upstairs to lie down. Don't you worry, my dear. M. Poirot will do everything he can for you—be sure of that."

"I ought to go back to Fernly," said Ursula uncertainly.

But Caroline silenced her protests with a firm hand. "Nonsense. You're in my hands for the time being. You'll stay here for the present, anyway—eh, M. Poirot?"

"It will be the best plan," agreed the little Belgian. "This evening I shall want mademoiselle—I beg her pardon, madame—to attend my little reunion. Nine o'clock at my house. It is most necessary that she should be there."

Caroline nodded, and went with Ursula out of the room. The door shut behind them. Poirot dropped down into a chair again. "So far, so good," he said. "Things are straightening themselves out."

"They're getting to look blacker and blacker against Ralph Paton," I observed gloomily.

Poirot nodded. "Yes, that is so. But it was to be expected, was it not?"

I looked at him, slightly puzzled by the remark. He was leaning back in the chair, his eyes half closed, the tips of his fingers just touching each other. Suddenly he sighed and shook his head.

"What is it?" I asked.

"Is it that there are moments when a great longing for my friend Hastings comes over me. That is the friend of whom I spoke to you—the one who resides now in the Argentine. Always, when I have had a big case, he has been by my side. And he has helped me—yes, often he has helped me. For he had a knack, that one, of stumbling over the truth unawares—without noticing it himself, *bien entendu.* At times he has said something particularly foolish, and behold that foolish remark has revealed the truth to me! And then, too, it, was his practice to keep a written record of the cases that proved interesting."

I gave a slight embarrassed cough. "As far as that goes," I began, and then stopped.

Poirot sat upright in his chair. His eyes sparkled. "But yes? What is it that you would say?"

"Well, as a matter of fact, I've read some of Captain Hasting's narratives, and I thought, why not try my hand at something of the same kind? Seemed a pity not to—unique opportunity—probably the only time I'll be mixed up with anything of this kind." I felt myself getting hotter and hotter, and more and more incoherent, as I floundered through the above speech.

Poirot sprang from his chair. I had a moment's terror that he was going to embrace me French fashion, but mercifully he refrained. "But this is magnificent—you have then written down your impressions of the case as you went along?"

I nodded.

"Épatant!"[1] cried Poirot. "Let me see them—this instant."

I was not quite prepared for such a sudden demand. I racked my brains to remember certain details. "I hope you won't mind," I stammered. "I may have been a little—er—*personal* now and then."

"Oh! I comprehend perfectly; you have referred to me as comic—as, perhaps, ridiculous now and then? It matters not at all. Hastings, he also was not always polite. Me, I have the mind above such trivialities."

Still somewhat doubtful, I rummaged in the drawers of my desk and produced an untidy pile of manuscript which I handed over to him. With an eye on possible publication in the future, I had divided the work into chapters, and the night before I had brought it up to date with an account of Miss Russell's visit. Poirot had therefore twenty chapters.

I left him with them. I was obliged to go out to a case at some distance away, and it was past eight o'clock when I got back, to be greeted with a plate of hot dinner on a tray, and the announcement that Poirot and my sister had supped together at half-past seven, and that the former had then gone to my workshop to finish his reading of the manuscript.

"I hope, James," said my sister, "that you've been careful in what you say about me in it?"

My jaw dropped. I had not been careful at all.

"Not that it matters very much," said Caroline, reading my expression correctly. "M. Poirot will know what to think. He understands me much better than you do."

I went into the workshop. Poirot was sitting by the window. The manuscript lay neatly piled on a chair beside him. He laid his hand on it and spoke. *"Eh bien,"* he said, "I congratulate you—on your modesty!"

"Oh!" I said, rather taken aback.

"And on your reticence," he added.

I said "Oh!" again.

"Not so did Hastings write," continued my friend. "On every page, many, many times was the word 'I.' What *he* thought—what *he* did. But you—you have kept your personality in the background; only once or twice does it obtrude—in scenes of home life, shall we say?"

I blushed a little before the twinkle in his eye. "What do you really think of the stuff?" I asked nervously.

"You want my candid opinion?"

"Yes."

Poirot laid his jesting manner aside. "A very meticulous and accurate account," he said kindly. "You have recorded all the facts faithfully and exactly—though you have shown yourself becoming reticent at to your own share in them."

"And it has helped you?"

"Yes. I may say that it has helped me considerably. Come, we must go over to my house and set the stage for my little performance."

---

[1] Splendid!—EDITOR.

Caroline was in the hall. I think she hoped that she might be invited to accompany us. Poirot dealt with the situation tactfully. "I should much like to have had you present, mademoiselle," he said regretfully, "but at this juncture it would not be wise. See you, all these people tonight are suspects. Amongst them, I shall find the person who killed Mr. Ackroyd."

"You really believe that?" I said incredulously.

"I see that you do not," said Poirot dryly. "Not yet do you appreciate Hercule Poirot at his true worth."

At that minute Ursula came down the staircase.

"You are ready, my child," asked Poirot. "That is good. We will go to my house together. Mademoiselle Caroline, believe me, I do everything possible to render you service. Good-evening." We went out, leaving Caroline, rather like a dog who has been refused a walk, standing on the front door step gazing after us.

The sitting-room at The Larches had been got ready. On the table were various *sirops* and glasses. Also a plate of biscuits. Several chairs had been brought in from the other room.

Poirot ran to and fro rearranging things. Pulling out a chair here, altering the position of a lamp there, occasionally stooping to straighten one of the mats that covered the floor. He was specially fussy over the lighting. The lamps were arranged in such a way as to throw a clear light on the side of the room where the chairs were grouped, at the same time leaving the other end of the room, where I presumed Poirot himself would sit, in a dim twilight.

Ursula and I watched him. Presently a bell was heard.

"They arrive," said Poirot. "Good, all is in readiness."

The door opened and the party from Fernly filed in. Poirot went forward and greeted Mrs. Ackroyd and Flora. "It is most good of you to come," he said. "And Major Blunt and Mr. Raymond."

The secretary was debonair as ever. "What's the great idea?" he said, laughing. "Some scientific machine? Do we have bands round our wrists which register guilty heart-beats? There is such an invention, isn't there?"

"I have read of it, yes," admitted Poirot. "But me, I am old-fashioned. I use the old methods. I work only with the little gray cells. Now let us begin—but first I have an announcement to make to you all." He took Ursula's hand and drew her forward. "This lady is Mrs. Ralph Paton. She was married to Captain Paton last March."

A little shriek burst from Mrs. Ackroyd. "Ralph! Married! Last March! Oh! But it's absurd. How could he be?" She stared at Ursula as though she had never seen her before. "Married to Bourne?" she said. "Really, M. Poirot, I don't believe you."

Ursula flushed and began to speak, but Flora forestalled her. Going quickly to the other girl's side, she passed her hand through her arm. "You must not mind our being surprised," she said. "You see, we had no idea of such a thing. You and Ralph have kept your secret very well. I am—very glad about it."

"You are very kind, Miss Ackroyd," said Ursula in a low voice, "and you have every right to be exceedingly angry. Ralph behaved very badly—especially to you."

"You needn't worry about that," said Flora, giving her arm a consoling pat. "Ralph was in a corner and took the only way out. I should probably have done the same in his place. I do think he might have trusted me with the secret, though. I wouldn't have let him down."

Poirot rapped gently on a table and cleared his throat significantly. "The board meeting's going to begin," said Flora. "M. Poirot hints that we mustn't talk. But just tell me one thing. Where is Ralph? You must know if anyone does."

"But I don't," cried Ursula, almost in a wail. "That's just it, I don't."

"Isn't he detained at Liverpool?" asked Raymond. "It said so in the paper."

"He is not at Liverpool," said Poirot shortly.

"In fact," I remarked, "no one knows where he is."

"Excepting Hercule Poirot, eh?" said Raymond.

Poirot replied seriously to the other's banter. "Me, I know everything. Remember that."

Geoffrey Raymond lifted his eyebrows. "Everything?" He whistled. "Whew! That's a tall order."

"Do you mean to say you can really guess where Ralph Paton is hiding?" I asked incredulously.

"You call it guessing. I call it knowing, my friend."

"In Cranchester?" I hazarded.

"No," replied Poirot gravely, "not in Cranchester." He said no more, but at a gesture from him the assembled party took their seats. As they did so, the door opened once more and two other people came in and sat down near the door. They were Parker and the housekeeper.

"The number is complete," said Poirot. "Everyone is here." There was a ring of satisfaction in his tone. And with the sound of it I saw a ripple of something like uneasiness pass over all those faces grouped at the other end of the room. There was a suggestion in all this as of a trap—a trap that had closed.

Poirot read from a list in an important manner. "Mrs. Ackroyd, Miss Flora Ackroyd, Major Blunt, Mr. Geoffrey Raymond, Mrs. Ralph Paton, John Parker, Elizabeth Russell." He laid the paper down on the table.

"What's the meaning of all this?" began Raymond.

"The list I have just read," said Poirot, "is a list of suspected persons. Everyone of you present had the opportunity to kill Mr. Ackroyd—"

With a cry Mrs. Ackroyd sprang up, her throat working. "I don't like it," she wailed. "I don't like it. I would much prefer to go home."

"You cannot go home, madame," said Poirot sternly, "until you have heard what I have to say."

He paused a moment, then cleared his throat. "I will start at the beginning. When Miss Ackroyd asked me to investigate the case, I went up to Fernly Park with the good Dr. Sheppard. I walked with him along the terrace, where I was shown the footprints on the window-sill. From there Inspector Raglan took me along the path which leads to the drive. My eye was caught by a little summerhouse, and I searched it thoroughly. I found two things—a scrap of starched cambric and an empty goose quill. The scrap of cambric immediately suggested to me a maid's apron. When Inspector Raglan showed me his list of the people in the house, I noticed at once that one of the maids—Ursula Bourne, the parlormaid—had no real alibi. According to her own story, she was in her bedroom from nine-thirty until ten. But supposing that instead she was in the summer-house? If so, she must have gone there to meet someone. Now we know from Dr. Sheppard that someone from outside *did* come to the house that night—the stranger whom he met just by the gate. At a first glance it would seem that our problem was solved, and that the stranger went to the summerhouse to meet Ursula Bourne. It was fairly certain that he *did* go to the summerhouse because of the goose quill. That suggested at once to my mind a taker of drugs—and one who had acquired the habit on the other side of the Atlantic where sniffing 'snow' is more common than in this country. The man who Dr. Sheppard met had an American accent, which fitted in with that supposition.

"But I was held up by one point. *The times did not fit.* Ursula Bourne could certainly not have gone to the summerhouse before nine-thirty, whereas the man must have got there by a few minutes past nine. I could, of course, assume that he waited there for half an hour. The only alternative supposition was that there had been two separate meetings in the summerhouse that night. *Eh bien,* as soon as I went into that alternative I found several significant facts. I discovered that Miss Russell, the housekeeper, had visited Dr. Sheppard that morning, and had displayed a good deal of interest in cures for victims of the drug habit. Taking that in conjunction with the goose quill, I assumed that the man in question came to Fernly to meet the housekeeper, and not Ursula Bourne. Who, then, did Ursula Bourne come to the rendezvous to meet? I was not long in doubt. First I found a ring—a wedding ring—with 'From R.' and a date inside it. Then I learnt that Ralph Paton had been seen coming up the path which led to the summer house at twenty-five minutes past nine, and I also heard of a certain conversation which had taken place in the wood near the village that very afternoon—a conversation between Ralph Paton and some unknown girl. So I had my facts succeeding each other in a neat and orderly manner. A secret marriage, an engagement announced on the day of the tragedy, the stormy interview in the wood, and the meeting arranged for the summerhouse that night.

"Incidentally this proved to me one thing, that both Ralph Paton and Ursula Bourne (or Paton) had the strongest motives for wishing Mr. Ackroyd out of the way. And it also made one other point unexpectedly clear. It could not have been Ralph Paton who was with Mr. Ackroyd in the study at nine-thirty.

"So we come to another and most interesting aspect of the crime. Who was it in the room with Mr. Ackroyd at nine-thirty? Not Ralph Paton, who was in the summerhouse with his wife. Not Charles Kent, who had already left. Who, then? I posed my cleverest—my most audacious question: *Was anyone with him?*"

Poirot leaned forward and shot the last words triumphantly at us, drawing back afterward with the air of one who has made a decided hit.

Raymond, however, did not seem impressed, and lodged a mild protest. "I don't know if you're trying to make me out a liar, M. Poirot, but the matter does not rest on my evidence alone—except perhaps as to the exact words used. Remember, Major Blunt also heard Mr. Ackroyd talking to someone. He was on the terrace outside, and couldn't catch the words clearly, but he distinctly heard the voices."

Poirot nodded. "I have not forgotten," he said quietly. "But Major Blunt was under the impression that it was *you* to whom Mr. Ackroyd was speaking."

For a moment Raymond seemed taken aback. Then he recovered himself. "Blunt knows now that he was mistaken, he said."

"Exactly," agreed the other man.

"Yet there must have been some reason for his thinking so," mused Poirot. "Oh! No," he held up his hand in protest, "I know the reason you will give—but it is not enough. We must seek elsewhere. I will put it this way. From the beginning of the case I have been struck by one thing—the nature of those words which Mr. Raymond overheard. It has been amazing to me that no one has commented on them—has seen anything odd about them."

He paused a minute, and then quoted softly: "*. . . The calls on my purse have been so frequent of late that I fear it is impossible for me to accede to your request.* Does nothing strike you as odd about that?"

"I don't think so," said Raymond. "He has frequently dictated letters to me, using almost exactly those same words."

"Exactly," cried Poirot. "That is what I seek to arrive at. Would any man use such a phrase in *talking* to another? Impossible that that should be part of a real conversation. Now if he had been dictating a letter—"

"You mean he was reading a letter aloud," said Raymond slowly. "Even so, he must have been reading to someone."

"But why? We have no evidence that there was anyone else in the room. No other voice but Mr. Ackroyd's was heard, remember."

"Surely a man wouldn't read letters of that type aloud to himself—not unless he was—well—going balmy."

"You have forgotten one thing," said Poirot softly: "the stranger who called at the house the preceding Wednesday."

They all stared at him.

"But yes," said Poirot, nodding encouragingly, "on Wednesday. The young man was not of himself important. But the firm he represented interested me very much."

"The Dictaphone Company," gasped Raymond. "I see it now. A dictaphone. That's what you think?"

Poirot nodded. "Mr. Ackroyd had promised to invest in a dictaphone, you remember. Me, I had the curiosity to inquire of the company in question. Their reply is that Mr. Ackroyd *did* purchase a dictaphone from their representative. Why he concealed the matter from you, I do not know."

"He must have meant to surprise me with it," murmured Raymond. "He had quite a childish love of surprising people. Meant to keep it up his sleeve for a day or so. Probably was playing with it like a new toy. Yes, it fits in. You're quite right—no one would use quite those words in casual conversation."

"It explains too," said Poirot, "why Major Blunt thought it was you who was in the study. Such scraps as came to him were fragments of dictation, and so his subconscious mind deduced that you were with him. His conscious mind was occupied with something quite different—the white figure he had caught a glimpse of. He fancied it was Miss Ackroyd. Really, of course, it was Ursula Bourne's white apron he saw as she was stealing down to the summerhouse."

Raymond had recovered from his first surprise. "All the same," he remarked, "this discovery of yours, brilliant though it is (I'm quite sure I should never have thought of it), leaves the essential position unchanged. Mr. Ackroyd was alive at nine-thirty, since he was speaking into the dictaphone. It seems clear that the man Charles Kent was really off the premises by then. As to Ralph Paton—?" He hesitated, glancing at Ursula.

Her color flared up, but she answered steadily enough. "Ralph and I parted just before a quarter to ten. He never went near the house, I am sure of that. He had no intention of doing so. The last thing on earth he wanted was to face his stepfather. He would have funked it badly."

"It isn't that I doubt your story for a moment," explained Raymond. "I've always been quite sure Captain Paton was innocent. But one has to think of a court of law—and the questions that would be asked. He is in a most unfortunate position, but if he were to come forward—"

Poirot interrupted. "That is your advice, yes? That he should come forward?"

"Certainly. If you know where he is—"

"I perceive that you do not believe that I do know. And yet I have told you just now that I know everything. The truth of the telephone call, of the footprints on the window sill, of the hiding place of Ralph Paton—"

"Where is he?" said Blunt sharply.

"Not very far away," said Poirot, smiling.

"In Cranchester?" I asked.

Poirot turned toward me. "Always you ask me that. The idea of Cranchester it is with you an *idée fixe*. No, he is not in Cranchester. He is—*there!*" He pointed a dramatic forefinger. Everyone's head turned. Ralph Paton was standing in the doorway.

24
Ralph Paton's Story

IT WAS A very uncomfortable minute for *me*. I hardly took in what happened next, but there were exclamations and cries of surprise! When I was sufficiently master of myself to be able to realize what was going on, Ralph Paton was standing by his wife, her hand in his, and he was smiling across the room at me.

Poirot, too, was smiling, and at the same time shaking an eloquent finger at me. "Have I not told you at least thirty-six times that it is useless to conceal things from Hercule Poirot?" he demanded. "That in such a case he finds out?"

He turned to the others. "One day, you remember, we held a little séance about the table—just the six of us. I accused the other five persons present of concealing something from me. Four of them gave up their secret. Dr. Sheppard did not give up his. But all along I have had my suspicions. Dr. Sheppard went to the Three Boars that night hoping to find Ralph. He did not find him there; but supposing, I said to myself, that he met him in the street on his way home? Dr. Sheppard was a friend of Captain Paton's, and he had come straight from the scene of the crime. He must know that things looked very black against him. Perhaps he knew more than the general public did—"

"I did," I said ruefully. "I suppose I might as well make a clean breast of things now. I went to see Ralph that afternoon. At first he refused to take me into his confidence, but he later told me about his marriage, and the hole he was in. As soon as the murder was discovered, I realized that once the facts were known, suspicion could not fail to attach to Ralph—or, if not to him, to the girl he loved. That night I put the facts plainly before him. The thought of having possibly to give evidence which might incriminate his wife made him resolve at all costs to—to—"

I hesitated, and Ralph filled up the gap. "To do a bunk," he said graphically. "You see, Ursula left me to go back to the house. I thought it possible she might have attempted to have another interview with my stepfather. He had already been very rude to her that afternoon. It occurred to me that he might have so insulted her—in such an unforgivable manner—that without knowing what she was doing—"

He stopped. Ursula released her hand from his, and stepped back. "You thought that, Ralph! You actually thought that I might have done it?"

"Let us get back to the culpable conduct of Dr. Sheppard," said Poirot dryly. "Dr. Sheppard consented to do what he could to help him. He was successful in hiding Captain Paton from the police."

"Where?" said Raymond. "In his own house?"

"Ah, no, indeed," said Poirot. "You should ask yourself the question that I did. If the good doctor is concealing the young man, what place would he choose? It must necessarily be somewhere near at hand. I think of Cranchester. A hotel? No. Lodgings? Even more emphatically, no. Where, then? Ah! I have it. A nursing home. A home for the mentally unfit. I test my theory. I invent a nephew with mental trouble. I consult Mademoiselle Sheppard as to suitable homes. She gives me the names of two near Cranchester to which her brother has sent patients. I make inquiries. Yes, at one of them a patient was brought there by the doctor himself early on Saturday morning. That patient, though known by another name, I had no difficulty in identifying as Captain Paton. After certain necessary formalities, I was allowed to bring him away. He arrived at my house in the early hours of yesterday morning."

I looked at him ruefully. "Caroline's Home Office expert," I murmured. "And to think I never guessed!"

"You see now why I drew attention to the reticence of your manuscript," murmured Poirot. "It was strictly truthful as far as it went—but it did not go very far, eh, my friend?"

I was too abashed to argue.

"Dr. Sheppard has been very loyal," said Ralph. "He has stood by me through thick and thin. He did what he thought was the best. I see now, from what M. Poirot has told me, that it was not really the best. I should have come forward and faced the music. You see, in the home, we never saw a newspaper. I knew nothing of what was going on."

"Dr. Sheppard has been a model of discretion," said Poirot dryly. "But me, I discover all the little secrets. It is my business."

"Now we can have your story of what happened that night," said Raymond impatiently.

"You know it already," said Ralph. "There's very little for me to add. I left the summer-house about nine-forty-five, and tramped about the lanes, trying to make up my mind as to what to do next—what line to take. I'm bound to admit that I've not the shadow of an alibi, but I give you my solemn word that I never went to the study, that I never saw my stepfather alive—or dead. Whatever the world thinks, I'd like all of you to believe me."

"No alibi," murmured Raymond. "That's bad. I believe you, of course, but—it's bad business."

"It makes things very simple, though," said Poirot, in a cheerful voice. "Very simple indeed."

We all stared at him.

"You see what I mean? No? Just this—to save Captain Paton the real criminal must confess." He beamed round at us all. "But yes—I mean what I say. See now. I did not invite Inspector Raglan to be present. That was for a reason. I did not want to tell him all that I knew—at least I did not want to tell him tonight."

He leaned forward, and suddenly his voice and his whole personality changed. He suddenly became dangerous. "I who speak to you—I know the murderer of Mr. Ackroyd is in this room now. It is to the murderer I speak. *Tomorrow the truth goes to Inspector Raglan.* You understand?"

There was a tense silence. Into the midst of it came the old Breton woman with a telegram on a salver. Poirot tore it open.

Blunt's voice abrupt and resonant. "The murderer is amongst us, you say? You know—which?"

Poirot had read the message. He crumpled it up in his hand. "I know—now." He tapped the crumpled ball of paper.

"What is that?" said Raymond sharply.

"A wireless message—from a steamer now on her way to the United States."

There was a dead silence, Poirot rose to his feet bowing. "Messieurs et Mesdames, this reunion of mine is ended. Remember—*the truth goes to Inspector Raglan in the morning.*"

25
The Whole Truth

A SLIGHT GESTURE from Poirot enjoined me to stay behind the rest. I obeyed, going over to the fire and thoughtfully stirring the big logs on it with the toe of my boot.

I was puzzled. For the first time I was absolutely at sea as to Poirot's meaning. For a moment I was inclined to think that the scene I had just witnessed was a gigantic piece of bombast—that he had been what he called "playing the comedy" with a view to making himself interesting and important. But, in spite of myself, I was forced to believe in an underlying reality. There had been real menace in his words—a certain indisputable sincerity. But I still believed him to be on entirely the wrong tack.

When the door shut behind the last of the party he came over to the fire. "Well, my friend," he said quietly, "and what do you think of it all?"

"I don't know what to think," I said frankly. "What was the point? Why not go straight to Inspector Raglan with the truth instead of giving the guilty person this elaborate warning?"

Poirot sat down and drew out his case of tiny Russian cigarettes. He smoked for a minute or two in silence. Then: "Use your little gray cells," he said. "There is always a reason behind my actions."

I hesitated for a moment, and then I said slowly: "The first one that occurs to me is that you yourself do not know who the guilty person is, but that you are sure that he is to be found amongst the people here tonight. Therefore your words were intended to force a confession from the unknown murderer."

Poirot nodded approvingly. "A clever idea, but not the truth."

"I thought, perhaps, that by making him believe you knew, you might force him out into the open—not necessarily by confession. He might try to silence you as he formerly silenced Mr. Ackroyd—before you could act tomorrow morning."

"A trap with myself as the bait! *Merci, mon ami*, but I am not sufficiently heroic for that."

"Then I fail to understand you. Surely you are running the risk of letting the murderer escape by thus putting him on his guard?"

Poirot shook his head. "He cannot escape," he said gravely. "There is only one way out—and that way does not lead to freedom."

"You really believe that one of those people here tonight committed the murder?" I asked incredulously.

"Yes, my friend."

"Which one?"

There was a silence for some minutes. Then Poirot tossed the stump of his cigarette into the grate and began to speak in a quiet, reflective tone. "I will take you the way that I have traveled myself. Step by step you shall accompany me, and see for yourself that all the facts point indisputably to one person. Now, to begin with, there were two facts and one little discrepancy in time which especially attracted my attention. The first fact was the telephone call. If Ralph Paton were indeed the murderer, the telephone call became meaningless and absurd. Therefore, I said to myself, Ralph Paton is not the murderer.

"I have satisfied myself that the call could not have been sent by anyone in the house, yet I was convinced that it was amongst those present on the fatal evening that I had to look for my criminal. Therefore I concluded that the telephone call must have been sent by an accomplice. I was not quite pleased with that deduction, but I let it stand for the minute.

"I next examined the *motive* for the call. That was difficult. I could only get at it by judging its *result*. Which was—that the murder was discovered that night instead of—in all probability—the following morning. You agree with that?"

"Ye-es," I admitted. "Yes. As you say, Mr. Ackroyd, having given orders that he was not to be disturbed, nobody would have been likely to go to the study that night."

"*Très bien.* The affair marches, does it not? But matters were still obscure. What was the advantage of having the crime discovered that night in preference to the following morning? The only idea I could get hold of was that the murderer, knowing the crime was to be discovered at a certain time, could make sure of being present when the door was broken in—or at any rate immediately afterward. And now we come to the second fact—the chair pulled out from the wall. Inspector Raglan dismissed that as of no importance. I, on the contrary, have always regarded it as of supreme importance."

"In your manuscripts you have drawn a neat little plan of the study. If you had it with you this minute you would see that—the chair being drawn out in the position indicated by Parker—it would stand in a direct line between the door and the window."

"The window," I said quickly.

"You, too, have my first idea. I imagined that the chair was drawn out so that something connected with the window should not be seen by one entering through the door. But I soon abandoned that supposition, for though the chair was a grandfather with a high back, it obscured very little of the window—only the part between the sash and the ground. No, *mon ami*—but remember that just in front of the window there stood a table with books and magazines upon it. Now that table *was* completely hidden by the drawn-out chair—and immediately I had my first shadowy suspicion of the truth.

"Supposing that there had been something on that table not intended to be seen? Something placed there by the murderer? As yet I had no inkling of what that something might be. But I knew certain very interesting facts about it. For instance, it was something that the murderer had not been able to take away with him at the time that he committed the crime. At the same time it was vital that it should be removed as soon as possible after the crime had been discovered. And so—the telephone message, and the opportunity for the murderer to be on the spot when the body was discovered.

"Now four people were on the scene before the police arrived. Yourself,

Parker, Major Blunt, and Raymond. Parker I eliminated at once, since at whatever time the crime was discovered, he was the one person certain to be on the spot. Also it was he who told me of the pulled-out chair. Parker, then, was cleared (of the murder, that is. I still thought it possible that he had been blackmailing Mrs. Ferrars). Raymond and Blunt, however, remained under suspicion since, if the crime had been discovered in the early hours of the morning, it was quite possible that they might have arrived on the scene too late to prevent the object on the round table being discovered.

"Now what was that object? You heard my arguments tonight in reference to the scrap of conversation overheard? As soon as I learned that a representative of a dictaphone company had called, the idea of the dictaphone took root in my mind. You heard what I said in this room not half an hour ago? They all agreed with my theory—but one vital fact seems to have escaped them. Granted that a dictaphone was being used by Mr. Ackroyd that night—why was no dictaphone found?"

"I never thought of that," I said.

"We know that a dictaphone was supplied to Mr. Ackroyd. But no dictaphone has been found among his effects. So, if something was taken from that table—why should not that something be the dictaphone? But there were certain difficulties in the way. The attention of everyone was, of course, focused on the murdered man. I think anyone could have gone to the table unnoticed by the other people in the room. But a dictaphone has certain bulk—it cannot be slipped casually into a pocket. There must have been a receptacle of some kind capable of holding it.

"You see where I am arriving? The figure of the murderer is taking shape. A person who was on the scene straightaway, but who might not have been if the crime had been discovered the following morning. A person carrying a receptacle into which the dictaphone might be fitted—"

I interrupted. "But why remove the dictaphone? What was the point?"

"You are like Mr. Raymond. You take it for granted that what was heard at nine-thirty was Mr. Ackroyd's voice speaking into a dictaphone. But consider this useful invention for a little minute. You dictate into it, do you not? And at some later time a secretary or a typist turns it on, and the voice speaks again."

"You mean—" I gasped.

Poirot nodded. "Yes, I mean that. *At nine-thirty Mr. Ackroyd was already dead.* It was the dictaphone speaking—not the man."

"And the murderer switched it on. Then he must have been in the room at that minute?"

"Possibly. But we must not exclude the likelihood of some mechanical device having been applied—something after the nature of a time lock, or even of a simple alarm clock. But in that case we must add two qualifications to our imaginary portrait of the murderer. It must be someone who knew of Mr. Ackroyd's purchase of the dictaphone and also someone with the necessary mechanical knowledge.

"I had got thus far in my own mind when we came to the footprints on the window ledge. Here there were three conclusions open to me. (1) They might really have been made by Ralph Paton. He had been at Fernly that night, and might have climbed into the study and found his uncle dead there. That was one hypothesis. (2) There was the possibility that the footmarks might have been made by somebody else who happened to have the same kind of studs in his shoes. But the inmates of the house had shoes soled with crepe rubber, and I declined to believe in the coincidence of someone from outside having the same kind of shoes as Ralph Paton wore. Charles Kent, as we know from the barmaid of the Dog and Whistle, had on a pair of boots 'clean dropping off him.' (3) Those prints were made by someone deliberately trying to throw suspicion on Ralph Paton. To test this last conclusion, it was necessary to ascertain certain facts. One pair of Ralph's shoes had been obtained from the Three Boars by the police. Neither Ralph nor anyone else could have worn them that evening, since they were downstairs being cleaned. According to the police theory, Ralph was wearing another pair of the same kind, and I found out that it was true that he had two pairs. Now for my theory to be proved correct it was necessary for the murderer to have worn Ralph's shoes that evening—in which case Ralph must have been wearing yet a *third* pair of footwear of some kind. I could hardly suppose that he would bring three pairs of shoes all alike—the third pair of footwear were more likely to be boots. I got your sister to make inquiries on this point—laying some stress on the color, in order—I admit it frankly—to obscure the real reason for my asking.

"You know the result of her investigations. Ralph Paton *had* had a pair of boots with him. The first question I asked him when he came to my house yesterday morning was what he was wearing on his feet on the fatal night. He replied at once that he had worn *boots*—he was still wearing them, in fact—having nothing else to put on.

"So we get a step further in our description of the murderer—a person who had the opportunity to take these shoes of Ralph Paton's from the Three Boars that day."

He paused, and then said, with a slightly raised voice:

"There is one further point. The murderer must have been a person who had the opportunity to purloin that dagger from the silver table. You might argue that anyone in the house might have done so, but I will recall to you that Miss Ackroyd was very positive that the dagger was not there when she examined that silver table."

He paused again. "Let us recapitulate—now that all is clear. A person who was at the Three Boars earlier that day, a person who knew Ackroyd well enough to know that he had purchased a dictaphone, a person who was of a mechanical turn of mind, who had the opportunity to take the dagger from the silver table before Miss Flora arrived, who had with him a receptacle suitable for hiding the dictaphone—such as a black bag, and who had the study to himself for a few minutes after the crime was discovered while Parker was telephoning for the police. In fact—*Dr. Sheppard!*"

26
And Nothing but the Truth

THERE WAS A dead silence for a minute and a half.

Then I laughed. "You're mad," I said.

"No," said Poirot placidly. "I am not mad. It was the little discrepancy in time that first drew my attention to you—right at the beginning."

"Discrepancy in time?" I queried, puzzled.

"But yes. You will remember that everyone agreed—you yourself included—that it took five minutes to walk from the lodge to the house—less if you took the short cut to the terrace. But you left the house at ten minutes to nine—both by your own statement and that of Parker, and yet it was nine o'clock as you passed through the lodge gates. It was a chilly night—not an evening a man would be inclined to dawdle; why had you taken ten minutes to do a five-minutes' walk? All along I realized that we had only your statement for it that the study window was ever fastened. Ackroyd asked you if you had done so—he never looked to see. Supposing, then, that the study window was unfastened? Would there be time in that ten minutes for you to round the outside of the house, change your shoes, climb in through the window, kill Ackroyd, and get to the gate by nine o'clock? I decided against that theory since in all probability a man as nervous as Ackroyd was that night would hear you climbing in, and then there would have been a struggle. But supposing that you killed Ackroyd *before* you left—as you were standing beside his chair? Then you go out of the front door, run round to the summer-house, take Ralph Paton's shoes out of the bag you brought up with you that night, slip them on, walk through the mud in them, and leave prints on the window ledge, you climb in, lock the study door on the inside, run back to the summer-house, change back into your own shoes, and race down to the gate. (I went through similar actions the other day, when you were with Mrs. Ackroyd—it took ten minutes exactly.) Then home—and an alibi—since you had timed the dictaphone for half-past nine."

"My dear Poirot," I said in a voice that sounded strange and forced to my own ears, "you've been brooding over this case too long. What on earth had I to gain by murdering Ackroyd?"

"Safety. It was you who blackmailed Mrs. Ferrars. Who could have had a better knowledge of what killed Mr. Ferrars than the doctor who was attending him? When you spoke to me that first day in the garden, you mentioned a legacy received about a year ago. I have been unable to discover any trace of a legacy. You had to invent some way of accounting for Mrs. Ferrars's twenty thousand pounds. It has not done you much good. You lost most of it in speculation—then you put the screw on too hard, and Mrs. Ferrars took a way out that you had not expected. If Ackroyd had learnt the truth he would have had no mercy on you—you were ruined forever."

"And the telephone call?" I asked, trying to rally. "You have a plausible explanation of that also, I suppose?"

"I will confess to you that it was my greatest stumbling block when I found that a call had actually been put through to you from King's Abbot station. I at first believed that you had simply invented the story. It was a very clever touch, that. You must have some excuse for arriving at Fernly, finding the body, and so getting a chance to remove the dictaphone on which your alibi depended. I had a very vague notion of how it was worked when I came to see your sister that first day and inquired as to what patients you had seen on Friday morning. I had no thought of Miss Russell in my mind at that time. Her visit was a lucky coincidence, since it distracted your mind from the real object of my questions. I found what I was looking for. Among your patients that morning was the steward of an American liner. Who more suitable than he to be leaving for Liverpool by the train that evening? And afterward he would be on the high seas, well out of the way. I noted that the *Orion* sailed on Saturday, and having obtained the name of the steward I sent him a wireless message asking a certain question. This is his reply you saw me receive just now."

He held out the message to me. It ran as follows— *"Quite correct. Dr. Sheppard asked me to leave a note at a patient's house. I was to ring him up from the station with the reply. Reply was 'No answer.'"*

"It was a clever idea," said Poirot. "The call was genuine. Your sister saw you take it. But there was only one man's word as to what was actually said—your own!"

I yawned. "All this," I said, "is very interesting—but hardly in the sphere of practical politics."

"You think not? Remember what I said—the truth goes to Inspector Raglan in the morning. But, for the sake of your good sister, I am willing to give you the chance of another way out. There might be, for instance, an overdose of a sleeping draught. You comprehend me? But Captain Ralph Paton must be cleared—*ça va sans dire.*[1] I should suggest that you finish that very interesting manuscript of yours—but abandoning your former reticence."

"You seem to be very prolific of suggestions," I remarked. "Are you sure you've quite finished?"

"Now that you remind me of the fact, it is true that there is one thing more. It would be most unwise on your part to attempt to silence me as you silenced M. Ackroyd. That kind of business does not succeed against Hercule Poirot, you understand?"

"My dear Poirot," I said, smiling a little, "whatever else I may be, I am not a fool," I rose to my feet. "Well, well," I said, with a slight yawn, "I must be off home. Thank you for a most interesting and instructive evening."

Poirot also rose and bowed with his accustomed politeness as I passed out of the room.

---

[1] That goes without saying.—EDITOR.

27
Apologia

FIVE A.M. I am very tired—but I have finished my task. My arm aches from writing.

A strange end to my manuscript. I meant it to be published some day as the history of one of Poirot's failures! Odd, how things pan out.

All along I've had a premonition of disaster, from the moment I saw Ralph Paton and Mrs. Ferrars with their heads together. I thought then that she was confiding in him; as it happened I was quite wrong there, but the idea persisted even after I went into the study with Ackroyd that night, until he told me the truth.

Poor old Ackroyd. I'm always glad that I gave him a chance. I urged him to read that letter before it was too late. Or let me be honest—didn't I subconsciously realize that with a pigheaded chap like him, it was my best chance of getting him *not* to read it? His nervousness that night was interesting psychologically. He knew danger was close at hand. And yet he never suspected *me.*

The dagger was an afterthought. I'd brought up a very handy little weapon of my own, but when I saw the dagger lying in the silver table, it occurred to me at once how much better it would be to use a weapon that couldn't be traced to me.

I suppose I must have meant to murder him all along. As soon as I heard of Mrs. Ferrars's death, I felt convinced that she would have told him everything before she died. When I met him and he seemed so agitated, I thought that perhaps he knew the truth, but that he couldn't bring himself to believe it, and was going to give me the chance of refuting it.

So I went home and took my precautions. If the trouble were after all only something to do with Ralph—well, no harm would have been done. The dictaphone he had given me two days before to adjust. Something had gone a little wrong with it, and I persuaded him to let me have a go at it, instead of sending it back. I did what I wanted to it, and took it up with me in my bag that evening.

I am rather pleased with myself as a writer. What could be neater, for instance, than the following: *"The letters were brought in at twenty minutes to nine. It was just on ten minutes to nine when I left him, the letter still unread. I hesitated with my hand on the door handle, looking back and wondering if there was anything I had left undone."*

All true, you see. But suppose I had put a row of stars after the first sentence! Would somebody than have wondered what exactly happened in that blank ten minutes?

When I looked round the room from the door, I was quite satisfied. Nothing had been left undone. The dictaphone was on the table by the window, timed to go off at nine-thirty (the mechanism of that little device was rather clever—based on the principle of an alarm clock), and the armchair was pulled out so as to hide it from the door.

I must admit that it gave me rather a shock to run into Parker just outside the door. I have faithfully recorded that fact.

Then later, when the body was discovered, and I had sent Parker to telephone for the police, what a judicious use of words: *"I did what little had to be done!"* It was quite little—just to shove the dictaphone into my bag and push back the chair against the wall in its proper place. I never dreamed that Parker would have noticed that chair. Logically, he ought to have been so agog over the body as to be blind to everything else. But I hadn't reckoned with the trained-servant complex.

I wish I could have known beforehand that Flora was going to say she'd seen her uncle alive at a quarter to ten. That puzzled me more than I can say. In fact, all through the case there have been things that puzzled me hopelessly. Everyone seems to have taken a hand.

My greatest fear all though has been Caroline. I have fancied she might guess. Curious the way she spoke that day of my "strain of weakness." Well, she will never know the truth. There is, as Poirot said, one way out . . .

I can trust him. He and Inspector Raglan will manage it between them. I should not like Caroline to know. She is fond of me, and then, too, she is proud. . . . My death will be a grief to her, but grief passes.

When I have finished writing, I shall enclose this whole manuscript in an envelope and address it to Poirot.

And then—what shall it be? Veronal? There would be a kind of justice. Not that I take any responsibility for Mrs. Ferrars's death. It was the direct consequence of her own actions. I feel no pity for her.

I have no pity for myself either.

So let it be veronal.

But I wish Hercule Poirot had never retired from work and come here to grow vegetable marrows.

THE END

The Boomerang Clue

1
The Accident

BOBBY JONES TEED up his ball, gave a short preliminary waggle, took the club back slowly, then brought it down and through with the rapidity of lightning.

Did the ball fly down the fairway straight and true, rising as it went and soaring over the bunker to land within an easy machine shot of the fourteenth green?

No, it did not. Badly topped, it scudded along the ground and embedded itself firmly in the bunker!

There were no eager crowds to groan with dismay. The solitary witness of the shot manifested no surprise. And that is easily explained—for it was not the American-born master of the game who had played the shot but merely the fourth son of the Vicar of Marchbolt, a small seaside town on the coast of Wales.

Bobby uttered a decidedly profane ejaculation.

He was an amiable-looking young man of about eight-and-twenty. His best friend could not have said that he was handsome, but his face was an eminently likable one, and his eyes had the honest brown friendliness of a dog's.

"I get worse every day," he muttered dejectedly.

"You press," said his companion.

Dr. Thomas was a middle-aged man with gray hair and a red, cheerful face. He himself never took a full swing. He played short, straight shots down the middle and usually beat more brilliant but more erratic players.

Bobby attacked his ball fiercely with a niblick. The third time was successful. The ball lay a short distance from the green which Dr. Thomas had reached with two creditable iron shots.

"Your hole," said Bobby.

They proceeded to the next tee.

The doctor drove first—a nice straight shot, but with no great distance about it.

Bobby sighed, teed his ball, reteed it, waggled his club a long time, took back stiffly, shut his eyes, raised his head, depressed his right shoulder, did everything he ought not to have done—and hit a screamer down the middle of the course!

He drew a deep breath of satisfaction. The well-known golfer's gloom passed from his eloquent face to be succeeded by the equally well-known golfer's exultation.

"I know now what I've been doing," said Bobby—quite untruthfully.

A perfect iron shot, a little chip with a mashie, and Bobby lay dead. He achieved a birdie four, and Dr. Thomas was reduced to one up.

Full of confidence, Bobby stepped onto the sixteenth tee. He again did everything he should not have done, and this time no miracle occurred. A terrific, a magnificent, an almost superhuman slice happened! The ball went round at right angles.

"If that had been straight—whew!" said Dr. Thomas.

"*If*—" said Bobby bitterly. "Hullo, I thought I heard a shout! Hope the ball didn't hit anyone."

He peered out to the right. It was a difficult light. The sun was on the point of setting, and looking straight into it, it was hard to see anything distinctly. Also there was a slight mist rising from the sea. The edge of the cliff was a few hundred yards away.

"The footpath runs along there," said Bobby. "But the ball can't possibly have traveled as far as that. All the same, I did think I heard a cry. Did you?"

But the Doctor had heard nothing.

Bobby went after his ball. He had some difficulty in finding it, but ran it to earth at last. It was practically unplayable—embedded in a furze bush. He had a couple of hacks at it, then picked it up and called out to his companion that he gave up the hole.

The Doctor came over toward him since the next tee was right on the edge of the cliff.

The seventeenth was Bobby's particular bugbear. At it you had to drive over a chasm. The distance was not actually so great, but the attraction of the depths below was overpowering.

They had crossed the footpath, which now ran inland to their left skirting the very edge of the cliff.

The Doctor took an iron and just landed on the other side.

Bobby took a deep breath and drove. The ball scudded forward and disappeared over the lip of the abyss.

"Every single dashed time," said Bobby bitterly, "I do the same dashed idiotic thing!"

He skirted the chasm, peering over. Far below the sea sparkled, but not every ball was lost in its depths. The drop was sheer at the top, but below it shelved gradually.

Bobby walked slowly along. There was, he knew, one place where one could scramble down fairly easily. Caddies did so, hurling themselves over the edge and reappearing triumphant and panting with the missing ball.

Suddenly Bobby stiffened and called to his companion: "I say, Doctor, come here. What do you make of that?"

Some forty feet below was a dark heap of something that looked like old clothes.

The Doctor caught his breath. "By Jove!" he said. "Somebody's fallen over the cliff. We must get down to him."

Side by side the two men scrambled down the rock, the more athletic Bobby helping the other. At last they reached the ominous dark bundle. It was a man of about forty—and he was still breathing, though unconscious.

The Doctor examined him, touching his limbs, feeling his pulse, drawing down the lids of his eyes. He knelt down beside him and completed his examination. Then he looked up at Bobby, who was standing there feeling rather sick, and slowly shook his head.

"Nothing to be done," he said. "His number's up, poor fellow. His back's broken. Well, well. I suppose he wasn't familiar with the path and when the mist came up he walked over the edge. I've told the council more than once there ought to be a railing just here."

He stood up again. "I'll go off and get help," he said. "Make arrangements to have the body got up. It'll be dark before we know where we are. Will you stay here?"

Bobby nodded. "There's nothing to be done for him, I suppose?" he asked.

The Doctor shook his head. "Nothing. It won't be long—the pulse is weakening fast. He'll last another twenty minutes at most. Just possible he may recover consciousness before the end—but very likely he won't. Still—"

"Rather," said Bobby quickly. "I'll stay. You get along. If he does come to, there's no drug or anything—?" He hesitated.

The Doctor shook his head. "There'll be no pain," he said. "No pain at all."

Turning away he began rapidly to climb up the cliffs again. Bobby watched him till he disappeared over the top with a wave of the hand.

Bobby moved a step or two along the narrow ledge, sat down on a projection in the rock and lit a cigarette. The business had shaken him. Up to now he had never come in contact with illness or death.

What rotten luck there was in the world! A swirl of mist on a fine evening, a false step—and life came to an end. Fine, healthy-looking fellow too—probably never known a day's illness in his life. The pallor of approaching death couldn't disguise the deep tan of the skin. A man who had lived an out-of-door life—abroad perhaps. Bobby studied him more closely—the crisp curling chestnut hair just touched with gray at the temples, the big nose, the strong jaw, the white teeth just showing through the parted lips. Then the broad shoulders and the fine sinewy hands. The legs were twisted at a curious angle. Bobby shuddered and brought his eyes up again to the face. An attractive face, humorous, determined, resourceful. The eyes, he thought, were probably blue—

And just as he reached that point in his thoughts, the eyes suddenly opened.

They *were* blue, a clear deep blue. They looked straight at Bobby. There was nothing uncertain or hazy about them. They seemed completely conscious. They were watchful and at the same time they seemed to be asking a question.

Bobby got up quickly and came toward the man. Before he got there the other spoke. His voice was not weak—it came out clear and resonant.

"Why didn't they ask Evans?" he said.

And then a queer little shudder passed over him, the eyelids dropped, the jaw fell. . . .

The man was dead.

2

Concerning Fathers

BOBBY KNELT DOWN beside him, but there was no doubt. The man was dead. A last moment of consciousness, that sudden question and then—the end.

Rather apologetically Bobby put his hand into the dead man's pocket and drawing out a silk handkerchief he spread it reverently over the dead face. There was nothing more he could do.

Then he noticed that in his action he had jerked something else out of the pocket. It was a photograph, and in the act of replacing it he glanced at the pictured face.

It was a woman's face, strangely haunting in quality. A fair woman with wide-apart eyes. She seemed little more than a girl, certainly under thirty, but it was the arresting quality of her beauty rather than the beauty itself that seized upon the boy's imagination. It was the kind of face, he thought, not easy to forget.

Gently and reverently, he replaced the photograph in the pocket from which it had come. Then he sat down again to wait for the Doctor's return.

The time passed very slowly—or at least so it seemed to the waiting boy. Also he had just remembered something. He had promised his father to play the organ at the evening service at six o'clock, and it was now ten minutes to six. Naturally his father would understand the circumstances, but all the same he wished that he had remembered to send a message by the Doctor. The Rev. Thomas Jones was a man of extremely nervous temperament. He was *par excellence* a fusser, and when he fussed, his digestive apparatus collapsed and he suffered agonizing pain. Bobby, though he considered his father a pitiful old ass, was nevertheless extremely fond of him. The Rev. Thomas, on the other hand, considered his fourth son a pitiful young ass, and with less tolerance than Bobby sought to effect improvement in the young man.

"The poor old gov'nor," thought Bobby. "He'll be ramping up and down. He won't know whether to start the service or not. He'll work himself up till he gets that pain in the tummy, and then he won't be able to eat his supper. He won't have the sense to realize that I wouldn't let him down unless it were quite unavoidable. And anyhow, what does it matter? But he'll never see it that way. Nobody over fifty has got any sense—they worry themselves to death about tuppenny-ha'penny things that don't matter. They've been brought up all wrong. I suppose, and now they can't help themselves. Poor old Dad, he's got less sense than a chicken!"

He sat there thinking of his father with mingled affection and exasperation. His life at home seemed to him to be one long sacrifice to his father's peculiar ideas. To Mr. Jones, the same life seemed to be one long sacrifice on *his* part, ill understood or appreciated by the younger generation. So many ideas on the same subject differ.

What an age the Doctor was! Surely he might have been back by this time?

Bobby got up and stamped his feet moodily. At that moment he heard something above him and looked up, thankful that help was at hand and that his own services were no longer needed.

But it was not the Doctor. It was a man in plus-fours whom Bobby did not know.

"I say," said the newcomer. "Is anything the matter? Has there been an accident? Can I help in any way?"

He was a tall man with a pleasant tenor voice. Bobby could not see him very clearly, for it was now fast growing dusk.

He explained what had happened, while the stranger made shocked comments.

"There's nothing I can do?" he asked. "Get help or anything?"

Bobby explained that help was on the way and asked if the other could see any signs of its arriving.

"There's nothing at present."

"You see," went on Bobby, "I've got an appointment at six."

"And you don't like to leave—"

"No, I don't quite," said Bobby. "I mean, the poor chap's dead and all that, and of course one can't do anything, but all the same—"

He paused, finding it, as usual, difficult to put confused emotions into words.

The other, however, seemed to understand.

"I know," he said. "Look here, I'll come down—that is, if I can see my way—and I'll stay till these fellows arrive."

"Oh! Would you?" said Bobby gratefully. "You see, it's my father. He's not a bad sort really, and things upset him. Can you see your way? A bit more to the left—now to the right—that's it. It's not really difficult."

He encouraged the other with directions until the two men were face to face on the narrow plateau. The newcomer was a man of about thirty-five. He had a rather indecisive face which seemed to be calling for a monocle and a little mustache.

"I'm a stranger down here," he explained. 'My name's Bassington-ffrench, by the way. Came down to see about a house. I say, what a beastly thing to happen! Did he walk over the edge?"

Bobby nodded.

"Bit of mist got up," he explained. "It's a dangerous bit of path. Well, so long. Thanks very much. I've got to hurry. It's awfully good of you."

"Not at all," the other protested. "Anybody would do the same. Can't leave the poor chap lying—well, I mean, it wouldn't be decent somehow."

Bobby was scrambling up the precipitous path. At the top he waved his hand to the other then set off at a brisk run across country. To save time he vaulted the churchyard wall instead of going round to the gate on the road—a proceeding observed by the Vicar from the vestry window and deeply disapproved of by him.

It was five minutes past six, but the bell was still tolling.

Explanations and recriminations were postponed until after the service. Breathless, Bobby sank into his seat and manipulated the stops of the ancient organ. Association of ideas led his fingers into Chopin's funeral march.

Afterward, more in sorrow than in anger (as he expressly pointed out), the Vicar took his son to task.

"If you cannot do a thing properly, my dear Bobby," he said, "it is better not to do it at all. I know that you and all your young friends seem to have no idea of time, but there is One whom we should not keep waiting. You offered to play the organ of your own accord. I did not coerce you. Instead, faint-hearted, your preferred playing a game—"

Bobby thought he had better interrupt before his father got too well away.

"Sorry, Dad," he said, speaking cheerfully and breezily as was his habit no matter what the subject. "Not my fault this time. I was keeping guard over a corpse."

"You were what?"

"Keeping guard over a blighter who stepped over the cliff. You know—the place where the chasm is, by the seventeenth tee. There was a bit of mist just then, and he must have gone straight on and over."

"Good heavens," cried the Vicar. "What a tragedy! Was the man killed outright?"

"No. He was unconscious. He died just after Dr. Thomas had gone off. But of course I felt I had to squat there—couldn't just push off and leave him. And then another fellow came along, so I passed the job of chief mourner on to him and legged it here as fast as I could."

The Vicar sighed.

"Oh, my dear Bobby!" he said. "Will nothing shake your deplorable callousness? It grieves me more than I can say. Here you have been brought face to face with death—with sudden death. And you can joke about it! It leaves you unmoved. Everything—everything, however solemn, however sacred, is merely a joke to your generation."

Bobby shuffled his feet.

If his father couldn't see that of course you joked about a thing because you had felt badly about it—well, he couldn't see it! It wasn't the sort of thing you could explain. With death and tragedy about, you had to keep a stiff upper lip.

But what could you expect? Nobody over fifty understood anything at all. They had the most extraordinary ideas.

"I expect it was the War," thought Bobby loyally. "It upset them and they never got straight again."

"Sorry, Dad," he said with a clear-eyed realization that explanation was impossible.

The Vicar felt sorry for his son—he looked so abashed; but he also felt ashamed of him. The boy had no conception of the seriousness of life. Even his apology was cheery and impenitent.

They moved toward the Vicarage, each making enormous efforts to find excuses for the other.

The Vicar thought, "I wonder when Bobby will find something to do . . ."

Bobby thought, "Wonder how much longer I can stick it down here . . ."

Yet they were both extremely fond of each other.

3

A Railway Journey

BOBBY DID NOT see the immediate sequel of his adventure. On the following morning he went up to town, there to meet a friend who was thinking of starting a garage and who fancied that Bobby's cooperation might be valuable.

After settling things to everybody's satisfaction, Bobby caught the 11:30 train home two days later. He caught it, true, but only by a very narrow margin. He arrived at Paddington when the clock announced the time to be 11:28, dashed down the subway, emerged on No. 3 platform just as the train was moving, and hurled himself at the first carriage he saw, heedless of indignant ticket collectors and porters in his immediate rear.

Wrenching open the door, he fell in on hands and knees, picked himself up, the door was shut with a slam by an agile porter, and Bobby found himself looking at the sole other occupant of the compartment.

It was a first-class carriage and in the corner facing the engine sat a dark girl smoking a cigarette. She had on a red skirt, a short green jacket and a brilliant blue béret, and despite a certain resemblance to an organ-grinder's monkey (she had long, sorrowful, dark eyes and a puckered-up face) she was distinctly attractive.

In the midst of an apology, Bobby broke off.

"Why, it's you, Frankie!" he said. "I haven't seen you for ages."

"Well, I haven't seen you. Sit down and talk."

Bobby grinned. "My ticket's the wrong color."

"That doesn't matter," said Frankie kindly. "I'll pay the difference for you."

"My manly indignation rises at the thought," said Bobby. "How could I let a lady pay for me?"

"It's about all we seem to be good for these days," said Frankie.

"I will pay the difference myself," said Bobby heroically as a burly figure in blue appeared at the door from the corridor.

"Leave it to me," said Frankie.

She smiled graciously at the ticket-collector, who touched his hat as he took the piece of white cardboard from her and punched it.

"Mr. Jones has just come in to talk to me for a bit," she said. "That won't matter, will it?"

"That's alright, your ladyship. The gentleman won't be staying long, I expect." He coughed tactfully. "I shan't be round again till after Bristol," he added significantly.

"What can be done with a smile!" said Bobby as the official withdrew.

Lady Frances Derwent shook her head thoughtfully.

"I'm not so sure it's the smile," she said. "I rather think it's Father's habit of tipping everybody five shillings whenever he travels that does it."

"I thought you'd given up Wales for good, Frankie."

Frances sighed. "My dear, you know what it is. You know how mouldy parents can be. What with that, and the bathrooms in the state they are, and nothing to do and nobody to see—and people simply won't come to the country to stay nowadays! They say they're economizing and they can't go so far. Well, I mean, what's a girl to do?"

Bobby shook his head, sadly recognizing the problem.

"However," went on Frankie, "after the party I went to last night, I thought even home couldn't be worse."

"What was wrong with the party?"

"Nothing at all. It was just like any other party only more so. It was to start at the Savoy at half-past eight. Some of us rolled up about a quarter past nine, and of course we got entangled with other people, but we got sorted out about ten. And we had dinner and then after a bit we went on to the 'Marionette'—there was a rumor it was going to be raided. But nothing happened—it was just moribund. And we drank a bit, and then we went on to the 'Bullring'—and that was even deader. And then we went to a coffee stall, and then we went to a fried-fish place, and then we thought we'd go and breakfast with Angela's uncle and see if he'd be shocked—but he wasn't—only bored. And then we sort of fizzled home. Honestly, Bobby, it isn't good enough."

"I suppose not," said Bobby, stifling a pang of envy. Never in his wildest moments did he dream of being able to be a member of the "Marionette" or the "Bullring."

His relationship with Frankie was a peculiar one. As children he and his brothers had played with the children at the Castle. Now that they were all grown up, they seldom came across each other. When they did, they still used Christian names. On the rare occasions when Frankie was at home, Bobby and his brothers would go up and play tennis. But Frankie and her two brothers were not asked to the Vicarage. It seemed to be tacitly recognized that it would not be amusing for them. On the other hand extra men were always wanted for tennis. There may have been a trace of constraint in spite of the Christian names. The Derwents were perhaps a shade more friendly than they need have been, as though to show that "there was no difference." The Joneses, on their side, were a shade formal as though determined not to claim more friendship than was offered them. The two families had now nothing in common save certain childish memories. Yet Bobby was very fond of Frankie and was always pleased on the rare occasions when Fate threw them together.

"I'm so tired of everything," said Frankie in a weary voice. "Aren't you?"

Bobby considered. "No, I don't think I am."

"My dear, how wonderful!" said Frankie.

"I don't mean I'm hearty," said Bobby, anxious not to create a painful impression. "I just can't stand people who are hearty."

Frankie shuddered at the mere mention of the word. "I know," she murmured. "They're dreadful."

They looked at each other sympathetically.

"By the way," said Frankie suddenly, "what's all this about a man falling over the cliffs?"

"Dr. Thomas and I found him," said Bobby. "How did you know about it, Frankie?"

"Saw it in the paper. Look."

She indicated with her finger a small paragraph headed "Fatal Accident in Sea Mist."

> The victim of the tragedy at Marchbolt was identified late last night by means of a photograph which he was carrying. The photograph proved to be that of Mrs. Leo Cayman. Mrs. Cayman was communicated with and journeyed at once to Marchbolt, where she identified the deceased as her brother, Alex Pritchard. Mr. Pritchard had recently returned from Siam. He had been out of England for ten years and was just starting upon a walking tour. The inquest will be held at Marchbolt tomorrow.

Bobby's thoughts flew back to the strangely haunting face of the photograph. "I believe I shall have to give evidence at the inquest," he said.

"How thrilling! I shall come and hear you."

"I don't suppose there will be anything thrilling about it," said Bobby. "We just found him, you know."

"Was he dead?"

"No—not then. He died about a quarter of an hour later. I was alone with him." He paused.

"Rather grim," said Frankie with that immediate understanding that Bobby's father had lacked.

"Of course he didn't feel anything—"

"No?"

"But all the same—well—you see, he looked awfully alive—that sort of person—rather a rotten way to finish—just stepping off a cliff in a silly little bit of mist."

"I get you, Steve," said Frankie and again the queer phrase represented sympathy and understanding. "Did you see the sister?" she asked presently.

"No. I've been up in town two days. Had to see a friend of mine about a garage business we're going in for. You remember him. Badger Beadon."

"Do I?"

"Of course you do. You must remember good old Badger. He squints."

Frankie wrinkled her brows.

"He's got an awfully silly kind of laugh—*Haw, haw, haw*—like that," continued Bobby helpfully.

Still Frankie wrinkled her brows.

"Fell off his pony when we were kids," continued Bobby. "Stuck in the mud head-down, and we had to pull him out by the legs."

"Oh!" said Frankie in a flood of recollection. "I know now. He stammered."

"He still does," said Bobby proudly.

"Didn't he run a chicken farm and it went bust?" inquired Frankie.

"That's right."

"And then he went into a stockbroker's office and they fired him after a month?"

"That's it."

"And then they sent him to Australia and he came back?"

"Yes."

"Bobby," said Frankie, "you're not putting any money into this business venture, I hope?"

"I haven't got any money to put," said Bobby.

"That's just as well," said Frankie.

"Naturally," went on Bobby, "Badger has tried to get hold of someone with a little capital to invest. But it isn't so easy as you'd think."

"When you look round you," said Frankie, "you wouldn't believe people had any sense at all, but they have."

The point of these remarks seemed at last to strike Bobby.

"Look here, Frankie," he said. "Badger's one of the best—one of the very best."

"They always are," said Frankie.

"Who are?"

"The ones who go to Australia and come back again. How did he get hold of the money to start this business?"

"An aunt or something died and left him a garage for six cars, with three rooms over, and his people stumped up a hundred pounds to buy second-hand cars with. You'd be surprised what bargains there are to be had in second-hand cars."

"I bought one once," said Frankie. "It's a painful subject. Don't let's talk of it. What did you want to leave the Navy for? They didn't ax you, did they? Not at your age?"

Bobby flushed. "Eyes," he said gruffly.

"You always had trouble with your eyes, I remember."

"I know. But I just managed to scrape through. Then foreign service—the strong light, you know—that rather did for them. So—well—I had to get out."

"Grim," murmured Frankie, looking out of the window.

There was an eloquent pause.

"All the same, it's a shame," burst out Bobby. "My eyes aren't really bad—they won't get any worse, they say. I could have carried on perfectly."

"They look alright," said Frankie. She looked straight into their honest brown depths.

"So you see," said Bobby, "I'm going in with Badger."

Frankie nodded.

An attendant opened the door and said, "First luncheon."

"Shall we?" said Frankie.

They passed along to the dining car.

Bobby made a short strategic retreat during the time when the ticket-collector might be expected.

"We don't want him to strain his conscience too much," he said.

But Frankie said she didn't expect ticket-collectors had any consciences.

It was just after five o'clock when they reached Sileham, which was the station for Marchbolt.

"The car's meeting me," said Frankie. "I'll give you a lift."

"Thanks. That will save me carrying this beastly thing for two miles." He kicked his suitcase disparagingly.

"Three miles, not two," said Frankie.

"Two miles if you go by the footpath over the links."

"The one where—"

"Yes—where that fellow went over."

"I suppose nobody pushed him over, did they?" asked Frankie as she handed her dressing-case to her maid.

"Pushed him over? Good Lord, no. Why?"

"Well, it would make it much more exciting, wouldn't it?" said Frankie idly.

4

The Inquest

THE INQUEST ON the body of Alex Pritchard was held on the following day. Dr. Thomas gave evidence as to the finding of the body.

"Life was not then extinct?" asked the Coroner.

"No, deceased was still breathing. There was, however, no hope of recovery. The—" Here the Doctor became highly technical.

The Coroner came to the rescue of the jury. "In ordinary, everyday language, the man's back was broken?"

"If you like to put it that way," said Dr. Thomas sadly.

He described how he had gone off to get help, leaving the dying man in Bobby's charge.

"Now as to the cause of this disaster, what is your opinion, Dr. Thomas?"

"I should say that in all probability (failing any evidence as to his state of mind, that is to say) the deceased stepped inadvertently over the edge of the cliff. There was a mist rising from the sea, and at that particular point the path turns abruptly inland. Owing to the mist the deceased may not have noticed the danger and walked straight on—in which case two steps would take him over the edge."

"There were no signs of violence? Such as might have been administered by a third party?"

"I can only say that all the injuries present are fully explained by the body's striking the rocks fifty or sixty feet below."

"There remains the question of suicide?"

"That is, of course, perfectly possible. Whether the deceased walked over the edge or threw himself over is a matter on which I can say nothing."

Robert Jones was called next.

Bobby explained that he had been playing golf with the Doctor and had sliced his ball toward the sea. A mist was rising at the time and it was difficult to see. He thought he heard a cry, and for a moment wondered if his ball could have hit anybody coming along the footpath. He had decided, however, that it could not possibly have travelled so far.

"Did you find the ball?"

"Yes, it was about a hundred yards short of the footpath."

He then described how they had driven from the next tee and how he himself had driven into the chasm.

Here the Coroner stopped him, since his evidence would have been a repetition of the Doctor's. He questioned him closely, however, as to the cry he had heard or thought he heard.

"It was just a cry."

"A cry for help?"

"Oh, no. Just a sort of shout, you know. In fact I wasn't quite sure I heard it."

"A startled kind of cry?"

"That's more like it," said Bobby gratefully. "Sort of noise a fellow might let out if a ball hit him unexpectedly."

"Or if he took a step into nothingness when he thought he was on a path?"

"Yes."

Then, having explained that the man actually died about five minutes after the Doctor left to get help, Bobby's ordeal came to an end.

The Coroner was by now anxious to get on with a perfectly straightforward business. Mrs. Leo Cayman was called.

Bobby gave a gasp of acute disappointment. Where was the face of the photograph that had tumbled from the dead man's pocket? Photograpers, thought Bobby disgustedly, were the worst kind of liars. The photograph obviously must have been taken some years ago, but even then it was hard to believe that that charming wide-eyed beauty could have become this brazen-looking woman with plucked eyebrows and obviously dyed hair. Time, thought Bobby suddenly, was a very frightening thing. What would Frankie, for instance, look like in twenty years' time? He gave a little shiver.

Meanwhile, Amelia Cayman of 17 St. Leonard's Gardens, Paddington, was giving evidence. Deceased was her only brother, Alexander Pritchard. She had last seen him the day before the tragedy, when he had announced his intention of going for a walking tour in Wales. He had recently returned from the East.

"Did he seem in a happy and normal state of mind?"

"Oh, quite! Alex was always cheerful."

"So far as you know he had nothing on his mind?"

"Oh, I'm sure he hadn't. He was looking forward to his trip."

"There have been no money troubles, or other troubles of any kind, in his life recently?"

"Well, really, I couldn't say as to that," said Mrs. Cayman. "You see, he'd only just come back, and before that I hadn't seen him for ten years, and he was never one much for writing. But he took me out to theaters and lunches in

London and gave me one or two presents, so I don't think he could have been short of money, and he was in such good spirits that I don't think there could have been anything else."

"What was your brother's profession, Mrs. Cayman?"

The lady seemed slightly embarrassed.

"Well, I can't say I rightly know. Prospecting—that's what he called it. He was very seldom in England."

"You know of no reason which might cause him to take his own life?"

"Oh, no, and I can't believe that he did such a thing. It must have been an accident."

"How do you explain the fact that your brother had no luggage with him—not even a knapsack?"

"He didn't like carrying a knapsack. He meant to post parcels alternate days. He posted one the day before he left with his night things and a pair of socks—only he addressed it to Derbyshire instead of Denbighshire, so it only got here today."

"Ah, that clears up a somewhat curious point."

Mrs. Cayman went on to explain how she had been communicated with through the photographers whose name was on the photograph her brother had carried. She had come down with her husband to Marchbolt and had at once recognized the body as that of her brother. As she said the last words she sniffed audibly and began to cry.

The Coroner said a few soothing words and dismissed her. Then he addressed the jury. Their task was to state how this man came by his death. Fortunately the matter appeared to be quite simple. There was no suggestion that Mr. Pritchard had been worried or depressed or in a state of mind where he would be likely to take his own life. On the contrary he had been in good health and spirits and he had been looking forward to his holiday. It was unfortunately the case that when a sea mist was rising, the path along the cliff was a dangerous one, and possibly they might agree with him that it was time something was done about it.

The jury's verdict was prompt.

"We find that the deceased came to his death by misadventure, and we wish to add a rider that in our opinion the Town Council should immediately take steps to put a fence or rail on the sea side of the path where it skirts the chasm."

The Coroner nodded approval. The inquest was over.

5
Mr. and Mrs. Cayman

On arriving back at the Vicarage about half an hour later, Bobby found that his connection with the death of Alex Pritchard was not yet quite over. He was informed that Mr. and Mrs. Cayman had called to see him and were in the study with his father. Bobby made his way there and found his father gravely making suitable conversation without, apparently, much enjoying his task.

"Ah!" he said with some slight relief. "Here is Bobby."

Mr. Cayman rose and advanced toward the young man with outstretched hand. Mr. Cayman was a big florid man with a would-be hearty manner and a cold and somewhat shifty eye that rather belied the manner. As for Mrs. Cayman, though she might be considered attractive in a bold, coarse fashion, she had little now in common with that early photograph of herself, and no trace of that wistful expression remained. In fact, Bobby reflected, if she had not recognized her own photograph it seemed doubtful if anyone else would have done so.

"I came down with the wife," said Mr. Cayman, enclosing Bobby's hand in a firm and painful grip. "Had to stand by, you know. Amelia's naturally upset."

Mrs. Cayman sniffed.

"We came round to see you," continued Mr. Cayman. "You see, my poor wife's brother died, practically speaking, in your arms. Naturally, she wanted to know all you could tell her of his last moments."

"Absolutely," said Bobby unhappily. "Oh, absolutely." He grinned nervously and was immediately aware of his father's sigh—a sigh of Christian resignation.

"Poor Alex!" said Mrs. Cayman, dabbing her eyes. "Poor, poor Alex!"

"I know," said Bobby. "Absolutely grim." He wriggled uncomfortably.

"You see," said Mrs. Cayman, looking hopefully at Bobby, "if he left any last words or messages—naturally I want to know."

"Oh, rather," said Bobby. "But as a matter of fact he didn't."

"Nothing at all?" Mrs. Cayman looked disappointed and incredulous. Bobby felt apologetic.

"No—well—as a matter of fact, nothing at all."

"It was best so," said Mr. Cayman solemnly. "To pass away unconscious, without pain—why, you must think of it as a mercy, Amelia."

"I suppose I must," said Mrs. Cayman. "You don't think he felt any pain?"

"I'm sure he didn't," said Bobby.

Mrs. Cayman sighed deeply. "Well, that's something to be thankful for. Perhaps I did hope he'd left a last message, but I can see that it's best as it is. Poor Alex. Such a fine out-of-door man."

"Yes, wasn't he?" said Bobby. He recalled the bronze face, the deep blue eyes. An attractive personality, that of Alex Pritchard, attractive even so near death. Strange that he should be the brother of Mrs. Cayman and the brother-in-law of Mr. Cayman! He had been worthy, Bobby felt, of better things.

"Well, we're very much indebted to you, I'm sure," said Mrs. Cayman.

"Oh, that's alright," said Bobby. "I mean—well, I couldn't do anything else—I mean—" He floundered hopelessly.

"We shan't forget it," said Mr. Cayman. Bobby suffered once more that painful grip. He received a flabby hand from Mrs. Cayman. His father made further adieus. Bobby accompanied the Caymans to the front door.

"And what do you do with yourself, young man?" inquired Cayman. "Home on leave—something of that kind?"

"I spend most of my time looking for a job," said Bobby. He paused. "I was in the Navy."

"Hard times—hard times nowadays," said Mr. Cayman, shaking his head. "Well, I wish you luck, I'm sure."

"Thank you very much," said Bobby politely.

He watched them down the weed-grown drive. Standing there, he fell into a brown study. Various ideas flashed chaotically through his mind, confused reflections—the photograph—that girl's face with the wide-apart eyes and the misty hair—and ten or fifteen years later, Mrs. Cayman with her heavy make-up, her plucked eyebrows, those wide-apart eyes sunk in between folds of flesh till they looked like pigs' eyes, and her violent henna-tinted hair. All traces of youth and innocence had vanished. The pity of things! It all came perhaps of marrying a hearty bounder like Mr. Cayman. If she had married someone else she might possibly have grown older gracefully. A touch of gray in her hair, eyes still wide-apart looking out from a smooth pale face. But perhaps anyway—

Bobby sighed and shook his head. "That's the worst of marriage," he said gloomily.

"What did you say?"

Bobby awoke from meditation to become aware of Frankie, whose approach he had not heard.

"Hullo," he said.

"Hullo. Why marriage? And whose?"

"I was making a reflection of a general nature," said Bobby.

"Namely—?"

"On the devastating effects of marriage."

"Who is devastated?"

Bobby explained. He found Frankie unsympathetic.

"Nonsense. The woman's exactly like her photograph."

"When did you see her? Were you at the inquest?"

"Of course I was at the inquest. What do you think? There's little enough to do down here. An inquest is a perfect godsend. I'd never been to one before. I was thrilled to the teeth. Of course it would have been better if it had been a mysterious poisoning case with analysts' reports and all that sort of thing—but one mustn't be too exacting when these simple pleasures come one's way. I hoped up to the end for a suspicion of foul play, but it all seemed most regrettably straightforward."

"What bloodthirsty instincts you have, Frankie."

"I know. It's probably atavism (however do you pronounce it?—I've never been sure). Don't you think so? I'm sure I'm atavistic. My nickname at school was Monkey Face."

"Do monkeys like murder?" queried Bobby.

"You sound like a correspondence in a Sunday paper," said Frankie. "'Our correspondents' views on this subject are solicited.'"

"You know," said Bobby, reverting to the original topic, "I don't agree with you about the female Cayman. Her photograph was lovely."

"Touched up, that's all," interrupted Frankie.

"Well, then, it was so much touched up that you wouldn't have known them for the same person."

"You're blind," said Frankie. "The photographer had done all that the art of photography could do, but it was still a nasty bit of work."

"I absolutely disagree with you," said Bobby coldly. "Anyway, where did you see it?"

"In the local *Evening Echo*."

"It probably reproduced badly."

"It seems to me you're absolutely batty," said Frankie crossly. "Over a painted-up raddled bitch—yes, I said *bitch*—like the Cayman."

"Frankie," said Bobby, "I'm surprised at you. In the Vicarage drive too. Semi-holy ground, so to speak."

"Well, you shouldn't have been so ridiculous."

There was a pause, then Frankie's sudden fit of temper abated.

"What is ridiculous," she said, "is to quarrel about the damned woman. I came to suggest a round of golf. What about it?"

"O.K., Chief," said Bobby happily.

They set off amicably together, and their conversation was of such things as slicing and pulling and how to perfect a chip shot onto the green.

The recent tragedy passed quite out of mind until Bobby, holing a long putt at the eleventh to halve the hole, suddenly gave an exclamation.

"What is it?"

"Nothing. I've just remembered something."

"What?"

"Well, these people, the Caymans—they came round and asked if the fellow had said anything before he died—and I told them he hadn't."

"Well?"

"And now I've just remembered that he did."

"Not one of your brightest mornings, in fact."

"Well, you see, it wasn't the sort of thing they meant. That's why, I suppose, I didn't think of it."

"What did he say?" asked Frankie curiously.

"He said: '*Why didn't they ask Evans?*'"

"What a funny thing to say. Nothing else?"

"No. He just opened his eyes and said that—quite suddenly—and then died, poor chap."

"Oh, well," said Frankie, turning it over in her mind, "I don't see that you need worry. It wasn't important."

"No, of course not. Still I wish I'd just mentioned it. You see, I said he'd said nothing at all."

"Well, it amounts to the same thing," said Frankie. "I mean it isn't like 'Tell Gladys I always loved her,' or 'The will is in the walnut bureau,' or any of the proper romantic Last Words there are in books."

"You don't think it's worthwhile writing about it to them?"

"I shouldn't bother. It couldn't be important."

"I expect you're right," said Bobby and turned his attention with renewed vigor to the game.

But the matter did not really dismiss itself from his mind. It was a small point but it fretted him. He felt very faintly uncomfortable about it. Frankie's point of view was, he felt sure, the right and sensible one. The thing was of no importance—let it go. But his conscience continued to reproach him faintly. He had said that the dead man had said nothing. That wasn't true. It was all very trivial and silly, but he couldn't feel quite comfortable about it.

Finally that evening on an impulse he sat down and wrote to Mr. Cayman.

DEAR MR. CAYMAN:

I have just remembered that your brother-in-law did actually say something before he died. I think the exact words were "Why didn't they ask Evans?" I apologize for not mentioning this this morning, but I attached no importance to the words at the time and so, I suppose, they slipped my memory.

Yours truly,
ROBERT JONES

On the next day but one he received a reply.

DEAR MR. JONES:

Your letter of 6th instant to hand. Many thanks for repeating my poor brother-in-law's last words so punctiliously in spite of their trivial character. What my wife hoped was that her brother might have left her some last message. Still, thank you for being so conscientious.

Yours faithfully,
LEO CAYMAN

Bobby felt snubbed.

6

End of a Picnic

ON THE FOLLOWING day Bobby received a letter of quite a different nature.

It's all fixed, old boy [wrote Badger in an illiterate scrawl which reflected no credit on the expensive public school which had educated him]. Actually got five cars yesterday for fifteen pounds the lot—an Austin, two Morrises and a couple of Rovers. At the moment they won't exactly go, but we can tinker them up sufficiently. I think. Dash it all, a car's a car, after all. So long as it takes the purchaser home without breaking down, that's all he can expect. I thought of opening up Monday week and am relying on you. So don't let me down, will you, old boy? I must say old Aunt Carrie was a sport. I once broke the window of an old boy next door to her who'd been rude to her about her cats, and she never got over it. Sent me a fiver every Christmas, and now this.

We're bound to succeed. The thing's a dead cert. I mean, a car's a car after all. You can pick 'em up for nothing. Put a lick of paint on, and that's all the ordinary fool notices. The thing will go with a Bang. Now don't forget. Monday week. I'm relying on you.

Yours ever,
BADGER

Bobby informed his father that he would be going up to town on Monday week to take up a job. The description of the job did not rouse the Vicar to anything like enthusiasm. He had, it may be pointed out, come across Badger Beadon in the past. He merely treated Bobby to a long lecture on the advisability of not making himself Liable for Anything. Since he was not an authority on financial or business matters, his advice was technically vague, but its meaning was unmistakable.

On the Wednesday of that week Bobby received another letter. It was addressed in a foreign, slanting handwriting. Its contents were somewhat surprising to the young man.

It was from the firm of Henriquez & Dallo in Buenos Aires and, to put it concisely, it offered Bobby a job in the firm with a salary of a thousand a year.

For the first minute or two the young man thought he must be dreaming. A thousand a year. He reread the letter more carefully. There was mention of an ex-Naval man's being preferred, a suggestion that Bobby's name had been put forward by someone (not named). Acceptance must be immediate, and Bobby must be prepared to start for Buenos Aires within a week.

"Well, I'm damned," said Bobby, giving vent to his feelings in a somewhat unfortunate manner.

"Bobby!"

"Sorry, Dad. Forgot you were there."

Mr. Jones cleared his throat. "I should like to point out to you—"

Bobby felt that this process—usually a long one—must at all costs be avoided. He achieved this by a simple statement.

"Someone's offered me a thousand a year."

The Vicar remained openmouthed, unable for the moment to make any comment.

"That's put him off his drive alright," thought Bobby with satisfaction.

"My dear Bobby, did I understand you to say that someone has offered you a thousand a year? *A thousand?*"

"Holed it in one, Dad," said Bobby.

"It's impossible," said the Vicar.

Bobby was not hurt by this frank incredulity. His estimate of his own monetary value differed little from that of his father.

"They must be complete mutts," he agreed heartily.

"Who—er—are these people?"

Bobby handed him the letter. The Vicar, fumbling for his pince-nez, peered at it suspiciously. Finally he read it twice.

"Most remarkable," he said at last. "*Most* remarkable."

"Lunatics," said Bobby.

"Ah, my boy," said the Vicar, "it is, after all, a great thing to be an Englishman. Honesty. That's what we stand for. The Navy has carried that ideal all over the world. An Englishman's word! This South American firm realizes the value of a young man whose integrity will be unshaken and of whose fidelity his employers will be assured. You can always depend on an Englishman to play the game—"

"And keep a straight bat," said Bobby.

The Vicar looked at his son doubtfully. The phrase, an excellent one, had actually been on the tip of his tongue, but there was something in Bobby's tone that struck him as not quite sincere.

The young man, however, appeared to be perfectly serious. "All the same, Dad," he said, "why me?"

"What do you mean—why you?"

"There are a lot of Englishmen in England," said Bobby. "Hearty fellows, full of cricketing qualities. Why pick on me?"

"Probably your late commanding officer may have recommended you."

"Yes, I suppose that's true," said Bobby doubtfully. "It doesn't matter anyway since I can't take the job."

"Can't take it? My dear boy, what do you mean?"

"Well, I'm fixed up, you see. With Badger."

"Badger? Badger Beadon? Nonsense, my dear Bobby. This is serious."

"It's a bit hard, I own," said Bobby with a sigh.

"Any childish arrangement you have made with young Beadon cannot count for a moment."

"It counts with me."

"Young Beadon is completely irresponsible. He has already, I understand, been a source of considerable trouble and expense to his parents."

"He's not had much luck. Badger's so infernally trusting."

"Luck—luck! I should say that young man had never done a hand's turn in his life."

"Nonsense, Dad. Why, he used to get up at five in the morning to feed those beastly chickens. It wasn't his fault they all got the roup or the croup or whatever it was."

"I have never approved of this garage project. Mere folly. You must give it up."

"Can't, sir. I've promised. I can't let old Badger down. He's counting on me."

The discussion proceeded. The Vicar, biased by his views on the subject of Badger, was quite unable to regard any promise made to that young man as binding. He looked on Bobby as obstinate and determined at all costs to lead an idle life in company with one of the worst of possible companions. Bobby, on the other hand, stolidly repeated without originality that he "couldn't let old Badger down."

The Vicar finally left the room in anger, and Bobby then and there sat down to write to the firm of Henriquez & Dallo refusing their offer.

He sighed as he did so. He was letting a chance go here which was never likely to occur again. But he saw no alternative.

Later, on the links, he put the problem to Frankie. She listened attentively.

"You'd have had to go to South America?"

"Yes."

"Would you have liked that?"

"Yes, why not?"

Frankie sighed. "Anyway," she said with decision, "I think you did quite right."

"About Badger, you mean?"

"Yes."

"I couldn't let the old bird down, could I?"

"No, but be careful that the old bird, as you call him, doesn't let you in."

"Oh! I shall be careful. Anyway I shall be alright. I haven't got any assets."

"That must be rather fun," said Frankie.

"Why?"

"I don't know why. It just sounded rather nice and free and irresponsible. I suppose, though, when I come to think of it, that I haven't got many assets either. I mean, Father gives me an allowance, and I've got lots of houses to live in and clothes and maids and some hideous family jewels and a good deal of credit at shops—but that's all the family, really. It's not *me*."

"No, but all the same—" Bobby paused.

"Oh, it's quite different, I know."

"Yes," said Bobby. "It's quite different." He felt suddenly very depressed.

They walked in silence to the next tee.

"I'm going up to town tomorrow," said Frankie as Bobby teed up his ball.

"Tomorrow. Oh—and I was going to suggest you should come for a picnic."

"I'd have liked to. However, it's arranged. You see, Father's got the gout again."

"You ought to stay and minister to him," said Bobby.

"He doesn't like being ministered to. It annoys him frightfully. He likes the second footman best. He's sympathetic and doesn't mind having things thrown at him and being called a damned fool."

Bobby topped his drive and it trickled into the bunker.

"Hard lines," said Frankie and drove a nice straight ball that sailed over it.

"By the way," she remarked, "we might do something together in London. You'll be up soon?"

"On Monday. But—well—it's no good, is it?"

"What do you mean—no good?"

"Well, I mean I shall be working as a mechanic most of the time. I mean—"

"Even then," said Frankie, "I suppose you're just as capable of coming to a cocktail party and getting tight as any other of my friends."

Bobby merely shook his head.

"I'll give a beer-and-sausage party if you prefer it," said Frankie encouragingly.

"Oh, look here, Frankie, what's the good? I mean, you can't mix your crowds. Your crowd's a different crowd from mine."

"I assure you," said Frankie, "that my crowd is a very mixed one."

"You're pretending not to understand."

"You can bring Badger if you like. *There's* friendship for you."

"You've got some sort of prejudice against Badger."

"I daresay it's his stammer. People who stammer always make me stammer too."

"Look here, Frankie, it's no good and you know it isn't. It's alright down here. There's not much to do and I suppose I'm better than nothing. I mean, you're always awfully decent to me and all that, and I'm grateful. But I know I'm just nobody—I mean—"

"When you've quite finished expressing your inferiority complex," said Frankie coldly, "perhaps you'll try getting out of the bunker with a niblick instead of a putter."

"Have I—oh, damn!" He replaced the putter in his bag and took out the niblick. Frankie watched with malicious satisfaction as he hacked at the ball five times in succession. Clouds of sand rose round them.

"Your hole," said Bobby, picking up the ball.

"I think it is," said Frankie. "And that gives me the match."

"Shall we play the bye?"

"No. I don't think so. I've got a lot to do."

"Of course. I suppose you have."

They walked together in silence to the clubhouse.

"Well," said Frankie, holding out her hand. "Goodbye, my dear. It's been too marvelous to have you to make use of while I've been down here. See something of you again, perhaps, when I've nothing better to do."

"Look here, Frankie—"

"Perhaps you'll condescend to come to my coster party. I believe you can get pearl buttons quite cheaply at Woolworth's."

"Frankie—"

His words were drowned in the noise of the Bentley's engine which Frankie had just started. She drove away with an airy wave of her hand.

"Damn!" said Bobby in a heartfelt tone.

Frankie, he considered, had behaved outrageously. Perhaps he hadn't put things very tactfully, but dash it all, what he had said was true enough. Perhaps, though, he shouldn't have put it into words.

The next three days seemed interminably long. The Vicar had a sore throat which necessitated his speaking in a whisper when he spoke at all. He spoke very little and was obviously bearing his fourth son's presence as a Christian should. Once or twice he quoted Shakespeare on how sharper than a serpent's tooth, etc.

On Saturday Bobby felt that he could bear the strain of home life no longer. He got Mrs. Roberts, who with her husband "ran" the Vicarage, to give him a packet of sandwiches, and supplementing this with a bottle of beer which he bought in Marchbolt he set off for a solitary picnic.

He had missed Frankie abominably these last few days. These older people were the limit. They harped on things so.

Bobby stretched himself out on a brackeny bank and debated with himself whether he should eat his lunch first and go to sleep afterward, or sleep first and eat afterward. While he was cogitating, the matter was settled for him by his falling asleep without noticing it.

When he awoke it was half-past three! Bobby grinned as he thought how his father would disapprove of this way of spending a day. A good walk across country—twelve miles or so—that was the kind of thing that a healthy young man should do. It led inevitably to that famous remark, "And now, I think, I've earned my lunch."

"Idiotic," thought Bobby., "Why earn lunch by doing a lot of walking you don't particularly want to do? What's the merit in it? If you enjoy it, then it's pure self-indulgence, and if you don't enjoy it you're a fool to do it."

Whereupon he fell to upon his unearned lunch and ate it with gusto. With a sigh of satisfaction he unscrewed the bottle of beer. Unusually bitter beer, but decidedly refreshing . . .

He lay back again, having tossed the empty beer bottle into a clump of heather.

He felt rather godlike lounging there. The world was at his feet. A phrase. But a good phrase. He could do anything—anything if he tried! Plans of great splendor and daring initiative flashed through his mind.

Then he grew sleepy again. Lethargy stole over him.

He slept . . .

Heavy, numbing sleep . . .

7
An Escape from Death

DRIVING HER LARGE green Bentley, Frankie drew up to the curb outside a large old-fashioned house over the doorway of which was inscribed "St. Asaph's."

Frankie jumped out and, turning, extracted a large bunch of lilies. Then she rang the bell. A woman in nurse's dress answered the door.

"Can I see Mr. Jones?" inquired Frankie.

The nurse's eyes took in the Bentley, the lilies and Frankie with intense interest.

"What name shall I say?"

"Lady Frances Derwent."

The nurse was thrilled, and her patient went up in her estimation. She guided Frankie upstairs into a room on the first floor.

"You've a visitor to see you, Mr. Jones. Now who do you think it is? Such a nice surprise for you."

All this in the "bright" manner usual to nursing homes.

"Gosh!" said Bobby, very much surprised. "If it isn't Frankie!"

"Hullo, Bobby. I've brought the usual flowers. Rather a graveyard suggestion about them, but the choice was limited."

"Ooh, Lady Frances," said the nurse, "they're lovely. I'll put them into water."

She left the room.

Frankie sat down in an obvious "visitor's" chair. "Well, Bobby," she said. "What's all this?"

"You may well ask," said Bobby. "I'm the complete sensation of this place. Eight grains of morphia, no less. They're going to write about me in the *Lancet* and the *B.M.J.*"

"What's the *B.M.J.*?" interrupted Frankie.

"The *British Medical Journal*."

"Alright. Go ahead. Rattle off some more initials."

"Do you know, my girl, that half a grain is a fatal dose? I ought to be dead about sixteen times over. It's true that recovery has been known after sixteen grains—still, eight is pretty good, don't you think? I'm the hero of this place. They've never had a case like me before."

"How nice for them!"

"Isn't it? Gives them something to talk about to all the other patients."

The nurse re-entered, bearing lilies in vases.

"It's true, isn't it, nurse?" demanded Bobby. "You've never had a case like mine?"

"Oh, you oughtn't to be here at all," said the nurse. "In the churchyard, you ought to be. But it's only the good die young, they say." She giggled at her own wit and went out.

"There you are," said Bobby. "You'll see, I shall be famous all over England."

He continued to talk. Any signs of inferiority complex that he had displayed at his last meeting with Frankie had now quite disappeared. He took a firm and egotistical pleasure in recounting every detail of his case.

"That's enough," said Frankie, quelling him. "I don't really care terribly for stomach pumps. To listen to you one would think nobody had ever been poisoned before."

"Jolly few have been poisoned with eight grains of morphia and got over it," Bobby pointed out. "Dash it all, you're not sufficiently impressed."

"Pretty sickening for the people who poisoned you," said Frankie.

"I know. Waste of perfectly good morphia."

"It was in the beer, wasn't it?"

"Yes. You see, someone found me sleeping like the dead, tried to wake me and couldn't. Then they got alarmed, carried me to farmhouse, and sent for a doctor—"

"I know all the next part," said Frankie hastily.

"At first they had the idea that I'd taken the stuff deliberately. Then when they heard my story, they went off and looked for the beer bottle and found it where I'd thrown it and had it analyzed—the dregs of it were quite enough for that apparently."

"No clue as to how the morphia got in the bottle?"

"None whatever. They've interviewed the pub where I bought it, and opened other bottles, and everything's been quite alright."

"Someone must have put the stuff in the beer while you were asleep?"

"That's it. I remember that the paper across the top wasn't still sticking properly."

Frankie nodded thoughtfully. "Well," she said, "it shows that what I said in the train that day was quite right."

"What did you say?"

"That that man—Pritchard—had been pushed over the cliff."

"That wasn't in the train. You said that at the station," said Bobby feebly.

"Same thing."

"But why—"

"Darling—it's obvious. Why should anyone want to put *you* out of the way? You're not the heir to a fortune or anything."

"I may be. Some great-aunt I've never heard of in New Zealand or somewhere may have left me all her money."

"Nonsense. Not without knowing you. And if she didn't know you, why leave money to a fourth son? Why, in these hard times even a clergyman mightn't have a fourth son! No, it's all quite clear. No one benefits by your death, so that's ruled out. Then there's revenge. You haven't seduced a chemist's daughter by any chance?"

"Not that I can remember," said Bobby with dignity.

"I know. One seduces so much that one can't keep count. But I should say offhand that you've never seduced anyone at all."

"You're making me blush, Frankie. And why must it be a chemist's daughter, anyway?"

"Free access to morphia? It's not so easy to get hold of morphia."

"Well, I haven't seduced a chemist's daughter."

"And you haven't got any enemies that you know of?"

Bobby shook his head.

"Well, there you are," said Frankie triumphantly. "It must be the man who was pushed over the cliff. What do the police think?"

"They think it must have been a lunatic."

"Nonsense. Lunatics don't wander about with unlimited supplies of morphia looking for odd bottles of beer to put it into. No, somebody pushed Pritchard over the cliff. A minute or two later you come along, and he thinks you saw him do it and so determines to put you out of the way."

"I don't think that will hold water, Frankie."

"Why not?"

"Well, to begin with, I didn't see anything."

"Yes, but he didn't know that."

"And if I had seen anything I should have said so at the inquest."

"I suppose that's so," said Frankie unwillingly. She thought for a minute or two.

"Perhaps he thought you'd seen something that you didn't think was anything but which really *was* something. That sounds pure gibberish, but you get the idea?"

Bobby nodded. "Yes, I see what you mean, but it doesn't seem very probable somehow."

"I'm sure that cliff business had something to do with this. You were on the spot—the first person to be there—"

"Thomas was there too," Bobby reminded her. "And nobody's tried to poison him."

"Perhaps they're going to," said Frankie cheerfully. "Or perhaps they've tried and failed."

"It all seems very farfetched."

"I think it's logical. If you get two out-of-the-way things happening in a stagnant pond like Marchbolt—Wait—there's a third thing."

"What?"

"That job you were offered. That, of course, is quite a small thing, but it was odd, you must admit. I've never heard of a foreign firm that specialized in seeking out undistinguished ex-Naval officers."

"Did you say undistinguished?"

"You hadn't got into the *B.M.J.* then. But you see my point. You've seen something you weren't meant to see—or so they (whoever they are) think. Very well. They first try to get rid of you by offering you a job abroad. Then, when that fails, they try to put you out of the way altogether."

"Isn't that rather drastic? And anyway a great risk to take?"

"Oh, but murderers are always frightfully rash. The more murders they do, the more murders they want to do."

"Like *The Third Bloodstain*," said Bobby, remembering one of his favorite works of fiction.

"Yes, and in real life too—Smith and his wives, and Armstrong, and other people."

"Well, but, Frankie, what on earth is it I'm supposed to have seen?"

"That, of course, is the difficulty," admitted Frankie. "I agree that it can't have been the actual pushing, because you would have told about that. It must be something about the man himself. Perhaps he had a birthmark or double-jointed fingers or some strange physical peculiarity."

"Your mind is running on Dr. Thorndyke, I see. It couldn't be anything like that because whatever I saw the police would see as well."

"So they would. That was an idiotic suggestion. It's very difficult, isn't it?"

"It's a pleasing theory," said Bobby. "And it makes me feel important. But all the same, I don't believe it's much more than a theory."

"I'm sure I'm right." Frankie rose. "I must be off now. Shall I come and see you again tomorrow?"

"Oh, do. The arch chatter of the nurses gets very monotonous. By the way, you're back from London very soon?"

"My dear, as soon as I heard about you, I tore back. It's more exciting to have a romantically poisoned friend."

"I don't know whether morphia is so very romantic," said Bobby reminiscently.

"Well, I'll come tomorrow. Do I kiss you or don't I?"

"It's not catching," said Bobby encouragingly.

"Then I'll do my duty to the sick thoroughly." She kissed him lightly. "See you tomorrow."

The nurse came in with Bobby's tea as she went out.

"I've seen her pictures in the paper often. She's not so very like them, though. And of course I've seen her driving about in her car. But I've never seen her before close to, so to speak. Not a bit haughty, is she?"

"Oh, no," said Bobby. "I should never call Frankie haughty."

"I said to Sister, I said, she's as natural as anything. Not a bit stuck-up. I said to Sister, she's just like you or me, I said."

Dissenting violently though silently from this view, Bobby returned no reply. The nurse, disappointed by his lack of response, left the room, and Bobby was left to his own thoughts.

He finished his tea. Then he went over in his mind the possibilities of Frankie's amazing theory, and ended by deciding reluctantly against it. He then cast about for other distractions.

His eye was caught by the vases of lilies. Frightfully sweet of Frankie to bring him all these flowers, and of course they were lovely, but he wished it had occurred to her to bring him a few detective stories instead. He cast his eye over the table beside him. There was a novel of Ouida's and a copy of *John Halifax, Gentleman*, and last week's *Marchbolt Weekly Times*. He picked up *John Halifax, Gentleman*.

After five minutes he put it down. To a mind nourished on *The Third Bloodstain*, *The Case of the Murdered Archduke*, and *The Strange Adventure of the Florentine Dagger*, Mrs. Mulock Craik's *John Halifax* somehow lacked pep. With a sigh he picked up last week's *Weekly Times*.

A moment or two later he was pressing the bell beneath his pillow with a vigor which brought a nurse into the room at a run.

"Whatever's the matter, Mr. Jones? Are you taken bad?"

"Ring up the Castle," cried Bobby. "Tell Lady Frances she must come back here at once."

"Oh, Mr. Jones—you can't send a message like that."

"Can't I?" said Bobby. "If I were allowed to get up from this blasted bed, you'd soon see whether I could or couldn't. As it is, you've got to do it for me."

"But she'll hardly be back."

"You don't know that Bentley."

"She won't have had her tea."

"Now look here, my dear girl," said Bobby, "don't stand there arguing with me. Ring up as I tell you. Tell her she's got to come here at once because I've got something very important to say to her."

Overborne, though unwilling, the nurse went. She took some liberties with Bobby's message. If it was no inconvenience to Lady Frances, Mr. Jones wondered if she would mind coming, as he had something he would like to say to her. But of course Lady Frances was not to put herself out in any way.

Lady Frances replied curtly that she would come at once.

"Depend upon it," said the nurse to her colleagues, "she's sweet on him! That's what it is."

Frankie arrived all agog. "What's this desperate summons?" she demanded.

Bobby was sitting up in bed, a bright red spot in each cheek. In his hand he waved the copy of the *Marchbolt Weekly Times*.

"Look at this, Frankie."

Frankie looked. "Well?" she demanded.

"This is the picture you meant when you said it was touched up but quite like the Cayman woman?" Bobby's finger pointed to a somewhat blurred reproduction of a photograph. Underneath it were the words *Portrait found on the dead man by which he was identified: Mrs. Amelia Cayman, the dead man's sister.*

"That's what I said—and it's true, too. I can't see anything to rave over in it."

"No more can I."

"But you said—"

"I know I 'said.' But you see, Frankie—" Bobby's voice became very impressive— "*this isn't the photograph that I put back in the dead man's pocket . . .*"

They looked at each other.

"Then, in that case—" began Frankie slowly.

"Either there must have been two photographs—"

"—which isn't likely—"

"—or else—"

They paused.

"*That man*—what's his name?" said Frankie.

"Bassington-ffrench!" said Bobby.

8
Riddle of a Photograph

THEY STARED AT each other as they tried to adjust themselves to the altered situation

"It couldn't be anyone else," said Bobby. "He was the only person who had the chance."

"Unless, as we said, there were *two* photographs?"

"We agreed that that wasn't likely. If there had been two photographs they'd have tried to identify him by means of both of them—not by only one."

"Anyway that's easily found out," said Frankie. "We can ask the police. We'll assume for the moment that there was just the one photograph—the one you saw, that you put back again in the man's pocket. It was there when you left him, and it *wasn't* there when the police came. Therefore the only person who *could* have taken it away and put the other one in its place is this man Bassington-ffrench. What was he like, Bobby?"

Bobby frowned in the effort to remember. "A sort of nondescript fellow. Pleasant voice. A gentleman and all that. I really didn't notice him particularly. He said he was a stranger down here—and something about looking for a house."

"We can verify that anyway," said Frankie. "Wheeler & Owen are the only house agents." Suddenly she gave a shiver. "Bobby, have you thought? If Pritchard was pushed over—*Bassington-ffrench must be the man who did it . . .*"

"That's pretty grim," said Bobby. "He seemed such a nice, pleasant sort of fellow. But you know, Frankie, we can't be sure Pritchard really was pushed over."

"*I'm* quite sure!"

"You have been, all along."

"No, I just wanted it to be that way because it made things more exciting. But now it's more or less proved. If it was murder everything fits in. Your unexpected appearance which upsets the murderer's plans. Your discovery of the photograph and, in consequence, the need to put you out of the way."

"There's a flaw there," said Bobby.

"Why? You were the only person who saw that photograph. As soon as Bassington-ffrench was left alone with the body he changed the photograph, which only you had seen."

But Bobby continued to shake his head. "No, that won't do. Let's grant for the moment that that photograph was so important that I had to be 'got out of the way,' as you put it. Sounds absurd, but I suppose it's just possible. Well then, whatever was going to be done would have to be done *at once*. The fact that I went to London and never saw the *Weekly Times* or the other papers with the photograph in them was just pure chance—a thing nobody could count on. The probability was that I should say at once, 'That isn't the photograph I saw.' Why wait till after the inquest when everything was nicely settled?"

"There's something in that," admitted Frankie.

"And there's another point. I can't be absolutely sure, of course, but I could almost swear that when I put the photograph back in the dead man's pocket Bassington-ffrench wasn't there. He didn't arrive till about five or ten minutes later."

"He might have been watching you all the time," argued Frankie.

"I don't see very well how he could have," said Bobby slowly. "There's really only one place where you can see down to exactly the spot we were. Farther round, the cliff bulges and then recedes underneath, so that you can't see over. There's just the one place, and when Bassington-ffrench did arrive there I heard him at once. Footsteps echo down below. He may have been near at hand, but he wasn't looking over till then—that I'll swear."

"Then you think that he didn't know about your seeing the photograph?'

"I don't see how he could have known."

"And he can't have been afraid you'd seen him doing it—the murder, I mean—because, as you say, that's absurd. You'd never have held your tongue about it. It looks as though it must have been something else altogether."

"Only I don't see what it could have been."

"Something they didn't know about till after the inquest. I don't know why I say *they*—"

"Why not? After all, the Caymans must have been in it too. It's probably a gang. I like gangs."

"That's a low taste," said Frankie absently. "A single-handed murder is much higher class. Bobby!"

"Yes?"

"What was it Pritchard said just before he died? You know, you told me about it that day on the links. That funny question?"

"Why didn't they ask Evans?"

"Yes. Suppose *that* was it?"

"But that's ridiculous."

"It sounds so, but it might be important really. Bobby, I'm *sure* it's that. Oh, no, I'm being an idiot—you never told the Caymans about it."

"I did, as a matter of fact," said Bobby slowly.

"You *did?*"

"Yes. I wrote to them that evening. Saying that of course it was probably quite unimportant."

"And what happened?"

"Cayman wrote back politely agreeing that of course there was nothing in it, but thanking me for taking the trouble. I felt rather snubbed."

"And two days later you got this letter from a strange firm bribing you to go out to South America?"

"Yes."

"Well," said Frankie, "I don't know what more you want. They try that first. You turn it down. And the next thing is that they follow you round and seize a good moment to empty a lot of morphia into your bottle of beer."

"Then the Caymans *are* in it?"

"Of course the Caymans are in it!"

"Yes," said Bobby thoughtfully. "If your reconstruction is correct, they must be in it. According to our present theory it goes like this. Dead man X is deliberately pushed over cliff—presumably by B.F. (pardon the initials). It is important that X should not be correctly identified, so the portrait of Mrs. C. is put in his pocket and the portrait of Fair Unknown removed. Who was she, I wonder?"

"Keep to the point," said Frankie sternly.

"Mrs. C. waits for photograph to appear. Then turns up as grief-stricken sister and identifies X as her brother from foreign parts."

"You don't believe he could really have been her brother?"

"Not for a moment! You know, it puzzled me all along. The Caymans were a different class altogether. The dead man was—well, it sounds a most awful thing to say and just like some deadly old retired Anglo-Indian—but the dead man was a pukka sahib."

"And the Caymans emphatically weren't?"

"*Most* emphatically."

"And then, just when everything has gone off well from the Caymans' point of view—body successfully identified, verdict of accidental death, everything in the garden lovely—*you* come along and mess things up," mused Frankie.

"*'Why didn't they ask Evans?'*" Bobby repeated the phrase thoughtfully. "You know I can't see what on earth there can be in that to put the wind up anybody."

"Ah! That's because you don't know. It's like making crossword puzzles. You write down a clue and you think it's too idiotically simple and that everyone will guess it straight off, and you're frightfully surprised when they simply can't get it in the least. *'Why didn't they ask Evans?'* must have been a most frightfully significant phrase to them, and they couldn't realize that it meant nothing at all to you."

"More fools they."

"Oh, quite so. But it's just possible they thought that if Pritchard said that, he might have said something more which would also recur to you in due time. Anyway they weren't going to take chances. You were safer out of the way."

"They took a lot of risk. Why didn't they engineer another 'accident'?"

"No, no. That would have been stupid. Two accidents within a week of each other? It might have suggested a connection between the two, and then people would have begun inquiring into the first one. No, I think there's a kind of bald simplicity about their method which is really rather clever."

"And yet you said just now that morphia wasn't easy to get hold of."

"No more it is. You have to sign poison books and things. Oh—of course, that's a clue! Whoever did it had easy access to supplies of morphia."

"A doctor, a hospital nurse, or a chemist," suggested Bobby.

"Well, I was thinking more of illicitly imported drugs."

"You can't mix up too many different sorts of crime," said Bobby.

"You see, the strong point would be the absence of motive. Your death doesn't benefit anyone. So what will the police think?"

"A lunatic," said Bobby. "And that's what they do think."

"You see? It's awfully simple really."

Bobby began to laugh suddenly.

"What's amusing you?"

"Just the thought of how sick-making it must be for them! All that morphia—enough to kill five or six people—and here I am alive and kicking."

"One of Life's little ironies that one can't foresee," agreed Frankie.

"The question is, what do we do next?" said Bobby practically.

"Oh! Lots of things," said Frankie promptly.

"Such as—?"

"Well—finding out about the photograph—that there was only one, not two. And about Bassington-ffrench's house-hunting."

"That will probably be quite alright and aboveboard."

"Why do you say that?"

"Look here, Frankie, think a minute. Bassington-ffrench *must* be above suspicion. He *must* be all clear and aboveboard. Not only must there be nothing to connect him in any way with the dead man, but he must have a proper reason for being down here. He may have invented house-hunting on the spur of the moment, but I bet he carried out something of the kind. There must be no suggestion of a 'mysterious stranger seen in the neighborhood of the accident.' I fancy that Bassington-ffrench is his real name, and that he's the sort of person who would be quite above suspicion."

"Yes," said Frankie thoughtfully. "That's a very good deduction. There will be nothing whatever to connect Bassington-ffrench with Alex Pritchard. Now if we knew who the dead man really was—"

"Ah! Then it might be different."

"So it was very important that the body should not be recognized. Hence all the Cayman camouflage. And yet it was taking a big risk."

"You forget that Mrs. Cayman identified him as soon as was humanly possible. After that, even if there had been pictures of him in the papers (you know how blurry these things are) people would only say, 'Curious, this man Pritchard who fell over a cliff is really extraordinarily like Mr. X.'"

"There must be more to it than that," said Frankie shrewdly. "X must have been a man who wouldn't easily be missed. I mean, he couldn't have been the sort of family man whose wife or relations would go to the police at once and report him missing."

"Good for you, Frankie. No, he must have been just going abroad, or perhaps just come back (he was marvelously tanned, like a big-game hunter—he looked that sort of person), and he can't have had any very near relations who knew all about his movements."

"We're deducing beautifully," said Frankie. "I hope we're not deducing all wrong."

"Very likely," said Bobby. "But I think what we've said so far is fairly sound sense—granted, that is, the wild improbability of the whole thing."

Frankie waved away the wild improbability with an airy gesture. "The thing is—what to do next?" she said. "It seems to me we've got three angles of attack."

"Go on, Sherlock."

"The first is *you*. They've made one attempt on your life. They'll probably try again. This time we might get what they call a 'line' on them. Using you as a decoy, I mean."

"No, thank you, Frankie," said Bobby with feeling. "I've been very lucky this time, but I mightn't be so lucky again if they changed the attack to a blunt instrument. I was thinking of taking a great deal of care of myself in the future. The decoy idea can be washed out."

"I was afraid you'd say that," said Frankie with a sigh. "Young men are sadly degenerate nowadays. Father says so. They don't enjoy being uncomfortable and doing dangerous and unpleasant things any longer. It's a pity."

"A great pity," said Bobby, but he spoke with firmness. "What's the second plan of campaign?"

"Working from the *'Why didn't they ask Evans?'* clue," said Frankie. "Presumably the dead man came down here to see Evans—whoever *he* was. Now, if we could find Evans—"

"How many Evanses," Bobby interrupted, "do you think there are in Marchbolt?"

"Several hundred, I should think," admitted Frankie.

"At least! We might do something that way, but I'm rather doubtful."

"We could list all the Evanses and visit the likely ones."

"And ask them—what?"

"That's the difficulty," said Frankie.

"We need to know a little more," said Bobby. "Then that idea of yours might come in useful. What's Number 3?"

"This man Bassington-ffrench. There we *have* got something tangible to go upon. It's an uncommon name. I'll ask Father. He knows all these county family names and their various branches."

"Yes," said Bobby, "we might do something that way."

"At any rate we are going to do something?"

"Of course we are. Do you think I'm going to be given eight grains of morphia and do nothing about it?"

"That's the spirit!" said Frankie.

"And besides that," added Bobby, "there's the indignity of the stomach pump to be washed out."

"That's enough," said Frankie. "You'll be getting morbid and indecent again if I don't stop you."

"You have no true womanly sympathy," Bobby retorted.

9
Concerning Mr. Bassington-ffrench

FRANKIE LOST NO time in setting to work. She attacked her father that same evening.

"Father," she said, "do you know any Bassington-ffrenches?"

Lord Marchington, who was reading a political article, did not quite take in the question. "It's not the French so much as the Americans," he said severely. "All this tomfoolery and Conferences—wasting the nation's time and money—"

Frankie abstracted her mind until Lord Marchington, running like a railway train along an accustomed line, came as it were to a halt at a station.

"The Bassington-ffrenches," repeated Frankie.

"What about 'em?" asked Lord Marchington.

Frankie didn't know what about them. She made a statement, knowing well enough that her father enjoyed contradicting.

"They're a Yorkshire family, aren't they?"

"Nonsense—Hampshire. There's the Shropshire branch, of course, and then there's the Irish lot. Which are your friends?"

"I'm not sure," said Frankie, accepting the implication of friendship with several unknown people.

"Not sure? What do you mean? You must be sure."

"People drift about so, nowadays," said Frankie.

"Drift—drift—that's about all they do do. In my day we asked people. Then one knew where one was—fellow said he was the Hampshire branch—very well, your grandmother married my second cousin. It made a link."

"It must have been too sweet," said Frankie. "But there really isn't time for genealogical and geographical research nowadays."

"No—you've no time nowadays for anything but drinking these poisonous cocktails." Lord Marchington gave a sudden yelp of pain as he moved his gouty leg which some free imbibing of the family port had not improved.

"Are they well off?" asked Frankie.

"The Bassington-ffrenches? Couldn't say. The Shropshire lot have been hard hit, I believe. Death duties and one thing or another. One of the Hampshire ones married an heiress. An American woman."

"One of them was down here the other day," said Frankie. "Looking for a house, I believe."

"Funny idea. What should anyone want with a house down here?"

That, thought Frankie, was the question.

On the following day she walked into the office of Messrs. Wheeler & Owen, House and Estate Agents.

Mr. Owen himself sprang up to receive her. Frankie gave him a gracious smile and dropped into a chair.

"And what can we have the pleasure of doing for you, Lady Frances? You don't want to sell the Castle, I suppose. Ha, ha!" Mr. Owen laughed at his own wit.

"I wish we could," said Frankie. "No, as a matter of fact, I believe a friend of mine was down here the other day—a Mr. Bassington-ffrench. He was looking for a house."

"Ah, yes, indeed! I remember the name perfectly. Two small f's."

"That's right," said Frankie.

"He was making inquiries about various small properties with a view to purchase. He was obliged to return to town the next day so could not view many of the houses, but I understand he is in no great hurry. Since he left, one or two suitable properties have come into the market, and I have sent him on particulars but have had no reply."

"Did you write to London—or to the—er—country address?" inquired Frankie.

"Let me see now." He called to a junior clerk. "Frank, Mr. Bassington-ffrench's address."

"Roger Bassington-ffrench, Esq., Merroway Court, Staverley, Hants," said the junior clerk glibly.

"Ah!" said Frankie. "Then it wasn't my Mr. Bassington-ffrench. This must be his cousin. I thought it was odd his being here and not looking me up."

"Quite so—quite so," said Mr. Owen intelligently.

"Let me see, it must have been the Wednesday he came to see you."

"That's right. Just before six-thirty. We close at six-thirty. I remember particularly because it was the day when that sad accident happened. Man fell over the cliff. Mr. Bassington-ffrench had actually stayed by the body till the police came. He looked quite upset when he came in here. Very sad tragedy, that, and high time something was done about that bit of path. The Town Council have been criticized very freely, I can tell you, Lady Frances. Most dangerous. Why we haven't had more accidents than we have, I can't imagine."

"Extraordinary," said Frankie.

She left the office in a thoughtful mood. As Bobby had prophesied, all Mr. Bassington-ffrench's actions seemed clear and aboveboard. He was one of the Hampshire Bassington-ffrenches, he had given his proper address, he had actually mentioned his part in the tragedy to the house agent. Was it possible that, after all, Mr. Bassington-ffrench was the completely innocent person he seemed?

Frankie had a qualm of doubt. Then she refuted it.

"No," she said to herself. "A man who wants to buy a little place would either get here earlier in the day, or else stay over the next day. You wouldn't go into a house agent's at six-thirty in the evening and go up to London the following day. Why make the journey at all? Why not write?"

No, she decided, Bassington-ffrench was the guilty party.

Her next call was the police station.

Inspector Williams was an old acquaintance, having succeeded in tracking down a maid with a false reference who had absconded with some of Frankie's jewelry.

"Good afternoon, Inspector."

"Good afternoon, your ladyship. Nothing wrong, I hope."

"Not as yet, but I'm thinking of holding up a bank soon because I'm getting so short of money."

The Inspector gave a rumbling laugh in acknowledgment of this witticism.

"As a matter of fact I've come to ask questions out of sheer curiosity," said Frankie.

"Is that so, Lady Frances?"

"Now do tell me this, Inspector—that man who fell over the cliff—Pritchard or whatever his name was—"

"Pritchard, that's right."

"He only had *one* photograph on him, didn't he? Somebody told me he had *three!*"

"One's right," said the Inspector. "Photograph of his sister, it was. She came down and identified him."

"How absurd to say there were three!"

"Oh, that's easy, your ladyship. These newspaper reporters don't mind how much they exaggerate, and as often as not they get the whole thing wrong."

"I know," said Frankie. "I've heard the wildest stories." She paused a moment, then drew freely on her imagination. "I've heard that his pockets were stuffed with papers proving him to be a Bolshevik agent. And there's another story that his pockets were full of dope, and another again about his having pockets full of counterfeit banknotes."

The Inspector laughed heartily. "That's a good one."

"I suppose really he had just the usual things in his pockets?"

"And very few at that. A handkerchief, not marked. Some loose change, a packet of cigarettes and a couple of Treasury notes—loose, not in a case. No letters. We'd have had a job to identify him if it hadn't been for the photo. Providential, you might call it."

"I wonder," said Frankie.

In view of her private knowledge, she considered "providential" a singularly inapposite word. She changed the conversation.

"I went to see Mr. Jones, the Vicar's son, yesterday. The one who's been poisoned. What an extraordinary thing that was!"

"Ah!" said the Inspector. "Now that is extraordinary, if you like. Never heard of anything like it happening before. A nice young gentleman without an enemy in the world, or so you'd say. You know, Lady Frances, there are some queer customers going about. All the same I never heard of a homicidal maniac who acted just this way."

"Is there any clue at all to who did it?" Frankie was all wide-eyed inquiry. "It's so interesting to hear all this," she added.

The Inspector swelled with gratification. He enjoyed this friendly conversation with an Earl's daughter. Nothing stuck up or snobbish about Lady Frances.

"There was a car seen in the vicinity," said the Inspector. "Dark-blue Talbot. A man on Lock's Corner reported dark-blue Talbot No. *GG 8282* passed going direction St. Botolph's."

"And you think—"

"*GG 8282* is the number of the Bishop of St. Botolph's car."

Frankie toyed for a minute or two with the idea of a homicidal bishop who offered sacrifices of clergymen's sons but rejected it with a sigh. "You don't suspect the Bishop, I suppose?" she said.

"We've found out that the Bishop's car never left the Palace garage that afternoon."

"So it was a false number."

"Yes. We've got that to go on alright."

With expressions of admiration Frankie took her leave. She made no damping remark, but she thought to herself, "There must be a large number of dark-blue Talbots in England."

On her return home she took a directory of Marchbolt from its place on the writing-table in the library and removed it to her own room. She worked over it for some hours. The result was not satisfactory. There were four hundred and eighty-two Evanses in Marchbolt.

"Damn!" said Frankie.

She began to make plans for the future.

10
Preparations for an Accident

A WEEK LATER Bobby had joined Badger in London. He had received several enigmatical communications from Frankie, mostly in such an illegible scrawl that he was quite unable to do more than guess at their meaning. However, their general purport seemed to be that Frankie had a plan and that he (Bobby) was to do nothing until he heard from her. This was as well, for Bobby would certainly have had no leisure to do anything, since the unlucky Badger had already succeeded in embroiling himself and his business in every way ingenuity could suggest, and Bobby was kept busy disentangling the extraordinary mess his friend seemed to have got into.

Meanwhile the young man remained very strictly on his guard. The effect of eight grains of morphia was to render their taker extremely suspicious of food and drink and had also induced him to bring to London a Service revolver, the possession of which was extremely irksome to him.

He was just beginning to feel that the whole thing had been an extravagant nightmare when Frankie's Bentley roared down the mews and drew up outside the garage. Bobby, in grease-stained overalls, came out to receive it. Frankie was at the wheel and beside her sat a rather gloomy-looking young man.

"Hullo, Bobby," said Frankie. "This is George Arbuthnot. He's a doctor and we shall need him."

Bobby winced slightly as he and George Arbuthnot made faint acknowledgment of each other's presence.

"Are you sure we're going to need a doctor?" he asked. "Aren't you being a bit pessimistic?"

"I didn't mean we should need him in that way," said Frankie. "I need him for a scheme that I've got on. Look here, is there anywhere we can go and talk?"

Bobby looked doubtfully round him. "Well, there's my bedroom," he said doubtfully.

"Excellent," said Frankie.

She got out of the car, and she and George Arbuthnot followed Bobby up some outside steps and into a microscopic bedroom.

"I don't know," said Bobby, looking round dubiously, "if there's anywhere to sit."

There was not. The only chair was loaded with, apparently, the whole of Bobby's wardrobe.

"The bed will do," said Frankie.

She plumped down on it. George Arbuthnot did the same and the bed groaned protestingly.

"I've got everything planned out," said Frankie. "To begin with we want a car. One of yours will do."

"Do you mean you want to buy one of our cars?"

"Yes."

"That's really very nice of you, Frankie," said Bobby with warm appreciation. "But you needn't. I really do draw the line at sticking my friends."

"You've got it all wrong," said Frankie. "It isn't like that at all. I know what you mean—it's like buying perfectly appalling clothes and hats from one's friends who are just starting in business. A nuisance, but it's got to be done. But this isn't like that at all. I really need a car."

"What about the Bentley?"

"The Bentley's no good."

"You're mad," said Bobby.

"No, I'm not. The Bentley's no good for what I want it for."

"What do you want it for?"

"Smashing it up."

Bobby groaned and put a hand to his head. "I don't seem very well this morning."

George Arbuthnot spoke for the first time. His voice was deep and melancholy. "She means," he said, "that she's going to have an accident."

"How does she know?" said Bobby wildly.

Frankie gave an exasperated sigh. "Somehow or other," she said, "we seem to have started wrong. Now just listen quietly, Bobby, and try and take in what I'm going to say. I know your brains are practically negligible, but you ought to be able to understand if you really concentrate."

She paused, then resumed.

"I am on the trail of Bassington-ffrench."

"Hear, hear!"

"Bassington-ffrench—our particular Bassington-ffrench—lives at Merroway Court at the village of Staverley in Hampshire. Merroway Court belongs to our Bassington-ffrench's brother, and our Bassington-ffrench lives there with the brother and his wife."

"Whose wife?"

"The brother's wife of course. That isn't the point. The point is, how are you or I—or both of us—going to worm ourselves into the household? I've been down and reconnoitered the ground. Staverley's a mere village. Strangers arriving there to stay would stick out a mile. It would be the sort of thing that simply isn't done. So I've evolved a plan. This is what is going to happen. Lady Frances Derwent, driving her car more recklessly than well, crashes into the wall near the gates of Merroway Court. Complete wreckage of car, less complete wreckage of Lady Frances, who is carried to the house suffering from concussion and shock and must emphatically not be moved."

"Who says so?"

"George. Now you see where George comes in. We can't risk a strange doctor's saying there is nothing the matter with me. Or perhaps some officious person might pick up my prostrate form and take it to some local hospital. No, what happens is this. George is passing, also in a car (you'd better sell us a second one), sees the accident, leaps out and takes charge. 'I am a doctor. Stand back, everybody!'—That is, if there is anybody to stand back.—'We must take her into that house—what is it, Merroway Court? That will do. I must be able to make a thorough examination!' I am carried to the best spare room, the Bassington-ffrenches either sympathetic or bitterly resisting; but in any case, George will overbear them. George makes his examination and emerges with his verdict. Happily, it is not so serious as he thought. No bones broken, but danger of concussion. I must on no account be moved for two or three days. After that I shall be able to return to London.

"And then George departs, and it's up to me to ingratiate myself with the household."

"And where do I come in?"

"You don't."

"But look here—"

"My dear child, do remember that Bassington-ffrench knows you. He doesn't know me from Adam. And I'm in a frightfully strong position because I've got a title. You see how useful that is. I'm not just a stray young woman gaining admission to the house for mysterious purposes. I am an Earl's daughter and therefore highly respectable. And George is a real doctor, and everything is quite above suspicion."

"Oh, I suppose it's alright," said Bobby unhappily.

"It's a remarkably well-planned scheme, I think," said Frankie with pride.

"And I don't do anything at all?" asked Bobby. He still felt injured—much like a dog who has been unexpectedly deprived of a bone. This, he felt, was his own particular crime, and now he was being ousted.

"Of course you do, darling. You grow a mustache."

"Oh, I grow a mustache, do I?"

"Yes. How long will it take?"

"Two or three weeks, I expect."

"Heavens! I'd no idea it was such a slow process. Can't you speed it up?"

"No. Why can't I wear a false one?"

"They always *look* so false, and they twist or come off or smell of spirit-gum. Wait a minute, though—I believe there is a kind you can get stuck on hair by hair, so to speak, that absolutely defies detection. I expect a theatrical wigmaker would do it for you."

"He'd probably think I was trying to escape from justice."

"It doesn't matter what he thinks."

"Once I've got the mustache, what do I do?"

"Put on a chauffeur's uniform and drive the Bentley down to Staverley."

"Oh, I see." Bobby brightened.

"You see my idea is this," said Frankie. "Nobody looks at a chauffeur in the way they look at a *person*. In any case Bassington-ffrench only saw you for a minute or two, and he must have been too rattled wondering if he could change the photographs in time to look at you much. You were just a young golfing ass to him. It isn't like the Caymans, who sat opposite you and talked to you and who were deliberately trying to sum you up. I'd bet anything that seeing you in chauffeur's uniform, Bassington-ffrench wouldn't recognize you even without the mustache. He might just possibly think that your face reminded him of somebody—no more than that. And with the mustache it ought to be perfectly safe. Now tell me, what do you think of the plan?"

Bobby turned it over in his mind. "To tell you the truth, Frankie," he said generously, "I think it's pretty good."

"In that case," said Frankie briskly, "let's go and buy some cars. I say, I think George has broken your bed."

"It doesn't matter," said Bobby hospitably. "It was never a particularly good bed."

They descended to the garage where a nervous-looking young man with a curious lack of chin and an agreeable smile greeted them with a vague haw-haw-haw. His general appearance was slightly marred by the fact that his eyes had a distinct disinclination to look in the same direction.

"Hullo, Badger," said Bobby. "You remember Frankie, don't you?"

Badger clearly didn't, but he said "Haw haw haw" again in an amiable manner.

"Last time I saw you," said Frankie, "you were head downward in the mud, and we had to pull you out by the legs."

"No, not really?" said Badger. "Why, that m-m-must have been in W-w-w-wales."

"Quite right," said Frankie. "It was."

"I always was a p-p-putrid r-r-r-rider," said Badger. "I s-s-s-still am," he added mournfully.

"Frankie wants to buy a car," said Bobby.

"Two cars," said Frankie. "George has got to have one too. He's crashed his at the moment."

"We can hire him one," said Bobby.

"Well, come and look at what we've got in s-s-s-stock," said Badger.

"They look very smart," said Frankie, dazzled by lurid hues of scarlet and apple green.

"They *look* alright," said Bobby darkly.

"That's r-r-r-remarkably good value in a s-s-second-hand Chrysler," said Badger.

"No, not that one," said Bobby. "Whatever she buys has got to go at least forty miles."

Badger cast his partner a look of reproach.

"That Standard is pretty much on its last legs," mused Bobby. "But I think it would just get you there. The Essex is a bit too good for the job. She'll go at least two hundred before breaking down."

"Alright," said Frankie. "I'll have the Standard."

Badger drew his colleague a little aside. "W-w-what do you think about p-p-price?' he murmured. "Don't want to s-s-stick a friend of yours too much. T-t-t-ten pounds?"

"Ten pounds is alright," said Frankie, entering the discussion. "I'll pay for it now."

"Who is she really?" asked Badger in a loud whisper.

Bobby whispered back.

"F-f-f-first time I ever knew anyone with a t-t-t-title who c-c-could pay cash," said Badger with respect.

Bobby followed the other two out to the Bentley.

"When is this business going to take place?" he demanded.

"The sooner the better," said Frankie. "We thought tomorrow afternoon."

"Look here, can't I be there? I'll put on a beard if you like."

"Certainly not," said Frankie. "A beard would probably ruin everything by falling off at the wrong moment. But I don't see why you shouldn't be a motorcyclist—with a lot of cap and goggles. What do you think, George?"

George Arbuthnot spoke for the second time. "Alright," he said. "The more the merrier."

His voice was even more melancholy than before.

11
The Accident Happens

THE RENDEZVOUS FOR the great accident party was fixed at a spot about a mile from Staverley village where the road to Staverley branched off from the main road to Andover.

All three arrived there safely, though Frankie's Standard had shown unmistakable signs of decrepitude at every hill. The time fixed had been one o'clock.

"We don't want to be interrupted when we're staging the thing," Frankie had said. "Hardly anything ever goes down this road, I should imagine, but at lunch time we ought to be perfectly safe."

They proceeded for half a mile on the side road and then Frankie pointed out the place she had selected for the accident to take place.

"It couldn't be better in my opinion," she said. "Straight down this hill, and then, as you see, the road gives a sudden very sharp turn round that bulging bit of wall. The wall is actually the wall of Merroway Court. If we start the car and let it run down the hill it will crash straight into the wall and something pretty drastic ought to happen to it."

"I should say so," Bobby agreed. "But one of us ought to be on the lookout at the corner to be sure nobody is coming round it from the opposite direction."

"Quite right," said Frankie. "We don't want to involve anybody else in a mess up and perhaps maim them for life. George can take his car down there and turn it as though he were coming from the other direction. Then when he waves a handkerchief it will show that all is clear."

"You're looking very pale, Frankie," said Bobby anxiously. "Are you sure you're alright?"

"I'm made up pale," explained Frankie. "Ready for the concussion. You don't want me to be carried into the house blooming with health."

"How wonderful women are!" said Bobby appreciatively. "You look exactly like a sick monkey."

"I think you're very rude," said Frankie. "Now then, I shall go and prospect at the gate into Merroway Court. It's just this side of the bulge. There's no lodge fortunately. When George waves his handkerchief and I wave mine you start her off."

"Right," said Bobby. "I'll stay on the running board to guide her until the pace gets too hot and then I'll jump off."

"Don't hurt yourself," said Frankie anxiously.

"I shall be extremely careful not to. It would complicate matters to have a real accident on the spot of the faked one."

"Well, start off, George," said Frankie.

George nodded, jumped into the second car and ran slowly down the hill. Bobby and Frankie stood looking after him.

"You'll—look after yourself, won't you, Frankie?" said Bobby with sudden gruffness. "I mean—don't go doing anything foolish."

"I shall be alright. Most circumspect. By the way, I don't think I'd better write to you direct. I'll write to George or my maid or someone or other to pass on to you."

"I wonder if George is going to be a success in his profession?"

"Why shouldn't he?"

"Well, he doesn't seem to have acquired a chatty bedside manner yet."

"I expect that will come," said Frankie. "I'd better be going now. I'll let you know when I want you to come down with the Bentley."

"I'll get busy with the mustache. So long, Frankie."

They looked at each other for a moment and then Frankie nodded and began to walk down the hill.

George had turned the car and then backed it round the bulge.

Frankie disappeared for a moment, then reappeared in the road waving a handkerchief. A second handkerchief waved from the bottom of the road at the turn.

Bobby put the car into third gear, then standing on the footboard he released the brake. The car moved grudgingly forward—impeded by being in gear. The slope, however, was sufficiently steep. The engine started. The car gathered way. Bobby steadied the steering wheel. At the last possible moment he jumped off.

The car went on down the hill and crashed into the wall with considerable force. All was well—the accident had taken place successfully.

Bobby saw Frankie run quickly to the scene of the crime and plop down amid the wreckage. George in his car came round the corner and pulled up.

With a sigh Bobby mounted his motorcycle and rode away in the direction of London.

At the scene of the accident things were busy.

"Shall I roll about in the road a bit?" asked Frankie. "To get myself dusty."

"You might as well," said George. "Here, give me your hat."

He took it and inflicted a terrific dent on it. Frankie gave a faint anguished cry.

"That's the concussion," explained George. "Now then, lie doggo just where you are. I think I heard a bicycle bell."

Sure enough, at that moment, a boy of about seventeen came whistling round the corner. He stopped at once, delighted with the pleasurable spectacle that met his eyes.

"Ooer!" he ejaculated, "'as there been an accident?"

"No," said George sarcastically. "The young lady ran her car into the wall on purpose."

Accepting, as he was meant to do, this remark as irony rather than the simple truth which it was, the boy said with relish, "Looks bad, don't she? Is she dead?"

"Not yet," said George. "She must be taken somewhere at once. I'm a doctor. What's this place in here?"

"Merroway Court. Belongs to Mr. Bassington-ffrench. He's a J.P., he is."

"She must be carried there at once," said George authoritatively. "Here, leave your bicycle, and lend me a hand."

Only too willing, the boy propped his bicycle against the wall and came to assist. Between them George and the boy carried Frankie up the drive to a pleasant, old-fashioned-looking manor house.

Their approach had been observed, for an elderly butler came out to meet them.

"There's been an accident," said George curtly. "Is there a room I can carry this lady into? She must be attended to at once."

The butler went back into the hall in a flustered way. George and the boy followed him up closely, still carrying the limp body of Frankie. The butler had gone into a room on the left and from there a woman emerged. She was tall, with red hair, and about thirty years of age. Her eyes were a light, clear blue.

She dealt with the situation quickly.

"There is a spare bedroom on the ground floor," she said. "Will you bring her in there? Ought I to telephone for a doctor?"

"I am a doctor," explained George. "I was passing in my car and saw the accident occur."

"Oh! How very fortunate. Come this way, will you?"

She showed them the way into a pleasant bedroom with windows giving on the garden.

"Is she badly hurt?" she inquired.

"I can't tell yet."

Mrs. Bassington-ffrench took the hint and retired. The boy accompanied her and launched out into a description of the accident as though he had been an actual witness of it.

"Run smack into the wall, she did. Car's all smashed up. There she was lying on the ground with her hat all dinted in. The gentleman he was passing in his car—" He proceeded ad lib till got rid of with a half-crown.

Meanwhile Frankie and George were conversing in careful whispers.

"George, darling, this won't blight your career, will it? They won't strike you off the register, or whatever it is, will they?"

"Probably," said George gloomily. "That is, if it ever comes out."

"It won't," said Frankie. "Don't worry, George. I shan't let you down." She added thoughtfully, "You did it very well. I've never heard you talk so much before."

George sighed. He looked at his watch. "I shall give my examination another three minutes," he said.

"What about the car?"

"I'll arrange with a garage to have that cleared up."

"Good."

George continued to study his watch. Finally he said with an air of relief, "Time!"

"George," said Frankie, "you've been an angel. I don't know why you did it."

"No more do I," said George. "Damn fool thing to do."

He nodded to her.

"Bye-bye. Enjoy yourself."

"I wonder if I shall," said Frankie. She was thinking of that cool impersonal voice with the slight American accent.

George went in search of the owner of it, whom he found waiting for him in the drawing-room.

"Well," he said abruptly. "I'm glad to say it's not so bad as I feared. Concussion very slight and already passing off. She ought to stay quietly where she is for a day or so, though." He paused. "She seems to be a Lady Frances Derwent."

"Oh, fancy!" said Mrs. Bassington-ffrench. "Then I know some cousins of hers, the Draycotts, quite well."

"I don't know if it's inconvenient for you to have her here," said George. "But if she *could* stay where she was for a day or two—" Here George paused.

"Oh, of course. That will be quite alright, Dr.—?"

"Arbuthnot. By the way, I'll see to the car business. I shall be passing a garage."

"Thank you very much, Dr. Arbuthnot. How very lucky you happened to be passing! I suppose a doctor ought to see her tomorrow just to see she's getting on alright."

"Don't think it's necessary," said George. "All she needs is quiet."

"But I should feel happier. And her people ought to know."

"I'll attend to that," said George. "And as to the doctoring business—well, it seems she's a Christian Scientist and won't have doctors at any price. She wasn't too pleased at finding me in attendance."

"Oh, dear!" said Mrs. Bassington-ffrench.

"But she'll be quite alright," said George reassuringly. "You can take my word for it."

"If you really think so, Dr. Arbuthnot," said Mrs. Bassington-ffrench rather doubtfully.

"I do," said George. "Good-bye. Dear me, I left one of my instruments in the bedroom."

He came rapidly into the room and up to the bedside.

"Frankie," he said in a quick whisper, "you're a Christian Scientist. Don't forget."

"But why?"

"I had to do it. Only way."

"Alright," said Frankie. "I won't forget."

12

In the Enemy's Camp

"WELL, HERE I AM," thought Frankie. "Safely in the enemy's camp. Now it's up to me."

There was a tap on the door and Mrs. Bassington-ffrench entered.

Frankie raised herself a little on her pillows.

"I'm so frightfully sorry," she said in a faint voice. "Causing you all this bother."

"Nonsense," said Mrs. Bassington-ffrench. Frankie heard anew that cool, attractive, drawling voice with a slight American accent, and remembered that Lord Marchington had said that one of the Hampshire Bassington-ffrenches had married an American heiress. "Dr. Arbuthnot says you will be quite alright in a day or two if you just keep quiet."

Frankie felt that she ought at this point to say something about "error" or "mortal mind" but was frightened of saying the wrong thing.

"He seems nice," she said. "He was very kind."

"He seemed a most capable young man," said Mrs. Bassington-ffrench. "It was very fortunate that he just happened to be passing."

"Yes, wasn't it? Not, of course, that I really needed him."

"But you mustn't talk," continued her hostess. "I'll send my maid along with some things for you and then she can get you properly into bed."

"It's frightfully kind of you."

"Not at all."

Frankie felt a momentary qualm as the other woman withdrew.

"A nice kind creature," she said to herself. "And beautifully unsuspecting."

For the first time she felt that she was playing a mean trick on her hostess. Her mind had been so taken up with the vision of a murderous Bassington-ffrench pushing an unsuspecting victim over a precipice that lesser characters in the drama had not entered her imagination.

"Oh, well," thought Frankie, "I've got to go through with it now. But I wish she hadn't been so nice about it."

She spent a dull afternoon and evening lying in her darkened room. Mrs. Bassington-ffrench looked in once or twice to see how she was, but she did not stay.

The next day, however, Frankie admitted the daylight and expressed a desire for company and her hostess came and sat with her for some time. They discovered many common acquaintances and friends, and by the end of that day Frankie felt, with a guilty qualm, that they had become friends.

Mrs. Bassington-ffrench referred several times to her husband and to her small boy, Tommy. She seemed a simple woman, deeply attached to her home; yet for some reason or other Frankie fancied that she was not quite happy. There was an anxious expression in her eyes sometimes that did not argue a mind at peace with itself.

On the third day Frankie got up and was introduced to the master of the house.

He was a big man, heavy-jowled, with a kindly but rather abstracted air. He seemed to spend a good deal of his time shut up in his study. Yet Frankie judged him to be very fond of his wife, though interesting himself very little in her concerns.

Tommy, the small boy, was seven, and a healthy, mischievous child. Sylvia Bassington-ffrench obviously adored him.

"It's so nice down here," said Frankie with a sigh. She was lying out on a long chair in the garden. "I don't know whether it's the bang on the head, or what it is, but I just don't feel I want to move. I'd like to lie here for days and days."

"Well, do," said Sylvia Bassington-ffrench in her calm, incurious tones. "No, really, I mean it. Don't hurry back to town. You see," she went on, "it's a great pleasure to me to have you here. You're so bright and amusing. It quite cheers me up."

"So she needs cheering up," flashed across Frankie's mind. At the same time she felt ashamed of herself.

"I feel we really have become friends," continued the other woman.

Frankie felt still more ashamed. It was a mean thing she was doing—mean—mean—mean. She would give it up! Go back to town—

Her hostess went on. "It won't be too dull here. Tomorrow my brother-in-law is coming back. You'll like him, I'm sure. Everyone likes Roger."

"He lives with you?"

"Off and on. He's a restless creature. He calls himself the ne'er-do-well of the family, and perhaps it's true in a way. He never sticks to a job for long—in fact I don't believe he's ever done any real work in his life. But some people just are like that—especially in old families. And they're usually people with a great charm of manner. Roger is wonderfully sympathetic. I don't know what I should have done without him this Spring when Tommy was ill."

"What was the matter with Tommy?"

"He had a bad fall from the swing. It must have been tied on to a rotten branch, and the branch gave way. Roger was very much upset because he was swinging the child at the time—you know, giving him high ones such as children love. We thought at first Tommy's spine was hurt, but it turned out to be a very slight injury and he's quite alright now."

"He certainly looks it," said Frankie, smiling, as she heard faint yells and whoops in the distance.

"I know. He seems in perfect condition. It's such a relief. He's had bad luck in accidents. He was nearly drowned last winter."

"Was he really?" said Frankie thoughtfully.

She no longer meditated returning to town. The feeling of guilt had abated. Accidents! Did Roger Bassington-ffrench specialize in accidents, she wondered.

She said: "If you're sure you mean it, I'd love to stay a little longer. But won't your husband mind my butting in like this?"

"Henry?" Mrs. Bassington-ffrench's lips curled in a strange expression. "No, Henry won't mind. Henry never minds anything—nowadays."

Frankie looked at her curiously.

"If she knew me better she'd tell me something," she thought to herself. "I believe there are lots of odd things going on in this household."

Henry Bassington-ffrench joined them for tea, and Frankie studied him closely. There was certainly something odd about the man. His type was an obvious one—a jovial, sport-loving, simple country gentleman. But such a man ought not to sit twitching nervously, his nerves obviously on edge, now sunk in an abstraction from which it was impossible to rouse him, now giving out bitter and sarcastic replies to anything said to him. Not that he was always like that. Later that evening, at dinner, he showed out in quite a new light. He joked, laughed, told stories, and was, for a man of his abilities, quite brilliant. Too brilliant, Frankie felt. The brilliance was just as unnatural and out of character.

"He has such queer eyes," she thought. "They frighten me a little."

And yet surely she did not suspect *Henry* Bassington-ffrench of anything? It was his brother, not he, who had been in Marchbolt on that fatal day.

As for the brother, Frankie looked forward to seeing him with eager interest. According to her and to Bobby, the man was a murderer. She was going to meet a murderer face to face.

She felt momentarily nervous. Yet, after all, how could he guess? How could he, in any way, connect her with a successfully accomplished crime?

"You're making a bogy for yourself out of nothing," she reflected.

Roger Bassington-ffrench arrived just before tea on the following afternoon. Frankie did not meet him till teatime. She was still supposed to "rest" in the afternoon.

When she came out onto the lawn where tea was laid, Sylvia said, smiling: "Here is our invalid. This is my brother-in-law—Lady Frances Derwent."

Frankie saw a tall, slender young man of something over thirty with very pleasant eyes. Although she could see what Bobby meant by saying he ought to have a monocle and a toothbrush mustache, she herself was more inclined to notice the intense blue of his eyes. They shook hands.

He said, "I've been hearing all about the way you tried to break down the park wall."

"I'll admit," said Frankie, "that I'm the world's worst driver. But I was driving an awful old rattle-trap. My own car was laid up, and I bought a cheap one second-hand."

"She was rescued from the ruins by a very good-looking young doctor," said Sylvia.

"He was rather sweet," agreed Frankie.

Tommy arrived at this moment and flung himself upon his uncle with squeaks of joy.

"Have you brought me a Hornby train? You said you would. You said you would!"

"Oh, Tommy, you mustn't ask for things!" said Sylvia.

"That's alright, Sylvia. It was a promise. I've got your train alright, old man." He looked casually at his sister-in-law. "Isn't Henry coming to tea?"

"I don't think so." A constrained note was in her voice. "He isn't feeling awfully well today, I imagine." Then she said impulsively, "Oh, Roger, I'm glad you're back!"

He put his hand on her arm for a minute. "That's alright, Sylvia, old girl."

After tea, Roger played trains with his nephew. Frankie watched them, her mind in a turmoil. Surely this wasn't the sort of man to push people over cliffs! This charming young man couldn't be a cold-blooded murderer!

But then—she and Bobby must have been wrong all along. Wrong, that is, about this part of it.

She felt sure now that it wasn't Bassington-ffrench who had pushed Pritchard over the cliff.

Then who was it? She was still convinced he had been pushed over. Who had done it? And who had put the morphia in Bobby's beer?

With the thought of morphia suddenly the explanation of Henry Bassington-ffrench's peculiar eyes came to her, with their pinpoint pupils. Was Henry Bassington-ffrench a drug fiend?

13

Alan Carstairs

STRANGELY ENOUGH, SHE received confirmation of this theory no later than the following day, and it came from Roger.

They had been playing a single at tennis against each other and, sitting afterward sipping iced drinks, had been talking about various indifferent subjects. Frankie had become more and more sensible of the charm of someone who had, like Roger Bassington-ffrench, traveled about all over the world. The family ne'er-do-well, she could not help thinking, contrasted very favorably with his heavy, serious-minded brother.

A pause had fallen while these thoughts were passing through Frankie's mind. It was broken by Roger—speaking this time in an entirely different tone of voice.

"Lady Frances, I'm going to do a rather peculiar thing. I've known you less than twenty-four hours, but I feel instinctively that you're the one person I can ask advice from."

"Advice?" said Frankie, surprised.

"Yes. I can't make up my mind between two different courses of action." He paused. He was leaning forward, swinging a racket between his knees, a light frown on his forehead. He looked worried and upset. "It's about my brother, Lady Frances."

"Yes?"

"He is taking drugs. I am sure of it."

"What makes you think so?" asked Frankie.

"Everything. His appearance. His extraordinary changes of mood. And have you noticed his eyes? The pupils are like pin-points."

"I had noticed that," admitted Frankie. "What do you think it is?"

"Morphia or some form of opium."

"Has it been going on for long?"

"I date the beginning of it from about six months ago. I remember that he complained of sleeplessness a good deal. How he first came to take the stuff I don't know, but I think it must have begun soon after then."

"How does he get hold of it?" inquired Frankie practically.

"I think it comes to him by post. Have you noticed that he is particularly nervous and irritable some days at teatime?"

"Yes, I have."

"I suspect that that is when he has finished up his supply and is waiting for more. Then, after the six o'clock post has come, he goes into his study and emerges for dinner in quite a different mood."

Frankie nodded. She remembered that unnatural brilliance of conversation sometimes at dinner.

"But where does the supply come from?" she asked.

"Ah, that I don't know. No reputable doctor would give it to him. There are, I suppose, various sources where one could get it in London by paying a big price."

Frankie nodded thoughtfully. She was remembering having said to Bobby something about a gang of drug-smugglers and his replying that one could not mix up too many crimes. It was queer that so soon in their investigations they should have come upon the traces of such a thing. And it was queerer that it should be the chief suspect who had drawn her attention to the fact. It made her more inclined than ever to acquit Roger Bassington-ffrench of the charge of murder.

And yet there was the inexplicable matter of the changed photograph. The evidence against him, she reminded herself, was still exactly what it had been. On the other side was only the personality of the man himself. And everyone always said that murderers were charming people!

She shook off these reflections and turned to her companion.

"Why exactly are you telling me this?" she asked frankly.

"Because I don't know what to do about Sylvia," he said simply.

"You think she doesn't know?"

"Of course she doesn't know. Ought I to tell her?"

"It's very difficult—"

"It *is* difficult. That's why I thought you might be able to help me. Sylvia has taken a great fancy to you. She doesn't care much for any of the people round about, but she liked you at once, she tells me. What ought I to do, Lady Frances? By telling her I shall add a great burden to her life."

"If she knew, she might have some influence," suggested Frankie.

"I doubt it. When it's a case of drug-taking, nobody, even the nearest and dearest, has any influence."

"That's rather a hopeless attitude, isn't it?"

"It's a fact. There are ways, of course. If Henry would only consent to go in for a cure—there's a place actually near here. Run by a Dr. Nicholson."

"But he'd never consent, would he?"

"He might. You can catch a morphia-taker in a mood of extravagant remorse sometimes when he'd do anything to cure himself. I'm inclined to think that Henry might be got to that frame of mind more easily if he thought Sylvia didn't know—if her knowing were held over him as a kind of threat. If the cure were successful—they'd call it 'nerves,' of course—she would never need to know."

"Would he have to go away for the cure?"

"The place I mean is about three miles from here, the other side of the village. It's run by a Canadian, Dr. Nicholson. A very clever man, I believe. And fortunately Henry likes him. Hush—here comes Sylvia."

Mrs. Bassington-ffrench joined them, observing, "Have you been very energetic?"

"Three sets," said Frankie. "And I was beaten every time."

"You play a very good game," said Roger.

"I'm terrible lazy about tennis," said Sylvia. "We must ask the Nicholsons over one day. She's very fond of a game. Why—what is it?" She had caught the glance the other two had exchanged.

"Nothing—only I just happened to be talking about the Nicholsons to Lady Frances."

"You'd better call her Frankie as I do," said Sylvia. "Isn't it odd how whenever one talks of any person or thing, somebody else does the same immediately afterward?"

"They are Canadians, aren't they?" inquired Frankie.

"He is, certainly. I rather fancy she is English, but I'm not sure. She's a very pretty little thing—quite charming, with the loveliest big wistful eyes. Somehow or other I fancy she isn't terribly happy. It must be a depressing life."

"He runs a kind of sanitarium, doesn't he?"

"Yes, nerve cases and people who take drugs. He's very successful, I believe. He's rather an impressive man."

"You like him?"

"No," said Sylvia abruptly. "I don't." And rather vehemently, after a moment or two, she added, "Not at all."

Later on, she pointed out to Frankie a photograph of a charming, large-eyed woman which stood on the piano.

"That's Moira Nicholson. An appealing face, isn't it? A man who came down here with some friends of ours some time ago was quite struck with it. He wanted an introduction to her, I think." She laughed. "I'll ask them to dinner tomorrow night. I'd like to know what you think of him."

"Him?"

"Yes. As I told you, I dislike him, and yet he's quite an attractive-looking man."

Something in her tone made Frankie look at her quickly, but Sylvia Bassington-ffrench had turned away and was taking some dead flowers out of a vase.

"I must collect my ideas," thought Frankie as she drew a comb through her thick dark hair when dressing for dinner that night. "And," she added resolutely, "it's time I made a few experiments."

Was, or was not, Roger Bassington-ffrench the villain she and Bobby assumed him to be?

She and Bobby had agreed that whoever had tried to put him out of the way must have easy access to morphia. Now in a way this held good for Roger Bassington-ffrench. If his brother received supplies of morphia by post, it would be easy enough for Roger to abstract a packet and use it for his own purposes.

"Mem.," wrote Frankie on a sheet of paper. "One—find out where Roger was on 16th—day when Bobby was poisoned."

She thought she saw her way to doing that fairly clearly.

"Two," she wrote. "Produce picture of dead man and observe reactions, if any. Also note whether R.B.F. admits being in Marchbolt then."

She felt slightly nervous over the second resolution. It meant coming out into the open. On the other hand the tragedy had happened in her own part of the world, and to mention it casually would be the most natural thing in the world. She crumpled up the sheet of paper and burnt it.

She managed to introduce the first point fairly naturally at dinner.

"You know," she said frankly to Roger, "I can't help feeling that we've met before. And it wasn't very long ago either. It wasn't, by any chance, at that party of Lady Shane's at Claridge's? On the 16th it was."

"It couldn't have been on the 16th," said Sylvia quickly. "Roger was here then. I remember, because we had a children's party that day, and what I should have done without Roger, I simply don't know."

She gave a grateful glance at her brother-in-law and he smiled back at her.

"I don't feel I've ever met you before," he said thoughtfully to Frankie and added, "I'm sure, if I had, I'd remember it." He said it rather nicely.

"One point settled," thought Frankie. "Roger Bassington-ffrench was not in Wales on the day that Bobby was poisoned."

The second point came up fairly easily later. Frankie led the talk to country places, their dullness, and the interest aroused by any local excitement.

"We had a man fall over the cliff last month," she remarked. "We were all thrilled to the core. I went to the inquest full of excitement, but it was all rather dull really."

"Was that at a place called Marchbolt?" asked Sylvia suddenly.

Frankie nodded. "Derwent Castle is only about seven miles from Marchbolt," she explained.

"Roger, that must have been your man!" cried Sylvia.

Frankie looked inquiringly at him.

"I was actually in at the death," said Roger. "I stayed with the body till the police came."

"I thought one of the Vicar's sons did that," said Frankie.

"He had to go off to play the organ or something—so I took over."

"How perfectly extraordinary!" said Frankie. "I did hear somebody else had been there too, but I never heard the name. So it was *you.*"

There was a general atmosphere of "How curious! Isn't the world small?" Frankie felt she was doing this rather well.

"Perhaps that's where you saw me before—in Marchbolt?" suggested Roger.

"I wasn't there actually at the time of the accident," said Frankie. "I came back from London a couple of days afterward. Were you at the inquest?"

"No. I went back to London the morning after the tragedy."

"He had some absurd idea of buying a house down there," said Sylvia.

"Utter nonsense," said Henry Bassington-ffrench.

"Not at all," said Roger good-humoredly.

"You know perfectly well, Roger, that as soon as you'd bought it, you'd get a fit of wanderlust and go off abroad again."

"Oh! I shall settle down some day, Sylvia."

"When you do, you'd better settle down near us," said Sylvia. "Not go off to Wales."

Roger laughed. Then he turned to Frankie. "Any points of interest about the accident? It didn't turn out to be suicide or anything?"

"Oh, no, it was all painfully aboveboard, and some appalling relations came and identified the man. He was on a walking tour, it seems. Very sad really, because he was awfully good-looking. Did you see his picture in the papers?"

"I think I did," said Sylvia vaguely, "but I don't remember."

"I've got a cutting upstairs from our local paper."

Frankie was all eagerness. She ran upstairs and came down with the cutting in her hand. She gave it to Sylvia. Roger came and looked over Sylvia's shoulder.

"Don't you think he's good-looking?" Frankie demanded.

"He is, rather," said Sylvia. "He looks very like that man Alan Carstairs. Don't you think so, Roger? I believe I remember saying so at the time."

"He's got quite a look of him here," agreed Roger. "But there wasn't much real resemblance, you know."

"You can't tell from newspaper pictures, can you?" said Sylvia as she handed the cutting back.

Frankie agreed that you couldn't, and the conversation passed to other matters.

She went to bed undecided. Everyone seemed to have reacted with perfect naturalness. Roger's house-hunting stunt had been no secret.

The only thing she had succeeded in getting was a name—the name of Alan Carstairs.

14
Dr. Nicholson

FRANKIE ATTACKED SYLVIA the following morning. She started by asking carelessly:

"What was that man's name you mentioned last night? Alan Carstairs, was it? I feel sure I've heard that name before."

"I dare say you have. He's rather a celebrity in his way, I believe. He's a Canadian—a naturalist and big-game hunter and explorer. I don't really know him. Some friends of ours, the Rivingtons, brought him down here one day for lunch. A very attractive man—big and bronzed and nice blue eyes."

"I was sure I'd heard of him."

"He'd never been over to this country before, I believe. Last year he went a tour through Africa with that millionaire man, John Savage—the one who thought he had cancer and killed himself in that tragic way. Carstairs has been all over the world. East Africa, South America—simply everywhere, I believe."

"Sounds a nice adventurous person," said Frankie.

"Oh, he was. Distinctly attractive."

"Funny—his being so like the man who fell over the cliff at Marchbolt," said Frankie.

"I wonder if everyone has a double."

They compared instances, citing Adolf Beck and refering lightly to the Lyons Mail. Frankie was careful to make no further references to Alan Carstairs. To show too much interest in him would be fatal. In her mind, however, she felt she was getting on now. She was quite convinced that the victim of the cliff tragedy at Marchbolt had been Alan Carstairs. He fulfilled all the conditions. He had no intimate friends or relations in this country, and his disappearance was unlikely to be noticed for some time. A man who frequently ran off to East Africa and South America was not likely to be missed at once. Moreover, Frankie noted, although Sylvia Bassington-ffrench had commented on the resemblance in the newspaper reproduction, it had not occurred to her for a moment that it actually *was* the man. That, Frankie thought, was rather an interesting bit of psychology. We seldom suspect people who are "news" of being people we have actually seen or met.

Very good then. The dead man was Alan Carstairs. The next step was to learn more about Alan Carstairs. His connection with the Bassington-ffrenches seemed to have been of the slightest. He had been brought down there quite by chance by friends. What was the name?—Rivington. Frankie stored it in her memory for future use.

That certainly was a possible avenue of inquiry. But it would be well to go slowly. Inquiries about Alan Carstairs must be very discreetly made.

"I don't want to be poisoned or knocked on the head," thought Frankie with a grimace. "They were ready enough to bump off Bobby for practically nothing at all—"

Her thoughts flew off at a tangent to that tantalizing phrase that had started the whole business. Evans! Who was Evans? Where did Evans fit in?

"A dope gang," decided Frankie. Perhaps some relative of Carstairs was being victimized, and he had determined to bust it up. Perhaps he had come to England for that purpose. Evans may have been one of the gang who had retired and gone to Wales to live. Carstairs had bribed Evans to give the others away, and Evans had consented and Carstairs went there to see him, and someone followed him and killed him.

Was that somebody Roger Bassington-ffrench? It seemed very unlikely. The Caymans, now, were far more what Frankie imagined a gang of dope-smugglers would be likely to be.

And yet—that photograph. If only there were some explanation of that photograph!

That evening Dr. Nicholson and his wife were expected to dinner. Frankie was finishing dressing when she heard their car drive up to the front door. Her window faced that way, and she looked out.

A tall man was just alighting from the driver's seat of a dark-blue Talbot.

Frankie withdrew her head thoughtfully.

Carstairs had been a Canadian. Dr. Nicholson was a Canadian. And Dr. Nicholson had a dark-blue Talbot.

Absurd to build anything upon that, of course, but wasn't it just faintly suggestive?

Dr. Nicholson was a big man with a manner that suggested great reserves of power. His speech was slow, and on the whole he said very little, but he contrived somehow to make every word sound significant. He wore strong glasses, and behind them his very pale blue eyes glittered reflectively.

His wife was a slender creature of perhaps twenty-seven, pretty, indeed beautiful. She seemed, Frankie thought, slightly nervous and chattered rather feverishly as though to conceal the fact.

"You had an accident, I hear, Lady Frances," said Dr. Nicholson as he took his seat beside her at the dinner table.

Frankie explained the catastrophe. She wondered why she should feel so nervous in doing so. The Doctor's manner was simple and interested. Why should she feel as though she were rehearsing a defence to a charge that had never been made? Was there any earthly reason why the Doctor should disbelieve in her accident?

"That was too bad," he said, as she finished, having perhaps made a more detailed story of it than seemed strictly necessary. "But you seem to have made a very good recovery."

"We won't admit she's cured yet. We're keeping her with us," said Sylvia.

The Doctor's gaze went to Sylvia. Something like a very faint smile came to his lips, but passed almost immediately.

"I should keep her with you as long as possible," he said gravely.

Frankie was sitting between her host and Dr. Nicholson. Henry Bassington-ffrench was decidedly moody tonight. His hands twitched, he ate next to nothing, and he took no part in the conversation.

Mrs. Nicholson, opposite, had a difficult time with him, and turned to Roger with obvious relief. She talked to him in a desultory fashion, but Frankie noticed that her eyes were never long absent from her husband's face.

Dr. Nicholson was talking about life in the country. "Do you know what a culture is, Lady Frances?"

"Do you mean book-learning?" asked Frankie, rather puzzled.

"No, no. I was referring to germs. They develop, you know, in specially prepared serum. The country, Lady Frances, is a little like that. There is time, and space, and infinite leisure—suitable conditions, you see, for development."

"Do you mean bad things?" asked Frankie.

"That depends, Lady Frances, on the kind of germ cultivated."

Idiotic conversation, thought Frankie. Why should it make her feel creepy? Yet it did! She said flippantly, "I expect I'm developing all sorts of dark qualities."

He looked at her and said calmly: "Oh, no, I don't think so, Lady Frances. I think you would always be on the side of law and order."

Was there a faint emphasis on the word *law?*

Suddenly, across the table Mrs. Nicholson said, "My husband prides himself on summing up character."

Dr. Nicholson nodded his head gently. "Quite right, Moira. Little things interest me." He turned to Frankie again. "I had heard of your accident, you know. One thing about it intrigued me very much."

"Yes?" said Frankie, her heart beating suddenly.

"The doctor who was passing. The one who brought you in here."

"Yes?"

"He must have had a curious character—to turn his car before going to the rescue."

"I don't understand."

"Of course not. You were unconscious. But young Reeves, the message boy, came from Staverley on his bicycle, and no car passed him. Yet he comes round the corner, finds the smash, and the doctor's car pointing the same way he was going—toward London. You see the point? The Doctor did not come from the direction of Staverley, so he must have come the other way, down the hill. But in that case, his car should have been pointing toward Staverley. But it wasn't. Therefore he must have turned it."

"Unless he had come from Staverley some time before," said Frankie.

"Then his car would have been standing there as you came down the hill. Was it?"

The pale-blue eyes were looking at her very intently through the thick glasses.

"I don't remember," said Frankie. "I don't think so."

"You sound like a detective, Jasper," said Mrs. Nicholson. "And all about nothing at all."

"Little things interest me," said Nicholson. He turned to his hostess and Frankie drew a breath of relief.

Why had he catechized her like that? How had he found out all about the accident? "Little things interest me," he had said. Was that all there was to it? Frankie remembered the dark-blue Talbot saloon, and the fact that Carstairs had been a Canadian. It seemed to her that Dr. Nicholson was a sinister man.

She kept out of his way after dinner, attaching herself to the gentle, fragile Mrs. Nicholson. She noticed that all the time Mrs. Nicholson's eyes still watched her husband. Was it love, Frankie wondered, or fear?

Nicholson devoted himself to Sylvia, and at half-past ten he caught his wife's eye and they rose to go.

"Well," said Roger after they had gone, "what do you think of our Dr. Nicholson? A very forceful personality, hasn't he?"

"I'm like Sylvia," said Frankie. "I don't think I like him very much. I like her better."

"Good-looking but rather a little idiot," said Roger. "She either worships him or is scared to death of him, I don't know which."

"That's just what I wondered," agreed Frankie.

"I don't like him," said Sylvia, "But I must admit that he's got a lot of—of *force*. I believe he's cured drug-takers in the most marvelous way. People whose relatives despaired utterly. They've gone there as a last hope and come out absolutely cured."

"Yes," cried Henry Bassington-ffrench suddenly. "And do you know what goes on there? Do you know the awful suffering and mental torment? A man's used to a drug and they cut him off it—cut him off it—till he goes raving mad for the lack of it and beats his head against the wall. That's what he does, your 'forceful' doctor, tortures people—tortures them—sends them to Hell—drives them mad . . ."

He was shaking violently. Suddenly he turned and left the room.

Sylvia Bassington-ffrench looked startled. "What is the matter with Henry?" she said wonderingly. "He seems very much upset."

Frankie and Roger dared not look at each other.

"He's not looked well all the evening," ventured Frankie.

"No. I noticed that. He's very moody lately. I wish he hadn't given up riding. Oh, by the way, Dr. Nicholson invited Tommy over tomorrow, but I don't like his going there very much—not with all those queer nerve cases and dope-takers."

"I don't suppose the Doctor would allow him to come into contact with them," said Roger. "He seems very fond of children."

"Yes, I think it's a disappointment he hasn't got any of his own. Probably to her, too. She looks very sad—and terribly delicate."

"She's like a sad Madonna," said Frankie.

"Yes, that describes her very well."

"If Dr. Nicholson is so fond of children, I suppose he came to your children's party?" said Frankie carelessly.

"Unfortunately he was away for a day or two just then. I think he had to go to London for some conference."

"I see."

They went up to bed. Before she went to sleep Frankie wrote to Bobby.

15
A Discovery

BOBBY HAD HAD an irksome time. His enforced inaction was exceedingly trying. He hated staying quietly in London and doing nothing.

He had been rung up on the telephone by George Arbuthnot, who in a few laconic words told him that all had gone well. A couple of days later he had a letter from Frankie delivered to him by her maid, the letter having gone under cover to her at Lord Marchington's town house. Since then he had heard nothing.

"Letter for you!" called out Badger.

Bobby came forward excitedly, but the letter was one addressed in his father's handwriting and postmarked Marchbolt. At that moment, however, he caught sight of the neat, black-gowned figure of Frankie's maid approaching down the mews. Five minutes later he was tearing open Frankie's second letter.

DEAR BOBBY.

I think it's about time you came down. I've given them instructions at home that you're to have the Bentley whenever you ask for it. Get a chauffeur's livery—dark green ours always are. Put it down to Father at Harrod's. It's best to be correct in details. Concentrate on making a good job of the mustache. It makes a frightful difference to anyone's face.

Come down here and ask for me. You might bring me an ostensible note from Father. Report that the car is now in working order again. The garage here only holds two cars and as it's got the family Daimler and Roger Bassington-ffrench's two-seater in it, it is fortunately full up, so you will go to Staverley and put up there.

Get what local information you can when there—particularly about a Dr. Nicholson who runs a place for dope patients. Several suspicious circumstances about him: he has a dark-blue Talbot saloon, he was away from home on the 16th when your beer was doctored, and he takes altogether too detailed an interest in the circumstances of my accident.

I think I've identified the corpse!!!

Au revoir, my fellow sleuth.

Love from your successfully concussed

FRANKIE.

P.S. I shall post this myself.

Bobby's spirits rose with a bound.

Discarding his overalls and braking the news of his immediate departure to Badger, he was about to hurry off when he remembered that he had not yet opened his father's letter. He did so with a rather qualified enthusiasm since the Vicar's letters were actuated by a spirit of duty rather than pleasure and breathed an atmosphere of Christian forbearance which was highly depressing.

The Vicar gave conscientious news of doings in Marchbolt, described his own troubles with the organist and commented on the unchristian spirit of one of his churchwardens. The rebinding of the hymnbooks was also touched upon. And the Vicar hoped that Bobby was sticking manfully to his job and trying to make good, and remained his ever affectionate Father.

There was a postscript.

> By the way, someone called who asked for your address in London. I was out at the time, and he did not leave his name. Mrs. Roberts described him as a tall, stooping gentleman with pince-nez. He seemed very sorry to miss you and very anxious to see you again.

A tall stooping man with pince-nez—Bobby tried to think of anyone he knew who was likely to fit that description, but could not. Suddenly a quick suspicion darted into his mind. Was this the forerunner of a new attempt upon his life? Was this mysterious enemy—one or more—trying to track him down?

He sat still and did some serious thinking. They, whoever they were, had only just discovered that he had left the neighborhood. All unsuspecting, Mrs. Roberts had given his new address. So that already they—whoever they were—might be keeping a watch upon the place. If he went out he would be followed—and just as things were at the moment that would never do.

"Badger," said Bobby.

"Yes, old lad."

"Come here."

The next five minutes were spent in genuine hard work. At the end of ten minutes Badger could repeat his instructions by heart.

When he was word-perfect, Bobby got into a two-seater Fiat dating from 1902 and drove dashingly down the mews. He parked the Fiat in St. James's Square and walked straight from there to his club. There he did some telephoning, and a couple of hours later certain parcels were delivered to him. Finally, about half-past three a chauffeur in dark-green livery walked to St. James's Square and went rapidly up to a large Bentley which had been parked there about half an hour previously. The parking attendant nodded to him—the gentleman who had left the car had remarked, stammering slightly as he did so, that his chauffeur would be fetching it shortly.

Bobby let in the clutch and drew neatly out. The abandoned Fiat still stood demurely awaiting its owner. Bobby, despite the intense discomfort of his upper lip, began to enjoy himself. He headed north, not south, and before long, the powerful engine was forging ahead on the Great North Road.

It was only an extra precaution that he was taking. He was pretty sure that he was not being followed. Presently he turned off to the left, and made his way by circuitous roads to Hampshire.

It was just after tea that the Bentley purred up the drive of Merroway Court, a stiff and correct chauffeur at the wheel.

"Hullo," said Frankie lightly. "There's the car."

She went out to the front door. Sylvia and Roger came with her.

"Is everything alright, Hawkins?"

The chauffeur touched his cap. "Yes, m'lady. She's been thoroughly overhauled."

"That's alright, then."

The chauffeur produced a note. "From his lordship, m'lady."

Frankie took it. "You'll put up at the—what is it—Anglers' Arms in Staverley, Hawkins. I'll telephone in the morning if I want the car."

"Very good, your ladyship." Bobby backed, turned and sped down the drive.

"I'm so sorry we haven't room here," said Sylvia. "It's a lovely car."

"You get some pace out of that," said Roger.

"I do," admitted Frankie.

She was satisfied that no faintest quiver of recognition had shown on Roger's face. She would have been surprised if it had. She would not have recognized Bobby herself had she met him casually. The small mustache had a perfectly natural appearance, and that, with the stiff demeanor so uncharacteristic of the natural Bobby, completed the disguise enhanced by the chauffeur's livery.

The voice, too, had been excellent, and quite unlike Bobby's own. Frankie began to think that Bobby was far more talented than she had given him credit for being.

Meanwhile Bobby had successfully taken up his quarters at the Anglers' Arms. It was up to him to create the part of Edward Hawkins, chauffeur to Lady Frances Derwent.

As to the behavior of chauffeurs in private life Bobby was singularly ill-informed, but he imagined that a certain haughtiness would not come amiss. He tried to feel himself a superior being and to act accordingly. The admiring attitude of various young women employed in the Anglers' Arms had a distinctly encouraging effect, and he soon found that Frankie and her accident had provided the principal topic of conversation in Staverley ever since it had happened. Bobby unbent toward the landlord, a stout genial person of the name of Thomas Askew, who permitted information to leak from him.

"Young Reeves, he was there and saw it happen," declared Mr. Askew.

Bobby blessed the natural mendacity of the young. The famous accident was now vouched for by an eyewitness.

"Thought his last moment had come, he did," went on Mr. Askew. "Straight for him down the hill it come—and then took the wall instead. A wonder the young lady wasn't killed."

"Her ladyship takes some killing," said Bobby.

"Had many accidents, has she?"

"She's been lucky," said Bobby. "But I assure you, Mr. Askew, that when her ladyship's taken over the wheel from me as she sometimes does—well, I've made sure my last hour has come."

Several persons present shook their heads wisely and said they didn't wonder and it's just what they would have thought.

"Very nice little place you have here, Mr. Askew," said Bobby kindly and condescendingly. "Very nice and snug."

Mr. Askew expressed gratification.

"Merroway Court the only big place in the neighborhood?"

"Well, there's the Grange, Mr. Hawkins. Not that you'd call that a place exactly. There's no family living there. No, it had been empty for years until this American doctor took it."

"An American doctor?"

"That's it—Nicholson his name is. And if you ask me, Mr. Hawkins, there are some very queer goings on there."

The barmaid at this point remarked that Dr. Nicholson gave her the shivers, he did.

"Goings on, Mr. Askew?" said Bobby. "Now what do you mean by goings on?"

Mr. Askew shook his head darkly. "There's those there that don't want to be there. Put away by their relations. I assure you, Mr. Hawkins, the moanings and the shrieks and the groans that go on there you wouldn't believe."

"Why don't the police interfere?"

"Oh, well, you see, it's supposed to be alright. Nerve cases, and such-like. Loonies that aren't so very bad. The gentleman's a doctor and it's all alright, so to speak—" Here the landlord buried his face in a pint pot and emerged again to shake his head in a very doubtful fashion.

"Ah!" said Bobby in a dark and meaning way. "If we knew everything that went on in these places. . . ." And he too applied himself to a pewter pot.

The barmaid chimed in eagerly: "That's what I say, Mr. Hawkins. What goes on there? Why, one night a poor young creature escaped—in her nightgown she was—and the Doctor and a couple of nurses out looking for her. 'Oh! Don't let them take me back!'—that's what she was crying out. Pitiful it was. And about her being rich really and her relations having her put away. But they took her back they did, and the Doctor he explained that she'd got a persecution mania—that's what he called it. Kind of thinking everyone was against her. But I've often wondered—yes, I have. I've often wondered. . . ."

"Ah!" said Mr. Askew. "It's easy enough to say—"

Somebody present said that there was no knowing what went on in places.

And someone else said that was right.

Finally the meeting broke up and Bobby announced his intention of going for a stroll before turning in.

The Grange was, he knew, on the other side of the village from Merroway Court, so he turned his footsteps in that direction. What he had heard that evening seemed to him worthy of attention. A lot of it could, of course, be discounted. Villages are usually prejudiced against newcomers, and still more so if the newcomer is of a different nationality. If Nicholson ran a place for curing drug-takers, there would naturally be strange sounds issuing from it—groans and even shrieks might be heard without any sinister reason for them. But all the same the story of the escaping girl struck Bobby unpleasantly. Supposing the Grange were really a place where people were kept against their will? A certain number of genuine cases might be taken as camouflage.

At this point in his meditations Bobby arrived at a high wall with an entrance of wrought-iron gates. He stepped up to the gates and tried one gently. It was locked. Well, after all, why not?

And yet somehow the touch of that locked gate gave him a faintly sinister feeling. The place was like a prison.

He moved a little farther along the road, measuring the wall with his eye. Would it be possible to climb over? The wall was smooth and high and presented no accommodating crannies. He shook his head. Suddenly he came upon a little door. Without much real hope he tried it. To his surprise it yielded. It was not locked.

"Bit of an oversight here," thought Bobby with a grin. He slipped through, closing the door softly behind him.

He found himself on a path leading through a shrubbery. He followed the path, which twisted a good deal—in fact it reminded Bobby of the one in *Alice Through the Looking-Glass*. Suddenly without any warning it gave a sharp turn and emerged into an open space close to the house. It was a moonlit night and the space was clearly lit. Bobby had stepped full into the moonlight before he could stop himself.

At the same moment a woman's figure came round the corner of the house. She was treading very softly, glancing from side to side with—or so it seemed to the watching Bobby—the nervous alertness of a hunted animal. Suddenly she stopped dead and stood swaying as though she would fall.

Bobby rushed forward and caught her. Her lips were white and it seemed to him that never had he seen such awful fear on any human countenance.

"It's alright," he said reassuringly in a very low voice. "It's quite alright."

The girl, for she was little more, moaned faintly, her eyelids half closed. "I'm so frightened," she murmured. "I'm so terribly frightened."

"What's the matter?" asked Bobby.

The girl only shook her head and repeated faintly, "I'm so frightened. I'm so horribly frightened."

Suddenly some sound seemed to come to her ears. She sprang upright, away from Bobby. Then she turned to him.

"Go away," she said. "Go away at once!"

"I want to help you," said Bobby.

"Do you?" She looked at him for a minute or two, a strange searching and moving glance. It was as though she explored his soul. Then she shook her head.

"No one can help me."

"I can," said Bobby. "I'd do anything. Tell me what it is that frightens you so."

She shook her head. "Not now. Oh, quick! They're coming. You can't help me unless you go now. At once—at once."

Bobby yielded to her urgency. With a whispered "I'm at the Anglers' Arms," he plunged back along the path. The last he saw of her was an urgent gesture bidding him hurry.

Suddenly he heard footsteps on the path from the little door. Bobby plunged abruptly into the bushes at the side of the path.

He had not been mistaken. A man was coming along the path. He passed close to Bobby, but it was too dark for the young man to see his face.

When he had passed Bobby resumed his retreat. He felt that he could do nothing more that night. Anyway, his head was in a whirl.

For he had recognized the girl—recognized her beyond any possible doubt.

She was the original of the photograph which had so mysteriously disappeared.

16

Bobby Becomes a Solicitor

"MR. HAWKINS?"

"Yes," said Bobby—his voice slightly muffled owing to a large mouthful of bacon and eggs.

"You're wanted on the telephone."

Bobby took a hasty gulp of coffee, wiped his mouth and rose. The telephone was in a small dark passage. He took up the receiver.

"Hullo," said Frankie's voice.

"Hullo, Frankie," said Bobby incautiously.

"This is Lady Frances Derwent speaking," said the voice coldly. "Is that Hawkins?"

"Yes, m'lady."

"I shall want the car at ten o'clock to take me up to London."

"Very good, your ladyship." Bobby replaced the receiver.

"When does one say 'my lady' and when does one say 'your ladyship'?" he cogitated. "I ought to know, but I don't. It's the sort of thing that will lead a real chauffeur or butler to catch me out."

At the other end, Frankie hung up the receiver and turned to Roger Bassington-ffrench.

"It's a nuisance," she observed lightly, "to have to go up to London today. All owing to Father's fuss."

"Still," said Roger, "you'll be back this evening?"

"Oh, yes."

"I'd half thought of asking you if you'd give me a lift to town," said Roger carelessly.

Frankie paused for an infinitesimal second before her answer—given with an apparent readiness.

"Why, of course," she said.

"But on second thoughts I don't think I will go up today," went on Roger. "Henry's looking even odder than usual. Somehow I don't very much like leaving Sylvia alone with him."

"I know," said Frankie.

"Are you driving yourself?" asked Roger casually as they moved away from the telephone.

"Yes, but I shall take Hawkins. I've got some shopping to do as well and it's a nuisance if you're driving yourself—you can't leave the car anywhere."

"Yes, of course."

He said no more, but when the car came around, Bobby at the wheel very stiff and correct of demeanor, he came out on the doorstep to see her off.

"Good-bye," said Frankie.

Under the circumstances she did not think of holding out a hand, but Roger took hers and held it a minute.

"You *are* coming back?" he said with curious insistence.

Frankie laughed. "Of course. I only meant good-bye till this evening."

"Don't have any more accidents."

"I'll let Hawkins drive if you like."

She sprang in beside Bobby, who touched his cap. The car moved off down the drive, Roger still standing on the steps looking after it.

"Bobby," said Frankie, "do you think it possible that Roger might fall for me?"

"Has he?" inquired Bobby.

"Well, I just wondered."

"I expect you know the symptoms pretty well," said Bobby. But he spoke absently.

Frankie shot him a quick glance. "Has anything—happened?" she asked.

"Yes, it has. Frankie, I've found the original of the photograph!"

"You mean—*the* one—the one you talked so much about—the one that was in the dead man's pocket?"

"Yes."

"*Bobby!* I've got a few things to tell you, but nothing to this. Where did you find her?"

Bobby jerked his head back over his shoulder. "In Dr. Nicholson's nursing home."

"Tell me."

Carefully and meticulously Bobby described the events of the previous night. Frankie listened breathlessly.

"Then we *are* on the right track," she said. "And Dr. Nicholson *is* mixed up in all this! Bobby, I'm afraid of that man."

"What is he like?"

"Oh! Big and forceful—and he watches you. Very intently behind glasses. And you feel he knows all about you."

"When did you meet him?"

"He came to dinner."

She described the dinner party and Dr. Nicholson's insistent dwelling on the details of her "accident."

"I felt he was suspicious," she ended up.

"It's certainly queer his going into details like that," said Bobby. "What do you think is at the bottom of all this business, Frankie?"

"Well, I'm beginning to think that your suggestion of a dope gang—which I was so haughty about at the time—isn't such a bad guess after all."

"With Dr. Nicholson as the head of the gang?"

"Yes. This nursing home business would be a very good cloak for that sort of thing. He'd have a certain supply of drugs on the premises quite legitimately. While pretending to cure drug cases he might really be supplying them with the stuff."

"That seems plausible enough," agreed Bobby.

"I haven't told you yet about Henry Bassington-ffrench."

Bobby listened attentively to her description of her host's idiosyncrasies. "His wife doesn't suspect?"

"I'm sure she doesn't."

"What is she like? Intelligent?"

"I never thought exactly. No, I suppose she isn't very. And yet in some ways she seems quite shrewd. A frank, pleasant woman."

"And our Bassington-ffrench?"

"There I'm puzzled," said Frankie slowly. "Do you think, Bobby, that just possibly we might be all wrong about him?"

"Nonsense!" said Bobby. "We worked it all out and decided that he must be the villain of the piece."

"Because of the photograph?"

"Because of the photograph. No one else *could* have changed that photograph for the other."

"I know," said Frankie. "But that one incident is all that we have against him."

"It's quite enough."

"I suppose so. And yet—"

"Well?"

"I don't know. But I have a queer sort of feeling that he's innocent—that he's not concerned in the matter at all."

Bobby looked at her coldly. "Did you say that he had fallen for you, or that you had fallen for him?" he inquired politely.

Frankie flushed. "Don't be so absurd, Bobby. I just wondered if there couldn't be some innocent explanation—that's all."

"I don't see that there can be. Especially now that we've actually found the girl in the neighborhood. That seems to clinch matters. If we only had some inkling as to who the dead man was—"

"Oh, but I have. I told you so in my letter. I'm nearly sure that the murdered man was somebody called Alan Carstairs."

Once more she plunged into narrative.

"You know," said Bobby, "we really are getting on. Now we must try, more or less, to reconstruct the crime. Let's spread out our facts and see what sort of job we can make of it."

He paused for a moment and the car slackened speed as though in sympathy. Then he pressed his foot down once more on the accelerator and at the same time spoke.

"First, we'll assume that you are right about Alan Carstairs. He certainly fulfills the conditions. He's the right sort of man, he led a wandering life, he had very few friends and acquaintances in England, and if he disappeared he wasn't likely to be missed or sought after. So far, so good. Alan Carstairs comes down to Staverley with these people—what did you say their name was—?"

"Rivington. There's a possible channel of inquiry there. In fact I think we ought to follow it up."

"We will. Very well, Carstairs comes down to Staverley with the Rivingtons. Now, is there anything in that?"

"You mean did he get them to bring him down here deliberately?"

"That's what I mean. Or was it just a casual chance? Was he brought down here by them, and did he then come across the girl by accident just as I did? I presume he knew her before or he wouldn't have had her photograph on him."

"The alternative being," said Frankie thoughtfully, "that he was already on the track of Nicholson and his gang."

"And used the Rivingtons as a means of getting to this part of the world naturally?"

"That's quite a possible theory," said Frankie. "He may have been on the track of this gang."

"Or simply on the track of the girl."

"The girl?"

"Yes. She may have been abducted. He may have come over to England to find her."

"Well, but if he had tracked her down to Staverley why should he go off to Wales?"

"Obviously, there's a lot we don't know yet," said Bobby.

"Evans," said Frankie thoughtfully. "We don't get any clues as to Evans. The Evans part of it must have to do with Wales."

They were both silent for a moment or two. Then Frankie woke up to her surroundings.

"My dear, we're actually at Putney Hill. It seems like five minutes. Where are we going and what are we doing?"

"That's for you to say. I don't even know why we've come up to town."

"The journey to town was only an excuse for getting a talk with you. I couldn't very well risk being seen walking the lanes at Staverley deep in conversation with my chauffeur. I used the pseudo-letter from Father as an excuse for driving up to town and talking to you on the way, and even that was nearly wrecked by Bassington-ffrench's suggestion that he should come too."

"That would have torn it severely."

"No really. We'd have dropped him wherever he liked and then we'd have gone on to Brook Street and talked there. I think we'd better do that anyway. Your garage place may be watched."

Bobby agreed and related the episode of the inquiries made about him at Marchbolt.

"Better go to our town house," suggested Frankie. "There's no one there but my maid and a couple of caretakers."

They drove to Brook Street. Frankie rang the bell and was admitted, Bobby remaining outside. Presently Frankie opened the door again and beckoned him in. They went upstairs to the big drawing-room and pulled up some of the blinds and removed the swathing from one of the sofas.

"There's one other thing I forgot to tell you," said Frankie. "On the 16th, the day you were poisoned, Bassington-ffrench was at Staverley, but Nicholson was away—supposedly at a conference in London. And his car is a dark-blue Talbot."

"And he has access to morphia," said Bobby.

They exchanged significant glances.

"It's not exactly evidence, I suppose," said Bobby, "but it fits in nicely."

Frankie went to a side table and returned with a telephone directory.

"What are you going to do?"

"I'm looking up the name Rivington."

She turned pages rapidly.

"A. Rivington & Sons, builders, B .A. C. Rivington, dental surgeon. D. Rivington, Shooter's hill—I think not. Miss Florence Rivington. Col. H. Rivington, D.S.O.—that's more like it—Tite Street, Chelsea."

She continued her search.

"There's M. R. Rivington, Onslow Square. He's possible. And there's a William Rivington at Hampstead. I think Onslow Square and Tite Street are the most likely ones. The Rivingtons, Bobby, have got to be seen without delay."

"I think you're right. But what are we going to say? Think up a few good lies, Frankie. I'm not much good at that sort of thing."

Frankie reflected for a minute or two. "I think," she said, "that you'll have to go. Do you feel you could be the junior partner of a solicitor's firm?"

"That seems a most gentlemanly role," said Bobby. "I was afraid you might think of something much worse than that. All the same, it's not quite in character, is it?"

"How do you mean?"

"Well, solicitors never do make personal visits, do they? Surely they always write letters at six-and-eight-pence a time, or else write and ask someone to keep an appointment at their office."

"This particular firm of solicitors is unconventional," said Frankie. "Wait a minute."

She left the room and returned with a card.

"*Mr. Frederick Spragge*," she said, handing it to Bobby. "You are a young member of the firm of Spragge, Spragge, Jenkinson and Spragge of Bloomsbury Square."

"Did you invent that firm, Frankie?"

"Certainly not. They're Father's solicitors."

"And suppose they have me up for impersonation?"

"That's alright. There isn't any young Spragge. The only Spragge is about a hundred, and anyway he eats out of my hand. I'll fix him if things go wrong. He's a great snob—he loves lords and dukes however little money he makes out of them."

"What about clothes? Shall I ring up Badger to bring some along?"

Frankie looked doubtful. "I don't want to insult your clothes, Bobby," she said, "or throw your poverty in your teeth, or anything like that. But will they carry conviction? I think, myself, that we'd better raid Father's wardrobe. His clothes won't fit you too badly."

A quarter of an hour later, Bobby, attired in a morning coat and striped trousers of exquisitely correct cut and passable fit, stood surveying himself in Lord Marchington's pier glass.

"Your father does himself well in clothes," he remarked graciously. "With the might of Savile Row behind me, I feel a great increase of confidence."

"I suppose you'll have to stick to your mustache," said Frankie.

"It's sticking to me," said Bobby. "It's a work of art that couldn't be repeated in a hurry."

"You'd better keep it then. Though it's more legal-looking to be clean-shaven."

"It's better than a beard," said Bobby. "Now then, Frankie, do you think your father could lend me a hat?"

17

Mrs. Rivington Talks

"SUPPOSING," SAID BOBBY, pausing on the doorstep, "that Mr. M. R. Rivington of Onslow Square is himself a solicitor? That would be a blow."

"You'd better try the Tite Street colonel first," said Frankie. "He won't know anything about solicitors."

Accordingly Bobby took a taxi to Tite Street. Colonel Rivington was out. Mrs. Rivington, however, was at home. Bobby delivered over to the smart parlormaid his card on which he had written *"From Messrs. Spragge, Spragge, Jenkinson & Spragge. Very urgent."*

The card and Lord Marchington's clothes produced their effect upon the parlormaid. She did not for an instant suspect that Bobby had come to sell miniatures or tout for insurance. He was shown into a beautifully and expensively furnished drawing room, and presently Mrs. Rivington beautifully and expensively dressed and made up, came into the room.

"I must apologize for troubling you, Mrs. Rivington," said Bobby. "But the matter was rather urgent and we wished to avoid the delay of letters."

That any solicitor could ever wish to avoid delay seemed so transparently impossible that Bobby for a moment wondered anxiously whether Mrs. Rivington would see through the pretence.

Mrs. Rivington, however, was clearly a woman of more looks than brains, who accepted things as they were presented to her.

"Oh, do sit down," she said. "I got the telephone message just now from your office saying that you were on your way here."

Bobby mentally applauded Frankie for this last-minute flash of brilliance. He sat down and endeavored to look legal.

"It is about our client, Mr. Alan Carstairs," he said.

"Oh, yes?"

"He may have mentioned that we were acting for him."

"Did he now? I believe he did," said Mrs. Rivington, opening very large blue eyes. She was clearly of a suggestible type. "But of course I know about you. You acted for Dolly Maltravers, didn't you, when she shot that dreadful dressmaker man? I suppose you know all the details?"

She looked at him with frank curiosity. It seemed to Bobby that Mrs. Rivington was going to be easy meat.

"We know a lot that never comes into court," he said, smiling.

"Oh, I suppose you must." Mrs. Rivington looked at him enviously. "Tell me, did she really—I mean—was she dressed as that woman said?"

"The story was contradicted in court," said Bobby solemnly. He slightly dropped the corner of his eyelid.

"Oh, I see," breathed Mrs. Rivington, enraptured.

"About Mr. Carstairs," said Bobby, feeling that he had now established friendly relations and could get on with his job. "He left England very suddenly, as perhaps you know?"

Mrs. Rivington shook her head. "Has he left England? I didn't know. We haven't seen him for some time."

"Did he tell you how long he expected to be over here?"

"He said he might be here for a week or two, or it might be six months or a year."

"Where was he staying?"

"At the Savoy."

"And you saw him last—when?"

"Oh, about three weeks or a month ago. I can't remember."

"You took him down to Staverley one day?"

"Of course! I believe that's the last time we saw him. He rang up to know when he could see us. He'd just arrived in London, and Hubert was very put out because we were going up to Scotland the next day, and we were going down to Staverley to lunch and dining out with some dreadful people that we couldn't get out of, and he wanted to see Carstairs because he liked him so much, and so I said, 'My dear, let's take him down to the Bassington-ffrenches with us. They won't mind.' And we did. And, of course, they didn't." She came breathlessly to a pause.

"Did he tell you his reasons for being in England?" asked Bobby.

"No. Did he have any? Oh, yes, I know. We thought it was something to do with that millionaire man, that friend of his, who had such a tragic death. Some doctor told him he had cancer, and he killed himself. A very wicked thing for a doctor to do, don't you think so? And they're often quite wrong. Our doctor said the other day that my little girl has measles, and it turned out to be a sort of heat rash. I told Hubert I should change him."

Ignoring Mrs. Rivington's treatment of doctors as though they were library books, Bobby returned to the point.

"Did Mr. Carstairs know the Bassington-ffrenches?"

"Oh, no. But I think he liked them. Though he was very queer and moody on the way back. I suppose something that had been said must have upset him. He's a Canadian, you know, and I often think Canadians are so touchy."

"You don't know what it was that upset him?"

"I haven't the least idea. The silliest things do it sometimes, don't they?"

"Did he take any walks in the neighborhood?" asked Bobby.

"Oh, no. What a very odd idea!" She stared at him.

Bobby tried again. "Was there a party? Did he meet any of the neighbors?"

"No, it was just ourselves and them. But it's odd your saying that—"

"Yes," said Bobby eagerly, as she paused.

"Because he asked a most frightful lot of questions about some people who lived near there."

"Do you remember the name?"

"No, I don't. It wasn't anyone very interesting—some doctor or other."

"Dr. Nicholson?"

"I believe that was the name. He wanted to know all about him and his wife and when they came there—all sorts of things. It seemed so odd when he didn't know them, and he wasn't a bit a curious man as a rule. But, of course, perhaps he was only making conversation and couldn't think of anything to say. One does do things like that sometimes."

Bobby agreed that one did and asked how the subject of the Nicholsons had come up, but this Mrs. Rivington was unable to tell him. She had been out with Henry Bassington-ffrench in the garden and had come in to find the others discussing the Nicholsons.

So far the conversation had proceeded easily, Bobby pumping the lady without any camouflage, but she now displayed a sudden curiosity.

"But what is it you want to know about Mr. Carstairs?" she asked.

"I really wanted his address," explained Bobby. "As you know, we act for him and we've just had a rather important cable from New York—you know there's rather a serious fluctuation in the dollar just now—"

Mrs. Rivington nodded with desperate intelligence.

"And so," continued Bobby rapidly, "we wanted to get into touch with him—to get his instructions. And he hasn't left an address—and having heard him mention he was a friend of yours, I thought you might possibly have news of him."

"Oh, I see," said Mrs. Rivington, completely satisfied. "What a pity! But he's always rather a vague man, I should think."

"Oh, distinctly so," said Bobby. "Well—" He rose. "I apologize for taking up so much of your time."

"Oh, not at all," said Mrs. Rivington. "And it's so interesting to know that Dolly Maltravers really did—as you say she did."

"I said nothing at all," said Bobby.

"Yes, but then lawyers are so discreet, aren't they?" said Mrs. Rivington with a little gurgle of laughter.

"So that's alright," thought Bobby, as he walked away down Tite Street. "I seem to have taken Dolly What's-her-name's character away for good, but I daresay she deserves it. And that charming idiot of a woman will never wonder why, if I wanted Carstairs' address, I didn't simply ring up and ask for it!"

Back in Brook Street he and Frankie discussed the matter from every angle.

"It looks as though it were really pure chance that took him to the Bassington-ffrenches," said Frankie thoughtfully.

"I know. But evidently when he was down there some chance remark directed his attention to the Nicholsons."

"So that, really, it is Nicholson who is at the heart of the mystery, not the Bassington-ffrenches?"

Bobby looked at her. "Still intent on whitewashing your hero?" he inquired coldly.

"My dear, I'm only pointing out what it looks like. It's the mention of Nicholson and his nursing home that excited Carstairs. Being taken down to the Bassington-ffrenches was a pure matter of chance. You must admit that."

"It seems like it."

"Why only 'seems'?"

"Well, there is just one other possibility. In some way, Carstairs may have found out that the Rivingtons were going down to lunch with the Bassington-ffrenches. He may have overheard some chance remark in a restaurant—at the Savoy perhaps. So he rings them up, very urgent to see them, and what he hopes may happen does happen. They're very booked up and they suggest his coming down with them—their friends won't mind and they do so want to see him. That is possible, Frankie."

"It is *possible*, I suppose. But it seems a very roundabout method of doing things."

"No more roundabout than your accident," said Bobby.

"My accident was vigorous direct action," said Frankie coldly.

Bobby removed Lord Marchington's clothes and replaced them where he had found them. Then he donned his chauffeur's uniform once more, and they were soon speeding back to Staverley.

"If Roger has fallen for me," said Frankie demurely, "he'll be pleased I've come back so soon. He'll think I can't bear to be away from him for long."

"I'm not sure that you can bear it, either," said Bobby. "I've always heard that really dangerous criminals are singularly attractive."

"Somehow I can't believe he is a criminal."

"So you remarked before."

"Well, I feel like that."

"You can't get over the photograph."

"Damn the photograph!" said Frankie.

Bobby drove up the drive in silence. Frankie sprang out and went into the house without a backward glance. Bobby drove away.

The house seemed very silent. Frankie glanced at the clock. It was half-past two.

"They don't expect me back for hours yet," she thought. "I wonder where they are."

She opened the door of the library and went in, stopping suddenly on the threshold.

Dr. Nicholson was sitting on the sofa holding both Sylvia Bassington-ffrench's hands in his.

Sylvia jumped to her feet and came across the room toward Frankie.

"He's been telling me," she said. Her voice was stifled. She put both hands to her face as though to hide it from view.

"It's too terrible!" she sobbed, and brushing past Frankie, she ran out of the room.

Dr. Nicholson had risen. Frankie advanced a step or two toward him. His eyes, watchful as ever, met hers.

"Poor lady!" he said suavely. "It has been a great shock to her."

The muscles at the corner of his mouth twitched. For a moment or two Frankie fancied that he was amused. And then, quite suddenly, she realized that it was quite a different emotion.

The man was angry. He was holding himself in, hiding his anger behind a suave, bland mask, but the emotion was there. It was all he could do to hold that emotion in.

There was a moment's pause.

"It was best that Mrs. Bassington-ffrench should know the truth," said the Doctor. "I want her to induce her husband to place himself in my hands."

"I'm afraid," said Frankie gently, "that I interrupted you." She paused. "I came back sooner than I meant."

18

The Girl of the Photograph

ON BOBBY'S RETURN to the inn he was greeted with the information that someone was waiting to see him.

"It's a lady. You'll find her in Mr. Askew's little sitting room."

Bobby made his way there slightly puzzled. Unless she had flown there on wings he could not see how Frankie could possibly have got to the Anglers' Arms ahead of him, and that his visitor could be anyone but Frankie never occurred to him.

He opened the door of the small room which Mr. Askew kept as his private sitting room. Sitting bolt upright in a chair was a slender figure dressed in black—the girl of the photograph.

Bobby was so astonished that for a moment or two he could not speak. Then he noticed that the girl was terribly nervous. Her small hands were trembling and closed and unclosed themselves on the arm of the chair. She seemed too nervous even to speak, but her large eyes held a kind of terrified appeal.

"So it's you," said Bobby at last. He shut the door behind him and came forward to the table.

Still the girl did not speak—still those large, terrified eyes looked into his. At last words came—a mere hoarse whisper.

"You said—you said—you'd help me. Perhaps I shouldn't have come—"

Here Bobby broke in, finding words and assurance at the same time. "Shouldn't have come? Nonsense! You did quite right to come. Of course you should have come. And I'll do anything—anything in the world to help you. Don't be frightened. You're quite safe now."

The color rose a little in the girl's face. She said abruptly: "Who are you? You're—you're—not a chauffeur. I mean you may be a chauffeur, but you're not one really."

Bobby understood her meaning in spite of her confused words.

"One does all sorts of jobs nowadays," he said. "I used to be in the Navy. As a matter of fact I'm not exactly a chauffeur—but that doesn't matter now. Anyway, I assure you you can trust me and—tell me all about it."

Her flush had deepened. "You must think me mad," she murmured. "You must think me quite mad."

"No, no."

"Yes—coming here like this. But I was so frightened—so terribly frightened—" Her voice died away. Her eyes widened as though they saw some vision of terror.

Bobby siezed her hand firmly.

"Look here," he said. "It's quite alright. Everything's going to be alright. You're safe now—with—with a friend. Nothing shall happen to you."

He felt the answering pressure of her fingers.

"When you stepped out into the moonlight the other night," she said in a low hurried voice, "it was—it was like a dream—a dream of deliverance. I didn't know who you were or where you came from. But it gave me hope and I determined to come and find you—and—and tell you."

"That's right," said Bobby encouragingly. "Tell me. Tell me everything."

She drew her hand away suddenly. "If I do, you'll think I'm mad—that I've gone wrong in my head from being in that place with those others."

"No, I shan't. I shan't really."

"You will. It *sounds* mad."

"I shall know it isn't. Tell me. Please tell me."

She drew a little farther away from him, sitting very upright, her eyes staring straight in front of her. "It's just this," she said. "I'm afraid I'm going to be murdered."

Her voice was dry and hoarse. She was speaking with obvious self-restraint, but her hands were trembling.

"Murdered?"

"Yes, that sounds mad, doesn't it? Like—what do they call it?—persecution mania."

"No," said Bobby. "You don't sound mad at all—just frightened. Tell me who wants to murder you and why?"

She was silent a minute or two, twisting and untwisting her hands. Then she said in a low voice, "My husband."

"Your husband?" Thoughts whirled round in Bobby's head. "Who are you?" he said abruptly.

It was her turn to look surprised. "Don't you know?"

"I haven't the least idea."

She said: "I'm Moira Nicholson. My husband is Dr. Nicholson."

"Then you're not a patient there?"

"A patient? Oh, no." Her face darkened suddenly. "I suppose you think I speak like one."

"No, no, I didn't mean that at all." He was at pains to reassure her. "Honestly, I didn't mean it that way. I was only surprised at finding you married—and—all that. Now go on with what you're telling me. About your husband wanting to murder you."

"It sounds mad, I know. But it isn't—it isn't! I see it in his eyes when he looks at me. And queer things have happened—accidents."

"Accidents?" said Bobby sharply.

"Yes. Oh, I know it sounds hysterical and as though I were making it all up—"

"Not a bit," said Bobby. "It sounds perfectly reasonable. Go on. About these accidents."

"They were just accidents. He backed the car, not seeing I was there—I just jumped aside in time. And some stuff that was in the wrong bottle—oh, stupid things—and things that people would think quite alright, but they weren't—they were *meant*. I know it. And it's wearing me out—watching for them—being on my guard—trying to save my life." She swallowed convulsively.

"Why does your husband want to do away with you?" asked Bobby.

Perhaps he hardly expected a definite answer—but the answer came promptly.

"Because he wants to marry Sylvia Bassington-ffrench."

"What? But she's married already."

"I know. But he's arranging for that."

"How do you mean?"

"I don't know exactly. But I know that he's trying to get Mr. Bassington-ffrench brought to the Grange as a patient."

"And then?"

"I don't know, but I think something would happen." She shuddered. "He's got some hold over Mr. Bassington-ffrench. I don't know what it is."

"Bassington-ffrench takes morphia," said Bobby.

"Is that it? Jasper gives it to him, I suppose."

"It comes by post."

"Perhaps Jasper doesn't do it directly—he's very cunning. Mr. Bassington-ffrench mayn't know it comes from Jasper—but I'm sure it does. And then Jasper would have him at the Grange and pretend to cure him—and once he was there—" She paused and shivered. "All sorts of things happen at the Grange," she went on. "Queer things. People come there to get better, and they don't get better—they get worse."

As she spoke Bobby was aware of a glimpse into a strange evil atmosphere. He felt something of the terror that had enveloped Moira Nicholson's life so long.

He said abruptly, "You say your husband wants to marry Mrs. Bassington-ffrench?"

Moira nodded. "He's crazy about her."

"And she?"

"I don't know," said Moira slowly. "I can't make up my mind. On the surface she seems fond of her husband and little boy, and content and peaceful. She seems a very simple woman. But sometimes I fancy that she isn't so simple as she seems. I've even wondered sometimes whether she is an entirely different woman from what we all think she is . . . whether perhaps she isn't playing a part and playing it very well. But really, I think, that's nonsense—foolish imagination on my part. When you've lived at a place like the Grange your mind gets distorted and you do begin imagining things."

"What about the brother Roger?" asked Bobby.

"I don't know much about him. He's nice, I think, but he's the sort of person who would be very easily deceived. He's quite taken in by Jasper, I know. Jasper is working on him to persuade Mr. Bassington-ffrench to come to the Grange. I believe he thinks it's all his own idea." She leaned forward suddenly and caught Bobby's sleeve. "Don't let him come to the Grange," she implored. "If he does, something awful will happen. I know it will."

Bobby was silent a minute or two, turning over the amazing story in his mind.

"How long have you been married to Nicholson?" he said at last.

"Just over a year—" She shivered.

"Haven't you ever thought of leaving him?"

"How could I? I've nowhere to go. I've no money. If anyone took me in, what sort of story could I tell? A fantastic tale that my husband wanted to murder me? Who would believe me?"

"Well, I believe you," said Bobby.

He paused a moment, as though making up his mind to a certain course of action. Then he went on.

"Look here," he said bluntly. "I'm going to ask you a question straight out. Did you know a man called Alan Carstairs?"

He saw the color come up in her cheeks. "Why do you ask me that?"

"Because it's rather important that I should know. My idea is that you did know Alan Carstairs, that perhaps at some time or other you gave him your photograph."

She was silent a moment, her eyes downcast. Then she lifted her head and looked him in the face. "That's quite true," she said.

"You knew him before you were married?"

"Yes."

"Has he been down here to see you since you were married?"

She hesitated, then said, "Yes, once."

"About a month ago, would that be?"

"Yes. I suppose it would be about a month."

"He knew you were living down here?"

"I don't know how he knew—I hadn't told him. I had never even written to him since my marriage."

"But he found out and came here to see you. Did your husband know that?"

"No."

"You think not. But he might have known all the same?"

"I suppose he might, but he never said anything."

"Did you discuss your husband at all with Carstairs? Did you tell him of your fears as to your safety?"

She shook her head. "I hadn't begun to suspect them."

"But you were unhappy?"

"Yes."

"And you told him so?"

"No, I tried not to show in any way that my marriage hadn't been a success."

"But he might have guessed it all the same," said Bobby gently.

"I suppose he might," she admitted in a low voice.

"Do you think—I don't know how to put it—but do you think that he knew anything about your husband—that he suspected, for instance, that this nursing home place mightn't be quite what it seemed to be?"

Her brows furrowed as she tried to think.

"It's possible," she said at last. "He asked one or two rather peculiar questions—but—no—I don't think he can really have known anything about it."

Bobby was silent again for a few minutes. Then he asked, "Would you call your husband a jealous man?"

Rather to his surprise she answered, "Yes. Very jealous."

"Jealous, for instance, of you?"

"You mean even though he doesn't care? But yes, he would be jealous, just the same. I'm his property, you see. He's a queer man—a very queer man."

She shivered. Then she asked suddenly, "You're not connected with the police in any way, are you?"

"I? Oh, no."

"I wondered. I mean—"

Bobby looked down at his chauffeur's livery.

"It's rather a long story," he said.

"You are Lady Frances Derwent's chauffeur, aren't you? So the landlord here said. I met her at dinner the other night."

"I know." He paused. "We've got to get hold of her," he said. "And it's a bit difficult for me to do. Do you think you could ring up and ask to speak to her and then get her to come and meet you somewhere outdoors?"

"I suppose I could," said Moira slowly.

"I know it must seem frightfully odd to you. But it won't when I've explained. We must get hold of her as soon as possible. It's essential."

Moira rose. "Very well," she said.

With her hand on the door-handle she hesitated. "Alan," she said. "Alan Carstairs. Did you say you'd seen him?"

"I have seen him," said Bobby slowly. "But not lately." And he thought, with a shock, "Of course—she doesn't know he's dead . . ."

He said, "Ring up Lady Frances. Then I'll tell you everything."

19
A Council of Three

MOIRA RETURNED A few minutes later.

"I got her," she said. "I've asked her to come and meet me at a little summerhouse down near the river. She must have thought it very odd, but she said she'd come."

"Good," said Bobby. "Now just where is this place exactly?"

Moira described it carefully, and the way to get to it.

"That's alright," said Bobby. "You go first. I'll follow on."

They adhered to this program, Bobby lingering to have a word with Mr. Askew.

"Odd thing," he said casually. "That lady—Mrs. Nicholson—I used to work for an uncle of hers. Canadian gentleman."

Moira's visit to him might, he felt, give rise to gossip, and the last thing he wanted was to let gossip of that kind get about and possibly find its way to Dr. Nicholson's ears.

"So that's it, is it?" said Mr. Askew. "I rather wondered."

"Yes," said Bobby. "She recognized me and came along to hear what I was doing now. A nice, pleasant-spoken lady."

"Very pleasant indeed. She can't have much of a life living at the Grange."

"It wouldn't be *my* fancy," agreed Bobby.

Feeling that he had achieved his object, he strolled out into the village and with an aimless air betook himself in the direction indicated by Moira.

He reached the rendezvous successfully and found her there waiting for him. Frankie had not yet put in an appearance.

Moira's glance was frankly inquiring and Bobby felt he must attempt the somewhat difficult task of explanation.

"There's an awful lot I've got to tell you," he said, and stopped awkwardly.

"Yes."

"To begin with," said Bobby, plunging, "I'm not really a chauffeur although I do work in a garage in London. And my name isn't Hawkins—it's Jones—Bobby Jones. I come from Marchbolt in Wales."

Moira was listening attentively, but clearly the name Marchbolt meant nothing to her. Bobby set his teeth and went bravely to the heart of the matter.

"Look here, I'm afraid I'm going to give you rather a shock. This friend of yours, Alan Carstairs—he's—well, you've got to know—he's dead."

He felt the start she gave and tactfully he averted his eyes from her face. Did she mind very much? Had she been—dash it all—keen on the fellow?

She was silent a moment or two, then she said in low thoughtful voice, "So that's why he never came back. I wondered."

Bobby ventured to steal a look at her. His spirits rose. She looked sad and thoughtful—but that was all.

"Tell me about it," she said.

Bobby complied.

"He fell over the cliff at Marchbolt—the place where I live. I and the doctor there happened to be the ones to find him." He paused and then added: "He had your photograph in his pocket."

"Did he?" She gave a sweet, rather sad smile. "Dear Alan, he was—very faithful."

There was silence for a moment or two and then she asked, "When did all this happen?"

"About a month ago. October 3rd, to be exact."

"That must have been just after he came down here."

"Yes. Did he mention that he was going to Wales?"

She shook her head.

"You don't know anyone called Evans, do you?" said Bobby.

"Evans?" Moira frowned, trying to think. "No, I don't think so. It's a very common name, of course, but I can't remember anybody. What is he?"

"That's just what we don't know—Oh, hullo! Here's Frankie."

Frankie came hurrying along the path. Her face, at the sight of Bobby and Mrs. Nicholson sitting chatting together, was a study in conflicting expressions.

"Hullo, Frankie," said Bobby. "I'm glad you've come. We've got to have a great powwow. To begin with, it's Mrs. Nicholson who is the original of *the* photograph."

"Oh!" said Frankie blankly. She looked at Moira and suddenly laughed.

"My dear," she said to Bobby, "now I see why the sight of Mrs. Cayman at the inquest was such a shock to you!"

"Exactly," said Bobby.

What a fool he had been! However could he have imagined for one moment that any space of time could turn a Moira Nicholson into an Amelia Cayman?

"Lord, what a fool I've been!" he exclaimed.

Moira was looking bewildered.

"There's such an awful lot to tell," said Bobby. "And I don't quite know how to put it all."

He described the Caymans and their identification of the body.

"But I don't understand," said Moira, bewildered. "Whose body was it really, her brother's, or Alan Carstairs'?"

"That's where the dirty work comes in," explained Bobby.

"And then," continued Frankie, "Bobby was poisoned."

"Eight grains of morphia," said Bobby reminiscently.

"Don't start on that," said Frankie. "You're capable of going on for hours on the subject, and it's really very boring to other people. Let me explain."

She took a long breath.

"You see," she said, "these Cayman people came to see Bobby after the inquest, to ask him if the brother (supposed) had said anything before he died, and Bobby said 'No.' But afterward he remembered that the man had said something about somebody called Evans—so Bobby wrote and told them so. And a few days afterward he got a letter offering him a job in Peru or somewhere, and when he wouldn't take it, the next thing was that someone put a lot of morphia—"

"Eight grains," said Bobby.

"—in his beer. Only, as Bobby has a most extraordinary inside or something, it didn't kill him. And so then we saw at once that Pritchard—or Carstairs, you know—must have been pushed over the cliff."

"But why?" asked Moira.

"Don't you see? Why, it seems perfectly clear to us. I expect I haven't told it very well. Anyway, we decided that he had been, and that Roger Bassington-ffrench had probably done it."

"Roger Bassington-ffrench?" Moira spoke in tones of the liveliest amazement.

"We worked it out that way. You see he was there at the time, and your photograph disappeared, and he seemed to be the only one who could have taken it."

"I see," said Moira thoughtfully.

"And then," continued Frankie, "I happened to have an accident just here. An amazing coincidence, wasn't it?" She looked hard at Bobby with an admonishing eye. "So I telephoned to Bobby and suggested that he should come down here pretending to be my chauffeur and we'd look into the matter."

"So now you see how it was," said Bobby, accepting Frankie's one discreet departure from the truth. "And the climax was when last night I strolled into the grounds of the Grange and ran right into you—the original of the mysterious photograph!"

"You recognized me very quickly," said Moira with a faint smile.

"Yes," said Bobby. "I would have recognized the original of that photograph anywhere."

For no particular reason Moira blushed. Then an idea seemed to strike her and she looked sharply from one to the other.

"Are you telling me the truth?" she asked. "Is it really true that you came down here—by accident? Or did you come because—because—" her voice quavered in spite of herself—"You suspected my husband?"

Bobby and Frankie looked at each other. Then Bobby said:

"I give you my word of honor that we'd never even heard of your husband till we came down here."

"Oh, I see." She turned to Frankie. "I'm sorry, Lady Frances, but you see I remembered that, on the evening when we came to dinner, Jasper—my husband—went on and on at you, asking you things about your accident. I couldn't think why. But I think now that perhaps he suspected it wasn't genuine."

"Well, if you really want to know, it wasn't," said Frankie. "Whoof—now I feel better! It was all camouflaged very carefully. But it had nothing to do with your husband. The whole thing was staged because we wanted to—to—what does one call it?—get a line on Roger Bassington-ffrench."

"Roger?" Moira frowned and smiled perplexedly. "It seems absurd," she said frankly.

"All the same, facts are facts," said Bobby.

"Roger? Oh, no." She shook her head. "He might be weak—or wild. He might get into debt or get mixed up in a scandal. But pushing someone over a cliff?—no, I simply can't imagine it."

"Do you know," said Frankie, "I can't very well imagine it either."

"But he must have taken that photograph," said Bobby stubbornly. "Listen, Mrs. Nicholson, while I go over the facts."

He did so slowly and carefully. When he had finished, she nodded her head comprehendingly.

"I see what you mean. It seems very queer." She paused a minute and then asked unexpectedly, "Why don't you ask him?"

20
Council of Two

FOR A MOMENT the bold simplicity of the question quite took their breaths away. Both Frankie and Bobby started to speak at once.

"That's impossible—" began Bobby, just as Frankie said, "That would never do."

Then they both stopped dead as the possibilities of the idea sank in.

"You see," said Moira eagerly, "I do understand what you mean. It does seem as though Roger *must* have taken that photograph. But I don't believe for one moment that he pushed Alan over. Why should he? He didn't even know him. They'd only met once—at lunch down here. They'd never come across each other in any way. There's no motive."

"Then who *did* push him over?" asked Frankie bluntly.

A shadow crossed Moira's face. "I don't know," she said constrainedly.

"Look here," said Bobby. "Do you mind if I tell Frankie what you told me? About what you're afraid of?"

Moira turned her head away. "If you like. But it sounds so melodramatic and hysterical. I can't believe it myself this minute."

And indeed the bald statement, made unemotionally in the open air of the quiet English countryside, did seem curiously lacking in reality.

Moira got up abruptly. "I really feel I've been terribly silly," she said, her lip trembling. "Please don't pay any attention to what I said, Mr. Jones. It was just—nerves. Anyway, I must be going now. Good-bye."

She moved rapidly away. Bobby sprang up to follow her, but Frankie pushed him firmly back.

"Stay there, idiot, leave this to me."

She went rapidly off after Moira. She returned a few minutes later.

"Well," queried Bobby anxiously.

"That's alright. I calmed her down. It was a bit hard on her, having her private fears blurted out in front of her to a third person. I made her promise we'd have a meeting—all three of us—again soon. Now that you're not hampered by her being here, tell us all about it."

Bobby did so. Frankie listened attentively. Then she said:

"It fits in with two things. First of all, I came back just now to find Nicholson holding both Sylvia Bassington-ffrench's hands—and didn't he look daggers at me! If looks could kill, I feel sure he'd have made me a corpse then and there."

"What's the second thing?" asked Bobby.

"Oh, just an incident. Sylvia described how Moira's photograph had made a great impression on some stranger who had come to the house. Depend upon it, that was Carstairs. He recognizes the photograph, Mrs. Bassington-ffrench tells him that it is a portrait of a Mrs. Nicholson, and that explains how he came to find out where she was. But you know, Bobby, I don't see yet where Nicholson comes in. Why should he want to do away with Alan Carstairs?"

"You think it was he and not Bassington-ffrench? Rather a coincidence if he and Bassington-ffrench should both be in Marchbolt on the same day."

"Well, coincidences do happen. But if it was Nicholson, I don't yet see the motive. Was Carstairs on the track of Nicholson as the head of a dope gang? Or is your new lady friend the motive for the murder?"

"It might be both," suggested Bobby. "He may know that Carstairs and his wife had an interview, and he may have believed that his wife gave him away somehow."

"Now that is a possibility," said Frankie. "But the first thing is to make sure about Roger Bassington-ffrench. The only thing we've got against him is the photograph business. If he can clear that up satisfactorily—"

"You're going to tackle him on the subject? Frankie, is that wise? If he is the villain of the piece, as we decided he must be, it means that we're going to show him our hand."

"Not quite—not the way I shall do it. After all, in every other way he's been perfectly straightforward and aboveboard. We've taken that to be super-cunning—but suppose it just happens to be innocence? *If* he can explain the photograph—and I shall be watching him when he does explain—and if there's the least sign of hesitation or guilt, I shall see it—as I say, *if* he can explain the photograph, then he may be a very valuable ally."

"How do you mean, Frankie?"

"My dear, your little friend may be an emotional scaremonger who likes to exaggerate, but supposing she isn't—that all she says is gospel truth—that her husband wants to get rid of her and marry Sylvia. Don't you realize that in that case, Henry Bassington-ffrench is in mortal danger too? At all costs, we've got to prevent his being sent to the Grange. And at present, Roger Bassington-ffrench is on Nicholson's side."

"Good for you, Frankie," said Bobby quietly. "Go ahead with your plan."

Frankie got up to go, but before departing she paused for a moment.

"Isn't it odd?" she said. "We seem somehow to have got in between the covers of a book. We're in the middle of someone else's story. It's a frightfully queer feeling."

"I know what you mean," said Bobby. "There is something rather uncanny about it. I should call it a play rather than a book. It's as though we'd walked onto the stage in the middle of the second act, and we haven't really got parts in the play at all, but we have to pretend, and what makes it so frightfully hard is that we haven't the faintest idea what the first act was about."

Frankie nodded eagerly. "I'm not even sure it's the second act—I think it's more like the third. Bobby, I'm sure we've got to go back a long way . . . And we've got to be quick because I fancy the play is frightfully near the final curtain."

"With corpses strewn everywhere," said Bobby. "And what brought us into the show was a regular cue—five words, quite meaningless as far as we are concerned."

"'Why didn't they ask Evans?' Isn't it odd, Bobby, that though we've found out a good deal, and more and more characters come into the thing, we never get any nearer to the mysterious Evans?"

"I've got an idea about Evans. I've a feeling that Evans doesn't really matter at all—that although he's been the starting point as it were, in himself he's probably quite unessential. It will be like that story of Wells' where a prince built a marvelous palace or temple round the tomb of his beloved. And when it was finished there was just one little thing that jarred. So he said, 'Take it away'—and the thing was actually the tomb itself."

"Sometimes," said Frankie, "I don't believe there is an Evans."

Saying which she nodded to Bobby and retraced her steps toward the house.

21

Roger Answers a Question

FORTUNE FAVORED HER, for she fell in with Roger not far from the house.

"Hullo," he said. "You're back early from London."

"I wasn't in the mood for London," said Frankie.

"Have you been to the house yet?" he asked. His face grew grave.

"Nicholson, I find, has been telling Sylvia the truth about poor old Henry. Poor girl, she's taken it hard. It seems she had absolutely no suspicion."

"I know," said Frankie. "They were both together in the library when I came in. She was—very much upset."

"Look here, Frankie," said Roger. "Henry has absolutely got to be cured. It isn't as though this drug habit had a real hold on him. He hasn't been taking it so very long. And he's got every incentive in the world to make him keen on being cured—Sylvia, Tommy, his home. He's got to be made to see the position clearly. Nicholson is just the man to put the thing through. He was talking to me the other day. He's had some amazing successes—even with people who have been slaves for years to the beastly stuff. If Henry will only consent to go to the Grange—"

Frankie interrupted.

"Look here," she said. "There's something I want to ask you. Just a question. I hope you won't think I'm simply frightfully impertinent."

"What is it?" asked Roger, his attention arrested.

"Do you mind telling me whether you took a photograph out of that man's pocket—the one who fell over the cliff at Marchbolt?"

She was studying him closely, watching every detail of his expression. She was satisfied with what she saw.

Slight annoyance, a trace of embarrassment—no flash of guilt or dismay.

"Now how on earth did you come to guess that?" he said. "Or did Moira tell you?—But then, she doesn't know—"

"You did then?"

"I suppose I'll have to admit it."

"Why?"

Roger seemed embarrassed again. "Well, look at it as I did. Here I am mounting guard over a strange dead body. Something is sticking out of his pocket. I look at it. By an amazing coincidence it's the photograph of a woman I know—a married woman—and a woman who I guess is not too happily married. What's going to happen? An inquest. Publicity. Possibly the wretched girl's name in all the papers. I acted on impulse. Took the photograph and tore it up. I dare say I acted wrongly, but Moira Nicholson is a nice little soul and I didn't want her to get landed in a mess."

Frankie drew a deep breath. "So that was it," she said. "If you only knew—"

"Knew what?" said Roger, puzzled.

"I don't know that I can tell you just now," said Frankie. "I may later. It's all rather complicated. I can quite see why you took the photograph, but was there any objection to your saying you recognized the man? Oughtn't you to have told the police who he was?"

"Recognized him?" said Roger. He looked bewildered. "How could I recognize him? I didn't know him."

"But you'd met him down here—only about a week before."

"My dear girl, are you quite mad?"

"Alan Carstairs—you did meet Alan Carstairs?"

"Oh, yes. Man who came down with the Rivingtons. But the dead man wasn't Alan Carstairs."

"But he *was!*"

They stared at each other. Then Frankie said, with a renewal of suspicion, "Surely you must have recognized him?"

"I never saw his face," said Roger.

"What?"

"No. There was a handkerchief spread over it."

Frankie stared at him. Suddenly she remembered that in Bobby's first account of the tragedy he had mentioned putting a handkerchief over the face of the dead man.

"You never thought of looking?" went on Frankie.

"No. Why should I?"

"Of course," thought Frankie. "If *I'd* found a photograph of somebody I knew in a dead person's pocket, I should simply have had to look at the person's face. How beautifully incurious men are!" She paused for a moment. "Poor little thing," she went on. "I'm so terribly sorry for her."

"Whom do you mean? Moira Nicholson? Why are you so sorry for her?"

"Because she's frightened," said Frankie slowly.

"She always looks half scared to death. But what is she frightened of?"

"Her husband."

"I don't know that I'd care to be up against Jasper Nicholson myself," admitted Roger.

"She's sure he's trying to murder her," said Frankie abruptly.

"Oh, my dear!" he protested.

"Sit down," said Frankie. "I'm going to tell you a lot of things. I've got to prove to you that Dr. Nicholson is a dangerous criminal."

"A criminal?" Roger's tone was frankly incredulous.

"Wait till you've heard the whole story."

She gave him a clear and careful narrative of all that had occurred since the day Bobby and Dr. Thomas had found the body. She kept back only the fact that her accident had not been genuine, but she let it appear that she had lingered at Merroway Court through her intense desire to get to the bottom of the mystery.

She could complain of no lack of interest on the part of her listener. Roger seemed quite fascinated by the story.

"Is this really true?" he demanded. "All this about the fellow Jones being poisoned and all that?"

"Absolute gospel truth."

"Sorry for my incredulity—but the facts do take a bit of swallowing, don't they?"

He was silent for a minute, frowning.

"Look here," he said at last. "Fantastic though the whole thing sounds, I think you must be right in your first deduction. This man, Alex Pritchard, or Alan Carstairs, must have been murdered. If he wasn't, there seems no point in the attack upon Jones. Whether or not the key to the situation is the phrase *'Why didn't they ask Evans?'* doesn't seem to me to matter much, since you've no clue to who Evans is or what he was to have been asked. Let's put it that the murderer or murderers assumed that Jones was in possession of some knowledge, whether he knew it himself or not, which was dangerous to them.

So they accordingly tried to eliminate him, and probably would try again if they got on his track. So far that seems sense—but I don't see by what process of reasoning you fix on Nicholson as the criminal."

"He's such a sinister man, and he's got a dark-blue Talbot, and he was away from here on the day that Bobby was poisoned."

"That's all pretty thin as evidence."

"There are all the things Mrs. Nicholson told Bobby."

She recited them—and once again they sounded melodramatic and unsubstantial repeated aloud against the background of the peaceful English landscape.

Roger shrugged his shoulders.

"She thinks he supplies Henry with the drug—but that's pure conjecture. She's not a particle of evidence that he does so. She thinks he wants to get Henry to the Grange as a patient—well, that's a very natural wish for a doctor to have. A doctor wants as many patients as he can get. She thinks he's in love with Sylvia. Well, as to that, of course, I can't say."

"If she thinks so, she's probably right," interrupted Frankie. "A woman would know alright about her own husband."

"Well, granting that that's the case, it doesn't necessarily mean that the man's a dangerous criminal. Lots of respectable citizens fall in love with other people's wives."

"There's her belief that he wants to murder her," urged Frankie.

Roger looked at her quizzically. "You take that seriously?"

"She believes it, anyhow."

Roger nodded and lit a cigarette. "The question is, how much attention to pay that belief of hers," he said. "It's a creepy sort of place, the Grange, full of queer customers. Living there would tend to upset a woman's balance, especially if she were of the timid, nervous type."

"Then you don't think it's true?"

"I don't say that. She probably believes quite honestly that he is trying to kill her. But is there any foundation in fact for that belief? There doesn't seem to be."

Frankie remembered with curious clearness Moira's saying, "It's just nerves." And somehow the mere fact that she had said that seemed to Frankie to point to the fact that it was *not* nerves; but she did not know how to explain her point of view to Roger.

Meanwhile the young man was going on:

"Mind you, if you could show that Nicholson had been in Marchbolt on the day of the cliff tragedy, that would be very different—or if we could find any definite motive linking him with Carstairs. But it seems to me you're ignoring the real suspects."

"What real suspects?"

"The—what did you call them—Haymans?"

"Caymans."

"That's it. Now, they are undoubtedly in it up to the hilt. First, there's the false identification of the body. Then there's their insistence on the point of whether the poor fellow said anything before he died. And I think it's logical to assume, as you did, that the Buenos Aires offer came from them or was arranged for by them."

"It's a bit annoying," said Frankie, "to have the most strenuous efforts made to get you out of the way because you know something—and not to know yourself what the something you know is. Bother—what a mess one gets into with words!"

"Yes," said Roger grimly, "that was a mistake on their part. A mistake that it's going to take them all their time to remedy."

"Oh!" cried Frankie, "I've just thought of something. Up to now, you see, I've been assuming that the photograph of Mrs. Cayman was substituted for the one of Moira Nicholson."

"I can assure you," said Roger gravely, "that I have never treasured the likeness of a Mrs. Cayman against my heart. She sounds a most repulsive creature."

"Well, she was handsome in a way," admitted Frankie. "A sort of bold, coarse, vampish way. But the point is this: Carstairs must have had *her* photograph on him as well as Mrs. Nicholson's."

Roger nodded. "And you think—" he suggested.

"I think one was love and the other was business! Carstairs was carrying about the Cayman's photograph for a reason. He wanted it identified by somebody, perhaps. Now listen—what happens? Someone, the male Cayman perhaps, is following him and seeing a good opportunity, steals up behind him in the mist and gives him a shove. Carstairs goes over the cliff with a startled cry. Male Cayman makes off as fast as he can—he doesn't know who may be about. We'll say that he doesn't know that Alan Carstairs is carrying about that photograph. What happens next? The photograph is published—"

"Consternation in the Cayman ménage," said Roger helpfully.

"Exactly. What is to be done? The bold thing—grasp the nettle. Who knows Carstairs as Carstairs? Hardly anyone in this country. Down goes Mrs. Cayman, weeping crocodile tears and recognizing the body as that of a convenient brother. The two also do a little hocus-pocus of posting parcels to bolster up the walking-tour story."

"You know, Frankie, I think that's positively brilliant," said Roger with admiration.

"I think it's pretty good myself," said Frankie. "And you're quite right. We ought to get busy on the track of the Caymans. I can't think why we haven't done so before."

This was not quite true, since Frankie knew the reason quite well—namely, that they had been on the track of Roger himself. However, she felt it would be tactless, just at this stage, to reveal the fact.

"What are we going to do about Mrs. Nicholson?" she asked abruptly.

"What do you mean—do about her?"

"Well, the poor thing is terrified to death. I do think you're callous about her, Roger."

"I'm not really, but people who can't help themselves always irritate me."

"Oh, but do be fair! What can she do? She's no money and nowhere to go."

Roger said unexpectedly, "If you were in her place, Frankie, you'd find something to do."

"Oh!" Frankie was rather taken aback.

"Yes, you would. If you really thought somebody was trying to murder you, you wouldn't just stay there tamely waiting to be murdered. You'd run away and make a living somehow, or you'd murder the other person first! You'd do *something.*"

Frankie tried to think what she would do.

"I'd certainly do something," she said thoughtfully.

"The truth of the matter is that you've got guts and she hasn't," said Roger with decision.

Frankie felt complimented. Moira Nicholson was not really the type of woman she admired, and she had also felt just slightly ruffled by Bobby's absorption in her. "Bobby," she thought to herself, "likes them helpless." And she remembered the curious fascination that the photograph had had for him from the start of the affair.

"Oh, well," thought Frankie, "at any rate Roger's different."

Roger, it was clear, did not like them helpless. Moira, on the other hand, clearly did not think very much of Roger. She had called him weak and had scouted the possibility of his having the guts to murder anyone. He was weak, perhaps—but undeniably he had charm. She had felt it from the first moment of arriving at Merroway Court.

Roger said quietly, "If you liked, Frankie, you could make anything you chose of a man . . ."

Frankie felt a sudden little thrill—and at the same time an acute embarrassment. She changed the subject hastily.

"About your brother," she said. "Do you still think he should go to the Grange?"

22
Another Victim

"NO," SAID ROGER. "I don't. After all, there are heaps of other places where he can be treated. The really important thing is to get Henry to agree."

"Do you think that will be difficult?" asked Frankie.

"I'm afraid it may be. You heard him the other night. On the other hand, if we just catch him in the repentant mood, that's very different. Hullo—here comes Sylvia."

Mrs. Bassington-ffrench emerged from the house and looked about her. Then seeing Roger and Frankie she walked across the grass toward them. They could see that she was looking terribly worried and strained.

"Roger," she began, "I've been looking for you everywhere." Then, as Frankie made a movement to leave them—"No, my dear, don't go. Of what use are concealments? In any case, I think you know all there is to know. You've suspected this business for some time, haven't you?"

Frankie nodded.

"While I've been blind—blind," said Sylvia bitterly. "Both of you saw what I never even suspected. I only wondered why Henry had changed so to all of us. It made me very unhappy, but I never suspected the reason."

She paused, then went on again with a slight change of tone.

"As soon as Dr. Nicholson told me the truth, I went straight to Henry. I've only just left him now." She paused, swallowing a sob. "Roger—it's going to be alright. He's agreed. He will go to the Grange and put himself in Dr. Nicholson's hands tomorrow."

"Oh, no!" The exclamation came from Roger and Frankie simultaneously. Sylvia looked at them, astonished.

Roger spoke awkwardly. "Do you know, Sylvia, I've been thinking it over, and I don't believe the Grange would be a good plan, after all."

"You think he can fight it by himself?" asked Sylvia doubtfully.

"No, I don't. But there are other places—places not—so—well, not so near at hand. I'm convinced that staying in this district would be a mistake."

"I'm sure of it," said Frankie, coming to his rescue.

"Oh, I don't agree," said Sylvia. "I couldn't bear to have him go away somewhere. And Dr. Nicholson has been so kind and understanding. I shall feel happy about Henry's being under his charge."

"I thought you didn't like Nicholson, Sylvia," said Roger.

"I've changed my mind." She spoke simply. "Nobody could have been nicer or kinder than he was this afternoon. My silly prejudice against him has quite vanished."

There was a moment's silence. The position was awkward. Neither Roger nor Sylvia knew quite what to say next.

"Poor Henry," said Sylvia. "He broke down. He was terribly upset at my knowing. He agreed that he must fight this awful craving for my sake and Tommy's, but he said I hadn't a conception of what it meant. I suppose I haven't, though Dr. Nicholson explained very fully. It becomes a kind of obsession—people aren't responsible for their actions, so he said. Oh, Roger, it seems so awful! But Dr. Nicholson was really kind. I trust him."

"All the same, I think it would be better—" began Roger.

Sylvia turned on him. "I don't understand you, Roger. Why have you changed your mind? Half an hour ago you were all for Henry's going to the Grange."

"Well—I've—I've had time to think the matter over since—"

Again Sylvia interrupted. "Anyway, I've made up my mind. Henry shall go to the Grange and nowhere else."

They confronted her in silence. Then Roger said: "Do you know, I think I will ring up Nicholson. He will be home now. I'd like—just to have a talk with him about matters."

Without waiting for her reply he turned away and went rapidly into the house. The two women stood looking after him.

"I cannot understand Roger," said Sylvia impatiently. "About a quarter of an hour ago he was positively urging me to arrange for Henry to go to the Grange." Her tone held a distinct note of anger.

"All the same," said Frankie, "I agree with him. I'm sure I've read somewhere that people ought always to go for a cure somewhere far away from their homes."

"I think that's just nonsense," said Sylvia.

Frankie felt in a dilemma. Sylvia's unexpected obstinacy was making things difficult, and also she seemed suddenly to have become as violently pro-Nicholson as she formerly had been against him. It was very hard to know what arguments to use. Frankie considered telling the whole story to Sylvia—but would Sylvia believe it? Even Roger had not been very impressed by the theory of Dr. Nicholson's guilt. Sylvia, with her newfound partisanship where the Doctor was concerned, would probably be even less so. She might even go and repeat the whole thing to him. It was certainly difficult.

An airplane passed low overhead in the gathering dusk, filling the air with its loud beat of engines. Both Sylvia and Frankie stared up at it, glad of the respite it afforded, since neither of them quite knew what to say next. It gave Frankie time to collect her thoughts, and Sylvia time to recover from her fit of sudden anger.

As the airplane disappeared over the trees and its roar receded into the distance, Sylvia turned abruptly to Frankie.

"It's been so awful—" she said brokenly. "And you all seem to want to send Henry far away from me."

"No, no," said Frankie. "It wasn't that at all."

She cast about for a minute.

"It was only that I thought he ought to have the best treatment. And I do think that Dr. Nicholson is rather—well, rather a quack."

"I don't believe it," said Sylvia. "I think he's a very clever man and just the kind of man Henry needs."

She looked defiantly at Frankie. Frankie marveled at the hold Dr. Nicholson had acquired over her in such a short time. All her former distrust of the man seemed to have vanished completely.

At a loss what to say or do next, Frankie relapsed into silence. Presently Roger came out again from the house. He seemed slightly breathless.

"Nicholson isn't in yet," he said. "I left a message."

"I don't see why you want to see Dr. Nicholson so urgently," said Sylvia. "You suggested this plan, and it's all arranged, and Henry has consented."

"I think I've got some say in the matter, Sylvia," said Roger gently. "After all, I'm Henry's brother."

"You suggested the plan yourself," said Sylvia obstinately.

"Yes, but I've heard a few things about Nicholson since."

"What things? Oh, I don't believe you!"

She bit her lip, turned away, and went into the house.

Roger looked at Frankie. "This is a bit awkward," he said.

"Very awkward indeed."

"Once Sylvia has made her mind up she can be obstinate as the devil."

"What are we going to do?"

They sat down again on the garden seat and went into the matter carefully. Roger agreed with Frankie that to tell the whole story to Sylvia would be a mistake. The best plan, in his opinion, would be to tackle the Doctor.

"But what are you going to say exactly?"

"I don't know that I shall say much—but I shall hint a good deal. At any rate, I agree with you about one thing—Henry mustn't go to the Grange. Even if we come right out into the open, we've got to stop that."

"We give the whole show away if we do," Frankie reminded him.

"I know. That's why we've got to try everything else first. Curse Sylvia, why must she turn obstinate just at this minute?"

"It shows the power of the man," Frankie said.

"Yes. You know, it inclines me to believe that, evidence or no evidence, you may be right about him after all—What's that?"

They both sprang up.

"It sounded like a shot," said Frankie. "From the house."

They looked at each other, then raced toward the building. They went in by the French window of the drawing-room and passed through into the hall. Sylvia Bassington-ffrench was standing there, her face white as paper.

"Did you hear?" she said. "It was a shot—from Henry's study."

She swayed, and Roger put an arm round her to steady her. Frankie went to the study and turned the handle.

"It's locked," she said.

"The window," said Roger.

He deposited Sylvia, who was in a half-fainting condition, on a convenient settee and raced out again through the drawing-room, Frankie on his heels. They went round the house till they came to the study window. It was closed but they put their faces close to the glass and peered in. The sun was setting and there was not much light—but they could see plainly enough.

Henry Bassington-ffrench was lying sprawled out across his desk. There was a bullet wound plainly visible in his temple, and a revolver lay on the floor where it had dropped from his hand.

"He's shot himself," said Frankie. "How ghastly . . ."

"Stand back a little," said Roger. "I'm going to break the window."

He wrapped his hand in his coat and struck the pane of glass a heavy blow that shattered it. Roger picked out the pieces carefully, then he and Frankie stepped into the room. As they did so, Mrs. Bassington-ffrench and Dr. Nicholson came hurrying along the terrace.

"Here's the Doctor," said Sylvia. "He's just come. Has—has anything happened to Henry?"

Then she saw the sprawling figure and uttered a cry.

Roger stepped quickly out again through the window, and Dr. Nicholson thrust Sylvia into his arms.

"Take her away," he said briefly. "Look after her. Give her some brandy if she'll take it. Don't let her see more than you can help." He himself stepped through the window and joined Frankie.

He shook his head slowly. "This is a tragic business," he said. "Poor fellow. So he felt he couldn't face the music. Too bad. Too bad."

He bent over the body, then straightened himself up again.

"Nothing to be done. Death must have been instantaneous. I wonder if he wrote something first. They usually do."

Frankie advanced till she stood beside them. A piece of paper with a few scrawled words on it, evidently freshly written, lay at Bassington-ffrench's elbow. Their purport was clear enough.

> I feel this is the best way out [Henry Bassington-ffrench had written]. This fatal habit has taken too great a hold on me for me to fight it now. Want to do the best I can for Sylvia—Sylvia and Tommy. God bless you both, my dears. Forgive me.

Frankie felt a lump rise in her throat.

"We mustn't touch anything," said Dr. Nicholson. "There will have to be an inquest, of course. We must ring up the police."

In obedience to his gesture, Frankie went toward the door. Then she stopped.

"The key's not in the lock," she said.

"No?" Perhaps it's in his pocket."

He knelt down, investigating delicately. From the dead man's coat pocket he drew out a key. He tried it in the lock and it fitted. Together they passed out into the hall. Dr. Nicholson went straight to the telephone.

Frankie, her knees shaking under her, felt suddenly sick.

23
Moira Disappears

FRANKIE RANG UP Bobby about an hour later.

"Is that Hawkins? Hullo, Bobby—have you heard what has happened? You have? Quick, we must meet somewhere. Early tomorrow morning would be best, I think. I'll stroll out before breakfast. Say eight o'clock—the same place we met today."

She rang off as Bobby uttered his third respectful "Yes, your ladyship," for the benefit of any curious ears.

Bobby arrived at the rendezvous first, but Frankie did not keep him waiting long. She looked pale and upset.

"Hullo, Bobby, isn't it awful? I wasn't able to sleep last night."

"I haven't heard any details," said Bobby. "Just that Mr. Bassington-ffrench had shot himself. That's right, I suppose?"

"Yes. Sylvia had been talking to him—persuading him to agree to a course of treatment, and he had said he would. Afterward, I suppose, his courage must have failed him. He went into his study, locked the door, wrote a few words on a sheet of paper—and—and shot himself. Bobby, it's too ghastly. It's—it's grim."

"I know," said Bobby quietly.

They were both silent for a little.

"I shall have to leave today, of course," said Frankie presently.

"Yes, I suppose you will. How is she—Mrs. Bassington-ffrench, I mean?"

"She's collapsed, poor soul. I haven't seen her since we—we found the body. The shock to her must have been awful."

Bobby nodded.

"You'd better bring the car round about eleven," continued Frankie.

Bobby did not answer. Frankie looked at him impatiently.

"What's the matter with you, Bobby? You look as though you were miles away."

"Sorry. As a matter of fact—"

"Yes?"

"Well, I was just wondering. I suppose—well, I suppose it's alright?"

"What do you mean—alright?"

"I mean it's quite certain that he *did* commit suicide?"

"Oh!" said Frankie. "I see." She thought a minute. "Yes," she said, "it was suicide alright."

"You're quite sure? You see, Frankie, we have Moira's word for it that Nicholson wanted two people out of the way. Well, *here's one of them gone.*"

Frankie thought again, but once more she shook her head.

"It must be suicide," she said. "I was in the garden with Roger when we heard the shot. We both ran straight in through the drawing-room to the hall. The study door was locked on the inside. We went round to the window. That was fastened also and Roger had to smash it. It wasn't till then that Nicholson appeared upon the scene."

Bobby reflected upon this information.

"It looks alright," he agreed. "But Nicholson seems to have appeared on the scene very suddenly."

"He'd left a stick behind earlier in the afternoon and had come back for it."

Bobby was frowning with the process of thought.

"Listen, Frankie. Suppose that actually Nicholson shot Bassington-ffrench—"

"Having induced him first to write a suicide's letter of farewell?"

"I should think that would be the easiest thing in the world to fake. Any alteration in handwriting would be put down to agitation."

"Yes, that's true. Go on with your theory."

"Nicholson shoots Bassington-ffrench, leaves the farewell letter, and nips out, locking the door—to appear again a few minutes later as though he had just arrived."

Frankie shook her head regretfully.

"It's a good idea—but it won't work. To begin with, the key was in Henry Bassington-ffrench's pocket—"

"Who found it there?"

"Well, as a matter of fact, Nicholson did."

"There you are! What's easier for him than to pretend to find it there?"

"I was watching him—remember. I'm sure the key was in the pocket."

"That's what one says when one watches a conjurer. You *see* the rabbit being put into the hat! If Nicholson is a high-class criminal a simple little bit of sleight-of-hand like that would be child's play to him."

"Well, you may be right about that, but honestly, Bobby, the whole thing's impossible. Sylvia Bassington-ffrench was actually in the house when the shot was fired. The moment she heard it she ran out into the hall. If Nicholson had fired the shot and come out through the study door she would have been bound to see him. Besides, she told us that he actually came up the drive to the front door. She saw him coming as we ran round the house, and went to meet him and brought him round to the study window. No, Bobby, I hate to say it, but the man has an alibi."

"On principle I distrust people who have alibis," said Bobby.

"So do I. But I don't see how you can get round this one."

"No. Sylvia Bassington-ffrench's word ought to be good enough."

"Yes, indeed."

"Well," said Bobby with a sigh, "I suppose we'll have to leave it at suicide. Poor devil. What's the next angle of attack, Frankie?"

"The Caymans," said Frankie. "I can't think how we've been so remiss as not to have looked them up before. You've kept the address Cayman wrote from, haven't you?"

"Yes. It's the same they gave at the inquest. Number 17 St. Leonard's Gardens, Paddington."

"Don't you agree that we've rather neglected that channel of inquiry?"

"Absolutely. All the same, you know, Frankie, I've got a very shrewd idea that you'll find the birds flown. I should imagine that the Caymans weren't exactly born yesterday."

"Even if they have gone off, I may find out something about them."

"Why *I*?"

"Because, once again, I don't think you'd better appear in the matter. It's like coming down here when we thought Roger was the bad man of the show. You are known to them and I am not."

"And how do you propose to make their acquaintance?" asked Bobby.

"I shall be something political," said Frankie. "Canvassing for the Conservative party. I shall arrive with leaflets."

"Good enough," said Bobby. "But, as I said before, I think you'll find the birds flown. Now there's another thing that requires to be thought of—Moira."

"Goodness!" said Frankie. "I'd forgotten all about her."

"So I noticed," said Bobby with a trace of coldness in his manner.

"You're right," said Frankie thoughtfully. "Something must be done about her."

Bobby nodded. The strange haunting face came up before his eyes. There was something tragic about it. He had always felt this from the first moment when he had taken the photograph from Alan Carstairs' pocket.

"If you'd seen her that night when I first went to the Grange!" he said. "She was crazy with fear—and I tell you Frankie, *she's right*. It's not nerves nor imagination nor anything like that. If Nicholson wants to marry Sylvia Bassington-ffrench, two obstacles have got to go. One's gone. I've a feeling that Moira's life is hanging by a hair and that any delay may be fatal."

Frankie was sobered by the earnestness of his words.

"My dear, you're right," she said. "We must act quickly. What shall we do?"

"We must persuade her to leave the Grange—at once."

Frankie nodded. "I tell you what," she said. "She'd better go down to Wales—to the Castle. Heaven knows she ought to be safe enough there."

"If you can fix that, Frankie, nothing could be better."

"Well, it's simple enough. Father never notices who goes or comes. He'll like Moira—nearly any man would, she's so feminine. It's extraordinary how men like helpless women."

"I don't think Moira is particularly helpless," said Bobby.

"Nonsense. She's like a little bird that sits and waits to be eaten by a snake without doing anything about it."

"What could she do?"

"Heaps of things," said Frankie vigorously.

"Well, I don't see it. She's got no money, no friends—"

"My dear, don't drone on as though you were recommending a case to the Girls' Friendly Society."

"Sorry," said Bobby.

There was an offended pause.

"Well," said Frankie, recovering her temper. "As you were. I think we'd better get on to this business as soon as possible."

"So do I," said Bobby. "Really, Frankie, it's awfully decent of you to—"

"That's alright," said Frankie, interrupting him. "I don't mind befriending the girl so long as you don't drivel on about her as though she had no hands or feet or tongue or brains."

"I simply don't know what you mean," said Bobby.

"Well, we needn't talk about it," said Frankie. "Now my idea is that whatever we're going to do we'd better do it quickly. Is that a quotation?"

"It's a paraphrase of one. Go on, Lady Macbeth."

"You know I've always thought," said Frankie, suddenly digressing wildly from the matter in hand, "that Lady Macbeth incited Macbeth to do all those murders simply and solely because she was so frightfully bored with life—and incidentally with Macbeth. I'm sure he was one of those meek, inoffensive men who drive their wives distracted with boredom. But having once committed a murder for the first time in his life he felt the hell of a fine fellow and began to develop egomania as a compensation for his former inferiority complex."

"You ought to write a book on the subject, Frankie."

"I can't spell. Now, where were we? Oh, yes, rescue of Moira. You'd better bring the car round at half-past ten. I'll drive over to the Grange, ask for Moira, and, if Nicholson's there when I see her, I'll remind her of her promise to come and stay with me and carry her off then and there."

"Excellent, Frankie. I'm glad we're not going to waste any time. I've a horror of another accident happening."

"Half-past ten, then," said Frankie.

By the time she got back to Merroway Court it was half-past nine. Breakfast had just been brought in, and Roger was pouring himself out some coffee. He looked ill and worn.

"Good morning," said Frankie. "I slept awfully badly. In the end I got up about seven and went for a walk."

"I'm frightfully sorry you should have been let in for all this worry," said Roger.

"How's Sylvia?"

"They gave her an opiate last night. She's still asleep, I believe. Poor girl, I'm most terribly sorry for her. She was simply devoted to Henry."

"I know."

Frankie paused, and then explained her plans for departure.

"I suppose you'll have to go," said Roger resentfully. "The inquest's on Friday. I'll let you know if you're wanted for it. It all depends on the Coroner."

He swallowed a cup of coffee and a piece of toast and then went off to see to the many things requiring his attention. Frankie felt very sorry for him. The amount of gossip and curiosity created by a suicide in a family she could imagine only too well. Tommy appeared and she devoted herself to amusing the child.

Bobby brought the car round at half-past ten. Frankie's luggage was brought down. She said goodbye to Tommy and left a note for Sylvia. The Bentley drove away.

They covered the distance to the Grange in a very short time. Frankie had never been there before, and the big iron gates and the overgrown shrubbery depressed her spirits.

"It's a creepy place," she observed. "I don't wonder Moira gets the horrors here."

They drove up to the front door and Bobby got down and rang the bell. It was not answered for some minutes. Finally a woman in nurse's kit opened it.

"Mrs. Nicholson?" said Bobby.

The woman hesitated, then withdrew into the hall and opened the door wider. Frankie jumped out of the car and passed into the house. The door closed behind her. It had a nasty echoing clang as it shut. Frankie noticed that it had heavy bolts and bars across it. Quite irrationally she felt afraid—as though she were here, in this sinister house, a prisoner.

"Nonsense!" she told herself. "Bobby's outside in the car. I've come here openly. Nothing can happen to me." And, shaking off the ridiculous feeling, she followed the nurse upstairs and along a passage. The nurse threw open a door and Frankie passed into a small sitting-room daintily furnished with cheerful chintzes and flowers in vases. Her spirits rose. Murmuring something, the nurse withdrew.

About five minutes passed and then the door opened and Dr. Nicholson came in.

Frankie was quite unable to control a slight nervous start, but she masked it by a welcoming smile and shook hands.

"Good morning," she said.

"Good morning, Lady Frances. You have not come to bring me bad news of Mrs. Bassington-ffrench, I hope?"

"She was still asleep when I left," said Frankie.

"Poor lady. Her own doctor is, of course, looking after her?"

"Oh, yes." She paused, then said, "I'm sure you're busy. I mustn't take up your time, Dr. Nicholson. I really called to see your wife."

"To see Moira? That was very kind of you."

Was it only a fancy, or did the pale-blue eyes behind the strong glasses harden ever so slightly?

"Yes," he repeated. "That was very kind."

"If she isn't up yet," said Frankie, smiling pleasantly, "I'll sit down and wait."

"Oh, she's up," said Dr. Nicholson.

"Good," said Frankie. "I want to persuade her to come to me for a visit. She's practically promised to." She smiled again.

"Why, now, that's really very kind of you, Lady Frances—very kind indeed. I'm sure Moira would have enjoyed that very much."

"'Would have'?" asked Frankie sharply.

Dr. Nicholson smiled, showing his fine set of even white teeth.

"Unfortunately my wife went away this morning."

"Went away?" said Frankie blankly. "Where?"

"Oh, just for a little change. You know what women are, Lady Frances. This is rather a gloomy place for a young woman. Occasionally Moira feels she must have a little excitement and then off she goes."

"You don't know where she has gone?" said Frankie.

"London, I imagine. Shops and theaters. You know the sort of thing."

Frankie felt that his smile was the most disagreeable thing she had ever come across.

"I am going up to London today," she said lightly. "Will you give me her address?"

"She usually stays at the Savoy," said Dr. Nicholson. "But in any case I shall probably hear from her in a day or so. She's not a very good correspondent, I'm afraid, and I believe in perfect liberty between husband and wife. But I think the Savoy is the most likely place for you to find her."

He held the door open and Frankie found herself shaking hands with him and being ushered to the front door. The nurse was standing there to let her out. The last thing Frankie heard was Dr. Nicholson's voice—suave and perhaps just a trifle ironical.

"So very kind of you to think of asking my wife to stay, Lady Frances."

24
On the Track of the Caymans

BOBBY HAD SOME ado to preserve his impassive chauffeur's demeanor as Frankie came out alone.

She said: "Back to Staverley, Hawkins," for the benefit of the nurse.

The car swept down the drive and out through the gates. Then, when they came to an empty bit of road, Bobby pulled up and looked inquiringly at his companion.

"What about it?" he asked.

Rather pale, Frankie replied, "Bobby, I don't like it. Apparently, she's gone away."

"Gone *away?* This morning?"

"Or last night."

"Without a word to us?"

"Bobby, I just don't believe it. The man was lying, I'm sure of it."

Bobby looked distressed. He murmured: "Too late! Idiots that we've been! We should never have let her go back there yesterday."

"You don't think she's—dead, do you?" whispered Frankie in a shaky voice.

"No," said Bobby in a violent voice, as though to reassure himself.

They were both silent for a minute or two, then Bobby stated his deductions in a calmer tone.

"She must be still alive because of disposing of the body and all that. Her death would have to seem natural and accidental. No, she's either been spirited away somewhere against her will, or else—and this is what I believe—she's still there."

"At the Grange?"

"At the Grange."

"Well," said Frankie, "what are we going to do?"

Bobby thought for a minute. "I don't think you can do anything," he said at last. "You'd better go back to London. You suggested trying to trace the Caymans. Go on with that."

"Oh, Bobby!"

"My dear, you can't be of any use down here. You're known—very well known by now. You've announced that you're going—what can you do? You can't stay on at Merroway. You can't come and stay at the Anglers' Arms. You'd set every tongue in the neighborhood wagging. No, you must go. Nicholson may suspect, but he can't be *sure* that you know anything. You go back to town and I'll stay."

"At the Anglers' Arms?"

"No, I think your chauffeur will now disappear. I shall take up my headquarters at Ambledever—that's ten miles away—and if Moira's still in that beastly house I shall find her."

Frankie demurred a little. "Bobby, you will be careful?"

"I shall be cunning as the serpent."

With rather a heavy heart Frankie gave in. What Bobby said was certainly sensible enough. She herself could do no further good down here. Bobby drove her up to town and Frankie, letting herself into the Brook Street house, felt suddenly forlorn.

She was not one, however, to let the grass grow under her feet. At three o'clock that afternoon, a fashionably but soberly dressed young woman with pince-nez and an earnest frown might have been seen approaching St.

Leonard's Gardens, a sheaf of pamphlets and papers in her hand.

St. Leonard's Gardens, Paddington, was a distinctly gloomy collection of houses, most of them in a somewhat dilapidated condition. The place had a general air of having seen "better days" a long time ago.

Frankie walked along looking up at the numbers. Suddenly she came to a halt with a grimace of vexation.

No. 17 had a board up announcing that it was to be sold or let unfurnished.

Frankie immediately removed the pince-nez and the earnest air.

It seemed that the political canvasser would not be required.

The names of several house agents were given. Frankie selected two and wrote them down. Then, having determined on her plan of campaign, she proceeded to put it into action.

The first agents were Messrs. Gordon & Porter of Praed Street.

"Good-morning," said Frankie. "I wonder if you can give me the address of a Mr. Cayman? He was until recently at 17 St. Leonard's Gardens."

"That's right," said the young man to whom Frankie had addressed herself. "Only there a short time, though, wasn't he? We act for the owners, you see. Mr. Cayman took it on a quarterly tenancy as he might have to take up a post abroad any moment. I believe he's actually done so."

"Then you haven't got his address?"

"I'm afraid not. He settled up with us and that was all."

"But he must have had some address originally when he took the house."

"A hotel—I think it was the G.W.R. Paddington Station, you know."

"References?" suggested Frankie.

"He paid the quarter's rent in advance and a deposit to cover the electric light and gas."

"Oh!" said Frankie, feeling despairing.

She saw the young man looking rather curiously at her. House agents are adepts at summing up the "class" of clients. He obviously found Frankie's interest in the Caymans rather unexpected.

"He owes me a good deal of money," said Frankie mendaciously.

The young man's face immediately assumed a shocked expression. Thoroughly sympathetic with beauty in distress, he hunted up files of correspondence and did all he could, but no trace of Mr. Cayman's present or late abode could be found.

Frankie thanked him and departed. She took a taxi to the next firm of house agents. She wasted no time in repeating the process. The first agents were the ones who had let Cayman the house. These people would be merely concerned to let it again on behalf of the owner. Frankie asked for an order to view.

This time, to counteract the expression of surprise that she saw appear on the clerk's face, she explained that she wanted a cheap property to open as a hostel for girls. The surprised expression disappeared, and Frankie emerged with the key of 17 St. Leonard's Gardens, the keys of two more "properties" which she had no wish to see, and an order to view yet a fourth.

It was a bit of luck, Frankie thought, that the clerk had not wished to accompany her, but perhaps they only did that when it was a question of a furnished tenancy.

The musty smell of a closed-up house assailed Frankie's nostrils as she unlocked and pushed open the front door of No. 17.

It was an unappetizing house, cheaply decorated, and with blistered, dirty paint. Frankie went over it methodically from garret to basement. The house had not been cleaned up on departure. There were bits of string, old newspapers and some odd nails and tools. But as for anything of a personal nature, Frankie could not find so much as the scrap of a torn-up letter.

The only thing that struck her as having a possible significance was an A.B.C. railway guide which lay open on one of the window seats. There was nothing to indicate that any of the names on the open page was of special significance, but Frankie copied the lot down in a little notebook as a poor substitute for all she had hoped to find.

As far as tracing the Caymans was concerned she had drawn a blank.

She consoled herself with the reflection that this was only to be expected. If Mr. and Mrs. Cayman were associated with the wrong side of the law they would take particularly good care that no one should be able to trace them. It was at least a kind of negative confirmatory evidence.

Still, Frankie felt definitely disappointed as she handed back the keys to the house agents and uttered mendacious statements as to communicating with them in a few days.

She walked down toward the Park feeling rather depressed and wondering what on earth she was going to do next. These fruitless meditations were interrupted by a sharp and violent squall of rain. No taxi was in sight and Frankie hurriedly preserved a favorite hat by hurrying into the Tube which was close at hand. She took a ticket to Piccadilly Circus and bought a couple of papers at the bookstall.

When she had entered the train—almost empty at this time of day—she resolutely banished thoughts of the vexing problem and opening her paper strove to concentrate her attention on its contents.

She read desultory snippets here and there.

Number of Road Deaths. Mysterious Disappearance of a Schoolgirl. Lady Peterhampton's Party at Claridge's. Sir John Milkington's convalescence after his yachting accident on the *Astradora*, the famous yacht which had belonged to the late Mr. John Savage, the millionaire. Was she an unlucky boat? The man who had designed her had met with a tragic death—Mr. Savage had committed suicide—Sir John Milkington had just escaped death by a miracle.

Frankie lowered the paper, frowning in an effort of remembrance.

Twice before, the name of John Savage had been mentioned—once by Sylvia Bassington-ffrench when she was speaking of Alan Carstairs, and once by Bobby when he was repeating the conversation he had had with Mrs. Rivington.

Alan Carstairs had been a friend of John Savage's. Mrs. Rivington had had a vague idea that Carstairs' presence in England had something to do with the death of Savage. Savage had—what was it?—he had committed suicide because he thought he had cancer.

Supposing—supposing Alan Carstairs had not been satisfied with the account of his friend's death? Supposing he had come over to inquire into the whole thing? Supposing that here, in the circumstances surrounding Savage's death, was the first act of the drama that she and Bobby were acting in?

"It's possible," thought Frankie. "Yes, it's possible."

She thought deeply, wondering how best to attack this new phase of the matter. She had no idea who John Savage's friends or intimates had been.

Then an idea struck her—his will. If there had been something suspicious about the way he met his death, his will would give a possible clue. Somewhere in London, Frankie knew, was a place where you went and read wills if you paid a shilling. But she couldn't remember where it was.

The train drew up at a station and Frankie saw that it was the British Museum. She had overshot Oxford Circus, where she had meant to change, by two stations.

She jumped up and left the train. As she emerged into the street an idea came to her. Five minutes' walk brought her to the office of Messrs. Spragge, Spragge, Jenkinson & Spragge.

Frankie was received with deference and was at once ushered into the private fastness of Mr. Spragge, the senior member of the firm.

Mr. Spragge was exceedingly genial. He had a rich, mellow, persuasive voice which his aristocratic clients had found extremely soothing when they had come to him to be extricated from some mess. It was rumored that Mr. Spragge knew more discreditable secrets about noble families than any other man in London.

"This is a pleasure indeed, Lady Frances," he said. "Do sit down. Now are you sure that chair is quite comfortable? Yes, yes. The weather is very delightful just now, is it not?—a St. Martin's summer. And how is Lord Marchington? Well, I trust?"

Frankie answered these and other inquiries in a suitable manner.

Then Mr. Spragge removed his pince-nez from his nose and became more definitely the legal guide and adviser.

"And now, Lady Frances," he said, "what is it gives me the pleasure of seeing you in my—hm—dingy office this afternoon?"

("Blackmail?" asked his eyebrows. "Indiscreet letters? An entanglement with an undesirable young man? Sued by your dressmaker?" But the eyebrows asked these questions in a very discreet manner as befitted a solicitor of Mr. Spragge's experience and income.)

"I want to look at a will," said Frankie. "And I don't know where you go and what you do. But there is some place where you can pay a shilling, isn't there?"

"Somerset House," said Mr. Spragge. "But what will is it? I think I can probably tell you anything you want to know about—er—wills in your family. I may say that I believe our firm has had the honor of drawing them up for many years past."

"It isn't a family will," said Frankie.

"No?" said Mr. Spragge.

And so strong was his almost hypnotic power of drawing confidences out of his clients that Frankie, who had not meant to do so, succumbed to the manner and told him.

"I wanted to see the will of Mr. Savage—John Savage."

"In-deed." A very real astonishment showed in Mr. Spragge's voice. He had not expected this. "Now that is very extraordinary—very extraordinary indeed."

There was something so unusual in his voice that Frankie looked at him in surprise.

"Really," said Mr. Spragge, "really I do not know what to do. Perhaps, Lady Frances, you can give me your reasons for wanting to see that will?"

"No," said Frankie slowly. "I'm afraid I can't."

It struck her that Mr. Spragge was, for some reason, behaving quite unlike his usual benign omniscient self. He looked actually worried.

"I really believe," said Mr. Spragge, "that I ought to warn you."

"Warn me?" said Frankie.

"Yes. The indications are vague, very vague—but clearly there is something afoot. I would not for the world have you involved in any questionable business."

As far as that went Frankie could have told him that she was already involved up to the neck in a business of which he would have decidedly disapproved. But she merely stared at him inquiringly.

"The whole thing is rather an extraordinary coincidence," Mr. Spragge was going on. "Something is clearly afoot—clearly. But what it is I am not at present at liberty to say."

Frankie continued to look inquiring.

"A piece of information has just come to my knowledge," continued Mr. Spragge. His chest swelled with indignation. "I have been impersonated, Lady Frances. Deliberately impersonated. What do you say to that?"

But for just one panic-stricken minute Frankie could say nothing at all.

25

Mr. Spragge Talks

AT LAST SHE stammered, "How did you find out?"

It was not at all what she meant to say. She could, in fact, have bitten out her tongue for stupidity a moment later, but the words had been said, and Mr. Spragge would have been no lawyer had he failed to perceive that they contained an admission.

"So you know something of this business, Lady Frances?"

"Yes," said Frankie.

She paused, drew a deep breath and said, "The whole thing is really my doing, Mr. Spragge."

"I am amazed," said Mr. Spragge.

There was a struggle in his voice—the outraged lawyer was at war with the fatherly family solicitor.

"How did this come about?" he asked.

"It was just a joke," said Frankie weakly. "We—we wanted something to do."

"And who," demanded Mr. Spragge, "had the idea of passing himself off as Me?"

Frankie looked at him and, her wits working once more, made a rapid decision.

"It was the young Duke of—no—" she broke off. "I—really mustn't mention names. It isn't fair."

But she knew that the tide had turned in her favor. It was doubtful whether Mr. Spragge could have forgiven a mere vicar's son such audacity, but his weakness for noble names led him to look softly on the impertinences of a duke. His benign manner returned.

"Oh! you Bright Young People—you Bright Young People," he murmured, wagging a forefinger. "What trouble you land yourselves in! You would be surprised, Lady Frances, at the amount of legal complications that may ensue from an apparently harmless practical joke determined upon the spur of the moment. Just high spirits—but sometimes extremely difficult to settle out of court."

"I think you're too marvelous, Mr. Spragge," said Frankie earnestly. "I do really. Not one person in a thousand would have taken it as you have done. I feel really terribly ashamed."

"No, no, Lady Frances," said Mr. Spragge paternally.

"Oh, but I do. I suppose it was the Rivington woman—what exactly did she tell you?"

"I think I have the letter here. I opened it only half an hour ago."

Frankie held out a hand, and Mr. Spragge put the letter into it with the air of one saying: "There, see for yourself what your foolishness has led you into."

DEAR MR. SPRAGGE, [Mrs. Rivington had written]

It's really too stupid of me, but I've just remembered something that might have helped you the day you called on me. Alan Carstairs mentioned that he was going down to a place called Chipping Somerton. I don't know whether this will be any help to you?

I was *so* interested in what you told me about the Maltravers case.

With kind regards,
Yours sincerely,
EDITH RIVINGTON

"You can see that the matter might have been very grave," said Mr. Spragge severely—but with a severity tempered by benevolence. "I took it that some extremely questionable business was afoot. Whether connected with the Maltravers case or with my client, Mr. Carstairs—"

Frankie interrupted him.

"Was Alan Carstairs a client of yours?" she inquired excitedly.

"He was. He consulted me when he was last in England a month ago. You know Mr. Carstairs, Lady Frances?"

"I think I may say I do," replied Frankie.

"A most attractive personality," said Mr. Spragge. "He brought quite a breath of the—er—wide open spaces into my office."

"He came to consult you about Mr. Savage's will, didn't he?" said Frankie.

"Ah!" said Mr. Spragge. "So it was you who advised him to come to me? He couldn't remember just who it was. I'm sorry I couldn't do more for him."

"Just what did you advise him to do?" asked Frankie. "Or would it be unprofessional to tell me?"

"Not in this case," said Mr. Spragge, smiling. "My opinion was that there was nothing to be done—nothing, that is, unless Mr. Savage's relatives were prepared to spend a lot of money on fighting the case—which I gather they were not prepared, or indeed in a position, to do. I never advise bringing a case into court unless there is every hope of success. The law, Lady Frances, is an uncertain animal. It has twists and turns that surprise the nonlegal mind. Settle out of court has always been my motto."

"The whole thing was very curious," said Frankie thoughtfully.

She had a little the sensation of walking barefoot over a floor covered with tin tacks. At any minute she might step on one—and the game would be up.

"Such cases are less uncommon than you might think," said Mr. Spragge.

"Cases of suicide?" inquired Frankie.

"No, no, I meant cases of undue influence. Mr. Savage was a hard-headed business man, and yet he was clearly as wax in this woman's hands. I've no doubt she knew her business thoroughly."

"I wish you'd tell me the whole story properly," said Frankie boldly. "Mr. Carstairs was—well, was so heated, that I never seemed to get the thing clearly."

"The case was extremely simple," said Mr. Spragge. "I can run over the facts to you—they are accessible to everyone—so there is no objection to my doing so."

"Then tell me all about it," said Frankie.

"Mr. Savage happened to be traveling back from the United States to England in November of last year. He was, as you know, an extremely wealthy man with no near relatives. On this voyage he made the acquaintance of a certain lady—a—er—Mrs. Templeton. Nothing much is known about Mrs. Templeton except that she was a very good-looking woman and had a husband somewhere conveniently in the background."

"The Caymans," thought Frankie.

"These ocean trips are dangerous," went on Mr. Spragge, smiling and shaking his head. "Mr. Savage was clearly very much attracted. He accepted the lady's invitation to come down and stay at her little cottage at Chipping Somerton. Exactly how often he went there I have not been able to ascertain, but there is no doubt that he came more and more under this Mrs. Templeton's influence.

"Then came the tragedy. Mr. Savage had for some time been uneasy about his state of health. He feared that he might be suffering from a certain disease—"

"Cancer?" said Frankie.

"Well, yes, as a matter of fact, cancer. The idea became quite an obsession with him. He was staying with the Templetons at the time. They persuaded him to go up to London and consult a specialist. He did so. Now here, Lady

Frances, I preserve an open mind. That specialist, a very distinguished man who has been at the top of his profession for many years, swore at the inquest that Mr. Savage was not suffering from cancer and that he had told him so, but that Mr. Savage was so obsessed by his own belief that he could not accept the truth when he was told it. Now, strictly without prejudice, Lady Frances, and knowing the medical profession, I think things may have gone a little differently. If Mr. Savage's symptoms puzzled the doctor he may have spoken seriously, pulled a long face, talked of certain expensive treatments, and while reassuring him as to cancer yet have conveyed the impression that something was seriously wrong. Mr. Savage, having heard that doctors usually conceal from a patient the fact that he *is* suffering from that disease, would interpret this according to his own lights. The doctor's reassuring words were *not* true—he *had* got the disease he thought he had.

"Anyway, Mr. Savage came back to Chipping Somerton in a state of great mental distress. He saw ahead of him a painful and lingering death. I understand some members of his family had died of cancer, and he determined not to go through what he had seen them suffer. He sent for a solicitor—a very reputable member of an eminently respectable firm, and the latter drew up a will there and then which Mr. Savage signed and which he then delivered over to the solicitor for safe-keeping. On that same evening Mr. Savage took a large overdose of chloral, leaving a letter behind in which he explained that he preferred a quick and painless death to a long and painful one.

"By his will Mr. Savage left the sum of seven hundred thousand pounds free of legacy duty to Mrs. Templeton, and the remainder to certain specified charities."

Mr. Spragge leaned back in his chair. He was now enjoying himself.

"The jury brought in the usual sympathetic verdict of 'suicide while of unsound mind,' but I do not think that we can argue from that that he was necessarily of unsound mind when he made the will. I do not think that any jury would take it so. The will was made in the presence of a solicitor in whose opinion the deceased was undoubtedly sane and in possession of his senses. Nor do I think we can prove undue influence. Mr. Savage did not disinherit anyone near and dear to him—his only relatives were distant cousins whom he seldom saw. They actually live in Australia, I believe."

Mr. Spragge paused.

"Mr. Carstairs' contention was that such a will was completely uncharacteristic of Mr. Savage. Mr. Savage had no liking for organized charities and had always held very strong opinions as to money passing by blood relationship. However, Mr. Carstairs had no documentary proof of these assertions and, as I pointed out to him, men change their opinions. In contesting such a will there would be the charitable organizations to deal with as well as Mrs. Templeton. Also the will had been admitted to probate."

"There was no fuss made at the time?" asked Frankie.

"As I say, Mr. Savage's relatives were not living in this country and they knew very little about the matter. It was Mr. Carstairs who took the matter up. He returned from a trip into the interior of Africa, gradually learnt the details of this business and came over to this country to see if something could be done about it. I was forced to tell him that in my view there was nothing to be done. Possession is nine points of the law, and Mrs. Templeton was in possession. Moreover, she had left the country and gone, I believe, to the south of France to live. She refused to enter into any communication on the matter. I suggested getting counsel's opinion, but Mr. Carstairs decided that it was not necessary and took my view that there was nothing to be done—or, alternatively, that though something might have been done at the time (and in my opinion that was exceedingly doubtful) it was now too late to do it."

"I see," said Frankie. "And nobody knows anything about this Mrs. Templeton?"

Mr. Spragge shook his head and pursed his lips.

"A man like Mr. Savage, with his knowledge of life, ought to have been less easily taken in, but—" Mr. Spragge shook his head sadly as a vision of innumerable clients, who ought to have known better and who had come to him to have their cases settled out of court, passed across his mind.

Frankie rose.

"Men are extraordinary creatures," she said.

She held out a hand.

"Good-bye, Mr. Spragge," she said. "You've been wonderful—simply wonderful. I feel too ashamed."

"You Bright Young People must be more careful," said Mr. Spragge, shaking his head at her.

"You've been an angel," said Frankie.

She squeezed his hand fervently and departed.

Mr. Spragge sat down again before his table.

He was thinking. "The young Duke of—"

There were only two dukes who could be so described. Which was it?

He picked up a *Peerage*.

26
Nocturnal Adventure

THE INEXPLICABLE ABSENCE of Moira worried Bobby more than he cared to admit. He told himself repeatedly that it was absurd to jump to conclusions—that it was fantastic to imagine that Moira had been done away with in a house full of possible witnesses—that there was probably some perfectly simple explanation and that at the worst she could only be a prisoner in the Grange.

That she had left Staverley of her own free will Bobby did not for one minute believe. He was convinced that she would never have gone off like that without sending him a word of explanation. Besides, she had stated emphatically that she had nowhere to go.

No, the sinister Dr. Nicholson was at the bottom of this. Somehow or other he must have become aware of Moira's activities, and this was his counter-move. Somewhere within the sinister walls of the Grange, Moira was a prisoner, unable to communicate with the outside world.

But she might not remain a prisoner long. Bobby believed implicitly every word Moira had uttered. Her fears were neither the result of a vivid imagination nor the result of nerves. They were simple stark truth.

Nicholson meant to get rid of his wife. Several times his plans had miscarried. Now Moira, by communicating her fears to others, had forced his hand. He must act quickly or not at all. Would he have the nerve to act?

Bobby believed he would. He must know that, even if these strangers had listened to his wife's fears, they had no evidence. Also, he would believe that he had only Frankie to deal with. It was possible that he had suspected her from the first—his pertinent questioning as to her "accident" seemed to point to that. But as Lady Frances' chauffeur Bobby did not believe that he himself was suspected of being anything other than he appeared to be.

Yes, Nicholson would act. Moira's body would probably be found in some district far from Staverley. It might, perhaps, be washed up by the sea. Or it might be found at the foot of a cliff. The thing would appear to be, Bobby was almost sure, an "accident." Nicholson specialized in "accidents."

Nevertheless, Bobby believed that the planning and carrying out of such an accident would need time—not much time, but a certain amount. Nicholson's hand was being forced—he had to act more quickly than he had anticipated. It seemed reasonable to suppose that twenty-four hours at least must elapse before he could put any plan into operation.

Before that interval had elapsed Bobby meant to have found Moira if she were in the Grange.

After he had left Frankie in Brook Street, he started to put his plans into operation. He judged it wise to give the mews a wide berth. For all he knew a watch might be being kept on it. As Hawkins, he believed himself to be still unsuspected. Now "Hawkins" in turn was about to disappear.

That evening a young man with a mustache, dressed in a cheap dark-blue suit, arrived at the bustling little town of Ambledever. He put up at a hotel near the station, registering as George Parker. Having deposited his suitcase there, he strolled out and entered into negotiations for hiring a motorcycle.

At ten o'clock that evening a motorcyclist in cap and goggles passed through the village of Staverley and came to a halt at a deserted part of the road not far from the Grange.

Hastily shoving the bicycle behind some convenient bushes, Bobby looked up and down the road. It was quite deserted.

Then he sauntered along the wall till he came to the little door. As before it was unlocked. With another look up and down the road to make sure he was not observed, Bobby slipped quietly inside. He put his hand into the pocket of his coat where a bulge showed the presence of his Service revolver. The feel of it was reassuring.

Inside the grounds of the Grange everything seemed quiet.

Bobby grinned to himself as he recalled bloodcurdling stories where the villain of the piece kept a cheetah or some exciting beast of prey about the place to deal with intruders.

Dr. Nicholson seemed content with mere bolts and bars, and even there he seemed to be somewhat remiss. Bobby felt certain that this little door should not have been left open. As the villain of the piece Dr. Nicholson seemed regrettably careless.

"No tame pythons," thought Bobby, "no cheetahs, no electrically charged wires—the man is shamefully behind the times."

He made these reflections more to cheer himself up than for any other reason. Every time he thought of Moira a queer constriction seemed to tighten round his heart.

Her face rose in the air before him—the trembling lips—the wide terrified eyes. It was just about here that he had first seen her in the flesh. A little thrill ran through him as he remembered how he had put his arm round her to steady her. . . .

Moira—where was she now? What had that sinister doctor done with her? If only she were still alive . . .

"She must be," said Bobby grimly between set lips. "I'm not going to think anything else."

He made a careful reconnaissance round the house. Some of the upstairs windows had lights in them and there was one lighted window on the ground floor. Toward this window Bobby crept. The curtains were drawn across it, but there was a slight chink between them. Bobby put a knee on the window-sill and hoisted himself noiselessly up. He peered through the slit.

He could see a man's arm and shoulder moving along as though writing. Presently the man shifted his position and his profile came into view. It was Dr. Nicholson.

It was a curious situation. Quite unconscious that he was being watched, the Doctor wrote steadily on. A queer sort of fascination stole over Bobby. The man was so near him that, but for the intervening glass, Bobby could have stretched out his arm and touched him.

For the first time, Bobby felt, he was really seeing the man. It was a forceful profile—the big bold nose, the jutting chin, the crisp, well-shaven line of the jaw. The ears, Bobby noted, were small and laid flat to the head, and the lobe of the ear was actually joined to the cheek. He had an idea that ears like these were said to have some special significance.

The Doctor wrote on, calm and unhurried. Now pausing for a moment or two as though to think of the right word—then setting to once more. His pen moved over the paper, precisely and evenly. Once he took off his pince-nez, polished them, and put them on again.

At last with a sigh, Bobby let himself slide noiselessly to the ground. From the look of it Nicholson would be writing for some time to come. Now was the moment to gain admission to the house.

If Bobby could force an entrance by an upstairs window while the Doctor was writing in his study, he could explore the building at his leisure later in the night.

He made a circuit of the house again and singled out a window on the first floor. The sash was open at the top, but there was no light in the room, so that it was probably unoccupied at the moment. Moreover a very convenient tree seemed to promise an easy means of access.

In another minute Bobby was swarming up the tree. All went well and he was just stretching out his hand to take a grip of the window ledge when an ominous crack came from the branch he was on, and the next minute the bough, a rotten one, had snapped and Bobby was pitchforked head-first into a clump of hydrangea bushes below, which fortunately broke his fall.

The window of Nicholson's study was farther along on the same side of the house. Bobby heard an exclamation in the Doctor's voice, and the window was flung up. Bobby, recovering from the first shock of his fall, sprang up, disentangled himself from the hydrangeas and bolted across a dark patch of shadow into the pathway leading to the little door. He went a short way along it, then dived into the bushes.

He heard the sound of voices and saw lights moving near the trampled and broken hydrangeas. Bobby kept still and held his breath. They might come along the path. If so, finding the door open, they would probably conclude that the intruder had escaped that way and would not prosecute the search further.

However, the minutes passed, and nobody came. Presently Bobby heard Nicholson's voice raised in a question. He did not hear the words but he heard an answer given in a hoarse, rather uneducated voice.

"All present and correct, sir. I've been the rounds."

The sounds gradually died down, the lights disappeared. Everyone seemed to have returned to the house.

Very cautiously Bobby came out of his hiding place. He emerged onto the path listening. All was still. He took a step or two toward the house.

And then out of the darkness, something struck him on the back of the neck. He fell forward . . . into darkeness.

27

"My Brother Was Murdered"

ON FRIDAY MORNING the green Bentley drew up outside the Station Hotel at Ambledever.

Frankie had wired Bobby under the name they had agreed upon—George Parker—that she would be required to give evidence at the inquest on Henry Bassington-ffrench and would call in at Ambledever on the way down from London. She had expected a wire in reply appointing some rendezvous, but nothing had come, so she had come to the hotel.

"Mr. Parker, miss?" said the boots. "I don't think there's any gentlemen of that name stopping here, but I'll see."

He returned a few minutes later.

"Come here Wednesday evening, miss. Left his bag and said he mightn't be in till late. His bag's still here but he hasn't been back to fetch it."

Frankie felt suddenly rather sick. She clutched at a table for support. The man was looking at her sympathetically.

"Feeling bad, miss?" he inquired.

Frankie shook her head. "It's alright," she managed to say. "He didn't leave any message?"

The man went away again and returned shaking his head.

"There's a telegram come for him," he said. "That's all."

He looked at her curiously. "Anything I can do, miss?" he asked.

Frankie shook her head. At the moment she only wanted to get away. She must have time to think what to do next.

"It's alright," she said, and getting into the Bentley she drove away.

The man nodded his head wisely as he looked after her.

"He's done a bunk, he has," he said to himself. "Disappointed her. Given her the slip. A fine rakish piece of goods she is. Wonder what he was like?"

He asked the young lady in the reception office, but the young lady couldn't remember.

"A couple of nobs," said the boots wisely. "Going to get married on the quiet—and he's hooked it."

Meanwhile Frankie was driving in the direction of Staverley, her mind a maze of conflicting emotions.

Why had Bobby not returned to the Station Hotel? There could be only two reasons. Either he was on the trail—and that trail had taken him away somewhere; or else—or else something had gone wrong. The Bentley swerved dangerously. Frankie recovered control just in time.

She was being an idiot—imagining things. Of course Bobby was alright. He was on the trail—that was all—on the trail.

But why, asked another voice, hadn't he sent her a word of reassurance?

That was more difficult to explain, but there were explanations. Difficult circumstances—no time or opportunity—Bobby would know that she, Frankie, wouldn't get the wind up about him. Everything was alright—bound to be.

The inquest passed like a dream. Roger was there, and Sylvia—looking quite beautiful in her widow's weeds. She made an impressive figure and a moving one. Frankie found herself admiring her as though she were admiring a performance at a theater.

The proceedings were very tactfully conducted. The Bassington-ffrenches were popular locally and everything was done to spare the feelings of the widow and the brother of the dead man.

Frankie and Roger gave their evidence—Dr. Nicholson gave his—the dead man's farewell letter was produced. The thing seemed over in no time, and the verdict was given as "Suicide while of unsound mind." The "sympathetic" verdict, as Mr. Spragge had called it.

The two events connected themselves in Frankie's mind. Two suicides "while of unsound mind." Was there—could there be a connection between them?

That this suicide was genuine enough she knew, for she had been on the scene. Bobby's theory of murder had had to be dismissed as untenable. Dr.

Nicholson's alibi was cast-iron—vouched for by the widow herself.

Frankie and Dr. Nicholson remained behind after the other people departed, the Coroner having shaken hands with Sylvia and uttered a few words of sympathy.

"I think there are some letters for you, Frankie dear," said Sylvia. "You won't mind if I leave you now and go and lie down. It's all been so awful."

She shivered and left the room. Nicholson went with her, murmuring something about a sedative.

Frankie turned to Roger. "Roger, Bobby's disappeared."

"Disappeared?"

"Yes!"

"Where and how?"

Frankie explained in a few rapid words.

"And he's not been seen since?" said Roger.

"No. What do you think?"

"I don't like the sound of it," said Roger slowly.

Frankie's heart sank. "You don't think—?"

"Oh! It may be alright, but— Sh, here comes Nicholson."

The Doctor entered the room with his noiseless tread. He was rubbing his hands together and smiling.

"That went off very well," he said. "Very well indeed. Dr. Davidson was most tactful and considerate. We may consider ourselves very lucky to have had him as our local Coroner."

"I suppose so," said Frankie mechanically.

"It makes a lot of difference, Lady Frances. The conduct of an inquest is entirely in the hands of the Coroner. He has wide powers. He can make things easy or difficult as he pleases. In this case everything went off perfectly."

"A good stage performance, in fact," said Frankie in a hard voice.

Nicholson looked at her in surprise.

"I know what Lady Frances is feeling," said Roger. "I feel the same. My brother was murdered, Dr. Nicholson."

He was standing behind the other and did not see, as Frankie did, the startled expression that sprang into the Doctor's eyes.

"I mean what I say," said Roger, interrupting Nicholson as he was about to reply. "The law may not regard it as such, but murder it was. The criminal brutes who induced my brother to become a slave to that drug murdered him just as truly as if they had struck him down."

He had moved a little and his angry eyes now looked straight into the Doctor's.

"I mean to get even with them," he said, and the words sounded like a threat.

Dr. Nicholson's pale-blue eyes fell before his. He shook his head sadly.

"I cannot say I disagree with you," he said. "I know more about drug-taking than you do, Mr. Bassington-ffrench. To induce a man to take drugs is indeed a most terrible crime."

Ideas were whirling through Frankie's head—one idea in particular.

"It can't be," she was saying to herself. "That would be too monstrous. And yet—his whole alibi depends on her word. But in that case—"

She roused herself to find Nicholson speaking to her.

"You came down by car, Lady Frances? No accident this time?"

Frankie felt she simply hated that smile.

"No," she said. "I think it's a pity to go in too much for accidents—don't you?"

She wondered whether she had imagined it, or whether his eyelids really flickered for a moment.

"Perhaps your chauffeur drove you this time?"

"My chauffeur," said Frankie, "has disappeared."

She looked straight at Nicholson.

"Indeed?"

"He was last seen heading for the Grange," went on Frankie.

Nicholson raised his eyebrows.

"Really? Have I—some attraction in the kitchen?" His voice sounded amused. "I can hardly believe it."

"At any rate that is where he was last seen," said Frankie.

"You sound quite dramatic," said Nicholson. "Possibly you are paying too much attention to local gossip. Local gossip is very unreliable. I have heard the wildest stories." He paused. His voice altered slightly in tone. "I have even had a story brought to my ears that my wife and your chauffeur had been seen talking together down by the river." Another pause. "He was, I believe, a very superior young man, Lady Frances."

"Is that it?" thought Frankie. "Is he going to pretend that his wife has run off with my chauffeur? Is that his little game?"

Aloud she said, "Hawkins is quite above the average chauffeur."

"So it seems," said Nicholson. He turned to Roger. "I must be going. Believe me, all my sympathies are with you and Mrs. Bassington-ffrench."

Roger went out into the hall with him. Frankie followed. On the hall table were a couple of letters addressed to her. One was a bill. The other—

Her heart gave a leap.

The other was in Bobby's handwriting.

Nicholson and Roger were on the doorstep.

She tore it open.

DEAR FRANKIE, [wrote Bobby]

I'm on the trail at last. Follow me as soon as possible to Chipping Somerton. You'd better come by train and not by car. The Bentley is too noticeable. The trains aren't too good, but you can get there alright. You're to come to a house called Tudor Cottage. I'll explain to you just exactly how to find it. Don't ask the way. [Here followed some minute directions.] Have you got that clear? Don't tell *anyone*. [This was heavily underlined.] *No one at all.*

Yours ever,
BOBBY

Frankie crushed the letter excitedly in the palm of her hand. So it was alright! Nothing dreadful had overtaken Bobby.

He was on the trail—and by a coincidence on the same trail as herself. She had been to Somerset House to look up the will of John Savage. "Rose Emily Templeton" was given as the wife of Edgar Templeton of Tudor Cottage, Chipping Somerton. And that again had fitted in with the open A.B.C. in the St. Leonard's Gardens house. Chipping Somerton had been one of the stations on the open page. The Caymans had gone to Chipping Somerton.

Everything was falling into place. They were nearing the end of the chase.

Roger Bassington-ffrench turned and came toward her.

"Anything interesting in your letter?" he inquired casually.

For a moment Frankie hesitated. Surely Bobby had not meant Roger when he adjured her to tell nobody?

Then she remembered the heavy underlining—remembered, too, her recent monstrous idea. If *that* were true, Roger might betray them both in all innocence. She dared not hint to him her own suspicions.

So she made up her mind. "No," she said. "Nothing at all."

She was to repent her decision bitterly before twenty-four hours had passed.

More than once in the course of the next few hours did she regret Bobby's dictum that the car was not to be used. Chipping Somerton was no very great distance as the crow flies, but the journey involved changing three times, with a long, dreary wait at a country station each time, and to one of Frankie's impatient temperament this slow method of procedure was extremely hard to endure with fortitude.

Still, she felt bound to admit that there was something in what Bobby had said. The Bentley *was* a noticeable car. Her excuses for leaving it at Merroway had been of the flimsiest, but she had been unable to think of anything brilliant on the spur of the moment.

It was getting dark when Frankie's train, an extremely deliberate and thoughtful train, drew into the little station of Chipping Somerton. To Frankie it seemed more like midnight. The train seemed to her to have been ambling on for hours and hours. It was just beginning to rain, too, which was additionally trying.

She buttoned up her coat to her neck, took a last look at Bobby's letter by the light of the station lamp, got the directions clearly in her head and set off.

The instructions were quite easy to follow. Frankie saw the lights of the village ahead and turned off to the left up a lane which led steeply up hill. At the top of the lane she took the right-hand fork and presently saw the little cluster of houses that formed the village lying below her and a belt of pine trees ahead. Finally, she came to a neat wooden gate and striking a match saw "Tudor Cottage" written on it.

There was no one about. Frankie slipped up the latch and passed inside. She could make out the outlines of the house behind a belt of pine trees. She took up her post within the trees where she could get a clear view of the house. Then, her heart beating a little faster, she gave the best imitation she could of the hoot of an owl. A few minutes passed and nothing happened. She repeated the call.

The door of the cottage opened and she saw a figure in chauffeur's dress peer cautiously out. Bobby! He made a beckoning gesture, then withdrew inside, leaving the door ajar.

Frankie came out from the trees and up to the door. There was no light in any window. Everything was perfectly dark and silent.

Frankie stepped gingerly over the threshold into a dark hall. She stopped, peering about her.

"Bobby?" she whispered.

It was her nose that gave her warning. Where had she known that smell before—that heavy, sweet odor?

Just as her brain gave the answer "Chloroform," strong arms seized her from behind. She opened her mouth to scream and a wet pad was clapped over it. The sweet, cloying smell filled her nostrils.

She fought desperately, twisting and turning, kicking. But it was of no avail. Despite the fight she put up she felt herself succumbing. There was a drumming in her ears, she felt herself choking. And then she knew no more . . .

28
At the Eleventh Hour

WHEN FRANKIE CAME to herself the immediate reactions were depressing. There is nothing romantic about the aftereffects of chloroform. She was lying on an extremely hard wooden floor, and her hands and feet were tied. She managed to roll herself over, and her head nearly collided violently with a battered coalbox. Various distressing events then occurred.

A few minutes later Frankie was able, if not to sit up, at least to take notice.

Close at hand she heard a faint groan. She peered about her. As far as she could make out she seemed to be in a kind of attic. The only light came from a skylight in the roof, and at this moment there was very little of that. In a few minutes it would be quite dark. There were a few broken pictures lying against the wall—a dilapidated iron bed, and some broken chairs, and the coal scuttle before mentioned.

The groan seemed to have come from the corner.

Frankie's bonds were not very tight. They permitted motion of a somewhat crablike type. She wormed her way across the dusty floor.

"Bobby!" she ejaculated.

Bobby it was, also tied hand and foot. In addition he had a piece of cloth bound round his mouth. This he had almost succeeded in working loose. Frankie came to his assistance. In spite of being bound together her hands were still of some use, and a final vigorous pull with the teeth finally did the job.

Rather stiffly Bobby managed to ejaculate, "Frankie!"

"I'm glad we're together," said Frankie. "But it does look as though we'd been had for mugs."

"I suppose," said Bobby gloomily, "it's what they call a 'fair cop.'"

"How did they get you?" demanded Frankie. "Was it after you wrote that letter to me?"

"What letter? I never wrote any letter!"

"Oh, I see!" said Frankie, her eyes opening. "What an idiot I have been! And all that stuff in it about not telling a soul."

"Look here, Frankie, I'll tell you what happened to me and then you carry on the good work and tell me what happened to you."

He described his adventures at the Grange and their sinister sequel.

"I came to in this beastly hole," he said. "There was some food and drink on a tray. I was frightfully hungry and I had some. I think it must have been doped for I fell asleep almost immediately. What day is it?"

"Friday."

"And I was knocked out on Wednesday evening. Dash it all, I've been pretty well unconscious all the time. Now tell me what happened to you."

Frankie recounted her adventures beginning with the story she had heard from Mr. Spragge and carrying on until she thought she recognized Bobby's figure in the doorway.

"And then they chloroformed me," she finished. "And, oh, Bobby, I've just been sick in a coal-bucket!"

"I call that very resourceful of you, Frankie," said Bobby approvingly. "With your hands tied and everything. The thing is—what are we going to do now? We've had it our own way for a long time, but now the tables are turned."

"If only I'd told Roger about your letter," lamented Frankie. "I did think of it and wavered—and then I decided to do exactly what you said and tell nobody at all."

"With the result that no one knows where we are," said Bobby, gravely. "Frankie, my dear, I'm afraid I've landed you in a mess."

"We got a bit too sure of ourselves," said Frankie somberly.

"The only thing I can't make out is why they didn't knock us both on the head straight away," mused Bobby. "I don't think Nicholson would stick at a little trifle like that."

"He's got a plan," said Frankie with a slight shiver.

"Well, we'd better have one too. We've got to get out of this, Frankie. How are we going to do it?"

"We can shout," said Frankie.

"Ye-es," said Bobby. "Somebody might be passing and hear. But from the fact that Nicholson didn't gag you I should say that the chances in that direction are pretty poor. Your hands are more loosely tied than mine. Let's see if I can get them undone with my teeth."

The next five minutes were spent in a struggle that did credit to Bobby's dentist.

"Extraordinary how easy these things sound in books," he panted. "I don't believe I'm making the slightest impression."

"You are," said Frankie. "It's loosening. Look out, there's somebody coming."

She rolled away from him. A step could be heard mounting a stair, a ponderous tread. A gleam of light appeared under the door. Then there was the sound of a key being turned in the lock. The door swung slowly open.

"And how are my two little birds?" said the voice of Dr. Nicholson.

He carried a candle in one hand, and though he was wearing a hat pulled down over his eyes and a heavy overcoat with the collar turned up, his voice would have betrayed him anywhere. His eyes glittered palely behind the strong glasses.

He shook his head at them playfully.

"Unworthy of you, my dear young lady," he said. "To fall into the trap so easily."

Neither Bobby nor Frankie made any reply. The honors of the situation so obviously lay with Nicholson that it was difficult to know what to say.

Nicholson put the candle down on a chair.

"At any rate," he said, "let me see if you are comfortable."

He examined Bobby's fastenings, nodded his head approvingly and passed on to Frankie. There he shook his head.

"As they truly used to say to me in my youth," he remarked, "fingers were made before forks—and teeth were used before fingers. Your young friend's teeth, I see, have been active."

A heavy, broken-backed oak chair was standing in a corner.

Nicholson picked up Frankie, deposited her on the chair and tied her securely to it.

"Not too uncomfortable, I trust?" he said. "Well, it isn't for long."

Frankie found her tongue. "What are you going to do with us?" she demanded.

Nicholson walked to the door and picked up his candle.

"You taunted me, Lady Frances, with being too fond of accidents. Perhaps I am. At any rate, I am going to risk one more accident."

"What do you mean?" said Bobby.

"Shall I tell you? Yes, I think I will. Lady Frances Derwent, driving her car, her chauffeur beside her, mistakes a turning and takes a disused road leading to a quarry. The car crashes over the edge. Lady Frances and her chauffeur are killed."

There was a slight pause, then Bobby said:

"But we mightn't be. Plans go awry sometimes. One of yours did down in Wales."

"Your tolerance of morphia was certainly very remarkable, and—from our point of view—regrettable," said Nicholson. "But you need have no anxiety on my behalf this time. You and Lady Frances will be quite dead when your bodies are discovered."

Bobby shivered in spite of himself. There had been a queer note in Nicholson's voice—it was the tone of an artist contemplating a masterpiece.

"He enjoys this," thought Bobby. "Really enjoys it."

He was not going to give Nicholson any more cause for enjoyment than he had to, so he said in a casual tone of voice, "You're making a mistake—especially where Lady Frances is concerned."

"Yes," said Frankie. "In that very clever letter you forged you told me to tell nobody. Well, I made just one exception. I told Roger Bassington-ffrench. He knows all about you. If anything happens to us, he will know who is responsible for it. You'd better let us go and clear out of the country as fast as you can."

Nicholson was silent for a moment. Then he said, "A good bluff—but I call it."

He turned to the door.

"What about your wife, you swine?" cried Bobby. "Have you murdered her too?"

"Moira is still alive," said Nicholson. "How much longer she will remain so, I do not really know. It depends on circumstances."

He made them a mocking little bow.

"Au revoir," he said. "It will take me a couple of hours to complete my arrangements. You may enjoy talking the matter over. I shall not gag you unless it becomes necessary. You understand? Any calls for help and I return and deal with the matter."

He went out and closed and locked the door behind him.

"It isn't true," said Bobby. "It can't be true. These things don't happen."

But he could not help feeling that they were going to happen—and to him and Frankie.

"In books there's always an eleventh-hour rescue," said Frankie, trying to speak hopefully.

But she was not feeling very hopeful. In fact, her morale was decidedly low.

"The whole thing's so impossible," said Bobby as though pleading with someone. "So fantastic. Nicholson himself was absolutely unreal. I wish an eleventh-hour rescue were possible, but I can't see who's going to rescue us."

"If only I'd told Roger!" wailed Frankie.

"Perhaps in spite of everything Nicholson believes you have," suggested Bobby.

"No," said Frankie. "The suggestion didn't go down at all. The man's too damned clever."

"He's been too clever for us," said Bobby gloomily. "Frankie, do you know what annoys me most about this business?"

"No. What?"

"That even now, when we're going to be hurled into the next world, we still don't know who Evans is."

"Let's ask him," said Frankie. "You know—a last-minute boon. He can't refuse to tell us. I agree with you that I simply can't die without having my curiosity satisfied."

There was a silence, then Bobby asked: "Do you think we ought to yell for help—a sort of last chance? It's about the only chance we've got."

"Not yet," said Frankie. "In the first place I don't believe anyone would hear—he would never have risked keeping us here if anybody could—and in the second place I feel I just can't bear waiting here to be killed without being able to speak or be spoken to. Let's leave shouting till the last possible moment. It's—it's so comforting having you to talk to." Her voice wavered a little over the last words.

"I've got you into an awful mess, Frankie."

"Oh, that's alright. You couldn't have kept me out. I wanted to come in. Bobby, do you think he'll really pull it off? Us, I mean."

"I'm terribly afraid he will. He's so damnably efficient."

"Bobby, do you believe now that it was he who killed Henry Bassington-ffrench?"

"If it were possible—"

"It *is* possible, granted one thing—*that Sylvia Bassington-ffrench is in it too.*"

"Frankie!"

"I know. I was just as horrified when the idea occurred to me. But it fits. Why was Sylvia so dense about the morphia? Why did she resist so obstinately when we wanted her to send her husband somewhere else instead of the Grange? And then she was in the house when the shot was fired—"

"She might have done it herself."

"Oh, no—surely!"

"Yes, she might. And then have given the key of the study to Nicholson to put in Henry's pocket."

"It's all crazy," said Frankie in a hopeless voice. "Like looking through a distorting mirror. All the people who seemed most alright are really all wrong—all the nice, everyday people. There ought to be some way of telling criminals—eyebrows or ears or something."

"My God!" cried Bobby.

"What is it?"

"Frankie, that wasn't Nicholson who came here just now!"

"Have you gone quite mad? Who was it then?"

"I don't know—but it wasn't Nicholson. All along I felt there was something wrong—but couldn't spot it, and your saying 'ears' has given me the clue. When I was watching Nicholson the other evening through the window I specially noticed his ears—the lobes are joined to his face. But this man tonight—his ears weren't like that."

"But what does it mean?" Frankie asked hopelessly.

"This is a very clever actor impersonating Nicholson."

"But why—and who could it be?"

"Bassington-ffrench," breathed Bobby. "*Roger Bassington-ffrench.* We spotted the right man at the beginning and then—like idiots, we went astray after red herrings."

"Bassington-ffrench?" whispered Frankie. "Bobby, you're right. It must be. He was the only person there when I taunted Nicholson about accidents."

"Then it really *is* all up," said Bobby. "I've still had a kind of sneaking hope that possibly Roger Bassington-ffrench might nose out our trail by some miracle. But now the last hope's gone. Moira's a prisoner, you and I are tied hand and foot. Nobody else has the least idea where we are. The game's up, Frankie."

As he finished speaking there was a sound overhead. The next minute, with a terrific crash, a heavy body fell through the skylight.

It was too dark to see anything.

"What the devil—" began Bobby.

From amidst a pile of broken glass a voice spoke.

"B-B-B-Bobby," it said.

"Well, I'm damned," said Bobby. "It's Badger!"

29
Badger's Story

THERE WAS NOT a minute to be lost. Already sounds could be heard on the floor below.

"Quick, Badger, you fool!" said Bobby. "Pull one of my boots off. Don't argue or ask questions! Haul it off somehow. Chuck it down in the middle there and crawl under that bed. *Quick*—I tell you."

Steps were ascending the stairs. The key turned.

Nicholson—the pseudo-Nicholson—stood in the doorway, candle in hand.

He saw Bobby and Frankie as he had left them, but in the middle of the floor was a pile of broken glass and in the middle of the broken glass was a boot!

Nicholson stared in amazement from the boot to Bobby. Bobby's left foot was bootless.

"Very clever, my young friend," he said drily. "Extremely acrobatic."

He came over to Bobby, examined the ropes that bound him and tied a couple of extra knots. He looked at him curiously.

"I wish I knew how you managed to throw that boot through the skylight. It seems almost incredible. A touch of the Houdini about you, my friend."

He looked at them both, up at the broken skylight, then shrugging his shoulders he left the room.

"Quick, Badger."

Badger crawled out from under the bed. He had a pocket-knife and with its aid he soon cut the other two free.

"That's better," said Bobby, stretching himself "Whew! I'm stiff. Well, Frankie? What about our friend Nicholson?"

"You're right," said Frankie. "It's Roger Bassington-ffrench. Now that I *know* he's Roger playing the part of Nicholson, I can *see* it. But it's a pretty good performance all the same."

"Entirely voice and pince-nez," said Bobby.

"I was at Oxford with a B-B-B-Bassington-ffrench," said Badger. "M-m-m-marvelous actor. B-b-b-bad hat, though. B-b-b-bad business about forging his p-p-p-pater's n-n-n-name to a check. Old m-m-man hushed it up."

In the minds of both Bobby and Frankie was the same thought. Badger, whom they had judged it wiser not to take into their confidence, could all along have given them valuable information!

"Forgery," said Frankie thoughtfully. "That letter from you, Bobby, was remarkably well done. I wonder how he knew your handwriting?"

"If he's in with the Caymans he probably saw my letter about the Evans business."

The voice of Badger rose plaintively.

"W-w-w-what are we going to do next?" he inquired.

"We're going to take up a comfortable position behind this door," said

Bobby. "And when our friend returns—which I imagine won't be for a little while yet—you and I are going to spring on him from behind and give him the surprise of his life. How about it, Badger? Are you game?"

"Oh, absolutely!"

"As for you, Frankie, when you hear his step you'd better get back onto your chair. He'll see you as soon as he opens the door and will come in without any suspicion."

"Alright," said Frankie. "And once you and Badger have got him down I'll join in and bite his ankles or something."

"That's the true womanly spirit," said Bobby approvingly. "Now, let's all sit close together on the floor here and hear all about things. I want to know what miracle brought Badger through that skylight just in the nick of time."

"Well, you s-s-see," said Badger, "after you w-w-went off, I got into a bit of a m-m-m-mess."

He paused. Gradually the story was extracted—a tale of liabilities, creditors, and bailiffs—a typical Badger catastrophe. Bobby had gone off leaving no address, only saying that he was driving the Bentley down to Staverley. So to Staverley came Badger.

"I thought p-p-p-perhaps you m-m-m-might be able to let me have a f-f-fiver," he explained.

Bobby's heart smote him. To aid Badger in his enterprise he had come to London and had promptly deserted his post to go off sleuthing with Frankie. And even now the faithful Badger uttered no word of reproach.

Badger had no wish to endanger Bobby's mysterious enterprises, but he was of the opinion that a car like the green Bentley would not be difficult to find in a place the size of Staverley. As a matter of fact he came across the car before he got to Staverley, for it was standing outside a pub—empty.

"S-s-so I thought," went on Badger, "that I'd give you a little s-s-s-surprise, don't you know? There were some r-r-rugs and things in the b-b-back and nobody about. I g-g-got in and p-p-p-pulled them over me. I thought I'd give you the s-s-surprise of your life."

What actually happened was that a chauffeur in green livery had emerged from the pub and that Badger, peering from his place of concealment, was thunderstruck to perceive that this chauffeur was not Bobby. He had an idea that the face was in some way familiar to him but couldn't place the man. The stranger got into the car and drove off.

Badger was in a predicament. He did not know what to do next. Explanations and apologies were difficult, and in any case it is not easy to explain to someone who is driving a car at sixty miles an hour. Badger decided to lie low and sneak out of the car when it stopped.

The car finally reached its destination—Tudor Cottage. The chauffeur drove it into the garage and left it there, but on going out he shut the garage doors. Badger was a prisoner. There was a small window at one side of the garage and through this, about half an hour later, Badger had observed Frankie's approach, her whistle and her admission into the house.

The whole business puzzled Badger greatly. He began to suspect that something was wrong. At any rate he determined to have a look round for himself and see what it was all about.

With the help of some tools lying about in the garage he succeeded in picking the lock of the garage door and set out on a tour of inspection. The windows on the ground floor were all shuttered, but he thought that by getting onto the roof he might manage to have a look into some of the upper windows. The roof presented no difficulties. There was a convenient pipe running up the garage, and from the garage roof to the roof of the cottage was an easy climb. In the course of his prowling Badger had come upon the skylight. Nature and Badger's weight had done the rest.

Bobby drew a long breath as the narrative came to an end.

"All the same," he said reverently, "you are a miracle—a singularly beautiful miracle! But for you, Badger, my lad, Frankie and I would have been little corpses in about an hour's time."

He gave Badger a condensed account of the activities of himself and Frankie. Toward the end, he broke off.

"Someone's coming. Get to your post, Frankie. Now then, this is where our playacting Bassington-ffrench gets the surprise of his life."

Frankie arranged herself in a depressed attitude on the broken chair. Badger and Bobby stood ready behind the door.

The steps came up the stairs, a line of candle-light showed underneath the door. The key was put in the lock and turned, the door swung open. The light of the candle disclosed Frankie drooping dejectedly on her chair. Their jailor stepped through the doorway.

Then, joyously, Badger and Bobby sprang.

The proceedings were short and decisive. Taken utterly by surprise, the man was knocked down, the candle flew wide and was retrieved by Frankie, and a few seconds later the three friends stood looking down with malicious pleasure at a figure securely bound with the same ropes that had previously secured two of them.

"Good evening, Mr. Bassington-ffrench," said Bobby, and if the exultation in his voice was a little crude, who shall blame him?—"It's a nice night for the funeral."

30
Escape

THE MAN ON the floor stared up at them. His pince-nez had flown off and so had his hat. There could be no further attempt at disguise. Slight traces of makeup were visible about the eyebrows, but otherwise the face was the pleasant, slightly vacuous face of Roger Bassington-ffrench.

He spoke in his own agreeable tenor voice, its note that of pleasant solioquy.

"Very interesting," he said. "I really knew quite well that no man tied up as you were *could* have thrown a boot through that skylight. But because the boot was there among the broken glass I took it for cause and effect and assumed that, though it was impossible, the impossible had been achieved. An interesting light on the limitations of the brain."

As nobody spoke, he went on still in the same reflective voice.

"So, after all, you've won the round. Most unexpected and extremely regrettable. I thought I'd got you all fooled nicely."

"So you had," said Frankie. "You forged that letter from Bobby, I suppose?"

"I have a talent that way," said Roger modestly.

"And Bobby?"

Lying on his back, smiling agreeably, Roger seemed to take a positive pleasure in enlightening them.

"I knew he'd go to the Grange. I only had to wait about in the bushes near the path. I was just behind him there when he retreated after rather clumsily falling off a tree. I let the hubbub die down and then got him neatly on the back of the neck with a sandbag. All I had to do was to carry him out to where my car was waiting, shove him in the dickey and drive him here. I was at home again before morning."

"And Moira?" demanded Bobby. "Did you entice her away somehow?"

Roger chuckled. The question seemed to amuse him. "Forgery is a very useful art, my dear Jones," he said.

"You swine," said Bobby.

Frankie intervened. She was still full of curiosity, and their prisoner seemed in an obliging mood.

"Why did you pretend to be Dr. Nicholson?" she asked.

"Why did I now?" Roger seemed to be asking the question of himself. "Partly, I think, the fun of seeing whether I could spoof you both. You were so very sure that poor old Nicholson was in it up to the neck." He laughed, and Frankie blushed. "Just because he cross-questioned you a bit about the details of your accident—in his pompous way. It was an irritating fad of his—accuracy in details."

"And really," said Frankie slowly, "he was quite innocent?"

"As a child unborn," said Roger. "But he did *me* a good turn. He drew my attention to that accident of yours. That and another incident made me realize that you mightn't be quite the innocent young thing you seemed to be. And then I was standing by you when you telephoned one morning and I heard your chauffeur's voice say 'Frankie.' I've got pretty good hearing. I suggested coming up to town with you and you agreed—but you were very much relieved when I changed my mind. After that—" He stopped and as far as he was able shrugged his bound shoulders. "It was rather fun seeing you get all worked up about Nicholson. He's a harmless old ass, but he does look exactly like a scientific super-criminal on the films. I thought I might as well keep the deception up. After all, you never know. The best-laid plans go wrong, as my present predicament shows."

"There's one thing you *must* tell me," said Frankie. "I've been driven nearly mad with curiosity. Who is Evans?"

"Oh!" said Bassington-ffrench. "So you don't know that?"

He laughed—and laughed again.

"That's rather amusing," he said. "It shows what a fool one can be."

"Meaning us?" asked Frankie.

"No," said Roger. "In this case, meaning me. Do you know, if you don't know who Evans is, I don't think I shall tell you. I'll keep that to myself as my own little secret."

The position was a curious one. They had turned the tables on Bassington-ffrench, and yet, in some peculiar way, he had robbed them of their triumph. Lying on the floor, bound and a prisoner, it was he who dominated the situation.

"And what are your plans now, may I ask?" he inquired.

Nobody had as yet evolved any plans. Bobby rather doubtfully murmured something about police.

"Much the best thing to do," said Roger cheerfully. "Ring them up and hand me over to them. The charge will be abduction, I suppose. I can't very well deny that." He looked at Frankie. "I shall plead a guilty passion."

Frankie reddened. "What about murder?" she asked.

"My dear, you haven't any evidence. Positively none. Think it over and you'll see you haven't."

"Badger," said Bobby, "you'd better stay here and keep an eye on him. I'll go down and ring up the police."

"You'd better be careful," said Frankie. "We don't know how many of them there may be in the house."

"No one but me," said Roger. "I was carrying this through single-handed."

"I'm not prepared to take your word for that," said Bobby gruffly.

He bent over and tested the knots.

"He's alright," he said. "Safe as houses. We'd better all go down together. We can lock the door."

"Terribly distrustful, aren't you, my dear chap?" said Roger. "There's a pistol in my pocket if you'd like it. It may make you feel happier, and it's certainly no good to me in my present position."

Ignoring the other's mocking tone, Bobby bent down and extracted the weapon.

"Kind of you to mention it," he said. "If you want to know, it does make me feel happier."

"Good," said Roger. "It's loaded."

Bobby took the candle and they filed out of the attic, leaving Roger lying on the floor. Bobby locked the door and put the key in his pocket. He held the pistol in his hand.

"I'll go first," he said. "We've got to be quite sure and not make a mess of things now."

"He's a qu-qu-queer chap, isn't he?" said Badger with a jerk of his head backward in the direction of the room they had left.

"He's a damned good loser," said Frankie.

Even now, she was not quite free from the charm of that very remarkable young man, Roger Bassington-ffrench.

A rather rickety flight of steps led down to the main landing. Everything was quiet. Bobby looked over the banisters. The telephone was in the hall below.

"We'd better look into these rooms first," he said. "We don't want to be taken in the rear."

Badger flung open each door in turn. Of the four bedrooms, three were empty. In the fourth a slender figure was lying on the bed.

"It's Moira!" cried Frankie.

The others crowded in. Moira was lying like one dead except that her breast moved up and down ever so slightly.

"Is she asleep?" asked Bobby.

"She's drugged, I think," said Frankie.

She looked round. A hypodermic syringe lay on a little enamel tray on a table near the window. There was also a little spirit-lamp and a type of morphia hypodermic needle.

"She'll be alright, I think," she said. "But we ought to get a doctor."

"Let's go down and telephone," said Bobby.

They adjourned to the hall below. Frankie had a half fear that the telephone wires might be cut, but her fears proved quite unfounded. They got through to the police station quite easily, but found a good deal of difficulty in explaining matters. The local police were highly disposed to regard the summons as a practical joke.

However, they were convinced at last, and Bobby replaced the receiver with a sigh. He had explained that they also wanted a doctor, and the police constable promised to bring one along.

Ten minutes later a car arrived with an inspector, a constable, and an elderly man who had his profession stamped all over him.

Bobby and Frankie received them and after explaining matters once more in a somewhat perfunctory fashion led the way to the attic. Bobby unlocked the door—then stood dumbfounded in the doorway. In the middle of the floor was a heap of severed ropes. Underneath the broken skylight a chair had been placed on the bed which had been dragged out till it was under the skylight.

Of Roger Bassington-ffrench there was no sign.

"Talk of Houdini," said Bobby. "He must have out-Houdini'd Houdini. How the devil did he cut these cords?"

"He must have had a knife in his pocket," said Frankie.

"Even then, how could he get at it? Both hands were bound together behind his back."

The inspector coughed. All his former doubts had returned. He was more strongly disposed than ever to regard the whole thing as a hoax.

Frankie and Bobby found themselves telling a long story which sounded more impossible every minute.

The doctor was their salvation. On being taken to the room where Moira was lying he declared at once that she had been drugged with morphia or some preparation of opium. He did not consider her condition serious and thought she would awake naturally in four or five hours' time.

He suggested taking her off then and there to a good nursing home in the neighborhood.

To this Bobby and Frankie agreed, not seeing what else could be done. Having given their own names and addresses to the inspector, who appeared to disbelieve utterly in Frankie's, they themselves were allowed to leave

Tudor Cottage, and with the assistance of the inspector succeeded in gaining admission to the "Seven Stars" in the village.

Here, still feeling that they were regarded as criminals, they were only too thankful to go to their rooms, a double one for Bobby and Badger, and a very minute single one for Frankie.

A few minutes after they had all retired, a knock came on Bobby's door. It was Frankie.

"I've thought of something," she said. "If that fool of a police inspector persists in thinking that we made all this up, at any rate I've got evidence that I was chloroformed."

"Have you? Where?"

"In the coal-bucket," said Frankie with decision.

31
Frankie Asks a Question

EXHAUSTED BY ALL her adventures, Frankie slept late the next morning. It was half-past ten when she came down to the small coffee room to find Bobby waiting for her.

"Hullo, Frankie, here you are at last."

"Don't be so horribly vigorous, my dear!" Frankie subsided onto a chair.

"What will you have? They've got haddock and eggs and bacon and cold ham."

"I shall have some toast and weak tea," said Frankie, quelling him. "What is the matter with you?"

"It must be the sandbagging," said Bobby. "It's probably broken up adhesions in the brain. I feel absolutely full of pep and vim and bright ideas and a longing to dash out and do things."

"Well, why not dash?" said Frankie languidly.

"I have dashed. I've been with Inspector Hammond for the last half-hour. We'll have to let it go as a practical joke, Frankie, for the moment."

"Oh, but, Bobby—"

"I said *for the moment*. We've got to get to the bottom of this, Frankie. We're on the right spot and all we've got to do is to get down to it. We don't want Roger Bassington-ffrench for abduction. We want him for *murder*."

"And we'll get him," said Frankie with a revival of spirit.

"That's more like it," said Bobby approvingly. "Drink some more tea."

"How's Moira?"

"Pretty bad. She came round in the most awful state of nerves. Scared stiff apparently. She's gone up to London—to a nursing home place in Queen's Gate. She says she'll feel safe there. She was terrified here."

"She never did have much nerve," said Frankie.

"Well, anyone might be scared stiff with a queer cold-blooded murderer like Roger Bassington-ffrench loose in the neighborbood."

"He doesn't want to murder *her*. We're the ones he's after."

"He's probably too busy taking care of himself to worry about us for the moment," said Bobby. "Now, Frankie, we've got to get down to it. The start of the whole thing must be John Savage's death and will. There's something wrong about it. Either that will was forged or Savage was murdered or something."

"It's quite likely the will was forged if Bassington-ffrench was concerned," said Frankie thoughtfully. "Forgery seems to be his speciality."

"It may have been forgery *and* murder. We've got to find out."

Frankie nodded. "I've got the notes I made after looking at the will. The witnesses were Rose Chudleigh, cook, and Albert Mere, gardener. They ought to be quite easy to find. Then there are the lawyers who drew it up—Elford & Leigh—a very respectable firm, as Mr. Spragge said."

"Right, we'll start from there. I think you'd better take the lawyers. You'll get more out of them than I would. I'll hunt up Rose Chudleigh and Albert Mere."

"What about Badger?"

"Badger never gets up till lunch time—you needn't worry about him."

"We must get his affairs straightened out for him some time," said Frankie. "After all, he did save my life."

"They'll soon get tangled again," said Bobby. "Oh, by the way, what do you think of this?"

He held out a dirty piece of cardboard for her inspection. It was a photograph.

"Mr. Cayman," said Frankie immediately. "Where did you get it?"

"Last night. It had slipped down behind the telephone."

"Then it seems pretty clear who Mr. and Mrs. Templeton were. Wait a minute."

A waitress had just approached bearing toast. Frankie displayed the photograph.

"Do you know who that is?" she asked.

The waitress regarded the photograph, her head a little on one side. "Now, I've seen the gentleman—but I can't quite call to mind. Oh, yes—it's the gentleman who had Tudor Cottage—Mr. Templeton. They've gone away now—somewhere abroad, I believe."

"What sort of man was he?" asked Frankie.

"I really couldn't say. They didn't come down here very often—just weekends now and then. Nobody saw much of him. Mrs. Templeton was a very nice lady. But they hadn't had Tudor Cottage very long—only about six months—when a very rich gentleman died and left Mrs. Templeton all his money, and they went to live abroad. They never sold Tudor Cottage, though. I think they sometimes lend it to people for weekends. But I don't suppose with all that money they'll ever come back here and live in it themselves."

"They had a cook called Rose Chudleigh, didn't they?" asked Frankie.

But the girl seemed uninterested in cooks. Being left a fortune by a rich gentleman was what really stirred her imagination. In answer to Frankie's question she replied that she couldn't say, she was sure, and withdrew carrying an empty toast-rack.

"That's all plain sailing," said Frankie. "The Caymans have given up coming here, but they keep the place on for the convenience of the gang."

They agreed to divide the labor as Bobby had suggested. Frankie went off in the Bentley, having smartened herself up by a few local purchases, and Bobby went off in quest of Albert Mere, gardener.

They met at lunch time.

"Well?" demanded Bobby.

Frankie shook her head. "Forgery's out of the question." She spoke in a dispirited voice. "I spent a long time with Mr. Elford—he's rather an old dear. He'd got wind of some of our doings last night and was wild to hear a few details. I don't suppose they get much excitement down here. Anyway, I soon got him eating out of my hand. Then I discussed the Savage case—pretended I'd met some of the Savage relations and that they'd hinted at forgery. At that my old dear bristled up—absolutely out of the question! It wasn't a question of letters or anything like that. He saw Mr. Savage himself, and Mr. Savage insisted on the will's being drawn up then and there. Mr. Elford wanted to go away and do it properly—you know how they do—sheets and sheets all about nothing—"

"I don't know," said Bobby. "I've never made any wills."

"I have—two. The second was this morning. I had to have some excuse for seeing a lawyer."

"Whom did you leave your money to?"

"You."

"That was a bit thoughtless, wasn't it? If Roger Bassington-ffrench succeeded in bumping you off I should probably be hanged for it!"

"I never thought of that," said Frankie. "Well, as I was saying, Mr. Savage was so nervous and wrought up that Mr. Elford wrote out the will then and there, and the servant and the gardener came and witnessed it, and Mr. Elford took it away with him for safe keeping."

"That does seem to knock out forgery," agreed Bobby.

"I know. You can't have forgery when you've actually seen the man sign his name. As to the other business—murder, it's going to be hard to find out anything about that now. The doctor who was called in has died since. The man we saw last night is a new man. He's been here only about two months."

"We seem to have rather an unfortunate number of deaths," said Bobby.

"Why, who else is dead?"

"Albert Mere."

"Do you think they've *all* been put out of the way?"

"That seems rather wholesale. We might give Albert Mere the benefit of the doubt—he was seventy-two, poor old man."

"Alright," said Frankie. "I'll allow you Natural Causes in his case. Any luck with Rose Chudleigh?"

"Yes. After she left the Templetons she went to the north of England to a place, but she's come back and married a man down here whom it seems she's been walking out with for the last seventeen years. Unfortunately she's a a bit of a nitwit. She doesn't seem to remember anything about anyone. Perhaps you could do something with her."

"I'll have a go," said Frankie. "I'm rather good with nitwits. Where's Badger, by the way?"

"Good Lord, I've forgotten all about him." said Bobby.

He got up and left the room, returning a few minutes later.

"He was still asleep," he explained. "He's getting up now. A chambermaid seems to have called him four times, but it didn't make any impression."

"Well, we'd better go and see the nitwit," said Frankie, rising. "And then I *must* buy a toothbrush and a nightgown and a sponge and a few other necessities of civilized existence. I was so close to Nature last night that I didn't think about any of them. I just stripped off my outer covering and fell upon the bed."

"I know," said Bobby. "So did I."

"Let's go and talk to Rose Chudleigh," said Frankie.

Rose Chudleigh, now Mrs. Pratt, lived in a small cottage that seemed to be overflowing with china dogs and furniture. Mrs. Pratt herself was a bovine-looking woman of ample proportions, with fishlike eyes and every indication of adenoids.

"You see, I've come back," said Bobby breezily.

Mrs. Pratt breathed hard and looked at them both incuriously.

"We were so interested to hear that you had lived with Mrs. Templeton," explained Frankie.

"Yes, ma'am," said Mrs. Pratt.

"She's living abroad now, I believe," continued Frankie, trying to give an impression of being an intimate of the family.

"I've heard so," agreed Mrs. Pratt.

"You were with her for some time, weren't you?" asked Frankie.

"Were I which, ma'am?"

"With Mrs. Templeton for some time," said Frankie, speaking slowly and clearly.

"I wouldn't say that, ma'am. Only two months."

"Oh! I thought you'd been with her longer than that."

"That was Gladys, ma'am. The house-parlormaid. She was there six months."

"There were two of you?"

"That's right. House-parlormaid she was, and I was cook."

"You were there when Mr. Savage died, weren't you?"

"I beg your pardon, ma'am?"

"You were there when Mr. Savage died?"

"Mr. Templeton didn't die—at least I haven't heard so. He went abroad."

"Not Mr. Templeton—Mr. Savage," said Bobby.

Mrs. Pratt looked at him vacantly.

"The gentleman who left her all the money," said Frankie.

A gleam of something like intelligence passed across Mrs. Pratt's face.

"Oh, yes, ma'am—the gentleman there was the inquest on."

"That's right," said Frankie, delighted with her success. "He used to come and stay quite often, didn't he?"

"I couldn't say as to that, ma'am. I'd only just come, you see. Gladys would know."

"But you had to witness his will, didn't you?"

Mrs. Pratt looked blank.

"You went and saw him sign a paper, and you had to sign it too?"

Again the gleam of intelligence. "Yes, ma'am. Me and Albert. I'd never done such a thing before, and I didn't like it. I said to Gladys, 'I don't like signing a paper, and that's a fact,' and Gladys she said it must be alright because Mr. Elford was there and he was a very nice gentleman as well as being a lawyer."

"What happened exactly?" asked Bobby.

"I beg your pardon, sir?"

"Who called you to sign your name?" asked Frankie.

"The mistress, sir. She came into the kitchen and said would I go outside and call Albert, and would we both come up to the best bedroom (which she'd moved out of for Mr.—the gentleman—the night before), and there was the gentleman sitting up in bed—he'd come back from London and gone straight to bed—and a very ill-looking gentleman he was. I hadn't seen him before, but he looked something ghastly. And Mr. Elford was there too, and he spoke very nice and said there was nothing to be afraid of and I was to sign my name where the gentleman had signed his, and I did and put 'cook' after it, and the address. And Albert did the same, and I went down to Gladys all of a tremble and said I'd never seen a gentleman look so like death, and Gladys said he'd looked alright the night before, and that it must have been something in London that had upset him. He'd gone up to London very early before anyone was up. And then I said about not liking to write my name to anything, and Gladys said it was alright because Mr. Elford was there."

"And Mr. Savage—the gentleman—died—when?"

"Next morning as ever was, ma'am. He shut himself up in his room that night and wouldn't let anyone go near him, and when Gladys called him in the morning he was all stiff and dead, and a letter propped up by his bedside—'To the Coroner,' it said. Oh, it gave Gladys a regular turn! And then there was an inquest and everything. And two months later Mrs. Templeton told me she was going abroad to live. But she got me a very good place up north with big wages, and she gave me a nice present and everything. A very nice lady, Mrs. Templeton."

Mrs. Pratt was by now thoroughly enjoying her own loquacity.

Frankie rose.

"Well," she said, "it's been very nice to hear all this." She slipped a note out of her purse. "You must let me leave you a—er—little present. I've taken up so much of your time."

"Well, thank you kindly, I'm sure, ma'am. Goodday to you and your good gentleman."

Frankie blushed and retreated rather rapidly. Bobby followed her after a few minutes. He looked preoccupied.

"Well," he said, "we seem to have got at all she knows."

"Yes," said Frankie. "And it hangs together. There seems no doubt that Savage *did* make that will, and I suppose his fear of cancer was genuine enough. They couldn't very well bribe a Harley Street doctor. I suppose they just took advantage of his having made that will to do away with him quickly before he changed his mind. But how we or anyone else can prove they *did* make away with him I can't see."

"I know. We may suspect that Mrs. T. gave him 'something to make him sleep,' but we can't prove it. Bassington-ffrench may have forged the letter to the Coroner, but that again we can't prove by now. I expect the letter is destroyed long ago after being put in as evidence at the inquest."

"So we come back to the old problem—what on earth are Bassington-ffrench & Co. so afraid of our discovering?"

"Nothing strikes you as odd particularly?"

"No, I don't think so—or at least only one thing. Why did Mrs. Templeton send out for the gardener to come and witness the will, when the house-parlormaid was in the house? Why didn't they ask the parlormaid?"

"It's odd your saying that, Frankie," said Bobby.

His voice sounded so queer that Frankie looked at him in surprise. "Why?"

"Because I stayed behind to ask Mrs. Pratt for Gladys's name and address."

"Well?"

"The parlormaid's name was Evans."

32
Evans

FRANKIE GASPED.

Bobby's voice rose excitedly. "You see, you've asked the same question that Carstairs asked. *Why didn't they ask the parlormaid? Why didn't they ask Evans?*"

"Oh, Bobby, we're getting there at last!"

"The same thing must have struck Carstairs. He was nosing round, just as we were looking for something fishy—and this point struck him, just as it struck us. And moreover I believe he came to Wales for that reason. Gladys Evans is a Welsh name—Evans was probably a Welsh girl. He was following her to Marchbolt. And someone was following him—and so he never got to her."

"Why *didn't* they ask Evans?" said Frankie. "There *must* be a reason. It's such a silly little point—and yet it's important. With a couple of maids in the house, why send out for a gardener?"

"Perhaps because both Chudleigh and Albert Mere were chumps, whereas Evans was rather a sharp girl."

"It can't be only that. Mr. Elford was there and he's quite shrewd. Oh, Bobby, the whole situation is there—I know it is. If we could just get at the reason. Evans. Why Chudleigh and Mere and not Evans?"

Suddenly she stopped and put both hands over her eyes.

"It's coming," she said. "Just a sort of flicker. It'll come in a minute."

She stayed dead still for a minute or two, then removed her hands and looked at her companion with an odd flicker in her eyes.

"Bobby," she said, "if you're staying in a house with two servants which do you tip?"

"The house-parlormaid, of course," said Bobby, surprised. "One never tips a cook. One never sees her, for one thing."

"No, and she never sees you. At most she might catch a glimpse of you if you were there for some time. But a house-parlormaid waits on you at dinner and calls you and hands you coffee."

"What are you getting at, Frankie?"

"They couldn't have Evans witnessing that will—*because Evans would have known that it wasn't Mr. Savage who was making it.*"

"Good Lord, Frankie, what do you mean? Who was it then?"

"Bassington-ffrench, of course! Don't you see, he impersonated Savage? I bet it was Bassington-ffrench who went to that doctor and made all that fuss about having cancer. Then the lawyer is sent for—a stranger who doesn't know Mr. Savage but who will be able to swear that he saw 'Mr. Savage' sign that will, and it's witnessed by two people, one of whom hadn't seen him before and the other an old man who was probably pretty blind and who probably had never seen Savage either. Now do you see?"

"But where was the real Savage all that time?"

"Oh, he arrived alright, and then I suspect they drugged him and put him in the attic, perhaps, and kept him there for twelve hours while Bassington-ffrench did his impersonation stunt. Then he was put back in his bed and given chloral, and Evans finds him dead in the morning."

"My God, I believe you've hit it, Frankie! But can we prove it?"

"Yes—no—I don't know. Supposing Rose Chudleigh—Pratt, I mean—were shown a photograph of the real Savage? Would she be able to say, 'That wasn't the man who signed the will'?"

"I doubt it," said Bobby. "She is such a nitwit."

"Chosen for that purpose, I expect. But there's another thing: an expert ought to be able to detect that the signature is a forgery."

"They didn't before."

"Because nobody ever raised the question. There didn't seem any possible moment when the will *could* have been forged. But now it's different."

"One thing we must do," said Bobby. "Find Evans. She may be able to tell us a lot. She was with the Templetons for six months, remember."

Frankie groaned. "That's going to make it even more difficult."

"How about the post office?" suggested Bobby.

They were just passing it. In appearance it was more of a general store than a post office.

Frankie darted inside and opened the campaign. There was no one in the shop except the postmistress, a young woman with an inquisitive nose.

Frankie bought a two-shilling book of stamps, commented on the weather and then said:

"But I expect you always have better weather here than we do in my part of the world. I live in Wales—Marchbolt. You wouldn't believe the rain we have."

The young woman with the nose said that they had a good deal of rain themselves and last Bank Holiday it had rained something cruel.

Frankie said, "There's someone in Marchbolt who comes from this part of the world. I wonder if you know her. Her name was Evans—Gladys Evans."

The young woman was quite unsuspicious.

"Why, of course," she said. "She was in service here. At Tudor Cottage. But she didn't come from these parts. She came from Wales, and she went back there and married—Roberts her name is now."

"That's right," said Frankie. "You can't give me her address, I suppose? I borrowed a raincoat from her and forgot to give it back. If I had her address I'd post it to her."

"Well, now," the other replied, "I believe I can. I get a p.c. from her now and again. She and her husband have gone into service together. Wait a minute now."

She went away and rummaged in a corner. Presently she returned with a piece of paper in her hand.

"Here you are," she said, pushing it across the counter.

Bobby and Frankie read it together. It was the last thing in the world they would expect.

Mrs. Roberts,
The Vicarage,
Marchbolt,
Wales.

33

Sensation in the Orient Café

HOW BOBBY AND Frankie got out of the post office without disgracing themselves neither of them ever knew.

Outside, with one accord, they looked at each other and shook with laughter.

"At the Vicarage—all the time!" gasped Bobby.

"And I looked through four hundred and eight Evanses!" lamented Frankie.

"*Now* I see why Bassington-ffrench was so amused when he realized we didn't know in the least who Evans was!"

"And of course it was dangerous from their point of view. You and Evans were actually under the same roof."

"Come on," said Bobby. "Marchbolt's the next place."

"Like where the rainbow ends," said Frankie. "Back to the dear old home."

"Dash it all," said Bobby, "we must do something about Badger. Have you any money, Frankie?"

Frankie opened her bag and took out a handful of notes.

"Give these to him and tell him to make some arrangement with his creditors, and say that Father will buy the garage and put him in as manager."

"Alright," said Bobby. "The great thing is to get off quickly."

"Why this frightful haste?"

"I don't know—but I've a feeling something might happen."

"How awful! Let's go ever so quickly."

"I'll settle Badger. You go and start the car."

"I shall never buy that toothbrush," said Frankie.

Five minutes saw them speeding out of Chipping Somerton. Bobby had no occasion to complain of lack of speed.

Nevertheless, Frankie suddenly said, "Look here, Bobby, this isn't quick enough."

Bobby glanced at the speedometer needle, which was, at the moment, registering eighty, and remarked drily, "I don't see what more we can do."

"We can take an air taxi," said Frankie. "We're only about seven miles from Medeshot Aerodrome."

"My dear girl!" said Bobby.

"If we do that we'll be home in a couple of hours."

"Good," said Bobby. "Let's take an air taxi."

The whole proceeding was beginning to take on the fantastic character of a dream. Why this wild hurry to get to Marchbolt? Bobby didn't know. He suspected that Frankie didn't know either. It was just a feeling.

At Medeshot Frankie asked for Mr. Donald King, and an untidy-looking young man was produced who appeared languidly surprised at the sight of her.

"Hullo, Frankie," he said. "I haven't seen you for an age. What do you want?"

"I want an air taxi," said Frankie. "You do that sort of thing, don't you?"

"Oh, yes. Where do you want to go?"

"I want to get home quickly," said Frankie.

Mr. Donald King raised his eyebrows. "Is that all?" he asked.

"Not quite," said Frankie. "But it's the main idea."

"Oh, well, we can soon fix you up."

"I'll give you a check," said Frankie.

Five minutes later they were off.

"Frankie," said Bobby, "why are we doing this?"

"I haven't the faintest idea," said Frankie. "But I feel we must. Don't you?"

"Curiously enough, I do. But I don't know why. After all, our Mrs. Roberts won't fly away on a broomstick."

"She might. Remember, we don't know what Bassington-ffrench is up to."

"That's true," said Bobby thoughtfully.

It was growing late when they reached their destination. The plane landed them in the Park, and five minutes later Bobby and Frankie were driving into Marchbolt in Lord Marchington's Chrysler.

They pulled up outside the Vicarage gate, the Vicarage drive not lending itself to the turning of expensive cars.

Then jumping out they ran up the drive.

"I shall wake up soon," thought Bobby. "What are we doing and why?"

A slender figure was standing on the doorstep. Frankie and Bobby recognized her at the same minute.

"Moira!" cried Frankie.

Moira turned. She was swaying slightly. "Oh, I'm so glad to see you. I don't know what to do."

"But what on earth brings you here?"

"The same thing that has brought you, I expect."

"You have found out who Evans is?" asked Bobby.

Moira nodded. "Yes, it's a long story—"

"Come inside," said Bobby.

But Moira shrank back. "No, no," she said hurriedly. "Let's go somewhere and talk. There's something I must tell you—before we go into the house. Isn't there a café or some place like that in the town? Somewhere where we could go?"

"Alright," said Bobby, moving unwillingly away from the door. "But why—"

Moira stamped her foot. "You'll see when I tell you. Oh, do come! There's not a minute to lose."

They yielded to her urgency. About halfway down the main street was the Orient Café, whose somewhat grand name was not borne out by the interior decoration. The three of them filed in. It was a slack moment—half-past six.

They sat down at a small table in the corner, and Bobby ordered three coffees.

"Now then?" he said.

"Wait till she's brought the coffee," said Moira.

The waitress returned and listlessly deposited three cups of tepid coffee in front of them.

"Now then," said Bobby again.

"I hardly know where to begin," said Moira. "It was in the train going to London. Really the most amazing coincidence. I went along the corridor and—"

She broke off. Her seat faced the door and she leant forward staring.

"He must have followed me," she said.

"Who?" cried Frankie and Bobby together.

"Bassington-ffrench," whispered Moira.

"You've seen him?"

"He's outside. I saw him. With a woman with red hair."

"Mrs. Cayman," cried Frankie.

She and Bobby jumped and ran to the door. A protest came from Moira, but neither of them heeded it. They looked up and down the street but Bassington-ffrench was nowhere in sight.

Moira joined them.

"Has he gone?" she asked, her voice trembling. "Oh! Do be careful. He's dangerous—horribly dangerous."

"He can't do anything so long as we're all together," said Bobby.

"Brace up, Moira," said Frankie. "Don't be such a rabbit."

"Well, we can't do anything for the moment," said Bobby, leading the way back to the table. "Go on with what you were telling us, Moira."

He picked up his cup of coffee. Frankie lost her balance and fell against him, and the coffee poured over the table.

"Sorry," said Frankie.

She stretched over to the adjoining table, which was laid for possible diners. There was a cruet on it with two glass-stoppered bottles containing oil and vinegar.

The oddity of Frankie's proceedings riveted Bobby's attention. She took the vinegar bottle, emptied the vinegar into the slop-bowl and began to pour coffee into it from her cup.

"Have you gone batty, Frankie?" asked Bobby. "What the devil are you doing?"

"Taking a sample of this coffee for George Arbuthnot to analyze," said Frankie.

She turned to Moira.

"The game's up, Moira! The whole thing came to me in a flash as we stood at the door just now! When I jogged Bobby's elbow and made him spill his coffee I saw your face. You put something in our cups when you sent us running to the door to look for Bassington-ffrench. The game's up, *Mrs. Nicholson or Templeton or whatever you like to call yourself!"*

"Templeton?" cried Bobby.

"Look at her face," cried Frankie. "If she denies it, ask her to come to the Vicarage and see if Mrs. Roberts doesn't identify her."

Bobby did look at her. He saw that face—that haunting, wistful face—transformed by a demoniac rage. The beautiful mouth opened and a stream of foul and hideous curses poured out. She fumbled in her handbag.

Bobby was still dazed, but he acted in the nick of time. It was his hand that struck the pistol up.

The bullet passed over Frankie's head and buried itself in the wall of the Orient Café.

For the first time in its history one of the waitresses hurried. With a wild scream she shot out into the street calling: "Help! *Murder!* POLICE!"

34
Letter from South America

IT WAS SOME weeks later.

Frankie has just received a letter. It bore the stamp of one of the less-known South American republics.

After reading it through, she passed it to Bobby.

It ran as follows:

DEAR FRANKIE:

Really, I congratulate you! You and your young Naval friend have shattered the plans of a lifetime. I had everything so nicely arranged.

Would you really like to hear all about it? My lady friend has given me away so thoroughly (spite, I'm afraid—women are invariably spiteful!) that my most damaging admissions won't do me any further harm. Besides, I am starting life again. Roger Bassington-ffrench is dead.

I fancy I've always been what they call a "wrong 'un." Even at Oxford I had a little lapse. Stupid, because it was bound to be found out. The Pater didn't let me down. But he sent me to the Colonies.

I fell in with Moira and her lot fairly soon. She was the real thing. She was an accomplished criminal by the time she was fifteen. When I met her things were getting a bit too hot for her. The American police were on her trail.

She and I liked each other. We decided to make a match of it, but we'd a few plans to carry through first.

To begin with, she married Nicholson. By doing so she removed herself to another world, and the police lost sight of her. Nicholson was just coming over to England to start a place for nerve patients. He was looking for a suitable house to buy cheap. Moira got him on to the Grange.

She was still working in with her gang in the dope business. Without knowing it, Nicholson was very useful to her.

I had always had two ambitions. I wanted to be the owner of Merroway, and I wanted to command an immense amount of money. A Bassington-ffrench played a great part in the reign of Charles II. Since then the family has dwindled down to mediocrity. I felt capable of playing a great part again. But I had to have money.

Moira made several trips across to Canada to "see her people." Nicholson adored her and believed anything she told him. Most men did. Owing to the complications of the drug business she traveled under various names. She was traveling as Mrs. Templeton when she met Savage. She knew all about Savage and his enormous wealth, and she went all out for him. He was attracted, but he wasn't attracted enough to lose his common sense.

However, we concocted a plan. You know pretty well the story of that. The man you know as Cayman acted the part of the unfeeling husband. Savage was induced to come down and stay at Tudor Cottage more than once. The third time he came our plans were laid. I needn't go into all that—you know it. The whole thing went with a bang. Moira cleared the money and went off—ostensibly abroad—in reality back to Staverley and the Grange.

In the meantime I was perfecting my own plans. Henry and young Tommy had to be got out of the way. I had bad luck over Tommy. A couple of perfectly good accidents went wrong. I wasn't going to fool about with accidents in Henry's case. He had a good deal of rheumatic pain after an accident in the hunting field. I introduced him to morphia. He took it in all good faith. Henry was a simple soul. He soon became an addict. Our plan was that he should go to the Grange for treatment and should there either "commit suicide" or get hold of an overdose of morphia. Moira would do the business. I shouldn't be connected with it in any way.

And then that fool Carstairs began to be active. It seems that Savage had written him a line on board ship mentioning Mrs. Templeton and even enclosing a snapshot of her. Carstairs went on a shooting trip soon afterward. When he came back from the wilds and heard the news of Savage's death and will, he was frankly incredulous. The story didn't ring true to him. He was certain that Savage wasn't worried about his health and didn't believe he had any special fear of cancer. Also the wording of the will sounded to him highly uncharacteristic. Savage was a hard-headed businessman, and while he might be quite ready to have an affair with a pretty woman, Carstairs didn't believe he would leave a vast sum of money to her and the rest to charity. The charity touch was my idea. It sounded so respectable and unfishy.

Carstairs came over here determined to look into the business. He began to poke about.

And straightaway we had a piece of bad luck. Some friends brought him down to lunch, and he saw a picture of Moira on the piano—and recognized it as the woman of the snapshot that Savage had sent him. He went down to Chipping Somerton and started to poke about there.

Moira and I began to get the wind up—I sometimes think unnecessarily. But Carstairs was a shrewd chap.

I went down to Chipping Somerton after him. He failed to trace the cook—Rose Chudleigh. She'd gone to the north, but he tracked down Evans, found out her married name and started off for Marchbolt.

Things were getting serious. If Evans identified Mrs. Templeton and Mrs. Nicholson as one and the same person, matters were going to become difficult. Also she'd been in the house some time and we weren't sure quite how much she might know.

I decided that Carstairs had got to be suppressed. He was making a serious nuisance of himself. Chance came to my aid. I was close behind him when the mist came up. I crept up nearer and a sudden push did the job.

But I was still in a dilemma. I didn't know what incriminating matter he might have on him. However, your young Naval friend played into my hands very nicely. I was left alone with the body for a short time—quite enough for my purpose. He had a photograph of Moira—he'd got it from the photographers, presumably for identification. I removed that and any letters or identifying matter. Then I planted the photograph of one of the gang.

All went well. The pseudo-sister and brother-in-law came down and identified him. All seemed to have gone off satisfactorily. And then your friend Bobby upset things. It seemed that Carstairs had recovered consciousness before he died and that he had been saying things. He'd mentioned Evans—and Evans was actually in service at the Vicarage.

I admit we were getting rattled by now. We lost our heads a bit. Moira insisted that he must be put out of the way. We tried one plan, which failed. Then Moira said she'd see to it. She went down to Marchbolt in the car. She seized a chance very neatly—slipped some morphia into Bobby's beer when he was asleep. But the young devil didn't succumb. That was pure bad luck.

As I told you, it was Nicholson's cross-questioning that made me wonder if you were just what you seemed. But imagine the shock that Moira had when she was creeping out to meet me one evening and came face to face with Bobby! She recognized him at once—she'd had a good look when he was asleep that day. No wonder she was so scared she nearly passed out. Then she realized that it wasn't she whom he suspected, and she rallied and played up.

She came to the inn and told him a few tall stories. He swallowed them like a lamb. She pretended that Alan Carstairs was an old lover and she piled it on thick about her fear of Nicholson. Also she did her best to disabuse you of your suspicions concerning me. I did the same to you and disparaged her as a weak, helpless creature—Moira, who had the nerve to put any number of people out of the way without turning a hair!

The position was serious. We'd got the money. We were getting on well with the Henry plan. I was in no hurry for Tommy. I could afford to wait a bit. Nicholson could easily be got out of the way when the time came. But you and Bobby were a menace. You'd got your suspicions fixed on the Grange.

It may interest you to know that Henry didn't commit suicide. I killed him! When I was talking to you in the garden, I saw there was no time to waste—and I went straight in and saw to things.

The airplane that came over gave me my chance. I went into the study, sat down by Henry, who was writing, and said: "Look here, old man—" and shot him! The noise of the plane drowned the sound. Then I wrote a nice affecting letter, wiped off my fingerprints from the revolver, pressed Henry's hand round it and let it drop to the floor. I put the key of the study in Henry's pocket and went out, locking the door from the outside with the dining-room key, which fits the lock.

I won't go into details of the neat little squib arrangement in the chimney which was timed to go off four minutes later.

Everything went beautifully. You and I were in the garden together and heard the "shot." A perfect suicide! The only person who laid himself open to suspicion was poor old Nicholson. The ass came back for a stick or something!

Of course Bobby's knight-errantry was a bit difficult for Moira. So she just went off to the Cottage. We fancied that Nicholson's explanation of his wife's absence would be sure to make you suspicious.

Where Moira really showed her mettle was at the Cottage. She realized from the noise upstairs that I'd been knocked out, and she quickly injected a large dose of morphia into herself, and lay down on the bed. After you all went down to telephone she nipped up to the attic and cut me free. Then the morphia took effect and by the time the Doctor arrived she was genuinely off in a hypnotic sleep.

But all the same her nerve was going. She was afraid you'd get on to Evans and get the hang of how Savage's will and suicide were worked. Also she was afraid that Carstairs had written to Evans before he came to Marchbolt. She pretended to go up to a London nursing home. Instead she hurried down to Marchbolt—and met you on the doorstep! Then her one idea was to get you both out of the way. Her methods were crude to the last degree, but I believe she'd have got away with it. I doubt if the waitress would have been able to remember much about what the woman who came in with you was like. Moira would have got away back to London and lain low in a nursing home. With you and Bobby out of the way the whole thing would have died down.

But you spotted her—and she lost her head. And then at the trial she dragged *me* into it!

Perhaps I was getting a little tired of her . . . But I had no idea that she knew it.

You see, she had got the money—*my* money! Once I had married her I might have got tired of her. I like variety.

So here I am starting life again . . . And all owing to you and that extremely objectionable young man Bobby Jones. But I've no doubt I shall make good!

Or ought it to be *"bad"* not *"good"*?

I haven't reformed—yet.

But if at first you don't succeed, try, try, try again.

Goodbye, my dear—or perhaps au revoir. One never knows, does one?

Your affectionate enemy, the bold, bad villain of the piece,

ROGER BASSINGTON-FFRENCH

35
News from the Vicarage

BOBBY HANDED BACK the letter and with a sigh Frankie took it.

"He's really a very remarkable person," she said.

"You always had a fancy for him," said Bobby coldly.

"He had charm," said Frankie. "So had Moira," she added.

Bobby blushed. "It was very queer that all the time the clue to the whole thing should have been in the Vicarage," he said. "You do know, don't you, Frankie, that Carstairs had actually written to Evans—to Mrs. Roberts, that is?"

Frankie nodded. "Telling her that he was coming to see her and that he wanted information about Mrs. Templeton who he had reason to believe was a dangerous international crook wanted by the police."

"And then when he's pushed over the cliff she doesn't put two and two together!" said Bobby bitterly.

"That's because the man who went over the cliff was Pritchard," said Frankie. "That identification was a very clever bit of work. If a man called Pritchard is pushed over, how *could* it be a man called Carstairs? That's how the ordinary mind works."

"The funny thing is that she recognized Cayman," went on Bobby. "At least she caught a glimpse of him when Roberts was letting him in and asked him who it was. And he said it was a Mr. Cayman and she said, 'Funny—he's the dead spit of a gentleman I used to be in service with.'"

"Can you beat it?" said Frankie.

"Even Bassington-ffrench gave himself away once or twice," she continued. "But like an idiot I never spotted it."

"Did he?"

"Yes, when Sylvia said that the picture in the paper was very like Carstairs, he said there wasn't much likeness really—showing he'd seen the dead man. And then later he said to me that he never saw the dead man's face."

"How on earth did you spot Moira, Frankie?"

"I think it was the description of Mrs. Templeton," said Frankie dreamily. "Everyone said she was 'such a nice lady.' Now that didn't seem to fit with the Cayman woman. No servant would describe her as a 'nice lady.' And then we got to the Vicarage and Moira was there and it suddenly came to me—*Suppose Moira was Mrs. Templeton?*"

"Very bright of you."

"I'm sorry for Sylvia," said Frankie. "With Moira dragging Roger into it, it's been a terrible lot of publicity for her. But Dr. Nicholson has stuck by her and I shouldn'y be at all surprised if they ended by making a match of it."

"Everything seems to have ended very fortunately," said Bobby. "Badger's doing well at the garage, thanks to your father. And also thanks to your father, I've got this perfectly marvelous job."

"Is it a marvelous job?"

"Managing a coffee estate out in Kenya on a whacking big screw? I should think so. It's just the sort of thing I used to dream about."

He paused. "People come out to Kenya a good deal on trips," he said with intention.

"Quite a lot of people live out there," said Frankie demurely.

"Oh, Frankie you wouldn't!" He blushed, stammered, recovered himself. "W-w-would you?"

"I would," said Frankie. "I mean I will."

"I've been keen about you always," said Bobby in a stifled voice. "I used to be miserable—knowing, I mean, that it was no good."

"I suppose that's what made you so rude that day on the golf links."

"Yes, I was feeling pretty grim."

"H'm," said Frankie. "What about Moira?"

Bobby looked uncomfortable. "Her face did sort of get me," he admitted.

"It's a better face than mine," said Frankie generously.

"It isn't—but it sort of haunted me. And then, when we were up in the attic and you were so plucky about things—well, Moira just faded out. I was hardly interested in what happened to her. It was *you*—only you. You were simply splendid! So frightfully plucky."

"I wasn't feeling plucky inside," said Frankie. "I was all shaking. But I wanted you to admire me."

"I did, darling. I do. I always have. I always shall. Are you sure you won't hate it out in Kenya?"

"I shall adore it. I was fed up with England."

"Frankie."

"Bobby."

"If you will come in here," said the Vicar, opening the door and ushering in the advance guard of the Dorcas Society. He shut the door precipitately and apologized. "My—er—one of my sons. He is—er—engaged."

A member of the Dorcas Society said archly that it looked like it.

"A good boy," said the Vicar. "Inclined at one time not to take life seriously. But he has improved very much of late. He is going out to manage a coffee estate in Kenya."

Said one member of the Dorcas Society to another in a whisper: "Did you see? It was Lady Frances Derwent he was kissing!"

In an hour's time the news was all over Marchbolt.

THE END

The Moving Finger

1

I HAVE OFTEN recalled the morning when the first of the anonymous letters came.

It arrived at breakfast and I turned it over in the idle way one does when time goes slowly and every event must be spun out to its full extent. It was, I saw, a local letter with a typewritten address. I opened it before the two with London postmarks, since one of them was clearly a bill, and on the other I recognized the handwriting of one of my more tiresome cousins.

It seems odd, now, to remember that Joanna and I were more amused by the letter than anything else. We hadn't, then, the faintest inkling of what was to come—the trail of blood and violence and suspicion and fear.

One simply didn't associate that sort of thing with Lymstock.

I see that I have begun badly. I haven't explained Lymstock.

When I took a bad crash flying, I was afraid for a long time, in spite of soothing words from doctors and nurses, that I was going to be condemned to lie on my back all my life. Then at last they took me out of the plaster and I learned cautiously to use my limbs, and finally Marcus Kent, my doctor, clapped me on my back and told me that everything was going to be alright, but that I'd got to go and live in the country and lead the life of a vegetable for at least six months.

"Go to some part of the world where you haven't any friends. Get right away from things. Take an interest in local politics, get excited about village gossip, absorb all the local scandal. Small beer—that's the prescription for you. Absolute rest and quiet."

Rest and quiet! It seems funny to think of that now.

And so Lymstock—and Little Furze.

Lymstock had been a place of importance at the time of the Norman Conquest. In the twentieth century it was a place of no importance whatsoever. It was three miles from a main road—a little provincial market town with a sweep of moorland rising above it. Little Furze was situated on the road leading up to the moors. It was a prim, low, white house with a sloping Victorian veranda painted a faded green.

My sister Joanna, as soon as she saw it, decided that it was the ideal spot for a convalescent. Its owner matched the house, a charming little old lady, quite incredibly Victorian, who explained to Joanna that she would never have dreamed of letting her house if "things had not been so different nowadays—this terrible taxation."

So everything was settled, and the agreement signed, and in due course

Joanna and I arrived and settled in, while Miss Emily Barton went into rooms in Lymstock kept by a former parlormaid ("my faithful Florence") and we were looked after by Miss Barton's present maid, Partridge, a grim but efficient personage who was assisted by a daily "girl."

As soon as we had been given a few days to settle down, Lymstock came solemnly to call. Everybody in Lymstock had a label—"rather like happy families" as Joanna said. There was Mr. Symmington the lawyer, thin and dry, with his querulous bridge-playing wife. Dr. Griffith—the dark, melancholy doctor—and his sister who was big and hearty. The vicar, a scholarly absentminded elderly man and his erratic eager-faced wife. Rich dilettante Mr. Pye of Prior's End, and finally Miss Emily Barton herself, the perfect spinster of village tradition.

Joanna fingered the cards with something like awe. "I didn't know," she said in an awestruck voice, "that people really *called* —with *cards!*"

"That," I told her, "is because you know nothing about the country."

Joanna is very pretty and very gay, and she likes dancing and cocktails and love affairs and rushing about in high-powered cars. She is definitely and entirely urban.

"At any rate," said Joanna, "I look alright."

I studied her critically and was not able to agree.

Joanna was dressed (by Mirotin) for le sport. The effect was charming, but a bit startling for Lymstock.

"No," I said. "You're all wrong. You ought to be wearing an old faded tweed skirt with a nice cashmere jumper matching it and perhaps a rather baggy cardigan coat, and you'd wear a felt hat and thick stockings and old well-worn brogues. Your face is all wrong, too," I added.

"What's wrong with that? I've got on my Country Tan Make-Up No. 2."

"Exactly" I said. "If you lived here, you would have just a little powder to take the shine off the nose and you would almost certainly be wearing all your eyebrows instead of only a quarter of them."

Joanna laughed, and said that coming to the country was a new experience and she was going to enjoy it.

"I'm afraid you'll be terribly bored," I said remorsefully.

"No, I shan't. I really was fed up with all my crowd, and though you won't be sympathetic I really was very cut up about Paul. It will take me a long time to get over it."

I was skeptical over this. Joanna's love affairs always run the same course. She has a mad infatuation for some completely spineless young man who is a misunderstood genius. She listens to his endless complaints and works to get him recognition. Then, when he is ungrateful, she is deeply wounded and says her heart is broken—until the next gloomy young man comes along, which is usually about three weeks later.

I did not take Joanna's broken heart very seriously, but I did see that living in the country was like a new game to my attractive sister. She entered with zest into the pastime of returning calls. We duly received invitations to tea and to bridge, which we accepted, and issued invitations in our turn.

To us, it was all novel and entertaining—a new game.

And, as I say, when the anonymous letter came, it struck me, at first, as amusing too.

For a minute or two after opening the letter, I stared at it uncomprehendingly. Printed words had been cut out and pasted on a sheet of paper.

The letter, using terms of the coarsest character, expressed the writer's opinion that Joanna and I were not brother and sister.

"Hullo," said Joanna. "What is it?"

"It's a particularly foul anonymous letter," I said.

I was still suffering from shock. Somehow one didn't expect that kind of thing in the placid backwater of Lymstock.

Joanna at once displayed lively interest. "*No*? What does it say?"

In novels, I have noticed, anonymous letters of a foul and disgusting character are never shown, if possible, to women. It is implied that women must at all cost be shielded from the shock it might give their delicate nervous systems.

I am sorry to say it never occurred to me not to show the letter to Joanna. I handed it to her at once.

She vindicated my belief in her toughness by displaying no emotion but that of amusement. "What an awful bit of dirt! I've always heard about anonymous letters, but I've never seen one before. Are they always like this?"

"I can't tell you," I said. "It's my first experience, too."

Joanna began to giggle. "You must have been right about my makeup, Jerry. I suppose they think I just *must* be an abandoned female!"

"That," I said, "coupled with the fact that our father was a tall, dark, lantern-jawed man and our mother a fair-haired blue-eyed little creature, and that I take after him and you take after her."

Joanna nodded thoughtfully. "Yes, we're not a bit alike. Nobody would take us for brother and sister."

"Somebody certainly hasn't," I said with feeling.

Joanna said she thought it was frightfully funny. She dangled the letter thoughtfully by one corner and asked what we were to do with it.

"The correct procedure, I believe," I said, "is to drop it into the fire with a sharp exlamation of disgust."

I suited the action to the word, and Joanna applauded. "You did that beautifully," she said. "You ought to have been on the stage. It's lucky we still have fires, isn't it?"

"The wastepaper basket would have been much less dramatic," I agreed. "I could, of course, have set light to it with a match and slowly watched it burn—or watched it slowly burn."

"Things never burn when you want them to," said Joanna. "They go out. You'd probably have had to strike match after match."

She got up and went toward the window. Then standing there, she turned her head sharply. "I wonder," she said, "who wrote it?"

"We're never likely to know," I said.

"No—I suppose not." She was silent a moment, and then said: "I don't know when I come to think of it that it is so funny after all. You know, I thought they—they *liked* us down here."

"So they do," I said. "This is just some half-crazy brain on the borderline."

"I suppose so. Ugh—nasty!"

As she went out into the sunshine I thought to myself as I smoked my after-breakfast cigarette that she was quite right. It *was* nasty. Someone resented our coming here—someone resented Joanna's bright young sophisticated beauty—someone wanted to *hurt*. To take it with a laugh was perhaps the best way—but deep down it wasn't funny.

Dr. Griffith came that morning. I had fixed up for him to give me a weekly overhaul. I liked Owen Griffith. He was a dark, ungainly, with awkward ways of moving and deft very gentle hands. He had a jerky way of talking and was rather shy.

He reported progress to be encouraging. Then he added, "You're feeling alright, aren't you? Is it my fancy, or are you a bit under the weather this morning?"

"Not really," I said. "A particularly scurrilous anonymous letter arrived with the morning coffee, and it's left rather a nasty taste in the mouth."

He dropped his bag on the floor. His thin dark face was excited. "Do you mean to say that *you've* had one of them?"

I was interested. "They've been going about, then?"

"Yes. For some time."

"Oh," I said. "I see. I was under the impression that our presence as strangers was resented here."

"No, no, it's nothing to do with that. It's just—" He paused and then asked, "What did it say? At least"—he turned suddenly red and embarrassed—"perhaps I oughtn't to ask?"

"I'll tell you with pleasure," I said. "It just said that the fancy tart I'd brought down with me wasn't my sister—not 'alf! And that, I may say, is a shortened version."

His dark face flushed angrily. "How damnable! Your sister didn't—she's not upset, I hope?"

"Joanna," I said, "looks a little like the angel off the top of the Christmas tree, but she's eminently modern and quite tough. She found it highly entertaining. Such things haven't come her way before."

"I should hope not, indeed," said Griffith warmly.

"And anyway," I said firmly, "that's the best way to take it, I think. As something utterly ridiculous."

"Yes," said Owen Griffith, "only—"

He stopped, and I chimed in quickly. "Quite so," I said. "Only is the word!"

"The trouble is," he said, "that this sort of thing, once it starts, *grows*."

"So I should imagine."

"It's pathological, of course."

I nodded. "Any idea who's behind it?" I asked.

"No, I wish I had. You see, the anonymous letter pest arises from one of two causes. Either it's *particular*—directed at one person or set of people, that is to say it's *motivated*, it's someone who's got a definite grudge (or thinks he has) and who chooses a particularly nasty and underhand way of working it off. It's mean and disgusting but it's not necessarily crazy, and it's usually fairly easy to trace the writer—a discharged servant, a jealous woman, and so on. But if it's *general*, and not particular, then it's more serious.

"The letters are sent indiscriminately and serve the purpose of working off some frustration in the writer's mind. As I say, it's definitely pathological. And the craze grows. In the end, of course, you track down the person in question—(it's often someone extremely unlikely) and that's that. There was a bad outburst of the kind over the other side of the county last year—turned out to be the head of the millinery department in a big draper's establishment. Quiet, refined woman—had been there for years.

"I remember something of the same kind in my last practice up north. But that turned out to be purely personal spite. Still, as I say, I've seen something of this kind of thing, and, quite frankly, it frightens me!"

"Has it been going on long?" I asked.

"I don't think so. Hard to say, of course, because people who get these letters don't go round advertising the fact. They put them in the fire."

He paused.

"I've had one myself. Symmington, the solicitor, he's had one. And one or two of my poorer patients have told me about them."

"All much the same sort of thing?"

"Oh, yes. A definite harping on the sex theme. That's always a feature." He grinned. "Symmington was accused of illicit relations with his lady clerk—poor old Miss Ginch, who's forty at least, with pince-nez and teeth like a rabbit. Symmington took it straight to the police. My letters accused me of violating professional decorum with my lady patients, stressing the details. They're all quite childish and absurd, but horribly venomous." His face changed, grew grave. "But all the same, I'm *afraid.* These things can be *dangerous*, you know."

"I suppose they can."

"You see," he said, "crude, childish spite though it is, sooner or later *one of these letters will hit the mark.* And then, God knows what may happen! I'm afraid, too, of the effect upon the slow, suspicious, uneducated mind. If they see a thing written, they believe it's true. All sorts of complications may arise."

"It was an illiterate sort of letter," I said thoughtfully, "written by somebody practically illiterate, I should say."

"Was it?" said Owen and went away.

Thinking it over afterward, I found that "Was it?" rather disturbing.

I am not going to pretend that the arrival of our anonymous letter did not leave a nasty taste in the mouth. It did. At the same time, it soon passed out of my mind. I did not, you see, at that point, take it seriously. I think I remember saying to myself that these things probably happen fairly often in out-of-the-way villages. Some hysterical woman with a taste for dramatizing herself was probably at the bottom of it. Anyway, if the letters were as childish and silly as the one we had got, they couldn't do much harm.

The next *incident*, if I may put it so, occurred about a week later, when Partridge, her lips set tightly together, informed me that Beatrice, the daily help, would not be coming today.

"I gather, sir," said Partridge, "that the girl has been upset."

I was not very sure what Partridge was implying, but I diagnosed (wrongly) some stomach trouble to which Partridge was too delicate to allude more directly. I said I was sorry and hoped she would soon be better.

"The girl is perfectly well, sir," said Partridge. "She is upset in her feelings."

"Oh," I said rather doubtfully.

"Owing," went on Partridge, "to a letter she has received. Making, I understand, insinuations."

The grimness of Partridge's eye made me apprehensive that the insinuations were concerned with me. Since I could hardly have recognized Beatrice by sight if I had met her in the town, so unaware of her had I been, I felt a not unnatural annoyance. An invalid hobbling about on two sticks is hardly cast for the role of deceiver of village girls.

I said irritably, "What nonsense!"

"My very words, sir, to the girl's mother," said Partridge. " 'Goings-on in this house,' I said to her, 'there never have been and never will be while I am in charge. As to Beatrice,' I said, 'girls are different nowadays, and as to goings-on elsewhere I can say nothing.' But the truth is, sir, that Beatrice's friend from the garage as she walks out with got one of them nasty letters, too, and he isn't acting reasonable at all."

"I have never heard anything so preposterous in my life," I said angrily.

"It's my opinion, sir," said Partridge, "that we're well rid of the girl. What I say is, she wouldn't take on so if there wasn't *something* she didn't want found out. No smoke without fire, that's what I say."

I had no idea how horribly tired I was going to get of that particular phrase.

That morning, by way of adventure, I was to walk down to the village. The sun was shining, the air was cool and crisp and with the sweetness of spring in it. I assembled my sticks and started off, firmly refusing to permit Joanna to accompany me.

It was arranged that she should pick me up with the car and drive me back up the hill in time for lunch.

"That ought to give you time to pass the time of day with everyone in Lymstock."

"I have no doubt," I said, "that I shall have seen anybody who is anybody by then."

For morning in the High Street was a kind of rendezvous for shoppers, when news was exchanged.

I did not, after all, walk down to the town unaccompanied. I had gone about two hundred yards, when I heard a bicycle bell behind me, then a scrunching of brakes, and then Megan Hunter more or less fell off her machine at my feet.

"Hullo," she said breathlessly as she rose and dusted herself off.

I rather liked Megan and always felt oddly sorry for her.

She was Symmington the lawyer's stepdaughter, Mrs. Symmington's daughter by a first marriage. Nobody talked much about Mr. (or Captain)

Hunter, and I gathered that he was considered best forgotten. He was reported to have treated Mrs. Symmington very badly. She had divorced him a year or two after the marriage. She was a woman with means of her own and had settled down with her little daughter in Lymstock "to forget," and had eventually married the only eligible bachelor in the place, Richard Symmington.

There were two boys of the second marriage to whom their parents were devoted, and I fancied that Megan sometimes felt odd-man in the establishment. She certainly did not resemble her mother, who was a small anemic woman, fadedly pretty, who talked in a thin melancholy voice of servant difficulties and her health.

Megan was a tall awkward girl, and although she was actually twenty, she looked more like a schoolgirlish sixteen. She had a shock of untidy brown hair, hazel green eyes, a thin bony face, and an unexpectedly charming one-sided smile. Her clothes were drab and unattractive and she usually had on lisle-thread stockings with holes in them.

She looked, I decided this morning, much more like a horse than a human being. In fact, she would have been a very nice horse with a little grooming.

She spoke, as usual, in a kind of breathless rush:

"I've been up to the farm—you know, Lasher's—to see if they'd got any duck eggs. They've got an awfully nice lot of little pigs. Sweet! Do you like pigs? I do. I even like the smell."

"Well-kept pigs shouldn't smell," I said.

"Shouldn't they? They all do around here. Are you walking down to the town? I saw you were alone, so I thought I'd stop and walk with you, only I stopped rather suddenly."

"You've torn your stocking," I said.

Megan looked rather ruefully at her right leg. "So I have. But it's got two holes already, so it doesn't matter very much, does it?"

"Don't you ever mend your stockings, Megan?"

"Rather. When Mummie catches me. But she doesn't notice awfully what I do—so it's lucky in a way, isn't it?"

"You don't seem to realize you're grown up," I said.

"You mean I ought to be more like your sister? All dolled up?"

I rather resented this description of Joanna. "She looks clean and tidy and pleasing to the eye," I said.

"She's awfully pretty," said Megan. "She isn't a bit like you, is she? Why not?"

"Brothers and sisters aren't always alike."

"No. Of course I'm not very like Brian or Colin. And Brian and Colin aren't like each other." She paused and said, "It's very rum, isn't it?"

"What is?"

Megan replied briefly:

"Families."

I said thoughtfully, "I suppose they are."

I wondered just what was passing in her mind. We walked on in silence for a moment or two, then Megan said in a rather shy voice, "You fly, don't you?"

"Yes."

"That's how you got hurt?"

"Yes, I crashed."

Megan said, "Nobody down here flies."

"No," I said, "I suppose not. Would you like to fly, Megan?"

"Me?" Megan seemed surprised. "Goodness, no. I should be sick. I'm sick in a train even."

She paused and then asked with that directness which only a child usually displays: "Will you get alright and be able to fly again, or will you always be a bit of a crock?"

"My doctor says I shall be quite alright."

"Yes, but is he the kind of man who tells lies?"

"I don't think so," I replied. "In fact, I'm quite sure of it. I trust him."

"That's alright then. But a lot of people do tell lies."

I accepted this undeniable statement of fact in silence.

Megan said in a detached judicial kind of way, "I'm glad. I was afraid you looked bad-tempered because you were crocked up for life—but if it's just natural, it's different."

"I'm not bad-tempered," I said coldly.

"Well, irritable, then."

"I'm irritable because I'm in a hurry to get fit again—and these things can't be hurried."

"Then why fuss?"

I began to laugh. "My dear girl, aren't you ever in a hurry for things to happen?"

Megan considered the question. She said, "No. Why should I be? There's nothing to be in a hurry about. Nothing ever happens."

I was struck by something forlorn in the words. I said gently. "What do you do with yourself down here?"

She shrugged her shoulders. "What is there to do?"

"Haven't you any hobbies? Don't you play games? Haven't you got friends around about?"

"I'm stupid at games. There aren't many girls around here, and the ones there are I don't like. They think I'm awful."

"Nonsense. Why should they?"

Megan shook her head.

We were now entering the High Street. Megan said sharply:

"Here's Miss Griffith coming. Hateful woman. She's always at me to join her foul Guides. I hate Guides. Why dress up and go about in clumps and put badges on yourself for something you haven't really learned to do properly. I think it's all rot."

On the whole I rather agreed with Megan. But Miss Griffith had descended upon us before I could voice any assent.

The doctor's sister, who rejoiced in the singularly inappropriate name of Aimée, had all the positive assurance her brother lacked. She was a handsome woman in a masculine weather-beaten way, with a deep voice.

"Hullo, you two," she bayed at us. "Gorgeous morning, isn't it? Megan, you're just the person I want to see. I want some help. Addressing envelopes for the Conservative Association."

Megan muttered something elusive, propped up her bicycle against the curb and dived in a purposeful way into the International Stores.

"Extraordinary child," said Miss Griffith, looking after her. "Bone lazy. Spends her time mooning about. Must be a great trial to poor Mrs. Symmington. I know her mother's tried more than once to get her to take up something—shorthand-typing, you know, or cookery, or keeping Angora rabbits. She needs an *interest* in life."

I thought that was probably true, but felt that in Megan's place I should have withstood firmly any of Aimée Griffith's suggestions for the simple reason that her aggressive personality would have put my back up.

"I don't believe in idleness," went on Miss Griffith. "And certainly not for young people. It's not as though Megan was pretty or attractive or anything like that. Sometimes I think the girl's half-witted. A great disappointment to her mother. The father, you know," she lowered her voice slightly, "was definitely a wrong 'un. Afraid the child takes after him. Painful for her mother. Oh, well, it takes all sorts to make a world, that's what I say."

"Fortunately," I responded.

Aimée Griffith gave a "jolly" laugh.

"Yes, it wouldn't do if we were all made to one pattern. But I don't like to see anyone not getting all he can out of life. I enjoy life myself and I want everyone to enjoy it too. People say to me you must be bored to death living down there in the country all the year around. Not a bit of it, I say. I'm always busy, always happy! There's always something going on in the country. My time's taken up, what with my Guides, and the Institute and various committees—to say nothing of looking after Owen."

At this minute, Miss Griffith saw an acquaintance on the other side of the street, and uttering a bay of recognition she leaped across the road, leaving me free to pursue my course to the bank.

I always found Miss Griffith rather overwhelming.

My business at the bank transacted satisfactorily, I went on to the offices of Messrs. Galbraith, Galbraith and Symmington. I don't know if there were any Galbraith's extant. I never saw any. I was shown into Richard Symmington's inner office which had the agreeable mustiness of a long-established legal firm.

Vast numbers of deed boxes labeled Lady Hope, Sir Everard Carr, William Yatesby-Hoares Esq., Deceased, etc., gave the required atmosphere of decorous county families and legitimate, long-established business.

Studying Mr. Symmington as he bent over the documents I had brought, it occurred to me that if Mrs. Symmington had encountered disaster in her first marriage, she had certainly played safe in her second. Richard Symmington was the acme of calm respectability, the sort of man who would never give his wife a moment's anxiety. A long neck with a pronounced Adam's apple, a slightly cadaverous face and a long thin nose. A kindly man, no doubt, a good husband and father, but not one to set the pulses madly racing.

Presently Mr. Symmington began to speak. He spoke clearly and slowly, delivering himself of much good sense and shrewd acumen. We settled the matter in hand and I rose to go, remarking as I did so, "I walked down the hill with your stepdaughter."

For a moment Mr. Symmington looked as though he did not know who his stepdaughter was, then he smiled.

"Oh, yes, of course—Megan. She—er—has been back from school some time. We're thinking about finding her something to do—yes, to do. But, of course, she's very young still. And backward for her age, so they say. Yes, so they tell me."

I went out. In the outer office was a very old man on a stool writing slowing and laboriously, a small, cheeky-looking boy and a middle-aged woman with frizzy hair and pince-nez who was typing with some speed and dash.

If this was Miss Ginch I agreed with Owen Griffith that tender passages between her and her employer were exceedingly unlikely.

I went into the baker's and said my piece about the currant loaf. It was received with the exclamations and incredulity proper to the occasion, and a new currant loaf was thrust upon me in replacement—"fresh from the oven this minute"—as its indecent heat pressed against my chest proclaimed to be no less than truth.

I came out of the shop and looked up and down the street, hoping to see Joanna with the car. The walk had tired me a good deal and it was awkward getting along with my sticks and the currant loaf.

But there was no sign of Joanna as yet.

Suddenly my eyes were held in glad and incredulous surprise. Along the pavement toward me there came floating a goddess. There is really no other word for it. The perfect features, the crisply curling golden hair, the tall exquisitely shaped body. And she walked like a goddess, without effort, seeming to swim nearer and nearer. A glorious, an incredible, a breathtaking girl!

In my intense excitement something had to go. What went was the currant loaf. It slipped from my clutches. I made a dive after it and lost my stick, which clattered to the pavement, and I slipped and nearly fell myself.

It was the strong arm of the goddess that caught and held me.

I began to stammer: "Th-thanks awfully, I'm f-f-frightfully sorry."

She had retrieved the currant loaf and handed it to me together with the stick. And then she smiled kindly and said cheerfully, "Don't mention it. No trouble, I assure you," and the magic died completely before the flat, competent voice.

A nice, healthy-looking, well set-up girl; no more.

I fell to reflecting what would have happened if the gods had given Helen of Troy exactly those flat accents. How strange that a girl could trouble your inmost soul so long as she kept her mouth shut, and that the moment she spoke the glamor could vanish as though it had never been.

I had known the reverse happen, though. I had seen a little sad monkey-faced woman whom no one would turn to look at twice. Then she had opened her mouth and suddenly enchantment had lived and bloomed and Cleopatra had cast her spell anew.

Joanna had drawn up at the curb beside me without my noticing her arrival. She asked if there was anything the matter.

"Nothing," I said, pulling myself together. "I was reflecting on Helen of Troy and others."

"What a funny place to do it," said Joanna. "You looked *most* odd, standing there clasping currant bread to your breast with your mouth wide open."

"I've had a shock," I said. "I had been transplanted to Ilium and back again."

I added, indicating a retreating back that was swimming gracefully away, "Do you know who that is?"

Peering after the girl Joanna said that it was Elsie Holland, the Symmington's nursery governess.

"Is that what struck you all of a heap?" she asked. "She's good-looking, but a bit of a wet fish."

"I know," I said. "Just a nice kind girl. And I'd been thinking her Aphrodite."

Joanna opened the door of the car and I got in.

"It's funny, isn't it?" she said. "Some people have lots of looks and absolutely no S. A. That girl hasn't. It seems such a pity."

I said that if she was a nursery governess it was probably just as well.

That afternoon we went to tea with Mr. Pye.

Mr. Pye was an extremely ladylike plump little man, devoted to his *petit point* chairs, his Dresden shepherdesses and his collection of period furniture. He lived at Prior's Lodge in the grounds of which were the ruins of the old Priory dissolved at the Reformation.

It was hardly a man's house. The curtains and cushions were of pastel shades in the most expensive silks.

Mr. Pye's small plump hands quivered with excitement as he described and exhibited his treasures, and his voice rose to a falsetto squeak as he narrated the exciting circumstances in which he had brought his Italian bedstead home from Verona.

Joanna and I, both being fond of antiques, met with approval.

"It is really a pleasure, a great pleasure, to have such an acquisition to our little community. The dear good people down here, you know, so painfully bucolic—not to say *provincial.* Vandals—absolute vandals! And the inside of their houses—it would make you weep, dear lady, I assure you it would make you weep. Perhaps it has done so?"

Joanna said she hadn't gone quite so far as that.

"The house you have taken," went on Mr. Pye, "Miss Emily Barton's house. Now that is charming, and she has some quite nice pieces. Quite nice. One or two of them are really first-class. And she has taste, too—although I'm not quite so sure of that as I was. Sometimes, I am afraid, I think it's really sentiment. She likes to keep things as they were—but not for *le bon motif*—not because of the resultant harmony—but because it is the way her mother had them."

He transferred his attention to me, and his voice changed. It altered from that of the rapt artist to that of the born gossip:

"You didn't know the family at all? No, quite so—yes, through house agents. But, my dears, you *ought* to have known that family! When I came here the old mother was still alive. An incredible person—quite incredible! A *monster*, if you know what I mean. Positively a monster. The old-fashioned Victorian monster, devouring her young. Yes, that's what it amounted to. She was monumental, you know, must have weighed seventeen stone, and all the five daughters revolved around her. 'The girls!' That's how she always spoke of them. The girls! And the eldest was well over sixty then.

"'Those stupid girls!' she used to call them sometimes. Black slaves, that's all they were, fetching and carrying and agreeing with her. Ten o'clock they had to go to bed and they weren't allowed a fire in their bedroom, and as for asking their own friends to the house, that would have been unheard of. She despised them, you know, for not getting married, and yet so arranged their lives that it was practically impossible for them to meet anybody. I believe Emily, or perhaps it was Agnes, did have some kind of affair with a curate. But his family wasn't good enough and Mamma soon put a stop to *that!*"

"It sounds like a novel," said Joanna.

"Oh, my dear, it was. And then the dreadful old woman died, but of course, it was far too late *then.* They just went on living there and talking in hushed voices about what poor Mamma would have wished. Even repapering her bedroom they felt to be quite sacrilegious. Still they did enjoy themselves in the parish in a quiet way. . . . But none of them had much stamina, and they just died off one by one. Influenza took off Edith, and Minnie had an operation and didn't recover and poor Mabel had a stroke—Emily looked after her in the most devoted manner. Really that poor woman has done nothing but nursing for the last ten years. A charming creature, don't you think? Like a piece of Dresden. So sad for her having financial anxieties—but of course, all investments have depreciated."

"We feel rather awful being in her house," said Joanna.

"No, no, my dear young lady. You mustn't feel that way. Her dear good Florence is devoted to her and she told me herself how happy she was to have got such nice tenants." Here Mr. Pye made a little bow. "She told me she thought she had been most fortunate."

"The house," I said, "has a very soothing atmosphere."

Mr. Pye darted a quick glance at me.

"Really? You feel that? Now, that's very interesting. I wondered, you know. Yes, I wondered."

"What do you mean, Mr. Pye?" asked Joanna.

Mr. Pye spread out his plump hands. "Nothing, nothing. One wondered, that is all. I do believe in atmosphere, you know. People's thoughts and feelings. They give their impressions to the walls and the furniture."

I did not speak for a moment or two. I was looking around me and wondering how I would describe the atmosphere of Prior's Lodge. It seemed to me that the curious thing was that it hadn't any atmosphere! That was really very remarkable.

I reflected on this point so long that I heard nothing of the conversation going on between Joanna and her host. I was recalled to myself, however, by hearing Joanna uttering farewell preliminaries. I came out of my dream and added my quota.

We all went out into the hall. As we came toward the front door a letter came through the box and fell on the mat.

"Afternoon post," murmured Mr. Pye as he picked it up. "Now, my dear young people, you will come again, won't you? Such a pleasure to meet some broader minds, if you understand me, in this peaceful backwater where nothing ever happens."

Shaking hands with us twice over, he helped me with exaggerated care into the car. Joanna took the wheel, she negotiated with some care the circular sweep around a plot of unblemished grass, then with a straight drive ahead, she raised a hand to wave goodbye to our host where he stood on the steps of the house. I leaned forward to do the same.

But our gesture of farewell went unheeded. Mr. Pye had opened his mail. He was standing staring down at the open sheet in his hand.

Joanna had described him once as a plump pink cherub. He was still plump, but he was not looking like a cherub now. His face was a dark congested purple, contorted with rage and surprise. Yes, and fear, too.

And at that moment I realized that there had been something familiar about the look of that envelope. I had not realized it at the time—indeed, it had been one of those things that you note unconsciously without knowing that you do note them.

"Goodness," said Joanna, "what's bitten the poor pet?"

"I rather fancy," I said, "that it's the Hidden Hand again."

She turned an astonished face toward me and the car swerved.

"Careful, wench," I said.

Joanna refixed her attention on the road. She was frowning. "You mean a letter like the one you got."

"That's my guess."

"What is this place?" asked Joanna. "It looks the most innocent, sleepy harmless little bit of England you can imagine."

"Where, to quote Mr. Pye, nothing ever happens," I cut in. "He chose the wrong minute to say that. Something has happened."

"Jerry," said Joanna. "I—I don't think I like this." For the first time, there was a note of fear in her voice.

I did not answer, for I, too, did not like it. . . .

Such a peaceful smiling happy countryside—and down underneath something evil. . . .

It was as though at that moment I had a premonition of all that was to come. . . .

The days passed. We went and played bridge at the Symmingtons and Mrs. Symmington annoyed me a good deal by the way she referred to Megan.

"The poor child's so awkward. They are at that age, when they've left school and before they are properly grown up."

Joanna said sweetly, "But Megan's twenty, isn't she?"

"Oh, yes, yes. But of course, she's very young for her age. Quite a child still. It's so nice, I think, when girls don't grow up too quickly." She laughed. "I expect all mothers want their children to remain babies."

"I can't think why," said Joanna. "After all, it would be a bit awkward if one had a child who remained mentally six while his body grew up."

Mrs. Symmington looked annoyed and said Miss Burton mustn't take things so literally.

I was pleased with Joanna, and it occurred to me that I did not really much care for Mrs. Symmington. That anemic middle-aged prettiness concealed, I thought, a selfish, grasping nature.

Joanna asked maliciously if Mrs. Symmington were going to give a dance for Megan.

"A dance?" Mrs. Symmington seemed surprised and amused. "Oh, no, we don't do things like that down here."

"I see. Just tennis parties and things like that."

"Our tennis court has not been played on for years. Neither Richard nor I play. I suppose, later, when the boys grow up—oh, Megan will find plenty to do. She's quite happy just pottering about, you know. Let me see, did I deal? Two no trumps."

As we drove home, Joanna said with a vicious pressure on the accelerator pedal that made the car leap forward, "I feel awfully sorry for that girl."

"Megan?"

"Yes. Her mother doesn't like her."

"Oh, come now, Joanna, it's not as bad as that."

"Yes, it is. Lots of mothers don't like their children. Megan, I should imagine, is an awkward sort of creature to have about the house. She disturbs the pattern—the Symmington pattern. It's a complete unit without her—and that's a most unhappy feeling for a sensitive creature to have—and she *is* sensitive."

"Yes," I said, "I think she is."

I was silent for a moment.

Joanna suddenly laughed mischievously. "Bad luck for you about the governess."

"I don't know what you mean," I said with dignity.

"Nonsense. Masculine chagrin was written on your face every time you looked at her. I agree with you, it is a waste. And I don't see who else there is here for you. You'll have to fall back upon Aimée Griffith."

"God forbid," I said with a shudder. "And anyway," I added, "why all this concern about my love life? What about you, my girl? You'll need a little distraction down here, if I know you. No unappreciated genius, knocking about here. You'll have to fall back on Owen Griffith. He's the only unattached male in the place."

Joanna tossed her head. "Dr. Griffith doesn't like me."

"He's not seen much of you."

"He's seen enough apparently to make him cross over if he sees me coming along the High Street!"

"A most unusual reaction," I said sympathetically. "And one you're not used to."

Joanna drove in silence through the gate of Little Furze and around to the garage. Then she said, "There may be something in that idea of yours. I don't see why any man should deliberately cross the street to avoid me. It's rude apart from everything else."

"I see," I said. "You're going to hunt the man down in cold blood."

"Well, I don't like being avoided."

I got slowly and carefully out of the car and balanced my sticks. Then I offered my sister a piece of advice:

"Let me tell you this, girl. Owen Griffith isn't any of your tame, whining, artistic young men. Unless you're careful, you'll stir up a hornets' nest about your ears. That man could be dangerous."

"Oh, do you think so?" demanded Joanna with every symptom of pleasure at the prospect.

"Leave the poor devil alone," I said sternly.

"How dare he cross the street when he saw me coming?"

"All you women are alike. You harp on one theme. You'll have sister Aimée gunning for you, too, if I'm not mistaken."

"She dislikes me already," said Joanna. She spoke meditatively, but with a certain satisfaction.

"We have come down here," I said sternly, "for peace and quiet, and I mean to see we get it."

But peace and quiet were the last things we were to have.

2

IT WAS ABOUT a week later that I came back to the house to find Megan sitting on the veranda steps, her chin resting on her knees.

She greeted me with her usual lack of ceremony.

"Hullo," she said. "Do you think I could come to lunch?"

"Certainly," I said.

"If it's chops, or anything difficult like that and they won't go around, just tell me," shouted Megan as I went around to apprise Partridge of the fact that there would be three to lunch.

I fancy that Partridge sniffed. She certainly managed to convey without saying a word of any kind, that she didn't think much of that Miss Megan.

I went back to the veranda.

"Is it alright?" asked Megan anxiously.

"Quite alright," I said. "Irish stew."

"Oh, well, that's rather like dogs' dinner anyway isn't it? I mean it's mostly potato and flavor."

"Quite," I said.

We were silent while I smoked my pipe. It was quite a companionable silence.

Megan broke it by saying suddenly and violently, "I suppose you think I'm awful like everyone else."

I was so startled that my pipe fell out of my mouth. It was a meerschaum, just coloring nicely, and it broke. I said angrily to Megan, "Now see what you've done."

That most unaccountable of children, instead of being upset, merely grinned broadly. "I do like you," she said.

It was a most warming remark. It is the remark that one fancies perhaps erroneously that one's dog would say if he could talk. It occurred to me that Megan, for all she looked like a horse had the disposition of a dog. She was certainly not quite human.

"What did you say before the catastrophe?" I asked, carefully picking up the fragments of my cherished pipe.

"I said I supposed you thought me awful," said Megan but not at all in the same tone she had said it before.

"Why should I?"

Megan said gravely, "Because I am."

I said sharply. "Don't be stupid."

Megan shook her head. "That's just it. I'm not really stupid. People think I am. They don't know that inside I know just what they're like, and that all the time I'm hating them."

"*Hating* them?"

"Yes," said Megan.

Her eyes, those melancholy, unchildlike eyes stared straight into mine, without blinking. It was a long, mournful gaze.

"You would hate people if you were like me," she said. "If you weren't wanted."

"Don't you think you're being rather morbid?" I asked.

"Yes," said Megan. "That's what people always say when you're saying the truth. And it is true. I'm not wanted and I can quite see why. Mummie doesn't like me a bit. I remind her, I think, of my father, who was cruel to her and pretty dreadful from all I can hear. Only mothers can't say they don't want their children and just go away. Or eat them. Cats eat the kittens they don't like. Awfully sensible, I think. No waste or mess. But human mothers have to keep their children, and look after them. It hasn't been so bad while I could be sent away to school—but you see what Mummie would really like is to be just herself and my stepfather and the boys."

I said slowly, "I still think you're morbid, Megan, but accepting some of what you say as true, why don't you go away and have a life of your own?"

She gave me an odd unchildlike smile. "You mean take up a career. Earn my living?"

"Yes."

"What at?"

"You could train for something, I suppose. Shorthand, typing, book-keeping."

"I don't believe I could. I am stupid about doing things. And besides—"

"Well?"

She had turned her head away, now she turned it slowly back again. It was crimson and there were tears in her eyes. She spoke now with all the childishness back in her voice:

"Why should I go away? And be made to go away? They don't want me, but I'll *stay*. I'll stay and make everyone sorry. I'll make them all sorry. Hateful pigs! I hate everyone here in Lymstock. They all think I'm stupid and ugly. I'll show them! I'll show them! I'll—"

It was a childish, oddly pathetic rage.

I heard a step on the gravel around the corner of the house.

"Get up," I said savagely. "Go into the house through the drawing-room. Go up to the bathroom. Wash your face. Quick."

She sprang awkwardly to her feet and darted through the window as Joanna came around the corner of the house.

I told her Megan had come to lunch.

"Good," said Joanna. "I like Megan, though I rather think she's a changeling. Something left on a doorstep by the fairies. But she's interesting."

I see that so far I have made little mention of the Reverend and Mrs. Calthrop.

And yet both the vicar and his wife were distinct personalities. Dane Calthrop himself was perhaps a being more remote from everyday life than anyone I have ever met. His existence was in his books and in his study. Mrs. Dane Calthrop, on the other hand, was quite terrifying on the spot. Though she seldom gave advice and never interfered, yet she represented to the uneasy consciences of the village the Deity personified.

She stopped me in the High Street the day after Megan had come to lunch. I had the usual feeling of surprise, because Mrs. Dane Calthrop's progress resembled coursing more than walking, thus according with her startling resemblance to a greyhound, and as her eyes were always fixed on the distant horizon you felt sure that her real objective was about a mile and a half away.

"Oh!" she said. "Mr. Burton!"

She said it rather triumphantly, as someone might who had solved a particularly clever puzzle. I admitted that I was Mr. Burton and Mrs. Dane Calthrop stopped focusing on the horizon and seemed to be trying to focus on me instead.

"Now what," she said, "did I want to see you about?"

I could not help her there. She stood frowning, deeply perplexed. "Something rather nasty," she said.

"I'm sorry about that," I said startled.

"Ah," cried Mrs. Dane Calthrop. "*Anonymous letters!* What's this story you've brought down here about anonymous letters?"

"I didn't bring it," I said, "it was here already."

"Nobody got any until you came, though," said Mrs. Dane Calthrop accusingly.

"But they did, Mrs. Dane Calthrop. The trouble had already started."

"Oh, dear," said Mrs. Dane Calthrop. "I don't like that."

She stood there, her eyes absent and faraway again. She said:

"I can't help feeling it's all *wrong*. We're not like that here. Envy, of course, and malice, and all the mean spiteful little sins—but I didn't think there was anyone who would do that. No, I really didn't. And it distresses me, you see, because *I* ought to know."

Her fine eyes came back from the horizon and met mine. They were worried, and seemed to hold the honest bewilderment of a child's.

"Why ought you to know?" I said.

"I usually do. I've always felt that's my function. Caleb preaches good sound doctrine and administers the sacraments. That's a priest's duty, but if you admit marriage at all for a priest, then I think his wife's duty is to know what people are feeling and thinking, even if she can't do anything about it. And I haven't the least idea whose mind is—"

She broke off, adding absently, "They are such silly letters, too."

"Have you—er—had any yourself?"

I was a little diffident of asking, but Mrs. Dane Calthrop replied perfectly naturally, her eyes opening a little wider:

"Oh, yes, two—no three. I forget exactly what they said. Something very silly about Caleb and the schoolmistress, I think. Quite absurb, because Caleb has absolutely no taste for flirtation. He never has had. So lucky being a clergyman."

"Quite," I said, "oh, quite."

"Caleb would have been a saint," said Mrs. Dane Calthrop, "if he hadn't been just a little too intellectual."

I did not feel qualified to answer this criticism, and anyway Mrs. Dane Calthrop went on, leaping back from her husband to the letters in rather a puzzling way.

"There are so many things the letters might say, but don't. That's what is so curious."

"I should hardly have thought they erred on the side of restraint," I said bitterly.

"But they don't seem to *know* anything. None of the real things."

"You mean?"

Those fine vague eyes met mine.

"Well, of course. There's plenty of wrongdoing here—any amount of shameful secrets. Why doesn't the writer use those?" She paused and then asked abruptly, "What did they say in your letter?"

"They suggested that my sister wasn't my sister."

"And she is?"

Mrs. Dane Calthrop asked the question with unembarrassed friendly interest.

"Certainly Joanna is my sister."

Mrs. Dane Calthrop nodded her head. "That just shows you what I mean. I daresay there are other things—"

Her clear uninterested eyes looked at me thoughtfully, and I suddenly understood why Lymstock was afraid of Mrs. Dane Calthrop.

In everybody's life there are hidden chapters which they hope may never be known. I felt that Mrs. Dane Calthrop knew them.

For once in my life, I was positively delighted when Aimée Griffith's hearty voice boomed out:

"Hullo, Maud. Glad I've just caught you. I want to suggest an alteration of date for the Sale of Work. Morning, Mr. Burton."

She went on.

"I must just pop into the grocer's and leave my order, then I'll come along to the Institute if that suits you?"

"Yes, yes, that will do quite well," said Mrs. Dane Calthrop.

Aimée Griffith went into the International Stores.

Mrs. Dane Calthrop said, "Poor thing."

I was puzzled. Surely she could not be pitying Aimée?

She went on, however: "You know, Mr. Burton I'm rather afraid—"

"About this letter business?"

"Yes, you see it means—it must mean—" She paused, lost in thought, her eyes screwed up. Then she said slowly, as one who solves a problem, "Blind hatred . . . yes, blind hatred. But even a blind man might stab to the heart by pure chance. . . . And what would happen then, Mr. Burton?"

We were to know that before another day had passed.

Partridge, who enjoys calamity, came into Joanna's room at an early hour the following morning, and told her with considerable relish that Mrs. Symmington had committed suicide on the preceding afternoon.

Joanna, who had been lost in the mists of sleep, sat up in bed shocked wide awake.

"Oh, Partridge, how awful."

"Awful it is, Miss. It's wickedness taking your own life. Not but what she was drove to it, poor soul."

Joanna had an inkling of the truth then. She felt rather sick.

"Not—?" Her eyes questioned Partridge and Partridge nodded.

"That's right, Miss. One of them nasty letters."

"How beastly," said Joanna. "How absolutely beastly! All the same, I don't see why she should kill herself for a letter like that."

"Looks as though what was in the letter was true, Miss."

"What was in it?"

But that, Partridge couldn't or wouldn't say. Joanna came in to me, looking white and shocked. It seemed worse, somehow, that Mrs. Symmington was not the kind of person you associated with tragedy.

Joanna suggested that we might ask Megan to come to us for a day or two. Elsie Holland, she said, would be alright with the children, but was the kind of person who would, almost certainly, drive Megan half mad.

I agreed. I could imagine Elsie Holland uttering platitude after platitude and suggesting innumerable cups of tea. A kindly creature but not the right person for Megan.

We drove down to the Symmingtons' house after breakfast. We were both of us a little nervous. Our arrival might look like sheer ghoulish curiosity. Luckily we met Owen Griffith just coming out. He greeted me with some warmth, his worried face lighting up.

"Oh, hullo, Burton, I'm glad to see you. What I was afraid would happen sooner or later has happened. A damnable business!"

"Good morning, Dr. Griffith," said Joanna, using the voice she keeps for one of our deafer aunts.

Griffith started and flushed. "Oh—oh, good morning, Miss Burton."

"I thought perhaps," said Joanna, "that you didn't see me."

Owen Griffith got redder still. His shyness enveloped him like a mantle. "I'm—I'm so sorry—preoccupied—I didn't."

Joanna went on mercilessly.

"After all, I *am* life-size."

"Merely kit-kat," I said in a stern aside to her. Then I went on:

"My sister and I, Griffith, wondered whether it would be a good thing if the girl came and stopped with us for a day or two? What do you think? I don't want to butt in—but it must be rather grim for the poor child. What would Symmington feel about it, do you think?"

Griffith turned the idea over in his mind for a moment or two.

"I think it would be an excellent thing," he said at last. "She's a queer, nervous sort of girl, and it would be good for her to get away from the whole thing. Miss Holland is doing wonders—she's an excellent head on her shoulders, but she really has quite enough to do with the two children and Symmington himself. He's quite broken up—bewildered."

"It was"—I hesitated—"suicide?"

Griffith nodded.

"Oh, yes. No question of accident. She wrote, 'I can't go on,' on a scrap of paper. The letter must have come by yesterday afternoon's post. The envelope was down on the floor by her chair and the letter itself was screwed up into a ball and thrown into the fireplace."

"What did—"

I stopped, rather horrified at myself.

"I beg your pardon," I said.

Griffith gave a quick, unhappy smile.

"You needn't mind asking. That letter will have to be read at the inquest. No getting out of it, more's the pity. It was the usual kind of thing—couched in the same foul style. The specific accusation was that the second boy, Colin, was not Symmington's child."

"Do you think that was true?" I exclaimed incredulously.

Griffith shrugged his shoulders.

"I've no means of forming a judgment. I've only been here five years. As far as I've ever seen, the Symmingtons were a placid, happy couple devoted to each other and their children. It's true the boy doesn't particularly resemble his parents—he's got bright red hair, for one thing—but a child often throws back in appearance to a grandfather or grandmother."

"That lack of resemblance might have been what prompted the particular accusation. A foul and quite uncalled-for blow at a venture."

"But it happened to hit the bull's-eye," said Joanna. "After all, she wouldn't have killed herself otherwise, would she?"

Griffith said doubtfully:

"I'm not quite sure. She's been ailing in health for sometime—neurotic, hysterical. I've been treating her for a nervous condition. It's possible, I think, that the shock of receiving such a letter, couched in those terms, may have induced such a state of panic and despondency that she may have decided to take her life. She may have worked herself up to feel that her husband might not believe her if she denied the story, and the general shame and disgust might have worked upon her so powerfully as to unbalance her judgment temporarily."

"Suicide while of unsound mind," said Joanna.

"Exactly. I shall be quite justified, I think, in putting forward that point of view at the inquest."

Joanna and I went on into the house.

The front door was open and it seemed easier than ringing the bell, especially as we heard Elsie Holland's voice inside.

She was talking to Mr. Symmington who, huddled in a chair, was looking completely dazed.

"No, but really, Mr. Symmington, you must take something. You haven't had any breakfast, not what I call a proper breakfast, and nothing to eat last night, and what with the shock and all, you'll be getting ill yourself, and you'll need all your strength. The doctor said so before he left."

Symmington said in a toneless voice, "You're very kind, Miss Holland, but—"

"A nice cup of hot tea," said Elsie Holland, thrusting the beverage on him firmly.

Personally I should have given the poor devil a whiskey-and-soda. He looked as though he needed it. However he accepted the tea, and looking up at Elsie Holland:

"I can't thank you for all you've done and are doing, Miss Holland. You've been perfectly splendid."

The girl flushed and looked pleased.

"It's nice of you to say that, Mr. Symmington. You must let me do all I can to help. Don't worry about the children—I'll see to them, and I've got the servants calmed down, and if there's anything I can do, letter-writing or telephoning, don't hesitate to ask me."

"You're very kind," Symmington said again.

Elsie Holland, turning, caught sight of us and came hurrying out into the hall.

"Isn't it terrible?" she said in a hushed whisper.

I thought, as I looked at her, that she was really a very nice girl. Kind, competent, practical in an emergency. Her magnificent blue eyes were just faintly rimmed with pink, showing that she had been soft-hearted enough to shed tears for her employer's death.

"Can we speak to you a minute?" asked Joanna. "We don't want to disturb Mr. Symmington."

Elsie Holland nodded comprehendingly and led the way into the dining-room on the other side of the hall.

"It's been awful for him," she said. "Such a shock. Who ever would have thought a thing like this could happen? But of course, I do realize now that she had been queer for some time. Awfully nervous and weepy. I thought it was her health, though Dr. Griffith always said there was nothing really wrong with her. But she was snappy and irritable and some days you wouldn't know just how to take her."

"What we really came for," said Joanna, "was to know whether we could have Megan for a few days—that is, if she'd like to come."

Elsie Holland looked rather surprised.

"Megan?" she said doubtfully. "I don't know, I'm sure. I mean, it's ever so kind of you, but she's such a queer girl. One never knows what she's going to say or feel about things."

Joanna said rather vaguely, "We thought it might be a help, perhaps."

"Oh, well, as far as that goes, it would. I mean, I've got the boys to look after (they're with cook just now) and poor Mr. Symmington—he really needs looking after as much as anyone, and such a lot to do and see to. I really haven't had time to say much to Megan. I think she's upstairs in the old nursery at the top of the house. She seems to want to get away from everyone. I don't know if—"

Joanna gave me the faintest of looks. I slipped quickly out of the room and upstairs.

The old nursery was at the top of the house. I opened the door and went in. The room downstairs had given on to the garden behind and the blinds had not been down there. But in this room which faced the road they were decorously drawn down.

Through a dim gray gloom I saw Megan. She was crouching on a divan set against the far wall, and I was reminded at once of some terrified animal, hiding. She looked petrified with fear.

"Megan," I said.

I came forward, and unconsciously I adopted the tone one does adopt when you want to reassure a frightened animal. I'm really surprised I didn't hold out a carrot or a piece of sugar. I felt like that.

She stared at me, but she did not move, and her expression did not alter.

"Megan," I said again. "Joanna and I have come to ask you if you would like to come and stay with us for a little."

Her voice came hollowly out of the dim twilight:

"Stay with you? In your house?"

"Yes."

"You mean, you'll take me away from here?"

"Yes, my dear."

Suddenly she began to shake all over. It was frightening and very moving.

"Oh, do take me away!—Please do. It's so awful, being here, and feeling so wicked."

I came over to her and her hands fastened on my coat sleeve.

"I'm an awful coward. I didn't know what a coward I was."

"It's alright, funnyface," I said. "These things are a bit shattering. Come along."

"Can we go at once? Without waiting a minute?"

"Well, you'll have to put a few things together, I suppose."

"What sort of things? Why?"

"My dear girl" I said. "We can provide you with a bed and bath and the rest of it, but I'm darned if I lend you my toothbrush."

She gave a very faint weak little laugh.

"I see. I'll go and pack some things. You—you won't go away? You'll wait for me?"

"I'll be on the mat."

"Thank you. Thank you very much. I'm sorry I'm so stupid. But you see it's rather dreadful when your mother dies."

"I know," I said.

I gave her a friendly pat on the back and she flashed me a grateful look and disappeared into a bedroom. I went on downstairs.

"I found Megan," I said. "She's coming."

"Oh, now, that *is* a good thing," exclaimed Elsie Holland. "It will take her out of herself. She's rather a nervy girl, you know. Difficult. It will be a great relief to feel I haven't got her on my mind as well as everything else. It's very kind of you, Miss Burton. I hope she won't be a nuisance. Oh, dear, there's the telephone. I must go and answer it. Mr. Symmington isn't fit."

She hurried out of the room.

Joanna said, "Quite the ministering angel!"

"You said that rather nastily," I observed. "She's a nice, kind girl, and obviously most capable."

"Most. And she knows it."

"This is unworthy of you, Joanna," I said.

"Meaning why shouldn't the girl do her stuff?"

"Exactly."

"I never can stand seeing people pleased with themselves," said Joanna. "It arouses all my worst instincts. How did you find Megan?"

"Crouching in a darkened room looking rather like a stricken gazelle."

"Poor kid. She was quite willing to come?"

"She leaped at it."

A series of thuds out in the hall announced the descent of Megan and her suitcase. I went out and took it from her.

Joanna, behind me, said urgently, "Come on. I've already refused some nice hot tea twice."

We went out to the car. It annoyed me that Joanna had to sling the suitcase in. I could get along with one stick now, but I couldn't do any athletic feats.

"Get in," I said to Megan.

She got in, I followed her. Joanna started the car and we drove off.

We got to Little Furze and went into the drawing room.

Megan dropped into a chair and burst into tears. She cried with the hearty fervor of a child—bawled, I think, is the right word. I left the room in search of a remedy. Joanna stood by feeling rather helpless, I think.

Presently I heard Megan say in a thick choked voice, "I'm sorry for doing this. It seems idiotic."

Joanna said kindly. "Not at all. Have another handkerchief."

I gather she supplied the necessary article. I reentered the room and handed Megan a brimming glass.

"What is it?"

"A cocktail," I said.

"Is it? Is it really?" Megan's tears were instantly dried. "I've never drunk a cocktail."

"Everything has to have a beginning," I said.

Megan sipped her drink gingerly, then a beaming smile spread over her face, she tilted her head back and gulped it down at a draught.

"It's lovely," she said. "Can I have another?"

"No," I said.

"Why not?"

"In about ten minutes you'll probably know."

"Oh!"

Megan transferred her attention to Joanna.

"I really am awfully sorry for having made such a nuisance of myself howling away like that. I can't think why. It seems awfully silly when I'm so glad to be here."

"That's alright," said Joanna. "We're very pleased to have you."

"You can't be really. It's just kindness on your part. But I am grateful."

"Please don't be grateful," said Joanna, "it will embarrass me. You're our friend and we're glad to have you here. That's all there is to it. . . ."

She took Megan upstairs to unpack.

Partridge came in, looking sour, and said she had made two cup custards for lunch and what should she do about it?

The inquest was held three days later.

The time of Mrs. Symmington's death was put at between three and four o'clock. She was alone in the house, Symmington was at his office, the maids were having their day out, Elsie Holland and the children were out walking and Megan had gone for a bicycle ride.

The letter must have come by the afternoon post. Mrs. Symmington must have taken it out of the box, read it—and then in a state of agitation she had gone to the potting shed, fetched some of the cyanide kept there for taking wasps' nests, dissolved it in water and drunk it after writing those last agitated words, "I can't go on . . ."

Owen Griffith gave medical evidence and stressed the view he had outlined to us of Mrs. Symmington's nervous condition and poor stamina. The coroner was suave and discreet. He spoke with bitter condemnation of people who write those despicable things, anonymous letters. Whoever had written that wicked and lying letter was morally guilty of murder, he said. He hoped the police would soon discover the culprit and take action against him or her. Such a dastardly and malicious piece of spite deserved to be punished with the utmost rigor of the law. Directed by him, the jury brought in the inevitable verdict: Suicide while temporarily insane.

The coroner had done his best—Owen Griffith also, but afterward, jammed in the crowd of eager village women, I heard the same hateful sibilant whisper I had begun to know so well: "No smoke without fire, that's what *I* say!" "Must 'a been something in it for certain sure. She wouldn't never have done it otherwise . . ."

Just for a moment I hated Lymstock and its narrow boundaries, and its gossiping and whispering women.

Outside Aimée Griffith said with a sigh:

"Well, that's over. Bad luck on Dick Symmington, its all having to come out. I wonder whether he'd ever had any suspicion."

I was startled.

"But surely you heard him say most emphatically that there wasn't a word of truth in that lying letter?"

"Of course he said so. Quite right. A man's got to stick up for his wife. Dick would." She paused and then explained: "You see, I've known Dick Symmington a long time."

"Really?" I said surprised. "I understood from your brother that he only bought this practice a few years ago."

"Yes, but Dick Symmington used to come and stay in our part of the world up north. I've known him for years."

I looked at Aimée curiously. She went on, still in that softened tone, "I know Dick very well . . . He's a proud man and very reserved. But he's the sort of man who could be very jealous."

"That would explain," I said deliberately, "why Mrs. Symmington was afraid to show him or tell him about the letter. She was afraid that, being a jealous man, he might not believe her denials."

Miss Griffith looked at me angrily and scornfully. "Good Lord," she said. "Do you think any woman would go and swallow a lot of cyanide of potassium for an accusation that wasn't true?"

"The coroner seemed to think it was possible. Your brother, too—"

Aimée interrupted me:

"Men are all alike. All for preserving the decencies. But you don't catch *me* believing that stuff. If an innocent woman gets some foul anonymous letter, she laughs and chucks it away. That's what I—" she paused suddenly, and then finished—"would do."

But I had noticed the pause. I was almost sure that what she had been about to say was "That's what I did."

I decided to take the war into the enemy's country.

"I see," I said pleasantly. "So you've had one, too?"

Aimée Griffith was the type of woman who scorns to lie. She paused a minute—flushed, then said, "Well, yes. But I didn't let it worry me!"

"Nasty?" I inquired sympathetically, as a fellow sufferer.

"Naturally. These things always are. The ravings of a lunatic! I read a few words of it, realized what it was and chucked it straight into the wastepaper basket."

"You didn't think of taking it to the police?"

"Not then. Least said soonest mended—that's what I felt."

An urge came over me to say solemnly, "No smoke without fire!" but I restrained myself.

I asked her if she had any idea how her mother's death would affect Megan financially. Would it be necessary for the girl to earn her own living?

"I believe she has a small income left her by her grandmother and of course Dick would always give her a home. But it would be much better for her to do something—not just slack about the way she does."

"I should have said Megan is at the age when a girl wants to enjoy herself—not to work."

Aimée flushed and said sharply, "You're like all men—you dislike the idea of women competing. It is incredible to you that women should want a career. It was incredible to my parents. I was anxious to study for a doctor. They would not hear of paying the fees. But they paid them readily for Owen. Yet I should have made a better doctor than my brother."

"I'm sorry about that," I said. "It was tough on you. If one wants to do a thing—"

She went on quickly.

"Oh, I've got over it now. I've plenty of willpower. My life is busy and active. I'm one of the happiest people in Lymstock. Plenty to do. But I go up in arms against the silly old-fashioned prejudice that woman's place is always the home."

"I'm sorry if I offended you," I said. I had had no idea that Aimée Griffith could be so vehement.

3

I MET SYMMINGTON in the town later in the day.

"Is it quite alright for Megan to stay on with us for a bit?" I asked. "It's company for Joanna—she's rather lonely sometimes with none of her own friends."

"Oh—er—Megan? Oh, yes, very good of you."

I took a dislike to Symmington then which I never quite overcame. He had so obviously forgotten all about Megan. I wouldn't have minded if he had actively disliked the girl—a man may sometimes be jealous of a first husband's child—but he didn't dislike her, he just hardly noticed her. He felt toward her much as a man who doesn't care much for dogs would feel about a dog in the house. You notice it when you fall over it and swear at it, and you give it a vague pat sometimes when it presents itself to be patted. Symmington's complete indifference to his stepdaughter annoyed me very much.

I said, "What are you planning to do with her?"

"With Megan?" He seemed rather startled. "Well, she'll go on living at home. I mean, naturally, it is her home."

My grandmother, of whom I had been very fond, used to sing old-fashioned songs to her guitar. One of them, I remember, ended thus:

"Oh, maid most dear, I am not here,
I have no place, no part,
No dwelling more, by sea nor shore,
But only in your heart."

I went home humming it.

Emily Barton came just after tea had been cleared away.

She wanted to talk about the garden.

We talked garden for about half an hour. Then we turned back toward the house.

It was then that lowering her voice, she murmured, "I do hope that that child—that she hasn't been too much *upset* by this dreadful business?"

"Her mother's death, you mean?"

"That, of course. But I really meant, the—the unpleasantness *behind* it."

I was curious. I wanted Miss Barton's reaction.

"What do you think about that? Was it true?"

"Oh, no, no, surely not. I'm quite sure that Mrs. Symmington never—that he wasn't—" little Emily Barton was pink and confused—"I mean it's quite untrue—although of course it may have been a judgment."

"A judgment?" I said, staring.

Emily Barton was very pink, very Dresden china shepherdesslike.

"I cannot help feeling that all these dreadful letters, all the sorrow and pain they have caused, may have been sent for a *purpose*."

"They were sent for a purpose, certainly," I said grimly.

"No, no, Mr. Burton, you misunderstand me. I'm not talking of the misguided creature who wrote them—someone quite abandoned that must be. I mean that they have been permitted—by Providence! To awaken us to a sense of our shortcomings."

"Surely," I said, "the Almighty could choose a less unsavory weapon."

Miss Emily murmured that God moved in a mysterious way.

"No," I said. "There's too much tendency to attribute to God the evils that man does of his own free will. I might concede you the Devil. God doesn't really need to punish us, Miss Barton. We're so very busy punishing ourselves."

"What I can't make out is *why* should anyone want to do such a thing?"

I shrugged my shoulders. "A warped mentality."

"It seems very sad."

"It doesn't seem to me sad. It seems to me just damnable. And I don't apologize for the word. I mean just that."

The pink had gone out of Miss Barton's cheeks. They were very white.

"But why, Mr. Burton, *why?* What pleasure can anyone get out of it?"

"Nothing you and I can understand, thank goodness."

Emily Barton lowered her voice; "Nothing of this kind has ever happened before—never in my memory. It has been such a happy little community. What would my dear mother have said? Well, one must be thankful that she has been spared."

I thought from all I heard that old Mrs. Barton had been sufficiently tough to have taken anything, and would probably have enjoyed this sensation.

Emily went on, "It distresses me deeply."

"You've not—er—had anything yourself?"

She flushed crimson. "Oh, no—oh, no, indeed. Oh! That would be dreadful."

I apologized hastily, but she went away looking rather upset.

I went into the house. Joanna was standing by the drawing-room fire which she had just lit, for the evenings were still chilly. She had an open letter in her hand.

She turned her head quickly as I entered.

"Jerry! I found this in the letter box—dropped in by hand. It begins: 'You painted trollop . . .'"

"What else does it say?"

Joanna gave a wide grimace. "Same old muck."

She dropped it on to the fire. With a quick gesture that hurt my back I jerked it off again just before it caught.

"Don't," I said. "We may need it."

"Need it?"

"For the police."

Superintendent Nash came to see me the following morning. From the first moment I saw him I took a great liking to him. He was the best type of C.I.D. County Superintendent. Tall, soldierly, with quiet, reflective eyes and a straightforward, unassuming manner.

"Good morning, Mr. Burton," he said. "I expect you can guess what I've come to see you about."

"Yes, I think so. This letter business."

He nodded.

"I understand you had one of them?"

"Yes, soon after we got here."

"What did it say exactly?"

I thought a minute, then conscientiously repeated the wording of the letter as closely as possible.

The superintendent listened with an immovable face, showing no signs of any kind of emotion.

When I had finished, he said, "I see. You didn't keep the letter, Mr. Burton?"

"I'm sorry. I didn't. You see, I thought it was just an isolated instance of spite against newcomers to the place."

The superintendent inclined his head comprehendingly.

"A pity," he said briefly.

"However," I said, "my sister got one yesterday. I just stopped her putting it in the fire."

"Thank you, Mr. Burton, that was thoughtful of you."

I went across to my desk and unlocked the drawer in which I had put it. It was not, I thought, very suitable for Partridge's eyes. I gave it to Nash.

He read it through. Then he looked up and asked:

"Is this the same in appearance as the last one?"

"I think so—as far as I can remember."

"The same difference between the envelope and the text?"

"Yes," I said. "The envelope was typed. The letter itself had printed words pasted on to a sheet of paper."

Nash nodded and put it in his pocket. Then he said:

"I wonder, Mr. Burton, if you would mind coming down to the station with me? We could have a conference there and it would save a good deal of time and overlapping."

"Certainly," I said. "You would like me to come now?"

"If you don't mind."

There was a police car at the door. We drove down in it.

I said, "Do you think you'll be able to get to the bottom of this?"

Nash nodded with easy confidence. "Oh, yes, we'll get to the bottom of it alright. It's a question of time and routine. They're slow, these cases, but they're pretty sure. It's a matter of narrowing things down."

"Elimination?" I said.

"Yes. And general routine."

"Watching post boxes, examining typewriters, fingerprints, all that?"

He smiled. "As you say."

At the police station I found Symmington and Griffith were already there. I was introduced to a tall, lantern-jawed man in plain clothes, Inspector Graves.

"Inspector Graves," explained Nash, "has come down from London to help us. He's an expert on anonymous letter cases."

Inspector Graves smiled mournfully. I reflected that a life spent in the pursuit of anonymous letter writers must be singularly depressing. Inspector Graves, however, showed a kind of melancholy enthusiasm.

"They're all the same, these cases," he said in a deep lugubrious voice like a depressed bloodhound. "You'd be surprised. The wording of the letters and the things they say."

"We had a case just on two years ago," said Nash. "Inspector Graves helped us then."

Some of the letters, I saw, were spread out on the table in front of Graves. He had evidently been examining them.

"Difficulty is," said Nash, "to get hold of the letters. Either people put them in the fire, or they won't admit to having received anything of the kind. Stupid, you see, and afraid of being mixed up with the police. They're a backward lot here."

"Still we've got a fair amount to get on with," said Graves. Nash took the letter I had given him from his pocket and tossed it over to Graves.

The latter glanced through it, laid it with the others and observed approvingly, "Very nice—very nice indeed."

It was not the way I should have chosen to describe the epistle in question, but experts, I suppose, have their own point of view. I was glad that that screed of vituperative and obscene abuse gave *somebody* pleasure.

"We've got enough, I think, to go on with," said Inspector Graves, "and I'll ask all you gentlemen, if you should get any more, to bring them along at once. Also, if you hear of someone else getting one (you, in particular, doctor, among your patients) do your best to get them to come along here with them. I've got"—he sorted with deft fingers among his exhibits—"one to Mr. Symmington, received as far back as two months ago, one to Dr. Griffith, one to Miss Ginch, one written to Mrs. Mudge, the butcher's wife, one to Jennifer Clark, barmaid at the Three Crowns, the one received by Mrs. Symmington, this one now to Miss Burton—oh, yes, and one to the bank manager."

"Quite a representative collection," I remarked.

"And not one I couldn't match from other cases! This one here is as near as nothing to one written by that milliner woman. This one is the dead spit of an outbreak we had up in Northumberland—written by a schoolgirl, they were. I can tell you, gentlemen, I'd like to see something *new* sometimes, instead of the same old treadmill."

"There is nothing new under the sun," I murmured.

"Quite so, sir. You'd know that if you were in our profession."

Nash sighed and said, "Yes, indeed."

Symmington asked. "Have you come to any definite opinion as to the writer?"

Graves cleared his throat and delivered a small lecture:

"There are certain similarities shared by all these letters. I shall enumerate them, gentlemen, in case they suggest anything to your minds. The text of the letters is composed of words made up from individual letters cut out of a printed book. It's an old book, printed, I should say, about the year 1830. This has obviously been done to avoid the risk of recognition through handwriting which is, as most people know nowadays, a fairly easy matter . . . the so-called disguising of a hand not amounting to much when faced with expert tests. There are no fingerprints on the letters and envelopes of a distinctive character. That is to say, they have been handled by the postal authorities, the recipient, and there are other stray fingerprints, but no set common to all, showing therefore that the person who put them together was careful to wear gloves.

"The envelopes are typewritten by a Windsor 7 machine, well worn, with the *a* and the *t* out of alignment. Most of them have been posted locally, or put in the box of a house by hand. It is therefore evident that they are of local provenance. They were written by a woman, and in my opinion a woman of middle age or over, and probably, though not certainly, unmarried."

We maintained a respectful silence for a minute or two. Then I said, "The typewriter's your best bet, isn't it? That oughtn't to be difficult in a little place like this."

Inspector Graves shook his head sadly and said, "That's where you're wrong, sir."

"The typewriter," said Superintendent Nash, "is unfortunately too easy. It is an old one from Mr. Symmington's office, given by him to the Women's Institute where, I may say, it's fairly easy of access. The ladies here all often go into the Institute."

"Can't you tell something definite from the—er—the touch, don't you call it?"

Again Graves nodded. "Yes, that can be done—but these envelopes have all been typed by someone using one finger."

"Someone, then, unused to the typewriter?"

"No, I wouldn't say that. Someone, perhaps, who can type but doesn't want us to know the fact."

"Whoever writes these things has been very cunning," I said slowly.

"She is, sir, she is," said Graves. "Up to every trick of the trade."

"I shouldn't have thought one of these bucolic women down here would have had the brains," I said.

Graves coughed. "I haven't made myself plain, I'm afraid. Those letters were written by an educated woman."

"What, by a lady?"

The word slipped out involuntarily. I hadn't used the term "lady" for years. But now it came automatically to my lips, re-echoed from days long ago, and my grandmother's faint unconsciously arrogant voice saying, "Of course, she isn't a *lady*, dear."

Nash understood at once. The word lady still meant something to him.

"Not necessarily a lady," he said. "But certainly not a village woman. They're mostly pretty illiterate down here, can't spell, and certainly can't express themselves with fluency."

I was silent, for I had had a shock. The community was so small. Unconsciously I had visualized the writer of the letters as a Mrs. Cleat or her like, some spiteful, cunning half-wit.

Symmington put my thoughts into words. He said sharply, "But that narrows it down to about half a dozen people in the whole place! I can't believe it."

Then, with a slight effort, and looking straight in front of him as though the mere sound of his own words was distasteful, he said:

"You have heard what I stated at the inquest. In case you may have thought that that statement was actuated by a desire to protect my wife's memory, I should like to repeat now that I am firmly convinced that the subject matter of the letter my wife received was absolutely false. I *know* it was false. My wife was a very sensitive woman, and—er—well, you might call it *prudish* in some respects. Such a letter would have been a great shock to her, and she was in poor health."

Graves responded instantly:

"That's quite likely to be right, sir. None of these letters show any signs of intimate knowledge. They're just blind accusations. There's been no attempt to blackmail. And there doesn't seem to be any religious bias—such as we sometimes get. It's just sex and spite! And that's going to give us quite a good pointer toward the writer."

Symmington got up. Dry and unemotional as the man was, his lips were trembling.

"I hope you find the devil who writes these soon. She murdered my wife as surely as if she'd put a knife into her." He paused. "How does she feel now, I wonder?"

He went out, leaving that question unanswered.

"How does she feel, Griffith?" I asked. It seemed to me the answer was in his province.

"God knows. Remorseful, perhaps. On the other hand, it may be that she's enjoying her power. Mrs. Symmington's death may have fed her mania."

"I hope not," I said, with a slight shiver. "Because if so, she'll—"

I hesitated and Nash finished the sentence for me:

"She'll try it again? That, Mr. Burton, would be the best thing that could happen, for us. The pitcher goes to the well once too often, remember."

"She'd be mad to go on with it," I exclaimed.

"She'll go on," said Graves. "They always do. It's a vice, you know, they can't let it alone."

I shook my head with a shudder. I asked if they needed me any longer, I wanted to get out into the air. The atmosphere seemed tinged with evil.

"There's nothing more, Mr. Burton," said Nash. "Only keep your eyes open, and do as much propaganda as you can—that is to say, urge on everyone that they've got to report any letter they receive."

I nodded.

"I should think everyone in the place has had one of the foul things by now," I said.

"I wonder," said Graves. He put his sad head a little on one side and asked, "You don't know, definitely, of anyone who *hasn't* had a letter?"

"What an extraordinary question! The population at large isn't likely to take me into their confidence."

"No, no, Mr. Burton, I didn't mean that. I just wondered if you knew of any one person who quite definitely, to your certain knowledge, has not received an anonymous letter."

"Well, as a matter of fact," I hesitated, "I do, in a way."

And I repeated my conversation with Emily Barton and what she had said.

Graves received the information with a wooden face and said, "Well, that may come in useful. I'll note it down."

I went out into the afternoon sunshine with Owen Griffith. Once in the street, I swore aloud.

"What kind of place is this for a man to come to to lie in the sun and heal his wounds? It's full of festering poison, this place, and it looks as peaceful and as innocent as the Garden of Eden."

"Even there," said Owen drily, "there was one serpent."

"Look here, Griffith, do they know anything? Have they got any idea?"

"I don't know. They've got a wonderful technique, the police. They're seemingly so frank, and they tell you nothing."

"Yes. Nash is a nice fellow."

"And a very capable one."

"If anyone's batty in this place, you ought to know it," I said accusingly.

Griffith shook his head. He looked discouraged. But he looked more than that—he looked worried. I wondered if he had an inkling of some kind.

We had been walking along the High Street. I stopped at the door of the house agents.

"I believe my second installment of rent is due—in advance. I've got a good mind to pay it and clear out with Joanna right away. Forfeit the rest of the tenancy."

"Don't go," said Owen.

"Why not?"

He didn't answer. He said slowly after a minute or two, "After all—I dare say you're right. Lymstock isn't healthy just now. It might—it might harm you or—or your sister."

"Nothing harms Joanna," I said. "She's tough. I'm the weakly one. Somehow this business makes me sick."

"It makes *me* sick," said Owen.

I pushed the door of the house agents' place half open.

"But I shan't go," I said. "Vulgar curiosity is stronger than pusillanimity. I want to know the solution."

I went in.

A woman who was typing got up and came toward me. She had frizzy hair and simpered, but I found her more intelligent than the spectacled youth who had previously held sway in the outer office.

A minute or two later something familiar about her penetrated through to my consciousness. It was Miss Ginch, lately Symmington's lady clerk.

I commented on the fact.

"You used to be with Galbraith, Galbraith and Symmington, weren't you?" I said.

"Yes. Yes, indeed. But I thought it was better to leave. This is quite a good post, though not quite so well paid. But there are things that are more valuable than money, don't you think so?"

"Undoubtedly," I said.

"Those awful letters," breathed Miss Ginch in a sibilant whisper. "I got a dreadful one. About me and Mr. Symmington—oh, terrible it was, saying the most *awful* things! I knew my duty and I took it to the police, though of course it wasn't exactly *pleasant* for me, was it?"

"No, no, most unpleasant."

"But they thanked me and said I had done quite right. But I felt that, after that, if people were talking—and evidently they *must* have been, or where did the writer get the idea from?—then I must avoid even the appearance of evil, though there has never been anything at all *wrong* between me and Mr. Symmington."

I felt rather embarrassed.

"No, no, of course not."

"But people have such evil minds. Yes, alas, such evil minds!"

Nervously trying to avoid it, I nevertheless met her eye, and I made a most unpleasant discovery.

Miss Ginch was thoroughly enjoying herself.

Already once today I had come across someone who reacted pleasurably to anonymous letters. Inspector Graves' enthusiasm was professional. Miss Ginch's enjoyment I found merely suggestive and disgusting.

An idea flashed across my startled mind.

Had Miss Ginch written these letters herself?

When I got home I found Mrs. Dane Calthrop sitting talking to Joanna. She looked, I thought, gray and ill.

"This has been a terrible shock to me, Mr. Burton," she said. "Poor thing, poor thing."

"Yes," I said. "It's awful to think of someone being driven to the stage of taking their own life."

"Oh, you mean Mrs. Symmington?"

"Didn't you?"

Mrs. Dane Calthrop shook her head. "Of course one is sorry for her, but it would have been bound to happen anyway, wouldn't it?"

"Would it?" said Joanna drily.

Mrs. Dane Calthrop turned to her.

"Oh, I think so, dear. If suicide is your idea of escape from trouble then it doesn't very much matter what the trouble is. Whenever some very unpleasant shock had to be faced, she'd have done the same thing. What it really comes down to is that she was that kind of woman. Not that one would have guessed it. She always seemed to me a selfish rather stupid woman, with a good firm hold on life. Not the kind to panic, you would think—but I'm beginning to realize how little I really know about anyone."

"I'm still curious as to whom you meant when you said 'Poor thing,'" I remarked.

She stared at me. "The woman who wrote the letters, of course."

"I don't think," I said drily, "I shall waste sympathy on her."

Mrs. Dane Calthrop leaned forward. She laid a hand on my knee.

"But don't you realize—can't you *feel?* Use your imagination. Think how desperately, violently unhappy anyone must be to sit down and write those things. How lonely, how cut off from human kind. Poisoned through and through, with a dark stream of poison that finds its outlet in this way. That's why I feel so self-reproachful. Somebody in this town has been racked with that terrible unhappiness, and I've had no idea of it. I should have had. You can't interfere with actions—I never do. But that black inward unhappiness—like a septic arm physically, all black and swollen. If you could cut it and let the poison out it would flow away harmlessly. Yes, poor soul, poor soul."

She got up to go.

I did not feel like agreeing with her. I had no sympathy for our anonymous letter writer whatsoever. But I did ask curiously:

"Have you any idea at all, Mrs. Calthrop, who this woman is?"

She turned her fine perplexed eyes on me. "Well, I can guess," she said. "But then I might be wrong, mightn't I?

She went swiftly out through the door, popping her head back to ask: "Do tell me, why have you never married, Mr. Burton?"

In anyone else it would have been impertinence, but with Mrs. Dane Calthrop you felt that the idea had suddenly come into her head and she had really wanted to know.

"Shall we say," I said, rallying, "that I have never met the right woman?"

"We can say so," Mrs. Dane Calthrop, "but it wouldn't be a very good answer, because so many men have obviously married the wrong woman."

This time she really departed.

Joanna said, "You know I really do think she's mad. But I like her. The people in the village here are afraid of her."

"So am I, a little."

"Because you never know what's coming next?"

"Yes. And there's a careless brilliancy about her guesses."

Joanna said slowly, "Do you really think whoever wrote these letters is very unhappy?"

"I don't know what the damned hag is thinking or feeling! And I don't care. It's her victims I'm sorry for."

It seems odd to me now that in our speculations about Poison Pen's frame of mind, we missed the most obvious one. Griffith had pictured her as possibly exultant. I had envisaged her as remorseful—appalled by the result of her handiwork. Mrs. Dane Calthrop had seen her as suffering.

Yet the obvious, the inevitable reaction we did not consider—or perhaps I should say, I did not consider. That reaction was Fear.

For with the death of Mrs. Symmington, the letters had passed out of one category into another. I don't know what the legal position was—Symmington knew, I suppose, but it was clear that with a death resulting, the position of the writer of the letters was much more serious. There could now be no question of passing it off as a joke if the identity of the writer was discovered. The police were active, a Scotland Yard expert was called in. It was vital now for the anonymous author to remain anonymous.

And granted that Fear was the principal reaction, other things followed. Those possibilities also I was blind to. Yet surely they should have been obvious.

Joanna and I came down rather late to breakfast the next morning. That is to say, late by the standards of Lymstock. It was nine-thirty, an hour at which, in London, Joanna was just unclosing an eyelid, and mine would probably be still tight shut.

However when Partridge had said, "Breakfast at half past eight, or nine o'clock?" neither Joanna nor I had had the nerve to suggest a later hour.

To my annoyance, Aimée Griffith was standing on the doorstep talking to Megan.

She gave tongue with her usual heartiness at the sight of us:

"Hello, there, slackers! I've been up for hours."

That, of course, was her own business. A doctor, no doubt, has to have early breakfast, and a dutiful sister is there to pour out his tea or coffee. But it is no excuse for coming and butting in on one's more somnolent neighbors. Nine-thirty is not the time for a morning call.

Megan slipped back into the house and into the dining-oom, where I gathered she had been interrupted in her breakfast.

"I said I wouldn't come in," said Aimée Griffith—"though why it is more of a merit to force people to come and speak to you on the doorstep, than to talk to them inside the house I do not know. Just wanted to ask Miss Burton if she'd any vegetables to spare for our Red Cross stall on the main road. If so, I'd get Owen to call for them in the car."

"You're out and about very early," I said.

"The early bird catches the worm," said Aimée. "You have a better chance of finding people in this time of day. I'm off to Mr. Pye's next. Got to go over to Brenton this afternoon. Guides."

"Your energy makes me quite tired," I said, and at that moment the telephone rang and I retired to the back of the hall to answer it, leaving Joanna murmuring rather doubtfully something about rhubarb and French beans and exposing her ignorance of the vegetable garden.

"Yes?" I said into the telephone mouthpiece.

A confused noise of deep breathing came from the other end of the wire and a doubtful female voice said, "Oh!"

"Yes?" I said again encouragingly.

"Oh," said the voice again, and then it inquired adenoidally, "Is that—what I mean—is that Little Furze?"

"This is Little Furze."

"Oh!" This clearly a stock beginning to every sentence. The voice inquired cautiously: "Could I speak to Miss Partridge just a minute?"

"Certainly," I said. "Who shall I say?"

"Oh. Tell her it's Agnes, would you? Agnes Waddle."

"Agnes Waddle?"

"That's right."

Resisting the temptation to say "Donald Duck to you," I put down the telephone receiver and called up the stairs to where I could hear the sound of Partridge's activities overhead.

"Partridge! Partridge!"

Partridge appeared at the head of the stairs, a long mop in one hand, and a look of "What is it *now?*" clearly discernible behind her invariably respectful manner.

"Yes, sir?"

"Agnes Waddle wants to speak to you on the telephone."

"I beg your pardon, sir?'

I raised my voice: "Agnes Waddle."

I have spelled the name as it presented itself to my mind. But I will now spell it as it was actually written:

"Agnes Woddell—whatever can she want now?"

Very much put out of countenance Partridge relinquished her mop and rustled down the stairs, her print dress crackling with agitation.

I beat an unobtrusive retreat into the dining room where Megan was wolfing down kidneys and bacon. Megan, unlike Aimée Griffith, was displaying no "glorious morning face." In fact she replied very gruffly to my morning salutations and continued to eat in silence.

I opened the morning paper and a minute or two later Joanna entered looking somewhat shattered.

"Whew!" she said. "I'm so tired. And I think I've exposed my utter ignorance of what grows when. Aren't there runner beans this time of year?"

"August," said Megan.

"Well, one has them any time in London," said Joanna defensively.

"Tins, sweet fool," I said. "And cold storage on ships from the far-flung limits of Empire."

"Like ivory, apes and peacocks?" asked Joanna.

"Exactly."

"I'd rather have peacocks," said Joanna thoughtfully.

"I'd like a monkey of my own as a pet," said Megan.

Meditatively peeling an orange, Joanna said:

"I wonder what it would feel like to be Aimée Griffith, all bursting with health and vigor and enjoyment of life. Do you think she's ever tired, or depressed, or—or wistful?"

I said I was quite certain Aimée Griffith was never wistful, and followed Megan out of the open French window onto the veranda.

Standing there, filling my pipe, I heard Partridge enter the dining-room from the hall and heard her voice say grimly, "Can I speak to you a minute, Miss?"

"Dear me," I thought. "I hope Partridge isn't going to give notice. Emily Barton would be very annoyed with us if so."

Partridge went on:

"I must apologize, Miss, for being rung up on the telephone. That is to say, the young person who did so should have known better. I have never been in the habit of using the telephone or of permitting my friends to ring me up on it, and I'm very sorry indeed that it should have occurred, and the master taking the call and everything."

"Why, that's quite alright, Partridge," said Joanna soothingly, "why shouldn't your friends use the phone if they want to speak to you?"

Partridge's face, I could feel, though I could not see it, was more dour than ever as she replied coldly:

"It is not the kind of thing that has ever been done in this house. Miss Emily would never permit it. As I say, I am sorry it occurred, but Agnes Woddell, the girl who did it, was upset and she's young too, and doesn't know what's fitting in a gentleman's house."

"That's one for you, Joanna," I thought gleefully.

"This Agnes who rung me up, Miss," went on Partridge, "she used to be in service here under me. Sixteen she was, then, and come straight from the orphanage. And you see, not having a home, or a mother or any relations to advise her, she's been in the habit of coming to me. I can tell her what's what, you see."

"Yes?" said Joanna and waited. Clearly there was more to follow.

"So I am taking the liberty of asking you, Miss, if you would allow Agnes to come here to tea this afternoon in the kitchen. It's her day out, you see, and she's got something on her mind she wants to consult me about it. I wouldn't dream of suggesting such a thing in the usual way."

Joanna said bewildered, "But why shouldn't you have anyone to tea with you?"

Partridge drew herself up at this, so Joanna said afterward and really looked most formidable, as she replied:

"It has never been the custom of this house, Miss. Old Mrs. Barton never allowed visitors in the kitchen, excepting as it should be our own day out, in which case we were allowed to entertain friends here instead of going out, but otherwise, on ordinary days, no. And Miss Emily keeps to the old ways."

Joanna is very nice to servants and most of them like her but she has never cut any ice with Partridge.

"It's no good, my girl," I said when Partridge had gone and Joanna had joined me outside. "Your sympathy and leniency are not appreciated. The good old overbearing ways for Partridge and things done the way they should be done in a gentleman's house."

"I never heard of such tyranny as not allowing them to have their friends to see them," said Joanna. "It's all very well, Jerry, but they can't *like* being treated like black slaves."

"Evidently they do," I said. "At least the Partridges of this world do."

"I can't imagine why she doesn't like me. Most people do."

"She probably despises you as an inadequate housekeeper. You never draw your hand across a shelf and examine it for traces of dust. You don't look under the mats. You don't ask what happened to the remains of the chocolate soufflé, and you never order a nice bread pudding."

"Ugh!" said Joanna.

She went on sadly: "I'm a failure all around today. Despised by our Aimée for ignorance of the vegetable kingdom. Snubbed by Partridge for being a human being. I shall now go out into the garden and eat worms."

"Megan's there already," I said.

For Megan had wandered away a few minutes previously and was now standing aimlessly in the middle of a patch of lawn looking not unlike a meditative bird waiting for nourishment.

She came back however toward us and said abruptly, "I say, I must go home today."

"What?" I was dismayed.

She went on, flushing, but speaking with nervous determination:

"It's been awfully good of you having me and I expect I've been a fearful nuisance, but I have enjoyed it awfully, only now I must go back, because after all, well, it's my home and one can't stay away for ever, so I think I'll go this morning."

Both Joanna and I tried to make her change her mind, but she was quite adamant, and finally Joanna got out the car and Megan went upstairs and came down a few minutes later with her belongings packed up again.

The only person pleased seemed to be Partridge, who had almost a smile on her grim face. She had never liked Megan much.

I was standing in the middle of the lawn when Joanna returned.

She asked me if I thought I was a sundial.

"Why?"

"Standing there like a garden ornament. Only one couldn't put on you the motto of only marking the sunny hours. You looked like thunder!"

"I'm out of humor. First Aimée Griffith"—('Gracious!' murmured Joanna, 'I must speak about those vegetables!') "and then Megan beetling off. I'd thought of taking her for a walk up to Legge Tor."

"With a collar and lead, I suppose," said Joanna.

"What?"

Joanna repeated loudly and clearly as she moved off around the corner of the house to the kitchen garden:

"I said 'With a collar and lead, I suppose?' Master's lost his dog, that's what's the matter with you!"

4

I WAS ANNOYED, I must confess, at the abrupt way in which Megan had left us. Perhaps she had suddenly got bored with us.

After all, it wasn't a very amusing life for a girl. At home she had the kids and Elsie Holland.

I heard Joanna returning and hastily moved in case she should make more rude remarks about sundials.

Owen Griffith called in his car just before lunch time, and the gardener was waiting for him with the necessary garden produce.

While Old Adams was stowing it in the car I brought Owen indoors for a drink. He wouldn't stay to lunch.

When I came in with the sherry I found Joanna had begun doing her stuff.

No signs of animosity now. She was curled up in the corner of the sofa and was positively purring, asking Owen questions about his work, if he liked being a G.P., if he wouldn't rather have specialized? She thought doctoring was one of the most fascinating things in the world.

Say what you will of her, Joanna is a lovely, a heaven-born listener. And after listening to so many would-be geniuses telling her how they had been unappreciated, listening to Owen Griffith was easy money. By the time we had got to the third glass of sherry, Griffith was telling her about some obscure reaction or lesion in such scientific terms that nobody could have understood a word of it except a fellow medico.

Joanna was looking intelligent and deeply interested.

I felt a moment's qualm. It was really too bad of Joanna. Griffith was too good a chap to be played fast and loose with. Women really were devils.

Then I caught a sideways view of Griffith, his long, purposeful chin and the grim set of his lips, and I was not so sure that Joanna was going to have it her own way after all. And anyway a man has no business to let himself be made a fool of by a woman. It's his own lookout if he does.

Then Joanna said:

"Do change your mind and stay to lunch with us, Dr. Griffith," and Griffith flushed a little and said he would, only his sister would be expecting him back—

"We'll ring her up and explain," said Joanna quickly and went out into the hall and did so.

I thought Griffith looked a little uneasy, and it crossed my mind that he was probably a little afraid of his sister.

Joanna came back smiling and said that that was alright.

And Owen Griffith stayed to lunch and seemed to enjoy himself. We talked about books and plays and world politics, and about music and painting and modern architecture.

We didn't talk about Lymstock at all, or about anonymous letters, or Mrs. Symmington's suicide.

We got right away from everything, and I think Owen Griffith was happy. His dark sad face lighted up, and he revealed an interesting mind.

When he had gone I said to Joanna, "That fellow's too good for your tricks."

"That's what *you* say!" Joanna said. "You men all stick together!"

"Why are you out after his hide, Joanna? Wounded vanity?"

"Perhaps," said my sister.

That afternoon we were to go to tea with Miss Emily Barton at her rooms in the village.

We strolled down there on foot, for I felt strong enough now to manage the hill back again.

We must actually have allowed too much time and got there early, for the door was opened to us by a tall, raw-boned, fierce-looking woman who told us that Miss Barton wasn't in yet.

"But she's expecting you, I know, so if you'll come up and wait, please."

This was evidently faithful Florence.

We followed her up the stairs and she threw open a door and showed us into what was quite a comfortable sitting room, though perhaps a little over-furnished. Some of the things, I suspected, had come from Little Furze.

The woman was clearly proud of her room.

"It's nice, isn't it?" she demanded.

"Very nice," said Joanna warmly.

"I make her as comfortable as I can. Not that I can do for her as I'd like to and in the way she ought to have. She ought to be in her own house, properly, not turned out into rooms."

Florence, who was clearly a dragon, looked from one to the other of us reproachfully. It was not, I felt, our lucky day. Joanna had been ticked off by Aimée Griffith and Partridge and now we were both being ticked off by the dragon Florence.

"Parlormaid I was for nine years there," she added.

Joanna, goaded by injustice, said, "Well, Miss Barton wanted to let the house. She put it down at the house agents."

"Forced to it," said Florence. "And she living so frugal and careful. But even then, the government can't leave her alone! Has to have its pound of flesh just the same."

I shook my head sadly.

"Plenty of money there was in the old lady's time," said Florence. "And then they all died off one after another, poor dears. Miss Emily nursing of them one after the other. Wore herself out she did, and always so patient and uncomplaining. But it told on her, and then to have worry about money on top of it all! Shares not bringing in what they used to, so she says, and why not, I should like to know? They ought to be ashamed of themselves. Doing down a lady like her who's got no head for figures and can't be up to their tricks."

"Practically everyone has been hit that way," I said, but Florence remained unsoftened.

"It's alright for some as can look after themselves, but not for *her*. She needs looking after, and as long as she's with me I'm going to see no one imposes on her or upsets her in any way. I'd do anything for Miss Emily."

And glaring at us for some moments in order to drive that point thoroughly home, the indomitable Florence left the room, carefully shutting the door behind her.

"Do you feel like a bloodsucker, Jerry?" inquired Joanna. "Because I do. What's the matter with us?"

"We don't seem to be going down very well," I said. "Megan gets tired of us, Partridge disapproves of you, faithful Florence disapproves of both of us."

Joanna murmured, "I wonder why Megan *did* leave?"

"She got bored.'

"I don't think she did at all. I wonder—do you think, Jerry, it could have been something that Aimée Griffith said?"

"You mean this morning, when they were talking on the doorstep?"

"Yes. There wasn't much time, of course, but—"

I finished the sentence: "But that woman's got the tread of a cow elephant! She might have—"

The door opened and Miss Emily came in. She was pink and a little out of breath and seemed excited. Her eyes were very blue and shining.

She chirruped at us in quite a distracted manner:

"Oh, dear, I'm sorry I'm late. Just doing a little shopping in the town, and the cakes at the Blue Rose didn't seem to me quite fresh, so I went on to Mrs. Lygon's. I always like to get my cakes the last thing, then one gets the newest batch just out of the oven, and one isn't put off with the day before's. But I am so distressed to have kept you waiting—really unpardonable—"

Joanna cut in:

"It's our fault, Miss Barton. We're early. We walked down and Jerry strides along so fast now that we arrive everywhere too soon."

"Never too soon, dear. Don't say that. One cannot have too much of a good thing, you know."

And the old lady petted Joanna affectionately on the shoulder.

Joanna brightened up. At last, so it seemed, she was being a success. Emily Barton extended her smile to include me, but with a slight timidity in it, rather as one might approach a man-eating tiger guaranteed for the moment harmless.

"It's very good of you to come to such a feminine meal as tea, Mr. Burton."

Emily Barton, I think, has a mental picture of men as interminably consuming whiskey-and-sodas and smoking cigars, and in the intervals dropping out to do a few seductions of village maidens, or to conduct a liaison with a married woman.

When I said this to Joanna later, she replied that it was probably wishful thinking, that Emily Barton would have liked to come across such a man, but alas, had never done so.

In the meantime, Miss Emily was fussing around the room, arranging Joanna and myself with little tables, and carefully providing ashtrays, and a minute later the door opened and Florence came in bearing a tray of tea with some fine Crown Derby cups on it, which I gathered Miss Emily had brought with her. The tea was China and delicious and there were plates of sandwiches and thin bread and butter, and a quantity of little cakes.

Florence was beaming now, and looked at Miss Emily with a kind of maternal pleasure, as at a favorite child enjoying a doll's tea party.

Joanna and I ate far more than we wanted to, our hostess pressed us so earnestly. The little lady was clearly enjoying her tea party and I perceived that to Emily Barton, Joanna and I were a big adventure, two people from the mysterious world of London and sophistication.

Naturally, our talk soon dropped into local channels. Miss Barton spoke warmly of Dr. Griffith, his kindness and his cleverness as a doctor. Mr. Symmington, too, was a very clever lawyer, and had helped Miss Barton to get some money back from the Income Tax which she would never have known about. He was so nice to his children, too, devoted to them and to his wife—she caught herself up. "Poor Mrs. Symmington, it's so dreadfully sad, with those young children left motherless. Never, perhaps, a very strong woman—and her health had been bad of late.

"A brain storm, that is what it must have been. I read about such a thing in the paper. People really do not know what they are doing under those circumstances. And she can't have known what she was doing or else she would have remembered Mr. Symmington and the children."

"That anonymous letter must have shaken her up very badly," said Joanna.

Miss Barton flushed. She said, with a tinge of reproof in her voice:

"Not a very nice thing to discuss, do you think, dear? I know there have been—er—letters, but we won't talk about them. Nasty things. I think they are better just ignored."

Well, Miss Barton might be able to ignore them, but for some people it wasn't so easy. However I obediently changed the subject and we discussed Aimée Griffith.

"Wonderful, quite wonderful," said Emily Barton. "Her energy and her organizing powers are really splendid. She's so good with girls too. And she's so practical and up to date in every way. She really runs this place. And absolutely devoted to her brother. It's very nice to see such devotion between brother and sister."

"Doesn't he ever find her a little overwhelming?" asked Joanna.

Emily Barton stared at her in a startled fashion.

"She has sacrificed a great deal for his sake," she said with a touch of reproachful dignity.

I saw a touch of Oh, Yeah? in Joanna's eye and hastened to divert the conversation to Mr. Pye.

Emily Barton was a little dubious about Mr. Pye.

All she could say was, repeated rather doubtfully, that he was very kind—yes, very kind. Very well off, too, and most generous. He had very strange visitors sometimes, but then, of course, he had traveled a lot.

We agreed that travel not only broadened the mind, but occasionally resulted in the forming of strange acquaintances.

"I have often wished, myself, to go on a cruise," said Emily Barton wistfully. "One reads about them in the papers and they sound so attractive."

"Why don't you go?" asked Joanna.

This turning of a dream into a reality seemed to alarm Miss Emily.

"Oh, no, no, that would be *quite* impossible."

"But why? They're fairly cheap."

"Oh, it's not only the expense. But I shouldn't like to go alone. Traveling alone would look very peculiar, don't you think?"

"No," said Joanna.

Miss Emily looked at her doubtfully.

"And I don't know how I would manage about my luggage—and going ashore at foreign ports—and all the different currencies—"

Innumerable pitfalls seemed to rise up before the little lady's affrighted gaze, and Joanna hastened to calm her by a question about an approaching garden fete and sale of work. This led us quite naturally to Mrs. Dane Calthrop.

A faint spasm showed for a minute on Miss Barton's face. "You know, dear," she said, "she is really a very *odd* woman. The things she says sometimes."

I asked what things.

"Oh, I don't know. Such very *unexpected* things. And the way she looks at you, as though you weren't there but somebody else was—I'm expressing it badly but it is so hard to convey the impression I mean. And then she won't—well, *interfere* at all. There are so many cases where a vicar's wife could advise and—perhaps *admonish*. Pull people up, you know, and make them mend their ways. Because people would listen to her, I'm sure of that, they're all quite in awe of her. But she insists on being aloof and far away, and has such a curious habit of feeling sorry for the most unworthy people."

"That's interesting," I said, exchanging a quick glance with Joanna.

"Still, she is a very well-bred woman. She was a Miss Farroway of Bellpath, very good family, but these old families sometimes *are* a little peculiar, I believe. But she is devoted to her husband who is a man of very fine intellect—wasted, I am sometimes afraid, in this country circle. A good man, and most sincere, but I always find his habit of quoting Latin a little confusing."

"Hear, hear," I said fervently.

"Jerry had an expensive public school education, so he doesn't recognize Latin when he hears it," said Joanna.

This led Miss Barton to a new topic.

"The schoolmistress here is a most unpleasant young woman," she said. "Quite *Red*, I'm afraid." She lowered her voice over the word "Red."

Later, as we walked home up the hill, Joanna said to me:

"She's rather sweet."

At dinner that night Joanna said to Partridge that she hoped her tea party had been a success.

Partridge got rather red in the face and held herself even more stiffly. "Thank you, Miss, but Agnes never turned up after all."

"Oh, I'm sorry."

"It didn't matter to *me,*" said Partridge.

She was so swelling with grievance that she condescended to pour it out to us:

"It wasn't me who thought of asking her! She rang up herself, said she'd something on her mind and could she come here, it being her day off. And I said, yes, subject to your permission which I obtained. And after that, not a sound or sign of her! And no word of apology either, though I should hope I'll get a postcard tomorrow morning. These girls nowadays—don't know their place—no idea of how to behave."

Joanna attempted to soothe Partridge's wounded feelings:

"She mightn't have felt well. You didn't ring up to find out?"

Partridge drew herself up again. "No, I did *not,* Miss! No, indeed. If Agnes likes to behave rudely that's her lookout, but I shall give her a piece of my mind when we meet."

Partridge went out of the room still stiff with indignation, and Joanna and I laughed.

"Probably a case of 'Advice from Aunt Nancy's Column,'" I said. "'*My boy is very cold in his manner to me, what shall I do about it?*' Failing Aunt Nancy, Partridge was to be applied to for advice, but instead there has been a reconciliation and I expect at this minute that Agnes and her boy are one of those speechless couples suddenly standing by a dark hedge. They embarrass you horribly, but you don't embarrass them."

Joanna laughed and said she expected that was it.

We began talking of the anonymous letters and wondered how Nash and the melancholy Graves were getting on.

"It's a week today exactly," said Joanna, "since Mrs. Symmington's suicide. I should think they must have got on to something by now. Fingerprints, or handwriting, or *something.*"

I answered her absently. Somewhere behind my conscious mind, a queer uneasiness was growing. It was connected in some way with the phrase that Joanna had used, "a week exactly."

I ought, I dare say, to have put two and two together earlier. Perhaps, unconsciously, my mind was already suspicious.

Anyway the leaven was working now. The uneasiness was growing—coming to a head.

Joanna noticed suddenly that I wasn't listening to her spirited account of a village encounter.

"What's the matter, Jerry?"

I did not answer because my mind was busy piecing things together.

Mrs. Symmington's suicide. . . . She was alone in the house that afternoon. . . . Alone in the house *because the maids were having their day out*. . . . A week ago exactly. . . .

"Jerry, what—"

I interrupted:

"Joanna, maids have days out once a week, don't they?"

"And alternate Sundays," said Joanna. "What on—"

"Never mind Sundays. They go out the same day every week?"

"Yes. That's the usual thing."

Joanna was staring at me curiously. Her mind had not taken the track mine had.

I crossed the room and rang the bell.

Partridge came.

"Tell me," I said, "this Agnes Woddell. She's in service?"

"Yes, sir. At Mrs. Symmington's. At Mr. Symmington's I should say now."

I drew a deep breath. I glanced at the clock. It was half past ten.

"Would she be back now, do you think?"

Partridge was looking disapproving. "Yes, sir. The maids have to be in by ten there. They're old-fashioned."

I said, "I'm going to ring up."

I went out to the hall. Joanna and Partridge followed me. Partridge was clearly furious. Joanna was puzzled. She said as I was trying to get the number, "What are you going to do, Jerry?"

"I'd like to be sure that the girl has come in alright."

Partridge sniffed. Just sniffed, nothing more. But I did not care twopence about Partridge's sniffs.

Elsie Holland answered the telephone from the other end.

"Sorry to ring you up," I said. "This is Jerry Burton speaking. Is—has—your maid Agnes come in?"

It was not until after I had said it that I suddenly felt a bit of a fool. For if the girl had come in and it was alright, how on earth was I going to explain my ringing up and asking. It would have been better if I had let Joanna ask the question, though even that would need a bit of explaining. I foresaw a new trail of gossip started in Lymstock, with myself and the unknown Agnes Woddell as its center.

Elsie Holland sounded, not unnaturally, very much surprised: "Agnes? Oh, she's sure to be in by now."

I felt a fool, but I went on with it: "Do you mind just seeing if she has come in, Miss Holland?"

There is one thing to be said for a nursery governess; she is used to doing things when told. Hers not to reason why! Elsie Holland put down the receiver and went off obediently.

Two minutes later I heard her voice:

"Are you there, Mr. Burton?"

"Yes."

"Agnes isn't in yet, as a matter of fact."

I knew then that my hunch had been right.

I heard a noise of voices vaguely from the other end, then Symmington himself spoke:

"Hello, Burton, what's the matter?"

"Your maid Agnes isn't back yet."

"No. Miss Holland has just been to see. What's the matter? There's not been an accident, has there?"

"Not an *accident*," I said.

"Do you mean you have reason to believe something has happened to the girl?"

I said grimly, "I shouldn't be surprised."

I slept badly that night.

I think that, even then, there were pieces of the puzzle floating about in my mind. I believe that if I had given my mind to it, I could have solved the whole thing then and there. Otherwise why did those fragments tag along so persistently?

How much do we know at any time? Much more, or so I believe, than we know we know! But we cannot break through to that subterranean knowledge. It is there, but we cannot reach it.

I lay on my bed, tossing uneasily, and only vague bits of the puzzle came to torture me.

There was a pattern, if only I could get hold of it. I ought to know who wrote those damned letters. There was a trail somewhere if only I could follow it. . . .

As I dropped off to sleep, words danced irritatingly through my drowsy mind:

"No smoke without fire. No fire without smoke. Smoke. . . . Smoke? Smoke screen. . . . No, that was the war—a war phrase. War. Scrap of paper. . . . Only a scrap of paper. Belgium—Germany. . . ."

I fell asleep. I dreamed that I was taking Mrs. Dane Calthrop, who had turned into a greyhound, for a walk with a collar and lead.

It was the ringing of the telephone that roused me. A persistent ringing.

I sat up in bed, glanced at my watch. It was half past seven. I had not yet been called. The telephone was ringing in the hall downstairs.

I jumped out of bed, pulled on a dressing gown, and raced down. I beat Partridge coming through the back door from the kitchen by a short head. I picked up the receiver.

"Hello?"

"Oh—" It was a sob of relief. "It's *you!*" Megan's voice. Megan's voice indescribably forlorn and frightened. "Oh, please do come—*do* come. Oh, please do! Will you?"

"I'm coming at once," I said. "Do you hear? *At once.*"

I took the stairs two at a time and burst in on Joanna.

"Look here, Jo, I'm going off to the Symmingtons'."

Joanna lifted a curly blond head from the pillow and rubbed her eyes like a small child.

"Why—what's happened?"

"I don't know. It was the child—Megan. She sounded all in."

"What do you think it is?"

"The girl Agnes, unless I'm very much mistaken."

As I went out of the door, Joanna called after me, "Wait. I'll get up and drive you down."

"No need. I'll drive myself."

"You can't drive the car."

"Yes, I can."

I did, too. It hurt, but not too much. I'd washed, shaved, dressed, got the car out and driven to the Symmingtons' in half an hour. Not bad going.

Megan must have been watching for me. She came out of the house at a run and clutched me. Her poor little face was white and twitching.

"Oh, you've come—you've *come!*"

"Hold up, funnyface," I said. "Yes, I've come. Now what is it?"

She began to shake. I put my arm around her.

"I—I found her."

"You found Agnes? Where?"

The trembling grew.

"Under the stairs. There's a cupboard there. It has fishing rods and gold clubs and things. You know."

I nodded. It was the usual cupboard.

Megan went on:

"She was there—all huddled up—and—and *cold*—horribly cold. She was—she was *dead,* you know!"

I asked curiously. "What made you look there?"

"I—I don't know. You telephoned last night. And we all began wondering where Agnes was. We waited up some time, but she didn't come in, and at last we went to bed. I didn't sleep very well and I got up early. There was only Rose (the cook, you know) about. She was very cross about Agnes not having come back. She said she'd been before somewhere when a girl did a flit like that. I had some milk and bread and butter in the kitchen—and then suddenly Rose came in looking queer and she said that Agnes' outdoor things were still in her room. Her best ones that she goes out in. And I began to wonder if—if she'd ever left the house, and I started looking around, and I opened the cupboard under the stairs and—and she was there . . ."

"Somebody's rung up the police, I suppose?"

"Yes, they're here now. My stepfather rang them up straightaway. And then I—I felt I couldn't bear it, and I rang *you* up. You don't mind?"

"No," I said. "I don't mind."

I looked at her curiously.

"Did anybody give you some brandy, or some coffee, or some tea after—after you found her?"

Megan shook her head.

I cursed the whole Symmington *ménage.* That stuffed shirt, Symmington, thought of nothing but the police. Neither Elsie Holland nor the cook seemed to have thought of the effect on the sensitive child who had made that gruesome discovery.

"Come on, slabface," I said. "We'll go to the kitchen."

We went around the house to the back door and into the kitchen. Rose, a plump pudding-faced woman of forty, was drinking strong tea by the kitchen fire. She greeted us with a flow of talk and her hand to her heart.

She'd come all over queer, she told me, awful the palpitations were! Just think of it, it might have been *her,* it might have been any of them, murdered in their beds they might have been.

"Dish out a good strong cup of that tea for Miss Megan," I said. "She's had a shock, you know. Remember it was she who found the body."

The mere mention of a body nearly sent Rose off again, but I quelled her with a stern eye and she poured out a cup of inky fluid.

"There you are, young woman," I said to Megan. "You drink that down. You haven't got any brandy, I suppose, Rose?"

Rose said rather doubtfully that there was a drop of cooking brandy left over from the Xmas puddings.

"That'll do," I said, and put a dollop of it into Megan's cup. I saw by Rose's eyes that she thought it a good idea.

I told Megan to stay with Rose.

"I can trust you to look after Miss Megan?" I said, and Rose replied in a gratified way, "Oh, yes, sir."

I went through into the house. If I knew Rose and her kind, she would soon find it necessary to keep her strength up with a little food, and that would be good for Megan too. Confound these people, why couldn't they look after the child?

Fuming inwardly I ran into Elsie Holland in the hall. She didn't seem surprised to see me. I suppose that the gruesome excitement of the discovery made one oblivious of who was coming and going. The constable, Bert Rundle, was by the front door.

Elsie Holland gasped out, "Oh, Mr. Burton, isn't it *awful?* Whoever can have done such a dreadful thing?"

"It was murder, then?"

"Oh, yes. She was struck on the back of the head. It's all blood and hair— oh! It's *awful*—and bundled into that cupboard. Who can have done such a wicked thing? And why? Poor Agnes, I'm sure she never did anyone any harm."

"No," I said. "Somebody saw to that pretty promptly."

She stared at me. Not, I thought, a quick-witted girl. But she had good nerves. Her color was as usual, slightly heightened by excitement, and I even fancied that in a macabre kind of way, and in spite of a naturally kind heart, she was enjoying the drama.

She said apologetically, "I must go up to the boys. Mr. Symmington is so anxious that they shouldn't get a shock. He wants me to keep them right away."

"Megan found the body, I hear," I said. "I hope somebody is looking after her."

I will say for Elsie Holland that she looked conscience-stricken.

"Oh, dear," she said. "I forgot all about her. I do hope she's alright. I've been so rushed, you know, and the police and everything—but it was remiss of me. Poor girl, she must be feeling bad. I'll go and look for her at once."

I relented.

"She's alright," I said. "Rose is looking after her. You get along to the kids."

She thanked me with a flash of white tombstone teeth and hurried upstairs. After all, the boys were her job, and not Megan—Megan was nobody's job. Elsie was paid to look after Symmington's blinking brats. One could hardly blame her for attending to it.

As she flashed around the corner of the stairs, I caught my breath. For a minute I caught a glimpse of a Winged Victory, deathless and incredibly beautiful, instead of a conscientious nursery governess.

Then a door opened and Superintendent Nash stepped out into the hall with Symmington behind him.

"Oh, Mr. Burton," he said, "I was just going to telephone you. I'm glad you are here."

He didn't ask me—then—why I was here.

He turned his head and said to Symmington, "I'll use this room if I may."

It was a small morning room with a window on the front of the house.

"Certainly, certainly."

Symmington's poise was pretty good, but he looked desperately tired. Superintendent Nash said gently:

"I should have some breakfast if I were you, Mr. Symmington. You and Miss Holland and Miss Megan will feel much better after coffee and eggs and bacon. Murder is a nasty business on an empty stomach."

He spoke in a comfortable family-doctor kind of way.

Symmington gave a faint attempt at a smile and said, "Thank you,

Superintendent, I'll take your advice."

I followed Nash into the little morning room and he shut the door.

He said then, "You've got here very quickly? How did you hear?"

I told him that Megan had rung me up. I felt well-disposed toward Superintendent Nash. He, at any rate, had not forgotten that Megan, too, would be in need of breakfast.

"I hear that you telephoned last night, Mr. Burton, asking about this girl? Why was that?"

I suppose it did seem odd. I told him about Agnes' telephone call to Partridge and her nonappearance. He said, "Yes, I see. . . ."

He said it slowly and reflectively, rubbing his chin.

Then he sighed.

"Well," he said. "It's murder now, right enough. Direct physical action. The question is, what did the girl know? Did she say anything to this Partridge? Anything definite?"

"I don't think so. But you can ask her."

"Yes, I shall come up and see her when I've finished here."

"What happened exactly?" I asked. "Or don't you know yet?"

"Near enough. It was the maids' day out—"

"Both of them?"

"Yes, it seems that there used to be two sisters here who liked to go out together, so Mrs. Symmington arranged it that way. Then when these two came, she kept to the same arrangement. They used to have cold supper laid out in the dining room, and Miss Holland used to get tea."

"I see."

"It's pretty clear up to a point. The cook, Rose, comes from Nether Mickford, and in order to get there on her day out she has to catch the half-past-two bus. So Agnes has to finish clearing up lunch always. Rose used to wash up the supper things in the evenings to even things up.

"That's what happened today. Rose went off to catch the bus at two-twenty-five, Symmington left for his office at twenty-five to three. Elsie Holland and the children went out at a quarter to three. Megan Hunter went out on her bicycle about five minutes later. Agnes would then be alone in the house. As far as I can make out, she normally left the house between three o'clock and half past three."

"The house being then left empty?"

"Oh, they don't worry about that down here. There's not much locking up done in these parts. As I say, at ten minutes to three Agnes was alone in the house. That she never left it is clear, for she was in her cap and apron still when we found her body."

"I suppose you can tell roughly the time of death?"

"Doctor Griffith won't commit himself. Between two o'clock and four-thirty is his official medical verdict."

"How was she killed?"

"She was first stunned by a blow on the back of the head. Afterward an ordinary kitchen skewer, sharpened to a fine point, was thrust into the base of the skull, causing instantaneous death."

I lit a cigarette. It was not a nice picture.

"Pretty cold-blooded," I said.

"Oh, yes, yes, that was indicated."

I inhaled deeply.

"Who did it?" I said. "And why?"

"I don't suppose," said Nash slowly, "that we shall ever know exactly why. But we can guess."

"She knew something?"

"She knew something."

"She didn't give anyone here a hint?"

"As far as I can make out, no. She's been upset, so the cook says, ever since Mrs. Symmington's death, and according to this Rose, she's been getting more and more worried, and kept saying she didn't know what she ought to do."

He gave a short exasperated sigh.

"It's always the way. They won't come to us. They've got that deep-seated prejudice against 'being mixed up with the police.' If she'd come along and told us what was worrying her, she'd be alive today."

"Didn't she give the other women *any* hint?"

"No, or so Rose says, and I'm inclined to believe her. For if she had, Rose would have blurted it out at once with a good many fancy embellishments of her own."

"It's maddening," I said, "not to know."

"We can still guess, Mr. Burton. To begin with, it can't be anything very definite. It's got to be the sort of thing that you think over, and as you think it over, your uneasiness grows. You see what I mean?"

"Yes."

"Actually, I think I know what it was."

I looked at him with respect.

"That's good work, Superintendent."

"Well, you see, Mr. Burton, I know something that you don't. On the afternoon that Mrs. Symmington committed suicide both maids were supposed to be out. It was their day out. But actually Agnes came back to the house."

"You know that?"

"Yes. Agnes has a boyfriend—young Rendell from the fish shop. Wednesday is early closing and he comes along to meet Agnes and they go for a walk, or to the pictures if it's wet. That Wednesday they had a row practically as soon as they met. Our letter writer had been active, suggesting that Agnes had other fish to fry, and young Fred Rendell was all worked up. They quarreled violently and Agnes bolted back home and said she wasn't coming out unless Fred said he was sorry."

"Well?"

"Well, Mr. Burton, the kitchen faces the back of the house, but the pantry looks out where we are looking now. There's only one entrance gate. You come through it and either up to the front door, or else along the path at the side of the house to the back door."

He paused.

"Now I'll tell you something: That letter that came to Mrs. Symmington that afternoon *didn't come by post*. It had a used stamp affixed to it, and the postmark faked quite convincingly in lamp black, so that it would seem to have been delivered by the postman with the afternoon letters. But actually *it had not been through the post*. You see what that means?"

"It means," I said slowly, "that it was left *by hand*, pushed through the letter box some time before the afternoon post was delivered, so that it should be among the other letters."

"Exactly. The afternoon post comes around about a quarter to four. My theory is this: The girl was in the pantry looking through the window (it's masked by shrubs but you can see through them quite well) watching out for her young man to turn up and apologize."

I said, *"And she saw whoever it was delivered that note?"*

"That's my guess, Mr. Burton. I may be wrong, of course."

"I don't think you are. . . . It's simple—and convincing—and it means that Agnes knew *who the anonymous letter writer was.*"

5

"YES," NASH SAID. "Agnes knew who wrote those letters."

"But then why didn't she—?" I paused, frowning.

Nash said quickly, "As I see it, the girl *didn't realize what she had seen*. Not at first. Somebody had left a letter at the house, yes—but that somebody was nobody she would dream of connecting with the anonymous letters. It was somebody, from that point of view, quite above suspicion."

"But the more she thought about it, the more uneasy she grew. Ought she, perhaps, to tell someone about it? In her perplexity she thinks of Miss Barton's Partridge who, I gather, is a somewhat dominant personality and whose judgment Agnes would accept unhesitatingly. She decides to ask Partridge what she ought to do."

"Yes," I said thoughtfully. "It fits well enough. And somehow or other, Poison Pen found out. How did she find out, Superintendent?"

"You're not used to living in the country, Mr. Burton. It's a kind of miracle how things get around. First of all there's the telephone call. Who overheard it on your end?"

I reflected.

"I took the call originally. I called up to Partridge."

"Mentioning the girl's name?"

"Yes—yes, I did."

"Anyone overhear you?"

"My sister or Miss Griffith might have done so."

"Ah, Miss Griffith. What was she doing up there?"

I explained.

"Was she going back to the village?"

"She was going to Mr. Pye first."

Superintendent Nash sighed. "That's two ways it could have gone all over the place."

I was incredulous. "Do you mean that either Miss Griffith or Mr. Pye would bother to repeat a meaningless little bit of information like that?"

"Anything's news in a place like this. You'd be surprised. If the dressmaker's mother has got a bad corn everybody hears about it! And then there is this end. Miss Holland, Rose—they could have heard what Agnes said. And there's Fred Rendell. It may have got around through him that Agnes went back to the house that afternoon."

I gave a slight shiver. I was looking out of the window. In the front of me was a neat square of grass and a path and the low prim gate.

Someone had opened the gate, had walked very correctly and quietly up to the house, and had pushed a letter through the letter box. I saw, hazily, in my mind's eye, that vague woman's shape. The face was blank—but it must be a face that I knew . . .

Superintendent Nash was saying:

"All the same, this narrows things down. That's always the way we get 'em in the end. Steady, patient elimination. There aren't so very many people it could be now."

"You mean—?"

"It knocks out any women clerks who were at their work all afternoon. It knocks out the schoolmistress. She was teaching. And the district nurse. I know where she was yesterday. Not that I ever thought it was any of *them*, but now we're *sure*. You see, Mr. Burton, we've got two definite times now on which to concentrate—yesterday afternoon, and the week before. On the day of Mrs. Symmington's death from, say, a quarter past three (the earliest possible time at which Agnes could have been back in the house after her quarrel) and four o'clock when the post must have come (but I can get that fixed more accurately with the postman). And yesterday from ten minutes to three (when Miss Megan Hunter left the house) until half past three or more probably a quarter past three as Agnes hadn't begun to change."

"What do you think happened yesterday?"

Nash made a grimace.

"What do I think? I think a certain lady walked up to the front door and rang the bell, quite calm and smiling, the afternoon caller. . . . Maybe she asked for Miss Holland, or for Miss Megan, or perhaps she had brought a parcel. Anyway Agnes turns around to get a salver for cards, or to take the parcel in, and our ladylike caller bats her on the back of her unsuspecting head."

"What with?"

Nash said. "The ladies around here usually carry large sizes in handbags. No saying what mightn't be inside it."

"And then stabs her through the back of the neck and bundles her into the cupboard? Wouldn't that be a hefty job for a woman?"

Superintendent Nash looked at me with rather a queer expression. "The woman we're after isn't normal—not by a long way—and that type of mental instability goes with surprising strength. Agnes wasn't a big girl!" He paused and then asked, "What made Miss Megan Hunter think of looking in that cupboard?"

"Sheer instinct," I said.

Then I asked, "Why drag her out of the way? What was the point?"

"The longer it was before the body was found, the more difficult it would be to fix the time of death accurately. If Miss Holland, for instance, fell over the body as soon as she came in, a doctor might be able to fix it within ten minutes or so—which might be awkward for our lady friend."

I said, frowning, "But if Agnes was suspicious of this person—"

Nash interrupted me: "She wasn't. Not to this pitch. She just thought it 'queer' shall we say? She was a slow-witted girl, I imagine, and she was only vaguely suspicious with a feeling that something was wrong. She certainly didn't suspect that she was up against a woman who would do murder."

"Did you suspect that?" I asked.

Nash shook his head. He said, with feeling:

"I ought to have known. That suicide business, you see, frightened Poison Pen. She got the wind up. Fear, Mr. Burton, is an incalculable thing."

Yes, fear. That was the thing we ought to have foreseen. Fear—in a lunatic brain. . . .

"You see," said Superintendent Nash, and somehow his words made the whole thing seem absolutely horrible. "We're up against someone who's respected and thought highly of—someone, in fact, of good social position!"

Presently Nash said that he was going to interview Rose once more. I asked him, rather diffidently, if I might come too. Rather to my surprise he assented cordially.

"I'm very glad of your cooperation, Mr. Burton, if I may say so."

"That sounds suspicious," I said. "In books when a detective welcomes someone's assistance, that someone is usually the murderer."

Nash laughed shortly. He said, "You're hardly the type to write anonymous letters, Mr. Burton." He added: "Frankly, you can be useful to us."

"I'm glad, but I don't see how."

"You're a stranger down here, that's why. You've got no preconceived ideas about the people here. But at the same time, you've got the opportunity of getting to know things in what I may call a social way."

"The murderer is a person of good social position," I murmured.

"Exactly."

"I'm to be the spy within the gates?"

"Have you any objection?"

I thought it over. "No," I said, "frankly I haven't. If there's a dangerous lunatic about, driving inoffensive women to suicide and hitting miserable little maidservants on the head, then I'm not adverse to doing a bit of dirty work to put that lunatic under restraint."

"That's sensible of you, sir. And let me tell you, the person we're after is dangerous. She's about as dangerous as a rattlesnake and a cobra and a black mamba rolled into one."

I gave a slight shiver. I said, "In fact, we've got to make haste?"

"That's right. Don't think we're inactive in the force. We're not. We're working on several different lines."

He said it grimly.

I had a vision of a fine, far-flung spider's web . . .

Nash wanted to hear Rose's story again, so he explained to me, because she had already told him two different versions, and the more versions he got from her, the more likely it was that a few grains of truth might be incorporated.

We found Rose washing up breakfast, and she stopped at once and rolled her eyes and clutched her heart and explained again how she'd been coming over queer all the morning.

Nash was patient with her but firm. He'd been soothing the first time, so he told me, and peremptory the second, and he now employed a mixture of the two.

Rose enlarged pleasurably on the details of the last week, of how Agnes had gone about in deadly fear, and had shivered and said "Don't ask me" when Rose had urged her to say what was the matter. "It would be death if she told me, that's what she said," finished Rose, rolling her eyes happily.

"Had Agnes given no hint of what was troubling her?"

No, except that she went in fear of her life.

Superintendent Nash sighed and abandoned the theme, contenting himself with extracting an exact account of Rose's own activities the preceding afternoon.

This, put baldly, was that Rose had caught the 2:30 bus and spent the afternoon and evening with her family, returning by the 8:40 bus from Nether Mickford. The recital was complicated by the extraordinary presentiments of evil that Rose had had all the afternoon and how her sister had commented on it and how she hadn't been able to touch a morsel of seed cake.

From the kitchen we went in search of Elsie Holland, who was superintending the children's lessons.

As always, Elsie Holland was competent and obliging. She rose and said, "Now, Colin, you and Brian will do these three sums and have the answers ready for me when I come back."

She then led us into the night nursery.

"Will this do? I thought it would be better not to talk before the children."

"Thank you, Miss Holland. Just tell me, once more, are you *quite* sure that Agnes never mentioned to you being worried over anything—since Mrs. Symmington's death, I mean?"

"No, she never said anything. She was a very quiet girl, you know, and didn't talk much."

"A change from the other one, then!"

"Yes, Rose talks much too much. I have to tell her not to be impertinent sometimes."

"Now, will you tell me exactly what happened yesterday afternoon? Everything you can remember."

"Well, we had lunch as usual. One o'clock, and we hurried just a little. I don't let the boys dawdle. Let me see. Mr. Symmington went back to the office, and I helped Agnes by laying the table for supper—the boys ran out in the garden till I was ready to take them."

"Where did you go?"

"Toward Combe Acre, by the field path—the boys wanted to fish. I forgot their bait and had to go back for it."

"What time was that?"

"Let me see, we started about twenty to three—or just after. Megan was coming but changed her mind. She was going out on her bicycle. She's got quite a craze for bicycling."

"I mean what time was it when you went back for the bait? Did you go into the house?"

"No. I'd left it in the conservatory at the back. I don't know what time it was then—about ten minutes to three, perhaps."

"Did you see Megan or Agnes?"

"Megan must have started, I think. No, I didn't see Agnes. I didn't see anyone."

"And after that you went fishing?"

"Yes, we went along by the stream. We didn't catch anything. We hardly ever do, but the boys enjoy it. Brian got rather wet. I had to change his things when we got in."

"You attend to tea on Wednesdays?"

"Yes. It's all ready in the drawing room for Mr. Symmington. I just make the tea when he comes in. The children and I have ours in the schoolroom—and Megan, of course. I have my own tea things and everything in the cupboard up there."

"What time did you get in?"

"At ten minutes to five. I took the boys up and started to lay tea. Then when Mr. Symmington came in at five I went down to make his but he said he would have it with us in the schoolroom. The boys were so pleased. We played Animal Grab afterward. It seems so awful to think of now—with that poor girl in the cupboard all the time."

"Would anybody go to that cupboard normally?"

"Oh, no, it's only used for keeping junk. The hats and coats hang in the little cloakroom to the right of the front door as you come in. No one might have gone to the other cupboard for months."

"I see. And you noticed nothing unusual, nothing abnormal at all when you came back?"

The blue eyes opened very wide. "Oh, no, Inspector, nothing at all. Everything was just the same as usual. That's what was so awful about it."

"And the week before?"

"You mean the day Mrs. Symmington—"

"Yes."

"Oh, that was terrible—terrible!"

"Yes, yes, I know. You were out all that afternoon also?"

"Oh, yes, I always take the boys out in the afternoon—if it's fine enough. We do lessons in the morning. We went up on the moor, I remember—quite a long way. I was afraid I was late back because as I turned in at the gate I saw Mr. Symmington coming from his office at the other end of the road, and I hadn't even put the kettle on, but it was just ten minutes to five."

"You didn't go up to Mrs. Symmington?"

"Oh, no. I never did. She always rested after lunch. She had attacks of neuralgia—and they used to come on after meals. Dr. Griffith had given her some powders to take. She used to lie down and try to sleep."

Nash said in a casual voice, "So no one would take her up the post?"

"The afternoon post? No, I'd look in the letter box and put the letters on the hall table when I came in. But very often Mrs. Symmington used to come down and get it herself. She didn't sleep all the afternoon. She was usually up again by four."

"You didn't think anything was wrong because she wasn't up that afternoon?"

"Oh, no, I never dreamed of such a thing. Mr. Symmington was hanging up his coat in the hall and I said, 'Tea's not quite ready, but the kettle's nearly boiling,' and he nodded and called out, 'Mona, Mona!'—and then as Mrs. Symmington didn't answer he went upstairs to her bedroom, and it must have been the most terrible shock to him. He called me and I came, and he said, 'Keep the children away,' and then he phoned Dr. Griffith and we forgot all about the kettle and it burned the bottom out! Oh, dear, it *was* dreadful, and she'd been so happy and cheerful at lunch."

Nash said abruptly, "What is your own opinion of that letter she received, Miss Holland?"

Elsie Holland said indignantly, "Oh, I think it was wicked—wicked!"

"Yes, yes, I don't mean that. Did you think it was true?"

Elsie Holland said firmly:

"No, indeed I don't. Mrs. Symmington was very sensitive—very sensitive indeed. She had to take all sorts of things for her nerves. And she was very—well, *particular*." Elsie flushed. "Anything of that sort—*nasty*, I mean—would have given her a great shock."

Nash was silent for a moment, then he asked: "Have you had any of these letters, Miss Holland?"

"No. No, I haven't had any."

"Are you sure? Please"—he lifted a hand—"don't answer in a hurry. They're not pleasant things to get, I know. And sometimes people don't like to admit they've had them. But it's very important in this case that we should know. We're quite aware that the statements in them are just a tissue of lies, so you needn't feel embarrassed."

"But I haven't, Superintendent. Really I haven't. Not anything of the kind."

She was indignant, and almost tearful, and her denials seemed genuine enough.

When she went back to the children, Nash stood looking out of the window.

"Well," he said, "that's that! She says she hasn't received any of these letters. And she sounds as though she's speaking the truth."

"She did certainly. I'm sure she was."

"H'm," said Nash. "Then what I want to know is, why the devil hasn't she?"

He went on rather impatiently, as I stared at him:

"She's a pretty girl, isn't she?"

"Rather more than pretty."

"Exactly. As a matter of fact, she's uncommonly good-looking. And she's young. In fact she's just the meat an anonymous letter writer would like. Then why has she been left out?"

I shook my head.

"It's interesting, you know. I must mention it to Graves. He asked if we could tell him definitely of anyone who hadn't had one."

"She's the second person," I said. "There's Emily Barton, remember."

Nash gave a faint chuckle. "You shouldn't believe everything you're told, Mr. Burton. Miss Barton had one alright—more than one."

"How do you know?"

"That devoted dragon she's lodging with told me—her late parlormaid or cook. Florence Elford. Very indignant she was about it. Would like to have the writer's blood."

"Why did Miss Emily say she hadn't had any?"

"Delicacy. Their language isn't nice. Little Miss Barton has spent her life avoiding the coarse and unrefined."

"What did the letter say?"

"The usual. Quite ludicrous in her case. And incidentally insinuated that she poisoned off her old mother and most of her sisters!"

I said incredulously, "Do you mean to say there's really this dangerous lunatic going about and we can't spot her right away?"

"We'll spot her," said Nash, and his voice was grim. "She'll write just one letter too many."

"But, my goodness, man, she won't go on writing these things—not now."

He looked at me.

"Oh, yes, she will. You see, *she can't stop now.* It's a morbid craving. The letters will go on, make no mistake about that."

I went and found Megan before leaving the house. She was in the garden and seemed almost back to her usual self. She greeted me quite cheerfully.

I suggested that she should come back to us again for a while, but after a momentary hesitation she shook her head.

"It's nice of you—but I think I'll stay here. After all, it is—well, I suppose it's my home. And I dare say I can help with the boys a bit."

"Well," I said, "It's as you like."

"Then I think I'll stay. I could—I could—"

"Yes?" I prompted.

"If—if anything awful happened, I could ring you up, couldn't I, and you'd come."

I was touched. "Of course. But what awful thing do you think might happen?"

"Oh, I don't know." She looked vague. "Things seem rather like that just now, don't they?"

"Stop it!" I said. "And don't go nosing out any more bodies! It's not good for you."

She gave me a brief flash of a smile. "No, it isn't. It made me feel awfully sick."

I didn't much like leaving her there, but after all, as she had said, it was her home. And I fancied now that Elsie Holland would feel more responsible for her.

Nash and I went up together to Little Furze. While I gave Joanna an account of the morning's doings, Nash tackled Partridge. He rejoined us, looking discouraged.

"Not much help there. According to this woman, the girl only said she was worried about something and didn't know what to do and that she'd like Miss Partridge's advice."

"Did Partridge mention the fact to anyone?" asked Joanna.

Nash nodded, looking grim.

"Yes, she told Mrs. Emory—your daily woman—on the lines, as far as I can gather, that there were *some* young women who were willing to take advice from their elders and didn't think they could settle everything for themselves offhand! Agnes mightn't be very bright, but she was a nice respectful girl and knew her manners."

"Partridge preening herself, in fact," murmured Joanna. "And Mrs. Emory could have passed it around the town?"

"That's right, Miss Burton."

"There's one thing rather surprises me," I said. "Why were my sister and I included? We were strangers down here—nobody could have had a grudge against us."

"You're failing to allow for the mentality of a Poison Pen—all is grist that comes to their mill. Their grudge, you might say, is against humanity."

"I suppose," said Joanna thoughtfully, "that that is what Mrs. Dane Calthrop meant."

Nash looked at her inquiringly, but she did not enlighten him.

The superintendent said:

"I don't know if you happened to look closely at the envelope of the letter you got, Miss Burton. If so, you may have noticed that it was actually addressed to Miss Barton, and the *a* altered to a *u* afterward.

That remark, properly interpreted, ought to have given us a clue to the whole business. As it was, none of us saw any significance in it.

Nash went off, and I was left with Joanna. She actually said: "You don't think that letter can really have been meant for Miss Emily, do you?"

"It would hardly have begun 'You painted trollop,'" I pointed out, and Joanna agreed.

Then she suggested that I should go down to the town. "You ought to hear what everyone is saying. It will be *the* topic this morning!"

I suggested that she should come too, but rather to my surprise Joanna refused. She said she was going to mess about in the garden.

I paused in the doorway and said, lowering my voice, "I suppose Partridge is alright."

"Partridge!"

The amazement in Joanna's voice made me feel ashamed of my idea.

I said apologetically, "I just wondered. She's rather 'queer' in some ways—a grim spinster—the sort of person who might have religious mania."

"This isn't religious mania—or so you told me Graves said."

"Well, sex mania. They're very closely tied up together, I understand. She's repressed and respectable, and has been shut up here with a lot of elderly women for years."

"What put the idea into your head?"

"Well," I said slowly, "we've only her word for it, haven't we, as to what the girl Agnes said to her? Suppose Agnes asked Partridge to tell her why Partridge

came and left a note that day—and Partridge said she'd call around that afternoon and explain."

"And then camouflaged it by coming to us and asking if the girl could come here?"

"Yes."

"But she never went out that afternoon."

"You don't know that. We were out ourselves, remember."

"Yes, that's true. It's possible, I suppose." Joanna turned it over in her mind. "But I don't think so, all the same. I don't think Partridge has the mentality to cover her tracks over the letters. To wipe off fingerprints, and all that. It isn't only cunning you want—it's knowledge. I don't think she's got that. I suppose—" Joanna hesitated, then said slowly, "they are sure it is a woman, aren't they?"

"You don't think it's a man?" I exclaimed incredulously.

"Not—not an ordinary man—but a certain kind of man. I'm thinking, really, of Mr. Pye."

"So Pye is your selection?"

"Don't you feel yourself that he's a possibility? He's the sort of person who might be lonely—and unhappy—and spiteful. Everyone, you see, rather laughs at him. Can't you see him secretly hating all the normal happy people, and taking a queer, perverse, artistic pleasure in what he was doing?"

"Graves said a middle-aged spinster."

"Mr. Pye," said Joanna, "*is* a middle-aged spinster."

"A misfit," I said slowly.

"Very much so. He's rich, but money doesn't help. And I do feel he might be unbalanced. He is, really, rather a *frightening* little man."

"He got a letter himself, remember."

"We don't know that," Joanne pointed out. "We only thought so. And anyway, he might have been putting on an act."

"For our benefit?"

"Yes. He's clever enough to think of that—and not to overdo it."

"He must be a first-class actor."

"But of course, Jerry, whoever is doing this *must* be a first-class actor. That's partly where the pleasure comes in."

"For heaven's sake, Joanna, don't speak so understandingly! You make me feel that you—that you understand the mentality."

"I think I do. I can—just—get into the mood. If I wasn't Joanna Burton, if I wasn't young and reasonably attractive and able to have a good time, if I was—how shall I put it?—behind bars, watching other people enjoy life, would a black, evil tide rise in me, making me want to hurt, to torture—even to destroy?"

"Joanna!" I took her by the shoulders and shook her. She gave a little sigh and shiver, and smiled at me.

"I frightened you, didn't I, Jerry? But I have a feeling that that's the right way to solve this problem. You've got to be the person, knowing how they feel and what makes them act, and then—and then perhaps you'll know what they're going to do next."

"Oh, gee!" I said. "And I came down here to be a vegetable and get

interested in all the dear little local scandals. Dear little local scandals! Libel, vilification, obscene language and murder!"

Joanna was quite right. The High Street was full of interesting groups. I was determined to get everyone's reactions in turn.

I met Griffith first. He looked terribly ill and tired. So much so that I wondered. Murder is not, certainly, all in the day's work to a doctor, but his profession does equip him to face most things including suffering, the ugly side of human nature, and the fact of death.

"You look all in," I said.

"Do I?" He was vague. "Oh! I've had some worrying cases lately."

"Including our lunatic at large?"

"That, certainly." He looked away from me across the street. I saw a fine nerve twitching in his eyelid.

"You've no suspicions as to—*who*?"

"No. No. I wish I had."

He asked abruptly after Joanna and said, hesitatingly, that he had some photographs she'd wanted to see.

I offered to take them to her.

"Oh, it doesn't matter. I shall be passing that way actually later in the morning."

I began to be afraid that Griffith had got it badly. Curse Joanna! Griffith was too good a man to be dangled as a scalp.

I let him go, for I saw his sister coming and I wanted, for once, to talk to her.

Aimée Griffith began, as it were, in the middle of conversation. "Absolutely shocking!" she boomed. "I hear you were there—quite early?"

There was a question in the words, and her eyes glinted as she stressed the word "early." I wasn't going to tell her that Megan had rung me up. I said instead, "You see, I was a bit uneasy last night. The girl was due to tea at our house and didn't turn up."

"And so you feared the worst? Very smart of you!"

"Yes," I said. "I'm quite the human bloodhound."

"It's the first murder we've ever had in Lymstock. Excitement is terrific. Hope the police can handle it alright."

"I shouldn't worry," I said. "They're an efficient body of men."

"Can't even remember what the girl looked like, although I suppose she's opened the door to me dozens of times. Quiet, insignificant little thing. Knocked on the head and then stabbed through the back of the neck, so Owen tells me. Looks like a boyfriend to me. What do you think?"

"That's your solution?"

"Seems the most likely one. Had a quarrel, I expect. They're very inbred around here—bad heredity, a lot of them." She paused, and then went on: "I hear Megan Hunter found the body? Must have given her a bit of a shock."

I said shortly, "It did."

"Not too good for her, I should imagine. In my opinion she's not too strong in the head—and a thing like this might send her completely off her onion."

I took a sudden resolution. I had to know something.

"Tell me, Miss Griffith, was it you who persuaded Megan to return home yesterday?"

"Well, I wouldn't say exactly persuaded."

I stuck to my guns. "But you did say something to her?"

Aimée Griffith planted her feet firmly and stared me in the eyes. She was, just slightly, on the defensive. She said:

"It's no good—that young woman shirking her responsibility. She's young and she doesn't know how tongues wag, so I felt it my duty to give her a hint."

"Tongues—?" I broke off because I was too angry to go on.

Aimée Griffith continued with that maddeningly complacent confidence in herself which was her chief characteristic:

"Oh, I dare say you don't hear all the gossip that goes around. I do! I know what people are saying. Mind you, I don't for a minute think there's anything in it—not for a minute! But you know what people are—if they can say something ill-natured, they do! And it's rather hard lines on the girl when she's got her living to earn."

"Her living to earn?" I said, puzzled.

Aimée went on:

"It's a difficult position for her, naturally. And I think she did the right thing. I mean, she couldn't go off at a moment's notice and leave the children with no one to look after them. She's been splendid—absolutely splendid. I say so to everybody! But there it is, it's an invidious position, and people will talk."

"Who are you talking about?" I asked.

"Elsie Holland, of course," said Aimée Griffith impatiently. "In my opinion, she's a thoroughly nice girl and has only been doing her duty."

"And what are people saying?"

Aimée Griffith laughed. It was, I thought, rather an unpleasant laugh.

"They're saying that she's already considering the possibility of becoming Mrs. Symmington No. 2—that she's all out to console the widower and make herself indispensable."

"But," I said, shocked, "Mrs. Symmington's only been dead a week!"

Aimée Griffith shrugged her shoulders.

"Of course. It's absurd! But you know what people are! The Holland girl is young and she's good-looking—that's enough. And mind you, being a nursery governess isn't much of a prospect for a girl. I wouldn't blame her if she wanted a settled home and a husband who was playing her cards accordingly.

"Of course," she went on. "Poor Dick Symmington hasn't the least idea of all this! He's still completely knocked out by Mona Symmington's death. But you know what men are! If the girl is always there, making him comfortable, looking after him, being obviously devoted to the children—well, he gets to be dependent on her."

I said quietly, "So you do think that Elsie Holland is a designing hussy?"

Aimée Griffith flushed.

"Not at all. I'm sorry for the girl—with people saying nasty things! That's why I more or less told Megan that she ought to go home. It looks better than having Dick Symmington and the girl alone in the house."

I began to understand things.

Aimée Griffith gave her jolly laugh. "You're shocked, Mr. Burton, at hearing what our gossiping little town thinks. I can tell you this—they always think the worst!"

She laughed and nodded and strode away.

I came upon Mr. Pye by the church. He was talking to Emily Barton, who looked pink and excited.

Mr. Pye greeted me with every evidence of delight:

"Ah, Burton, good morning, good morning! How is your charming sister?"

I told him that Joanna was well.

"But not joining our village Parliament? We are all agog over the news. Murder! Real Sunday newspaper murder in our midst! Not the most interesting of crimes, I fear. Somewhat sordid. The brutal murder of a little serving maid. No finer points about the crime, but still undeniably news."

Miss Barton said tremulously, "It is shocking—quite shocking."

Mr. Pye turned on her: "But you enjoy it, dear lady, you enjoy it. Confess it now. You disapprove, you deplore, but there *is* the thrill. I insist, there *is* the thrill!"

"Such a nice girl," said Emily Barton. "She came to me from St. Clotilde's Home. Quite a raw girl. But most teachable. She turned into such a nice little maid. Partridge was very pleased with her."

I said quickly, "She was coming to tea with Partridge yesterday afternoon." I turned to Pye: "I expect Aimée Griffith told you."

My tone was quite casual. Pye responded apparently quite unsuspiciously:

"She did mention it, yes. She said, I remember, that it was something quite new for servants to ring up on their employers' telephones."

"Partridge would never dream of doing such a thing," said Miss Emily, "and I am really surprised at Agnes doing so."

"You are behind the times, dear lady," said Mr. Pye. "My two terrors use the telephone constantly and smoked all over the house until I objected. But one daren't say too much. Prescott is a divine cook, though temperamental, and Mrs. Prescott is an admirable house-parlormaid."

"Yes, indeed, we all think you're very lucky."

I intervened, since I did not want the conversation to become purely domestic.

"The news of the murder has got around very quickly," I said.

"Of course, of course," said Mr. Pye. "The butcher, the baker, the candlestick maker. Enter Rumor, painted full of tongues! Lymstock, alas! Is going to the dogs. Anonymous letters, murders, any amount of criminal tendencies."

Emily Barton said nervously, "They don't think—there's no idea—that—that the two are connected."

Mr. Pye pounced on the idea. "An interesting speculation. The girl knew something, therefore she was murdered. Yes, yes, most promising. How clever of you to think of it."

"I—I can't bear it."

Emily Barton spoke abruptly and turned away, walking very fast.

Pye looked after her. Her cherubic face was pursed up quizzically.

He turned back to me and shook his head gently.

"A sensitive soul. A charming creature, don't you think? Absolutely a period piece. She's not, you know, of her own generation, she's of the generation before that. The mother must have been a woman of very strong character. She kept the family time ticking at about 1870, I should say. The whole family preserved under a glass case. I do like to come across that sort of thing."

I did not want to talk about period pieces.

"What do you really think about all this business?" I asked.

"Meaning by that?"

"Anonymous letters, murder . . ."

"Our local crime wave? What do you ?"

"I asked you first," I said pleasantly.

Mr. Pye said gently:

"I'm a student, you know, of abnormalities. They interest me. Such apparently unlikely people do the most fantastic things. Take the case of Lizzie Borden. There's not really a reasonable explanation of that. In this case, my advice to the police would be—study *character*. Leave your fingerprints and your measuring of handwriting and your microscopes. Notice instead what people do with their hands, and their little tricks of manner, and the way they eat their food, and if they laugh sometimes for no apparent reason."

I raised my eyebrows.

"Mad?" I said.

"Quite, quite mad," said Mr. Pye, and added, "but you'd never know it!"

"Who?"

His eyes met mine. He smiled.

"No, no, Burton, that would be slander. We can't add slander to all the rest of it."

He fairly skipped off down the street.

6

AS I STOOD staring after Mr. Pye the church door opened and the Rev. Caleb Dane Calthrop came out.

He smiled vaguely at me. "Good—good morning, Mr.—er—er—"

I helped him.

"Burton."

"Of course, of course, you mustn't think I don't remember you. Your name had just slipped my memory for the moment. A beautiful day."

"Yes," I said rather shortly.

He peered at me.

"But something—something, ah, yes, that poor unfortunate child who was in service at the Symmington's. I find it hard to believe, I must confess, that we have a murderer in our midst, Mr.—er—Burton."

"It does seem a bit fantastic," I said.

"Something else has just reached my ears." He leaned toward me. "I learn that there have been anonymous letters going about. Have you heard any rumor of such things?"

"I have heard," I said.

"Cowardly and dastardly things." He paused and quoted an enormous stream of Latin. "Those words of Horace are very applicable, don't you think?" he said.

"Absolutely," I said.

There didn't seem anyone more I could profitably talk to, so I went home, dropping in for some tobacco and for a bottle of sherry, so as to get some of the humbler opinions on the crime.

"A narsty tramp," seemed to be the verdict.

"Come to the door, they do, and whine and ask for money, and then if it's a girl alone in the house, they turn nasty. My sister Dora, over to Combe Acre, she had a narsty experience one day—drunk, he was, and selling those little printed poems. . . ."

The story went on, ending with the intrepid Dora courageously banging the door in the man's face and taking refuge and barricading herself in some vague retreat, which I gathered from the delicacy in mentioning it, must be the lavatory. "And there she stayed till her lady came home!"

I reached Little Furze just a few minutes before lunch time. Joanna was standing in the drawing-room window doing nothing at all and looking as though her thoughts were miles away.

"What have you been doing with yourself?" I asked.

"Oh, I don't know. Nothing particular."

I went out on the veranda. Two chairs were drawn up to an iron table and there were two empty sherry glasses. On another chair was an object at which I looked with bewilderment for some time.

"What on earth is this?"

"Oh," said Joanna, "I think it's a photograph of a diseased spleen or something. Dr. Griffith seemed to think I'd be interested to see it."

I looked at the photograph with some interest. Every man has his own ways of courting the female sex. I should not, myself, choose to do it with photographs of spleens, diseased or otherwise. Still no doubt Joanna had asked for it!

"It looks most unpleasant," I said.

Joanna said it did, rather.

"How was Griffith?" I asked.

"He looked tired and very unhappy. I think he's got something on his mind."

"A spleen that won't yield to treatment?"

"Don't be silly. I mean something real."

"I should say the man's got *you* on his mind. I wish you'd lay off him, Joanna."

"Oh, do shut up. I haven't done anything."

"Women always say that."

Joanna whirled angrily out of the room.

The diseased spleen was beginning to curl up in the sun. I took it by one corner and brought it in to the drawing room. I had no affection for it myself, but I presumed it was one of Griffith's treasures.

I stooped down and pulled out a heavy book from the bottom shelf of the bookcase in order to press the photograph flat between its leaves. It was a ponderous volume of somebody's sermons.

The book came open in my hand in rather a surprising way. In another minute I saw why. *From the middle of it a number of pages had been neatly cut out.*

I stood staring at it. I looked at the title page. It has been published in 1840. There could be no doubt at all. I was looking at the book from the pages of which the anonymous letters had been put together. Who had cut them out?

Well, to begin with, it could be Emily Barton herself. She was, perhaps, the obvious person to think of. Or it could have been Partridge.

But there were other possibilities. The pages could have been cut out by anyone who had been alone in this room, any visitor, for instance, who had sat there waiting for Miss Emily. Or even anyone who called on business.

No, that wasn't so likely. I had noticed that when, one day a clerk from the bank had come to see me, Partridge had shown him into the little study at the back of the house. That was clearly the house routine.

A visitor, then? Someone "of good social position." Mr. Pye? Aimée Griffith? Mrs. Dane Calthrop?

The gong sounded and I went in to lunch. Afterward, in the drawing room I showed Joanna my find.

We discussed it from every aspect. Then I took it down to the police station.

They were elated at the find, and I was patted on the back for what was, after all, the sheerest piece of luck.

Graves was not there, but Nash was, and rang up the other man. They would test the book for fingerprints, though Nash was not hopeful of finding anything. I may say that he did not. There were mine, Partridge's and nobody else's merely showing that Partridge dusted conscientiously.

Nash walked back with me up the hill. I asked how he was getting on.

"We're narrowing it down, Mr. Burton. We've eliminated the people it couldn't be."

"Ah," I said. "And who remains?"

"Miss Ginch. She was to meet a client at a house yesterday afternoon by appointment. That house was situated not far along the Combe Acre road—that's the road that goes past the Symmingtons'. She would have to pass the house both going and coming . . . the week before, the day the anonymous letter was delivered and Mrs. Symmington committed suicide, was her last day at Symmington's office.

"Mr. Symmington thought at first she had not left the office at all that afternoon. He had Sir Henry Lushington with him all the afternoon and rang several times for Miss Ginch. I find, however, that she did leave the office between three and four. She went out to get some high denomination of stamp of which they had run short. The office boy could have gone, but Miss Ginch elected to go, saying she had a headache and would like the air. She was not gone long."

"But long enough?"

"Yes, long enough to hurry along to the other end of the village, slip the letter in the box and hurry back. I must say, however, that I cannot find anybody who saw her near the Symmington's house."

"Would they notice?"

"They might and they might not."

"Who else is in your bag?"

Nash looked very straight ahead of him. "You'll understand that we can't exclude anybody—anybody at all."

"No," I said. "I see that."

He said gravely, "Miss Griffith went to Brenton for a meeting of Girl Guides yesterday. She arrived rather late."

"You don't think—"

"No, I don't think. But I don't *know*. Miss Griffith seems an eminently sane, healthy-minded woman—but I say, I don't *know*."

"What about the previous week? Could she have slipped the letter in the box?"

"It's possible. She was shopping in the town that afternoon." He paused. "The same applies to Miss Emily Barton. She was out shopping early yesterday afternoon and she went for a walk to see some friends on the road past the Symmingtons' house the week before."

I shook my head unbelievingly. Finding the cut book in Little Furze was bound, I knew, to direct attention to the owner of that house, but when I remembered Miss Emily coming in yesterday so bright and happy and excited . . .

Damn it all—excited. . . . Yes, excited—pink cheeks—shining eyes—surely not because—not because—

I said thickly, "This business is bad for one! One sees things—one imagines things—"

Nash nodded sympathetically. "Yes, it isn't very pleasant to look upon the fellow creatures one meets as possible criminal lunatics."

He paused for a moment, then went on, "And there's Mr. Pye—"

I said sharply, "So you have considered him?"

Nash smiled. "Oh, yes, we've considered him alright. A very curious character—not, I should say, a very nice character. He has no alibi. He was in his garden, alone, on both occasions."

"So you're not only suspecting women?"

"I don't think a man wrote the letters—in fact, I'm sure of it—and so is Graves—always excepting our Mr. Pye, that is to say, who's got an abnormally female streak in his character. But we've checked up on *everybody* for yesterday afternoon. That's a murder case, you see. *You're* alright," he grinned, "and so's your sister, and Mr. Symmington didn't leave his office after he got there and Dr. Griffith was on a round in the other direction, and I've checked up on his visits."

He paused, smiled again, and said, "You see, we *are* thorough."

I said slowly: "So your case is eliminated down to those three? Mr. Pye, Miss Griffith, little Miss Barton?"

"Oh, no, no, we've got a couple more—besides the vicar's lady."

"You've thought of *her*?"

"We've thought of *everybody*, but Mrs. Dane Calthrop is a little too openly mad, if you know what I mean. Still she *could* have done it. She was in a wood watching birds yesterday afternoon—and the birds can't speak for her."

He turned sharply as Owen Griffith came into the police station.

"Hello, Nash. I heard you were around asking for me this morning. Anything important?"

"Inquest on Friday, if that suits you, Dr. Griffith."

"Right. Moresby and I are doing the P. M. tonight."

Nash said, "There's just one other thing, Dr. Griffith. Mrs. Symmington was taking some powders or something, that you prescribed for her—"

He paused.

Owen Griffith said interrogatively, "Yes?"

"Would an overdose of those powders have been fatal?"

"Certainly not," Griffith said drily. "Not unless she'd taken about twenty-five of them!"

"But you once warned her about exceeding the dose, so Miss Holland tells me."

"Oh, that, yes. Mrs. Symmington was the sort of woman who would go and overdo anything she was given—fancy that to take twice as much would do her twice as much good, and you don't want anyone to overdo even phenacetin or aspirin—bad for the heart. And anyway there's absolutely no doubt about the cause of death. It was cyanide."

"Oh, I know that—you don't get my meaning. I only thought that when committing suicide you'd prefer to take an overdose of a soporific rather than to feed yourself prussic acid."

"Oh, quite. On the other hand, prussic acid is more dramatic and is pretty certain to do the trick. With barbiturates, for instance, you can bring the victim around if only a short time has elapsed."

"I see; thank you, Dr. Griffith."

Griffith departed, and I said goodbye to Nash. I went slowly up the hill home. Joanna was out—at least there was no sign of her, and there was an enigmatical memorandum scribbled on the telephone block presumably for the guidance of either Partridge or myself:

"If Dr. Griffith rings up, I can't go on Tuesday, but could manage Wednesday or Thursday."

I raised my eyebrows and went into the drawing room. I sat down in the most comfortable armchair—(none of them were very comfortable, they tended to have straight backs and were reminiscent of the late Mrs. Barton)—stretched out my legs and tried to think the whole thing out.

With sudden annoyance, I remembered that Owen's arrival had interrupted my conversation with the inspector, and that he had mentioned two other people as being possibilities.

I wondered who they were.

Partridge, perhaps, for one? After all, the cut book had been found in this house. And Agnes could have been struck down quite unsuspectingly by her guide and mentor. No, you couldn't eliminate Partridge.

But who was the other?

Somebody, perhaps, that I didn't know? Mrs. Cleat? The original local suspect?

I closed my eyes. I considered the four people, these strangely unlikely people, in turn: Gentle, frail little Emily Barton? What points were there actually against her? A starved life? Dominated and repressed from early childhood? Too many sacrifices asked of her? Her curious horror of discussing anything "not quite nice"? Was that actually a sign of inner preoccupation with just these themes? Was I getting too horribly Freudian? I remembered a doctor once telling me that the mutterings of gentle maiden ladies when going off under an anesthetic were a revelation. "You wouldn't think they knew such words!"

Aimée Griffith?

Surely nothing repressed or "inhibited" about her. Cheery, mannish, successful. A full, busy life. Yet Mrs. Dane Calthrop had said, "Poor thing!"

And there was something—something—some remembrance . . . Ah! I'd got it. Owen Griffith saying something like, "We had an outbreak of anonymous letters up north where I had a practice."

Had that been Aimée Griffith's work, too? Surely rather a coincidence. Two outbreaks of the same thing.

Stop a minute, they'd tracked down the author of those. Griffith had said so. A schoolgirl.

Cold it was suddenly—must be a draft, from the window. I turned uncomfortably in my chair. Why did I suddenly feel so queer and upset?

Go on thinking . . . Aimée Griffith? Perhaps it was Aimée Griffith, *not* that other girl? And Aimée had come down here and started her tricks again. And that was why Owen Griffith was looking so unhappy and hag-ridden. He suspected. Yes, he suspected. . . .

Mr. Pye? Not, somehow, a very nice little man. I could imagine him staging the whole business, laughing . . .

That telephone message on the telephone pad in the hall—why did I keep thinking of it? Griffith and Joanna—he was falling for her. No, that wasn't why the message worried me. It was something else. . . .

My senses were swimming, sleep was very near. I repeated idiotically to myself: "No smoke without fire. No smoke without fire. . . . That's it . . . it all links up together. . . ."

And then I was walking down the street with Megan, and Elsie Holland passed. She was dressed as a bride, and people were murmuring, "She's going to marry Dr. Griffith at last. Of course, they've been engaged secretly for years . . ."

There we were, in the church, and Dane Calthrop was reading the service in Latin.

And in the middle of it Mrs. Dane Calthrop jumped up and cried energetically, "It's got to be stopped, I tell you. It's got to be stopped!"

For a minute or two I didn't know whether I was asleep or awake. Then my brain cleared, and I realized I was in the drawing-room of Little Furze and that Mrs. Dane Calthrop had just come through the window and was standing in front of me saying with nervous violence:

"It has got to be *stopped*, I tell you."

I jumped up. "I beg your pardon," I said. "I'm afraid I was asleep. What did you say?"

Mrs. Dane Calthrop beat one fist fiercely on the palm of her other hand. "It's got to be stopped. These letters! Murder! You can't go on having poor innocent children like Agnes Woddell *killed*!"

"You're quite right," I said. "But how do you propose to set about it?"

Mrs. Dane Calthrop said, "We've got to do something!"

I smiled, perhaps in rather a superior fashion. "And what do you suggest that we should do?"

"Get the whole thing cleared up! I said this wasn't a wicked place. I was wrong. It is."

I felt annoyed. "Yes, my dear woman," I said, not too politely, "but what are you going to *do*?"

Mrs. Dane Calthrop said, "Put a stop to it all, of course."

"The police are doing their best."

"If Agnes could be killed yesterday, their best isn't good enough."

"So you know better than they do?"

"Not at all. *I* don't know anything at all. That's why I'm going to call in an expert."

I shook my head. "You can't do that. Scotland Yard will only take over on a demand from the chief constable of the county. Actually they *have* sent Graves."

"I don't mean *that* kind of an expert. I don't mean someone who knows about anonymous letters or even about murder. I mean someone who knows *people*. Don't you see? We want someone who knows a great deal about *wickedness*!"

It was a queer point of view. But it was, somehow, stimulating.

Before I could say anything more, Mrs. Dane Calthrop nodded her head at me and said in a quick, confident tone:

"I'm going to see about it right away."

And she went out of the window again.

The next week, I think, was one of the queerest times I have ever passed through. It had an odd dream quality. Nothing seemed real.

The inquest on Agnes Woddell was held and the curious of Lymstock attended *en masse*. No new facts came to light and the only possible verdict was returned: "Murder by person or persons unknown."

So poor little Agnes Woddell, having had her hour of limelight, was duly buried in the quiet old churchyard and life in Lymstock went on as before.

No, that last statement is untrue. Not as before. . . .

There was a half-scared, half-avid gleam in almost everybody's eye. Neighbor looked at neighbor. One thing had been brought out clearly at the inquest—it was most unlikely that any stranger had killed Agnes Woddell. No tramps or unknown men had been noticed or reported in the district. Somewhere, then, in Lymstock, walking down the High Street, shopping, passing the time of day, was a person who had cracked a defenseless girl's skull and driven a sharp skewer home to her brain.

And no one knew who that person was.

As I say, the days went on in a kind of dream. I looked at everyone I met in a new light, the light of a possible murderer. It was not an agreeable sensation!

And in the evenings, with the curtain drawn, Joanna and I sat talking,

talking, arguing, going over in turn all the various possibilities that still seemed so fantastic and incredible.

Joanna held firm to her theory of Mr. Pye. I, after wavering a little, had gone back to my original suspect, Miss Ginch. But we went over the possible names again and again:

Mr. Pye?

Miss Ginch?

Mrs. Dane Calthrop?

Aimée Griffith?

Emily Barton?

Partridge?

And all the time, nervously, apprehensively, we waited for something to happen.

But nothing did happen. Nobody, so far as we knew, received any more letters. Nash made periodic appearances in the town but what he was doing and what traps the police were setting, I had no idea. Graves had gone again.

Emily Barton came to tea. Megan came to lunch. Owen Griffith went about his practice. We went and drank sherry with Mr. Pye. And we went to tea at the vicarage.

I was glad to find that Mrs. Dane Calthrop displayed none of the militant ferocity she had shown on the occasion of our last meeting. I think she had forgotten all about it.

She seemed now principally concerned with the destruction of white butterflies so as to preserve cauliflower and cabbage plants.

Our afternoon at the vicarage was really one of the most peaceful we had spent. It was an attractive old house and had a big, shabby, comfortable drawing room with faded rose cretonne. The Dane Calthrops had a guest staying with them, an amiable, elderly lady who was knitting something with white, fleecy wool. We had very good hot scones for tea, the vicar came in, and beamed placidly on us while he pursued his gentle erudite conversation. It was very pleasant.

I don't mean that we got away from the topic of the murder, because we didn't.

Miss Marple, the guest, was naturally thrilled by the subject. As she said apologetically:

"We have so little to talk about in the country!" She had made up her mind that the dead girl must have been just like her Edith.

"Such a nice little maid, and so willing, but sometimes just a *little* slow to take in things."

Miss Marple also had a cousin whose niece's sister-in-law had had a great deal of annoyance and trouble over some anonymous letters, so that, too, was very interesting to the charming old lady.

"But tell me, dear," she said to Mrs. Dane Calthrop, "what do the village people—I mean the townspeople—say? What do *they* think?"

"Mrs. Cleat still, I suppose," said Joanna.

"Oh, no," said Mrs. Dane Calthrop. "Not *now*."

Miss Marple asked who Mrs. Cleat was.

Joanna said she was the village witch.

"That's right, isn't it, Mrs. Dane Calthrop?"

The vicar murmured a long Latin quotation about, I think, the evil power of witches, to which we all listened in respectful and uncomprehending silence.

"She's a very silly woman," said his wife. "Likes to show off. Goes out to gather herbs and things at the full moon and takes care that everybody in the place knows about it."

"And silly girls go and consult her, I suppose?" said Miss Marple.

I saw the vicar getting ready to unload more Latin on us and I asked hastily, "But why shouldn't people suspect her of the murder now? They thought the letters were her doing."

Miss Marple said finally:

"Oh! But the girl was killed with a *skewer*, so I hear. Very unpleasant! Well, naturally, that takes *all* suspicion away from this Mrs. Cleat. Because, you see, she could ill-wish her, so that the girl would waste away and die from natural causes."

"Strange how those old beliefs linger," said the vicar. "In early Christian times, local superstitions were wisely incorporated with Christian doctrines and their most unpleasant attributes gradually eliminated."

"It isn't superstition we've got to deal with here," said Mrs. Dane Calthrop, "but *facts*."

"And very unpleasant facts," I said.

"As you say, Mr. Burton," said Miss Marple. "Now *you*—excuse me if I am being too personal—are a stranger here, and have a knowledge of the world and of various aspects of life. It seems to me that you ought to be able to find a solution to this distasteful problem."

I smiled.

"The best solution I have had was a dream. In my dream it all fitted in and panned out beautifully. Unfortunately when I woke up the whole thing was nonsense!"

"How interesting, though. Do tell me how the nonsense went."

"Oh, it all started with the silly phrase 'No smoke without fire.' People have been saying that *ad nauseam*. And then I got it mixed up with war terms. Smoke screen, scrap of paper, telephone messages—no, that was another dream."

"And what was that dream?"

The old lady was so eager about it, that I felt sure she was a secret reader of Napoleon's Book of Dreams, which had been the great standby of my old nurse.

"Oh! Only Elsie Holland—the Symmingtons' nursery governess, you know, was getting married to Dr. Griffith and the vicar here was reading the service in Latin—('Very appropriate, dear,' murmured Mrs. Dane Calthrop to her spouse) and then Mrs. Dane Calthrop got up and forbade the banns and said it had got to be stopped!

"But that part," I added with a smile, "was true. I woke up and found you standing over me saying it."

"And I was quite right," said Mrs. Dane Calthrop—but quite mildly, I was glad to note.

"But where did a telephone message come in?" asked Miss Marple, crinkling her brows.

"I'm afraid I'm being rather stupid. That wasn't in the dream. It was just before it. I came through the hall and noticed Joanna had written down a message to be given to someone if they rang up."

Miss Marple leaned forward. There was a pink spot in each cheek. "Will you think me *very* inquisitive and *very* rude if I ask just what that message was?" She cast a glance at Joanna. "I *do* apologize, my dear."

Joanna, however, was highly entertained.

"Oh, I don't mind," she assured the old lady. "I can't remember anything about it myself, but perhaps Jerry can. It must have been something quite trivial."

Solemnly I repeated the message as best I could remember it, enormously tickled at the old lady's rapt attention.

I was afraid the actual words were going to disappoint her, but perhaps she had some sentimental idea of a romance, for she nodded her head and smiled and seemed pleased.

"I see," she said. "I thought it might be something like that."

Mrs. Dane Calthrop said sharply, "Like what, Jane?"

"Something quite ordinary," said Miss Marple.

She looked at me thoughtfully for a moment or two, then she said unexpectedly, "I can see you are a very clever young man—but with not quite enough confidence in yourself. You ought to have!"

Joanna gave a loud hoot. "For goodness' sake don't encourage him to feel like that. He thinks quite enough of himself as it is."

"Be quiet, Joanna," I said. "Miss Marple understands me."

Miss Marple had resumed her fleecy knitting.

"You know," she observed pensively, "to commit a successful murder must be very much like bringing off a conjuring trick."

"The quickness of the hand deceives the eye?"

"Not only that. You've got to make people look at the wrong thing and in the wrong place—misdirection, they call it, I believe."

"Well," I remarked, "so far everybody seems to have looked in the wrong place for our lunatic at large."

"I should be inclined, myself," said Miss Marple, "to look for somebody very sane."

"Yes," I said thoughtfully, "that's what Nash said. I remember he stressed respectability, too."

"Yes," agreed Miss Marple. "That's *very* important."

Well, we all seemed agreed.

I addressed Mrs. Calthrop. "Nash thinks," I said, "that there will be more anonymous letters. What do you think?"

"There may be," she said slowly, "I suppose."

"If the police think that, there will have to be, no doubt," said Miss Marple.

I went on doggedly to Mrs. Dane Calthrop: "Are you still sorry for the writer?"

She flushed. "Why not?"

"I don't think I agree with you, dear," said Miss Marple. "Not in this case."

I said hotly, "They've driven one woman to suicide, and caused untold misery and heartburnings!"

"Have you had one, Miss Burton?" asked Miss Marple of Joanna.

Joanna gurgled: "Oh, yes! It said the most frightful things."

"I'm afraid," said Miss Marple, "that the people who are young and pretty are apt to be singled out by the writer."

"That's why I certainly think it's odd that Elsie Holland hasn't had any," I said.

"Let me see," said Miss Marple. "Is that the Symmingtons' nursery governess—the one you dreamed about, Mr. Burton?"

"Yes."

"She's probably had one and won't say so," said Joanna.

"No," I said, "I believe her. So does Nash."

"Dear me," said Miss Marple. "Now that's *very* interesting. That's the most interesting thing I've heard yet."

As we were going home Joanna told me that I ought not to have repeated what Nash said about more letters coming.

"Why not?"

"Because Mrs. Dane Calthrop might be It."

"You don't really believe that!"

"I'm not sure. She's a queer woman."

We began our discussion of probables all over again.

It was two nights later that I was coming back in the car from Exhampton. I had had dinner there and then started back and it was already dark before I got into Lymstock.

Something was wrong with the car lights, and after slowing up and switching on and off, I finally got out to see what I could do. I was some time fiddling, but I managed to fix them up finally.

The road was quite deserted. Nobody in Lymstock is about after dark. The first few houses were just ahead, among the the ugly gabled building of the Women's Institute. It loomed up in the dim starlight and something impelled me to go and have a look at it. I don't know whether I had caught a faint glimpse of a stealthy figure flitting through the gate—if so, it must have been so indeterminate that it did not register in my conscious mind, but I did suddenly feel a kind of overweening curiosity about the place.

The gate was slightly ajar, and I pushed it open and walked in. A short path and four steps led up to the door.

I stood there a moment hesitating. What was I really doing there? I didn't know, and then, suddenly, just near at hand, I caught the sound of a rustle. It sounded like a woman's dress.

I took a sharp turn and went around the corner of the building toward where the sound had come from.

I couldn't see anybody. I went on and again turned a corner. I was at the back of the house now and suddenly I saw, only two feet away from me, an open window.

I crept up to it and listened. I could hear nothing, but somehow or other I felt convinced that there was someone inside.

My back wasn't too good for acrobatics as yet, but I managed to hoist myself up and drop over the sill inside. I made rather a noise unfortunately.

I stood just inside the window listening. Then I walked forward, my hands outstretched. I heard then the faintest sound ahead of me to my right.

I had a torch in my pocket and I switched it on.

Immediately a low, sharp voice said, "Put that out."

I obeyed instantly, for in that brief second I had recognized Superintendent Nash.

I felt him take my arm and propel me through a door and into a passage. Here, where there was no window to betray our presence to anyone outside, he switched on a lamp and looked at me more in sorrow than in anger.

"You *would* have to butt in just that minute, Mr. Burton."

"Sorry," I apologized. "But I got a hunch that I was on to something."

"And so you were probably. Did you see anyone?"

I hesitated.

"I'm not sure," I said slowly. "I've got a vague feeling I saw someone sneak in through the front gate but I didn't really see anyone. Then I heard a rustle around the side of the house."

Nash nodded. "That's right. Somebody came around the house before you. He—or she—hesitated by the window, then went on quickly—heard *you*, I expect."

I apologized again. "What's the big idea?" I asked.

Nash said.

"I'm banking on the fact that an anonymous letter writer can't stop writing letters. She may know it's dangerous, but she'll have to do it. It's like a craving for drink or drugs."

I nodded.

"Now you see, Mr. Burton, I fancy whoever it is will want to keep the letters looking the same as much as possible. She's got the cutout pages of that book, and can go on using letters and words cut out of them. But the envelopes present a difficulty. She'll want to type them on the same machine. She can't risk using another typewriter or her own handwriting."

"Do you really think she'll go on with the game?" I asked incredulously.

"Yes, I do. And I'll bet you anything you like she's full of confidence. They're always vain as hell, these people! Well, then, I figured out that whoever it was would come to the Institute after dark so as to get at the typewriter."

"Miss Ginch," I said.

"Maybe."

"You don't know yet?"

"I don't *know*."

"But you suspect?"

"Yes. But somebody's very cunning, Mr. Burton. Somebody knows all the tricks of the game."

I could imagine some of the network that Nash had spread abroad. I had no doubt that every letter written by a suspect and posted or left by hand was immediately inspected. Sooner or later the criminal would slip up, would grow careless.

For the third time I apologized for my zealous and unwanted presence.

"Oh, well," said Nash philosophically, "it can't be helped. Better luck next time."

I went out into the night. A dim figure was standing beside my car. To my astonishment I recognized Megan.

"Hello!" she said. "I thought this was your car. What have you been doing?"

"What are you doing is much more to the point?" I said.

"I'm out for a walk. I like walking at night. Nobody stops you and says silly things, and I like the stars, and things smell better, and everyday things look all mysterious."

"All of that I grant you freely," I said. "But only cats and witches walk in the dark. They'll wonder about you at home."

"No, they won't. They never wonder where I am or what *I'm* doing."

"How are you getting on?" I asked.

"Alright, I suppose."

"Miss Holland look after you and all that?"

"Elsie's alright. She can't help being a perfect fool."

"Unkind—but probably true," I said. "Hop in and I'll drive you home."

It was not quite true that Megan was never missed.

Symmington was standing on the doorstep as we drove up.

He peered toward us.

"Hello, is Megan there?"

"Yes," I said. "I've brought her home."

Symmington said sharply. "You mustn't go off like this without telling us, Megan. Miss Holland has been quite worried about you."

Megan muttered something and went past him into the house.

Symmington sighed. "A grown-up girl is a great responsibility with no mother to look after her. She's too old for school, I suppose."

He looked toward me rather suspiciously.

"I suppose you took her for a drive?" I thought it best to leave it like that.

7

ON THE FOLLOWING day I went mad. Looking back on it, that is really the only explanation I can find.

I was due my monthly visit to Marcus Kent. . . . I went up by train. To my intense surprise Joanna elected to stay behind. As a rule she was eager to come and we usually stayed up for a couple of days.

This time, however, I proposed to return the same day by the evening train, but even so I was astonished at Joanna. She merely said enigmatically that she'd got plenty to do, and why spend hours in a nasty stuffy train when it was a lovely day in the country?

That, of course, was undeniable, but sounded very unlike Joanna.

She said she didn't want the car, so I was to drive it to the station and leave it parked there against my return.

The station of Lymstock is situated, for some obscure reason known to railway companies only, quite half a mile from Lymstock itself. Halfway along the road I overtook Megan shuffling along in an aimless manner. I pulled up.

"Hello, what are you doing?"

"Just out for a walk."

"But not what is called a good brisk walk, I gather. You were crawling along like a dispirited crab."

"Well, I wasn't going anywhere particular."

"Then you'd better come and see me off at the station." I opened the door of the car and Megan jumped in.

"Where are you going?" she asked.

"London. To see my doctor."

"Your back's not worse, is it?"

"No, it's practically alright again. I'm expecting him to be very pleased about it."

Megan nodded.

We drew up at the station. I parked the car and went in and bought my ticket at the booking office. There were very few people on the platform and nobody I knew.

"You wouldn't like to lend me a penny, would you?" said Megan. "Then I'd get a bit of chocolate out of the slot machine."

"Here you are, baby," I said, handing her the coin in question. "Sure you wouldn't like some clear gums or some throat pastilles as well?"

"I like chocolate best," said Megan without suspecting sarcasm.

She went off to the chocolate machine, and I looked after her with a feeling of mounting irritation.

She was wearing trodden-over shoes, and coarse unattractive stockings and a particularly shapeless jumper and skirt. I don't know why all this should have infuriated me, but it did.

I said angrily as she came back, "Why do you wear those disgusting stockings?"

Megan looked down at them, surprised. "What's the matter with them?"

"Everything's the matter with them. They're loathsome. And why wear a pullover like a decayed cabbage?"

"It's alright, isn't it? I've had it for years."

"So I should imagine. And why do you—"

At this minute the train came in and interrupted my angry lecture.

I got into an empty first-class carriage, let down the window and leaned out to continue the conversation.

Megan stood below me, her face upturned. She asked me why I was so cross.

"I'm not cross," I said untruly. "It just infuriates me to see you so slack, and not caring how you look."

"I couldn't look nice, anyway, so what does it matter?"

"Cut it!" I said. "I'd like to see you turned out properly. I'd like to take you to London and outfit you from tip to toe."

"I wish you could," said Megan.

The train began to move. I looked down into Megan's upturned, wistful face.

And then as I have said, madness came upon me.

I opened the door, grabbed Megan with one arm and fairly hauled her into the carriage.

There was an outraged shout from a porter, but all he could do was dexterously to bang shut the door again. I pulled Megan up from the floor where my impetuous action had landed her.

"What on earth did you do that for?" she demanded, rubbing one knee.

"Shut up," I said. "You're coming to London with me and when I've done with you you won't know yourself. I'll show you what you can look like if you try. I'm tired of seeing you mouch about down at heel and all anyhow."

"Oh!" said Megan in an ecstatic whisper.

The ticket collector came along and I bought Megan a return ticket. She sat in her corner looking at me in a kind of awed respect.

"I say," she said when the man had gone. "You are sudden, aren't you?"

"Very," I said. "It runs in our family."

How explain to Megan the impulse that had come over me?—She had looked like a wistful dog being left behind. She now had on her face the incredulous pleasure of the dog who has been taken on the walk after all.

"I suppose you don't know London very well?" I said to Megan.

"Yes, I do," said Megan. "I always went through it to school. And I've been to the dentist there and to a pantomime."

"This," I said darkly, "will be a different London."

We arrived with half an hour to spare before my appointment in Harley Street.

I took a taxi and we drove straight to Mirotin, Joanna's dressmaker. Mirotin is, in the flesh, an unconventional and breezy woman of forty-five, Mary Grey. She is a clever woman and very good company. I have always liked her.

I said to Megan, "You're my cousin."

"Why?"

"Don't argue," I said.

Mary Grey was being firm with a stout woman who was enamored of a skin-tight powder-blue evening dress. I detached her and took her aside.

"Listen," I said. "I've brought a little cousin of mine along. Joanna was coming up but was prevented. But she said I could leave it all to you. You see what the girl looks like now?"

"I most certainly do!" said Mary Grey with feeling.

"Well, I want her turned out right in every particular from head to foot. Carte blanche. Stockings, shoes, undies, everything! By the way, the man who does Joanna's hair is close around here, isn't he?"

"Antoine? Around the corner. I'll see to that too."

"You're a woman in a thousand."

"Oh, I shall enjoy it—apart from the money—and that's not to be sneezed at in these days—half my damned brutes of women never pay their bills. But as I say, I shall enjoy it." She shot a quick professional glance at Megan standing a little way off. "She's got a lovely figure."

"You must have X-ray eyes," I said. "She looks completely shapeless to me."

Mary Grey laughed.

"It's these schools," she said. "They seem to take a pride in turning out girls who preen themselves on looking like nothing on earth. They call it being sweet and unsophisticated. Sometimes it takes a whole season before a girl can pull herself together and look human. Don't worry, leave it all to me."

"Right," I said. "I'll come back and fetch her about six."

* * *

Marcus Kent was pleased with me. He told me that I surpassed his wildest expectations.

"You must have the constitution of an elephant," he said, "to make a comeback like this. Oh, well, wonderful what country air and no late hours or excitement will do for a man if he can only stick it."

"I grant you your first two," I said. "But don't think that the country is free from excitement. We've had a good deal in my part."

"What sort of excitement?"

"Murder," I said.

Marcus Kent pursed up his mouth and whistled. "Some bucolic love tragedy? Farm lad kills his lass?"

"Not at all. A crafty, determined lunatic killer."

"I haven't read anything about it. When did they lay him by the heels?"

"They haven't, and it's a she!"

"Whew! I'm not sure that Lymstock's quite the right place for you, old boy."

I said firmly, "Yes, it is. And you're not going to get me out of it."

Marcus Kent has a low mind. He said at once, "So that's it! Found a blonde?"

"Not at all," I said, with a guilty thought of Elsie Holland. "It's merely that the psychology of crime interests me a good deal."

"Oh, alright. It certainly hasn't done you any harm so far, but just make sure that your lunatic killer doesn't obliterate *you.*"

"No fear of that," I said.

"What about dining with me this evening? You can tell me all about your revolting murder."

"Sorry. I'm booked."

"Date with a lady—eh? Yes, you're definitely on the mend."

"I suppose you could call it that," I said, rather tickled at the idea of Megan in the role.

I was at Mirotin's at six o'clock when the establishment was officially closing. Mary Grey came to meet me at the top of the stairs outside the showroom. She had a finger to her lips.

"You're going to have a shock! If I say it myself, I've put in a good bit of work."

I went on into the big showroom. Megan was standing looking at herself in a long mirror. I give you my word I hardly recognized her! For the minute it took my breath away. Tall and slim as a willow with delicate ankles and feet shown off by sheer silk stockings and well-cut shoes. Yes, lovely feet and hands, small bones—quality and distinction in every line of her. Her hair had been trimmed and shaped to her head and it was glowing like a glossy chestnut. They'd had the sense to leave her face alone. She was not made up, or if she was it was so slight and delicate that it did not show. Her mouth needed no lipstick.

Moreover there was about her something that I had never seen before, a new innocent pride in the arch of her neck. She looked at me gravely with a small, shy smile.

"I do look—rather nice, don't I?" said Megan.

"Nice?" I said. "Nice isn't the word! Come on out to dinner and if every second man doesn't turn around to look at you I'll be surprised. You'll knock all the other girls into a cocked hat."

Megan was not beautiful, but she was unusual and striking-looking. She had personality. She walked into the restaurant ahead of me and as the head waiter hurried toward us, I felt the thrill of idiotic pride that a man feels when he has got something out of the ordinary with him.

We had cocktails first and lingered over them. Then we dined. And later we danced. Megan was keen to dance and I didn't want to disappoint her, but for some reason or other I hadn't thought she would dance well. But she did. She was light as a feather in my arms, and her body and feet followed the rhythm perfectly.

"Gosh!" I said. "You can dance!"

She seemed a little surprised.

"Well, of course I can. We had dancing class every week at school."

"It takes more than dancing class to make a dancer," I said.

We went back to our table.

"Isn't this food lovely?" said Megan. "And everything!"

She heaved a delighted sigh.

"Exactly my sentiments," I said.

It was a delirious evening. I was still mad. Megan brought me down to earth when she said doubtfully, "Oughtn't we to be going home?"

My jaw dropped. Yes, definitely I was mad. I had forgotten everything! I was in a world divorced from reality, existing in it with the creature I had created.

"Good Lord!" I said.

I realized that the last train had gone.

"Stay there," I said. "I'm going to telephone."

I rang up the Llewellyn Hire people and ordered their biggest and fastest car to come around as soon as possible.

I came back to Megan.

"The last train has gone," I said. "So we're going home by car."

"Are we? What fun!"

What a nice child she was, I thought. So pleased with everything, so unquestioning, accepting all my suggestions without fuss or bother.

The car came, and it was large and fast, but all the same it was very late when we came into Lymstock.

Suddenly conscience-stricken, I said, "They'll have been sending out search parties for you."

But Megan seemed in an equable mood. "Oh, I don't think so," she said vaguely. "I often go out and don't come home for lunch."

"Yes, my dear child, but you've been out for tea and dinner too."

However, Megan's lucky star was in the ascendant. The house was dark and silent. On Megan's advice, we went around to the back and threw stones at Rose's window.

In due course Rose looked out and with many suppressed exclamations and palpitations came down to let us in.

"Well now, and I saying you were asleep in your bed. The master and Miss Holland—" (slight sniff after Miss Holland's name) "had early supper and went for a drive. I said I'd keep an eye to the boys. I thought I heard you come in when I was up in the nursery trying to quiet Colin, who was playing up, but you weren't about when I came down so I thought you'd gone to bed. And that's what I said when the master came in and asked for you."

I cut short the conversation by remarking that that was where Megan had better go now.

"Good night," said Megan, "and thank you *awfully*. It's been the loveliest day I've ever had."

I drove home slightly lightheaded still, and tipped the chauffeur handsomely, offering him a bed if he liked. But he preferred to drive back through the night.

The hall door had opened during our colloquy and as he drove away it was flung wide open and Joanna said, "So it's you at last, is it?"

"Were you worried about me?" I asked, coming in and shutting the door.

Joanna went into the drawing room and I followed her. There was a coffeepot on the trivet and Joanna made herself coffee while I helped myself to a whiskey-and-soda.

"Worried about you? No, of course not. I thought you'd decided to stay in town and have a binge."

"I've had a binge—of a kind."

I grinned and then began to laugh.

Joanna asked what I was laughing at and I told her.

"But, Jerry, you must have been mad—quite mad."

"I suppose I was."

"But, my dear boy, you can't do things like that—not in a place like this. It will be all around Lymstock tomorrow."

"I suppose it will. But, after all, Megan's only a child."

"She isn't. She's twenty. You can't take a girl of twenty to London and buy her clothes without a most frightful scandal. Good gracious, Jerry, you'll probably have to marry the girl."

Joanna was half serious, half laughing.

It was at that moment that I made a very important discovery.

"Damn it all," I said. "I don't mind if I do. In fact—I should like it."

A very funny expression came over Joanna's face. She got up and said drily, as she went toward the door, "Yes, I've known that for some time . . ."

She left me standing, glass in hand, aghast at my new discovery.

I don't know what the usual reactions are of a man who goes to propose marriage.

In fiction his throat is dry and his collar feels too tight and he is in a pitiable state of nervousness.

I didn't feel at all like that. Having thought of a good idea I just wanted to get it all settled as soon as possible. I didn't see any particular need for embarrassment.

I went along to the Symmingtons' house about eleven o'clock. I rang the bell and when Rose came, I asked for Miss Megan.

It was the knowing look that Rose gave me that first made me feel slightly shy.

She put me in the little morning room and while waiting there I hoped uneasily that they hadn't been upsetting Megan.

When the door opened and I wheeled around, I was instantly relieved. Megan was not looking shy or upset at all. Her head was still like a glossy chestnut, and she wore that air of pride and self-respect that she had acquired yesterday. She was in her old clothes again but she had managed to make them look different. It's wonderful what knowledge of her own attractiveness will do for a girl. Megan, I realized suddenly, had grown up.

I suppose I must really have been rather nervous, otherwise I should not have opened the conversation by saying affectionately: "Hello, catfish!" It was hardly, in the circumstances, a loverlike greeting.

It seemed to suit Megan. She grinned and said, "Hello!"

"Look here," I said. "You didn't get into a row about yesterday, I hope?"

Megan said with assurance, "Oh, *no*," and then blinked, and said vaguely, "Yes, I believe I did. I mean, they said a lot of things and seemed to think it had been very odd—but then you know what people are and what fusses they make all about nothing."

I was relieved to see that shocked disapproval had slipped off Megan like water off a duck's back.

"I came around this morning," I said, "because I've a suggestion to make. You see I like you a lot, and I think you like me—"

"Frightfully," said Megan with rather disquieting enthusiasm.

"And we get on awfully well together, so I think it would be a good idea if we got married."

"Oh," said Megan.

She looked surprised. Just that. Not startled. Not shocked. Just mildly surprised.

"You mean you really want to marry me?" she asked with the air of one getting a thing perfectly clear.

"More than anything in the world," I said—and I meant it.

"You mean, you're in love with me?"

"I'm in love with you."

Her eyes were steady and grave. She said, "I think you're the nicest person in the world—but I'm not in love with you."

"I'll make you love me."

"That wouldn't do. I don't want to be *made*." She paused and then said gravely, "I'm not the sort of wife for you. I'm better at hating than at loving."

She said it with a queer intensity.

I said, "Hate doesn't last. Love does."

"Is that true?"

"It's what I believe."

Again there was a silence. Then I said, "So it's 'no,' is it?"

"Yes, it's 'No.'"

"And you don't encourage me to hope?"

"What would be the good of that?"

"None whatever," I agreed. "Quite redundant in fact—because I'm going to hope whether you tell me to or not."

Well, that was that.

I walked away from the house feeling slightly dazed but irritatingly conscious of Rose's passionately interested gaze following me.

Rose had had a good deal to say before I could escape.

That she'd never felt the same since that awful day! That she wouldn't have stayed except for the children and being sorry for poor Mr. Symmington. That she wasn't going to stay unless they got another maid quick—and they wouldn't be likely to do that when there had been a murder in the house! That it was all very well for that Miss Holland to say she'd do the housework in the meantime.

Very sweet and obliging she was—oh yes, but it was mistress of the house that she was fancying herself going to be one fine day! Mr. Symmington, poor man, never saw anything—but one knew what a widower was, a poor helpless creature made to be the prey of a designing woman. And that it wouldn't be for want of trying if Miss Holland didn't step into the dead mistress's shoes!

I assented mechanically to everything, yearning to get away and unable to do so because Rose was holding firmly on to my hat while she indulged in her flood of spite.

I wondered if there was any truth in what she said. Had Elsie Holland envisaged the possibility of becoming the second Mrs. Symmington? Or was she just a decent kindhearted girl doing her best to look after a bereaved household?

The result would quite likely be the same in either case. And why not? Symmington's young children needed a mother—Elsie was a decent soul—besides being quite indecently beautiful—a point which a man might appreciate—even such a stuffed fish as Symmington!

I thought all this, I know, because I was trying to put off thinking about Megan.

You may say that I had gone to ask Megan to marry me in an absurdly complacent frame of mind and that I deserved what I got—but it was not really like that. It was because I felt so assured, so certain, that Megan belonged to me—that she was my business, that to look after her and make her happy and keep her from harm was the only natural right way of life for me, that I had expected her to feel, too—that she and I—belonged to each other.

But I was not giving up. Oh, no! Megan was my woman and I was going to have her.

After a moment's thought, I went to Symmington's office. Megan might pay no attention to strictures on her conduct, but I would like to get things straight.

Mr. Symmington was disengaged, I was told, and I was shown into the room.

By a pinching of the lips, and an additional stiffness of manner, I gathered that I was not exactly popular at the moment.

"Good morning," I said. "I'm afraid this isn't a professional call, but a personal one. I'll put it plainly. I dare say you'll have realized that I'm in love with Megan. I've asked her to marry me and she has refused. But I'm not taking that as final."

I saw Symmington's expression change, and I read his mind with ludicrous ease. Megan was a disharmonious element in his house. He was, I felt sure, a just and kindly man, and he would never have dreamed of not providing a home for his dead wife's daughter. But her marriage to me would certainly be a relief. The frozen halibut thawed. He gave me a pale, cautious smile.

"Frankly, do you know, Burton, I had no idea of such a thing. I know you've taken a lot of notice of her, but we've always regarded her as such a child."

"She's not a child," I said shortly.

"No, no, not in years."

"She can be her age any time she's allowed to be," I said, still slightly angry. "She's not of age, I know, but she will be in a month or two. I'll let you have all the information about myself you want. I'm well off and have led quite a decent life. I'll look after her and do all I can to make her happy."

"Quite—quite. Still, it's up to Megan herself."

"She'll come round in time," I said. "But I just thought I'd like to get straight with you about it."

He said he appreciated that, and we parted amicably.

I ran into Miss Emily Barton outside. She had a shopping basket on her arm.

"Good morning, Mr. Burton, I hear you went to London yesterday."

Yes, she had heard alright. Her eyes were, I thought, kindly, but full of curiosity, too.

"I went to see my doctor," I said.

Miss Emily smiled.

That smile made little of Marcus Kent. She murmured, "I hear Megan nearly missed the train. She jumped in when it was going."

"Helped in by me," I said. "I hauled her in."

"How very lucky you were there. Otherwise there might have been an accident."

It is extraordinary how much of a fool one gentle, inquisitive, old maiden lady can make a man feel!

I was saved further suffering by the onslaught of Mrs. Dane Calthrop. She had her own tame elderly maiden lady in tow, but she herself was full of direct speech.

"Good morning," she said. "I hear you've made Megan buy herself some decent clothes? Very sensible of you. It takes a man to think of something really practical like that. I've been worried about that girl for a long time. Girls with brains are so liable to turn into morons, aren't they?"

With which remarkable statement, she shot into the fish shop.

Miss Marple, left standing by me, twinkled a little and said, "Mrs. Dane Calthrop is a very remarkable woman, you know. She's nearly always right."

"It makes her rather alarming," I said.

"Sincerity has that effect," said Miss Marple.

Mrs. Dane Calthrop shot out of the fish shop again and rejoined us. She was holding a large red lobster.

"Have you ever seen anything so unlike Mr. Pye?" she said. "Very virile and handsome, isn't it?"

I was a little nervous of meeting Joanna but I found when I got home that I needn't have worried. She was out and she did not return for lunch. This aggrieved Partridge a good deal, who said sourly as she proffered two loin chops in an entrée dish:

"Miss Burton said specially as she was going to be *in*."

I ate both chops in an attempt to atone for Joanna's lapse. All the same, I wondered where my sister was. She had taken to being very mysterious about her doings of late.

It was half past three when Joanna burst into the drawing-room. I had heard a car stop outside and I half expected to see Griffith, but the car drove on and Joanna came in alone.

Her face was very red and she seemed upset. I perceived that something had happened.

"What's the matter?" I asked.

Joanna opened her mouth, closed it again, sighed, plumped herself down in a chair and stared in front of her.

She said, "I've had the most awful day."

"What's happened?"

"I've done the most incredible things. It was awful—"

"But what—"

"I just started out for a walk, an ordinary walk—I went up over the hill and on to the moor. I walked miles—I felt like it. Then I dropped down into a hollow. There's a farm there—a God-forsaken lonely sort of spot. I was thirsty and I wondered if they had any milk or something. So I wandered into the farmyard and then the door opened and Owen came out."

"Yes?"

"He thought it might be the district nurse. There was a woman in there having a baby. He was expecting the nurse and he'd sent word to her to get hold of another doctor. It—things were going wrong."

"Yes?"

"So he said—to *me*. 'Come on, you'll do—better than nobody.' I said I couldn't, and he said what did I mean? I said I'd never done anything like that, that I didn't know anything—

"He asked me what the hell that mattered. And then he was *awful*. He turned on me. He said, 'You're a woman, aren't you? I suppose you can do your durndest to help another woman?' And he went on at me—said I'd talked as though I was interested in doctoring and had said I wished I was a nurse. 'All pretty talk, I suppose! You didn't mean anything real by it, but this *is* real and you're going to behave like a decent human being and not a useless ornamental nitwit.'

"I've done the most indiscernible things, Jerry. Held instruments and boiled them and handed things. I'm so tired I can hardly stand up. It was dreadful. But he saved her—and the baby. It was born alive. He didn't think at one time he could save it. Oh, dear!"

Joanna covered her face with her hands.

I contemplated her with a certain amount of pleasure and mentally took my hat off to Owen Griffith. He'd brought Joanna slap up against reality for once.

I said, "There's a letter for you in the hall. From Paul, I think."

"Eh?" She paused for a minute and then said, "I'd no idea, Jerry, what doctors had to do. The nerve they've got to have!"

I went out into the hall and brought Joanna her letter. She opened it, glanced vaguely at its contents, and let it drop.

"He was—really—rather wonderful. The way he fought—the way he wouldn't be beaten! He was rude and horrible to *me*—but he *was* wonderful!"

I observed Paul's disregarded letter with some pleasure. Plainly, Joanna was cured of Paul.

Things never come when they are expected.

I was full of Joanna's and my personal affairs and was quite taken aback the next morning when Nash's voice said over the telephone:

"*We've got her*, Mr. Burton!"

I was so startled I nearly dropped the receiver.

"You mean the—"

He interrupted: "Can you be overheard where you are?"

"No, I don't think so—well, perhaps—"

It seemed to me that the baize door to the kitchen had swung open a trifle.

"Perhaps you'd care to come down to the station?"

"I will. Right away."

I was at the police station in next to no time. In an inner room Nash and Sergeant Parkins were together. Nash was wreathed in smiles.

"It's been a long chase," he said. "But we're there at last."

He flicked a letter across the table. This time it was all typewritten. It was, of its kind, fairly mild:

"It's no use thinking you're going to step into a dead woman's shoes. The whole town is laughing at you. Get out now. Soon it will be too late. This is a warning. Remember what happened to that other girl. Get out and stay out."

It finished with some mildly obscene language.

"That reached Miss Holland this morning," said Nash.

"Thought it was funny she hadn't had one before," said Sergeant Parkins.

"Who wrote it?" I asked.

Some of the exultation faded out of Nash's face.

He looked tired and concerned. He said soberly:

"I'm sorry about it, because it will hit a decent man hard, but there it is. Perhaps he's had his suspicions already."

"Who wrote it?" I reiterated.

"Miss Aimée Griffith."

Nash and Parkins went to the Griffiths' house that afternoon with a warrant.

By Nash's invitation I went with them.

"The doctor," he said, "is very fond of you. He hasn't many friends in this place. I think if it is not too painful to you, Mr. Burton, that you might help him to bear up under the shock."

I said I would come. I didn't relish the job, but I thought I might be some good.

We rang the bell and asked for Miss Griffith and we were shown into the drawing room. Elsie Holland, Megan and Symmington were there having tea.

Nash behaved very circumspectly.

He asked Aimée if he might have a few words with her privately.

She got up and came toward us. I thought I saw just a faint hunted look in her eye. If so, it went again. She was perfectly normal and hearty.

"Want me? Not in trouble over my car lights again, I hope?"

She led the way out of the drawing room and across the hall into a small study.

As I closed the drawing-room door, I saw Symmington's head jerk up sharply. I supposed his legal training had brought him in contact with police cases, and he had recognized something in Nash's manner. He half rose.

That is all I saw before I shut the door and followed the others.

Nash was saying his piece. He was very quiet and correct. He cautioned her and then told her that he must ask her to accompany him. He had a warrant for her arrest and he read out the charge.

I forget now the exact legal term. It was the letters, not murder yet.

Aimée Griffith flung up her head and bayed with laughter. She boomed out:

"What ridiculous nonsense. As though I'd write a packet of indecent stuff like that. You must be mad. I've never written a word of the kind."

Nash had produced the letter to Elsie Holland. He said, "Do you deny having written this, Miss Griffith?"

If she hesitated it was only for a split second.

"Of course I do. I've never seen it before."

Nash said quietly:

"I must tell you, Miss Griffith, that you were observed to type that letter on the machine at the Women's Institute between eleven and eleven-thirty P.M. on the night before last. Yesterday you entered the post office with a bunch of letters in your hand—"

"I never posted this."

"No, you did not. While waiting for stamps, you dropped it inconspicuously on the floor, so that somebody should come along unsuspectingly and pick it up and post it."

"I never—"

The door opened and Symmington came in. He said sharply, "What's going on? Aimée, if there is anything wrong, you ought to be legally represented. If you wish me—"

She broke then. Covered her face with her hands and staggered to a chair. She said, "Go away, Dick, go away. Not you! Not *you*!"

"You need a solicitor, my dear girl."

"Not you. I—I couldn't bear it. I don't want you to know—all this."

He understood then, perhaps. He said quietly. "I'll get hold of Mildmay, of Exhampton. Will that do?"

She nodded. She was sobbing now.

Symmington went out of the room. In the doorway he collided with Owen Griffith.

"What's this?" said Owen violently. "My sister—"

"I'm sorry, Dr. Griffith. Very sorry. But we have no alternative."

"You think she—was responsible for those letters?"

"I'm afraid there is no doubt of it, sir," said Nash—he turned to Aimée: "You must come with us now, please, Miss Griffith—you shall have every facility for seeing a solicitor, you know."

Owen cried, "Aimée?"

She brushed past him without looking at him.

She said, "Don't talk to me. Don't say anything. And for heaven's sake don't *look* at me!"

They went out. Owen stood like a man in a dream.

I waited a bit, then I came up to him.

"If there's anything I can do, Griffith, tell me."

He said like a man in a dream, "Aimée? I don't believe it."

"It may be a mistake," I suggested feebly.

He said slowly, "She wouldn't take it like that if it were. But I would never have believed it. I *can't* believe it."

He sank down on a chair. I made myself useful by finding a stiff drink and bringing it to him. He swallowed it down and it seemed to do him good.

He said, "I couldn't take it in at first. I'm alright now. Thanks, Burton, but there's nothing you can do. Nothing *anyone* can do."

The door opened and Joanna came in. She was very white.

She came over to Owen and looked at me.

She said, "Get out, Jerry. This is my business."

As I went out of the door, I saw her kneel down by his chair.

8

I CAN'T TELL you coherently the events of the next twenty-four hours. Various incidents stand out, unrelated to other incidents.

I remember Joanna coming home, very white and drawn and of how I tried to cheer her up, saying:

"Now who's being a ministering angel?"

And of how she smiled in a pitiful twisted way and said, "He says he won't have me, Jerry. He's very *very* proud and stiff!"

And I said, "My girl won't have me either. . . ."

We sat there for a while, Joanna saying at last, "The Burton family isn't exactly in demand at the moment!"

I said, "Never mind, my sweet, we still have each other," and Joanna said, "Somehow or other, Jerry, that doesn't comfort me much just now. . . ."

Owen came the next day and rhapsodized in the most fulsome way about Joanna. She was wonderful, marvelous! The way she'd come to him, the way she was willing to marry him—at once if he liked. But he wasn't going to let her do that. No, she was too good, too fine to be associated with the kind of muck that would start as soon as the papers got hold of the news.

I was fond of Joanna, and knew she was the kind who's alright when standing by in trouble, but I got rather bored with all this highfalutin stuff. I told Owen rather irritably not to be so damned noble.

I went down to the High Street and found everybody's tongue wagging nineteen to the dozen. Emily Barton was saying that she had never really trusted Aimée Griffith. The grocer's wife was saying with gusto that she's always thought Miss Griffith had a queer look in her eye—

They had completed the case against Aimée, so I learned from Nash. A search of the house had brought to light the cut pages of Emily Barton's book—in the cupboard under the stairs, of all places, wrapped up in an old roll of wallpaper.

"And a jolly good place too," said Nash appreciatively. "You never know when a prying servant won't tamper with a desk or a locked drawer—but those junk cupboards full of last year's tennis balls and old wallpaper are never opened except to shove something more in."

"The lady would seem to have had a penchant for that particular hiding place," I said.

"Yes. The criminal mind seldom has much variety. By the way, talking of the dead girl, we've got one fact to go upon: There's a large heavy pestle missing from the doctor's dispensary. I'll bet anything you like that's what she was stunned with."

"Rather an awkward thing to carry about," I objected.

"Not for Miss Griffith. She was going to the Guides that afternoon, but she was going to leave flowers and vegetables at the Red Cross stall on the way, so she'd got a whopping great basket with her."

"You haven't found the skewer?"

"No, and I shan't. The poor devil may be mad, but she wasn't mad enough to keep a bloodstained skewer just to make it easy for us, when all she'd got to do was to wash it and return it to a kitchen drawer."

"I suppose," I conceded, "that you can't have everything."

The vicarage had been one of the last places to hear the news. Old Miss Marple was very much distressed by it. She spoke to me very earnestly on the subject:

"It isn't *true*, Mr. Burton. I'm sure it isn't true."

"It's true enough, I'm afraid. They were lying in wait, you know. They actually *saw* her type that letter."

"Yes, yes—perhaps they did. Yes, I can understand *that*."

"And the printed pages from which the letters were cut were found where she'd hidden them in her house."

Miss Marple stared at me. Then she said, in a very low voice, "But that is horrible—really *wicked*."

Mrs. Dane Calthrop came up with a rush and joined us and said, "What's the matter, Jane?"

Miss Marple was murmuring helplessly, "Oh, dear, oh, dear, what can one *do*?"

"What's upset you, Jane?"

Miss Marple said, "There must be *something*. But I am so old and so ignorant and, I am afraid, so foolish."

I felt rather embarrassed and was glad when Mrs. Dane Calthrop took her friend away.

I was to see Miss Marple again that afternoon, however. Much later when I was on my way home.

She was standing near the little bridge at the end of the village, near Mrs. Cleat's cottage, and talking to Megan, of all people.

I wanted to see Megan. I had been wanting to see her all day. I quickened my pace. But as I came up to them, Megan turned on her heel and went off in the other direction.

It made me angry and I would have followed her, but Miss Marple blocked my way.

"I wanted to speak to you," she said. "No, don't go after Megan now. It wouldn't be wise."

I was just going to make a sharp rejoinder when she disarmed me by saying, "That girl has great courage—a very high order of courage."

I still wanted to go after Megan, but Miss Marple said, "Don't try and see her now. I do know what I am talking about. She must keep her courage intact."

There was something about the old lady's assertion that chilled me. It was as though she knew something that I didn't.

I was afraid and didn't know why I was afraid.

I didn't go home. I went back into the High Street and walked up and down aimlessly. I don't know what I was waiting for, nor what I was thinking about. . . .

I got caught by that awful old bore Colonel Appleby. He asked after my pretty sister as usual and then went on:

"What's all this about Griffith's sister being mad as a hatter? They say she's been at the bottom of this anonymous letter business that's been such a confounded nuisance to everybody? Couldn't believe it at first, but they say it's quite true."

I said it was true enough.

"Well, well—I must say our police force is pretty good on the whole. Give 'em time, that's all, give 'em time. Funny business this anonymous letter stunt—these desiccated old women are always the ones who go in for it—though the Griffith woman wasn't bad-looking even if she was a bit long in the tooth. But there aren't any decent-looking girls in this part of the world—except that governess girl of the Symmingtons. She's worth looking at. Pleasant girl, too. Grateful if one does any little thing for her.

"Came across her having a picnic or something with those kids not long ago. They were romping about in the heather and she was knitting—ever so vexed she'd run out of wool. 'Well,' I said, 'like me to run into Lymstock? I've got to call for a rod of mine there. I shan't be more than ten minutes getting it, then I'll run you back again.' She was a bit doubtful about leaving the boys. 'They'll be alright,' I said. 'Who's to harm them?' Wasn't going to have the boys along, no fear! So I ran her in, dropped her at the wool shop, picked her up again later and that was that. Thanked me very prettily. Grateful and all that. Nice girl."

I managed to get away from him.

It was after that, that I caught sight of Miss Marple for the third time. She was coming out of the police station.

Where do one's fears come from? Where do they shape themselves? Where do they hide before coming out into the open?

Just one short phrase. Heard and noted and never quite put aside:

"Take me away—It's so awful being here—feeling so wicked . . ."

Why had Megan said that? What had she to feel wicked about?

There could be nothing in Mrs. Symmington's death to make Megan feel wicked.

Why had the child felt wicked? Why? Why?

Could it be because she felt responsible in any way?

Megan? Impossible! *Megan* couldn't have had anything to do with those letters—those foul obscene letters.

Owen Griffith had known a case up north—a schoolgirl . . .

What had Inspector Graves said?

Something about an *adolescent mind . . .*

Innocent middle-aged ladies on operating tables babbled words they hardly knew. Little boys chalking up things on walls.

No, no, not *Megan.*

Heredity? Bad blood? An unconscious inheritance of something abnormal? Her misfortune, not her fault, a curse laid upon her by a past generation?

"I'm not the wife for you. I'm better at hating than loving."

Oh, my Megan, my little child. Not *that*! Anything but that. And that old Tabby is after you, she suspects. She says you have courage. Courage to do *what*?

It was only a brainstorm. It passed. But I wanted to see Megan—I wanted to see her badly.

At half past nine that night I left the house and went down to the town and along to the Symmingtons'.

It was then that an entirely new idea came into my mind. The idea of a woman whom nobody had considered for a moment.

(Or had Nash considered her?)

Wildly unlikely, wildly improbable, and I would have said up to today impossible, too. But that was not so. No, not *impossible.*

I redoubled my pace. Because it was now even more imperative that I should see Megan straightaway.

I passed through the Symmingtons' gate and up to the house. It was a dark overcast night. A little rain was beginning to fall. The visibility was bad.

I saw a line of light from one of the windows. The little morning room?

I hesitated a moment or two, then instead of going up to the front door, I swerved and crept very quietly up to the window, skirting a big bush and keeping low.

The light came from a chink in the curtains, which were not quite drawn. It was easy to look through and see.

It was a strangely peaceful and domestic scene. Symmington in a big armchair, and Elsie Holland, her head bent, busily patching a boy's torn shirt.

I could hear as well as see, for the window was open at the top.

Elsie Holland was speaking:

"But I do think, really, Mr. Symmington, that the boys are quite old enough to go to boarding school. Not that I shan't hate leaving them because I shall. I'm ever so fond of them both."

Symmington said, "I think perhaps you're right about Brian, Miss Holland. I've decided that he shall start next term at Winhays—my old prep school. But Colin is a little young yet. I'd prefer him to wait another year."

"Well, of course I see what you mean. And Colin is perhaps a little young for his age—"

Quiet domestic talk—quiet domestic scene—and a golden head bent over needlework.

Then the door opened and Megan came in.

She stood very straight in the doorway, and I was aware at once of something tense and strung up about her. The skin of her face was tight and drawn and her

eyes bright and resolute. There was no diffidence about her tonight and no childishness.

She said, addressing Symmington, but giving him no title (and I suddenly reflected that I never had heard her call him anything. Did she address him as father or as Dick or what?):

"I would like to speak to you, please. Alone."

Symmington looked surprised and, I fancied, not best pleased. He frowned, but Megan carried her point with a determination unusual in her.

She turned to Elsie Holland and said, "Do you mind, Elsie?"

"Oh, of course." Elsie Holland jumped up. She looked startled and a little flurried.

She went to the door and Megan came farther in so that Elsie passed her.

Just for a minute Elsie stood motionless in the doorway looking over her shoulder.

Her lips were closed, she stood quite still, one hand stretched out, the other clasping her needlework to her.

I caught my breath, overwhelmed suddenly by her beauty.

When I think of her now, I always think of her like that—in arrested motion, with that matchless deathless perfection that belonged to ancient Greece.

Then she went out shutting the door.

Symmington said rather fretfully, "Well, Megan, what is it? What do you want?"

Megan had come right up to the table. She stood there looking down at Symmington. I was struck anew by the resolute determination of her face and by something else—a hardness new to me.

Then she opened her lips and said something that startled me to the core.

"I want some money," she said.

The request didn't improve Symmington's temper. He said sharply, "Couldn't you have waited until tomorrow morning? What's the matter, do you think your allowance is inadequate?"

A fair man, I thought even then, open to reason, though not to emotional appeal.

Megan said, "I want a good deal of money."

Symmington sat up straight in his chair. He said coldly:

"You will come of age in a few months' time. Then the money left you by your grandmother will be turned over to you by the Public Trustee."

Megan said:

"You don't understand. I want money from *you.*" She went on, speaking faster: "Nobody's ever talked much to me about my father. They've not wanted me to know about him. But I do know that he went to prison and I know why. It was for blackmail!"

She paused.

"Well, I'm his daughter. And perhaps I take after him. Anyway, I'm asking you to give me money because—if you don't—" She stopped and then went on very slowly and evenly—"if you don't—*I shall say what I saw you doing to the cachet that day in my mother's room.*"

There was a pause. Then Symmington said in a completely emotionless voice, "I don't know what you mean."

Megan said, "I think you do."

And she smiled. It was not a nice smile.

Symmington got up. He went over to the writing desk. He took a checkbook from his pocket and wrote out a check. He blotted it carefully and then came back. He held it out to Megan.

"You're grown up now," he said. "I can understand that you may feel you want to buy something rather special in the way of clothes and all that. I don't know what you're talking about. I didn't pay attention. But here's a check."

Megan looked at it, then she said, "Thank you. That will do to go on with."

She turned and went out of the room. Symmington stared after her and at the closed door, then he turned around and as I saw his face I made a quick uncontrolled movement forward.

It was checked in the most extraordinary fashion. The big bush that I had noticed by the wall stopped being a bush. Superintendent Nash's arms went around me and Superintendent Nash's voice just breathed in my ear:

"Quiet, Burton. For God's sake."

Then, with infinite caution he beat a retreat, his arm impelling me to accompany him.

Around the side of the house he straightened himself and wiped his forehead.

"Of course," he said, "You *would* have to butt in!"

"That girl isn't safe," I said urgently. "You saw his face? We've got to get her out of here."

Nash took a firm grip of my arm.

"Now, look here, Mr. Burton, you've got to *listen.*"

Well, I listened.

I didn't like it—but I gave in.

But I insisted on being on the spot and I swore to obey orders implicitly.

So that is how I came with Nash and Parkins into the house by the back door, which was already unlocked.

And I waited with Nash on the upstairs landing behind the velvet curtain masking the window alcove until the clocks in the house struck two, and Symmington's door opened and he went across the landing and into Megan's room.

I did not stir or make a move for I knew that Sergeant Parkins was inside masked by the opening door, and I knew that Parkins was a good man and knew his job, and I knew that I couldn't have trusted myself to keep quiet and not break out.

And waiting there, with my heart thudding, I saw Symmington come out with Megan in his arms and carry her downstairs, with Nash and myself a discreet distance behind him.

He carried her through to the kitchen and he had just arranged her comfortably with her head in the gas oven and had turned on the gas when Nash and I came through the kitchen door and switched on the light.

And that was the end of Richard Symmington. He collapsed. Even while I was hauling Megan out and turning off the gas I saw the collapse. He didn't even try to fight. He knew he'd played and lost.

Upstairs I sat by Megan's bed waiting for her to come around and

occasionally cursing Nash.

"How do you know she's alright? It was too big a risk."

Nash was very soothing.

"Just a soporific in the milk she always had by her bed. Nothing more. It stands to reason, he couldn't risk her being poisoned. As far as he's concerned the whole business is closed with Miss Griffith's arrest. He can't afford to have any mysterious death. No violence, no poison. But if a rather unhappy type of girl broods over her mother's suicide, and finally goes and puts her head in the gas oven—well, people just say that she was never quite normal and the shock of her mother's death finished her."

I said, watching Megan, "She's a long time coming around."

"You heard what Dr. Griffith said? Heart and pulse quite alright—she'll just sleep and wake naturally. Stuff he gives a lot of his patients, he says."

Megan stirred. She murmured something.

Superintendent Nash unobtrusively left the room.

Presently Megan opened her eyes.

"Jerry."

"Hello, sweet."

"Did I do it well?"

"You might have been blackmailing ever since your cradle!"

Megan closed her eyes again. Then she murmured:

"Last night—I was writing to you—in case anything went—[illegible]rong. But I was too sleepy to finish. It's over there."

I went across to the writing table. In a shabby little blotter I foun[illegible]an's unfinished letter.

"My dear Jerry," it began primly:

"I was reading my school Shakespeare and the sonnet that begins

> "*'So are you to my thoughts as food to life*
> *Or as sweet-season'd showers are to the*
> *ground'*

and I see that I am in love with you after all, because that is what I feel." . . .

"So you see," said Mrs. Dane Calthrop, "I was quite right to call in an expert."

I stared at her. We were all at the vicarage. The rain was pouring down outside and there was a pleasant log fire, and Mrs. Dane Calthrop had just wandered around, beat up a sofa cushion and put it for some reason of her own on the top of the grand piano.

"But did you?" I said, surprised. "Who was it? What did he do?"

"It wasn't a he," said Mrs. Dane Calthrop.

With a sweeping gesture she indicated Miss Marple. Miss Marple had finished the fleecy knitting and was now engaged with a crochet hook and a ball of cotton.

"That's my expert," said Mrs. Dane Calthrop. "Jane Marple. Look at her well. I tell you, that woman knows more about the different kinds of human wickedness than anyone I've ever known."

"I don't think you should put it quite like that, dear," murmured Miss Marple.

"But you do."

"One sees a good deal of human nature living in a village all the year around," said Miss Marple placidly.

Then, seeming to feel it was expected of her, she laid down her crochet, and delivered a gentle old-maidish dissertation on murder.

"The great thing in these cases is to keep an absolutely open mind. Most crimes, you see, are so absurdly simple. This one was. Quite sane and straightforward—and quite understandable—in an unpleasant way, of course."

"Very unpleasant!"

"The truth was really so very obvious. You saw it, you know, Mr. Burton."

"Indeed I did not."

"But you did. You indicated the whole thing to me. You saw perfectly the relationship of one thing to the other, but you just hadn't enough self-confidence to see what those feelings of yours meant. To begin with, that tiresome phrase 'No smoke without fire.' It irritated you, but you proceeded quite correctly to label it for what it was—a smoke screen. Misdirection, you see—everybody looking at the wrong thing—the anonymous letters, but the whole point was that there *weren't* any anonymous letters!"

"But, my dear Miss Marple, I can assure you that there *were.* I had one."

"Oh, yes, but they weren't real at all. Dear Maud here tumbled to that. Even in peaceful Lymstock there are plenty of scandals, and I can assure you any *woman* living in the place would have known about them and used them. But a man, you see, isn't interested in gossip in the same way—especially a detached logical man like Mr. Symmington. But a genuine woman writer of those letters would have made her letters much more to the point.

"So you see that if you disregard the smoke and come to the fire you know where you are. You just come down to the actual facts of what happened. And putting aside the letters, just one thing happened—Mrs. Symmington died.

"So then, naturally, one thinks of who might have wanted Mrs. Symmington to die, and of course the very first person one thinks of in such a case is, I am afraid, the *husband.* And one asks oneself is there any *reason?*—any *motive?*—for instance, *any other woman?*

"And the very first thing I hear is that there is a very attractive young governess in the house. So clear, isn't it? Mr. Symmington, a rather dry repressed unemotional man, tied to a querulous and neurotic wife and then suddenly this radiant young creature comes along.

"I'm afraid, you know, that gentlemen, when they fall in love at a certain age, get the disease very badly. It's quite a madness. And Mr. Symmington, as far as I can make out, was never actually a *good* man—he wasn't very kind or very affectionate or very sympathetic—his qualities were all negative—so he hadn't really the strength to fight his madness. And in a place like this, only his wife's death would solve his problem. He wanted to marry the girl, you see. She's very respectable and so is he. And besides, he's devoted to his children, his respectability and Elsie. And the price he would have to pay for that was murder.

"He chose, I do think, a very clever way. He knew so well from his experience of criminal cases how soon suspicion falls on the husband if a wife dies unexpectedly—and the possibility of exhumation in the case of poison. So he created a death which seemed only incidental to something else. He created a nonexistent anonymous letter writer. And the clever thing was that the police were certain to suspect a *woman*— and they were quite right in a way. All the letters were a woman's letters; he cribbed them very cleverly from the letters in the case last year and from a case Dr. Griffith told him about. I don't mean that he was so crude as to reproduce any letter verbatim, but he took phrases and expressios from them and mixed them up, and the net result was that the letters definitely represented a woman's mind—a half-crazy repressed personality.

"He knew all the tricks that the police use, handwriting, typewriting tests, etc. He's been preparing his crime for some time. He typed all the envelopes before he gave away the typewriter to the Women's Institute, and he cut the pages from the book at Little Furze probably quite a long time ago when he was waiting in the drawing room one day. People don't open books of sermons much!

"And finally, having got his false Poison Pen well established, he staged the real thing. A fine afternoon when the governess and the boys and his stepdaughter would be out, and the servants having their regular day out. He couldn't foresee that the little maid Agnes would quarrel with her boyfriend and come back to the house."

Joanna asked, "But what did she see? Do you know that?"

"I don't *know*. I can only guess. My guess would be that she didn't see anything."

"That it was all a mare's nest?"

"No, no, my dear, I mean that she stood at the pantry window all the afternoon waiting for the young man to come and make it up and that—quite literally she saw nothing. That is, *no one* came to the house at all, not the postman, nor anybody else.

"It would take her some time, being slow, to realize that that was very odd—because apparently Mrs. Symmington *had* received an anonymous letter that afternoon."

"Didn't she receive one?" I asked, puzzled.

"But of course not! As I say, this crime is so simple. Her husband just put the cyanide in the top cachet of the ones she took in the afternoon when her sciatica came on after lunch. All Symmington had to do was to get home before, or at the same time as Elsie Holland, call his wife, get no answer, go up to her room, drop a spot of cyanide in the plain glass of water she had used to swallow the cachet, toss the crumpled-up anonymous letter into the grate, and put by her hand the scrap of paper with *'I can't go on'* written on it."

Miss Marple turned to me.

"You were quite right about that, too, Mr. Burton. A 'scrap of paper' was all wrong. People don't leave suicide notes on small torn scraps of paper. They use a *sheet* of paper—and every often an envelope too. Yes, the scrap of paper was wrong and you knew it."

"You are rating me too high," I said. "I knew nothing."

"But you did, you really *did*, Mr. Burton. Otherwise why were you immediately impressed by the message your sister left scribbled on the telephone pad?"

I repeated slowly: "'Say that *I can't go on Friday*'—I see! *'I can't go on'?*"

Miss Marple beamed on me.

"Exactly. Mr. Symmington came across such a message and saw its possibilities. He tore off the words he wanted for when the time came—a message genuinely in his wife's handwriting."

"Was there any further brilliance on my part?"

Miss Marple twinkled at me.

"You put me on the track, you know. You assembled those facts together for me—in sequence—and on top of it you told me the most important thing of all—that Elsie Holland had never received any anonymous letters."

"Do you know," I said, "last night I thought that *she* was the letter writer and that that was why there had been no letters written to her?"

"Oh, dear me, no. . . . The person who writes anonymous letters practically always sends them to herself as well. That's part of the—well, the excitement, I suppose. No, no, the fact interested me for *quite* another reason. It was really, you see, Mr. Symmington's one weakness. He couldn't bring himself to write a foul letter to the girl he loved. It's a very interesting sidelight on human nature—and a credit to him, in a way—but it's where he gave himself away."

Joanna said, "And he killed Agnes? But surely that was quite unnecessary?"

"Perhaps it was, but what you don't realize, my dear (not having killed anyone), is that your judgment is distorted afterward and everything seems exaggerated. No doubt he heard the girl telephoning to Partridge, saying she'd been worried ever since Mrs. Symmington's death, that there was something she didn't understand. He can't take any chances—this stupid foolish girl has seen *something*, knows something."

"Yet apparently he was at his office all that afternoon?"

"I should imagine he killed her before he went. Miss Holland was in the dining-room and kitchen. He just went out into the hall, opened and shut the front door as though he was going out, then slipped into the little cloakroom.

"When only Agnes was left in the house, he probably rang the front-door bell, slipped back into the cloakroom, came out behind her and hit her on the head as she was opening the front door, and then after thrusting the body into the cupboard, he hurried along to his office, arriving just a little late if anyone had happened to notice it, but they probably didn't. You see, no one was suspecting a *man*."

"Abominable brute," said Mrs. Dane Calthrop.

"You're not sorry for him, Mrs. Dane Calthrop?" I inquired.

"Not in the least. Why?"

"I'm glad to hear it, that's all."

Joanna said:

"But why Aimée Griffith? I know that the police have found the pestle taken from Owen's dispensary—and the skewer too. I suppose it's not so easy for a man to return things to kitchen drawers. And guess where they were? Superintendent Nash only told me just now when I met him on my way here. In one of those musty old deed boxes in his office. Estate of Sir Jasper Harrington-West, deceased."

"Poor Jasper," said Mrs. Dane Calthrop. "He was a cousin of mine. Such a correct old boy. He would have had a fit!"

"Wasn't it madness to keep them?" I asked.

"Probably madder to throw them away," said Mrs. Dane Calthrop. "No one had any suspicions about Symmington."

"He didn't strike her with the pestle," said Joanna. "There was a clock weight there too, with hair and blood on it. He pinched the pestle, they think, on the day Aimée was arrested, and hid the book pages in her house. And that brings me back to my original question. What about Aimée Griffith? The police actually *saw* her write that letter."

"Yes, of course," said Miss Marple. "She did write *that* letter."

"But why?"

"Oh, my dear, surely you have realized that Miss Griffith had been in love with Symmington all her life?"

"Poor thing!" said Mrs. Dane Calthrop mechanically.

"They'd always been good friends, and I daresay she thought, after Mrs. Symmington's death, that some day, perhaps—well—" Miss Marple coughed delicately. "And then the gossip began spreading about Elsie Holland and I expect that upset her badly. She thought of the girl as a designing minx worming her way into Symmington's affections and quite unworthy of him. And so, I think, she succumbed to temptation. Why not add one more anonymous letter, and frighten the girl out of the place? It must have seemed quite safe to her and she took, as she thought, every precaution."

"Well?" said Joanna. "Finish the story."

"I should imagine," said Miss Marple slowly, "that when Miss Holland showed that letter to Symmington he realized at once who had written it, and he saw a chance to finish the case once and for all, and make himself safe. Not very nice—no, not very nice, but he was frightened, you see. The police wouldn't be satisfied until they'd got the anonymous letter writer. When he took the letter down to the police and he found they'd actually seen Aimée writing it, he felt he'd got a chance in a thousand of finishing the whole thing.

"He took the family to tea there that afternoon and as he came from the office with his attaché case, he could easily bring the torn-out book pages to hide under the stairs and clinch the case. Hiding them under the stairs was a neat touch. It recalled the disposal of Agnes' body, and, from the practical point of view, it was very easy for him. When he followed Aimée and the police, just a minute or two in the hall passing through would be enough."

"All the same," I said, "there's one thing I can't forgive you for, Miss Marple—roping in Megan."

Miss Marple put down her crochet which she had resumed. She looked at me over her spectacles and her eyes were stern.

"My dear young man, *something* had to be done. There was no evidence against this very clever and unscrupulous man. I needed someone to help me, someone of high courage and good brains. I found the person I needed."

"It was very dangerous for her."

"Yes, it was dangerous, but we are not put into this world, Mr. Burton, to avoid danger when an innocent fellow creature's life is at stake. You understand me?"

I understood.

It was morning in the High Street.

Miss Emily Barton came out of the grocer's with her shopping bag. Her cheeks were pink and her eyes were excited.

"Oh, dear, Mr. Burton, I really am in such a flutter. To think I really am going on a cruise at last!"

"I hope you'll enjoy it."

"Oh, I'm sure I shall. I should never have dared to go by myself. It does seem so *providential* the way everything has turned out. For a long time I've felt that I ought to part with Little Furze, that my means were really too straitened, but I couldn't bear the idea of *strangers* there.

"But now that you have bought it and are going to live there with Megan—it is quite different. And then dear Aimée, after her terrible ordeal, not quite knowing what to do with herself, and her brother getting married (how nice to think you have *both* settled down with us!), and agreeing to come with me. We mean to be away quite a long time. We might even"—Miss Emily dropped her voice—*"go around the world!* And Aimée is so splendid and so practical. I really do think—don't you?—that everything turns out for the *best*."

Just for a fleeting moment I thought of Mrs. Symmington and Agnes Woddell in their graves in the churchyard and wondered if they would agree, and then I remembered that Agnes' boyfriend hadn't been very fond of her and that Mrs. Symmington hadn't been very nice to Megan and, what the hell? We've all got to die some time! And I agreed with happy Miss Emily that everything was for the best in the best possible worlds.

I went along the High Street and in at the Symmingtons' gate and Megan came out to meet me.

It was not a romantic meeting because an outsize old English sheep dog came out with Megan and nearly knocked me over with his ill-timed exuberance.

"Isn't he *adorable*?" said Megan.

"A little overwhelming. Is he ours?"

"Yes, he's a wedding present from Joanna. We *have* had nice wedding presents, haven't we? That fluffy woolly thing that we don't know what it's for from Miss Marple, and the lovely Crown Derby tea set from Mr. Pye, and Elsie has sent me a toast rack—"

"How typical!" I interjected.

"And she's got a post with a dentist and is very happy. And—where was I?"

"Enumerating wedding presents. Don't forget if you change your mind you'll have to send them all back."

"I shan't change my mind. What else have we got? Oh, yes, Mrs. Dane Calthrop has sent an Egyptian scarab."

"Original woman," I said.

"Oh! Oh! But you don't know the best. *Partridge* has actually sent me a present. It's the most hideous tea cloth you've ever seen. But I think she *must* like me now because she says she embroidered it all with her own hands."

"In a design of sour grapes and thistles, I suppose?"

"No; true lover's knots."

"Dear, dear," I said, "Partride *is* coming on."

Megan had dragged me into the house.

She said:

"There's just one thing I can't make out. Besides the dog's own collar and lead, Joanna has sent an extra collar and lead. What do you think that's for?"

"That," I said, "is Joanna's little joke."

THE END

Death Comes as the End

To PROFESSOR S. R. K. GLANVILLE

DEAR STEPHEN,

It was you who originally suggested to me the idea of a detective story set in Ancient Egypt, and but for your active help and encouragement this book would never have been written.

I want to say here how much I have enjoyed all the interesting literature you have lent me and to thank you once more for the patience with which you have answered my questions and for the time and trouble you have expended. The pleasure and interest which the writing of the book have brought to me you already know.

Your affectionate and grateful friend,

AGATHA CHRISTIE

Author's Note

THE ACTION OF this book takes place on the west bank of the Nile at Thebes in Egypt about 2000 B.C. Both places and time are incidental to the story. Any other place at any other time would have served as well, but it so happened that the inspiration of both characters and plot was derived from two or three Egyptian letters of the XIth Dynasty, found during the 1920–1921 season by the Egyptian Expedition of the Metropolitan Museum of Art, New York, in a rock tomb opposite Luxor, and translated by Professor (then Mr.) Battiscombe Gunn in the Museum's Bulletin.

It may be of interest to the reader to note that an endowment for ka-service—an everyday feature of ancient Egyptian civilization—was very similar in principle to a medieval chantry bequest. Property was bequeathed to the ka-priest, in return for which he was expected to maintain the tomb of the testator, and to provide offerings at the tomb on certain feast days throughout the year for the repose of the deceased's soul.

The terms "Brother," "Sister," in Egyptian text regularly meaning "Lover," are frequently interchangeable with "Husband," "Wife." They are so used on occasion in this book.

The agricultural calendar of Ancient Egypt, consisting of three seasons of four months of thirty days, formed the background of peasant life, and with the addition of five intercalary days at the end of the year, was used as the official calendar of 365 days to the year. This "year" originally began with the arrival in Egypt of the flood-water of the Nile in the third week of July by our reckoning. The absence of a leap year caused this to lag through the centuries, so that at the time of our story, the official New Year's Day fell about six months earlier than the opening of the agricultural year, i.e. in January instead of July. To save the reader from continually having to make allowance for this six months, however, the dates here used as chapter headings are calculated by the agricultural year of the time, i.e., Inundation—late July to late November; Winter—late November to late March; and Summer—late March to late July.

Cast of Characters

RENISENB—Too young and lovely to remain a widow for very long, she had a fateful choice to make—life or death.

YAHMOSE—His nagging wife, Satipy, and overbearing father, Imhotep, had robbed him of the courage to assert his rights as eldest son.

SOBEK—A handsome braggart, the second of Imhotep's sons, he too resented his dependent status on the Nile farm lands.

IMHOTEP—Fussily pompous in his role as ka-priest and provider for his large household, he anticipated no trouble when he brought home a concubine.

SATIPY—A tall, energetic, loud-tongued woman who bullied her husband and outraged everyone else.

KAIT—One passion in life dominated her every act: love for her children.

HENET—In her self-pitying, cringing way, the housekeeper took malicious pleasure in fanning the flames of family discord.

ESA—The old lady called her son, Imhotep, a fool, and laughed at death. But even she learned the meaning of fear.

HORI—Imhotep's scribe and man of business. His concern for Renisenb's safety was based on logic—and love.

IPY—Only his doting father, Imhotep, could put up with his youngest son's adolescent arrogance.

NOFRET—The beautiful young concubine of the aging Imhotep touched off smoldering jealousies in the ka-priest's family.

KAMENI—He was a kinsman—broad-shouldered and handsome. When he sang songs of love, Renisenb's heart answered.

1

Second Month of Inundation, 20th Day

RENISENB STOOD LOOKING out over the Nile.

In the distance she could hear faintly the upraised voices of her brothers, Yahmose and Sobek, disputing as to whether or not the dikes in a certain place needed strengthening. Sobek's voice was high and confident as always. He had the habit of asserting his view with easy certainty. Yahmose's was low and grumbling in tone; it expressed doubt and anxiety. Yahmose was always in a state of anxiety over something or other. He was the eldest son and during his father's absence on the northern estates, the management of the farm lands was more or less in his hands. Yahmose was slow, prudent and prone to look for difficulties where none existed. He was a heavily built, slow-moving man with none of Sobek's gaiety and confidence.

From her early childhood Renisenb could remember hearing these elder brothers of hers arguing in just those selfsame accents. It gave her suddenly a feeling of security. . . . She was at home again. Yes, she had come home. . . .

Yet as she looked once more across the pale, shining river, her rebellion and pain mounted again. Khay, her young husband, was dead. . . . Khay with his laughing face and his strong shoulders. Khay was with Osiris in the Kingdom of the Dead—and she, Renisenb, his dearly loved wife, was left desolate. Eight years they had had together—she had come to him as little more than a child—and now she had returned widowed, with Khay's child, Teti, to her father's house.

It seemed to her at this moment as though she had never been away. . . .

She welcomed that thought. . . .

She would forget those eight years—so full of unthinking happiness, so torn and destroyed by loss and pain.

Yes, forget them, put them out of her mind. Become once more Renisenb, Imhotep the ka-priest's daughter, the unthinking, unfeeling girl. This love of a husband and brother had been a cruel thing, deceiving her by its sweetness. She remembered the strong bronze shoulders, the laughing mouth—now Khay was embalmed, swathed in bandages, protected with amulets in his journey through the other world. No more Khay in this world to sail on the Nile and catch fish and laugh up into the sun whilst she, stretched out in the boat with little Teti on her lap, laughed back at him. . . .

Renisenb thought: "I will not think of it. It is over! Here I am at home. Everything is the same as it was. I, too, shall be the same presently. It will all be as before. Teti has forgotten already. She plays with the other children and laughs."

Renisenb turned abruptly and made her way back toward the house, passing on the way some loaded donkeys being driven toward the riverbank. She passed by the cornbins and the outhouses and through the gateway into the courtyard. It was very pleasant in the courtyard. There was the artificial lake, surrounded by flowering oleanders and jasmines and shaded by sycamore fig trees. Teti and the other children were playing there now, their voices rising shrill and clear. They were running in and out of the little pavilion that stood at one side of the lake. Renisenb noticed that Teti was playing with a wooden lion whose mouth opened and shut by pulling a string, a toy which she herself had loved as a child. She thought again, gratefully, "I have come home. . . ." Nothing was changed here; all was as it had been. Here life was safe, constant, unchanging. Teti was now the child and she one of the many mothers enclosed by the home walls—but the framework, the essence of things, was unchanged.

A ball with which one of the children was playing rolled to her feet and she picked it up and threw it back, laughing.

Renisenb went on to the porch with its gaily colored columns, and then through into the house, passing through the big central chamber, with its colored frieze of lotus and poppies, and so on to the back of the house and the women's quarters.

Upraised voices struck on her ear and she paused again, savoring with pleasure the old familiar echoes. Satipy and Kait—arguing as always! Those well-remembered tones of Satipy's voice, high, domineering and bullying! Satipy was her brother Yahmose's wife, a tall, energetic, loud-tongued woman, handsome in a hard, commanding kind of way. She was eternally laying down the law, hectoring the servants, finding fault with everything, getting impossible things done by sheer force of vituperation and personality. Everyone dreaded her tongue and ran to obey her orders. Yahmose himself had the greatest admiration for his resolute, spirited wife, though he allowed himself to be bullied by her in a way that had often infuriated Renisenb.

At intervals, in the pauses in Satipy's high-pitched sentences, the quiet, obstinate voice of Kait was heard. Kait was a broad, plain-faced woman, the wife of the handsome, gay Sobek. She was devoted to her children and seldom thought or spoke about anything else. She sustained her side of the daily arguments with her sister-in-law by the simple expedient of repeating whatever statement she had originally made with quiet, immovable obstinacy. She displayed neither heat nor passion, and never considered for a moment any side of a question but her own. Sobek was extremely attached to his wife and talked freely to her of all his affairs, secure in the knowledge that she would appear to listen, make comforting sounds of assent or dissent, and would remember nothing inconvenient, since her mind was sure to have been dwelling on some problem connected with the children all the time.

"It's an outrage, that's what I say," shouted Satipy. "If Yahmose had the spirit of a mouse he would not stand it for a moment! Who is in charge here when Imhotep is absent? Yahmose! And as Yahmose's wife it is *I* who should have the first choice of the woven mats and cushions. That hippopotamus of a black slave should be—"

Kait's heavy, deep voice cut in: "No, no, my little one, do not eat your doll's hair. See, here is something better—a sweet—oh, how *good*. . . ."

"As for you, Kait, you have no courtesy; you don't even listen to what I say—you do not reply—your manners are atrocious."

"The blue cushion has always been mine. . . . Oh, look at little Ankh—she is trying to walk. . . ."

"You are as stupid as your children, Kait, and that is saying a good deal! But you shall not get out of it like this. I will have my rights, I tell you."

Renisenb started as a quiet footfall sounded behind her. She turned with a start and with the familiar feeling of dislike at seeing the woman Henet standing behind her.

Henet's thin face was twisted into its usual half-cringing smile.

"Things haven't changed much, you'll be thinking, Renisenb," she said. "How we all bear Satipy's tongue I don't know! Of course, Kait can answer back. Some of us aren't so fortunate! I know *my* place, I hope—and my gratitude to your father for giving me a home and food and clothing. Ah, he's a good man, your father. And I've always tried to do what I can. I'm always working—giving a hand here and a hand there—and I don't expect thanks or gratitude. If your dear mother had lived it would have been different. *She* appreciated me. Like sisters we were! A beautiful woman she was. Well, I've done my duty and kept my promise to her. "Look after the children, Henet," she said when she was dying. And I've been faithful to my word. Slaved for you all, I have, and never wanted thanks. Neither asked for them nor got them! 'It's only old Henet,' people say; 'she doesn't count.' Nobody thinks anything of me. Why should they? I just try to be helpful, that's all."

She slipped like an eel under Renisenb's arm and entered the inner room.

"About those cushions, you'll excuse me, Satipy, but I happened to hear Sobek say—"

Renisenb moved away. Her old dislike of Henet surged up. Funny how they all disliked Henet! It was her whining voice, her continual self-pity and the malicious pleasure she took in fanning the flames of a discussion.

"Oh, well," thought Renisenb, "why not?" It was, she supposed, Henet's way of amusing herself. Life must be dreary for her—and it was true that she worked like a drudge and that no one was ever grateful. You couldn't be grateful to Henet—she drew attention to her own merits so persistently that it chilled any generous response you might have felt.

Henet, thought Renisenb, was one of those people whose fate it is to be devoted to others and to have no one devoted to them. She was unattractive to look at, and stupid as well. Yet she always knew what was going on. Her noiseless way of walking, her sharp ears and quick, peering eyes made it a certainty that nothing could long be a secret from her. Sometimes she hugged her knowledge to herself—at other times she would go round from one person to another whispering and standing back delightedly to observe the results of her tale-telling.

At one time or another everyone in the household had begged Imhotep to get rid of Henet, but Imhotep would never hear of such a thing. He was perhaps the only person who was fond of her; and she repaid his patronage with a fulsome devotion that the rest of the family found quite nauseating.

Renisenb stood uncertainly for a moment, listening to the accelerated clamor of her sisters-in-law, fanned by the flame of Henet's interference, then she went slowly toward the small room where her grandmother, Esa, sat by herself, attended by two little black girls. She was busy now inspecting certain linen garments that they were displaying to her and scolding them in a characteristic, friendly fashion.

Yes, it was all the same. Renisenb stood unnoticed, listening. Old Esa had shrunk a little, that was all. But her voice was the same and the things she was saying were the same, word for word, almost, as Renisenb could remember them before she herself had left home eight years ago. . . .

Renisenb slipped out again. Neither the old woman nor the two little slave girls had noticed her. For a moment or two Renisenb paused by the open kitchen door. A smell of roasting ducks, a lot of talking and laughing and scolding all going on at once; a mound of vegetables waiting to be prepared.

Renisenb stood quite still, her eyes half-closed. From where she stood she could hear everything going on at once. The rich, varied noises of the kitchen, the high, shrill note of Esa's voice, the strident tones of Satipy and, very faintly, the deeper, persistent contralto of Kait. A babel of women's voices—chattering, laughing, complaining, scolding, exclaiming. . . .

And suddenly Renisenb felt stifled, encircled by this persistent and clamorous femininity. Women—noisy, vociferous women! A household of women—never quiet, never peaceful—always talking, exclaiming, *saying* things—not *doing* them!

And Khay—Khay silent and watchful in his boat, his whole mind bent on the fish he was going to spear.

None of this clack of tongues, this busy, incessant *fussiness*.

Renisenb went swiftly out of the house again into hot, clear stillness. She saw Sobek coming back from the fields and saw in the distance Yahmose going up toward the Tomb.

She turned away and took the path up the limestone cliffs where the Tomb was. It was the Tomb of the great noble Meriptah, and her father was the mortuary priest responsible for its upkeep. All the estate and land was part of the endowment of the Tomb.

When her father was away the duties of the ka-priest fell upon her brother Yahmose. When Renisenb, walking slowly up the steep path, arrived, Yahmose was in consultation with Hori, her father's man of business and affairs, in a little rock chamber of the Tomb.

Hori had a sheet of papyrus spread out on his knees and Yahmose and he were bending over it.

Both Yahmose and Hori smiled at Renisenb when she arrived and she sat near them in a patch of shade. She had always been fond of her brother Yahmose. He was gentle and affectionate to her and had a mild and kindly disposition. Hori, too, had always been gravely kind to the small Renisenb and had sometimes mended her toys for her. He had been a grave, silent young man when she went away, with sensitive, clever fingers. Renisenb thought that though he looked older he had changed hardly at all. The grave smile he gave her was just the same as she remembered.

Yahmose and Hori were murmuring together: "Seventy-three bushels of barley with Ipi the younger . . ."

"The total then is two hundred and thirty of spelt and one hundred and twenty of barley."

"Yes, but there is the price of the timber, and the crop was paid for in oil at Perhaa. . . ."

Their talk went on. Renisenb sat drowsily content with the men's murmuring voices as a background. Presently Yahmose got up and went away, handing back the roll of papyrus to Hori.

Renisenb sat on in a companionable silence.

Presently she touched a roll of papyrus and asked: "Is that from my father?"

Hori nodded.

'What does it say?" she asked curiously.

She unrolled it and stared at those marks that were so meaningless to her untutored eyes.

Smiling a little, Hori leaned over her shoulder and traced with his little finger as he read. The letter was couched in the ornate style of the professional letter writer of Heracleopolis.

"The servant of the estate, the ka-servant Imhotep, says:

"'May your condition be like that of one who lives a million times. May the God Herishaf, Lord of Heracleopolis, and all the Gods that are aid you. May the God Ptah gladden your heart as one who lives long. The son speaks to his mother, the ka-servant to his mother, Esa. How are you in your life, safety and health? To the whole household, how are you? To my son Yahmose, how are you in your life, safety and health? Make the most of my land. Strive to the uttermost, dig the ground with your noses in the work. See, if you are industrious I will praise God for you—'"

Renisenb laughed.

"Poor Yahmose! He works hard enough, I am sure."

Her father's exhortation had brought him vividly before her eyes—his pompous, slightly fussy manner; his continual exhortations and instructions.

Hori went on:

"'Take great care of my son Ipy. I hear he is discontented. Also see that Satipy treats Henet well. Mind this. Do not fail to write about the flax and the oil. Guard the produce of my grain—guard everything of mine, for I shall hold you responsible. If my land floods, woe to you and Sobek.'"

"My father is just the same," said Renisenb happily. "Always thinking that nothing can be done right if he is not here."

She let the roll of papyrus slip and added softly: *"Everything is just the same. . . ."*

Hori did not answer. He took up a sheet of papyrus and began to write. Renisenb watched him lazily for some time. She felt too contented to speak.

By and by she said dreamily: "It would be interesting to know how to write on papyrus. Why doesn't everyone learn?"

"It isn't necessary."

"Not necessary, perhaps, but it would be pleasant."

"You think so, Renisenb? What difference would it make to *you?*"

Renisenb considered for a moment or two. Then she said slowly: "When you ask me that, truly I do not know, Hori."

Hori said, "At present a few scribes are all that are needed on a large estate, but the day will come, I fancy, when there will be armies of scribes all over

Egypt. We are living at the beginning of great times."

"That will be a good thing," said Renisenb.

Hori said slowly: "I am not so sure."

"Why are you not so sure?"

"Because, Renisenb, it is so easy and it costs so little labor to write down ten bushels of barley, or a hundred head of cattle, or ten fields of spelt—and the thing that is written well come to seem like the real thing, and so the writer and the scribe will come to despise the man who plows the fields and reaps the barley and raises the cattle—but all the same the fields and the barley and the cattle are *real*—they are not just marks of ink on papyrus. And when all the records and all the papyrus rolls are destroyed and the scribes are scattered, the men who toil and reap will go on, and Egypt will still live."

Renisenb looked at him attentively. She said slowly: "Yes, I see what you mean. Only the things that you can *see* and *touch* and *eat* are real. . . . To write down 'I have two hundred and forty bushels of barley' means nothing unless you have the barley. One could write down lies."

Hori smiled at her serious face. Renisenb said suddenly: "You mended my lion for me—long ago, do you remember?"

"Yes, I remember, Renisenb."

"Teti is playing with it now. . . . It is the same lion."

She paused and then said simply: "When Khay went to Osiris I was very sad. But now I have come home and I shall be happy again and forget—for everything here is the same. Nothing is changed at all."

"You really think that?"

Renisenb looked up at him sharply. "What do you mean, Hori?"

"I mean there is always a change. Eight years is eight years."

"Nothing changes here," said Renisenb with confidence.

"Perhaps, then, there *should* be change."

Renisenb said sharply: "No, no, I want everything the same!"

"But you yourself are not the same Renisenb who went away with Khay."

"Yes, I am! Or if not, then I soon shall be again."

Hori shook his head.

"You cannot go back, Renisenb. It is like my measures here. I take a half and add it to a quarter, and then a tenth and then a twenty-fourth—and at the end, you see, it is a different quantity altogether."

"But I am just Renisenb."

"But Renisenb has something added to her all the time, so she becomes all the time a different Renisenb."

"No, no. You are the same Hori."

"You may think so, but it is not so."

"Yes, yes, and Yahmose is the same, so worried and so anxious, and Satipy bullies him just the same, and she and Kait were having their usual quarrel about mats or beads, and presently when I go back they will be laughing together, the best of friends, and Henet still creeps about and listens and whines about her devotion, and my grandmother was fussing with her little maid over some linen! It was all the same and presently my father will come home and there will be a great fuss and he will say, 'Why have you not done this?' and 'You should have done that,' and Yahmose will look worried and Sobek will laugh and be innocent about it, and my father will spoil Ipy, who is sixteen, just as he used to spoil him when he was eight, and nothing will be different at all!" She paused, breathless.

Hori sighed. Then he said gently: "You do not understand, Renisenb. There is an evil that comes from outside, that attacks so that all the world can see, but there is another kind of rottenness that breeds from within—that shows no outward sign. It grows slowly, day by day, till at last the whole fruit is rotten—eaten by disease."

Renisenb stared at him. He had spoken almost absently, not as though he were speaking to her, but more like a man who muses to himself.

She cried out sharply: "What do you mean, Hori? You make me afraid."

"I am afraid myself."

"But what do you *mean?* What is this evil you talk about?"

He looked at her then and suddenly smiled.

"Forget what I said, Renisenb. I was thinking of the diseases that attack the crops."

Renisenb sighed in relief.

"I'm glad. I thought—I don't know what I thought."

2

Third Month of Inundation, 4th Day

SATIPY WAS TALKING to Yahmose. Her voice had a high, strident note that seldom varied its tone.

"You must assert yourself. That is what I say? You will never be valued unless you assert yourself. Your father says this must be done and that must be done and why have you not done this? And you listen meekly and reply 'Yes, yes,' and excuse yourself for things that he says should have been done—and which, the Gods know, have often been quite impossible! Your father treats you as a child—as a young, irresponsible boy! You might be the age of Ipy."

Yahmose said quietly: "My father does not treat me in the least as he treats Ipy."

"No, indeed.' Satipy fell upon the new subject with renewed venom. "He is foolish about that spoiled brat! Day by day Ipy gets more impossible. He swaggers around and does no work that he can help and pretends that anything that is asked of him is too hard for him! It is a disgrace. And all because he knows that father will always indulge him and take his part. You and Sobek should take a strong line about it."

Yahmose shrugged his shoulders.

"What is the good?"

"You drive me mad, Yahmose—that is so like you! You have no *spirit.* You're as meek as a woman! Everything that your father says you agree with at once!"

"I have a great affection for my father."

"Yes, and he trades on that! You go on meekly accepting blame and excusing yourself for things that are no fault of yours! You should speak up and answer him back as Sobek does. Sobek is afraid of nobody!"

"Yes, but remember, Satipy, that it is *I* who am trusted by my father, not Sobeck. My father reposes no confidence in Sobeck. Everything is always left to my judgment, not his."

"And that is why you should be definitely associated as a partner in the estate! You represent your father when he is away, you act as ka-priest in his absence; everything is left in your hands—and yet you have no recognized authority. There should be a proper settlement. You are now a man of nearly middle age. It is not right that you should be treated still as a child."

Yahmose said doubtfully: "My father likes to keep things in his own hands."

"Exactly. It pleases him that everyone in the household should be dependent upon him—and upon his whim of the moment. It is bad, that, and it will get worse. This time when he comes home you must tackle him boldly—you must say that you demand a settlement in writing, that you insist on having a regularized position."

"He would not listen."

"Then you must *make* him listen. Oh, that I were a man! If I were in your place I would know what to do! Sometimes I feel that I am married to a worm."

Yahmose flushed.

"I will see what I can do—I might, yes, I might perhaps speak to my father—ask him—"

"Not *ask*—you must *demand!* After all, you have the whip hand of him. There is no one but you whom he can leave in charge here. Sobek is too wild, your father does not trust him; and Ipy is too young."

"There is always Hori."

"Hori is not a member of the family. Your father relies on his judgment but he would not leave authority except in the hands of his own kin. But I see how it is; you are too meek and mild—there is milk in your veins, not blood! You don't consider me or our children. Not till your father is dead shall we ever have our proper position."

Yahmose said heavily: "You despise me, don't you, Satipy?"

"You make me angry."

"Listen, I tell you that I will speak to my father when he comes. There, it is a promise."

Satipy murmured under her breath: "Yes—but *how* will you speak? Like a man—or like a mouse?"

II

Kait was playing with her youngest child, little Ankh. The baby was just beginning to walk and Kait encouraged her with laughing words, kneeling in front of her and waiting with outstretched arms until the child lurched precariously forward and toddled on uncertain feet into her mother's arms.

Kait had been displaying these accomplishments to Sobeck, but realized suddenly that he was not attending, but was sitting with his handsome forehead furrowed into a frown.

"Oh, Sobeck—you were not looking. You do not see. Little one, tell your father he is naughty not to watch you."

Sobeck said irritably: "I have other things to think of—yes, and worry about."

Kait leaned back on her heels, smoothing her hair back from her heavy dark brows where Ankh's fingers had clutched it.

"Why? Is there something wrong?"

Kait spoke without quite giving all her attention. The question was more than half mechanical.

Sobeck said angrily: "The trouble is that I am not trusted. My father is an old man, absurdly old-fashioned in his ideas, and he insists on dictating every single action here—he will not leave things to my judgment."

Kait shook her head and murmured vaguely: "Yes, yes, it is too bad."

"If only Yahmose had a little more spirit and would back me up there might be some hope of making my father see reason. But Yahmose is so timid. He carries out every single instruction my father gives him to the letter."

Kait jingled some beads at the child and murmured: "Yes, that is true."

"In this matter of the timber I shall tell my father when he comes that I used my judgment. It was far better to take the price in flax and not in oil."

"I am sure you are right."

"But my father is as obstinate over having his own way as anyone can be. He will make an outcry, will shout out, 'I told you to transact the business in oil. Everything is done wrong when I am not here. You are a foolish boy who knows nothing!' How old does he think I am? He doesn't realize that I am now a man in my prime and he is past his. His instructions and his refusals to sanction any unusual transactions mean that we do not do nearly as good business as we might do. To attain riches it is necessary to take a few risks. I have vision and courage. My father has neither."

Her eyes on the child, Kait murmured softly: "You are so bold and so clever, Sobek."

"But he shall hear some home truths this time if he dares to find fault and shout abuse at me! Unless I am given a free hand, I shall leave. I shall go away."

Kait, her hand stretched out to the child, turned her head sharply, the gesture arrested.

"Go away? Where would you go?"

"Somewhere! It is insupportable to be bullied and nagged at by a fussy, self-important old man who gives me no scope at all to show what I can do."

"No," said Kait sharply. "I say no, Sobek."

He stared at her, recalled by her tone into noticing her presence. He was so used to her as a merely soothing accompaniment to his talk that he often forgot her existence as a living, thinking, human woman.

"What do you mean, Kait?"

"I mean that I will not let you be foolish. All the estate belongs to your father—the lands, the cultivation, the cattle, the timber, the fields of flax—all! When your father dies it will be ours—yours and Yahmose's and our children's.

If you quarrel with your father and go off, then he may divide your share between Yahmose and Ipy—already he loves Ipy too much. Ipy knows that and trades on it. You must not play into the hands of Ipy. It would suit him only too well if you were to quarrel with Imhotep and go away. We have our children to think of."

Sobek stared at her. Then he gave a short surprised laugh.

"A woman is always unexpected. I did not know you had it in you, Kait, to be so fierce."

Kait said earnestly: "Do not quarrel with your father. Do not answer him back. Be wise for a little longer."

"Perhaps you are right—but this may go on for years. What my father should do is associated us with him in a partnership."

Kait shook her head.

"He will not do that. He likes too much to say that we are all eating his bread, that we are all dependent on him, that without him we should all be nowhere."

Sobek looked at her curiously.

"You do not like my father very much, Kait."

But Kait had bent once more to the toddling baby.

"Come, sweetheart—see, here is your doll. Come, then—come . . ."

Sobek looked down at her black bent head. Then, with a puzzled look, he went out.

III

Esa had sent for her grandson, Ipy.

The boy, a handsome, discontented-looking stripling, was standing before her whilst she rated him in a high shrill voice, peering at him out of her dim eyes that were shrewd although they could now see little.

"What is this I hear? You will not do this, and you will not do that? You want to look after the bulls, and you do not like going with Yahmose or seeing to the cultivating? What are things coming to when a child like you says what he will or will not do?"

Ipy said sullenly: "I am not a child. I am grown now—and why should I be treated like as a child? Put to this work or that with no say of my own and no separate allowance! Given orders all the time by Yahmose! Who does Yahmose think he is?"

"He is your older brother and he is in charge here when my son Imhotep is away."

"Yahmose is stupid—slow and stupid. I am much cleverer than he is. And Sobek is stupid too for all that he boasts and talks about how clever he is! Already my father has written and has said that I am to do the work that I myself choose—"

"Which is none at all," interpolated old Esa.

"And that I am to be given more food and drink and that if he hears I am discontented and have not been well treated he will be very angry."

He smiled as he spoke, a sly, upcurving smile.

"You are a spoiled brat," said Esa with energy. "And I shall tell Imhotep so."

"No, no, Grandmother, you would not do that."

His smile changed; it became caressing, if slightly impudent.

"You and I, Grandmother, we have the brains of the family."

"The impudence of you!"

"My father relies on your judgment—he knows you are wise."

"That may be—indeed it is so—but I do not need you to tell me so."

Ipy laughed.

"You had better be on my side, Grandmother."

"What is this talk of *sides?*"

"The big brothers are very discontented. Don't you know that? Of course you do. Henet tells you everything. Satipy harangues Yahmose all day and all night whenever she can get hold of him. And Sobek has made a fool of himself over the sale of the timber and is afraid my father will be furious when he finds out. You will see, Grandmother, in another year or two I shall be associated with my father and he will do everything that I wish."

"You, the youngest of the family?"

"What does age matter? My father is the one who has the power—and I am the one who knows how to manage my father!"

"This is evil talk," said Esa.

Ipy said softly: "You are not a fool, Grandmother, you know quite well that my father, in spite of all his big talk, is really a weak man—"

He stopped abruptly, noting that Esa had shifted her head and was peering over her shoulder. He turned his own head to find Henet standing close behind him.

"So Imhotep is a weak man?" said Henet in her soft whining voice. "He will not be pleased, I think, to hear that you have said that of him."

Ipy gave a quick uneasy laugh.

"But you will not tell him, Henet. . . . Come now, Henet—promise me. . . . Dear Henet . . ."

Henet glided toward Esa. She raised her voice with its slightly whining note.

"Of course, I never want to make trouble—you know that. . . . I am devoted to all of you. I never repeat anything unless I think it is my *duty*. . . ."

"I was teasing Grandmother, that was all," said Ipy. "I shall tell my father so. He will know I could not have said such a thing seriously."

He gave Henet a short, sharp nod and went out of the room.

Henet looked after him and said to Esa: "A fine boy—a fine, well-grown boy. And how bravely he speaks!"

Esa said sharply: "He speaks dangerously. I do not like the ideas he has in his head. My son indulges him too much."

"Who would not? He is such a handsome, attractive boy."

"Handsome is as handsome does," said Esa sharply.

She was silent a moment or two, then she said slowly: "Henet—I am worried."

"Worried, Esa? What should worry you? Anyway, the master will soon be here and then all will be well."

"Will it? I wonder."

She was silent once more, then she said: "Is my grandson Yahmose in the house?"

"I saw him coming toward the porch a few moments ago."

"Go and tell him I wish to speak with him."

Henet departed. She found Yahmose on the cool porch with its gaily colored columns and gave him Esa's message. Yahmose obeyed the summons at once.

Esa said abruptly: "Yahmose, very soon Imhotep will be here."

Yahmose's gentle face lighted up.

"Yes, that will indeed be good."

"All is in order for him? Affairs have prospered?"

"My father's instructions have been carried out as well as I could compass them."

"What of Ipy?"

Yahmose sighed.

"My father is overindulgent where that boy is concerned. It is not good for the lad."

"You must make that clear to Imhotep."

Yahmose looked doubtful.

Esa said firmly: "I will back you up."

"Sometimes," said Yahmose, sighing, "there seem to be nothing but difficulties. But everything will be right when my father comes. He can make his own decisions then. It is hard to act as he would wish in his absence—especially when I have no real authority and only act as his delegate."

Esa said slowly: "You are a good son—loyal and affectionate. You have been a good husband too; you have obeyed the proverb that says that a man should love his wife and make a home for her, that he should fill her belly and put clothes on her back, and provide expensive ointments for her toilet and that he should gladden her heart as long as she lives. But there is a further precept—it goes like this: *Prevent her from getting the mastery*. If I were you, Grandson, I should take that precept to heart. . . ."

Yahmose looked at her, flushed deeply, and turned away.

3

Third Month of Inundation, 14th Day

EVERYWHERE THERE WERE bustle and preparation. Hundreds of loaves had been baked in the kitchen, now ducks were roasting; there was a smell of leeks and garlic and various spices. Women were shouting and giving orders, servingmen ran to and fro.

Everywhere ran the murmur: "The master—the master is coming. . . ."

Renisenb, helping to weave garlands of poppies and lotus flowers, felt an excited happiness bubbling up in her heart. Her father was coming home! In the last few weeks she had slipped imperceptibly back into the confines of her old life. That first sense of unfamiliarity and strangeness, induced in her, she believed, by Hori's words, had gone. She was the same Renisenb—Yahmose, Satipy, Sobek and Kait were all the same—now, as in the past, there was all the bustle and fuss of preparations for Imhotep's return. Word had come ahead that he would be with them before nightfall. One of the servants had been posted on the riverbank to give warning of the master's approach, and suddenly his voice rang out loud and clear, giving the agreed call.

Renisenb dropped her flowers and ran out with the others. They all hastened toward the mooring place on the riverbank. Yahmose and Sobek were already there in a little crowd of villagers, fishermen and farm laborers, all calling out excitedly and pointing.

Yes, there was the barge with its great square sail coming fast up the river with the north wind bellying out the sails. Close behind it was the kitchen barge crowded with men and women. Presently Renisenb could make out her father sitting holding a lotus flower and with him someone whom she took to be a singer.

The cries on the bank redoubled, Imhotep waved a welcoming hand, the sailors were heaving and pulling on the halyards. There were cries of "Welcome to the master," calls upon the Gods, and thanks for his safe return, and a few moments later Imhotep came ashore, greeting his family and answering the loud salutations that etiquette demanded.

"Praise be to Sobek, the child of Neith, who has brought you safely on the water!" "Praise be to Ptah, south of the Memphite wall, who brings you to us!" "Thanks be to Re who illumines the Two Lands!"

Renisenb pressed forward, intoxicated with the general excitement.

Imhotep drew himself up importantly and suddenly Renisenb thought: "But he is a *small* man. I thought of him as much bigger than that."

A feeling that was almost dismay passed over her.

Had her father *shrunk?* Or was her own memory at fault? She had thought of him as rather a splendid being, tyrannical, often fussy, exhorting everybody right and left, and sometimes provoking her to quiet inward laughter, but nevertheless a *personage*. But this small, stout, elderly man, looking so full of his own importance and yet somehow failing to impress—What was wrong with her? What were these disloyal thoughts that came into her head?

Imhotep, having finished the sonorous and ceremonial phrases, had arrived at the stage of more personal greetings. He embraced his sons.

"Ah, my good Yahmose, all smiles, you have been diligent in my absence, I am sure. . . . And Sobek, my handsome son, still given to merriness of heart, I see. And here is Ipy—my dearest Ipy—let me look at you—stand away—so. Grown bigger, more of a man! How it rejoices my heart to hold you again! And Renisenb—my dear daughter—once more in the home. Satipy, Kait, my no less dear daughters. . . . And Henet—my faithful Henet—"

Henet was kneeling, embracing his knees, and ostentatiously wiping tears of joy from her eyes.

"It is good to see you, Henet—you are well—happy? As devoted as ever—that is pleasant to the heart. . . ."

"And my excellent Hori, so clever with his accounts and his pen! All has prospered? I am sure it has."

Then, the greetings finished and the surrounding murmur dying down,

Imhotep raised his hand for silence and spoke out loud and clear: "My son and daughters—friends. I have a piece of news for you. For many years, as you all know, I have been a lonely man in one respect. My wife—your mother, Yahmose and Sobek—and my sister—your mother, Ipy—have both gone to Osiris many years ago. So to you, Satipy and Kait, I bring a new sister to share your home. Behold, this is my concubine, Nofret, whom you shall love for my sake. She has come with me from Memphis in the north and will dwell here with you when I go away again."

As he spoke he drew forward a woman by the hand. She stood there beside him, her head flung back, her eyes narrowed, young, arrogant and beautiful.

Renisenb thought with a shock of surprise: "But she's quite young—perhaps not as old as I am."

Nofret stood quite still. There was a faint smile on her lips—it had more derision in it than any anxiety to please.

She had very straight black brows and a rich bronze skin, and her eyelashes were so long and thick that one could hardly see her eyes.

The family, taken aback, stared in dumb silence. With a faint edge of irritation in his voice, Imhotep said: "Come now, children, welcome Nofret. Don't you know how to greet your father's concubine when he brings her to his house?"

Haltingly and stumblingly the greetings were given.

Imhotep, affecting a heartiness that perhaps concealed some uneasiness, exclaimed cheerfully: "That is better! Nofret, Satipy and Kait and Renisenb will take you to the women's quarters. Where are the trunks? Have the trunks been brought ashore?"

The round-topped traveling trunks were being carried from the barge. Imhotep said to Nofret: "Your jewels and your clothes are here safely. Go and see to their bestowing."

Then, as the women moved away together, he turned to his sons.

"And what of the estate? Does all go well?"

"The lower fields that were rented to Nehkte—" began Yahmose, but his father cut him short.

"No details now, good Yahmose. They can wait. Tonight is rejoicing. Tomorrow you and I and Hori here will get to business. Come here, Ipy, my boy, let us walk to the house. How tall you have grown—your head is above mine."

Scowling, Sobek walked behind his father and Ipy. Into Yahmose's ear he murmured: "Jewels and clothes—did you hear? That is where the profits of the northern estate have gone. *Our* profits."

"Hush," whispered Yahmose. "Our father will hear."

Once in the house, Henet came to Imhotep's room to prepare the bath. She was all smiles.

Imhotep abandoned a little of his defensive heartiness. "Well, Henet, and what do you think of my choice?"

Although he had determined to carry things off with a high hand, he had known quite well that the arrival of Nofret would provoke a storm—at least in the women's part of the house. Henet was different—a singularly devoted creature. She did not disappoint him.

"She is beautiful! Quite beautiful! What hair, what limbs! She is worthy of you, Imhotep. What can I say more than that? Your dear wife who is dead will be glad that you have chosen such a companion to gladden your days."

"You think so, Henet?"

"I am sure of it, Imhotep. After mourning her so many years it is time that you once more enjoyed life."

"You knew her well. . . . I, too, felt it was time to live as a man should live. Er—ahem—my sons' wives and my daughter—they will take this with resentment perhaps?"

"They had better not," said Henet. "After all, do they not all depend upon you in this house?"

"Very true, very true," said Imhotep.

"Your bounty feeds and clothes them—their welfare is entirely the result of your efforts."

"Yes, indeed." Imhotep sighed. "I am continually active on their behalf. I sometimes doubt if they realize all they owe me."

"You must remind them of it." said Henet, nodding her head. "I, your humble devoted Henet, never forget what I owe you—but children are sometimes thoughtless and selfish, thinking, perhaps, that it is *they* who are important and not realizing that they only carry out the instructions that *you* give."

"That is indeed most true," said Imhotep. "I have always said you were an intelligent creature, Henet."

Henet sighed.

"If others only thought so."

"What is this? Has anyone been unkind to you?"

"No, no—that is, they do not mean it—it is a matter of course to them that I should work unceasingly—which I am glad to do—but a word of affection and appreciation, that is what makes all the difference."

"That you will always have from me," said Imhotep. "And this is always your home, remember."

"You are too kind, master." She paused and added: "The slaves are ready in the bathroom with the hot water—and when you have bathed and dressed your mother asks that you should go to her."

"Ah, my mother? Yes—yes, of course. . . ."

Imhotep looked suddenly slightly embarrassed. He covered his confusion by saying quickly: "Naturally—I had intended that—tell Esa I shall come."

II

Esa, dressed in her best pleated linen gown, peered across at her son with a kind of sardonic amusement.

"Welcome, Imhotep. So you have returned to us—and not alone, I hear."

Imhotep, drawing himself up, replied rather shamefacedly: "Oh, so you have heard?"

"Naturally. The house is humming with the news. The girl is beautiful, they say, and quite young."

"She is nineteen and—er—not ill-looking."

Esa laughed—an old woman's spiteful cackle.

"Ah, well," she said, "there's no fool like an old fool."

"My dear mother, I am really at a loss to understand what you mean."

Esa replied composedly: "You always were a fool, Imhotep."

Imhotep drew himself up and spluttered angrily. Though he was usually comfortably conscious of his own importance, his mother could always pierce the armor of his self-esteem. In her presence he felt himself dwindling. The faint sarcastic gleam of her nearly sightless eyes never failed to disconcert him. His mother, there was no denying, had never had an exaggerated opinion of his capabilities. And although he knew well that his own estimate of himself was the true one and his mother's a maternal idiosyncrasy of no importance—yet her attitude never failed to puncture his happy conceit of himself.

"Is it so unusual for a man to bring home a concubine?"

"Not at all unusual. Men are usually fools."

"I fail to see where the folly comes in."

"Do you imagine that the presence of this girl is going to make for harmony in the household? Satipy and Kait will be beside themselves and will inflame their husbands."

"What has it to do with them? What right have they to object?"

"None."

Imhotep began to walk up and down angrily.

"Can I not do as I please in my own house? Do I not support my sons and their wives? Do they not owe the very bread they eat to me? Do I not tell them so without ceasing?"

"You are too fond of saying so, Imhotep."

"It is the truth. They all depend on me. All of them!"

"And are you sure that that is a good thing?"

"Are you saying that it is not a good thing for a man to support his family?"

Esa sighed.

"They work for you, remember."

"Do you want me to encourage them in idleness? Naturally they work."

"They are grown men—at least Yahmose and Sobek are—more than grown."

"Sobek has no judgment. He does everything wrong. Also he is frequently impertinent, which I will not tolerate. Yahmose is a good obedient boy—"

"A good deal more than a boy!"

"But sometimes I have to tell him things two or three times before he takes them in. I have to think of everything—be everywhere! All the time I am away, I am dictating to scribes—writing full instructions so that my sons can carry them out. . . . I hardly rest—I hardly sleep! And now when I come home, having earned a little peace, there is to be fresh difficulty! Even you, my mother, deny my right to have a concubine like other men. You are angry—"

Esa interrupted him.

"I am not angry. I am amused. There will be good sport to watch in the household—but I say all the same that when you go north again you had best take the girl with you."

"Her place is here, in my household! And woe to any who dares ill-treat her."

"It is not a question of ill-treatment. But remember, it is easy to kindle a fire in dry stubble. It has been said of women that 'the place where they are is not good. . . .'"

Esa paused and said slowly: "Nofret is beautiful. But remember this: *Men are made fools by the gleaming limbs of women, and lo, in a minute they are become discolored carnelians. . . .*"

Her voice deepened as she quoted:

"A trifle, a little, the likeness of a dream, and death comes as the end. . . ."

4

Third Month of Inundation, 15th Day

IMHOTEP LISTENED TO Sobek's explanations of the sale of the timber in ominous silence. His face had grown very red and a small pulse was beating in his temple.

Sobek's air of easy nonchalance wore a little thin. He had intended to carry things off with a high hand, but in the face of his father's gathering frowns, he found himself stammering and hesitating.

Imhotep finally cut him short impatiently: "Yes, yes, yes—you thought that you knew more than I did—you departed from my instructions—it is always the same—unless I am here to see to everything." He sighed. "What would become of you boys without me, I cannot imagine!"

Sobek went on doggedly: "There was a chance of making a much bigger profit—I took the risk. One cannot always be pettifogging and cautious!"

"There is nothing cautious about you, Sobek! You are rash and much too bold and your judgment is always wrong."

"Do I ever have a chance to exercise my judgment?"

Imhotep said dryly: "You have done so this time—against my express orders—"

"Orders? Have I always got to take orders? I am a grown man."

Losing control of his temper, Imhotep shouted: "Who feeds you; who clothes you? Who thinks of the future? Who has your welfare—the welfare of all of you—constantly in mind? When the River was low and we were threatened with famine, did I not arrange for food to be sent south to you? You are lucky to have such a father—who thinks of everything! And what do I ask in return? Only that you should work hard, do your best, and obey the instructions I send you—"

"Yes," shouted Sobek. "We are to work for you like slaves—so that you can buy gold and jewels for your concubine!"

Imhotep advanced toward him, bristling with rage.

"Insolent boy—to speak like that to your father. Be careful or I will say that this is no longer your home—and you can go elsewhere!"

"And if *you* are not careful I *will* go! I have ideas, I tell you—good ideas—that would bring in wealth if I was not tied down by pettifogging caution and never allowed to act as I choose."

"Have you finished?"

Imhotep's tone was ominous. Sobek, a trifle deflated, muttered angrily: "Yes—yes—I have no more to say—*now.*"

"Then go and see after the cattle. This is no time for idling."

Sobek turned and strode angrily away. Nofret was standing not far away and as he passed her she looked sideways at him and laughed. At her laugh the blood came up in Sobek's face—he made an angry half-step toward her. She stood quite still, looking at him out of contemptuous half-closed eyes.

Sobek muttered something and resumed his former direction. Nofret laughed again, then walked slowly on to where Imhotep was now turning his attention to Yahmose.

"What possessed you to let Sobek act in that foolish fashion?" he demanded irritably. "You should have prevented it! Don't you know by now that he has no judgment in buying and selling? He thinks everything will turn out as he wants it to turn out."

Yahmose said apologetically: "You do not realize my difficulties, Father. You told me to entrust Sobek with the sale of the timber. It was necessary therefore that it should be left to him to use his judgment."

"Judgment? Judgment? He has no judgment! He is to do what I instruct him to do—and it is for *you* to see that he does exactly that."

Yahmose flushed.

"I? What authority have *I?*"

"What authority? The authority I give you."

"But I have no real status. If I were legally associated with you—"

He broke off as Nofret came in. She was yawning and twisting a scarlet poppy in her hands.

"Won't you come to the little pavilion by the lake, Imhotep? It is cool there and there is fruit waiting for you and Keda beer. Surely you have finished giving your orders by now."

"In a minute, Nofret—in a minute."

Nofret said in a soft, deep voice: "Come *now*. I want you to come now. . . ."

Imhotep looked pleased and a little sheepish. Yahmose said quickly before his father could speak: "Let us just speak of this first. It is important. I want to ask you—"

Nofret spoke directly to Imhotep, turning her shoulder on Yahmose: "Can you not do what you want in your own house?"

Imhotep said sharply to Yahmose: "Another time, my son. Another time."

He went with Nofret and Yahmose stood on the porch looking after them.

Satipy came out from the house and joined him.

"Well," she demanded eagerly, "have you spoken to him? What did he say?"

Yahmose sighed.

"Do not be so impatient, Satipy. The time was not—propitious."

Satipy gave an angry exclamation.

"Oh, yes—that's what you *would* say! That is what you will always say. The truth is you are *afraid* of your father—you are as timid as a sheep—you bleat at him—you will not stand up to him like a man! Do you not recall the things you promised me? I tell you I am the better man of us two? You promise—you say: 'I will ask my father—at once—the very first day.' And what happens—"

Satipy paused—for breath, not because she had finished—but Yahmose cut in mildly: "You are wrong, Satipy. I began to speak—but we were interrupted."

"Interrupted? By whom?"

"By Nofret."

"Nofret! That woman! Your father should not let his concubine interrupt when he is speaking of business to his eldest son. Women should not concern themselves with business."

Possibly Yahmose wished that Satipy herself would live up to the maxim she was enunciating so glibly, but he was given no opportunity to speak. His wife swept on: "Your father should have made that clear to her at once."

"My father," said Yahmose dryly, "showed no signs of displeasure."

"It is disgraceful," Satipy declared. "Your father is completely bewitched by her. He lets her say and do as she pleases."

Yahmose said thoughtfully: "She is very beautiful. . . ."

Satipy snorted.

"Oh, she has looks of a kind. But no manners! No upbringing! She does not care how rude she is to all of us."

"Perhaps *you* are rude to her?"

"I am the soul of politeness. Kait and I treat her with every courtesy. Oh, she shall have nothing of which to go complaining to your father. We can wait our time, Kait and I."

Yahmose looked up sharply.

"How do you mean—*wait your time?*"

Satipy laughed meaningly as she moved away.

"My meaning is woman's meaning—you would not understand. We have our ways—and our weapons! Nofret would do well to moderate her insolence. What does a woman's life come to in the end, after all? It is spent in the back of the house—amongst the other women."

There was a peculiar significance to Satipy's tone. She added: "Your father will not always be here. . . . He will go away again to his estates in the north. And then—we shall see."

"Satipy—"

Satipy laughed—a hard-sounding, high laugh—and went back into the house.

II

By the lake the children were running about and playing. Yahmose's two boys were fine, handsome little fellows, looking more like Satipy than like their father. Then there were Sobek's three—the youngest a mere toddling baby. And there was Teti, a grave, handsome child of four years.

They laughed and shouted, threw balls—occasionally a dispute broke out and a childish wail of anger rose high and shrill.

Sitting sipping his beer, with Nofret beside him, Imhotep murmured: "How fond children are of playing by water. It was always so, I remember. But, by Hathor, what a noise they make."

Nofret said quickly: "Yes—and it could be so peaceful. . . . Why do you not tell them to go away whilst you are here? After all, when the master of the house wants relaxation a proper respect should be shown. Don't you agree?"

"I—well—" Imhotep hesitated. The idea was new to him but pleasing. "I do not really mind them," he finished doubtfully.

He added rather weakly: "They are accustomed to play here always as they please."

"When you are away, yes," said Nofret quickly. "But I think, Imhotep, considering all that you do for your family, they should show more sense of your dignity—of your importance. You are too gentle—too easygoing."

Imhotep sighed placidly.

"It has always been my failing. I never insist on the outward forms."

"And therefore these women, your sons' wives, take advantage of your kindness. It should be understood that when you come here for repose, there must be silence and tranquillility. See, I will go and tell Kait to take her children away and the others too. Then you shall have peace and contentment here."

"You are a thoughtful girl, Nofret—yes, a good girl. You are always thinking of my comfort."

Nofret murmured: "Your pleasure is mine."

She got up and went to where Kait was kneeling by the water playing with a little model barge which her second child, a rather spoilt-looking boy, was trying to float.

Nofret said curtly: "Will you take the children away, Kait?"

Kait stared up at her uncomprehendingly.

"Away? What do you mean? This is where they always play."

"Not today. Imhotep wants peace. These children of yours are noisy."

Color flamed Kait's heavy face.

"You should mend your ways of speech, Nofret! Imhotep likes to see his sons' children playing here. He has said so."

"Not today," said Nofret. "He has sent me to tell you to take the whole noisy brood into the house so that he can sit in peace—with me."

"With *you* . . ." Kait stopped abruptly in what she has been about to say. Then she got up and walked to where Imhotep was half-sitting, half-lying. Nofret followed her.

Kait spoke without circumlocution.

"Your concubine says I am to take the children away from here? Why? What are they doing that is wrong? For what reason should they be banished?"

"I should have thought the wish of the master of the house was enough," said Nofret softly.

"Exactly—exactly," said Imhotep pettishly. "Why should I have to give *reasons?* Whose house is this?"

"I suppose it is *she* who wants them away." Kait turned and looked Nofret up and down.

"Nofret thinks of my comfort—of my enjoyment," said Imhotep. "No one else in this house ever considers it—except perhaps poor Henet."

"So the children are not to play here any more?"

"Not when I have come here to rest."

Kait's anger flamed forth suddenly: "Why do you let this woman turn you against your own blood? Why should she come and interfere with the ways of the house—with what has always been done?"

Imhotep began to shout. He felt a need to vindicate himself.

"It is *I* who say what is to be done here—not you! You are all in league to do as you choose—to arrange everything to suit yourselves. And when I, the master of the house, come home, no proper attention is paid to my wishes. But I *am* master here, let me tell you! I am constantly planning and working for your welfare—but am I given gratitude, are my wishes respected? No. First, Sobek is insolent and disrespectful, and now you, Kait, try to browbeat me! What am I supporting you all for? Take care—or I shall cease to support you. Sobek talks of going—then let him go and take you and your children with him."

For a moment Kait stood perfectly still. There was no expression at all on her heavy, rather vacant face.

Then she said in a voice from which all emotion had been eliminated: "I will take the children into the house. . . ."

She moved a step or two, pausing by Nofret.

In a low voice Kait said: "This is *your* doing, Nofret. I shall not forget. No, I shall not forget. . . ."

5

Fourth Month of Inundation, 5th Day

IMHOTEP BREATHED A sigh of satisfaction as he finished his ceremonial duties as mortuary priest. The ritual had been observed with meticulous detail—for Imhotep was in every respect a most conscientious man. He had poured the libations, burned incense, and offered the customary offerings of food and drink.

Now, in the cool shade of the adjacent rock chamber where Hori was waiting for him, Imhotep became once more the landowner and the man of affairs. Together the two men discussed business matters, prevailing prices, and the profits resulting from crops, cattle, and timber.

After half an hour or so, Imhotep nodded his head with satisfaction.

"You have an excellent head for business, Hori," he said.

The other smiled.

"I should have, Imhotep. I have been your man of affairs for many years now."

"And a most faithful one. Now, I have a matter to discuss with you. It concerns Ipy. He complains that his position is subordinate."

"He is still very young."

"But he shows great ability. He feels that his brothers are not always fair to him. Sobek, it seems, is rough and overbearing—and Yahmose's continual caution and timidity irk him. Ipy is high-spirited. He does not like taking orders. Moreover he says that it is only I, his father, who have the right to command."

"That is true," said Hori. "And it has struck me, Imhotep, that that is a weakness here on the estate. May I speak freely?"

"Certainly, my good Hori. Your words are always thoughtful and well-considered."

"Then I say this. When you are away, Imhotep, there should be someone here who has real authority."

"I trust my affairs to you and to Yahmose—"

"I know that we act for you in your absence—but that is not enough. Why not appoint one of your sons as a partner—associate him with you by a legal deed of settlement."

Imhotep paced up and down, frowning.

"Which of my sons do you suggest? Sobek has an authoritative manner—but he is insubordinate—I could not trust him. His disposition is not good."

"I was thinking of Yahmose. He is your eldest son. He has a gentle and affectionate disposition. He is devoted to you."

"Yes, he has a good disposition—but he is too timid—too yielding. He gives in to everybody. Now if Ipy were only a little older—"

Hori said quickly: "It is dangerous to give power to too young a man."

"True—true—well, Hori, I will think of what you have said. Yahmose is certainly a good son . . . an obedient son. . . ."

Hori said gently but urgently: "You would, I think, be wise."

Imhotep looked at him curiously.

"What is in your mind, Hori?"

Hori said slowly: "I said just now that it is dangerous to give a man power when he is too young. But it is also dangerous to give it to him too late."

"You mean that he has become too used to obeying orders and not to giving them? Well, perhaps there is something in that."

Imhotep sighed.

"It is a difficult task to rule a family! The women in particular are hard to manage. Satipy has an ungovernable temper; Kait is often sulky. But I have made it clear to them that Nofret is to be treated in a proper fashion. I think I may say that—"

He broke off. A slave was coming panting up the narrow pathway.

"What is this?"

"Master—a barge is here. A scribe called Kameni has come with a message from Memphis."

Imhotep got up fussily.

"More trouble," he exclaimed. "As sure as Re sails the Heavens this will be more trouble! Unless I am on hand to attend to things everything goes wrong."

He went stamping down the path and Hori sat quite still looking after him. There was a troubled expression on his face.

II

Renisenb had been wandering aimlessly along the bank of the Nile when she heard shouts and commotion and saw people running toward the landing stage.

She ran and joined them. In the boat that was pulling to shore stood a young man and just for a moment, as she saw him outlined against the bright light, her heart missed a beat.

A mad, fantastic thought leapt into her mind.

"It is Khay," she thought. "Khay returned from the Underworld."

Then she mocked herself for the superstitious fancy. Because, in her own remembrance, she always thought of Khay as sailing on the Nile, and this was indeed a young man of about Khay's build—she had imagined a fantasy. This man was younger than Khay, with an easy, supple grace, and had a laughing, gay face.

He had come, he told them, from Imhotep's estates in the north. He was a scribe and his name was Kameni.

A slave was dispatched for her father and Kameni was taken to the house where food and drink were put before him. Presently her father arrived and there was much consultation and talking.

The gist of it all filtered through into the women's quarters with Henet, as usual, as the purveyor of the news. Renisenb sometimes wondered how it was that Henet always contrived to know all about everything.

Kameni, it seemed, was a young scribe in Imhotep's employ—the son of one of Imhotep's cousins. Kameni had discovered certain fraudulent dispositions—a falsifying of the accounts, and since the matter had many ramifications and involved the stewards of the property, he had thought it best to come south in person to report.

Renisenb was not much interested. It was clever, she thought, of Kameni to have discovered all this. Her father would be pleased with him.

The immediate outcome of the matter was that Imhotep made hurried preparations for departure. He had not meant to leave for another two months, but now the sooner he was on the spot the better.

The whole household was summoned and innumerable exordiums and recommendations were made. This was to be done and that. Yahmose was on no account to do such and such a thing. Sobek was to exercise the utmost discretion over something else. It was all, Renisenb thought, very familiar. Yahmose was attentive, Sobek was sulky. Hori, as usual, was calm and efficient. Ipy's demands and importunities were put aside with more sharpness than usual.

"You are too young to have a separate allowance. Obey Yahmose. He knows my wishes and commands." Imhotep placed a hand on his eldest son's shoulder. "I trust you, Yahmose. When I return we will speak once more of a partnership."

Yahmose flushed quickly with pleasure. He drew himself a little more erect.

Imhotep went on: "See only that all goes well in my absence. See to it that my concubine is well-treated—and with due honor and respect. She is in your charge. It is for you to control the conduct of the women of the household. See that Satipy curbs her tongue. See also that Sobek duly instructs Kait. Renisenb, also, must act toward Nofret with courtesy. Then I will have no unkindness shown toward our good Henet. The woman, I know, find her tiresome sometimes. She has been here long and thinks herself privileged to say many things that are sometimes unwelcome. She has, I know, neither beauty not wit—but she is faithful, remember, and has always been devoted to my interests. I will not have her despised and abused."

"Everything shall be done as you say," said Yahmose. "But Henet sometimes makes trouble with her tongue."

"Pah! Nonsense! All women do. Not Henet more than another. Now as to Kameni, he shall remain here. We can do with another scribe and he can assist Hori. As for the land that we have rented to the woman Yaii—"

Imhotep went off into meticulous details.

When at last all was ready for the departure Imhotep felt a sudden qualm. He took Nofret aside and said doubtfully: "Nofret, are you content to remain here? Would it be, perhaps, best if, after all, you came with me?"

Nofret shook her head and smiled.

"You will not be long absent," she said.

"Three months—perhaps four. Who knows?"

"You see—it will not be long. I shall be content here."

Imhotep said fussily: "I have enjoined upon Yahmose—upon all my sons—that you are to have every consideration. On their heads be it if you have anything of which to complain!"

"They will do as you say, I am sure, Imhotep." Nofret paused. Then she said, "Who is there here whom I can trust absolutely? Someone who is truly devoted to your interest? I do not mean one of the family."

"Hori—my good Hori? He is in every way my right hand—and a man of good sense and discrimination."

Nofret said slowly: "He and Yahmose are like brothers. Perhaps—"

"There is Kameni. He, too, is a scribe. I will enjoin on him to place himself at your service. If you have anything of which to complain, he will write down your words with his pen and dispatch the complaint to me."

Nofret nodded appreciatively.

"That is a good thought. Kameni comes from the north. He knows my father. He will not be influenced by family considerations."

"And Henet," exclaimed Imhotep. "There is Henet."

"Yes," said Nofret reflectively. "There is Henet. Suppose that you were to speak to her now—in front of me?"

"An excellent plan."

Henet was sent for and came with her usual cringing eagerness. She was full of lamentations over Imhotep's departure. Imhotep cut her short with abruptness.

"Yes, yes, my good Henet—but these things must be. I am a man who can seldom count on any stretch of peace or rest. I must toil ceaselessly for my family—little though they sometimes appreciate it. Now I wish to speak to you very seriously. You love me faithfully and devotedly, I know. I can leave you in a position of trust. Guard Nofret here—she is very dear to me."

"Whoever is dear to you, master, is dear to me," Henet declared with fervor.

"Very good. Then you will devote yourself to Nofret's interests?"

Henet turned toward Nofret, who was watching her under lowered lids.

"You are to beautiful, Nofret," she said. "That is the trouble. That is why the others are jealous—but *I* will look after you—I will warn you of all they say and do. You can count on me!"

There was a pause whilst the eyes of the two women met.

"You can count on me," Henet repeated.

A slow smile came to Nofret's lips—a rather curious smile. "Yes," she said. "I understand you, Henet. I think I can count on you."

Imhotep cleared his throat noisily.

"Then I think all is arranged—yes—everything is satisfactory. Organization—that has always been my strong point."

There was a dry cackle of laughter and Imhotep turned sharply to see his mother standing in the entrance of the room. She was supporting her weight on a stick and looked more dried up and malevolent than ever.

"What a wonderful son I have!" she observed.

"I must not delay—there are some instructions to Hori—" Muttering importantly, Imhotep hurried from the room. He managed to avoid meeting his mother's eye.

Esa gave an imperious nod of her head to Henet—and Henet glided obediently out of the room.

Nofret had risen. She and Esa stood looking at each other.

Esa said: "So my son is leaving you behind? You had better go with him, Nofret."

"He wishes me to stay here."

Nofret's voice was soft and submissive. Esa gave a shrill chuckle.

"Little good that would do if you wanted to go! And why do you not want to go? I do not understand you. What is there for you here? You are a girl who has lived in cities—who has perhaps traveled. Why do you choose the monotony of day after day here—among those who—I am frank—do not like you—who in fact dislike you?"

"So you dislike me?"

Esa shook her head.

"No—I do not dislike you. I am old and though I can see but dimly—I can still see beauty and enjoy it. You are beautiful, Nofret, and the sight of you pleases my old eyes. Because of your beauty I wish you well. I am warning you. Go north with my son."

Again Nofret repeated: "He wishes me to stay here."

The submissive tone was now definitely impregnated with mockery. Esa said sharply: "You have a purpose in remaining here. What is it, I wonder? Very well, on your own head be it. But be careful. Act discreetly. And trust no one."

She wheeled abruptly and went out. Nofret stood quite still. Very slowly her lips curved upward in a wide, catlike smile.

6

First Month of Winter, 4th Day

RENISENB HAD GOT into the habit of going up to the Tomb almost every day. Sometimes Yahmose and Hori would be there together, sometimes Hori alone, sometimes there would be no one—but always Renisenb was aware of a curious relief and peace—a feeling almost of escape. She liked it best when Hori was there alone. There was something in his gravity, his incurious acceptance of her coming, that gave her a strange feeling of contentment. She would sit in the shade of the rock chamber entrance with one knee raised and her hands clasped around it, and stare out over the green belt of cultivation to where the Nile showed a pale gleaming blue and beyond it to a distance of pale soft fawns and creams and pinks, all melting hazily into each other.

She had come the first time, months ago now, on a sudden wish to escape from a world of intense femininity. She wanted stillness and companionship—and she found them here. The wish to escape was still with her but it was no longer a mere revulsion from the stress and fret of domesticity. It was something more definite, more alarming.

She said to Hori one day: "I am afraid. . . ."

"Why are you afraid, Renisenb?" He studied her gravely.

Renisenb took a minute or two to think. Then she said slowly: "Do you remember saying to me once that there were two evils—one that came from without and one from within?"

"Yes, I remember."

"You were speaking, so you said afterward, about diseases that attack fruit and crops, but I have been thinking—it is the same with *people.*"

Hori nodded slowly.

"So you have found that out. . . . Yes, you are right, Renisenb."

Renisenb said abruptly: "It is happening now—down there at the house. Evil has come—from outside! And I know who has brought it. It is Nofret."

Hori said slowly: "You think so?"

Renisenb nodded vigorously.

"Yes, yes, I know what I am talking about. Listen, Hori, when I came up to you here and said that everything was the same even to Satipy and Kait quarreling—that was true. But those quarrels, Hori, were not *real* quarrels. I mean Satipy and Kait *enjoyed* them—they made the time pass—neither of the women felt any real anger against each other! But now it is different. Now they do not just say things that are rude and unpleasant—they say things that they mean shall *hurt*—and when they have seen that a thing hurts, then they are glad! It is horrid, Hori—horrid! Yesterday Satipy was so angry that she ran a long gold pin into Kait's arm—and a day or two ago Kait dropped a heavy copper pan full of boiling fat over Satipy's foot. And it is the same everywhere—Satipy rails at Yahmose far into the night—we can all hear her. Yahmose looks sick and tired and haunted. And Sobek goes off to the village and stays there with women and comes back drunk and shouts and boasts and says how clever he is?"

"Some of these things are true, I know," said Hori slowly. "But why should you blame Nofret?"

"Because it is her doing! It is always the things she says—little things—clever things—that start it all. She is like the goad with which you prick oxen. She is clever, too, in knowing just *what* to say. Sometimes I think it is Henet who tells her. . . ."

"Yes," said Hori thoughtfully. "That might well be."

Renisenb shivered.

"I don't like Henet. I hate the way she creeps about. She is so devoted to us all, and yet none of us want her devotion. How *could* my mother have brought her here and been so fond of her?"

"We have only Henet's word for that," said Hori dryly.

"Why should Henet be so fond of Nofret and follow her round and whisper and fawn upon her? Oh, Hori, I tell you I am *afraid!* I hate Nofret! I wish she would go away. She is beautiful and cruel and *bad!*"

"What a child you are, Renisenb."

Then Hori added quietly: "Nofret is coming up here now."

Renisenb turned her head. Together they watched Nofret come slowly up the steep path that led up the cliff face. She was smiling to herself and humming a little tune under her breath.

When she reached the place where they were, she looked round her and smiled. It was a smile of amused curiosity.

"So this is where you slip away to every day, Renisenb."

Renisenb did not answer. She had the angry, defeated feeling of a child whose refuge had been discovered.

Nofret looked about her again.

"And this is the famous Tomb?"

"As you say, Nofret," said Hori.

She looked at him, her catlike mouth curving into a smile.

"I've no doubt you find it profitable, Hori. You are a good man of business, so I hear." There was a tinge of malice in her voice, but Hori remained unmoved, smiling his quiet, grave smile.

"It is profitable to all of us. . . . Death is always profitable. . . ."

Nofret gave a quick shiver as she looked round her, her eyes sweeping over the offering tables, the entrance to the shrine and the false door.

She cried sharply: "I hate death!"

"You should not." Hori's tone was quiet. "Death is the chief source of wealth here in Egypt. Death bought the jewels you wear, Nofret. Death feeds you and clothes you."

She stared at him.

"What do you mean?"

"I mean that Imhotep is a ka-priest—a mortuary priest—all his lands, all his cattle, his timber, his flax, his barley, are the endowment of a Tomb."

He paused and then went on reflectively: "We are a strange people, we Egyptians. We love life—and so we start very early to plan for death. That is where the wealth of Egypt goes—into pyramids, into tombs, into tomb endowments."

Nofret said violently: *"Will* you stop talking about death, Hori! I do not like it!"

"Because you are truly Egyptian—because you love life, because—sometimes—you feel the shadow of death very near. . . ."

"Stop!"

She turned on him violently. Then, shrugging her shoulders, she turned away and began to descend the path.

Renisenb breathed a sigh of satisfaction.

"I am glad she has gone," she said childishly. "You frightened her, Hori."

"Yes. . . . Did I frighten you, Renisenb?"

"N-no." Renisenb sounded a little unsure. "It is true what you said, only I had never thought of it that way before. My father *is* a mortuary priest."

Hori said with sudden bitterness: "All Egypt is obsessed with death? And do you know why, Renisenb? Because we have eyes in our bodies, but none in our minds. We cannot conceive of a life other than this one—of a life after death. We can visualize only a continuation of what we know. We have no real belief in a God."

Renisenb stared at him in amazement.

"How can you say that, Hori? Why, we have many, *many* Gods—so many that I could not name them all. Only last night we were saying, all of us, which Gods we preferred. Sobek was all for Sakhmet and Kait prays to Meskhent. Kameni swears by Thoth, as is natural, being a scribe. Satipy is for the falcon-headed Horus and also for our own Meresger. Yahmose says that Ptah is to be worshipped because he made all things. I myself love Isis. And Henet is all for our local God Amûn. She says that there are prophecies amongst the priests that one day Amûn will be the greatest God in all Egypt—so she takes him offerings now while he is still a small God. And there is Ra, the Sun God, and Osiris, before whom the hearts of the dead are weighed."

Renisenb paused, out of breath. Hori was smiling at her.

"And what is the difference, Renisenb, between a God and a man?"

She stared at him.

"The Gods are—they are *magic!"*

"That is all?"

"I don't know what you mean, Hori."

"I meant that to you a God is only a man or a woman who can do certain things that men and women cannot do."

"You say such odd things! I cannot understand you."

She looked at him with a puzzled face—then glanced down over the valley, her attention was caught by something else."

"Look," she exclaimed. "Nofret is talking to Sobek. She is laughing. Oh"—she gave a sudden gasp—"no, it is nothing. I thought he was going to strike her. She is going back to the house and he is coming up here."

Sobek arrived looking like a thundercloud.

"May a crocodile devour that woman!" he cried. "My father was more of a fool than usual when he took her for a concubine!"

"What did she say to you?" asked Hori curiously.

"She insulted me as usual! Asked if my father had entrusted me with the sale of any more timber. I'd like to strangle her."

He moved along the platform and, picking up a piece of rock, threw it down to the valley below. He levered up a larger piece, then sprang back as a snake that had been coiled up beneath it raised its head. It reared up, hissing, and Renisenb saw that it was a cobra.

Catching up a heavy staff, Sobek attacked it furiously. A well-directed blow broke its back, but Sobek continued to slash at it, his head thrown back, his eyes sparkling, and below his breath he muttered some word which Renisenb only half heard and did not recognize.

She cried out: "Stop, Sobek, stop—it is dead!"

Sobek paused, then he threw the staff away and laughed. "One poisonous snake the less in the world."

He laughed again, his good humour restored, and clattered off down the path again.

Renisenb said in a low voice: "I believe Sobek—*likes* killing things!"

"Yes."

There was no surprise in the word. Hori was merely acknowledging a fact which he evidently already knew well. Renisenb turned to stare at him. She said slowly: "Snakes are dangerous—but how beautiful that cobra looked. . . ."

She stared down at its broken, twisted body. For some unknown reason she felt a pang at her heart.

Hori said dreamily: "I remember when we were all small children—Sobek attacked Yahmose. Yahmose was a year older, but Sobek was the bigger and the stronger. He had a stone and he was banging Yahmose's head with it. Your mother came running and tore them apart. I remember how she stood looking down at Yahmose—and how she cried out: 'You must not do things like that, Sobek—it is dangerous! I tell you, it is *dangerous!*'" He paused and went on, "She was very beautiful. . . . I thought so as a child. You are like her, Renisenb."

"Am I?" Renisenb felt pleased—warmed. Then she asked: "Was Yahmose badly hurt?"

"No, it was not as bad as it looked. Sobek was very ill the next day. It might have been something he ate, but your mother said it was his rage and the hot sun—it was the middle of summer."

"Sobek has a terrible temper," said Renisenb thoughtfully.

She looked again at the dead snake and turned away with a shiver.

II

When Renisenb got back to the house Kameni was sitting on the front porch with a roll of papyrus. He was singing and she paused a minute and listened to the words.

"I will go to Memphis," sang Kameni, *"I will go to Ptah, Lord of Truth. I will say to Ptah, 'Give me my sister tonight.' The stream is wine, Ptah is its reeds, Sakhmet its lotus, Earit its bud, Nefertem its flower. I will say to Ptah, 'Give me my sister tonight. The dawn breaks through her beauty. Memphis is a dish of love apples set before the fair of face. . . .'"*

He looked up and smiled at Renisenb.

"Do you like my song, Renisenb?"

"What is it?"

"It is a love song from Memphis."

He kept his eyes on her, singing softly: *"Her arms are full of branches of the persea, her hair is weighed down with unguent. She is like a Princess of the Lord of the Two Lands."*

The color came up in Renisenb's face. She passed on quickly into the house and almost collided with Nofret.

"Why are you in such a hurry, Renisenb?"

Nofret's voice had a sharp edge to it. Renisenb looked at her in faint surprise. Nofret was not smiling. Her face looked grim and tense and Renisenb noticed that her hands were clenched at her sides.

"I am sorry, Nofret. I did not see you. It is dark in here when you come from the light outside."

"Yes, it is dark here. . . ." Nofret paused a moment. "It would be pleasanter outside—on the porch—with Kameni's singing to listen to. He sings well, does he not?"

"Yes—yes, I am sure he does."

"Yet you did not stay to listen? Kameni will be disappointed."

Renisenb's cheeks felt hot again. Nofret's cold, sneering glance made her uncomfortable.

"Do you not like love songs, Renisenb?"

"Does it matter to you, Nofret, what I like or do not like?"

"So little cats have claws."

"What do you mean?"

Nofret laughed. "You are not such a fool as you look, Renisenb. So you find Kameni handsome? Well, that will please him, no doubt."

"I think you are quite odious," said Renisenb passionately. She ran past Nofret toward the back of the house. She heard the girl's mocking laugh. But through that laugh, sounding clearly in her memory, was the echo of Kameni's voice and the song that he had sung with his eyes watching her face. . . .

III

That night Renisenb had a dream.

She was with Khay, sailing with him in the Barque of the Dead in the Underworld. Khay was standing in the bows of the boat—she could only see the back of his head. Then, as they drew near to sunrise, Khay turned his head and Renisenb saw that it was not Khay but Kameni. And at the same time the prow of the barque, the serpent's head, began to writhe. It was a live serpent, a cobra, and Renisenb thought. *"It is the serpent that comes out in the Tombs to eat the souls of the dead."* She was paralyzed with fear. And then she saw that the serpent's face was the face of Nofret and she woke up screaming: "Nofret—Nofret. . . ."

She had not really screamed—it was all in the dream. She lay still, her heart beating, telling herself that none of all this was real. And then she thought suddenly: "That was what Sobek said when he was killing the snake yesterday. He said: *'Nofret'*. . ."

7

First Month of Winter, 5th Day

RENISENB'S DREAM HAD left her wakeful. She slept after it only in snatches, and toward morning she did not sleep at all. She was obsessed by an obscure feeling of impending evil.

She rose early and went out of the house. Her steps led her, as they did so often, to the Nile. There were fishermen out already and a big barge rowing with powerful strokes toward Thebes. There were other boats with sails flapping in the faint puffs of wind.

Something turned over in Renisenb's heart—the stirring of a desire for something she could not name. She thought, "I feel—I feel—" But she did not know what it was that she felt! That is to say, she knew no words to fit the sensation. She thought, "I want—but what do I want?"

Was it Khay she wanted? Khay was dead—he would not come back. She said to herself, "I shall not think of Khay any more. What is the use? It is over, all that."

Then she noticed another figure standing looking after the barge that was making for Thebes, and something forlorn about that figure—some emotion it expressed by its very motionlessness—struck Renisenb, even as she recognized Nofret.

Nofret staring out at the Nile. Nofret—alone, Nofret thinking of—what?

With a little shock Renisenb suddenly realized how little they all knew about Nofret. They had accepted her as an enemy—a stranger—without interest or curiosity in her life or the surroundings from which she had come.

It must, Renisenb thought suddenly, be sad for Nofret alone here, without friends, surrounded only by people who disliked her.

Slowly, Renisenb went forward until she was standing by Nofret's side. Nofret turned her head for a moment, then moved it back again and resumed her study of the Nile. Her face was expressionless.

Renisenb said timidly: "There are a lot of boats on the River."

"Yes."

Renisenb went on, obeying some obscure impulse toward friendliness: "Is it like this, at all, where you come from?"

Nofret laughed, a short, rather bitter laugh.

"No, indeed. My father is a merchant in Memphis. It is gay and amusing in Memphis. There are music and singing and dancing. Then my father travels a good deal. I have been with him to Syria—to Byblos beyond the Gazelle's Nose. I have been with him in a big ship on the wide seas."

She spoke with pride and animation.

Renisenb stood quite still, her mind working slowly, but with growing interest and understanding.

"It must be very dull for you here," she said slowly.

Nofret laughed impatiently.

"It is dead here—dead—nothing but plowing and sowing and reaping and grazing—and talk of crops—and wrangling about the price of flax."

Renisenb was still wrestling with unfamiliar thoughts as she watched Nofret sideways.

And suddenly, as though it was something physical, a great wave of anger and misery and despair seemed to emanate from the girl at her side.

Renisenb thought: "She is as young as I am—younger. And she is the concubine of that old man, that fussy, kindly, but rather ridiculous old man, my father. . . ."

What did she, Renisenb, know about Nofret? Nothing at all. What was it Hori had said yesterday when she had cried out, "She is beautiful and cruel and bad?"

"You are a child, Renisenb." That was what he had said. Renisenb knew now what he meant. Those words of hers had meant nothing—you could not dismiss a human being so easily. What sorrow, what bitterness, what despair lay behind Nofret's cruel smile? What had Renisenb, what had any of them, done to make Nofret welcome?

Renisenb said stumblingly, childishly: "You hate us all—I see why—we have not been kind—but now—it is not too late. Can we not, you and I, Nofret, can we not be sisters to each other? You are far away from all you know—you are alone—can I help?"

Her words faltered into silence. Nofret turned slowly.

For a minute or two her face was expressionless—there was even, Renisenb thought, a momentary softening in her eyes. In that early morning stillness, with its strange clarity and peace, it was as though Nofret hesitated—as though Renisenb's words had touched in her some last core of irresolution.

It was a strange moment, a moment Renisenb was to remember afterward. . . .

Then, gradually, Nofret's expression changed. It became heavily malevolent, her eyes smoldered. Before the fury of hate and malice in her glance, Renisenb recoiled a step.

Nofret said in a low, fierce voice: "Go! I want nothing from any of you. Stupid fools, that is what you all are, every one of you. . . ."

She paused for a moment, then wheeled round and retraced her steps toward the house, walking with energy.

Renisenb followed her slowly. Curiously enough, Nofret's words had not made her angry. They had opened before her eyes a black abyss of hate and misery—something quite unknown as yet in her own experience, and in her mind was only a confused, groping thought of how dreadful it must be to feel like that.

II

As Nofret entered the gateway and crossed the courtyard, one of Kait's children came running across her path, chasing a ball.

Nofret pushed the child out of her way with an angry thrust that sent the little girl sprawling on the ground. The child set up a wail and Renisenb ran to her and picked her up, saying fiercely: "You should not have done that, Nofret! You have hurt her, see. She has cut her chin."

Nofret laughed stridently.

"So I should be careful not to hurt these spoiled brats? Why? Are their mothers so careful of *my* feelings?"

Kait had come running out of the house at the sound of her child's wails. She ran to it, examining the injured face. Then she turned to Nofret.

"Devil and serpent! Evil one! Wait and see what we will do to you."

With all the force of her arm she struck Nofret in the face. Renisenb gave a cry and caught her arm before she could repeat the blow.

"Kait—Kait—you must not do that."

"Who says so? Let Nofret look to herself. She is only one here among many."

Nofret stood quite still. The print of Kait's hand showed clear and red on her cheek. By the corner of the eye, where a bangle Kait wore on her wrist had cut the skin, a small trickle of blood was running down her face.

But it was Nofret's expression that puzzled Renisenb—yes, and frightened her. Nofret showed no anger. Instead there was a queer, exultant look in her eyes, and once more her mouth was curving up in its catlike, satisfied smile. "Thank you, Kait," she said.

Then she walked on into the house.

III

Humming softly under her breath, her eyelids lowered, Nofret called Henet.

Henet came running, stopped, exclaimed. Nofret cut short her exclamations.

"Fetch me Kameni. Tell him to bring his pen case and ink and papyrus. There is a letter to be written to the master."

Henet's eyes were fixed on Nofret's cheek.

"To the master . . . I see. . . ."

Then she asked: "Who did—that?"

"Kait." Nofret smiled quietly and reminiscently.

Henet shook her head and clicked her tongue.

"All this is very bad—very bad. . . . Certainly the master must know of it." She darted a quick, sideways look at Nofret. "Yes, certainly Imhotep must know."

Nofret said smoothly: "You and I, Henet, think alike. . . . I thought that we should do so."

From the corner of her linen robe she detached a jewel of amethyst set in gold and placed it in the woman's hand.

"You and I, Henet, have Imhotep's true welfare at heart."

"This is too good for me, Nofret. . . . You are too generous. . . . such a lovely bit of workmanship."

"Imhotep and I appreciate fidelity."

Nofret was still smiling, her eyes narrow and catlike.

"Fetch Kameni," she said. "And come with him. You and he together are witnesses of what has occurred."

Kameni came a little unwillingly, his brow puckered.

Nofret spoke imperiously: "You remember Imhotep's instructions—before he left?"

"Yes," said Kameni.

"The time has come," said Nofret. "Sit and take ink and write as I tell you." Then as Kameni still hesitated, she said impatiently, "What you write shall be what you have seen with your own eyes and heard with your own ears—and Henet shall confirm all I say. The letter must be dispatched with all secrecy and speed."

Kameni said slowly: "I do not like—"

Nofret flashed out at him: "I have no complaint against Renisenb. Renisenb is soft, weak and a fool, but she has not tried to harm me. Does that content you?"

The color of Kameni's bronze face deepened.

"I was not thinking of that—"

Nofret said smoothly: "I think you were. . . . Come now—fulfill your instructions—write."

"Yes, write," said Henet. "I'm so distressed by all this—so terribly distressed. Certainly Imhotep must know about it. It's only right that he should. However unpleasant a thing is, one has to do one's duty. I've always felt that."

Nofret laughed softly.

"I'm sure you have, Henet. You shall do your duty! And Kameni shall do his office. And I—I shall do what it is my pleasure to do. . . ."

But still Kameni hesitated. His face was sullen—almost angry.

"I do not like this," he said. "Nofret, you had better take a little time to think."

"You say that to *me!"* Kameni flushed at her tone. His eyes avoided hers, but his sullen expression remained.

"Be careful, Kameni," said Nofret smoothly. "I have great influence with Imhotep. He listens to what I say—so far he has been pleased with you—" She paused significantly.

"Are you threatening me, Nofret?" asked Kameni.

"Perhaps."

He looked angrily at her for a moment or two—then he bent his head.

"I will do as you say, Nofret, but I think—yes, I think—that you will be sorry."

"Are *you* threatening *me,* Kameni?"

"I am warning you. . . ."

8
Second Month of Winter, 10th Day

DAY FOLLOWED DAY, and Renisenb sometimes felt that she was living in a dream.

She had made no more timid overtures to Nofret. She was, now, afraid of Nofret. There was something about Nofret she did not understand.

After the scene in the courtyard that day, Nofret had changed. There was a complacency about her, an exultation that Renisenb could not fathom. Sometimes she thought that her own vision of Nofret as profoundly unhappy must have been ridiculously wrong. Nofret seemed pleased with life and herself and her surroundings.

And yet, actually, her surroundings had very definitely changed for the worse. In the days following Imhotep's departure, Nofret had quite deliberately, Renisenb thought, set out to sow dissension between the various members of Imhotep's family.

Now that family had closed its ranks solidly against the invader. There were no more dissensions between Satipy and Kait—no railing of Satipy against the unfortunate Yahmose. Sobek seemed quieter and boasted less. Ipy was less impudent and offhand with his elder brothers. There seemed a new harmony among the family—yet this harmony did not bring peace of mind to Renisenb—for with it went a curious, persistent undercurrent of ill will to Nofret.

The two women, Satipy and Kait, no longer quarreled with her—they avoided her. They never spoke to her and wherever she came, they immediately gathered the children together and went elsewhere. At the same time, queer, annoying little accidents began to happen. A linen dress of Nofret's was spoilt with an overhot iron—some dyestuff was spilt over another. Sometimes sharp thorns found their way into her clothing—a scorpion was discovered by her bed. The food that was served to her was overseasoned—or lacking in any seasoning. There was a dead mouse one day in her portion of bread.

It was a quiet, relentless, petty persecution—nothing overt, nothing to lay hold of—it was essentially a woman's campaign.

Then, one day, old Esa sent for Satipy, Kait and Renisenb. Henet was already there, shaking her head and rubbing her hands in the background.

"Ha!" said Esa, peering at them with her usual ironical expression. "So here are my clever granddaughters. What do you think you are doing, all of you? What is this I hear about Nofret's dress being ruined—and her food uneatable?"

Satipy and Kait both smiled. They were not nice smiles.

Satipy said: "Has Nofret complained?"

"No," said Esa. She pushed the wig she always wore, even in the house, a little awry with one hand. "No, Nofret has not complained. That is what worries me."

"It does not worry *me*," said Satipy, tossing her handsome head.

"Because you are a fool," snapped Esa. "Nofret has twice the brains of any of you three."

"That remains to be seen," said Satipy. She looked good-humored and pleased with herself.

"What do you think you are all doing?" inquired Esa.

Satipy's face hardened.

"You are an old woman, Esa. I do not speak with any lack of respect—but things no longer matter to you in the way they matter to us who have husbands and young children. We have decided to take matters into our own hands—we have ways of dealing with a woman whom we do not like and will not accept."

"Fine words," said Esa. "Fine words." She cackled. "But a good discourse can be found with slave girls over the millstone."

"A true and wise saying," sighed Henet from the background.

Esa turned on her.

"Come, Henet, what does Nofret say to all this that is going on? You should know—you are always waiting on her."

"As Imhotep told me to do. It is repugnant to me, of course—but I must do what the master ordered. You do not think, I hope—"

Esa cut into the whining voice: "We know all about you, Henet. Always devoted—and seldom thanked as you should be. What does Nofret say to all this? That is what I asked you."

Henet shook her head.

"She says nothing. She just—smiles."

"Exactly." Esa picked up a jujube from a dish at her elbow, examined it and put it in her mouth. Then she said with sudden, malevolent acerbity: "You are fools, all of you. The power is with Nofret, not with you. All you are doing is to play into her hands. I dare swear it even pleases her what you are doing."

Satipy said sharply: "Nonsense. Nofret is alone amongst many. What power has she?"

Esa said grimly: "The power of a young, beautiful woman married to an aging man. I know what I am talking about." With a quick turn of her head she said: "Henet knows what I am talking about!"

Henet started. She sighed and began to twist her hands.

"The master thinks a great deal of her—naturally—yes, quite naturally."

"Go to the kitchen," said Esa. "Bring me some dates and some Syrian wine—yes, and honey too."

When Henet had gone, the old woman said: "There is mischief brewing—I can smell it. Satipy, you are the leader in all of this. Be careful that while you are thinking yourself clever, you do not play into Nofret's hands."

She leaned back and closed her eyes.

"I have warned you—now go."

"We in Nofret's power, indeed!" said Satipy with a toss of her head as they went out to the lake. "Esa is so old she gets the most extraordinary ideas into her head. It is we who have got Nofret in *our* power! We will do nothing against her that can be reported—but I think, yes, I think that she will soon be sorry she ever came here."

"You are cruel—cruel—" cried Renisenb.

Satipy looked amused.

"Do not pretend you love Nofret, Renisenb!"

"I do not. But you sound so—so *vindictive.*"

"I think of my children—and Yahmose! I am not a meek woman or one who brooks insult—and I have ambition. I would wring that woman's neck with the greatest of pleasure. Unfortunately it is not so simple as that. Imhotep's anger must not be aroused. But I think—in the end—something may be managed."

II

The letter came like a spear thrust to a fish.

Dumfounded, silent, Yahmose, Sobek and Ipy stared at Hori as he read out the words from the papyrus scroll.

"Did I not tell Yahmose that I would hold him to blame if any harm came to my concubine? As you all live, I am against you and you are against me! I will no longer live with you in one house since you have not respected my concubine Nofret! You are no longer my sons of my flesh. Neither are Sobek and Ipy my sons of my flesh. Each one of you has done harm to my concubine. That is attested by Kameni and Henet. I will turn you out of my house—each of you! I have supported you—now I will no longer support you."

Hori paused and went on:

"'The ka-servant Imhotep addresses Hori. To you who have been faithful, how are you in your life, safety and health? Salute my mother Esa for me and my daughter Renisenb, and greet Henet. Look after my affairs carefully until I reach you and see that there be prepared for me a deed whereby my concubine Nofret shall share with me in all my property as my wife. Neither Yahmose nor Sobek shall be associated with me, nor will I support them, and hereby I denounce them that they have done harm to my concubine! Keep all safe till I come. How evil it is when a man's household do evil deeds to his concubine. As for Ipy, let him take warning, and if he does a single hurt to my concubine, he too shall depart from my house."

There was a paralyzed silence. Then Sobek rose up in a violent rage.

"How has this come about? What has my father heard? Who has been bearing false tales to him? Shall we endure this? My father cannot disinherit us so and give all his goods to his concubine!"

Hori said mildly: "It will cause unfavorable comment—and it will not be accepted as a right action—but legally it is in his power. He can make a deed of settlement in any way he wishes."

"She has bewitched him—that black, jeering serpent has put a spell upon him!"

Yahmose murmured as though dumbfounded: "It is unbelievable—it cannot be true."

"My father is mad—mad!" cried Ipy. "He turns even against *me* at this woman's bidding!"

Hori said gravely: "Imhotep will return shortly—that he says. By then his anger may have abated; he may not really mean to do as he says." There was a short, unpleasant laugh. It was Satipy who had laughed. She stood looking at them from the doorway into the women's quarters.

"So that is what we are to do, is it, most excellent Hori? Wait and see?"

Yahmose said slowly: "What else can we do?"

"What else?" Satipy's voice rose. She screamed out: "What have you got in your veins, all of you? Milk? Yahmose, I know, is not a man! But you, Sobek—have you no remedy for these ills? A knife in the heart and the girl could do us no more harm."

"Satipy," cried Yahmose. "My father would never forgive us!"

"So you say. But I will tell you a dead concubine is not the same as a live concubine! Once she was dead, his heart would return to his sons and their children. And besides, how should he know *how* she died? We could say a scorpion stung her! We are all together in this, are we not?"

Yahmose said slowly: "My father *would* know. Henet would tell him."

Satipy gave a hysterical laugh.

"Most prudent Yahmose! Most gentle, cautious Yahmose! It is *you* who should look after the children and do woman's work in the back of the house. Sakhmet help me! Married to a man who is not a man. And *you,* Sobek, for all your bluster, what courage have you, what determination? I swear by Re, I am a better man than either of you."

She swung round and went out.

Kait, who had been standing behind her, came a step forward.

She said, her voice deep and shaken: "It is true what Satipy says! She is a better man than any of you. Yahmose, Sobek, Ipy—will you all sit here doing nothing? What of our children, Sobek? Cast out to starve! Very well, if *you* will do nothing, *I* will. You are none of you *men!*"

As she in turn went out, Sobek sprang to his feet.

"By the Nine Gods of the Ennead, Kait is right! There is a man's work to be done—and we sit here talking and shaking our heads."

He strode toward the door. Hori called after him: "Sobek, Sobek, where are you going? What are you going to do?"

Sobek, handsome and fierce, shouted from the doorway: "I shall do *something*—that is clear. And what I do I shall *enjoy* doing!"

9

Second Month of Winter, 10th Day

RENISENB CAME OUT onto the porch and stood there for a moment, shielding her eyes against the sudden glare.

She felt sick and shaken and full of a nameless fear. She said to herself, repeating the words over and over again mechanically: "I must warn Nofret. . . . I must warn her. . . ."

Behind her, in the house, she could hear men's voices: those of Hori and

Yahmose blending into each other, and above them, shrill and clear, the boyish tones of Ipy.

"Satipy and Kait are right. There are no men in this family! But *I* am a man. Yes, I am a man in heart if not in years. Nofret has jeered at me, laughed at me, treated me as a child. I will show her that I am *not* a child. I am not afraid of my father's anger. I know my father. He is bewitched—the woman has put a spell on him. If she were destroyed his heart would come back to me—to *me! I* am the son he loves best. You all treat me as a child—but you shall see. Yes, you shall see!"

Rushing out of the house, he collided with Renisenb and almost knocked her down. She clutched at his sleeve.

"Ipy, Ipy, where are you going?"

"To find Nofret. She shall see whether she can laugh at me!"

"Wait a little. You must calm down. We must none of us do anything rash."

"Rash?" The boy laughed scornfully. "You are like Yahmose. Prudence! Caution! Nothing must be done in a hurry! Yahmose is an old woman. And Sobek is all words and boasting. Let go of me, Renisenb."

He twitched the linen of his sleeve from her grasp.

"Nofret, where *is* Nofret?"

Henet, who had just come bustling out from the house, murmured: "Oh, dear, this is a bad business—a very bad business. What will become of us all? What would my dear mistress say?"

"Where is Nofret, Henet?"

Renisenb cried: "Don't tell him," but Henet was already answering: "She went out the back way. Down toward the flax fields."

Ipy rushed back through the house and Renisenb said reproachfully: "You should not have told him, Henet."

"You don't trust old Henet. You never have confidence in me." The whine in her voice became more pronounced. "But poor old Henet knows what she is doing. The boy needs time to cool off. He won't find Nofret by the flax fields." She grinned. "Nofret is here—in the pavilion—with Kameni."

She nodded her head across the courtyard.

And she added with what seemed rather disproportionate stress: "With Kameni. . . ."

But Renisenb had already started to cross the courtyard.

Teti, dragging her wooden lion, came running from the lake to her mother and Renisenb caught her up in her arms. She knew, as she held the child to her, the force that was driving Satipy and Kait. These women were fighting for their children.

Teti gave a little fretful cry. "Not so tight, Mother, not so tight. You are hurting me."

Renisenb put the child down. She went slowly across the courtyard. On the far side of the pavilion Nofret and Kameni were standing together. They turned as Renisenb approached.

Renisenb spoke quickly and breathlessly: "Nofret, I have come to warn you. You must be careful. You must guard yourself."

A look of contemptuous amusement passed over Nofret's face.

"So the dogs are howling?"

"They are very angry—they will do some harm to you."

Nofret shook her head.

"No one can harm me," she said with superb confidence. "If they did, it would be reported to your father—and he would exact vengeance. They will know that when they pause to think." She laughed. "What fools they have been—with their petty insults and persecutions! It was *my* game they played all the time."

Renisenb said slowly: "So you have planned for this all along? And I was sorry for you—I thought we were unkind! I am not sorry any longer. . . . I think, Nofret, that you are *wicked*. When you come to deny the forty-two sins at the hour of judgment you will not be able to say, 'I have done no evil.' Nor will you be able to say, 'I have not been covetous,' and your heart that is being weighed in the scales against the feather of truth will sink in the balance."

Nofret said sullenly: "You are very pious all of a sudden. But I have not harmed *you*, Renisenb. I said nothing against you. Ask Kameni if that is not so."

Then she walked across the courtyard and up the steps to the porch. Henet came out to meet her and the two women went into the house.

Renisenb turned slowly to Kameni.

"So it was *you*, Kameni, who helped her to do this to us?"

Kameni said eagerly: "Are you very angry with me, Renisenb? But what could I do? Before Imhotep left he charged me solemnly that I was to write at Nofret's bidding at any time she might ask me to do so. Say you do not blame me, Renisenb. What else could I do?"

"I cannot blame you," said Renisenb slowly. "You had, I suppose, to carry out my father's orders."

"I did not like doing it—and it is true, Renisenb, there was not one word said against *you*."

"As if I cared about that!"

"But I do. Whatever Nofret had told me, I would not have written one word that might harm *you*. Renisenb—please believe me."

Renisenb shook her head perplexedly. The point Kameni was laboring to make seemed of little importance to her. She felt hurt and angry, as though Kameni, in some way, had failed her. Yet he was, after all, a stranger. Though allied by blood, he was nevertheless a stranger whom her father had brought from a distant part of the country. He was a junior scribe who had been given a task by his employer, and who had obediently carried it out.

"I wrote no more than truth," Kameni persisted. "There were no lies set down; that I swear to you."

"No," said Renisenb. "There would be no lies. Nofret is too clever for that."

Old Esa had, after all, been right. That persecution over which Satipy and Kait had gloated had been just exactly what Nofret had wanted. No wonder she had gone about smiling her catlike smile.

"She is bad," said Renisenb, following out her thoughts. "Yes!"

Kameni assented. "Yes," he said. "She is an evil creature."

Renisenb turned and looked at him curiously.

"You knew her before she came here, did you not? You knew her in Memphis?"

Kameni flushed and looked uncomfortable.

"I did not know her well. . . . I had heard of her. A proud girl, they said, ambitious and hard—and one who did not forgive."

Renisenb flung back her head in sudden impatience.

"I do not believe it," she said. "My father will not do what he threatens. He is angry at present—but he could not be so unjust. When he comes he will forgive."

"When he comes," said Kameni, "Nofret will see to it that he does not change his mind. You do not know Nofret, Renisenb. She is very clever and very determined—and she is, remember, very beautiful."

"Yes," admitted Renisenb. "She is beautiful."

She got up. For some reason the thought of Nofret's beauty hurt her. . . .

II

Renisenb spent the afternoon playing with the children. As she took part in their game, the vague ache in her heart lessened. It was not until just before sunset that she stood upright, smoothing back her hair and the pleats of her dress which had got crumpled and disarranged, and wondered vaguely why neither Satipy nor Kait had been out as usual.

Kameni had long gone from the courtyard. Renisenb went slowly across into the house. There was no one in the living room and she passed through to the back of the house and the women's quarters. Esa was nodding in the corner of her room and her little slave girl was marking piles of linen sheets. They were baking batches of triangular loaves in the kitchen. There was no one else about.

A curious emptiness pressed on Renisenb's spirits. Where was everyone?

Hori had probably gone up to the Tomb. Yahmose might be with him or out in the fields. Sobek and Ipy would be with the cattle or possibly seeing to the cornbins. But where were Satipy and Kait, and where, yes, where was Nofret?

The strong perfume of Nofret's unguent filled her empty room. Renisenb stood in the doorway staring at the little wood pillow, at a jewel box, at a heap of bead bracelets and a ring set with a blue glazed scarab. Perfumes, unguents, clothes, linens, sandals—all speaking of their owner, of Nofret who lived in their midst and who was a stranger and an enemy.

Where, Renisenb wondered, could Nofret herself be?

She went slowly toward the back entrance of the house and met Henet coming in.

"Where is everybody, Henet? The house is empty except for my grandmother."

"How should *I* know, Renisenb? I have been working—helping with the weaving, seeing to a thousand and one things. *I* have no time for going for walks."

That meant, thought Renisenb, that somebody had gone for a walk. Perhaps Satipy had followed Yahmose up to the Tomb to harangue him further? But where was Kait? Unlike Kait to be away from her children for so long.

And again, a strange disturbing undercurrent, there ran the thought.

"Where is Nofret?"

As though Henet had read the thought in her mind, she supplied the answer.

"As for Nofret, she went off a long time ago up to the Tomb. Oh, well, Hori is a match for her." Henet laughed spitefully: "Hori has brains too." She sidled a little closer to Renisenb. "I wish you knew, Renisenb, how unhappy I've been over all this. She came to me, you know, that day—with the mark of Kait's fingers on her cheek and the blood streaming down. And she got Kameni to write and me to say what I'd seen—and of course I couldn't say I *hadn't* seen it! Oh, she's a clever one. And I, thinking all the time of your dear mother—"

Renisenb pushed past her and went out into the golden glow of the evening sun. Deep shadows were on the cliffs—the whole world looked fantastic at this hour of sunset.

Renisenb's steps quickened as she took the way to the cliff path. She would go up to the Tomb—find Hori. Yes, find Hori. It was what she had done as a child when her toys had been broken—when she had been uncertain or afraid. Hori was like the cliffs themselves—steadfast, immovable, unchanging.

Renisenb thought confusedly: "Everything will be alright when I get to Hori. . . ."

Her steps quickened—she was almost running.

Suddenly she saw Satipy coming toward her. Satipy too must have been up to the Tomb.

What a very odd way Satipy was walking, swaying from side to side, stumbling as though she could not see. . . .

When Satipy saw Renisenb, she stopped short, her hand went to her breast. Renisenb, drawing close, was startled at the sight of Satipy's face.

"What's the matter, Satipy, are you ill?"

Satipy's voice in answer was a croak, her eyes were shifting from side to side.

"No, no, of course not."

"You look ill. You look frightened. What has happened?"

"What should have happened? Nothing, of course."

"Where have you been?"

"I went up to the Tomb—to find Yahmose. He was not there. No one was there."

Renisenb still stared. This was a new Satipy—a Satipy with all the spirit and resolution drained out of her.

"Come, Renisenb—come back to the house."

Satipy put a slightly shaking hand on Renisenb's arm, urging her back the way she had come and at that touch Renisenb felt a sudden revolt.

"No, I am going up to the Tomb."

"There is no one there, I tell you."

"I like to look out over the River. To sit there."

"But the sun is setting—it is too late."

Satipy's fingers closed viselike over Renisenb's arm. Renisenb wrenched herself loose.

"Don't! Let me go, Satipy."

"No. Come back. Come back with me."

But Renisenb had already broken loose, pushed past her, and was on her way to the cliff.

There was something—instinct told her there was *something*. . . . Her steps quickened to a run. . . .

Then she saw it—the dark bundle lying under the shadow of the cliff. . . . She hurried along until she stood close beside it.

There was no surprise in her at what she saw. It was as though already she had expected it. . . .

Nofret lay with her face upturned, her body broken and twisted. Her eyes were open and sightless. . . .

Renisenb bent and touched the cold stiff cheek, then stood up again looking down on her. She hardly heard Satipy come up behind her.

"She must have fallen," Satipy was saying. "She has fallen. She was walking along the cliff path and she fell. . . ."

Yes, Renisenb thought, that was what had happened. Nofret had fallen from the path above, her body bouncing off the limestone rocks.

"She may have seen a snake," said Satipy, "and been startled. There are snakes asleep in the sun on that path sometimes."

Snakes. Yes, snakes. *Sobek and the snake.* A snake, its back broken, lying dead in the sun. Sobek, his eyes gleaming. . . .

She thought: *"Sobek . . . Nofret . . ."*

Then sudden relief came to her as she heard Hori's voice.

"What has happened?"

She turned with relief. Hori and Yahmose had come up together. Satipy was explaining eagerly that Nofret must have fallen from the path above.

Yahmose said, "She must have come up to find us, but Hori and I have been out to look at the irrigation canals. We have been away at least an hour. As we came back we saw you standing here."

Renisenb said, and her voice surprised her, it sounded so different: *"Where is Sobek?"*

She felt rather than saw Hori's immediate sharp turn of the head at the question. Yahmose sounded merely puzzled as he said: "Sobek? I have not seen him all the afternoon. Not since he left us so angrily in the house."

But Hori was looking at Renisenb. She raised her eyes and met his. She saw him turn from their gaze and look down thoughtfully at Nofret's body and she knew with absolute certainty exactly what he was thinking.

He murmured questioningly: "Sobek?"

"Oh, no," Renisenb heard herself saying. "Oh, no . . . Oh, *no. . . .*"

Satipy said again urgently: *"She fell from the path.* It is narrow just above here—and dangerous. . . ."

Dangerous? What was it Hori had told her once? A tale of Sobek as a child attacking Yahmose, and of her dead mother prizing them apart and saying, "You must not do that, Sobek. It is *dangerous. . . .*"

Sobek liked killing. *"What I do, I shall enjoy doing. . . ."*

Sobek killing a snake . . .

Sobek meeting Nofret on that narrow path . . .

She heard herself murmuring brokenly: "We don't know—we don't *know. . . .*"

And then, with infinite relief, with the sense of a burden taken away, she heard Hori's grave voice giving weight and value to Satipy's asseveration.

"She must have fallen from the path. . . ."

His eyes met Renisenb's. She thought: "He and I know. . . . We shall always know. . . ."

Aloud she heard her voice saying shakily: "She fell from the path. . . ."
And like a final echo, Yahmose's gentle voice chimed in: "She must have fallen from the path."

10

Fourth Month of Winter, 6th Day

IMHOTEP SAT FACING ESA.
"They all tell the same story," he said fretfully.
"That is at least convenient," said Esa.
"Convenient—convenient? What extraordinary words you use!"
Esa gave a short cackle.
"I know what I am saying, my son."
"Are they speaking the truth, that is what *I* have to decide!" Imhotep spoke portentously.
"You are hardly the goddess Maat. Nor, like Anubis, can you weigh the heart in a balance!"
"Was it an accident?" Imhotep shook his head judicially. "I have to remember that the announcement of my intentions toward my ungrateful family may have aroused some passionate feelings."
"Yes, indeed," said Esa. "Feelings were aroused. They shouted so in the main hall that I could hear what was said in my room here. By the way, were those *really* your intentions?"
Imhotep shifted uneasily as he murmured: "I wrote in anger—in justifiable anger. My family needed teaching a sharp lesson."
"In other words," said Esa, "you were merely giving them a fright. Is that it?"
"My dear mother, does that matter now?"
"I see," said Esa. "You did not know what you meant to do. Muddled thinking, as usual."
Imhotep controlled his irritation with an effort.
"I simply mean that that particular point no longer arises. It is the facts of Nofret's death that are now in question. If I were to believe that anyone in my family could be so undutiful, so unbalanced in their anger, as wantonly to harm the girl—I—I really do not know what I should do!"
"So it is fortunate," said Esa, "that they all tell the same story! Nobody had hinted at anything else, have they?"
"Certainly not."
"Then why not regard the incident as closed? You should have taken the girl north with you. I told you so at the time."
"Then you *do* believe—"
Esa said with emphasis: "I believe what I am told unless it conflicts with what I have seen with my own eyes—which is very little nowadays—or heard with my

own ears. You have questioned Henet, I suppose? What has she to say of the matter?"

"She is deeply distressed—very deeply distressed. On my behalf."

Esa raised her eyebrows.

"Indeed. You surprise me."

"Henet," said Imhotep warmly, "has a lot of heart."

"Quite so. She has also more than the usual allowance of tongue. If distress at your loss is her only reaction, I should certainly regard the incident closed. There are plenty of other affairs to occupy your attention."

"Yes, indeed." Imhotep rose with a reassumption of his fussy, important manner. "Yahmose is waiting for me now in the main hall with all sorts of matters needing my urgent attention. There are many decisions awaiting my sanction. As you say, private grief must not usurp the main functions of life."

He hurried out.

Esa smiled for a moment, a somewhat sardonic smile, then her face grew grave again. She sighed and shook her head.

II

Yahmose was awaiting his father with Kameni in attendance. Hori, Yahmose explained, was superintending the work of the embalmers and undertakers who were busy with the first stages of the funeral preparations.

It had taken Imhotep some weeks to journey home after receiving the news of Nofret's death, and the furneral preparations were not completed. The body had received its long soaking in the brine bath, had been restored to some semblance of its normal appearance, had been oiled and rubbed with salts, and duly wrapped in its bandages and deposited in its coffin.

Yahmose explained that he had appointed a small funeral chamber near the rock tomb designed later to hold the body of Imhotep himself. He went into the details of what he had ordered and Imhotep expressed his approval.

"You have done well, Yahmose," he said kindly. "You seem to have shown very good judgment and to have kept your head well."

Yahmose colored a little at this unexpected praise.

"Ipi and Montu are, of course, expensive embalmers," went on Imhotep. "These canopic jars, for instance, seem to me unduly costly. There is really no need for such extravagance. Some of their charges seem to me too high. That is the worst of these embalmers who have been employed by the Governor's family. They think they can charge any fantastic prices they like. It would have come much cheaper to go to somebody less well-known."

"In your absence," said Yahmose, "I had to decide on these matters—and I was anxious that all honor should be paid to a concubine for whom you had so great a regard."

Imhotep nodded and patted Yahmose's sholder.

"It was a fault on the right side, my son. You are, I know, usually most prudent in money matters. I appreciate that in this matter any unnecessary expense was incurred in order to please me. All the same, I am not made of money, and a concubine is—eh, ahem!—only a concubine. We will cancel, I think, the more expensive of the amulets—and let me see, there are one or two other ways of cutting down the fees. . . . Just read out the items of the estimate, Kameni."

Kameni rustled the papyrus.

Yahmose breathed a sigh of relief.

III

Kait, coming slowly out from the house to the lake, paused where the children and their mothers were.

"You were right, Satipy," she said. "A live concubine is *not* the same as a dead concubine!"

Satipy looked up at her, her eyes vague and unseeing. It was Renisenb who asked quietly: "What do you mean, Kait?"

"For a live concubine, nothing was too good—clothes, jewels—even the inheritance of Imhotep's own flesh and blood! But now Imhotep is busy cutting down the cost of the funeral expenses! After all, why waste money on a dead woman? Yes, Satipy, you were right."

Satipy murmured: "What did I say? I have forgotten."

"It is best so," agreed Kait. "I too, have forgotten. And Renisenb also."

Renisenb looked at Kait without speaking. There had been something in Kait's voice—something faintly menacing, that impressed Renisenb disagreeably. She had always been accustomed to think of Kait as rather a stupid woman—someone gentle and submissive, but rather negligible. It struck her now that Kait and Satipy seemed to have changed places. Satipy the dominant and aggressive was subdued—almost timid. It was the quiet Kait who now seemed to domineer over Satipy.

But people, thought Renisenb, do not really change their characters—or do they? She felt confused. Had Kait and Satipy *really* changed in the last few weeks, or was the change in the one the result of the change in the other? Was it Kait who had grown aggressive? Or did she merely *seem* so because of the sudden collapse of Satipy?

Satipy definitely *was* different. Her voice was no longer upraised in the familiar shrewish accents. She crept round the courtyard and the house with a nervous, shrinking gait quite unlike her usual self-assured manner. Renisenb had put down the change in her to the shock of Nofret's death, but it was incredible that that shock could last so long. It would have been far more like Satipy, Renisenb could not but think, to have exulted opening in a matter-of-fact manner over the concubine's sudden and untimely death. As it was, she shrank nervously whenever Nofret's name was mentioned. Even Yahmose seemed to be exempt from her hectoring and bullying and had, in consequence begun to assume a more resolute demeanor himself. At any rate, the change in Satipy was all to the good—or at least so Renisenb supposed. Yet something about it made her vaguely uneasy. . . .

Suddenly, with a start, Renisenb became aware that Kait was looking at her, was frowning. Kait, she realized, was waiting for a word of assent to something she had said.

"Renisenb also," repeated Kait, "has forgotten."

Suddenly Renisenb felt a flood of revolt overwhelm her. Neither Kait, nor Satipy, nor anyone should dictate to her what she should or should not remember. She returned Kait's look steadily with a distinct hint of defiance.

"The women of a household," said Kait, "must stand together."

Renisenb found her voice. She said clearly and defiantly: "Why?"

"Because their interests are the same."

Renisenb shook her head violently. She thought confusedly, "I am a person as well as a woman. I am Renisenb."

Aloud she said: "It is not so simple as that."

"Do you want to make trouble, Renisenb?"

"No. And anyway, what do you mean by trouble?"

"Everything that was said that day in the big hall had best be forgotten."

Renisenb laughed.

"You are stupid, Kait. The servants, the slaves, my grandmother—everyone must have overheard! Why pretend that things did not happen that did happen?"

"We were angry," said Satipy in a dull voice. "We did not mean what we said."

She added with a feverish irritability: "Stop talking about it, Kait. If Renisenb wants to make trouble, let her."

"I don't want to make trouble," said Renisenb indignantly. "But it is stupid to *pretend.*"

"No," said Kait. "It is wisdom. You have Teti to consider."

"Teti is alright."

"Everything is alright—*now that Nofret is dead.*" Kait smiled.

It was a serene, quiet, satisfied smile—and again Renisenb felt a tide of revolt rise in her.

Yet what Kait said was quite true. Now that Nofret was dead everything was alright. Satipy, Kait, herself, the children—all secure—all at peace—with no apprehensions for the future. The intruder, the disturbing, menacing stranger, had departed—forever.

Then why this stirring of an emotion that she did not understand on Nofret's behalf? Why this feeling of championship for the dead girl whom she had not liked? Nofret was wicked and Nofret was dead. Could she not leave it at that? Why this sudden stab of pity—of something more than pity—something that was almost comprehension?

Renisenb shook her head perplexedly. She sat on there by the water after the others had gone in, trying vainly to understand the confusion in her mind.

The sun was low when Hori, crossing the courtyard, saw her and came to sit beside her.

"It is late, Renisenb. The sun is setting. You should go in."

His grave, quiet voice soothed her, as always. She turned to him with a question.

"*Must* all women of a household stick together?"

"Who has been saying that to you, Renisenb?"

"Kait. She and Satipy—"

Renisenb broke off.

"And you—want to think for yourself?"

"Oh, *think!* I do not know how to think, Hori. Everything is confused in my head. *People* are confused. Everybody is different from what I thought they were. Satipy I always thought was bold, resolute, domineering. But now she is weak, vacilating, even timid. Then which is the real Satipy? People cannot change like that in a day."

"Not in a day—no."

"And Kait—she who was always meek and submissive and let everybody bully her. Now she dominates us all! Even Sobek seems afraid of her. And even Yahmose is different—he gives orders and expects them to be obeyed!"

"And all this confuses you, Renisenb?"

"Yes. Because I do not *understand.* I feel sometimes that even Henet may be quite different from what she appears to be!"

Renisenb laughed as though at an absurdity, but Hori did not join her. His face remained grave and thoughtful.

"You have never thought very much about people, have you, Renisenb? If you had you would realize—" He paused and then went on. "You know that in all tombs there is always a false door?"

Renisenb stared. "Yes, of course."

"Well, people are like that too. They create a false door—to deceive. If they are conscious of weakness, of inefficiency, they make an imposing door of self-assertion, of bluster, of overwhelming authority—and, after a time, they get to believe in it themselves. They think, and everybody thinks, that they *are* like that. But behind that door, Renisenb, is bare rock. . . . And so when reality comes and touches them with the feather of truth—their true self reasserts itself. For Kait gentleness and submission brought her all she desired—a husband and children. Stupidity made life easier for her. But when reality in the form of danger threatened, her true nature appeared. She did not change, Renisenb—that strength and that ruthlessness were always there."

Renisenb said childishly: "But I do not like it, Hori. It makes me afraid. Everyone being different from what I thought them. And what about myself? *I* am always the same."

"Are you?" He smiled at her. "Then why have you sat here all these hours, your forehead puckered, brooding and thinking? Did the old Renisenb—the Renisenb who went away with Khay—ever do that?"

"Oh, no. There was no need—" Renisenb stopped.

"You see? You have said it yourself. That is the word of reality—*need!* You are not the happy, unthinking child you have always appeared to be, accepting everything at its face value. You are not just one of the women of the household. You are Renisenb who wants to think for herself, who wonders about other people. . . ."

Renisenb said slowly: "I have been wondering about Nofret. . . ."

"What have you been wondering?"

"I have been wondering why I cannot forget about her. . . . She was bad and cruel and tried to do us harm and she is dead. Why can I not leave it at that?"

"Can you not leave it at that?"

"No. I try to—but—" Renisenb paused. She passed her hand across her eyes perplexedly. "Sometimes I feel I *know* about Nofret, Hori."

"Know? What do you mean?"

"I can't explain. But it comes to me every now and then—almost as though she were here beside me. I feel—almost—as though I were she. I seem to know what she felt. She was very unhappy, Hori, I know that now, though I didn't at the time. She wanted to hurt us all *because* she was so unhappy."

"You cannot know that, Renisenb."

"No, of course I cannot *know* it, but it is what I *feel.* That misery, that bitterness, that black hate—I saw it in her face once, and I did not understand! She must have loved someone and then something went wrong—perhaps he died . . . or went away—but it left her like that—wanting to hurt—to wound. Oh! You may say what you like. I know I am right! She became a concubine to that old man, my father—and she came here, and we disliked her—and she thought she would make us all as unhappy as she was— Yes, that was how it was!"

Hori looked at her curiously.

"How sure you sound, Renisenb. And yet you did not know Nofret well."

"But I feel it is *true,* Hori. I feel *her*—Nofret. Sometimes I feel her quite close beside me. . . ."

"I see."

There was silence between them. It was almost dark now.

Then Hori said quietly: "You believe, do you not, that Nofret did not die by accident? You think she was thrown down?"

Renisenb felt a passionate repugnance at hearing her belief put into words.

"No, no, don't say it."

"But I think, Renisenb, we had better say it—since it is in your head. You *do* think so?"

"I—yes!"

Hori bent his head thoughtfully. He went on: "And you think it was Sobek who did it?"

"Who else could it have been? You remember him with the snake? And you remember what he said—that day—the day of her death—before he went out of the great hall?"

"I remember what he said, yes. But it is not always the people who *say* most who *do* most!"

"But don't you believe she *was* killed?"

"Yes, Renisenb, I do. . . . But it is, after all, only an opinion. I have no proof. I do not think there ever can be proof. That is why I have encouraged Imhotep to accept the verdict of accident. Someone pushed Nofret—we shall never know who it was."

"You mean you don't think it *was* Sobek?"

"*I* do not think so. But as I say, we can never know—so it is best not to think about it."

"But—if it was not Sobek—who do you think it was?"

Hori shook his head.

"If I have an idea—it may be the wrong idea. So it is better not to say. . . ."

"But then—we shall never know!"

There was dismay in Renisenb's voice.
"Perhaps"—Hori hesitated—"perhaps that may be the best thing."
"Not to know?"
"Not to know."
Renisenb shivered.
"But then—oh, Hori, I am afraid!"

11

First Month of Summer, 11th Day

THE FINAL CEREMONIES had been completed and the incantations duly spoken. Montu, a Divine Father of the Temple of Hathor, took the broom of *heden* grass and carefully swept out the chamber whilst he recited the charm to remove the footprints of all evil spirits before the door was sealed up forever.

Then the Tomb was sealed and all that remained of the embalmers' work, pots full of natron, salt and rags that had been in contact with the body, were placed in a little chamber near by, and that too was sealed.

Imhotep squared his shoulders and took a deep breath, relaxing his devout funeral expression. Everything had been done in a befitting manner. Nofret had been buried with all the prescribed rites and with no sparing of expense (somewhat undue expense, in Imhotep's opinion).

Imhotep exchanged courtesies with the priests who, their sacred office now finished, reassumed their men-of-the-world manner. Everyone descended to the house, where suitable refreshments were waiting. Imhotep discussed with the principal Divine Father the recent political changes. Thebes was rapidly becoming a very powerful city. It was possible that Egypt might once more be united under one ruler before very long. The Golden Age of the Pyramid builders might return.

Montu spoke with reverence and approval of the King Neb hepet-Re. A first-class soldier and a man of piety also. The corrupt and cowardly north could hardly stand against him. A unified Egypt—that was what was needed. And it would mean, undoubtedly, great things for Thebes. . . .

The men walked together, discussing the future.

Renisenb looked back at the cliff and the sealed tomb chamber.

"So that is the end," she murmured. A feeling of relief swept over her. She had feared she hardly knew what! Some last-minute outburst or accusation? But everything had gone with commendable smoothness. Nofret was duly buried with all the rites of religion.

It was the end.

Henet said below her breath: "I hope so; I'm sure I hope so, Renisenb."

Renisenb turned on her.

"What do you mean, Henet?"

as though—as though she were afraid of her own shadow. You must have ed it, Renisenb?"

es, indeed, we have all noticed it."

I have asked her if she is ill—if I should send for a physician—but she says re is nothing—that she is perfectly well."

"I know."

"So you have asked her that too? And she has said nothing to you—nothing at ll?"

He laid stress on the words. Renisenb sympathized with his anxiety, but she could say nothing to help.

"She insists that she is quite well."

Yahmose murmured: "She does not sleep well at night—she cries out in her sleep. Is she—could she have some sorrow that we know nothing about?"

Renisenb shook her head.

"I do not see how that is possible. There is nothing wrong with the children. othing has happened here—except, of course, Nofret's death—and Satipy ıld hardly grieve for that," she added dryly.

ahmose smiled faintly.

No, indeed. Quite the contrary. Besides, this has been coming on for some . It began, I think, before Nofret's death."

His tone was a little uncertain and Renisenb looked at him quickly. Yahmose l with mild persistence: "*Before* Nofret's death. Don't you think so?"

'I did not notice it until afterward," said Renisenb slowly.

"And she has said nothing to you—you are sure?"

Renisenb shook her head. "But you know, Yahmose, I do not think Satipy is It seems to me more that she is—afraid."

"Afraid?" exclaimed Yahmose in great astonishment. "But why should Saty be afraid? And of what? Satipy has always had the courage of a lion."

"I know," said Renisenb helplessly. "We have always thought so—but people hange—it is queer."

"Does Kait know anything, do you think? Has Satipy spoken to her?"

"She would be more likely to talk to her than to me—but I do not think so. In fact, I am sure of it."

"What does Kait think?"

"Kait? Kait never thinks about anything."

All Kait had done, Renisenb was reflecting, was to take advantage of Satipy's unusual meekness by grabbing for herself and her children the finest of the newly-woven linen—a thing she would never have been allowed to do had Satipy been her usual self. The house would have resounded with passionate disputings! The fact that Satipy had given it up with hardly a murmur had impressed Renisenb more than anything else that could have happened.

"Have you spoken to Esa?" Renisenb asked. "Our grandmother is wise about women and their ways."

"Esa," said Yahmose with some slight annoyance, "merely bids me be thankful for the change. She says it is too much to hope that Satipy will continue to be so sweetly reasonable."

Renisenb said with some slight hesitation: "Have you asked Henet?"

"Henet?" Yahmose frowned. "No, indeed. I would not speak of such things to

Henet avoided her eyes.

"I just said I hoped it *was* the end. Sometimes wha... a beginning. And that wouldn't do at all."

Renisenb said angrily: "What are you talking abou... hinting at?"

"I'm sure I never hint, Renisenb. I wouldn't do such a t... and everyone is satisfied. So everything is as it should be."

Renisenb demanded: "Did my father ask you what *you* thoug... death?"

"Yes, indeed, Renisenb. Most particular, he was, that I sh... exactly what I thought about it all."

"And what did you tell him?"

"Well, of course I said it was an accident. What else could it have be... don't think for a minute, I said, that anyone in your family would harm th... do you? They wouldn't dare, I said. They have far too much respect for ... Grumble they might, but nothing more, I said. You can take it from me, I sa... that there's been nothing of *that* kind!"

Henet nodded her head and chuckled.

"And my father believed you?"

Again Henet nodded with a good deal of satisfaction.

"Ah, your father knows how devoted I am to his interests. He'll always t... old Henet's word for anything. *He* appreciates me if none of the rest of you ... Ah, well, my devotion to all of you is its own reward. I don't expect thanks..."

"You were devoted to Nofret too," said Renisenb.

"I'm sure I don't know what gave you that idea, Renisenb. I had to obe... orders like everyone else."

"She thought you were devoted to her."

Henet chuckled again.

"Nofret wasn't quite as clever as she thought herself. A proud girl—and a gi... who thought she owned the earth. Well, she's got the judges in the Underworl... to satisfy now—and a pretty face won't help her there. At any rate we're quit o... her. At least," she added under her breath and touching one of the amulets she wore, "I hope so."

II

"Renisenb, I want to talk to you about Satipy."

"Yes, Yahmose?"

Renisenb looked up sympathetically into her brother's gentle, worried face.

Yahmose said slowly and heavily: "There is something very wrong with Satipy. I cannot understand it."

Renisenb shook her head sadly. She was at a loss to find anything comforting to say.

"I have noticed this change in her for some time," went on Yahmose. "She starts and trembles at any unaccustomed noise. She does not eat well. She creeps

Henet. She takes far too much upon herself as it is. My father spoils her."

"Oh, I know that. She is very tiresome. But all the same—well"—Renisenb hesitated—"Henet usually knows things."

Yahmose said slowly: "Would you ask her, Renisenb? And tell me what she says?"

"If you like."

Renisenb put her query at a moment when she had Henet to herself. They were on their way to the weaving sheds. Rather to her surprise the question seemed to make Henet uneasy. There was none of her usual avidity to gossip.

She touched an amulet she was wearing and glanced over her shoulder.

"It's nothing to do with me, I'm sure. . . . It's not for me to notice whether anyone's themselves or not. I mind my own business. If there's trouble I don't want to be mixed up in it."

"Trouble? What kind of trouble?"

Henet gave her a quick, sideways glance.

"None, I hope. None that need concern us, anyway. You and I, Renisenb, we've nothing to reproach ourselves with. That's a great consolation to me."

"Do you mean that Satipy— What *do* you mean?"

"I don't mean anything at all, Renisenb—and please don't start making out that I do. I'm little better than a servant in this house, and it's not my business to give my opinion about things that are nothing to do with me. If you ask me, it's a change for the better and if it stops at that, well, we'll all do nicely. Now, please, Renisenb. I've got to see that they are marking the date properly on the linen. So careless as they are, these women, always talking and laughing and neglecting their work."

Unsatisfied, Renisenb watched her dart away into the weaving shed. She herself walked slowly back to the house. Her entry into Satipy's room was unheard, and Satipy sprang round with a cry as Renisenb touched her shoulder.

"Oh, you startled me. I thought—"

"Satipy," said Renisenb. "What is the matter? Won't you tell me? Yahmose is worried about you and—"

Satipy's fingers flew to her lips. She said, stammering nervously, her eyes wide and frightened: "Yahmose? What—what did he say?"

"He is anxious. You have been calling out in your sleep—"

"Renisenb!" Satipy caught her by the arm. "Did I say—What did I say?"

Her eyes seemed dilated with terror.

"Does Yahmose think— What did he tell you?"

"We both think that you are ill—or—or unhappy."

"Unhappy?" Satipy repeated the word under her breath with a peculiar intonation.

"*Are* you unhappy, Satipy?"

"Perhaps. . . . I don't know. It is not that."

"No. You're frightened, aren't you?"

Satipy stared at her with sudden hostility.

"Why should you say that? Why should I be frightened? What is there to frighten me?"

"I don't know," said Renisenb. "But it is true, isn't it?"

With an effort Satipy recovered her old arrogant pose. She tossed her head.

"I'm not afraid of anything—or anyone! How dare you suggest such a thing to me, Renisenb? And I won't have you talking me over with Yahmose. Yahmose and I understand each other." She paused and then said sharply, "Nofret is dead—and a good riddance. That's what I say. And you can tell anyone who asks you that that's what I feel about it."

"Nofret?" Renisenb uttered the name questioningly.

Satipy flew into a passion that made her seem quite like her old self. "Nofret—Nofret—Nofret! I'm sick of the sound of that name. We don't need to hear it any more in this house—and thank goodness for that."

Her voice, which had been raised to its old shrill pitch, dropped suddenly as Yahmose entered. He said, with unusual sternness: "Be quiet, Satipy. If my father heard you, there would be fresh trouble. How can you behave so foolishly?"

If Yahmose's stern and displeased tone was unusual, so too was Satipy's meek collapse. She murmured: "I am sorry, Yahmose. . . . I did not think."

"Well, be more careful in future! You and Kait made most of the trouble before. You women have no sense!"

Satipy murmured again: "I am sorry. . . ."

Yahmose went out, his shoulders squared, and his walk far more resolute than usual, as though the fact of having asserted his authority for once had done him good. Renisenb went slowly along to old Esa's room. Her grandmother, she felt, might have some helpful counsel.

Esa, however, who was eating grapes with a good deal of relish, refused to take the matter seriously.

"Satipy? Satipy? Why all this fuss about Satipy? Do you all like being bullied and ordered about by her that you make such a to-do because she behaves herself properly for once?"

She spat out the pips of the grapes and remarked: "In any case, it's too good to last—unless Yahmose can keep it up."

"Yahmose?"

"Yes. I hoped Yahmose had come to his senses at last and given Satipy a good beating. It's what she needs—and she's the kind of woman who would probably enjoy it. Yahmose, with his meek, cringing ways, must have been a great trial to her."

"Yahmose is a dear," cried Renisenb indignantly. "He is kind to everybody—and as gentle as a woman—if women are gentle," she added doubtfully.

Esa cackled.

"A good afterthought, Granddaughter. No, there's nothing gentle about women—or if there is, Isis help them! And there are few women who care for a kind, gentle husband. They'd sooner have a handsome, blustering brute like Sobek—he's the one to take a girl's fancy. Or a smart young fellow like Kameni—hey, Renisenb? The flies in the courtyard don't settle on him for long! He's got a pretty taste in love songs, too. Eh? Hee, hee, hee."

Renisenb felt her cheeks going red.

"I don't know what you mean," she said with dignity.

"You all think old Esa doesn't know what's going on! I know alright." She peered at Renisenb with her semi-blind eyes. "I know, perhaps, before you do, child. Don't be angry. It's the way of life, Renisenb. Khay was a good brother to

you—but he sails his boat now in the Field of Offerings. The sister will find a new brother who spears his fish in our own River—not that Kameni would be much good. A reed pen and a papyrus roll are his fancy. A personable young man, though—with a pretty taste in songs. But for all that I'm not sure he's the man for you. We don't know much about him—he's a northerner. Imhotep approves of him—but then I've always thought Imhotep was a fool. Anyone can get round him by flattery. Look at Henet!"

"You are quite wrong," said Renisenb with dignity.

"Very well, then, I'm wrong. Your father is *not* a fool."

"I didn't mean that. I meant—"

"I know what you meant, child." Esa grinned. "But you don't know the real joke. You don't know how good it is to sit at ease like I do, and to be done with all this business of brothers and sisters, and loving and hating. To eat a well-cooked fat quail or a reed bird, and then a cake with honey, and some well-cooked leeks and celery and wash it down with wine from Syria—and have never a care in the world. And look on at all the turmoil and the heartaches and know that none of that can affect you anymore. To see your son make a fool of himself over a handsome girl, and to see her set the whole place by the ears—it made me laugh, I can tell you! In a way, you know, I liked that girl! She had the devil in her alright—the way she touched them all on the raw. Sobek like a pricked bladder—Ipy made to look a child—Yahmose shamed as a bullied husband. It's like the way you see your face in a pool of water. She made them see just how they looked to the world at large. But why did she hate *you,* Renisenb? Answer me that."

"Did she hate me?" Renisenb spoke doubtfully. "I—tried once to be friends."

"And she'd have none of it? She hated you alright, Renisenb."

Esa paused and then asked sharply: "Would it be because of Kameni?"

The color rose in Renisenb's face. "Kameni? I do not know what you mean."

Esa said thoughtfully: "She and Kameni both came from the north, but it was you Kameni watched cross the courtyard."

Renisenb said abruptly: "I must go and see to Teti."

Esa's shrill, amused cackle followed her. Her cheeks hot, Renisenb sped across the courtyard toward the lake. Kameni called to her from the porch: "I have made a new song, Renisenb. Stay and hear it."

She shook her head and hurried on. Her heart was beating angrily. Kameni and Nofret. Nofret and Kameni. Why let old Esa, with her malicious love of mischief, put these ideas into her head? And why should she care?

Anyway, what did it matter? She cared nothing for Kameni—nothing at all. An impertinent young man with a laughing voice and shoulders that reminded her of Khay.

Khay . . . Khay . . .

She repeated his name insistently—but for once no image came before her eyes. Khay was in another world. He was in the Field of Offerings . . .

On the porch Kameni was singing softly: *"I will say to Ptah: 'Give me my sister tonight. . . .'"*

III

"Renisenb!"

Hori had repeated her name twice before she heard him and turned from her contemplation of the Nile.

"You were lost in thought, Renisenb. What were you thinking about?"

Renisenb said with defiance: "I was thinking of Khay."

Hori looked at her for a minute or two—then he smiled.

"I see," he said.

Renisenb had an uncomfortable feeling that he did see!

She said with a sudden rush: "What happens when you are dead? Does anyone really know? All these texts—all these things are written in coffins—some of them are so obscure they seem to mean nothing at all. We know that Osiris was killed and that his body was joined together again, and that he wears the white crowns, and because of him we need not die—but sometimes, Hori, none of it seems *real*—and it is all so confused. . . ."

Hori nodded gently.

"But what really happens after you are dead—that is what I want to know."

"I cannot tell you, Renisenb. You should ask a priest these questions."

"He would just give me the usual answers. I want to *know.*"

Hori said gently: "We shall none of us know until we are dead ourselves. . . ."

Renisenb shivered. "Don't—don't say that!"

"Something has upset you, Renisenb?"

"It was Esa." She paused and then said, "Tell me, Hori, did—did Kameni and Nofret know each other well before—before they came here?"

Hori stood quite still for a moment, then as he walked by Renisenb's side, back toward the house, he said: "I see. So that is how it is. . . ."

"What do you mean—*'that is how it is'?* I only asked you a question.

"To which I do not know the answer. Nofret and Kameni knew each other in the north—how well, I do not know."

He added gently: "Does it matter?"

"No, of course not," said Renisenb. "It is of no importance at all."

"Nofret is dead."

"Dead and embalmed and sealed up in her Tomb! And that is that!"

Hori continued calmly: "And Kameni—does not seem to grieve. . . ."

"No," said Renisenb, struck by this aspect of the question. "That is true." She turned to him impulsively. "Oh, Hori, how—how *comforting* a person you are!"

He smiled.

"I mended little Renisenb's lion for her. Now—she has other toys."

Renisenb skirted the house as they came to it.

"I don't want to go in yet. I feel I hate them all. Oh, not *really,* you understand. But just because I am cross—and impatient and everyone is so *odd.* Can we not go up to your Tomb? It is so nice up there—one is—oh, *above* everything."

"That is clever of you, Renisenb. That is what I feel. The house and the cultivation and the farming lands—all that is below one, insignificant. One looks beyond all that—to the River—and beyond again—to the whole of Egypt.

For very soon now Egypt will be one again—strong and great as she was in the past."

Renisenb murmured vaguely: "Oh—does it matter?"

Hori smiled.

"Not to little Renisenb. Only her own lion matters to Renisenb."

"You are laughing at me, Hori. So it *does* matter to you?"

Hori murmured: "Why should it? Yes, why should it? I am only a ka-priest's man of business. Why should I care if Egypt is great or small?"

"Look." Renisenb drew his attention to the cliff above them. "Yahmose and Satipy have been up to the Tomb. They are coming down now."

"Yes," said Hori. "There were some things to be cleared away, some rolls of linen that the embalmers did not use. Yahmose said he would get Satipy to come up and advise him what to do about them."

The two of them stood there looking up at the two descending the path above.

It came to Renisenb suddenly that they were just approaching the spot from which Nofret must have fallen.

Satipy was ahead, Yahmose a little way behind her.

Suddenly Satipy turned her head to speak to Yahmose. Perhaps, Renisenb thought, she was saying to him that this must be the place where the accident had occurred.

And then, suddenly, Satipy stiffened in her tracks. She stood as though frozen, staring back along the path. Her arms went up as though at some dreadful sight or as though to ward off a blow. She cried out something, stumbled, swayed, and then, as Yahmose sprang toward her, she screamed, a scream of terror, and plunged forward off the edge headlong to the rocks below. . . .

Renisenb, her hand to her throat, watched the fall unbelievingly.

Satipy lay, a crumpled mass, just where the body of Nofret had lain.

Rousing herself, Renisenb ran forward to her. Yahmose was calling and running down the path.

Renisenb reached the body of her sister-in-law and bent over it. Satipy's eyes were open, the eyelids fluttering. Her lips were moving, trying to speak. Renisenb bent closer to her. She was appalled by the glazed terror in Satipy's eyes.

Then the dying woman's voice came. It was just a hoarse croak.

"Nofret . . ."

Satipy's head fell back. Her jaw dropped.

Hori had turned to meet Yahmose. The two men came up together.

Renisenb turned on her brother.

"What did she call out, up there, before she fell?"

Yahmose's breath was coming in short jerks—he could hardly speak. . . .

"She looked past me—*over my shoulder*—as though she saw someone coming along the path—but there was no one—*there was no one there."*

Hori assented: "There was no one. . . ."

Yahmose's voice dropped to a low, terrified whisper. "And then she called out—"

"What did she say?" Renisenb demanded impatiently.

"She said—she said"—his voice trembled—"'Nofret.' . . ."

12

First Month of Summer, 12th Day

"SO THAT IS WHAT YOU MEANT?"

Renisenb flung the words at Hori more as an affirmation than as a question.

She added softly under her breath with growing comprehension and horror: "It was Satipy who killed Nofret. . . ."

Sitting with her chin supported by her hands in the entrance to Hori's little rock chamber next to the Tomb, Renisenb stared down at the valley below.

She thought dreamily how true the words were she had uttered yesterday. Was it really only such a short time ago? From up here the house below and the busy hurrying figures had no more significance nor meaning than an ants' nest.

Only the sun, majestic in power, shining overhead—only the slim streak of pale silver that was the Nile in this morning light—only these were eternal and enduring. Khay had died, and Nofret and Satipy—and someday she and Hori would die. But Re would still rule the Heavens and travel by night in his barque through the Underworld to the dawning of the next day. And the River would still flow, flow from beyond Elephantine and down past Thebes and past the village and to lower Egypt where Nofret had lived and been gay and light of heart, and on to the great waters and so away from Egypt altogether.

Satipy and Nofret . . .

Renisenb pursued her thoughts aloud, since Hori had not answered her last demand.

"You see, I was so sure that Sobek—" She broke off.

Hori said thoughtfully: "The preconceived idea."

"And yet it was stupid of me," Renisenb went on. "Henet told me, or more or less told me, that Satipy had gone walking this way and she said that Nofret had come up here. I ought to have seen how obvious it was that Satipy had followed Nofret—that they had met on the path—and that Satipy had thrown her down. She had said, only a short while before, that she was a better man than any of my brothers."

Renisenb broke off and shivered.

"And when I met her," she resumed, "I should have known then. She was quite different—she was frightened. She tried to persuade me to turn back with her. She didn't want me to find Nofret's body. I must have been blind not to realize the truth. But I was so full of fear about Sobek . . ."

"I know. It was seeing him kill that snake."

Renisenb agreed eagerly.

"Yes, that was it. And then I had a dream. . . . Poor Sobek—how I have misjudged him. As you say, *threatening* is not *doing.* Sobek has always been full of boastful talk. It was Satipy who was always bold and ruthless and not afraid of action. And then ever since—the way she has gone about like a ghost—it has puzzled us all. Why did we not think of the true explanation?"

She added, with a quick upward glance: "But you did?"

"For some time," said Hori, "I have felt convinced that the clue to the truth of Nofret's death was in Satipy's extraordinary change of character. It was so remarkable that there had to be something to account for it."

"And yet you said nothing?"

"How could I, Renisenb? What could I ever *prove?*"

"No, of course not."

"Proofs must be solid brick walls of fact."

"Yet once you said," Reinsenb argued, "that people did not really change. But now you admit that Satipy *did* change."

Hori smiled at her.

"You should argue in the Nomarch's courts. No, Renisenb, what I said was true enough—people are always themselves. Satipy, like Sobek, was all bold words and talk. She, indeed, might go on from talk to action—but I think she is one of those who cannot know a thing or what it is like until it has happened. In her life up to that particular day, she had never had anything to *fear.* When fear came, it took her unawares. She learned then that courage is the resolution to face the unforeseen—and she had not got that courage."

Renisenb murmured in a low voice: *"When fear came* . . . Yes, that is what has been with us ever since Nofret died. Satipy has carried it in her face for us all to see. It was there, staring from her eyes when she died . . . when she said 'Nofret. . . .' It was as though she saw—"

Renisenb stopped herself. She turned her face to Hori, her eyes wide with a question.

"Hori, what did she see? There on the path. We saw nothing! There *was* nothing."

"Not for us—no."

"But for her? It was Nofret she saw—Nofret come to take her revenge. But Nofret is dead and her tomb is sealed. What then did she see?"

"The picture that her own mind showed her."

"You are sure? Because if not—"

"Yes, Renisenb, if not?"

"Hori—" Renisenb stretched out her hand. "Is it ended now? Now that Satipy is dead? Is it truly ended?"

He held her hand in both of his in a comforting clasp.

"Yes, yes, Renisenb—surely. And you at least need not be afraid."

Renisenb murmured under her breath: "But Esa says that Nofret hated me. . . ."

"Nofret hated *you?*"

"Esa says so."

"Nofret was good at hating," said Hori. "Sometimes I think she hated every person in this house. But you at least did nothing against her."

"No—no, that is true."

"And therefore, Renisenb, there is nothing in *your* mind to rise up against you in judgment."

"You mean, Hori, that if I were to walk down this path alone—at sunset—at the same time when Nofret died—and if I were to turn my head—I should see nothing? I should be safe?"

"You will be safe, Renisenb, because if you walk down the path, I will walk with you and no harm shall come to you."

But Renisenb frowned and shook her head.

"No, Hori. I will walk alone."

"But why, little Renisenb? Will you not be afraid?"

"Yes," said Renisenb, "I think I shall be afraid. But all the same that is what has to be done. They are all trembling and shaking in the house and running to the temples to buy amulets and crying out that it is not well to walk on this path at the hour of sundown. But it was not magic that made Satipy sway and fall—it was fear—fear because of an evil thing that she had done.

"For it is evil to take away life from someone who is young and strong and who enjoys living. But I have not done any evil thing, and so even if Nofret did hate me, her hate cannot harm me. That is what I believe. And anyway if one is to live always in fear it would be better to die—so I will overcome fear."

"Those are brave words, Renisenb."

"They are perhaps rather braver than I feel, Hori." She smiled up at him. She rose to her feet. "But it has been good to say them."

Hori rose and stood beside her.

"I shall remember these words of yours, Renisenb. Yes, and the way you threw back your head when you said them. They show the courage and the truth that I have always felt were in your heart."

He took her hand in his.

"Look, Renisenb. Look out from here across the valley to the River and beyond. That is Egypt, our land. Broken by war and strife for many long years, divided into petty kingdoms, but now—very soon—to come together and form once more a united land—Upper and Lower Egypt once again welded into one—I hope and believe to recover her former greatness! In those days, Egypt will need men and women of heart and courage—women such as you are, Renisenb. It is not men like Imhotep, forever preoccupied with his own narrow gains and losses, nor men like Sobek, idle and boastful, nor boys like Ipy, who thinks only of what he can gain for himself, no, nor even conscientious, honest sons like Yahmose whom Egypt will need in that hour. Sitting there, literally amongst the dead, reckoning up gains and losses, casting accounts, I have come to see gains that cannot be reckoned in terms of wealth, and losses that are more damaging than loss of a crop. . . . I look at the River and I see the lifeblood of Egypt that has existed before we lived and that will exist after we die. . . . Life and death, Renisenb, are not of such great account. I am only Hori, Imhotep's man of of business, but when I look out over Egypt I know a peace—yes, and an exultation that I would not exchange to be Governor of the Province. Do you understand at all what I mean, Renisenb?"

"I think so, Hori—a little. You are different from the others down there—I have known that for some time. And sometimes when I am with you here, I can feel what you feel—but dimly—not very clearly. But I do know what you mean. When I am *here* the things down *there*"—she pointed—"do not seem to matter any longer—the quarrels and the hatreds and the incessant bustle and fuss. Here one escapes from all that."

She paused, her brow puckering, and went on, stammering a little: "Sometimes I—I am glad to have escaped. And yet—I do not know—there is something—down there—that calls me back."

Hori dropped her hand and stepped back a pace.
He said gently: "Yes—I see—Kameni singing in the courtyard."
"What do you mean, Hori? I was not thinking of Kameni."
"You may have have been thinking of him. But all the same, Renisenb, I think it is his songs that you are hearing without knowing it."
Renisenb stared at him, her brow puckered.
"What extraordinary things you say, Hori. One could not possibly hear him singing up here. It is much too far away."
Hori sighed gently and shook his head. The amusement in his eyes puzzled her. She felt a little angry and bewildered because she could not understand.

13

First Month of Summer, 23rd Day

"CAN I SPEAK with you a minute, Esa?"
Esa peered sharply toward Henet, who stood in the doorway of the room, an ingratiating smile upon her face.
"What is it?" the old woman asked sharply.
"It's nothing, really—at least I don't suppose so—but I thought I'd just like to ask—"
Esa cut her short.
"Come in, then; come in. And you"—she tapped the little balck slave girl, who was threading beads, on the shoulder with her stick—"go to the kitchen. Get me some olives—and make me a drink of pomegranate juice."
The little girl ran off, and Esa beckoned Henet impatiently.
"It's just this, Esa."
Esa peered down at the article Henet was holding out to her. It was a small jewel box with a sliding lid, the top fastened with two buttons.
"What about it?"
"It's *hers*. And I found it now—in her room."
"Who are you talking about? Satipy?"
"No, no, Esa. *The other.*"
"Nofret, you mean? What of it?"
"All her jewels and her toilet vases and her perfume jars—everything—was buried with her."
Esa twirled the string from the buttons and opened the box. In it was a string of small carnelian beads and half of a green glazed amulet which had been broken in two.
"Pooh," said Esa. "Nothing much here. It must have been overlooked."
"The embalmers' men took everything away."
"Embalmers' men aren't any more reliable than anyone else. They forgot this."

"I tell you, Esa—this wasn't in the room when last I looked in."

Esa looked up sharply at Henet.

"What are you trying to make out? That Nofret has come back from the Underworld and is here in the house? You're not really a fool, Henet, though you sometimes like to pretend you're one. What pleasure do you get from spreading these silly magical tales?"

Henet was shaking her head portentously.

"We all know what happened to Satipy—and *why!*"

"Maybe we do," said Esa. "And maybe some of us knew it before! Eh, Henet? I've always had an idea you knew more about how Nofret came to her death than the rest of us."

"Oh, Esa, surely you wouldn't think for a moment—"

Esa cut her short.

"What wouldn't I think? I'm not afraid of thinking, Henet. I've seen Satipy creeping about the house for the last two months looking frightened to death—and it's occurred to me since yesterday that someone might have known what she'd done to Nofret, and that that someone might have been holding the knowledge over her head—threatening maybe to tell Yahmose—or Imhotep himself."

Henet burst into a shrill clamor of protestations and exclamations. Esa closed her eyes and leaned back in her chair.

"I don't suppose for a moment you'd ever admit you did such a thing. I'm not expecting you to."

"Why should I? That's what I ask you—why should I?"

"I've not the least idea," said Esa. "You do a lot of things, Henet, for which I've never been able to find a satisfactory reason."

"I suppose you think I was trying to make her bribe me to silence. I swear by the Nine Gods of the Ennead—"

"Do not trouble the Gods. You're honest enough, Henet—as honesty goes. And it may be that you knew nothing about how Nofret came to her death. But you know most things that go on in this house. And if I were going to do any swearing myself, I'd swear that you put this box in Nofret's room yourself—though why I can't imagine. But there's some reason behind it. . . . You can deceive Imhotep with your tricks, but you can't deceive me. And don't *whine!* I'm an old woman and I cannot stand people whining. Go and whine to Imhotep. He seems to like it, though Re alone knows why!"

"I will take the box to Imhotep and tell him—"

"I'll hand the box to him myself. Be off with you, Henet, and stop spreading these silly superstitious tales. The house is a more peaceful place without Satipy. Nofret dead has done more for us than Nofret living. But now that the debt is paid, let everyone return to their everyday tasks."

II

"What is all this?" Imhotep demanded as he came fussily into Esa's room a few minutes later. "Henet is deeply distressed. She came to me with the tears running down her face. Why nobody in the house can show that devoted woman the most ordinary kindness—"

Esa, unmoved, gave a cackle of laughter.

Imhotep went on: "You have accused her, I understand, of stealing a box—a jewel box."

"Is that what she told you? I did nothing of the sort. Here is the box. It seems it was found in Nofret's room."

Imhotep took it from her.

"Ah, yes, it is one I gave her." He opened it. "H'm, nothing much inside. Very careless of the embalmers not to have included it with the rest of her personal belongings. Considering the prices Ipi and Montu charge, one could at least expect no carelessness. Well, this all seems to me a great fuss about nothing—"

"Quite so."

"I will give the box to Kait—no, to Renisenb. She always behaved with courtesy toward Nofret."

He sighed.

"How impossible it seems for a man to get any peace. These women—endless tears or else quarrels and bickerings."

"Ah, well, Imhotep, there is at least one woman less now!"

"Yes, indeed. My poor Yahmose! All the same, Esa—I feel that—er—it may be all for the best. Satipy bore healthy children, it is true, but she was in many ways a most unsatisfactory wife. Yahmose, of course, gave in to her far too much. Well, well, all that is over now. I must say that I have been much pleased with Yahmose's behavior of late. He seems much more self-reliant—less timid—and his judgment on several points has been excellent—quite excellent. . . ."

"He was always a good, obedient boy."

"Yes, yes—but inclined to be slow and somewhat afraid of responsibility."

Esa said dryly: "Responsibility is a thing you have never allowed him to have!"

"Well, all that will be changed now. I am arranging a deed of association and partnership. It will be signed in a few days' time. I am associating with myself all my three sons."

"Surely not Ipy?"

"He would be hurt to be left out. Such a dear, warmhearted lad."

"There is certainly nothing slow about *him,*" observed Esa.

"As you say. And Sobek too—I have been displeased with him in the past, but he has really turned over a new leaf of late. He no longer idles his time away, and he defers more to my judgment and to that of Yahmose."

"This is indeed a hymn of praise," said Esa. "Well, Imhotep, I must say that I think you are doing the right thing. It was bad policy to make your sons discontented. But I still think that Ipy is too young for what you propose. It is ridiculous to give a boy of that age a definite position. What hold will you have over him?"

"There is something in that, certainly." Imhotep looked thoughtful.

Then he roused himself.

"I must go. There are a thousand things to see to. The embalmers are here—there are all the arrangements to make for Satipy's burial. These deaths are very costly—very costly. And following so quickly one upon the other!"

"Oh, well," said Esa consolingly, "we'll hope this is the last of them—until my time comes!"

"You will live many years yet, I hope, my dear mother."

"I'm sure you hope so," said Esa with a grin. "No economy over me, if you please! It wouldn't look well! I shall want a good deal of equipment to amuse me in the other world. Plenty of food and drink and lot of models of slaves—a richly ornamental gaming board, perfume sets and cosmetics, and I insist on the most expensive canopic jars—the alabaster ones."

"Yes, yes, of course." Imhotep changed his position nervously from one foot to the other. "Naturally all respect will be paid when the sad day comes. I must confess that I feel rather differently about Satipy. One does not want a scandal, but really, *in the circumstances*—"

Imhotep did not finish his sentence, but hurried away.

Esa smiled sardonically as she realized that that one phrase "in the circumstances" was the nearest Imhotep would ever get toward admitting that an accident did not fully describe the way his valued concubine had met her death.

14

First Month of Summer, 25th Day

WITH THE RETURN of the members of the family from the Nomarch's court, the deed of association duly ratified, a general spirit of hilarity was felt. The exception was undoubtedly Ipy who had, at the last moment, been excluded from participation on the ground of his extreme youth. He was sullen in consequence and purposely absented himself from the house.

Imhotep, in excellent spirits, called for a pitcher of wine to be brought out onto the porch where it was placed in the big wine stand.

"You shall drink, my son," he declared, clapping Yahmose on the shoulder. "Forget for the moment your sorrow in bereavement. Let us think only of the good days that are to come."

Imhotep, Yahmose, Sobek and Hori drank the toast. Then word was brought that an ox had been stolen and all four men went hurriedly off to verify the report.

When Yahmose reentered the courtyard, an hour later, he was tired and hot. He went to where the wine jar still stood in the stand. He dipped a bronze cup into it and sat down on the porch, gently sipping the wine. A little later Sobek came striding in and exclaimed with pleasure.

"Ha," he said. "Now for more wine! Let us drink to our future which is at last well-assured. Undoubtedly this is a joyful day for *us*, Yahmose!"

Yahmose agreed.

"Yes, indeed. It will make life easier in every way."

"You are always so moderate in your feelings, Yahmose."

Sobek laughed as he spoke and dipping a cup in the wine, he tossed it off, smacking his lips as he put it down.

"Let us see now whether my father will be as much of a stick-in-the-mud as ever, or whether I shall be able to convert him to up-to-date methods."

"I should go slowly if I were you," Yahmose counseled. "You are always so hotheaded."

Sobek smiled at his brother affectionately. He was in high good-humor.

"Old slow-and-sure," he said scoffingly.

Yahmose smiled, not at all put out.

"It is the best way in the end. Besides, my father has been very good to us. We must do nothing to cause him worry."

Sobek looked at him curiously.

"You are really fond of our father? You are an affectionate creature, Yahmose! Now I—I care for nobody—for nobody, that is, but Sobek, long life to him!"

He took another long draught of wine.

"Be careful," Yahmose said warningly. "You have eaten little today. Sometimes, then, when one drinks wine—"

He broke off with a sudden contortion of the lips.

"What is the matter, Yahmose?"

"Nothing—a sudden pain—I, it is nothing. . . ."

But he raised a hand to wipe his forehead which was suddenly bedewed with moisture.

"You do not look well."

"I was quite alright just now."

"So long as nobody has poisoned the wine." Sobek laughed at his own words and stretched out his arm toward the jar. Then, in the very act, his arm stiffened, his body bent forard in a sudden spasm of agony. . . .

"Yahmose," he gasped. "Yahmose . . . I—too . . ."

Yahmose, slipping forward, was bent double. A half-stifled cry came from him.

Sobek was now contorted with pain. He raised his voice.

"Help. Send for a physician—a physician. . . ."

Henet came running out of the house.

"You called? What was it that you said? What is it?"

Her alarmed cries brought others.

The two brothers were both groaning with pain.

Yahmose said faintly. "The wine—poison—send for a physician. . . ."

Henet uttered a shrill cry: "More misfortune. In truth this house is accursed. Quick! Hurry! Send to the Temple for the Divine Father Mersu, who is a skilled physician of great experience."

II

Imhotep paced up and down the central hall of the house. His fine linen robe was soiled and limp, he had neither bathed nor changed. His face was drawn with worry and fear.

From the back of the house came a low sound of keening and weeping—the women's contribution to the catastrophe that had overrun the household—Henet's voice led the mourners.

From a room at the side, the voice of the physician and priest Mersu was heard raised as he strove over the inert body of Yahmose. Renisenb, stealing quietly out of the women's quarters into the central hall, was drawn by the sound. Her feet took her to the open doorway and she paused there, feeling a healing balm in the sonorous words that the priest was reciting.

"O, Isis, great of magic, loose thou me, release thou me from all things bad, evil, and red, from the stroke of a God, from the stroke of a Goddess, from dead man or dead woman, from a male foe, or a female for who may oppose himself to me. . . ."

A faint sigh came fluttering from Yahmose's lips.

In her heart Renisenb joined in the prayer.

"O Isis—O great Isis—save him—save my brother Yahmose—thou who are great of magic. . . ."

Thoughts passed confusedly through her mind, raised there by the words of the incantation.

"From all things bad, evil, and red. . . . That is what has been the matter with us here in this house—yes, red thoughts, angry thoughts—the anger of a dead woman."

She spoke within the confines of her thoughts, directly addressing the person in her mind.

"It was not Yahmose who harmed you, Nofret—and though Satipy was his wife, you cannot hold him responsible for her actions—he never had any control over her—no one had. Satipy who harmed you is dead. Is that not enough? Sobek is dead—Sobek who only spoke against you, yet never actually harmed you. O Isis, do not let Yahmose also die—save him from the vengeful hatred of Nofret."

Imhotep, pacing distractedly up and down, looked up and saw his daughter and his face relaxed with affection.

"Come here, Renisenb, dear child."

She ran to him and he put his arm round her.

"Oh, Father, what do they say?"

Imhotep said heavily: "They say that in Yahmose's case there is hope. Sobek—you know?"

"Yes, yes. Have you not heard us wailing?"

"He died at dawn," said Imhotep. "Sobek, my strong, handsome son." His voice faltered and broke.

"Oh, it is wicked, cruel— Could nothing be done?"

"All was done that could be. Potions forcing him to vomit. Administration of the juice of potent herbs. Sacred amulets were applied and mighty incantations spoken. All was of no avail. Mersu is a skilled physician. If he could not save my son—then it was the will of the Gods that he should not be saved."

The priest-physician's voice rose in a final high chant and he came out from the chamber wiping the perspiration from his forehead.

"Well?" Imhotep accosted him eagerly.

The physician said gravely: "By the favor of Isis your son will live. He is weak but the crisis of the poison has passed. The evil influence is on the wane."

He went on, slightly altering his tone to a more everyday intonation.

"It is fortunate that Yahmose drank much less of the poisoned wine. He sipped his drink, whereas it seems your son Sobek tossed it off at a draught."

Imhotep groaned.

"You have there the difference between them. Yahmose timid, cautious and slow in his approach to everything, even eating and drinking. Sobek, always given to excess, generous, free-handed—alas! Impudent."

Then he added sharply: "And the wine was definitely poisoned?"

"'There is no doubt of that, Imhotep. The residue was tested by my young assistants—of the animals treated with it, all died more or less swiftly."

"And yet I who had drunk of the same wine not an hour earlier have felt no ill effects."

"It was doubtless not poisoned at that time—the poison was added afterward."

Imhotep struck the palm of one hand with his other hand clenched into a fist.

"No one," he declared, "no one living would dare to poison my sons here under my roof! Such a thing is impossible. No *living* person, I say!"

Mersu inclined his head slightly. His face became inscrutable. "Of that, Imhotep, you are the best judge."

Imhotep stood scratching nervously behind the ear.

"There is a tale I would like you to hear," he said abruptly.

He clapped his hands and as a servant ran in, he called: "Bring the herd boy here."

He turned back to Mersu, saying: "This is a boy whose wits are not at the best. He takes in what people say to him with difficulty and he has not full possession of his faculties. Nevertheless he has eyes and his eyesight is good, and he is moreover devoted to my son Yahmose, who has been gentle with him and kindly to his infirmity."

The servant came back, dragging by the hand a thin, almost black-skinned boy, clad in a loincloth, with slightly squinting eyes and a frightened, witless face.

"Speak," said Imhotep sharply. "Repeat what you have told me just now."

The boy hung his head, his fingers began kneading the cloth round his waist.

"Speak," shouted Imhotep.

Esa came hobbling in, supported by her stick and peering with her dim eyes.

"You are terrifying the child. Here, Renisenb, give him this jujube. There, boy, tell us what you saw."

The boy gazed from one to the other of them.

Esa prompted him.

"It was yesterday, as you passed the door of the courtyard—you saw— What did you see?"

The boy shook his head, glancing sideways. He murmured: "Where is my Lord Yahmose?"

The priest spoke with authority and kindliness.

"It is the wish of your Lord Yahmose that you tell us your tale. Have no fear. No one will hurt you."

A gleam of light passed over the boy's face.

"My Lord Yahmose has been good to me. I will do what he wishes."

He paused. Imhotep seemed about to break out, but a look from the physician restrained him.

Suddenly the boy spoke, nervously, in a quick gabble, and with a look from side to side as he spoke, as though he was afraid that some unseen presence would overhear him.

"It was the little donkey—protected by Set and always up to mischief. I ran after him with my stick. He went past the big gate of the courtyard, and I looked in through the gate at the house. There was no one on the porch but there was a wine stand there. And then a woman, a lady of the house, came out upon the porch from the house. She walked to the wine jar and she held out her hands over it and then—and then—she went back into the house, I think. I do not know. For I heard footsteps and turned and saw in the distance my Lord Yahmose coming back from the fields. So I went on seeking the little donkey, and my Lord Yahmose went into the courtyard."

"And you did not warn him," cried Imhotep angrily. "You said nothing."

The boy cried out, "I did not know anything was wrong. I saw nothing but the lady standing there smiling down as she spread out her hand over the wine jar. . . . I saw nothing. . . ."

"Who was this lady, boy?" asked the priest.

With a vacant expression the boy shook his head.

"I do not know. She must have been one of the ladies of the house. I do not know them. I have the herds at the far end of the cultivation. She wore a dress of dyed linen."

Renisenb started.

"A servant, perhaps?" suggested the priest, watching the boy.

The boy shook his head positively.

"She was not a servant. . . . She had a wig on her head and she wore jewels—a servant does not wear jewels."

"Jewels?" demanded Imhotep. "What jewels?"

The boy replied eagerly and confidently as though at last he had overcome his fear and was quite sure of what he was saying.

"Three strings of beads, with gold lions hanging from them in front . . ."

Esa's stick clattered to the floor. Imhotep uttered a stifled cry.

Mersu said threateningly: "If you are lying, boy—"

"It is the truth. I swear it is the truth." The boy's voice rose shrill and clear.

From the side chamber where the ill man lay, Yahmose cried feebly: "What is all this?"

The boy darted through the open door and crouched down by the couch on which Yahmose lay.

"Master, they will torture me."

"No, no." Yahmose turned his head with difficulty on the curved, wooden headrest. "Do not let the child be hurt. He is simple but honest. Promise me."

"Of course, of course," said Imhotep. "There is no need. It is clear the boy has told all that he knows—and I do not think he is inventing. Be off with you, child, but do not return to the far herds. Stay near the house so that we can summon you again if we need you."

The boy rose to his feet. He bent a reluctant glance upon Yahmose.

"You are ill, Lord Yahmose?"

Yahmose smiled faintly. "Have no fear. I am not going to die. Go now—and be obedient to what you have been told."

Smiling happily now, the boy went off. The priest examined Yahmose's eyes and felt the rate at which the blood was coursing under the skin. Then, recommending him to sleep, he went with the others out into the central hall again.

He said to Imhotep: "You recognize the description the boy gave?"

Imhotep nodded. His deep, bronze cheeks showed a sickly plum color.

Renisenb said: "Only Nofret ever wore a dress of dyed linen. It was a new fashion she brought with her from the cities in the north. But those dresses were buried with her."

Imhotep said: "And the three strings of beads with the lion's heads in gold were what I gave her. There is no other such ornament in the house. It was costly and unusual. All her jewelry, with the exception of a trumpery string of carnelian beads, was buried with her and is sealed in her tomb."

He flung out his arms.

"What persecution—what vindictiveness—is this! My concubine whom I treated well, to whom I paid all honor, whom I buried with the proper rites, sparing no expense. I have eaten and drunk with her in friendship—to that all can bear witness. She had had nothing of which to complain—I did indeed more for her than would have been considered right and fitting. I was prepared to favor her to the detriment of my sons who were born to me. Why, then, should she thus come back from the dead to persecute me and my family?"

Mersu said gravely: "It seems that it is not against you personally that the dead woman wishes evil. The wine when you drank it was harmless. Who in your family did injury to your dead concubine?"

"A woman who is dead," Imhotep answered shortly.

"I see. You mean the wife of your son Yahmose?"

"Yes." Imhotep paused, then broke out: "But what can be done, Reverend Father? How can we counteract this malice? Oh, evil day when I first took the woman into my house!"

"An evil day indeed," said Kait in a deep voice, coming forward from the entrance to the women's quarters.

Her eyes were heavy with the tears she had shed, and her plain face had a strength and resolution which made it noticeable. Her voice, deep and hoarse, was shaken with anger.

"It was an evil day when you brought Nofret here, Imhotep, to destroy the cleverest and most handsome of your sons! She has brought death to Satipy and death to my Sobek, and Yahmose has only narrowly escaped. Who will be next? Will she spare even children—she who struck my little Ankh? Something must be *done,* Imhotep!"

"Something *must* be done," Imhotep echoed, looking imploringly at the priest.

The latter nodded his head with calm assumption.

"There are ways and means, Imhotep. Once we are sure of our facts, we can go ahead. I have in mind your dead wife, Ashayet. She was a woman of influential family. She can invoke powerful interests in the Land of the Dead who can intervene on your behalf and against whom the woman Nofret will have no power. We must take counsel together."

Kait gave a short laugh.

"Do not wait too long. Men are always the same—Yes, even priests! Everything must be done according to law and precedent. But I say, act quickly—or there will be more dead beneath this room."

She turned and went out.

"An excellent woman," murmured Imhotep. "A devoted mother to her children, a dutiful wife—but her manners, sometimes, are hardly what they should be—to the head of the house. Naturally at such a time I forgive her. We are all distraught. We hardly know what we are doing."

He clasped his hands to his head.

"Some of us seldom do know what we are doing," remarked Esa.

Imhotep shot an annoyed glance at her. The physician prepared to take his leave and Imhotep went out with him onto the porch, receiving instructions for the care of the sick man.

Renisenb, left behind, looked inquiringly at her grandmother.

Esa was sitting very still. She was frowning and the expression on her face was so curious that Renisenb asked timidly: "What is it that you are thinking, Grandmother?"

"Thinking is the word, Renisenb. Such curious things are happening in this house that it is very necessary for someone to think."

"They are terrible," said Renisenb with a shiver. "They frighten me."

"They frighten *me,*" said Esa. "But not perhaps for the same reason."

With the old familiar gesture, she pushed the wig on her head askew.

"But Yahmose will not die now," said Renisenb. "He will live." Esa nodded.

"Yes, a master physician reached him in time. On another occasion, though, he may not be so lucky."

"You think—there will be other happenings like this?"

"I think that Yahmose and you and Ipy—and perhaps Kait too had better be very careful indeed what you eat and drink. See always that a slave tastes it first."

"And you, Grandmother?"

Esa smiled her sardonic smile.

"I, Renisenb, am an old woman, and I love life as only the old can, savoring every hour, every minute, that is left to them. Of you all I have the best chance of life—because I shall be more careful than any of you."

"And my father? Surely Nofret would wish no evil to my father?"

"Your father? I do not know. . . . No, I do not know. I cannot as yet see clearly. Tomorrow, when I have thought about it all, I must speak once more with that herd boy. There was something about his story—"

She broke off, frowning. Then, with a sigh, she rose to her feet, and helping herself with her stick, limped slowly back to her own quarters.

Renisenb went into her brother's room. He was sleeping and she crept out again softly. After a moment's hesitation she went to Kait's quarters. She stood in the doorway unnoticed, watching Kait sing one of the children to sleep. Kait's face was calm and placid again—she looked so much as usual that for a moment Renisenb felt that the tragic occurrences of the last twenty-four hours were a dream.

She turned slowly away and went to her own apartment. On the table, amongst her own cosmetic boxes and jars, was the little jewel case that had belonged to Nofret.

Renisenb picked it up and stood looking at it as it lay on the palm of her hand. Nofret had touched it, had held it—it was her possession.

And again a wave of pity swept over Renisenb, allied to the queer sense of understanding. Nofret had been unhappy. As she had held this little box in her hand perhaps she had deliberately forced that unhappiness into malice and hatred . . . and even now that hatred was unabated . . . was still seeking revenge. . . . Oh, no, surely not—surely not!

Almost mechanically, Renisenb twisted the two buttons and slid back the lid. The carnelian beads were there and the broken amulet and *something else*. . . .

Her heart beating violently, Renisenb drew out a necklace of gold beads with gold lions in front. . . .

15

First Month of Summer, 30th Day

THE FINDING OF the necklace frightened Renisenb badly.

On the impulse of the minute she replaced it quickly in the jewel box, slid home the lid and tied the string round the buttons again. Her instinct was to conceal her discovery. She even glanced fearfully behind her to make sure that no one had watched what she had been doing.

She passed a sleepless night, twisting to and fro uneasily and settling and resettling her head on the curved wooden headrest of her bed.

By the morning she had decided that she must confide in someone. She could not bear the weight of that disturbing discovery alone. Twice in the night she had started up, wondering if, perhaps, she might perceive Nofret's figure standing menacingly by her side. But there was nothing to be seen.

Taking the lion necklace from the jewel box, Renisenb hid it in the folds of her linen dress. She had only just done so when Henet come bustling in. Her eyes were bright and sharp with the pleasure of having fresh news to impart.

"Just imagine, Renisenb, isn't it terrible? That boy—the herd boy, you know—fast asleep this morning out by the cornbins and everyone shaking him and yelling in his ear—and now it seems that he'll never wake again. It's as though he'd drunk the poppy juice—and maybe he did—but if so, who gave it to him? Nobody here, that I'll be bound. And it's not likely he'd take it himself. Oh, we might have known how it would be yesterday." Henet's hand went to one of the many amulets she wore. "Amûn protect us against the evil spirits of the dead! The boy told what he saw. He told how he saw Her. And so She came back and gave him poppy juice to close his eyes forever. Oh, She's very powerful, that Nofret! She's been abroad, you know, out of Egypt. I dare swear she got to know all sorts of outlandish primitive magic. We're not safe in this house—none of us are safe. Your father should give several bulls to Amûn—a whole herd if necessary—this isn't a time for economy. We've got to protect ourselves. We must appeal to your mother—that's what Imhotep is planning to do. The priest Mersu says so. A solemn letter to the Dead. Hori is busy now drawing up the terms of it. Your father was for addressing it to Nofret—appealing to her. You know: 'Most excellent Nofret, what evil thing have I ever done to you—' etc. But as the Divine Father Mersu pointed out, it needs strongers measures than *that*. Now your mother, Ashayet, was a great lady. Her mother's brother was the Nomarch and her brother was Chief Butler to the Vizier at Thebes. If it's once brought to *her* knowledge, she'll see to it that a mere concubine isn't allowed to destroy her own children! Oh, yes, we'll get justice done. As I say, Hori is drawing up the plea to her now."

It had been Renisenb's intention to seek out Hori and tell him about her finding of the lion necklace. But if Hori were busy with the priests at the Temple of Isis it was hopeless to think of trying to get hold of him alone.

Should she go to her father? Dissatisfied, Renisenb shook her head. Her old childish belief in her father's omnipotence had quite passed away. She realized now how quickly in times of crisis he went to pieces—a fussy pomposity replacing any real strength. If Yahmose were not ill, she could have told him, though she doubted if he would have any very practical counsels to offer. He would probably insist on the matter being laid before Imhotep.

And that, Renisenb felt with increasing urgency, was at all costs to be avoided. The first thing Imhotep would do would be to blazon the whole thing abroad, and Renisenb had strong instinct for keeping it secret—though for what exact reason she would have been hard put to it to say.

No, it was Hori's advice she wanted. Hori would, as always, know the right thing to do. He would take the necklace from her and at the same time take her worry and perplexity away. He would look at her with those kind, grave eyes and instantly she would feel that now all was well. . . .

For a moment Renisenb was tempted to confide in Kait—but Kait was unsatifactory; she never listened properly. Perhaps if one got her away from the children—no, it wouldn't do. Kait was nice but stupid.

Renisenb thought. "There is Kameni . . . and there is my grandmother."

Kameni . . . ? There was something pleasurable in the thought of telling Kameni. She could see his face quite clearly in her thoughts—its expression changing from a merry challenge to interest—to apprehension on her behalf. . . . Or would it not be on her behalf?

Why this insidious lurking suspicion that Nofret and Kameni had been closer friends than had appeared on the surface? Because Kameni had helped Nofret in her campaign of detaching Imhotep from his family? He had protested that he could not help himself—but was that true? It was an easy thing to say. Everything Kameni said sounded easy and natural and right. His laugh was so gay that you wanted to laugh. The swing of his body was so graceful as he walked—the turn of his head on those smooth bronze shoulders—his eyes that looked at you—that looked at you—Renisenb's thought broke off confusedly. Kameni's eyes were not Hori's eyes, safe and kind. They demanded; they challenged.

Renisenb's thoughts had brought blood into her cheeks and a sparkle into her eye. But she decided that she would not tell Kameni about the finding of Nofret's necklace. No, she would go to Esa. Esa had impressed her yesterday. Old as she was, the old woman had a grasp of things and a shrewd practical sense that was unshared by anyone else in the family.

Renisenb thought: "She is old. But she will know."

II

At the first mention of the necklace, Esa glanced quickly round, placed a finger to her lips, and held out her hand. Renisenb fumbled in her dress, drew out the necklace and laid it in Esa's hand. Esa held it for a moment close to her dim eyes, then stowed it away in her dress. She said in a low, authoritative voice:

"No more now. Talking in this house is talking to a hundred ears. I have lain awake most of the night thinking, and there is much that must be done."

"My father and Hori have gone to the Temple of Isis to confer with the priest Mersu on the drawing up of a petition to my mother for her intervention."

"I know. Well, let your father concern himself with the spirits of the dead. My thoughts deal with the things of this world. When Hori returns, bring him here to me. There are things that must be said and discussed—and Hori I can trust."

"Hori will know what to do," said Renisenb happily.

Esa looked at her curiously.

"You go often up to see him at the Tomb, do you not? What do you talk about, you and Hori?"

Renisenb shook her head vaguely.

"Oh, the River—and Egypt—and the way the light changes and the colors of the sand below and the rocks. . . . But very often we do not talk at all. I just sit there and it is peaceful, with no scolding voices and no crying children and no bustle of coming and going. I can think my own thoughts and Hori does not interrupt them. And then, sometimes, I look up and find him watching me and we both smile. . . . I can be happy there."

Esa said slowly: "You are lucky, Renisenb. You have found the happiness that is inside everybody's own heart. To most women happiness means coming and going, busied over small affairs. It is care for one's children and laughter and conversation and quarrels with other women and alternate love and anger with a man. It is made up of small things strung together like beads on a string."

"Has your life been like that, Grandmother?"

"Most of it. But now that I am old and sit much alone and my sight is dim and I walk with difficulty—then I realize that there is a life within as well as a life without. But I am too old now to learn the true way of it—and so I scold my little maid and enjoy good food hot from the kitchen and savor all the many different kinds of bread that we bake and enjoy ripe grapes and the juice from pomegranates. These things remain when others go. The children that I have loved most are now dead. Your father, Re help him, was always a fool. I loved him when he was a toddling little boy but now he irritates me with his airs of importance. Of my grandchildren I love you, Renisenb—and talking of grandchildren, where is Ipy? I have not seen him today or yesterday."

"He is very busy superintending the storing of the grain. My father left him in charge."

Esa grinned.

"That will please our young gander. He will be strutting about full of his own importance. When he comes in to eat tell him to come to me."

"Yes, Esa."

"For the rest, Renisenb, *silence*. . . ."

III

"You wanted to see me, Grandmother?"

Ipy stood smiling and arrogant, his head held a little on one side, a flower held between his white teeth. He looked very pleased with himself and with life generally.

"If you can spare a moment of your valuable time," said Esa, screwing her eyes up to see better and looking him up and down.

The acerbity of her tone made no impression on Ipy.

"It is true that I am very busy today. I have to oversee everything since my father has gone to the Temple."

"Young jackals bark loud," said Esa.

But Ipy was quite imperturbable.

"Come, Grandmother, you must have more to say to me than that."

"Certainly I have more to say. And to begin with, this is a house of mourning. Your brother Sobek's body is already in the hands of the embalmers. Yet your face is as cheerful as though this was a festival day."

Ipy grinned.

"You are no hypocrite, Esa. Would you have me be one? You know very well that there was no love lost between me and Sobek. He did everything he could to thwart and annoy me. He treated me as a child. He gave me all the most humiliating and childish tasks in the fields. Frequently he jeered and laughed at me. And when my father would have associated me with him in partnership, together with my elder brothers, it was Sobek who persuaded him not to do so."

"What makes you think it was Sobek who persuaded him?" asked Esa sharply.

"Kameni told me so."

"Kameni?" Esa raised her eyebrows, pushed her wig on one side, and scratched her head. "Kameni indeed. Now I find that interesting."

"Kameni said he had it from Henet—and we all agree that Henet always knows everything."

"Nevertheless," said Esa dryly, "this is an occasion when Henet was wrong in her facts. Doubtless both Sobek and Yahmose were of the opinion that you were too young for business—but it was I—yes, I—who dissuaded your father from including you."

"You, Grandmother?" The boy stared at her in frank surprise. Then a dark scowl altered the expression of his face, the flower fell from his lips. "Why should you do that? What business was it of yours?"

"My family's business is my business."

"And my father listened to you?"

"Not at the moment," said Esa. "But I will teach you a lesson, my handsome child. Women work roundabout—and they learn—if they are not born with the knowledge—to play on the weaknesses of men. You may remember I sent Henet with the gaming board to the porch in the cool of the evening."

"I remember. My father and I played together. What of it?"

"This. You played three games. And each time being a much cleverer player, you beat your father."

"Yes."

"That is all," said Esa, closing her eyes. "Your father, like all inferior players, did not like being beaten—especially by a chit of a boy. So he remembered my words—and he decided that you were certainly too young to be given a share in the partnership."

Ipy stared at her for a moment. Then he laughed—not a very pleasant laugh.

"You are clever, Esa," he said. "Yes, you may be old, but you are clever. Decidedly you and I have the brains of the family. You have pegged out in the first match on our gaming board. But you will see, I shall win the second. So look to yourself, Grandmother."

"I intend to," said Esa. "And in return for your words, let me advise *you* to look to *yourself*. One of your brothers is dead, the other has been near to death. You also are your father's son—and you may go the same way."

Ipy laughed scornfully.

"There is little fear of that."

"Why not? You also threatened and insulted Nofret."

"Nofret!" Ipy's scorn was unmistakable.

"What is in your mind?" demanded Esa sharply.

"I have my ideas, Grandmother. And I can assure you that Nofret and her spirit tricks will not worry me. Let her do her worst."

There was a shrill wail behind him and Henet ran in crying out: "Foolish boy—imprudent child. Defying the dead! And after we've all had a taste of her quality! And not so much as an amulet on you for protection!"

"Protection? I will protect myself. Get out of my way, Henet. I've got work to do. Those lazy peasants shall know what it is to have a real master over them."

Pushing Henet aside, Ipy strode out of the room.

Esa cut short Henet's wails and lamentations.

"Listen to me, Henet, and stop exclaiming about Ipy. He may know what he is doing or he may not. His manner is very odd. But answer me this: Did you tell Kameni that it was Sobek who had persuaded Imhotep not to include Ipy in the deed of association?"

Henet's voice dropped to its usual whining key.

"I'm sure I'm far too busy in the house to waste my time running about telling people things—and telling Kameni, of all people. I'm sure I'd never speak a word to him if he didn't come and speak to me. He's got a pleasant manner, as you must admit yourself, Esa—and I'm not the only one who thinks so—oh, dear, no! And if a young widow wants to make a new contract, well, she usually fancies a handsome young man—though what Imhotep would say I'm sure I don't know. Kameni is only a junior scribe, when all is said and done."

"Never mind what Kameni is or isn't! Did you tell him that it was Sobek who opposed Ipy being made a partner in the association?"

"Well, really, Esa. I can't remember what I may or may not have said. I didn't actually go and tell anyone anything, that much is sure. But a word passes here and there, and you know yourself that Sobek was saying—and Yahmose too for that matter, though, of course, not so loud nor so often—that Ipy was a mere boy and that it would never do—and for all I know Kameni may have heard him say it himself and not got it from me at all. I never gossip—but after all, a tongue is given one to speak with, and I'm not a deaf mute."

"That you most certainly are not," said Esa. "A tongue, Henet, may sometimes be a weapon. A tongue may cause a death—may cause more than one death. I hope *your* tongue, Henet, has not caused a death."

"Why, Esa, the things you say! And what's in your mind? I'm sure I never say a word to anybody that I wouldn't be willing to let the whole world overhear. I'm so devoted to the whole family—I'd die for any one of them. Oh, they underestimate old Henet's devotion. I promised their dear mother—"

"Ha," said Esa, cutting her short, "here comes my plump reed bird, cooked with leeks and celery. It smells delicious—cooked to a turn. Since you're so devoted, Henet, you can take a little mouthful from one side—just in case it's poisoned."

"Esa!" Henet gave a squeal. "Poisoned! How can you say such things! And cooked in our very own kitchen."

"Well," said Esa, "someone's got to taste it—just in case. And it had better be you, Henet, since you're so willing to die for any member of the family. I don't suppose it would be too painful a death. Come on, Henet. Look how plump and juicy and tasty it is. No, thanks, I don't want to lose my little slave girl. She's young and merry. You've passed your best days, Henet, and it wouldn't matter so much what happened to you. Now then—open your mouth. . . . Delicious isn't it? I declare—you're looking quite green in the face. Didn't you like my little joke? I don't believe you did. Ha ha, he he!"

Esa rolled about with merriment, then composing herself suddenly, she set greedily to work to eat her favorite dish.

16

Second Month of Summer, 1st Day

THE CONSULTATION AT the Temple was over. The exact form of the petition had been drawn up and amended. Hori and two Temple scribes had been busily employed. Now at last the first step had been taken.

The priest signed that the draft of the petition should be read out.

"TO THE MOST EXCELLENT SPIRIT ASHAYET:

"This from your brother and husband. Has the sister forgotten her brother? Has the mother forgotten the children that were born to her? Does not the most excellent Ashayet know that a spirit of evil life menaces her children? Already is Sobek, her son, passed to Osiris by means of poison.

"I treated you in life with all honor. I gave you jewels and dresses, unguents and perfumes and oils for your limbs. Together we ate of good foods, sitting in peace and amity with tables loaded before us. When you were ill I spared no expense. I procured for you a master physician. You were buried with all honor and due with ceremonies and all things needful for your life in the hereafter were provided for you—servants and oxen and food and drink and jewels and raiment. I mourned for you for many years—and after long, long years only did I take a concubine so that I might live as befits a man not yet old.

"This concubine it is that now does evil to your children. Do you not know of this? Perchance you are in ignorance. Surely if Ashayet knows, she will be swift to come to the aid of the sons born to her.

"Is it that Ashayet knows, but that evil is still done because the concubine Nofret is strong in evil magic? Yet surely it is against your will, most excellent Ashayet. Therefore reflect that in the Field of Offerings you have great relatives and powerful helpers. The great and noble Ipi, Chief Butler to the Vizier. Invoke his aid! Also your mother's brother, the great and powerful Meriptah, the Nomarch of the Province. Acquaint him with the shameful truth! Let it be brought before his court. Let witnesses be summoned. Let them testify against Nofret that she has done this evil. Let judgment be given and may Nofret be condemned, and let it be decreed that she do no more evil to this house.

"Oh, excellent Ashayet, if you are angry with this your brother Imhotep in that he did listen to this woman's evil persuasions and did threaten to do injustice to your children that were born of you, then reflect that it is not he alone that suffers, but your children also. Forgive your brother Imhotep aught that he has done for the sake of your children."

The Chief Scribe stopped reading. Mersu nodded approval.

"It is well-expressed. Nothing, I think, has been left out."

Imhotep rose.

"I thank you, Reverend Father. My offering shall reach you before tomorrow's sun sets—cattle, oil and flax. Shall we fix the day after that for the ceremony—the placing of the inscribed bowl in the offering chamber of the Tomb?"

"Make it three days from now. The bowl must be inscribed and the preparations made for the necessary rites."

"As you will. I am anxious that no more mischief should befall.

"I can well understand your anxiety, Imhotep. But have no fear. The good spirit Ashayet will surely answer this appeal, and her kinsfolk have authority and power and can deal justice where it is so richly deserved."

"May Isis allow that it be so! I thank you, Mersu—and for your care and cure of my son, Yahmose. Come, Hori, we have much that must be seen to. Let us return to the house. Ah—this petition does indeed lift a weight off my mind. The excellent Ashayet will not fail her distracted brother."

II

When Hori entered the courtyard, bearing his rolls of papyrus, Renisenb was watching for him. She came running from the lake.

"Hori!"

"Yes, Renisenb?"

"Will you come with me to Esa? She has been waiting and wants you."

"Of course. Let me just see if Imhotep—"

But Imhotep had been buttonholed by Ipy and father and son were engaged in close conversation.

"Let me put down these scrolls and these other things and I will come with you, Renisenb."

Esa looked pleased when Renisenb and Hori came to her.

"Here is Hori, Grandmother. I brought him to you at once."

"Good. Is the air pleasant outside?"

"I—I think so," Renisenb was slightly taken aback.

"Then give me my stick. I will walk a little in the courtyard."

Esa seldom left the house, and Renisenb was surprised. She guided the old woman with a hand below her elbow. They went through the central hall and out onto the porch.

"Will you sit here, Grandmother?"

"No, child, I will walk as far as the lake."

Esa's progress was slow, but although she limped, she was strong on her feet and showed no signs of tiredness. Looking about her, she chose a spot where flowers had been planted in a little bed near the lake and where a sycamore fig tree gave welcome shade.

Then, once established, she said with a grim satisfaction: "There! Now we can talk and no one can overhear our talk."

"You are wise, Esa," said Hori approvingly.

"The things which have to be said must be known only to us three. I trust you, Hori. You have been with us since you were a little boy. You have always been faithful and discreet and wise. Renisenb here is the dearest to me of all my son's children. No harm must come to her, Hori."

"No harm shall come to her, Esa."

Hori did not raise his voice but the tone of it and the look in his face as his eyes met the old woman's amply satisfied her.

"That is well said, Hori—quietly and without heat—but as one who means what he says. Now tell us what has been arranged today?"

Hori recounted the drawing up of the petition and the gist of it. Esa listened carefully.

"Now listen to me, Hori, and look at this." She drew the lion necklace from her dress and handed it to him. She added: "Tell him, Renisenb, where you found this." Renisenb did so. Then Esa said: "Well, Hori, what do you think?"

Hori was silent for a moment, then he asked: "You are old and wise, Esa. What do you think?"

Esa said: "You are one of those, Hori, who do not like to speak rash words unaccompanied with facts. You knew, did you not, from the first how Nofret came to her death?"

"I suspected the truth, Esa. It was only suspicion."

"Exactly. And we have only suspicion now. Yet here, by the lake, between us three, suspicion can be spoken—and afterward not referred to again. Now it seems to me that there are three explanations of the tragic things that happened. The first is that the herd boy spoke truth and that what he saw was indeed Nofret's ghost returned from the dead and that she had an evil determination to revenge herself still further by causing increased sorrow and grief to our family. That may be so—it is said by priests and others to be possible and we do know that illnesses are caused by evil spirits. But it seems to me, who am an old woman and who am not inclined to believe all that priests and others say, that there are other possibilities."

"Such as?" asked Hori.

"Let us admit that Nofret was killed by Satipy, that some time afterward at that same spot Satipy had a vision of Nofret and that, in her fear and guilt, she fell and died. That is all clear enough. But now let us come to another assumption; and that is that after that someone, for a reason we have yet to discover, wished to cause the death of two of Imhotep's sons. That someone counted on a superstitious dread ascribing the deed to the spirit of Nofret—a singularly convenient assumption."

"Who would want to kill Yahmose or Sobek?" cried Renisenb.

"Not a servant," said Esa; "they would not dare. That leaves us with but few people from whom to choose."

"One of *ourselves?* But, Grandmother, that could not be!"

"Ask Hori," said Esa dryly. "You notice he makes no protest."

Renisenb turned to him.

"Hori—surely—"

Hori shook his head gravely.

"Renisenb, you are young and trusting. You think that everyone you know and love is just as they appear to you. You do not know the human heart and the bitterness—yes, and evil—it may contain."

"But who—which one—?"

Esa broke in briskly: "Let us go back to this tale told by the herd boy. He saw a woman dressed in a dyed linen dress wearing Nofret's necklace. Now if it was no spirit, then he saw exactly what he said he did—which means that he saw a woman who was deliberately trying to *appear* like Nofret. It might have been Kait—it might have been Henet—it might have been *you,* Renisenb! From that distance it might have been *anyone* wearing a woman's dress and a wig. Hush—let me go on. The other possibility is that the boy is lying. He told a tale that he had been *taught* to tell. He was obeying someone who had the right to command him and he may have been too dull-witted even to realize the point of the story he was bribed or cajoled to tell. We shall never know now because the boy is dead—in itself a suggestive point. It inclines me to the belief that the boy told a story he had been taught. Questioned closely, as he would have been today, that story could have been broken down—it is easy to discover with a little patience whether a child is lying."

"So you think we have a poisoner in our midst?" asked Hori.

"I do," said Esa, "And you?"

"I think so too," said Hori.

Renisenb glanced from one to the other of them in dismay.

Hori went on: "But the motive seems to me far from clear."

"I agree," said Esa. "That is why I am uneasy. *I do not know who is threatened next.*"

Renisenb broke in: "But one of *us?*" Her tone was still incredulous.

Esa said sternly: "Yes, Renisenb—one of us. Henet or Kait or Ipy, or Kameni, or Imhotep himself—yes, or Esa or Hori or even"—she smiled—"Renisenb."

"You are right, Esa," said Hori. "We must include ourselves."

"But *why?*" Renisenb's voice held wondering horror. *"Why?"*

"If we knew that, we'd know very nearly all we wanted to know," said Esa. "We can only go by who was attacked. Sobek, remember, joined Yahmose unexpectedly after Yahmose had commenced to drink. Therefore it is *certain* that whoever did it wanted to kill Yahmose, less certain that that person wished also to kill Sobek."

"But who could wish to kill Yahmose?" Renisenb spoke with skeptical intonation. "Yahmose, surely, of us all would have no enemies. He is always quiet and kindly."

"Therefore, clearly, the motive was not one of personal hate," said Hori. "As Renisenb says, Yahmose is not the kind of man who makes enemies."

"No," said Esa. "The motive there is more obscure than that. We have here either enmity against the family as a whole, or else there lies behind all these things that covetousness against which the Maxims of Ptahotep warn us. It is, he says, a bundle of every kind of evil and a bag of everything that is blameworthy!"

"I see the direction in which your mind is tending, Esa," said Hori. "But to arrive at any conclusion we shall have to make a forecast of the future."

Esa nodded her head vigorously and her large wig slipped over one ear. Grotesque though this made her appearance, no one was inclined to laugh.

"Make such a forecast, Hori," she said.

Hori was silent for a moment or two, his eyes thoughtful. The two women waited. Then, at last, he spoke.

"If Yahmose had died as intended, then the principal beneficiaries would have been Imhotep's remaining sons, Sobek and Ipy—some part of the estate would doubtless have been set aside for Yahmose's children, but the administration of it would have been in their hands—in Sobek's hands in particular. Sobek would undoubtedly have been the greatest gainer. He would presumably have functioned as ka-priest during Imhotep's absences and would succeed to that office after Imhotep's death. But though Sobek benefited, yet Sobek *cannot* be the guilty person, since he himself drank of the poisoned wine so heartily that he died. Therefore, as far as I can see, the deaths of these two can *benefit* only one person—at the moment, that is—and that person is Ipy."

"Agreed," said Esa. "But I note, Hori that you are farseeing—and I appreciate your qualifying phrase. But let us consider Ipy. He is young and impatient; he has in many ways a bad disposition; he is at the age when the fulfillment of what he desires seems to him the most important thing in life. He felt anger and resentment against his elder brothers and considered that he had been unjustly excluded from participation in the family partnership. It seems, too, that unwise things were said to him by Kameni—"

"Kameni?"

It was Renisenb who interrupted. Immediately she had done so she flushed and bit her lip. Hori turned his head to look at her. The long, gentle, penetrating look he gave her hurt her in some indefinable way. Esa craned her neck forward and peered at the girl.

"Yes," she said. "By Kameni. Whether or not inspired by Henet is another matter. The fact remains that Ipy is ambitious and arrogant, was resentful of his brothers' superior authority and that he definitely considers himself, as he told me long ago, the superior ruling intelligence of the family."

Esa's tone was dry.

Hori asked: "He said that to *you?*"

"He was kind enough to associate me with himself in the possession of a certain amount of intelligence."

Renisenb demanded incredulously: "You think Ipy deliberately poisoned Yahmose and Sobek?"

"I consider it a possibility, no more. This is suspicion that we talk now—we have not yet come to proof. Men have killed their brothers since the beginning of time, knowing that the Gods dislike such killing, yet driven by the evils of covetousness and hatred. And if Ipy did this thing, we shall not find it easy to get proof of what he did, for Ipy, I freely admit, is clever."

Hori nodded.

"But as I say, it is suspicion we talk here under the sycamore. And we will go on now to considering every member of the household in the light of suspicion. As I say, I exclude the servants because I do not believe for one moment that anyone of them dare do such a thing. But I do not exclude Henet."

"Henet?" cried Renisenb. "But Henet is devoted to us all. She never stops saying so."

'It is easy to utter lies as truth. I have known Henet for many years. I knew her when she came here as a young woman with your mother. She was a relative of hers—poor and unfortunate. Her husband had not cared for her—and indeed Henet was always plain and unattractive—and had divorced her. The one child she bore died in infancy. She came here professing herself devoted to your mother, but I have seen her eyes watching your mother as she moved about the house and courtyard—and I tell you, Renisenb, there was no love in them. No, sour envy was nearer the mark—and as to her professions of love for you all, I distrust them."

"Tell me, Renisenb," said Hori. "Do you yourself feel affection toward Henet?"

"N-no," said Renisenb unwillingly. "I cannot. I have often reproached myself because I dislike her."

"Don't you think that that is because, instinctively, you know her words are false? Does she ever show her reputed love for you by any real service? Has she not always fomented discord between you all by whispering and repeating things that are likely to wound and cause anger?"

"Yes—yes, that is true enough."

Esa gave a dry chuckle.

"You have both eyes and ears in your head, most excellent Hori."

Renisenb argued: "But my father believes in her and is fond of her."

"My son is a fool and always has been," said Esa. "All men like flattery—and Henet applies flattery as lavishly as unguents are applied at a banquet! She may be really devoted to him—sometimes I think she is—but certainly she is devoted to no one else in this house."

"But surely she would not—she would not *kill,*" Renisenb protested. "Why should she want to poison any of us? What good would it do her?"

"None. None. As to why—I know nothing of what goes on inside Henet's head. What she thinks, what she feels—that I do not know. But I think that strange things are brewing behind that cringing, fawning manner. And if so, her reasons are reasons that we, you and I and Hori, would not understand."

Hori nodded.

"There is a rottenness that starts from within. I spoke to Renisenb once of that."

"And I did not understand you," said Renisenb. "But I am beginning to understand better now. It began with the coming of Nofret—I saw then how none of us were quite what I had thought them to be. It made me afraid. . . . And now"—she made a helpless gesture with her hands—"everything is fear. . . ."

"Fear is only incomplete knowledge," said Hori. "When we *know,* Renisenb, then there will be no more fear."

"And then, of course, there is Kait," proceeded Esa.

"Not Kait," protested Renisenb. "Kait would not try to kill Yahmose. It is unbelievable."

"Nothing is unbelievable," said Esa. "That at least I have learned in the course of my life. Kait is a thoroughly stupid woman. and I have always mistrusted stupid women. They are dangerous. They can see only their own immediate surroundings and only one thing at a time. Kait lives at the core of a small world which is herself and her children and Sobek as her children's father. It might occur to her quite simply that to remove Yahmose would be to enrich her children. Sobek had always been unsatisfactory in Imhotep's eyes—he was rash, impatient of control and not amenable. Yahmose was the son on whom Imhotep relied. But with Yahmose gone, Imhotep would *have* to rely on Sobek. She would see it, I think, quite simply like that."

Renisenb shivered. In spite of herself she recognized a true description of Kait's attitude to life. Her gentleness, her tenderness, her quiet loving ways were all directed to her own children. Outside herself and her children and Sobek, the world did not exist for her. She looked at it without curiosity and without interest.

Renisenb said slowly: "But surely she would have realized that it was quite possible for Sobek to come back, as he did, thirsty and also drink the wine?"

"No," said Esa. "I don't think that she would. Kait, as I say, is stupid. She would see only what she wanted to see—Yahmose drinking and dying and the business being put down to the magical intervention of our evil and beautiful Nofret. She would see only one simple thing—not various possibilities or probabilities, and since she did not want Sobek to die, it would never occur to her that he might come back unexpectedly."

"And now Sobek is dead and Yahmose is living! How terrible that must be for her if what you suggest is true."

"It is the kind of thing that happens to you when you are stupid," said Esa. "Things go entirely differently from the way you planned them." She paused and then went on: "And now we come to Kameni."

"Kameni?" Renisenb felt it necessary to say the word quietly and without protest. Once again she was uncomfortably aware of Hori's eyes on her.

"Yes, we cannot exclude Kameni. He has no known motive for injuring us—but then what do we really know of him? He comes from the north—from the same part of Egypt as Nofret. He helped her—willingly or unwillingly, who can say?—to turn Imhotep's heart against the children that had been born to him. I have watched him sometimes and in truth I can make little of him. He seems to me, on the whole, a commonplace young man with a certain shrewdness of mind, and also, besides being handsome, with a certain something that draws after him the eyes of women. Yes, women will always like Kameni and yet I think—I may be wrong—that he is not one of those who have a real hold on their hearts and minds. He seems always gay and lighthearted and he showed no great concern at the time of Nofret's death.

"But all this is outward seeming. Who can tell what goes on in the human heart? A determined man could easily play a part. . . . Does Kameni in reality passionately resent Nofret's death, and does he seek to exact revenge for it? Since Satipy killed Nofret, must Yahmose, her huband, also die? Yes, and Sobek too, who threatened her—and perhaps Kait, who persecuted her in petty ways, and Ipy, who also hated her. It seems fantastic, but who can tell?"

Esa paused. She looked at Hori.

"Who can tell, Esa?"

Esa peered at him shrewdly.

"Perhaps you can tell, Hori? You think you know, do you not?"

Hori was silent for a moment, then he said: "I have an idea of my own, yes, as to who poisoned that wine and why—but it is not as yet very clear—and indeed I do not see—" He paused for a minute, frowning, then shook his head. "No, I could make no definite accusation."

"We talk only suspicion here. Go on, Hori, speak."

Hori shook his head.

"No, Esa. It is only a nebulous thought. . . . And if it were true, then it is better for you not to know. The knowledge might be dangerous. And the same applies to Renisenb."

"Then the knowledge is dangerous to you, too, Hori?"

"Yes, it is dangerous. . . . I think, Esa, that we are all in danger—though Renisenb, perhaps, least."

Esa looked at him for some time without speaking.

"I would give a great deal," she said at last, "to know what is in your mind."

Hori did not reply directly. He said, after a moment or two during which he seemed to be thinking: "The only clue to what is in people's minds is in their behavior. If a man behaves strangely, oddly, is not himself—"

"Then you suspect him?" asked Renisenb.

"No," said Hori. "That is just what I mean. A man whose mind is evil and whose intentions are evil is conscious of that fact and he knows that he must conceal it at all costs. He dare not, therefore, afford any unusual behavior. . . ."

"A man?" asked Esa.

"Man or woman—it is the same."

"I see," said Esa. She threw him a very sharp glance. Then she said: "And what of us— What of suspicion where we three are concerned?"

"That, too, must be faced," said Hori. "I have been much trusted. The making of contracts and the disposal of crops have been in my hands. As scribe I have dealt with all the accounts. It could be that I have falsified them—as Kameni discovered had been done in the north. Then Yahmose, it may be, might have been puzzled, he might have begun to suspect. Therefore it would be necessary for me to silence Yahmose." He smiled faintly at his own words.

"Oh, Hori," said Renisenb, "how can you say such things! No one who knew you would believe them."

"No one, Renisenb, knows anyone else. Let me tell you that yet once more."

"And I?" said Esa. "Where does suspicion point in my case? Well, I am old. When a brain grows old, it turns sick sometimes. It hates where it used to love. I may be weary of my children's children and seek to destroy my own blood. It is an affliction of an evil spirit that happens sometimes to those who are old."

"And I?" asked Renisenb. "Why should I try to kill my brother whom I love?"

Hori said: "If Yahmose and Sobek and Ipy were dead, then you would be the last of Imhotep's children. He would find you a husband and all here would come to you—and you and your husband would be guardians to Yahmose's and Sobek's children."

Then he smiled.

"But under the sycamore tree, we do not suspect you, Renisenb."

"Under the sycamore tree, or not under the sycamore tree, we love you," said Esa.

17

Second Month of Summer, 1st Day

"SO YOU HAVE been outside the house?" said Henet, bustling in as Esa limped into her room. "A thing you have not done for almost a year!"

Her eyes looked inquisitively at Esa.

"Old people," said Esa, "have whims."

"I saw you sitting by the lake—with Hori and Renisenb."

"Pleasant company, both of them. Is there ever anything you do *not* see, Henet?"

"Really, Esa, I don't know what you mean! You were sitting there plain enough for all the world to see."

"But not near enough for all the world to hear!"

Esa grinned and Henet bridled angrily.

"I don't know why you're so unkind to me, Esa! You're always suggesting things. I'm much too busy seeing that things are done as they should be in this house to listen to other people's conversations. What do *I* care what people say!"

"I've often wondered."

"If it were not for Imhotep, who *does* appreciate me—"

Esa cut in sharply: "Yes, if it were not for Imhotep! It is on Imhotep you depend, is it not? If anything were to happen to Imhotep—"

It was Henet's turn to interrupt.

"Nothing will happen to Imhotep!"

"How do you know, Henet? Is there such safety in this house? Something has happened to Yahmose and Sobek."

"That is true—Sobek died—and Yahmose nearly died."

"Henet!" Esa leaned forward. *"Why did you smile when you said that?"*

"I? Smile?" Henet was taken aback. "You are dreaming, Esa! Is it likely I should smile—at such a moment—talking of such a terrible thing?"

"It is true that I am nearly blind," said Esa. "But I am not quite blind. Sometimes, by a trick of light, by a screwing up of the eyelids, I see very well. It can happen that if anyone is talking to a person they know cannot see well, they are careless. They permit themselves an expression of fact that on other occasions they would not allow. So I ask you again: Why do you smile with such secret satisfaction?"

"What you say is outrageous—quite outrageous!"

"Now you are frightened."

"And who would not be with the things going on in this house?" cried Henet shrilly. "We're all afraid, I'm sure, with evil spirits returning from the dead to torment us! But I know what it is—you've been listening to Hori. What did he say about me?"

"What does Hori know about you, Henet?"

"Nothing—nothing at all. You'd better ask what do *I* know about *him?*"

Esa's eyes grew sharp.

"Well, what do you know?"

Henet tossed her head.

"Ah, you all despise poor Henet! You think she's ugly and stupid. But I know what's going on! There are a lot of things I know—indeed, there's not much I *don't* know of what goes on in this house. I may be stupid, but I can count how many beans are planted to a row. Maybe I see more than clever people like Hori do. When Hori meets me anywhere he has a trick of looking as though I didn't exist, as though he saw something behind me, something that isn't there. He'd better look *at* me, that's what I say. He may think me negligible and stupid—but it's not always the clever ones who know everything. Satipy thought she was clever, and where is she now, I should like to know?"

Henet paused triumphantly—than a qualm seemed to pass over her, and she visibly cringed a little, glancing nervously at Esa.

But Esa seemed lost in some train of thought of her own. She had a shocked, almost frightened look of bewilderment on her face. She said slowly and musingly: "Satipy . . ."

Henet said in her old whining tone: "I'm sorry, Esa, I'm sure, for losing my temper. Really, I don't know what came over me. I didn't mean anything of what I've been saying. . . ."

Looking up, Esa cut her short.

"Go away, Henet. Whether you meant what you said or did not mean what you said does not really matter. But you have uttered one phrase which has awakened new thoughts in my mind. . . . Go, Henet, and I warn you. Be careful of your words and actions. *We want no more deaths in this house.* I hope you understand."

II

Everything is fear. . . .

Renisenb had found those words rising to her lips automatically during the consultation by the lake. It was only afterward that she began to realize their truth.

She set out mechanically to join Kait and the children where they were clustered by the little pavilion, but found that her footsteps lagged and then ceased as if of their own volition.

She was afraid, she found, to join Kait, to look into that plain and placid face, in case she might fancy she saw there the face of a poisoner. She watched Henet bustle out on the porch and back again and her usual sense of repulsion was, she found, heightened. Desperately she turned toward the doorway of the courtyard, and a moment later encountered Ipy striding in, his head held high and a gay smile on his impudent face.

Renisenb found herself staring at him. Ipy, the spoilt child of the family, the handsome, willful little boy she remembered when she had gone away with Khay. . . .

"Why, Renisenb, what is it? Why are you looking at me so strangely?"

"Was I?"

Ipy laughed.

"You are looking as half-witted as Henet."

Renisenb shook her head.

"Henet is not half-witted. She is very astute."

"She has plenty of malice, that I know. In fact, she's a nuisance about the house. I mean to get rid of her."

Renisenb's lips opened and closed. She whispered, "Get rid of her?"

"My dear sister, what is the matter with you? Have you too been seeing evil spirits like that miserable, half-witted black child?"

"You think everyone is half-witted?"

"That child certainly was. Well, it's true I'm inclined to be impatient of stupidity. I've had too much of it. It's no fun, I can tell you, being plagued with two slow-going elder brothers who can't see beyond their own nose! Now that they are out of the way, and there is only my father to deal with, you will soon see the difference. My father will do what *I* say."

Renisenb looked up at him. He looked unusually handsome and arrogant. There was a vitality about him, a sense of triumphant life and vigor, that struck her as above the normal. Some inner consciousness seemed to be affording him this vital sense of well-being.

Renisenb said sharply: "My brothers are not both out of the way, as you put it. Yahmose is alive."

Ipy looked at her with an air of contemptuous mockery.

"And I suppose you think he will get quite well again?"

"Why not?"

Ipy laughed.

"Why not? Well, let us say simply that I disagree with you. Yahmose is finished, done for—he may crawl about for a little and sit and moan in the sun. But he is no longer a man. He has recovered from the first effects of the poison, but you can see yourself, he makes no further headway."

"Then why doesn't he?" Renisenb demanded. "The physician said it would only take a little time before he was quite strong and himself again."

Ipy shrugged his shoulders.

"Physicians do not know everything. They talk wisely and use long words. Blame the wicked Nofret if you like—but Yahmose, your dear brother Yahmose, is doomed."

"And have you no fear yourself, Ipy?"

"Fear? I?" The boy laughed, throwing back his handsome head.

"Nofret did not love you overwell, Ipy."

"Nothing can harm me, Renisenb, unless I choose to let it! I am young still, but I am one of those people who are born to succeed. As for you, Renisenb, you would do well to be on my side, do you hear? You treat me, often, as an irresponsible boy. But I am more than that now. Every month will show a difference. Soon there will be no will but mine in this place. My father may give the orders but though his voice speaks them, the brain that conceives them will be mine!" He took a step or two, paused, and said over his shoulder: "So be careful, Renisenb, that I do not become displeased with *you.*"

As Renisenb stood staring after him, she heard a footstep and turned to see Kait standing beside her.

"What was Ipy saying, Renisenb?"

Renisenb said slowly: "He says that he will be master here soon."

"Does he?" said Kait. "I think otherwise."

III

Ipy ran lightly up the steps of the porch and into the house. The sight of Yahmose lying on a couch seemed to please him. He said gaily: "Well, how goes it, Brother? Are we never to see you back on the cultivation? I cannot understand why everything has not gone to pieces without you?"

Yahmose said fretfully in a weak voice: "I do not understand it at all. The poison is now eliminated. Why do I not regain my strength? I tried to walk this morning and my legs would not support me. I am weak—weak—and what is worse, I seem to grow weaker every day."

Ipy shook his head with facile commiseration.

"That is indeed bad. And the physician's give no help?"

"Mersu's assistant comes every day. He cannot understand my condition. I drink strong decoctions of herbs. The daily incantations are made to the goddess. Special food full of nourishment is prepared for me. There is no reason, so the physician assures me, why I should not rapidly grow strong. Yet instead, I seem to waste away."

"That is too bad," said Ipy.

He went on, singing softly under his breath till he came upon his father and Hori engaged with a sheet of accounts.

Imhotep's face, anxious and careworn, lightened at the sight of his much-loved youngest son. "Here is my Ipy. What have you to report from the estate?"

"All goes well, Father. We have been reaping the barley. A good crop."

"Yes, thanks to Re, all goes well outside. Would it went as well inside. Still I must have faith in Ashayet—she will not refuse to aid us in our distress. I am worried about Yahmose. I cannot understand this lassitude—this unaccountable weakness."

"Yahmose was always a weakling," he said.

"That is not so," said Hori mildly. "His health has always been good."

Ipy said assertively: "Health depends upon the spirit of a man. Yahmose never had any spirit. He was afraid, even, to give orders."

"That is not so lately," said Imhotep. "Yahmose has shown himself to be full of authority in these last months. I have been surprised. But this weakness in the limbs worries me. Mersu assured me that once the effects of the poison had worn off, recovery should be swift."

Hori moved some of the papyrus aside.

"There are other poisons," he said quietly.

"What do you mean?" Imhotep wheeled round.

Hori spoke in a gentle, speculative voice.

"There are poisons known which do not act at once, with violence. They are insiduous. A little taken every day accumulates in the system. Only after long months of weakness, does death come. . . . There is a knowledge of such things among women—they use them sometimes to remove a husband and to make it seem as though his death were natural."

Imhotep grew pale.

"Do you suggest that that—*that*—is what is the matter with Yahmose?"

"I am suggesting that it is a possibility. Though his food is now tasted by a slave before he gets it, such a precaution means nothing, since the amount in any one dish on any one day would cause no ill effect."

"Folly," cried Ipy loudly. "Absolute folly! I do not believe there are such poisons. I have never heard of them."

Hori raised his eyes.

"You are very young, Ipy. There are still things you do not know."

Imhotep exclaimed, "But what can we do? We have appealed to Ashayet. We have sent offerings to the Temple—not that I have ever had much belief in temples. It is women who are credulous about such things. What more can be done?"

Hori said thoughtfully: "Let Yahmose's food be prepared by one trustworthy slave, and let that slave be watched all the time."

"But that means—that *here* in this house—"

"Rubbish," shouted Ipy. "Absolute rubbish."

Hori raised his eyebrows.

"Let it be tried," he said. "We shall soon see if it is rubbish."

Ipy went angrily out of the room. Hori stared thoughtfully after him with a perplexed frown on his face.

IV

Ipy went out of the house in such a rage that he almost knocked over Henet.

"Get out of my way, Henet. You are always creeping about and getting in the way."

"How rough you are, Ipy. You have bruised my arm."

"A good thing. I am tired of you and your sniveling ways. The sooner you are out of this house for good the better—and I shall see that you do go."

Henet's eyes flashed maliciously.

"So you would turn me out, would you? After all the care and love I have bestowed on you all. Devoted, I've been, to the whole family. Your father knows it well enough."

"He's heard about it enough, I'm sure! And so have we! In my opinion you're just an evil-tongued old mischief maker. You helped Nofret with her schemes—that I know well enough. Then she died and you came fawning round us again. But you'll see—in the end my father will listen to *me* and not to your lying tales."

"You're angry, Ipy. What has made you angry?"

"Never mind."

"You're not afraid of something, are you, Ipy? There are odd things going on here."

"You can't frighten me, you old cat."

He flung himself past her and out of the house.

Henet turned slowly inward. A groan from Yahmose attracted her attention. He had raised himself from the couch and was trying to walk. But his legs failed him almost at once and but for Henet's rapid assistance, he would have fallen to the ground.

"There, Yahmose, there. Lie back again."

"How strong you are, Henet. One would not think it to look at you." He settled back again with his head on the wooden headrest. "Thank you. But what is the matter with me? Why this feeling as though my muscles were turned to water?"

"The matter is that this house is bewitched. The work of a she-devil who came to us from the north. No good ever came out of the north."

Yahmose murmured with sudden despondency: "I am dying. Yes, I am dying. . . ."

"Others will die before you," said Henet grimly.

"What? What do you mean?" He raised himself on an elbow and stared at her.

"I know what I am saying." Henet nodded her head several times. "It is not you who will die next. Wait and see."

V

"Why do you avoid me, Renisenb?"

Kameni planted himself directly in Renisenb's way. She flushed and found it difficult to give a suitable answer. It was true that she had deliberately turned aside when she saw Kameni coming.

"Why, Renisenb, tell me why?"

But she had no answer ready—could only shake her head dumbly.

Then she glanced up at him as he stood facing her. She had had a faint dread that Kameni's face too might seem different. It was with a curious gladness that she saw it unchanged, his eyes looking at her gravely and for once no smile upon his lips.

Before the look in his eyes her own fell. Kameni could always disturb her. His nearness affected her physically. Her heart beat a shade faster.

"I know why you avoid me, Renisenb."

She found her voice.

"I—was not avoiding you. I did not see you coming."

"That is a lie." He was smiling now; she could hear it in his voice.

"Renisenb, beautiful Renisenb."

She felt his warm, strong hand round her arm and immediately she shook herself free.

"Do not touch me! I do not like to be touched."

"Why do you fight against me, Renisenb? You know well enough the thing that is between us. You are young and strong and beautiful. It is against nature that you should go on grieving for a husband all your life. I will take you away from this house. It is full of deaths and evil spells. You shall come away with me and be safe."

"And suppose I do not want to come?" said Renisenb with spirit.

Kameni laughed. His teeth gleamed white and strong.

"But you do want to come, only you will not admit it! Life is good, Renisenb, when a sister and brother are together. I will love you and make you happy and you shall be a glorious field to me, your lord. See, I shall no longer sing to Ptah, 'Give me my sister tonight,' but I shall go to Imhotep and say, 'Give me my sister Renisenb.' But I think it is not safe for you here, so I shall take you away. I am a good scribe and I can enter the household of one of the great nobles of Thebes if I wish, though actually I like the country life here—the cultivation and the cattle and the songs of the men who reap, and the little pleasure craft on the River. I would like to sail with you on the River, Renisenb. And we will take Teti with us. She is a beautiful strong child and I will love her and be a good father to her. Come, Renisenb, what do you say?"

Renisenb stood silent. She was conscious of her heart beating fast and she felt a kind of languor stealing over her senses. Yet with this feeling of softness, this yielding, went something else—a feeling of antagonism.

"The touch of his hand on my arm and I am all weakness . . ." she thought. "Because of his strength . . . of his square shoulders . . . his laughing mouth . . . But I know nothing of his mind, of his thoughts, of his heart. There is no peace between us and no sweetness. . . . What do I want? I do not know. . . . But not this . . . No, not this . . ."

She heard herself saying, and even to her own ears the words sounded weak and uncertain: "I do not want another husband . . . I want to be alone . . . to be myself. . . ."

"No, Renisenb, you are wrong. You were not meant to live alone. Your hand says so when it trembles within mine. . . . See?"

With an effort Renisenb drew her hand away.

"I do not love you, Kameni. I think I hate you."

He smiled.

"I do not mind your hating me, Renisenb. Your hate is very close to love. We will speak of this again."

He left her, moving with the swiftness and easy gait of a young gazelle.

Renisenb went slowly on to where Kait and the children were playing by the lake.

Kait spoke to her, but Renisenb answered at random.

Kait, however, did not seem to notice, or else, as usual, her mind was too full of the children to pay much attention to other things.

Suddenly, breaking the silence, Renisenb said: "Shall I take another husband? What do you say, Kait?"

Kait replied placidly without any great interest: "It would be as well, I think. You are strong and young, Renisenb, and you can have many more children."

"Is that all a woman's life is, Kait? To busy myself in the back of the house, to have children, to spend afternoons with them by the lake under the sycamore trees?"

"It is all that matters to a woman. Surely you know that. Do not speak as though you were a slave. Women have power in Egypt—inheritance passes through them to their children. Women are the lifeblood of Egypt."

Renisenb looked thoughtfully at Teti, who was busily making a garland of flowers for her doll. Teti was frowning a little with the concentration of what she was doing. There had been a time when Teti had looked so like Khay, pushing out her underlip, turning her head a little sideways, that Renisenb's heart had been turned over with pain and love. But now not only was Khay's face dim in Renisenb's memory, but Teti no longer had that trick of head-turning and pushing out her lip. There had been other moments when Renisenb had held Teti close to her, feeling the child still part of her own body, her own living flesh, with a passionate sense of ownership. "She is mine, all mine," she had said to herself.

Now, watching her, Renisenb thought: "She is *me*—and she is *Khay*. . . ."

Then Teti looked up, and seeing her mother, she smiled. It was a grave, friendly smile, with confidence in it and pleasure.

Renisenb thought: "No, she is not me and she is not Khay—she is *herself*. She is Teti. She is alone, as I am alone, as we are all alone. If there is love between us we shall be friends, all our life—but if there is not love she will grow up and we shall be strangers. She is Teti and I am Renisenb."

Kait was looking at her curiously.

"What *do* you want, Renisenb? I do not understand."

Renisenb did not answer. How put into words for Kait the things she hardly understood herself? She looked round her, at the courtyard walls, at the gaily colored porch of the house, at the smooth waters of the lake and the graceful little pleasure pavilion, the neat flower beds and the clumps of papyrus. All safe, shut in, nothing to fear, with around her the murmur of the familiar home sounds, the babble of children's voices, the raucous, far-off, shrill clamor of women in the house, the distant lowing of cattle.

She said slowly: "One cannot see the River from here."

Kait looked surprised.

"Why should one want to see it?"

Renisenb said slowly: "I am stupid. I do not know."

Before her eyes, very clearly, she saw spread out the panorama of green fields, rich and lush, and beyond, far away, an enchanted distance of pale rose and amethyst fading into the horizon, and cleaving the two, the pale silver of the Nile. . . .

She caught her breath—for with the vision, the sights and sounds around her faded—there came instead a stillness, a richness, an infinite satisfaction. . . .

She said to herself: "If I turn my head, I shall see Hori. He will look up from his papyrus and smile at me. . . . Presently the sun will set and there will be darkness and then I shall sleep. . . . That will be death."

"What did you say, Renisenb?"

Renisenb started. She was not aware she had spoken aloud. She came back from her vision to reality. Kait was looking at her curiously.

"You said *'death,'* Renisenb. What were you thinking?"

Renisenb shook her head.

"I don't know. I didn't mean—" She looked round her again. How pleasant it was, this family scene, with the splashing water and the children at play. She drew a deep breath.

"How peaceful it is here. One can't imagine anything—horrible—happening here."

But it was by the lake that they found Ipy the next morning. He was sprawled face downward with his face in the water where a hand had held him while he drowned.

18

Second Month of Summer, 10th Day

IMHOTEP SAT HUDDLED down upon himself. He looked very much older, a broken, shrunken old man. On his face was a piteous look of bewilderment.

Henet brought him food and coaxed him to take it.

"Yes, yes, Imhotep, you must keep up your strength."

"Why should I? What is strength? Ipy was strong—strong in youth and beauty—and now he lies in the brine bath. . . . My son, my dearly loved son. The last of my sons."

"No, no, Imhotep—you have Yahmose, your good Yahmose."

"For how long? No, he too is doomed. We are all doomed. What evil is this that has come upon us? Could I know that such things would come of taking a concubine into my house? It is an accepted thing to do—it is righteous and according to the law of men and gods. I treated her with honor. Why, then, should these things come upon me? Or is it Ashayet who wreaks vengeance upon me? Is it she who will not forgive? Certainly she has made no answer to my petition. The evil business still goes on."

"No, no, Imhotep. You must not say that. So short a time has passed since the bowl was placed in the offering-chamber. Does one not know how long affairs of law and justice take in this world—how endless are the delays in the Nomarch's court—and still more when a case goes up to the Vizier? Justice is justice in this world and the next, a business that moves slowly but is adjusted with righteousness in the end."

Imhotep shook his head doubtfully. Henet went on: "Besides, Imhotep, you must remember that Ipy was not Ashayet's son—he was born to your sister Ipi. Why, then, should Ashayet concern herself violently on his behalf? But with Yahmose, it will be different—Yahmose will recover because Ashayet will see to it that he does."

"I must admit, Henet, that your words comfort me. . . . There is much in what you say. Yahmose, it is true, recovers strength now every day. He is a good loyal son—but, oh! For my Ipy—such spirit—such beauty!" Imhotep groaned anew.

"Alas! Alas!" Henet wailed in sympathy.

"That accursed girl and her beauty! Would I had never set eyes on her."

"Yes, indeed, dear master. A daughter of Set if I ever saw one. Learned in magic and evil spells, there can be no doubt about it."

There was the tap of a stick on the floor and Esa came limping into the hall.

She gave a derisive snort.

"Has no one in this house any sense? Have you nothing better to do than bleat out curses against an unfortunate girl who took your fancy and who indulged in a little feminine spite and malice, goaded by the stupid behavior of the stupid wives of your stupid sons?"

"A little spite and malice—is that what you call it, Esa? When, of my three sons, two are dead and one is dying; Oh! That my mother should say such things to me!"

"It seems necessary that someone should say them, since you cannot recognize facts for what they are. Wipe out of your mind this silly superstitious belief that a dead girl's spirit is working this evil. It was a *live* hand that held Ipy's head down in the lake to drown, and a live hand that dropped poison into the wine that Yahmose and Sobek drank. You have an enemy, yes, Imhotep, but an enemy here in this house. And the proof is that since Hori's advice was taken and Renisenb herself prepares Yahmose's food, or a slave prepares it while she watches, and that her hand carries it to him, since then, I say, Yahmose has gained health and strength every day. Try to stop being a fool, Imhotep, and moaning and beating your head—in all of which Henet is being extremely helpful—"

"Oh, Esa, how you misjudge me!"

"In which, I say, Henet assists you—either because she is a fool, too, or for some other reason—"

"May Re forgive you, Esa, for your unkindness to a poor lonely woman!"

Esa swept on, shaking her stick in an impressive gesture.

"Pull yourself together, Imhotep, and *think*. Your dead wife Ashayet, who was a very lovely woman and *not* a fool, by the way, may exert her influnce for you in the other world, but can hardly be expected to do your thinking for you in this one! We have got to *act,* Imhotep, for if we do not, then there will be more deaths."

"A live enemy? An enemy in this house? You really believe that, Esa?"

"Of course I believe it, because it is the only thing that makes sense."

"But then we are all in danger?"

"Certainly we are. In danger, not of spells and spirit hands, but of human agency—of live fingers that drop poison in food and drink, of a human figure that steals up behind a boy who returns late at night from the village and forces his head down in the waters of the lake!"

Imhotep said thoughtfully, "Strength would be needed for that."

"On the face of it, yes, but I am not sure. Ipy had drunk much beer in the village. He was in a wild and boastful mood. It may be that he returned home unsteady on his feet and that, having no fear of the person who accosted him, he bent of his own accord to bathe his face in the lake. Little strength would be needed then."

"What are you trying to say, Esa? That a *woman* did this thing? But it is impossible—the whole thing is impossible—there can be no enemy in this house or we should know it. *I* should know it!"

"There is an evil of the heart, Imhotep, that does not show in the face."

"You mean that one of our servants, or a slave—"

"No servant and no slave, Imhotep."

"One of ourselves? Or else—do you mean Hori or Kameni? But Hori is one of the family. He has proved himself faithful and trustworthy.

"And Kameni—he is a stranger, true, but he is of our blood and he has proved his devotion by his zeal in my service. Moreover, he came to me only this morning and urged that I should consent to his marriage with Renisenb."

"Oh, he did, did he?" Esa showed interest. "And what did you say?"

"What could I say?" Imhotep was fretful. "Is this a time to talk of marriage? I said as much to him."

"And what did he say to that?"

"He said that in his opinion this *was* the time to talk of marriage. He said that Renisenb was not safe in this house."

"I wonder," said Esa. "I very much wonder. . . . Is she? I thought she was—and Hori thought so—but now . . ."

Imhotep went on.

"Can one have marriages and funeral ceremonies going on side by side? It is not decent. The whole Nome would talk about it."

"This is no time for convention," said Esa. "Especially since it would seem that the embalmers' men are with us permanently. All this must be a blessing to Ipi and Montu—the firm must be doing exceptionally well."

"They have put their charges up by ten per cent!" Imhotep was momentarily diverted. "Iniquitous! They say that labor is more expensive."

"They should give us a cut-rate price for quantity!" Esa smiled grimly at her own joke.

"My dear mother"—Imhotep looked at her in horror—"this is not a jest."

"All life is a jest, Imhotep—and it is death who laughs last. Do you not hear it at every feast? Eat, drink and be merry, for tomorrow you die? Well, that is very true for us here—it is a question only of *whose* death will come tomorrow."

"What you say is terrible—terrible! What can be done?"

"Trust no one," said Esa. "That is the first, the most vital thing." She repeated with emphasis: *"Trust no one."*

Henet began to sob.

"Why do you look at *me?* . . . I'm sure if anyone is worthy of trust, I am. I've proved it over all these years. Don't listen to her, Imhotep."

"There, there, my good Henet—naturally I trust you. I know only too well your true and devoted heart."

"You know nothing," said Esa. "None of us know anything. That is our danger."

"You accused *me,*" whined Henet.

"I cannot accuse. I have neither knowledge nor proof—only suspicion."

Imhotep looked up sharply.

"You have suspicion—of whom?"

Esa said slowly: "I have suspected once—and twice—and a third time. I will be honest. I suspected first Ipy—but Ipy is dead, so that suspicion was false. Then I suspected another person—but, on the very day of Ipy's death, yet a third idea came to me. . . ."

She paused.

"Are Hori and Kameni in the house? Send for them here—yes, and Renisenb too from the kitchen. And Kait and Yahmose. I have something to say and all the house should hear it."

II

Esa looked round at the assembled family. She met Yahmose's grave and gentle glance, Kameni's ready smile, the frightened inquiry in Renisenb's eyes, the placid incurious glance of Kait, the quiet inscrutability of Hori's thoughtful gaze, the irritable fear in Imhotep's twitching face and the avid curiosity and—yes—pleasure in Henet's eyes.

She thought: "Their faces tell me nothing. They show only the outward emotion. Yet surely, if I am right, there must be *some* betrayal."

Aloud she said: "I have something to say to you all—but first I will speak only to Henet—here in front of all of you."

Henet's expression changed—the avidity and the pleasure went out of it. She looked frightened. Her voice rose in a shrill protest. "You suspect me, Esa. I knew it! You will make a case against me and how am I, a poor woman with no great wits, to defend myself? I shall be condemned—condemned unheard."

"Not unheard," said Esa with irony, and saw Hori smile.

Henet went on, her voice growing more and more hysterical:

"I have done nothing . . . I am innocent . . . Imhotep, my dearest master, save me. . . ." She flung herself down and clasped him round the knees. Imhotep began to splutter indignantly, meanwhile patting Henet's head.

"Really, Esa, I protest—this is disgraceful. . . ."

Esa cut him short.

"I have made no accusation. I do not accuse without proof. I ask only that Henet shall explain to us here the meaning of certain things she has said."

"I have said nothing—nothing at all. . . ."

"Oh, yes, you have," said Esa. "These are words I heard with my own ears—and my ears are sharp even if my eyes are dim. You said that you knew something about Hori. Now what is it that you know about Hori?"

"Yes, Henet," Hori said. "What do you know about me? Let us have it."

Henet sat back on her haunches and wiped her eyes. She looked sullen and defiant.

"I know nothing," she said. "What should I know?"

"That is what we are waiting for you to tell us," said Hori.

Henet shrugged her shoulders.

"I was just talking. I meant nothing."

Esa said: "I will repeat to you your own words. You said that we all despised you, but that you knew a lot of what was going on in this house—and that you saw more than many clever people saw.

"And then you said this—that when Hori met you, he looked at you as though you didn't exist, as though he saw something behind you—*something that wasn't there.*"

"He always looks like that," said Henet sullenly. "I might be an insect, the way he looks at me—something that practically doesn't matter."

Esa said slowly: "That phrase has remained in my mind—something behind—*something that wasn't there*. Henet said, 'He should have looked *at* me.' And she went on to speak of Satipy—yes, of Satipy—and of how Satipy was clever, but where was Satipy now? . . ."

Esa looked around.

"Does that mean nothing to any of you? Think of Satipy—Satipy who is dead. . . . And remember one should look *at* a person—not at something that isn't there. . . ."

There was a moment's dead silence and then Henet screamed. It was a high, thin scream—a scream, it would seem, of sheer terror. She cried out incoherently: "I didn't— Save me—master. Don't let her . . . I've said nothing—nothing."

Imhotep's pent-up rage burst out.

"This is unpardonable," he roared. "I will not have this poor woman terrified and accused. What have you against her? By your own words, nothing at all."

Yahmose joined in without his usual timidity. "My father is right. If you have a definite accusation to bring against Henet, bring it."

"I do not accuse her," said Esa slowly.

She leaned on her stick. Her figure seemed to have shrunk. She spoke slowly and heavily.

Yahmose turned with authority to Henet.

"Esa is not accusing you of causing the evils that have happened, but if I understand her rightly, she thinks that you have certain knowledge which you are withholding. Therefore, Henet, if there is anything you know, about Hori or another, now is the time to speak. Here, before us all. Speak. What knowledge have you?"

Henet shook her head.

"None."

"Be very sure of what you are saying, Henet. Knowledge is dangerous."

"I know nothing. I swear it, I swear it by the Nine Gods of the Ennead, by the Goddess Maat, by Re himself."

Henet was trembling. Her voice had none of its usual whining affected quality. It sounded awed and sincere.

Esa gave a deep sigh. Her figure bent forward. She murmured: "Help me back to my room."

Hori and Renisenb came quickly to her.

Esa said: "Not you, Renisenb. I will have Hori."

She leaned on him as he helped her from the room toward her own quarters. Glancing up at him she saw his face was stern and unhappy.

She murmured: "Well, Hori?"

"You have been unwise, Esa; very unwise."

"I had to know."

"Yes—but you have taken a terrible risk."

"I see. So you too think the same."

"I have thought so for some time, but there is no proof—no shadow of proof. And even now, Esa, *you* have no *proof*. It is all in your mind."

"It is enough that I *know.*"

"It may be too much."

"What do you mean? Oh, yes, of course."

"Guard yourself, Esa. From now on you are in danger."

"We must try to act quickly."

"That, yes. But what can we do? There must be proof."

"I know."

They could say no more. Esa's little maid came running to her mistress. Hori relinquished her to the girl's care and turned away. His face was grave and perplexed.

The little maid chattered and fussed round Esa, but Esa hardly noticed her. She felt old and ill and cold. . . . Once again she saw that intent circle of faces watching her as she spoke.

Only a look—a momentary flash of fear and understanding. Could she have been wrong? Was she so sure of what she had seen? After all, her eyes were dim. . . .

Yes, she was sure. It was less an expression than the sudden tension of a whole body—a hardening—a rigidity. To one person, and one person only, her rambling words had made sense—that deadly, unerring sense which is truth. . . .

19

Second Month of Summer, 15th Day

"NOW THAT THE matter is laid before you, Renisenb, what have you to say?"

Renisenb looked doubtfully from her father to Yahmose. Her head felt dull and bemused.

"I do not know."

The words fell from her lips tonelessly.

"Under ordinary conditions," went on Imhotep, "there would be plenty of time for discussion. I have other kinsmen, and we could select and reject until we settled upon the most suitable as a husband for you. But as it is, life is uncertain—yes, life is uncertain."

His voice faltered. He went on: "That is how the matter stands, Renisenb. Death is facing all three of us today. Yahmose, yourself, myself. At which of us will the peril strike next? Therefore it behoves me to put my affairs in order. If anything should happen to Yahmose, you, my only daughter, will need a man to stand by your side and share your inheritance and perform such duties of my estate as cannot be administered by a woman. For who knows at what moment I may be taken from you? The trusteeship and guardianship of Sobek's children, I have arranged in my will, shall be administered by Hori if Yahmose is no longer alive—also the guardianship of Yahmose's children—since that is his wish—eh, Yahmose?"

Yahmose nodded.

"Hori has always been very close to me. He is as one of my own family."

"Quite, quite," said Imhotep. "But the fact remains he is *not* of the family. Now Kameni is. Therefore, all things considered, he is the best husband available at the moment for Renisenb. So what do you say? Renisenb?"

"I do not know," Renisenb repeated again.

She felt a terrible lassitude.

"He is handsome and pleasing, you will agree?"

"Oh, yes."

"But you do not want to marry him?" Yahmose asked gently.

Renisenb threw her brother a grateful glance. He was so resolved that she should not be hurried or badgered into doing what she did not want to do.

"I really do not know what I want to do." She hurried on: "It is stupid, I know, but I am stupid today. It is—it is the strain under which we are living."

"With Kameni at your side you will feel protected," said Imhotep.

Yahmose asked his father: "Have you considered Hori as a possible husband for Renisenb?"

"Well, yes, it is a possibility. . . ."

"His wife died when he was still a young man. Renisenb knows him well and likes him."

Renisenb sat in a dream while the two men talked. This was her marriage they were discussing, and Yahmose was trying to help her to choose what she herself wanted, but she felt as lifeless as Teti's wooden doll.

Presently she said abruptly, interrupting their speech without even hearing what they were saying: "I will marry Kameni since you think it is a good thing."

Imhotep gave an exclamation of satisfaction and hurried out of the hall. Yahmose came over to his sister. He laid a hand on her shoulder.

"Do you want this marriage, Renisenb? Will you be happy?"

"Why should I not be happy? Kameni is handsome and gay and kind."

"I know," Yahmose still looked dissatisfied and doubtful. "But your happiness is important, Renisenb. You must not let my father rush you into something you do not want. You know how he is."

"Oh, yes, yes, when he gets an idea into his head we all have to give way to it."

"Not necessarily." Yahmose spoke with firmness. "I will not give way here unless you wish it."

"Oh, Yahmose, you never stand out against our father."

"But I will in this case. He cannot force me to agree with him and I shall not do so."

Renisenb looked up at him. How resolute and determined his usually undecided face was looking!

"You are good to me, Yahmose," she said gratefully. "But indeed I am not yielding to compulsion. The old life here, the life I was so pleased to come back to, has passed away. Kameni and I will make a new life together and live as a good brother and sister should."

"If you are sure—"

"I am sure," said Renisenb, and smiling at him affectionately, she went out of the hall onto the porch.

From there she crossed the courtyard. By the edge of the lake Kameni was playing with Teti. Renisenb drew near very quietly and watched them whilst they were still unaware of her approach. Kameni, merry as ever, seemed to be enjoying the game as much as the child did. Renisenb's heart warmed to him. She thought: "He will make a good father to Teti."

Then Kameni turned his head and saw her and stood upright with a laugh.

"We have made Teti's doll a ka-priest," he said. "And he is making the offerings and attending to the ceremonies at the Tomb."

"His name is Meriptah," said Teti. She was very serious. "He has two children and a scribe like Hori." Kameni laughed.

"Teti is very intelligent," he said. "And she is strong and beautiful too."

His eyes went from the child to Renisenb and in their caressing glance Renisenb read the thought in his mind—of the children that she would one day bear him.

It sent a slight thrill through her—yet at the same time a sudden piercing regret. She would have liked in that moment to have seen in his eyes only her own image. She thought: "Why cannot it be only Renisenb he sees?"

Then the feeling passed and she smiled at him gently.

"My father has spoken to me," she said.

"And you consent?"

She hesitated a moment before she answered: "I consent."

The final words were spoken; that was the end. It was all settled. She wished she did not feel so tired and numb.

"Renisenb?"

"Yes, Kameni?"

"Will you sail with me on the River in a pleasure boat? That is a thing I have always wanted to do with you."

Odd that he should say that. The very first moment she had seen him she had thought of a square sail and the River and Khay's laughing face. And now she had forgotten Khay's face and in the place of it, against the sail and the River, it would be Kameni who sat and laughed into her eyes.

That was death. That was what death did to you. "I felt this," you said. "I felt that"—but you only said it, you did not now feel anything. The dead were dead. There was no such thing as resemblance.

Yes, but there was Teti. There were life and the renewing of life, as the waters of the yearly inundation swept away the old and prepared the soil for the new crops.

What had Kait said: "The women of the household must stand together?" What was she, after all, but a woman of a household—whether Renisenb or another, what matter? . . .

Then she heard Kameni's voice—urgent, a little troubled.

"What are you thinking, Renisenb? You go so far away sometimes. . . . Will you come with me on the River?"

"Yes, Kameni, I will come with you."

"We will take Teti too."

II

It was like a dream, Renisenb thought—the boat and the sail and Kameni and herself and Teti. They had escaped from death and the fear of death. This was the beginning of new life.

Kameni spoke and she answered as though in a trance. . . .

"This is my life," she thought, "there is no escape. . . ."

Then, perplexed: "But why do I say to myself 'escape'? What place is there to which I could fly?"

And again there rose before her eyes the little rock chamber beside the Tomb and herself sitting there with one knee drawn up and her chin resting on her hand. . . .

She thought: "But that was something outside life. *This* is life—and there is no escape now until death. . . ."

Kameni moored the boat and she stepped ashore. He lifted Teti out. The child clung to him and her hand at his neck broke the string of an amulet he wore. It fell at Renisenb'a feet. She picked it up. It was an Ankh sign of electrum and gold.

She gave a little regretful cry.

"It is bent. I am sorry. Be careful"—as Kameni took it from her—"it may break."

But his strong fingers, bending it still further, snapped it deliberately in two.

"Oh, what have you done?"

"Take half, Renisenb, and I will take the other. It shall be a sign between us—that we are halves of the same whole."

He held it out to her, and just as she stretched out her hand to take it, something clicked in her brain and she drew in her breath sharply.

"What is it, Renisenb?"

"*Nofret.*"

"What do you mean—*Nofret?*"

Renisenb spoke with swift certainty.

"The broken amulet in Nofret's jewel box. It was *you* who gave it to her. . . . *You and Nofret.* . . . I see everything now. Why she was so unhappy. And I know who put the jewel box in my room. I know everything. . . . Do not lie to me, Kameni, I tell you, I *know.*"

Kameni made no protest. He stood looking at her steadily and his gaze did not falter. When he spoke, his voice was grave and for once there was no smile on his face.

"I shall not lie to you, Renisenb."

He waited a moment, frowning a little as though trying to arrange his thoughts.

"In a way, Renisenb, I am glad that you do know—though it is not quite as you think."

"You gave the broken amulet to her—as you would have given it to me—as a sign that you were halves of the same whole. Those were your words."

"You are angry, Renisenb. I am glad because that shows that you love me. But all the same, I must make you understand. I did not give the Amulet to Nofret. *She* gave it to *me* . . ."

He paused.

"Perhaps you do not believe me, but it is true. I swear that it is true."

Renisenb said slowly: "I will not say that I do not believe you. . . . That may very well be true."

Nofret's dark, unhappy face rose up before her eyes.

Kameni was going on, eagerly, boyishly. . . .

"Try to understand, Renisenb. Nofret was very beautiful. I was flattered and pleased. Who would not be? But I never really loved her—"

Renisenb felt an odd pang of pity. No, Kameni had not loved Nofret—but Nofret had loved Kameni—had loved him despairingly and bitterly. It was at just this spot on the Nile bank that she has spoken to Nofret that morning, offering her friendship and affection. She remembered only too well the dark tide of hate and misery that had emanated from the girl then. The cause of it was clear enough now. Poor Nofret—the concubine of a fussy, elderly man—eating her heart out for love of a gay, careless, handsome young man who had cared little or nothing for her.

Kameni was going on eagerly: "Do you not understand, Renisenb, that as soon as I came here, I saw you and loved you? That from that moment I thought of no one else? Nofret saw it plainly enough."

Yes, Renisenb thought, Nofret had seen it. Nofret had hated her from that moment—and Renisenb did not feel inclined to blame her.

"I did not even want to write the letter to your father. I did not want to have anything to do with Nofret's schemes any more. But it was difficult—you must try to realize that it was difficult."

"Yes, yes." Renisenb spoke impatiently. "All that does not matter. It is only Nofret that matters. She was very unhappy. She loved you, I think, very much."

"Well, I did not love her." Kameni spoke impatiently.

"You are cruel," said Renisenb.

"No, I am a man, that is all. If a woman chooses to make herself miserable about me, it annoys me, that is the simple truth. I did not want Nofret. I wanted you. Oh, Renisenb, you cannot be angry with me for *that?*"

In spite of herself she smiled.

"Do not let Nofret who is dead make trouble between us who are living. I love you, Renisenb, and you love me and that all that matters."

Yes, Renisenb thought, that is all that matters. . . .

She looked at Kameni, who stood with his head a little on one side, a pleading expression on his gay, confident face. He looked very young.

Renisenb thought: "He is right. Nofret is dead and we are alive. I understand her hatred of me now—and I am sorry that she suffered—but it was not my fault. And it was not Kameni's fault that he loved me and not her. These things happen."

Teti, who had been playing on the riverbank, came up and pulled at her mother's hand.

"Shall we go home now? Mother—shall we go home?"

Renisenb gave a deep sigh.

"Yes," she said, "we will go home."

They walked toward the house, Teti running a little way in front of them.

Kameni gave a sign of satisfaction.

"You are generous, Renisenb, as well as lovely. All is the same as it was between us?"

"Yes, Kameni. All is the same."

He lowered his voice.

"Out there on the River—I was very happy. Were you happy too, Renisenb?"

"Yes, I was happy."

"You looked happy. But you looked as though you were thinking of something very far away. I want you to think of *me.*"

"I was thinking of you."

He took her hand and she did not draw it away. He sang very softly under his breath:

"My sister is like the persea tree. . . ."

He felt her hand tremble in his, and heard the quickened pace of her breathing, and was satisfied at last. . . .

III

Renisenb called Henet to her room.

Henet, hurrying in, came to an abrupt stop as she saw Renisenb standing by the open jewel box with the broken amulet in her hand. Renisenb's face was stern and angry.

"You put this jewel box in my room, didn't you, Henet? You wanted me to find that amulet. You wanted me one day—"

"To find out who had the other half? I see you have found out. Well, it's always as well to know, isn't it, Renisenb?"

Henet laughed spitefully.

"You wanted the knowledge to hurt me," said Renisenb, her anger still at white heat. "You like hurting people, don't you, Henet? You never say anything straight out. You wait and wait—until the best moment comes. You hate us all, don't you? You always have."

"The things you're saying, Renisenb! I'm sure you don't mean them!"

But there was no whine in Henet's voice now, only a sly triumph.

"You wanted to make trouble between me and Kameni. Well, there's no trouble."

"That's very nice and forgiving of you, I'm sure, Renisenb. You're quite different from Nofret, aren't you?"

"Do not let us talk of Nofret."

"No, better not, perhaps. Kameni's lucky as well as being good-looking, isn't he? It was lucky for him, I mean, that Nofret died when she did. She could have made a lot of trouble for him—with your father. She wouldn't have liked his marrying you—no, she wouldn't have liked it at all. In fact, I think she would have found some way of stopping it. I'm quite sure she would."

Renisenb looked at her with cold dislike.

"There is always poison in your tongue, Henet. It stings like a scorpion. But you cannot make me unhappy."

"Well, that's splendid, isn't it? You must be very much in love. Oh, he's a handsome young man is Kameni—and he knows how to sing a very pretty love song. He'll always get what he wants, never fear. I admire him, I really do. He always seems so simple and straightforward."

"What are you trying to say, Henet?"

"I'm just telling you that I admire Kameni. And I'm quite sure that he *is* simple and straightforward. It's not put on. The whole thing is quite like one of those tales the storytellers in the bazaars recite. The poor young scribe marrying the master's daughter and sharing the inheritance with her and living happily ever afterward. Wonderful, what good luck a handsome young man always has."

"I am right," said Renisenb. "You do hate us."

"Now how can you say that, Renisenb, when you know how I've slaved for you all ever since your mother died?"

But there was still the evil triumph in Henet's voice rather than the customary whine.

Renisenb looked down again at the jewel box and suddenly another certainty came in to her mind.

"It was *you* who put the gold lion necklace in this box. Don't deny it, Henet, I know, I tell you."

Henet's sly triumph died. She looked suddenly frightened.

"I couldn't help it, Renisenb. I was afraid. . . ."

"What do you mean—afraid?"

Henet came a step nearer and lowered her voice.

"*She* gave it to me—Nofret, I mean. Oh, some time before she died. She gave me one or two—presents. Nofret was generous, you know. Oh, yes, she was generous."

"I dare say she paid you well."

"That's not a nice way of putting it, Renisenb. But I'm telling you all about it. She gave me the gold lion necklace and an amethyst clasp and one or two other things. And then, when that boy came out with his story of having seen a woman with the necklace on—well, I was afraid. I thought maybe they'd think that it was I who poisoned Yahmose's wine. So I put the necklace in the box."

"Is that the truth, Henet? Do you ever speak the truth?"

"I swear it's the truth, Renisenb. I was afraid. . . ."

Renisenb looked at her curiously.

"You're shaking, Henet. You look as though you were afraid now."

"Yes, I am afraid. . . . I've reason to be."

"Why? Tell me."

Henet licked her thin lips. She glanced sideways behind her. Her eyes came back like a hunted animal's.

"Tell me," said Renisenb.

Henet shook her head. She said in an uncertain voice: "There's nothing to tell."

"You know too much, Henet. You've always known too much. You've enjoyed it, but now it's dangerous. That's it, isn't it?"

Henet shook her head again. Then she laughed maliciously.

"You wait, Renisenb. One day I shall hold the whip in this house—and crack it. Wait and see."

Renisenb drew herself up.

"You will not harm *me*, Henet. My mother will not let you harm me."

Henet's face changed—the eyes burned.

"I hated your mother," she said. "I always hated her. . . . And you who have her eyes—and her voice—her beauty and her arrogance—I hate *you*, Renisenb."

Renisenb laughed.

"And at last—I've made you say it!"

20

Second Month of Summer, 15th Day

OLD ESA LIMPED wearily into her room.

She was perplexed and very weary. Age, she realized, was at last taking toll of her. So far she had acknowledged her weariness of body but had been conscious of no weariness of mind. But now she had to admit that the strain of remaining mentally alert was taxing her bodily resources.

If she knew now, as she believed she did, from what quarter danger impended—yet that knowledge permitted of no mental relaxation. Instead she had to be more than ever on her guard since she had deliberately drawn attention to herself. Proof—proof—she must get proof. But how?

It was there, she realized, that her age told against her. She was too tired to improvise—to make the mental creative effort. All she was capable of was defense—to remain alert, watchful, guarding herself.

For the killer—she had no illusion about that—would be quite ready to kill again.

Well, she had no intention of being the next victim. Poison, she felt sure, was the vehicle that would be employed. Violence was not conceivable, since she was never alone, but was always surrounded by servants. So it would be poison. Well, she could counter that. Renisenb should cook her food and bring it to her. She had a wine stand and jar brought to her room, and after a slave had tasted it, she waited twenty-four hours to make sure that no evil results followed. She made Renisenb share her food and her wine—although she had no fear for Renisenb—yet. It might be that there was no fear for Renisenb—ever. But of that one could not be sure.

Between whiles she sat motionless, driving her weary brain to devise means of proving the truth, or watching her little maid starching and pleating her linen dresses, or restringing necklaces and bracelets.

This evening she was very weary. She had joined Imhotep at his request to discuss the question of Renisenb's marriage before he himself spoke to his daughter.

Imhotep, shrunken and fretful, was a shadow of his former self. His manner had lost its pomposity and assurance. He leaned now on his mother indomitable will and determination.

As for Esa, she had been fearful—very fearful—of saying the wrong thing. Lives might hang on an injudicious word.

Yes, she said at last, the idea of marriage was wise. And there was no time to go far afield for a husband amongst the more important members of the family clan. After all, the female line was the important one—her husband would be only the administrator of the inheritance that came to Renisenb and Renisenb's children.

So it came to a question of Hori—a man of integrity, of old and long-proved friendship, the son of a small landowner whose estate had adjoined their own—or young Kameni, with his claims of cousinship.

Esa had weighed the matter carefully before speaking. A false word now—and disaster might result.

Then she had made her answer, stressing it with the force of her indomitable personality. Kameni, she said, was undoubtedly the husband for Renisenb. Their declarations and the necessary attendant festivities—much curtailed owing to the recent bereavements—might take place in a week's time. That is, if Renisenb was willing. Kameni was a fine young man—together they would raise strong children. Moreover, the two of them loved each other.

Well, Esa thought, she had cast her die. The thing would be pegged out now on the gaming board. It was out of her hands. She had done what she thought expedient. If it was hazardous—well, Esa liked a match at the gaming board quite as well as Ipy had. Life was not a matter of safety—it must be hazarded to win the game.

She looked suspiciously round her room when she returned to it. Particularly she examined the big wine jar. It was covered over and sealed as she had left it. She always sealed it when she left the room, and the seal hung safely round her neck.

Yes—she was taking no risks of that kind. Esa chuckled with malicious satisfaction. Not to easy to kill an old woman. Old women knew the value of life—and knew most of the tricks too.

Tomorrow— She called her little maid.

"Where is Hori? Do you know?"

The girl replied that she thought Hori was up at the Tomb in the rock chamber.

Esa nodded satisfaction.

"Go up to him there. Tell him that tomorrow morning, when Imhotep and Yahmose are out on the cultivation, taking Kameni with them for the outing, and when Kait is at the lake with the children, he is to come to me here. Have you understood that? Repeat it."

The little maid did so, and Esa sent her off.

Yes, her plan was satisfactory. The consultation with Hori would be quite private, since she would send Henet on an errand to the weaving sheds. She would warn Hori of what was to come and they could speak freely together.

When the black girl returned with the message that Hori would do as she said, Esa gave a sigh of relief.

Now, these things settled, her weariness spread over her like a flood. She told the girl to bring the pot of sweet-smelling ointment and massage her limbs.

The rhythm soothed her, and the unguent eased the aching of her bones.

She stretched herself out at last, her head on the wooden pillow, and slept—her fears for the moment allayed.

She woke much later with a strange sensation of coldness. Her feet, her hands, were numbed and dead. . . . It was like a constriction stealing all over her body. She could feel it numbing her brain, paralyzing her will, slowing down the beat of her heart.

She thought: "This is death. . . ."

A strange death—death unheralded, with no warning signs.

This, she thought, is how the old die. . . .

And then a surer conviction came to her. This was *not* natural death! This was the enemy striking out of the darkness.

Poison . . .

But how? When? All she had eaten, all she had drunk—tasted, secured—there had been no loophole of error.

Then how? When?

With her last feeble flickers of intelligence, Esa sought to penetrate the mystery. She must know—she *must*—before she died.

She felt the pressure increasing on her heart—the deadly coldness—the slow painful indrawing of her breath.

How had the enemy done this thing?

And suddenly, from the past, a fleeting memory came to aid her understanding. The shaven skin of a lamb—a lump of smelling grease—an experiment of her father's—to show that some poisons could be absorbed by the skin. Wool fat—unguents made of wool fat.

That was how the enemy had reached her. Her pot of sweet-smelling unguent, so necessary to an Egyptian woman. The poison had been in that. . . .

And tomorrow—Hori—he would not know—she could not tell him. . . . It was too late.

In the morning a frightened little slave girl went running through the house crying out that her lady had died in her sleep.

II

Imhotep stood looking down on Esa's dead body. His face was sorrowful, but not suspicious.

His mother, he said, had died naturally enough of old age.

"She was old," he said. "Yes, she was old. It was doubtless time for her to go to Osiris, and all our troubles and sorrows have hastened the end. But it seems to have come peacefully enough. Thank Re in his mercy that here is a death unaided by man or by evil spirit. There is no violence here. See how peaceful she looks."

Renisenb wept and Yahmose comforted her. Henet went about sighing and shaking her head, and saying what a loss Esa would be and how devoted she, Henet, had always been to her. Kameni checked his singing and showed a proper mournful face.

Hori came and stood looking down at the dead woman. It was the hour of her summons to him. He wondered what, exactly, she had meant to say.

She had had something definite to tell him.

Now he would never know.

But he thought, perhaps, that he could guess. . . .

21

Second Month of Summer, 16th Day

"HORI, WAS SHE killed?"

"I think so, Renisenb."

"How?"

"I do not know."

"But she was so careful." The girl's voice was distressed and bewildered. "She was always on the watch. She took every precaution. Everything she ate and drank was proved and tested."

"I know, Renisenb. But all the same, I think she was killed.

"And she was the wisest of us all—the cleverest. She was so sure that no harm could befall her. Hori, it *must* be magic! Evil magic, the spell of an evil spirit."

"You believe that because it is the easiest thing to believe. People are like that. But Esa herself would not have believed it. If she knew—before she died, and did not die in her sleep—she knew it was a living person's work."

"And she knew whose?"

"Yes. She had shown her suspicion too openly. She became a danger to the enemy. The fact that she died proves that her suspicion was correct."

"And she told you—who it was?"

"No," said Hori. "She did not tell me. She never mentioned a name. Nevertheless, her thought and my thought were, I am convinced, the same."

"Then you must tell *me,* Hori, so that I may be on my guard."

"No, Renisenb, I care too much for your safety to do that."

"*Am* I so safe?"

Hori's face darkened. He said: "No, Renisenb, you are not safe. But you are much safer than if you were assured of the truth—for then you would become a definite menace, to be removed at once whatever the risk."

"What about you, Hori? *You* know."

He corrected her. "I *think* I know. But I have said nothing and shown nothing. Esa was unwise. She spoke out. She showed the direction in which her thoughts were tending. She should not have done that— I told her so afterward."

"But you—Hori . . . If anything happens to you . . ."

She stopped. She was aware of Hori's eyes looking into hers.

Grave, intent, seeing straight into her mind and heart. . . .

He took her hands in his and held them lightly.

"Do not fear for me, little Renisenb. . . . All will be well."

Yes, she thought, all will indeed be well if Hori says so. Strange, that feeling of content, of peace, of clear singing happiness—as lovely and as remote as the far distance seen from the Tomb—a distance in which there was no clamor of human demands and restrictions.

Suddenly, almost harshly, she heard herself saying: "I am to marry Kameni."

Hori let her hands go—quietly and quite naturally.

"I know, Renisenb."

"They—my father—they think it is the best thing."

"I know."

He moved away.

The courtyard walls seemed to come nearer, the voices within the house and from the cornbins outside seemed louder and noisier.

Renisenb had only one thought in her mind: "Hori is going. . . ."

She called to him timidly:

"Hori, where are you going?"

"Out to the fields with Yahmose. There is much work there to be done and recorded. The reaping is nearly finished."

"And Kameni?"

"Kameni comes with us."

Renisenb cried out: "I am afraid here. Yes, even in daylight with the servants all round and Re sailing across the heavens, I am afraid."

He came quickly back.

"Do not be afraid, Renisenb. I swear to you that you need not be afraid. Not today."

"But after today?"

"Today is enough to live through—and I swear to you you are not in danger today."

Renisenb looked at him and frowned.

"But we *are* in danger? Yahmose, my father, myself? It is not *I* who am threatened first . . . is that what you think?"

"Try not to think about it, Renisenb. I am doing all I can, though it may appear to you that I am doing nothing."

"I see—" Renisenb looked at him thoughtfully. "Yes, I see. It is to be Yahmose first. The enemy has tried twice with poison and failed. There is to be a third attempt. That is why you will be close beside him—to protect him. And after that it will be the turn of my father and myself. Who is there who hates our family so much that—"

"Hush. You would do well not to talk of these things. Trust me, Renisenb. Try to banish fear from your mind."

Renisenb threw her head back. She faced him proudly. "I do trust you, Hori. You will not let me die. . . . I love life very much and I do not want to leave it."

"You shall not leave it, Renisenb."

"Nor you either, Hori."

"Nor I either."

They smiled at each other and then Hori went away to find Yahmose.

II

Renisenb sat back on her haunches watching Kait.

Kait was helping the children to model toys out of clay, using the water of the lake. Her fingers were busy kneading and shaping, and her voice encouraged the two small serious boys at their task. Kait's face was the same as usual, affectionate, plain, expressionless. The surrounding atmosphere of violent death and constant fear seemed to affect her not at all. . . .

Hori had bidden Renisenb not to think, but with the best will in the world Renisenb could not obey. If Hori knew the enemy, if Esa had known the enemy, then there was no reason why she should not know the enemy too. She might be safer not knowing, but no human creature could be content to have it that way. She wanted to know.

And it must be very easy—very easy indeed. Her father, clearly, could not desire to kill his own children. So that left—who did it leave? It left, starkly and uncompromisingly, two people—Kait and Henet.

Women, both of them . . .

And surely with no reason for killing . . .

Yet Henet hated them all. . . . Yes, undoubtedly Henet hated them. She had admitted hating Renisenb. So why should she not hate the others equally?

Renisenb tried to project herself into the dim, tortured recesses of Henet's brain. Living here all these years, working, protesting her devotion, lying, spying, making mischief . . . Coming here, long ago, as the poor relative of a great and beautiful lady. Seeing that lovely lady happy with husband and children. Repudiated by her own husband, her only child dead . . . Yes, that might be the way of it. Like a wound from a spear thrust that Renisenb had once seen. It had healed quickly over the surface, but beneath evil matters had festered and raged and the arm had swollen and had gone hard to the touch. And then the physician had come and, with a suitable incantation, had plunged a small knife into the hard, swollen, distorted limb. It had been like the breaking down of an irrigation dike. A great stream of evil-smelling stuff had come welling out. . . .

That, perhaps, was like Henet's mind. Sorrow and injury smoothed over too quickly—and festering poison beneath, ever swelling in a great tide of hate and venom.

But did Henet hate Imhotep too? Surely not. For years she had fluttered round him, fawning on him, flattering him. . . . He believed in her implicitly. Surely that devotion could not be wholly feigned?

And if she were devoted to him, could she deliberately inflict all this sorrow and loss upon him?

Ah, but suppose she hated him too—had always hated him? Had flattered him deliberately with a view to bringing out his weaknesses? Supposing Imhotep was the one she hated *most?* Then to a distorted, evil-ridden mind, what better pleasure could there be than this—to let him see his children die off one by one?

"What is the matter, Renisenb?"

Kait was staring at her. "You look so strange."

Renisenb stood up.

"I feel as though I were going to vomit," she said.

In a sense it was true enough. The picture she had been conjuring up induced in her a strong feeling of nausea. Kait accepted the words at their face value.

"You have eaten too many green dates—or perhaps the fish had turned."

"No, no, it is nothing I have eaten. It is the terrible thing we are living through."

"Oh, that."

Kait's disclaimer was no nonchalant that Renisenb stared at her.

"But, Kait are you not afraid?"

"No, I do not think so." Kait considered. "If anything happens to Imhotep, the children will be protected by Hori. Hori is honest. He will guard their inheritance for them."

"Yahmose will do that too."

"Yahmose will die."

"Kait, you say that so calmly. Do you not mind at all? I mean, that my father and Yahmose should die?"

Kait considered a moment or two. Then she shrugged her shoulders.

"We are two women together. Let us be honest. Imhotep I have always considered tyrannical and unfair. He behaved outrageously in the matter of his concubine—letting himself be persuaded by her to disinherit his own flesh and blood. I have never liked Imhotep. As to Yahmose—he is nothing. Satipy ruled him in every way. Lately, since she is gone, he takes authority on himself, gives orders. He would always prefer his children before mine—that is natural. So, if he is to die, it is as well for my children that it should be so—that is how I see it. Hori has no children and he is just. All these happenings have been upsetting—but I have been thinking that very likely they are all for the best."

"You can talk like that, Kait—so calmly, so coldly—when your own husband, whom you loved, was the first to be killed?"

A faint expression of some indefinable nature passed over Kait's face. She gave Renisenb a glance which seemed to contain a certain scornful irony.

"You are very like Teti sometimes, Renisenb. Really, one would swear, no older!"

"You do not mourn for Sobek." Renisenb spoke the words slowly. "No, I have noticed that."

"Come, Renisenb, I have fulfilled all the conventions. I know how a newly made widow should behave."

"Yes—that was all there was to it. . . . So—it means—that you did not love Sobek?"

Kait shrugged her shoulders. "Why should I?"

"Kait! He was your husband—he gave you children."

Kait's expression softened. She looked down at the two small boys engrossed with the clay and then to where Ankh was rolling about chanting to herself and waving her little legs.

"Yes, he gave me my children. For that I thank him. But what was he, after all?

A handsome braggart—a man who was always going to other women. He did not take a sister, decently, into the household, some modest person who would have been useful to us all. No, he went to ill-famed houses, spending too much copper and gold there, drinking too and asking for all the most expensive dancing girls. It was fortunate that Imhotep kept him as short as he did and that he had to account so closely for the sales he made on the estate. What love and respect should I have for a man like that? And what are men anyway? They are necessary to breed children, that is all. But the strength of the race is in the women. It is *we,* Renisenb, who hand down to our children all that is ours. As for men, let them breed and die early. . . ." The scorn and contempt in Kait's voice rose in a note like some musical instrument. Her strong, ugly face was transfigured.

Renisenb thought with dismay: "Kait is strong. If she is stupid, it is with a stupidity that is satisfied with itself. She hates and despises men. I should have known. Once before I caught a glimpse of this—this *menacing* quality. Yes, Kait is strong—"

Unthinkingly, Renisenb's gaze fell on Kait's hands. They were squeezing and kneading clay—strong, muscular hands, and as Renisenb watched them pushing down the clay, she thought of Ipy and of strong hands pushing his head down into the water and holding it there inexorably. Yes, Kait's hands could have done that. . . .

The little girl, Ankh, rolled over onto a thorny spike and set up a wail. Kait rushed to her. She picked her up, holding her to her breast, crooning over her. Her face now was all love and tenderness.

Henet ran out from the porch. "Is anything wrong? The child yelled so loud. I thought perhaps—"

She paused, disappointed. Her eager, mean, spiteful face, hoping for some catastrophe, fell.

Renisenb looked from one woman to the other.

Hate in one face. Love in the other. Which, she wondered, was the more terrible?

III

"Yahmose, be careful of Kait."

"Of Kait!" Yahmose showed his astonishment. "My dear Renisenb—"

"I tell you, she is dangerous."

"Our quiet Kait? She has always been a meek, submissive woman, not very clever—"

Renisenb interrupted him.

"She is neither meek nor submissive. I am afraid of her, Yahmose. I want you to be on your guard."

"Against Kait!" He was still incredulous. "I can hardly see Kait dealing out death all round. She would not have the brains."

"I do not think that it is brains that are concerned. A knowledge of poisons—that is all that has been needed. And you know that such knowledge is often found amongst certain families. They hand it down from mother to daughter. They brew these concoctions themselves from potent herbs. It is the kind of lore that Kait might easily have. She brews medicines for the children when they are ill, you know."

"Yes, that is true." Yahmose spoke thoughtfully.

"Henet too is an evil woman," went on Renisenb.

"Henet—yes. We have never liked her. In fact, but for my father's protection—"

"Our father is deceived in her," said Renisenb.

"That may well be." Yahmose added in a matter-of-fact tone: "She flatters him."

Renisenb looked at him for a moment in surprise. It was the first time she had ever heard Yahmose utter a sentence containing criticism of Imhotep. He had always seemed overawed by his father.

But now, she realized, Yahmose was gradually taking the lead. Imhotep had aged by years in the last few weeks. He was incapable now of giving orders, of making decisions. Even his physical activity seemed impaired. He spent long hours staring in front of him, his eyes filmed and abstracted. Sometimes he seemed not to understand what was said to him.

"Do you think that she—" Renisenb stopped. She looked round and began, "Is it she, do you think, who has—who has—?"

Yahmose caught her by the arm. "Be quiet, Renisenb. These things are better not said—not even whispered."

"Then you think—"

Yahmose said softly and urgently: "Say nothing now. We have plans.

22

Second Month of Summer, 17th Day

The following day was the festival of the new moon. Imhotep was forced to go up to the Tomb to make the offerings. Yahmose begged his father to leave it to him on this occasion, but Imhotep was obdurate. With what seemed now a feeble parody of his old manner, he murmured, "Unless I see to things myself, how can I be sure they are properly done? Have I ever shirked my duties? Have I not provided for all of you, supported you all—"

His voice stopped. "All? *All?* Ah, I forget—my two brave sons—my handsome Sobek—my clever and beloved Ipy—gone from me. Yahmose and Renisenb—my dear son and daughter—you are still with me—but for how long—how long?"

"Many long years, we hope," said Yahmose.

He spoke rather loudly as to a deaf man.

"Eh? What?" Imhotep seemed to have fallen into a coma.

He said suddenly and surprisingly:

"It depends on Henet, does it not? Yes, it depends on Henet."

Yahmose and Renisenb exchanged glances.

Renisenb said gently and clearly: "I do not understand you, Father."

Imhotep muttered something they did not catch. Then, raising his voice a little, but with dull and vacant eyes, he said: "Henet understands me. She always has. She knows how great my responsibilities are—how great. Yes, how great . . . And always ingratitude . . . Therefore there must be retribution. That, I think, is a practice well-established. Presumption must be punished. Henet has always been modest, humble and devoted. She shall be rewarded. . . ."

He drew himself up and said pompously: "You understand, Yahmose. Henet is to have all she wants. Her commands are to be obeyed!"

"But why is this, Father?"

"Because I say so. Because if what Henet wants is done, there will be no more deaths. . . ."

He nodded his head sagely and went away—leaving Yahmose and Renisenb staring at each other in wonder and alarm.

"What does this mean, Yahmose?"

"I do not know, Renisenb. Sometimes I think my father no longer knows what he does or says."

"No—perhaps not. But I think, Yahmose, that *Henet* knows very well what she is saying and doing. She said to me, only the other day, that it would soon be *she* who would crack the whip in this house."

They looked at each other. Then Yahmose put his hand on Renisenb's arm.

"Do not anger her. You show your feelings too plainly, Renisenb. You heard what my father said? If what Henet wants is done—*there will be no more deaths. . . .*"

II

Henet was crouching down on her haunches in one of the storerooms counting out piles of sheets. They were old sheets, and she held the mark on the corner of one close up to her eyes.

"Ashayet," she murmured. "Ashayet's sheets. Marked with the year she came here—she and I together. . . . That's a long time ago. Do you know, I wonder, what your sheets are being used for now, Ashayet?" She broke off in the midst of a chuckle and gave a start as a sound made her glance over her shoulder.

It was Yahmose.

"What are you doing, Henet?"

"The embalmers need more sheets. Piles and piles of sheets they've used. Four hundred cubits they used yesterday alone. It's terrible the way these funerals use up the sheeting! We'll have to use these old ones. They're good quality and not much worn. Your mother's sheets, Yahmose. Yes, your mother's sheets. . . ."

"Who said you might take those?"

Henet laughed.

"Imhotep's given everything into my charge. I don't have to ask leave. He trusts poor old Henet. He knows she'll see to everything in the right way. I've seen to most things in this house for a long time. I think—now—I'm going to have my reward!"

"It looks like it, Henet." Yahmose's tone was mild. "My father said"—he paused—*"everything depends on you."*

"Did he now? Well, that's nice hearing—but perhaps *you* don't think so, Yahmose."

"Well—I'm not quite sure." Yahmose's tone was still mild, but he watched her closely.

"I think you'd better agree with your father, Yahmose. We don't want any more—*trouble,* do we?"

"I don't quite understand. You mean—we don't want any more deaths."

"There are going to be more deaths, Yahmose. Oh, yes—"

"Who is going to die next, Henet?"

"Why do you think I should know that?"

"Because I think you know a great deal. You knew the other day, for instance, that Ipy was going to die. . . . You are very clever, aren't you, Henet?"

Henet bridled.

"So you're beginning to realize that now! I'm not poor, stupid Henet any longer. I'm the one who *knows."*

"What do you know, Henet."

Henet's voice changed. It was low and sharp.

"I know that *at last* I can do as I choose in this house. There will be no one to stop me. Imhotep leans upon me already. And *you* will do the same, eh, Yahmose?"

"And Renisenb?"

Henet laughed, a malicious, happy chuckle.

"Renisenb will not be here."

"You think it is Renisenb who will die next?"

"What do *you* think, Yahmose?"

"I am waiting to hear what *you* say."

"Perhaps I only meant that Renisenb will marry—and go away."

"What *do* you mean, Henet?"

Henet chuckled.

"Esa once said my tongue was dangerous. Perhaps it is!"

She laughed shrilly, swaying to and fro on her heels.

"Well, Yahmose, what do you say? Am I at last to do as I choose in this house?"

Yahmose studied her for a moment before saying: "Yes, Henet. You are so clever. You shall do as you choose."

He turned to meet Hori, who was coming from the main hall and who said: "There you are, Yahmose. Imhotep is awaiting you. It is time to go up to the Tomb."

Yahmose nodded.

"I am coming." He lowered his voice. "Hori—I think Henet is mad—she is definitely afflicted by devils. I begin to believe that *she* has been responsible for all these happenings."

Hori paused for a moment before saying in his quiet, detached voice: "She is a strange woman—and an evil one, I think."

Yahmose lowered his voice still more: "Hori, I think Renisenb is in danger."

"From Henet?"

"Yes. She has just hinted that Renisenb may be the next to—go."

Imhotep's voice came fretfully: "Am I to wait all day? What conduct is this? No one considers me any more. No one knows what I suffer. Where is Henet? Henet understands."

From within the storeroom Henet's chuckle of triumph came shrilly. "Do you hear that, Yahmose? Henet is the one!"

Yahmose said fiercely: "Yes, Henet—I understand. You are the powerful one.

You and my father and I—we three together. . . ."

Hori went off to find Imhotep. Yahmose spoke a few more words to Henet, who nodded, her face sparkling with malicious triumph.

Then Yahmose joined Hori and Imhotep, apologizing for his delay, and the three men went up to the Tomb together.

III

The day passed slowly for Renisenb.

She was restless, passing to and fro from the house to the porch, then to the lake and then back again to the house.

At midday Imhotep returned, and after a meal had been served to him, he came out upon the porch and Renisenb joined him.

She sat with her hands clasped round her knees, occasionally looking up at her father's face. It still wore that absent, bewildered expression. Imhotep spoke little. Once or twice he sighed.

Once he roused himself and asked for Henet. But just at that time Henet had gone with linen to the embalmers.

Renisenb asked her father where Hori and Yahmose were.

"Hori has gone out to the far flax fields. There is a tally to be taken there. Yahmose is on the cultivation. It all falls on him now. . . . Alas for Sobek and Ipy. My boys—my handsome boys. . . ."

Renisenb tried quickly to distract him.

"Cannot Kameni oversee the workers?"

"Kameni? Who is Kameni? I have no son of that name."

"Kameni the scribe. Kameni who is to be my husband."

He stared at her.

"You, Renisenb? But you are to marry Khay."

She sighed, but said no more. It seemed cruel to try to bring him back to the present.

After a little while, however, he roused himself and exclaimed suddenly: "Of course. Kameni! He has gone to give some instructions to the overseer at the brewery. I must go and join him.

He strode away, muttering to himself, but with a resumption of his old manner, so that Renisenb felt a little cheered.

Perhaps this clouding of his brain was only temporary.

She looked round her. There seemed something sinister about the silence of the house and court today. The children were at the far side of the lake. Kait was not with them and Renisenb wondered where she was.

Then Henet came out onto the porch. She looked round her and then came sidling up to Renisenb. She had resumed her old wheedling, humble manner.

"I've been waiting till I could get you alone, Renisenb."

"Why, Henet?"

Henet lowered her voice.

"I've got a message for you—from Hori."

"What does he say?" Renisenb's voice was eager.

"He asks that you should go up to the Tomb."

"Now?"

"No. Be there an hour before sunset. That was the message. If he is not there then, he asks that you will wait until he comes. It is important, he says."

Henet paused—and then added: "I was to wait until I got you alone to say this—and no one was to overhear."

Henet glided away again.

Renisenb felt her spirits lightened. She felt glad at the prospect of going up to the peace and quietness of the Tomb. Glad that she would see Hori and be able to talk to him freely. The only thing that surprised her a little was that he should have entrusted his message to Henet.

Nevertheless, malicious though Henet was, she had delivered the message faithfully.

"And why should I fear Henet at any time?" thought Renisenb. "I am stronger than she is."

She drew herself up proudly. She felt young and confident and very much alive. . . .

IV

After giving the message to Renisenb, Henet went once more into the linen storeroom. She was laughing quietly to herself.

She bent over the disordered piles of sheets.

"We'll be needing more of you soon," she said to them gleefully. "Do you hear, Ashayet? I'm the mistress here now and I'm telling you that your linen will bandage yet another body. And whose body is that, do you think? Hee hee! You've not been able to do much about things, have you? You and your mother's brother, the Nomarch! Justice? What justice can you do in *this* world? Answer me that!"

There was a movement behind the bales of linen. Henet half turned her head.

Then a great width of linen was thrown over her, stifling her mouth and nose. An inexorable hand wound the fabric round and round her body, swathing her like a corpse until her struggles ceased. . . .

23

Second Month of Summer, 17th Day

RENISENB SAT IN the entrance of the rock chamber staring out at the Nile and lost in a queer dream fantasy of her own.

It seemed to her a very long time since the day when she had first sat here soon after her return to her father's house. That had been the day when she had declared so gaily that everything was unchanged, that all in the home was exactly as it had been when she left it eight years before.

She remembered now how Hori had told her that she herself was not the same

Renisenb who had gone away with Khay and how she had answered confidently that she soon would be.

Then Hori had gone on to speak of changes that came from within, of a rottenness that left no outward sign.

She knew now something of what had been in his mind when he said those things. He had been trying to prepare her. She had been so assured, so blind—accepting so easily the outward values of her family.

It had taken Nofret's coming to open her eyes. . . .

Yes, Nofret's coming. It had all hinged on that.

With Nofret had come death. . . .

Whether Nofret had been evil or not, she had certainly brought evil. . . .

And the evil was still in their midst.

For the last time, Renisenb played with the belief that Nofret's spirit was the cause of everything. . . .

Nofret, malicious and dead. . . .

Or Henet, malicious and living . . . Henet the despised, the sycophantic, fawning Henet . . .

Renisenb shivered, stirred, and then slowly rose to her feet.

She could wait for Hori no longer. The sun was on the point of setting. Why, she wondered, had he not come?

She got up, glanced round her, and started to descend the path to the valley below.

It was very quiet at this evening hour. Quiet and beautiful, she thought. What had delayed Hori? If he had come, they would at least have had this hour together. . . .

There would not be many such hours. In the near future, when she was Kameni's wife—

Was she really going to marry Kameni? With a kind of shock Renisenb shook herself free from the mood of dull acquiesence that had held her so long. She felt like a sleeper awakening from a feverish dream. Caught in that stupor of fear and uncertainty, she had assented to whatever had been proposed to her.

But now she was Renisenb again, and if she married Kameni it would be because she wanted to marry him, and not because her family arranged it. Kameni, with his handsome, laughing face! She loved him, didn't she? That was why she was going to marry him.

In this evening hour up here, there were clarity and truth. No confusion. She was Renisenb, walking here above the world, serene and unafraid, herself at last.

Had she not once said to Hori that she must walk down this path alone at the hour of Nofret's death—that whether fear went with her or not, she must still go alone?

Well, she was doing it now. This was just about the hour when she and Satipy had bent over Nofret's body. And it was about this same hour when Satipy in her turn had walked down the path and had suddenly looked back—to see doom overtaking her.

And just about this same point too. What was it that Satipy had heard to make her look suddenly behind her?

Footsteps?

Footsteps . . . but Renisenb heard footsteps now—*following her down the path.*

Her heart gave a sudden leap of fear. It *was* true then! Nofret was behind her, following her. . . .

Fear coursed through her, but her footsteps did not slacken. Nor did they race ahead. She must overcome fear, since there was, in her mind, no evil deed to regret. . . .

She steadied herself, gathered her courage, and, still, walking, turned her head.

Then she felt a great throb of relief. It was Yahmose following her. No spirit from the dead, but her own brother. He must have been busied in the offering chamber of the Tomb and have come out of it just after she had passed.

She stopped with a happy little cry.

"Oh, Yahmose, I'm so glad it's you."

He was coming up to her rapidly. She was just beginning another sentence—a recital of her foolish fears—when the words froze on her lips.

This was not the Yahmose she knew—the gentle, kindly brother. His eyes were very bright and he was passing his tongue quickly over dried lips. His hands, held a little in front of his body, were slightly curved, the fingers looking like talons.

He was looking at her, and the look in his eye was unmistakable. It was the look of a man who had killed and was about to kill again. There was a gloating cruelty, an evil satisfaction in his face. Yahmose—the hidden enemy was Yahmose! Behind the mask of that gentle, kindly face—*this!*

She had thought that her brother loved her—but there was no love in that inhuman, gloating face.

Renisenb screamed—a faint, hopeless scream.

This, she knew, was death. There was no strength in her to match Yahmose's strength. Here, where Nofret had fallen, where the path was narrow, she too would fall to death. . . .

"Yahmose!" It was a last appeal—in that uttering of his name was the love she had always given to this eldest brother. It pleaded in vain. Yahmose laughed, a soft, inhuman, happy little laugh.

Then he rushed forward, those cruel hands with talons curving as though they longed to fasten round her throat. . . .

Renisenb backed up against the cliff face, her hands outstretched in a vain attempt to ward him off. This was terror—death.

And then she heard a sound, a faint, twanging, musical sound. . . .

Something came singing through the air. Yahmose stopped, swayed, then with a loud cry he pitched forward on his face at her feet. She stared down stupidly at the feathered shaft of an arrow.

II

"Yahmose . . . Yahmose . . ."

Renisenb, numbed by shock, repeated the name again, and yet again. It was as though she could not believe it. . . .

She was outside the little rock chamber, Hori's arm still round her. She could hardly recollect how he had led her back up the path. She had been only able to repeat her brother's name in that dazed tone of wonder and horror.

Hori said gently: "Yes, Yahmose. All the time, Yahmose."

"But how? Why? And how *could* it be he? Why, he was poisoned himself. He nearly died."

"No, he ran no risk of dying. He was very careful of how much wine he drank.

He sipped enough to make him ill and he exaggerated his symptoms and his pains. It was the one way, he knew, to disarm suspicion."

"But *he* could not have killed Ipy. Why, he was so weak he could not stand on his feet."

"That, again, was feigned. Do you not remember that Mersu pronounced that once the poison was eliminated, he would regain strength quickly. So he did in reality."

"But *why*, Hori? That is what I cannot make out—why?"

Hori sighed.

"Do you remember, Renisenb, that I talked to you once of the rottenness that comes from within?"

"I remember. Indeed I was thinking of it only this evening."

"You said once that the coming of Nofret brought evil. That was not true. The evil was already here concealed within the hearts of the household. All that Nofret's coming did was to bring it from its hidden place into light. Her presence banished concealment. Kait's gentle motherliness had turned to ruthless egoism for herself and her young. Sobek was no longer the gay and charming young man, but the boastful, dissipated weakling. Ipy was not so much a spoilt, attractive child as a scheming, selfish boy. Through Henet's pretended devotion, the venom began to show clearly. Satipy showed herself as a bully and coward. Imhotep himself had degenerated into a fussy, pompous tyrant."

"I know—I know." Renisenb's hands went to her eyes. "You need not tell me. I have found out little by little for myself. . . . Why should these things happen? Why should this rottenness come, as you say, working from within ?"

Hori shrugged his shoulders.

"Who can tell? It may be that there must always be growth—and that if one does not grow kinder and wiser and greater, then the growth must be the other way, fostering the evil things. Or it may be that the life they all led was too shut in, too folded back upon itself—without breadth or vision. Or it may be that, like a disease of crops, it is contagious, that first one and then another sickened."

"But Yahmose—Yahmose seemed always the same."

"Yes, and that is one reason, Renisenb, why I came to suspect. For the others, by reason of their temperaments, could get relief. But Yahmose has always been timid, easily ruled, and with never enough courage to rebel. He loved Imhotep and worked hard to please him, and Imhotep found him well-meaning but stupid and slow. He despised him. Satipy, too, treated Yahmose with all the scorn of a bullying nature. Slowly his burden of resentment, concealed but deeply felt, grew heavier. The meeker he seemed, the more his inward anger grew.

"And then, just when Yahmose was hoping at last to reap the reward of his industry and diligence, to be recognized and associated with his father, Nofret came. It was Nofret, and perhaps Nofret's beauty, that kindled the final spark. She attacked the manhood of all three brothers. She touched Sobek on the raw by her scorn of him as a fool, she infuriated Ipy by treating him as a truculent child without any claim to manhood, and she showed Yahmose that he was something less than a man in her eyes. It was after Nofret came that Satipy's tongue finally goaded Yahmose beyond endurance. It was her jeers, her taunt that she was a better man than he, that finally sapped his self-control. He met Nofret on this path and—driven beyond endurance—he threw her down."

"But it was *Satipy*—"

"No, no, Renisenb. That is where you were all wrong. From down below

Satipy *saw it happen*. Now do you understand?"

"But Yahmose was with you on the cultivation."

"Yes, for the last hour. But do you not realize, Renisenb, that Nofret's body was *cold?* You felt her cheek yourself. You thought she had fallen a few moments before—but that was impossible. She had been dead at least two hours; otherwise, in that hot sun, her face could never have felt cold to your touch. Satipy saw it happen. Satipy hung around, fearful, uncertain what to do; then she saw you coming and tried to head you off."

"Hori, when did you know all this?"

"I guessed fairly soon. It was Satipy's behavior that told me. She was obviously going about in deadly fear of someone or something—and I was fairly soon convinced that the person she feared was *Yahmose*. She stopped bullying him and instead was eager to obey him in every way. It had been, you see, a terrible shock to her. Yahmose, whom she despised as the meekest of men, had actually been the one to kill Nofret. It turned Satipy's world upside down. Like most bullying women, she was a coward. This new Yahmose terrified her. In her fear she began to talk in her sleep. Yahmose soon realized that she was a danger to him. . . .

"And now, Renisenb, you can realize the truth of what you saw that day with your own eyes. It was not a spirit Satipy saw that caused her to fall. She saw what you saw today. She saw in the face of the man following her—her own husband—the intention to throw her down as he had thrown that other woman. In her fear she backed away from him and fell. And when, with her dying lips, she shaped the word *Nofret,* she was trying to tell you that Yahmose killed Nofret."

Hori paused and then went on: "Esa came on the truth because of an entirely irrelevant remark made by Henet. Henet complained that I did not look *at* her, but as though I saw something behind her that was not there. She went on to speak of Satipy. In a flash Esa saw how much simpler the whole thing was than we had thought. Satipy did not look at something *behind Yahmose*—it was *Yahmose himself* she saw. To test her idea, Esa introduced the subject in a rambling way which could mean nothing to anyone except Yahmose himself—and only to him if what she suspected was true. Her words surprised him and he reacted to them just for a moment, sufficiently for her to know that what she suspected was the truth. But Yahmose knew then that she *did* suspect. And once a suspicion had arisen, things would fit in too well, even to the story the herd boy told—a boy devoted to him who would do anything his Lord Yahmose commanded—even to swallowing a medicine that night which ensured that he would not wake again. . . ."

"Oh, Hori, it is so hard to believe that Yahmose could do such things. Nofret, yes, I can understand that. But why these other killings?"

"It is difficult to explain to you, Renisenb, but once the heart is opened to evil—evil blossoms like poppies amongst the corn. All his life Yahmose had had, perhaps, a longing for violence and had been unable to achieve it. He despised his own meek, submissive role. I think that the killing of Nofret gave him a great sense of *power*. He realized it first by Satipy. Satipy, who had browbeaten and abused him, was now meek and terrified. All the grievances that had lain buried in his heart so long reared their heads—as that snake reared up on the path here one day. Sobek and Ipy were, one handsomer, the other cleverer than he—so *they* must go. He, Yahmose, was to be the ruler of the house, and his father's only comfort and stay! Satipy's death increased the actual pleasure of killing. He felt more powerful as a result of it. It was after that that his mind began to give way—from then on evil possessed him utterly.

"You, Renisenb, were not a rival. So far as he still could, he loved you. But the idea that your husband should share with him in the estate was not one to be borne. I think Esa agreed to the idea of accepting Kameni with two ideas in her head—the first that if Yahmose struck again, it would be more likely to be at Kameni than at you—and in any case she trusted me to see that you were kept safe. The second idea—for Esa was a bold woman—was to bring things to a head. Yahmose, watched by me—whom he did not know suspected him—could be caught in the act."

"As you did," said Renisenb. "Oh, Hori. I was so frightened when I looked back and saw him."

"I know, Renisenb. But it had to be. So long as I stuck close to Yahmose's side, you would necessarily be safe—but that could not go on forever. I knew that if he had an opportunity of throwing you off the path *at the same place*, he would take it. It would revive the superstitious explanation of the deaths."

"Then the message Henet brought me was not from you?"

Hori shook his head.

"I sent you no message."

"But why did Henet—" Renisenb stopped and shook her head. "I cannot understand Henet's part in all this."

"I think Henet knows the truth," said Hori thoughtfully. "She was conveying as much to Yahmose this morning—a dangerous thing to do. He made use of her to lure you up here—a thing she would be willing to do—since she hates you, Renisenb—"

"I know."

"Afterward—I wonder? Henet would believe her knowledge would give her power. But I do not believe Yahmose would have let her live long. Perhaps even now—"

Renisenb shivered.

"Yahmose was mad," said Renisenb. "He was possessed by evil spirits, but he was not always like that."

"No, and yet— You remember, Renisenb, how I told you the story of Sobek and Yahmose as children, and how Sobek beat Yahmose's head against the ground and how your mother came, all pale and trembling and said, 'That is dangerous.' I think, Renisenb, that her meaning was that to do such things to *Yahmose* was dangerous. Remember that next day how Sobek was ill—food poisoning, they thought. I think your mother, Renisenb, knew something of the queer self-contained fury that dwelt within the breast of her gentle, meek little son and feared that someday it might be roused."

Renisenb shuddered. "Is no one what he seems?"

Hori smiled at her.

"Yes, sometimes. Kameni and I, Renisenb. Both of us, I think, are as you believe we are. Kameni and I . . ."

He said the last words with significance, and suddenly Renisenb realized that she stood at a moment of choice in her life.

Hori went on: "We both love you, Renisenb. You must know that."

"And yet," said Renisenb slowly, "you have let the arrangements be made for my marriage, and you have said nothing—not one word."

"That was for your protection. Esa had the same idea. I must remain disinterested and aloof, so that I could keep constant watch on Yahmose, and not arouse his animosity." Hori added with emotion: "You must understand, Renisenb, that

Yahmose had been my friend for many years. I loved Yahmose. I tried to induce your father to give him the status and authority he desired. I failed. All that came too late. But although I was convinced in my heart that Yahmose had killed Nofret, I tried *not* to believe it. I found excuses, even, for his action. Yahmose, my unhappy, tormented friend, was very dear to me. Then came Sobek's death, and Ipy's and finally Esa's. . . . I knew then that the evil in Yahmose had finally vanquished the good. And so Yahmose has come to his death at my hands—a swift, almost painless death."

"Death—always death."

"No, Renisenb. It is not death that faces you today, but life. With whom will you share that life? With Kameni or with me?"

Renisenb stared straight ahead of her out over the valley below and the silver streak of the Nile.

Before her, very clearly, there rose up the image of Kameni's smiling face as he had sat facing her that day in the boat.

Handsome, strong, gay . . . She felt again the throb and lilt of her blood. She had loved Kameni in that moment. She loved him now. Kameni could take the place that Khay had held in her life.

She thought: "We shall be happy together—yes, we shall be happy. We shall live together and take pleasure in each other and we shall have strong, handsome children. There will be busy days full of work . . . and days of pleasure when we sail on the River. . . . Life will be again as I knew it with Khay. . . . What could I ask more than that? What do I want more than that?"

And slowly, very slowly indeed, she turned her face toward Hori. It was as though, silently, she asked him a question.

As though he understood her, he answered.

"When you were a child, I loved you. I loved your grave face and the confidence with which you came to me, asking me to mend your broken toys. And then, after eight years' absence, you came again and sat here, and brought me the thoughts that were in your mind. And your mind, Renisenb, is not like the minds of the rest of your family. It does not turn in upon itself, seeking to encase itself in narrow walls. Your mind is like my mind, it looks out over the River, seeing a world of changes, of new ideas—seeing a world where all things are possible to those with courage and vision. . . ."

"I know, Hori, I know. I have felt these things with you. But not all the time. There will be moments when I cannot follow you, when I shall be alone. . . ."

She broke off, unable to find words to frame her struggling thoughts. What life would be with Hori, she did not know. In spite of his gentleness, in spite of his love for her, he would remain in some respects incalculable and imcomprehensible. They would share moments of great beauty and richness together—but what of their common daily life?

She stretched out her hands impulsively to him.

"Oh, Hori, decide for me. Tell me what to do!"

He smiled at her, at the child Renisenb speaking, perhaps, for the last time. But he did not take her hands.

"I cannot tell you what to do with your life, Renisenb—because it is your life—and only you can decide."

She realized then she was to have no help, no quickening appeal to her senses such as Kameni had made. If Hori would only have touched her—but he did not touch her.

And the choice suddenly presented itself to her in the simplest terms—the easy life or the difficult one. She was strongly tempted then to turn and go down the winding path, down to the normal, happy life she already knew—that she had experienced before with Khay. There was safety there—the sharing of daily pleasures and griefs, with nothing to fear but old age and death. . . .

Death . . . From thoughts of life she had come full circle again to death. Khay had died. Kameni, perhaps, would die, and his face, like Khay's, would slowly fade from her memory. . . .

She looked then at Hori, standing quietly beside her. It was odd, she thought, that she had never really known just what Hori looked like. . . . She had never needed to know. . . .

She spoke then, and the tone of her voice was the same as when she had announced, long before, that she would walk down the path at sunset alone.

"I have made my choice, Hori. I will share my life with you for good or evil, until death comes. . . ."

With his arms round her, with the sudden new sweetness of his face against hers, she was filled with an exultant richness of living.

"If Hori were to die," she thought, "I should *not* forget! Hori is a song in my heart forever. . . . That means—that there is no more death. . . ."

ABOUT THE AUTHOR

Agatha Christie's enormous success as a detective story writer and the excellence of her work caused her to be honored by Queen Elizabeth II of England as a Dame of the British Empire in 1971.

She knew, and described with humor and deadly accuracy, the world of culture, wealth, and breeding, laying bare, with devastating effectiveness, the passions that dwelt there, turning otherwise attractive men and women into killers. Her devilishly complex and daring plots have baffled and delighted mystery fans throughout the world for more than half a century.

After her marriage to the archaeologist Max Mallowan, she spent part of each year in the Middle East, which provided the exotic settings for several of her popular mysteries—among them *Death on the Nile.*

At the time of her death in 1976, Agatha Christie had written a total of 87 published works, over fifty of them mysteries, and had been translated more widely than any other British author, not excepting Shakespeare.